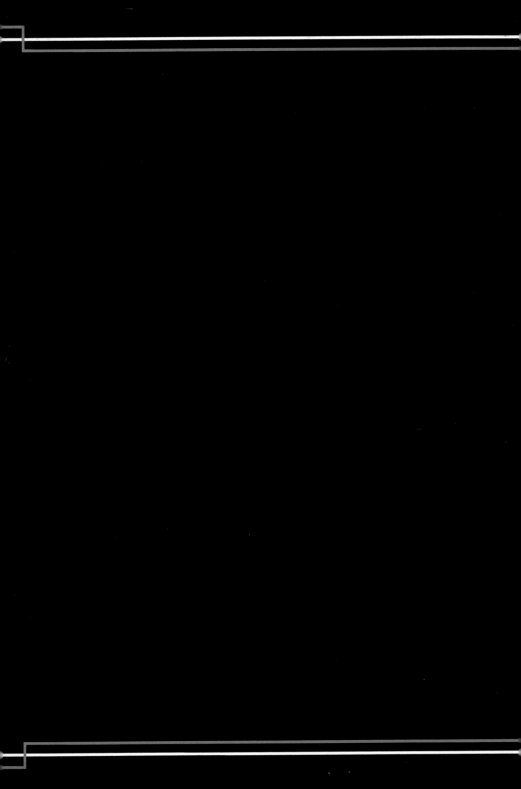

Thomas Siddell

Gunnerkrigg Court™

Dissolve

Published by
ARCHAIA™

Written & Illustrated by
Thomas Siddell

Designer
Marie Krupina

Editor
Jasmine Amiri

GUNNERKRIGG COURT Volume Six, January 2018. Published by Archaia, a division of Boom Entertainment, Inc. Gunnerkrigg Court is ™ and © 2018 Thomas Siddell. All Rights Reserved. Archaia™ and the Archaia logo are trademarks of Boom Entertainment, Inc., registered in various countries and categories. All characters, events, and institutions depicted herein are fictional. Any similarity between any of the names, characters, persons, events, and/or institutions in this publication to actual names, characters, and persons, whether living or dead, events, and/or institutions is unintended and purely coincidental.

BOOM! Studios, 5670 Wilshire Boulevard, Suite 450, Los Angeles, CA 90036-5679. Printed in China. First Printing.

ISBN: 978-1-60886-830-8, eISBN: 978-1-61398-501-4

Table of Contents

Gunnerkrigg Court

Chapter 50:

Totem

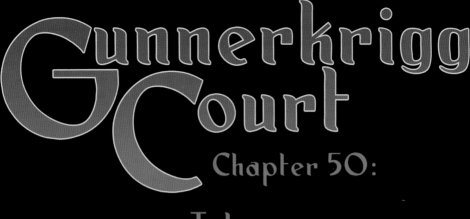

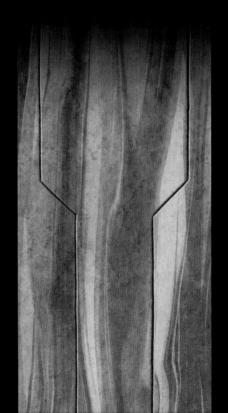

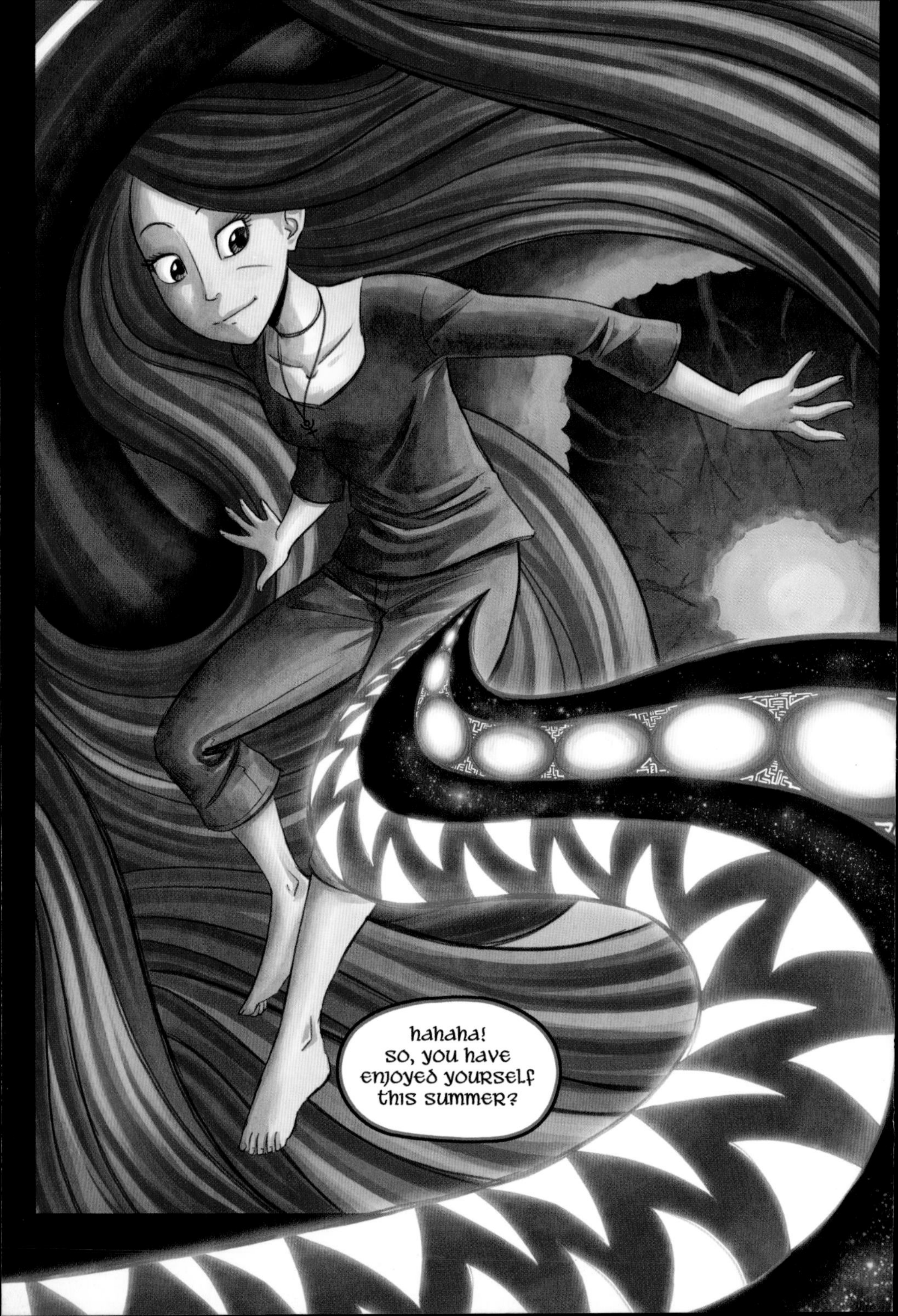
hahaha! so, you have enjoyed yourself this summer?

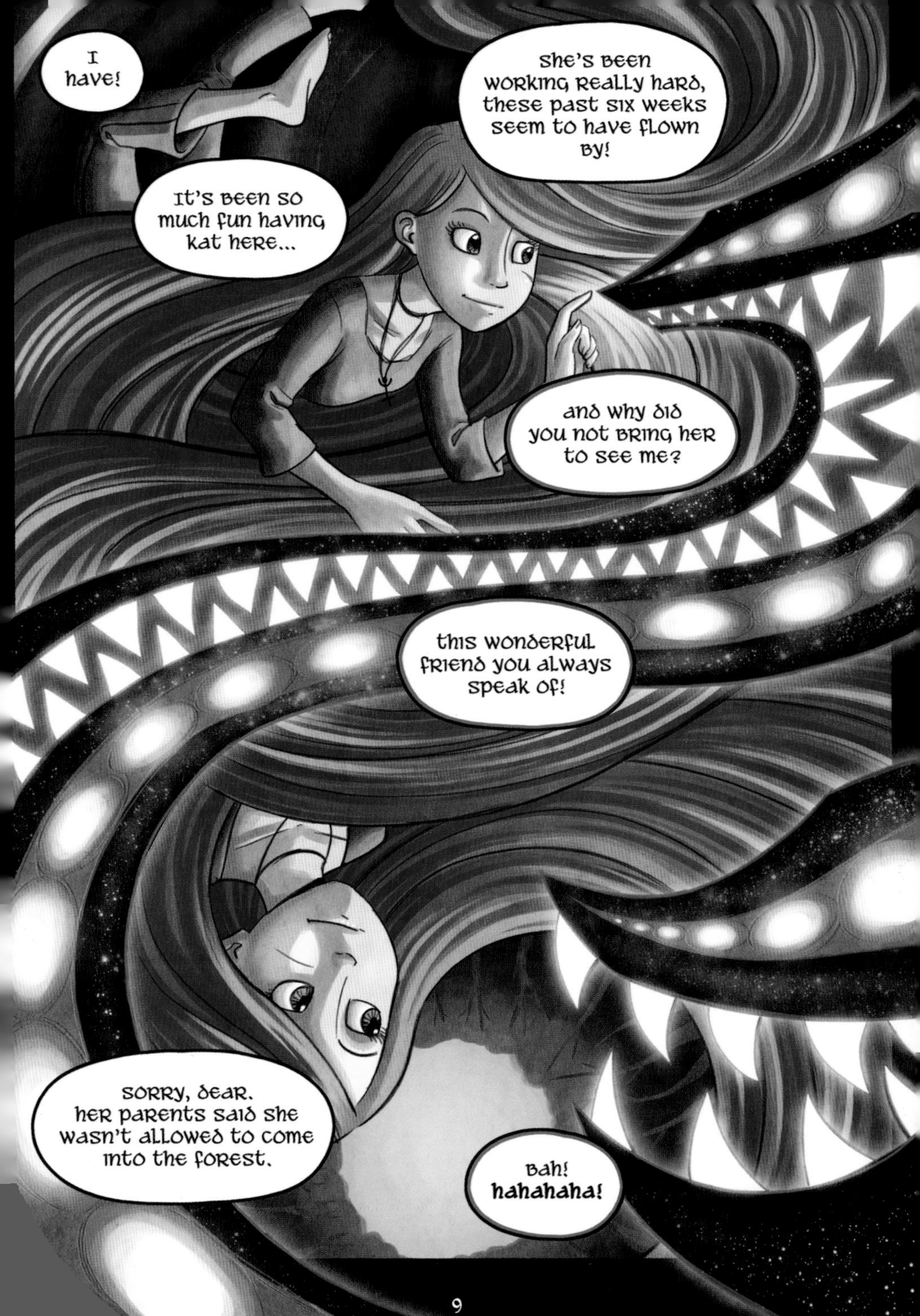
I have!
She's been working really hard, these past six weeks seem to have flown by!
It's been so much fun having Kat here...
And why did you not bring her to see me?
This wonderful friend you always speak of!
Sorry, dear. Her parents said she wasn't allowed to come into the forest.
Bah! Hahahaha!

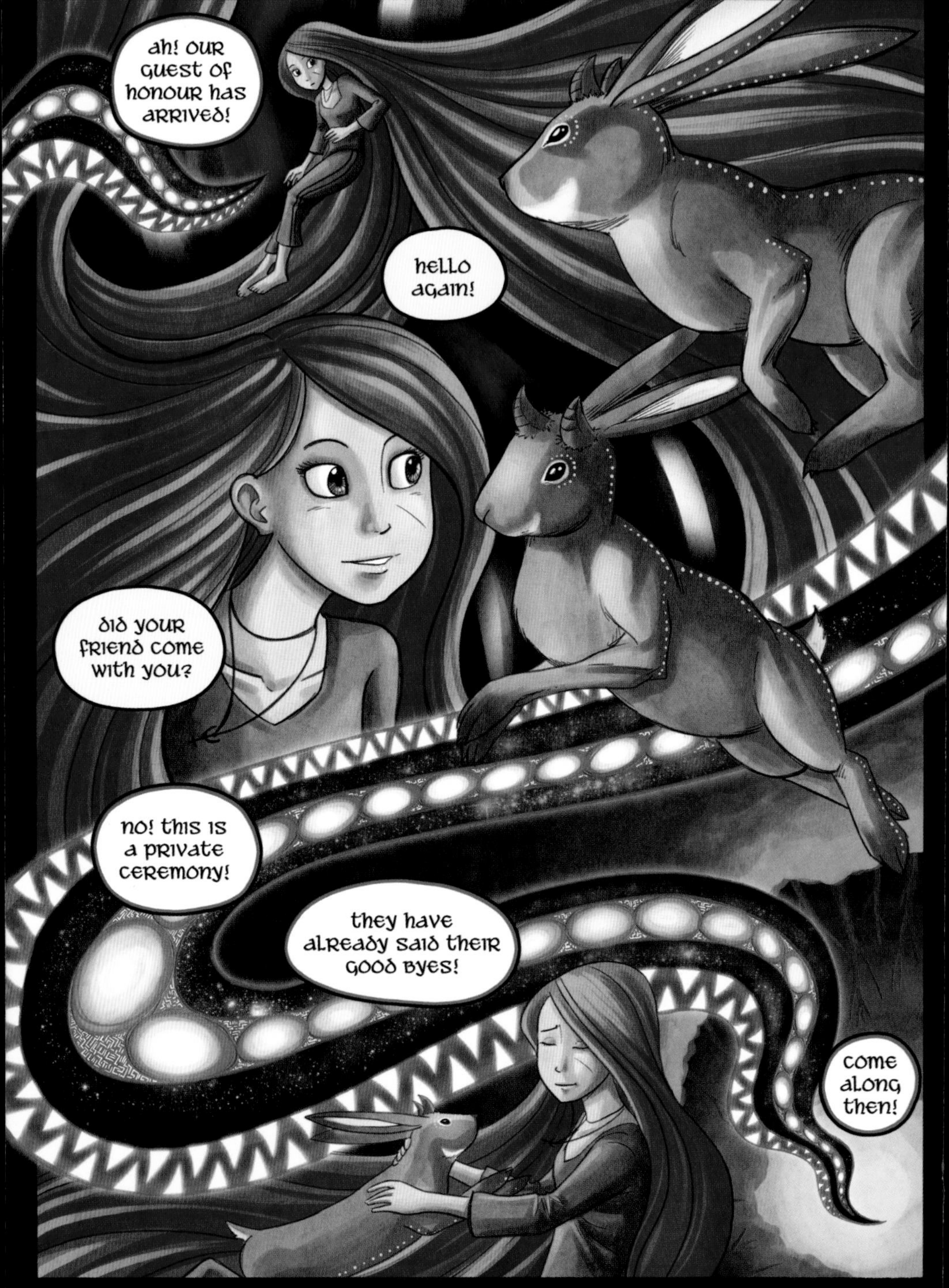
ah! our guest of honour has arrived!
hello again!
did your friend come with you?
no! this is a private ceremony!
they have already said their good byes!
come along then!

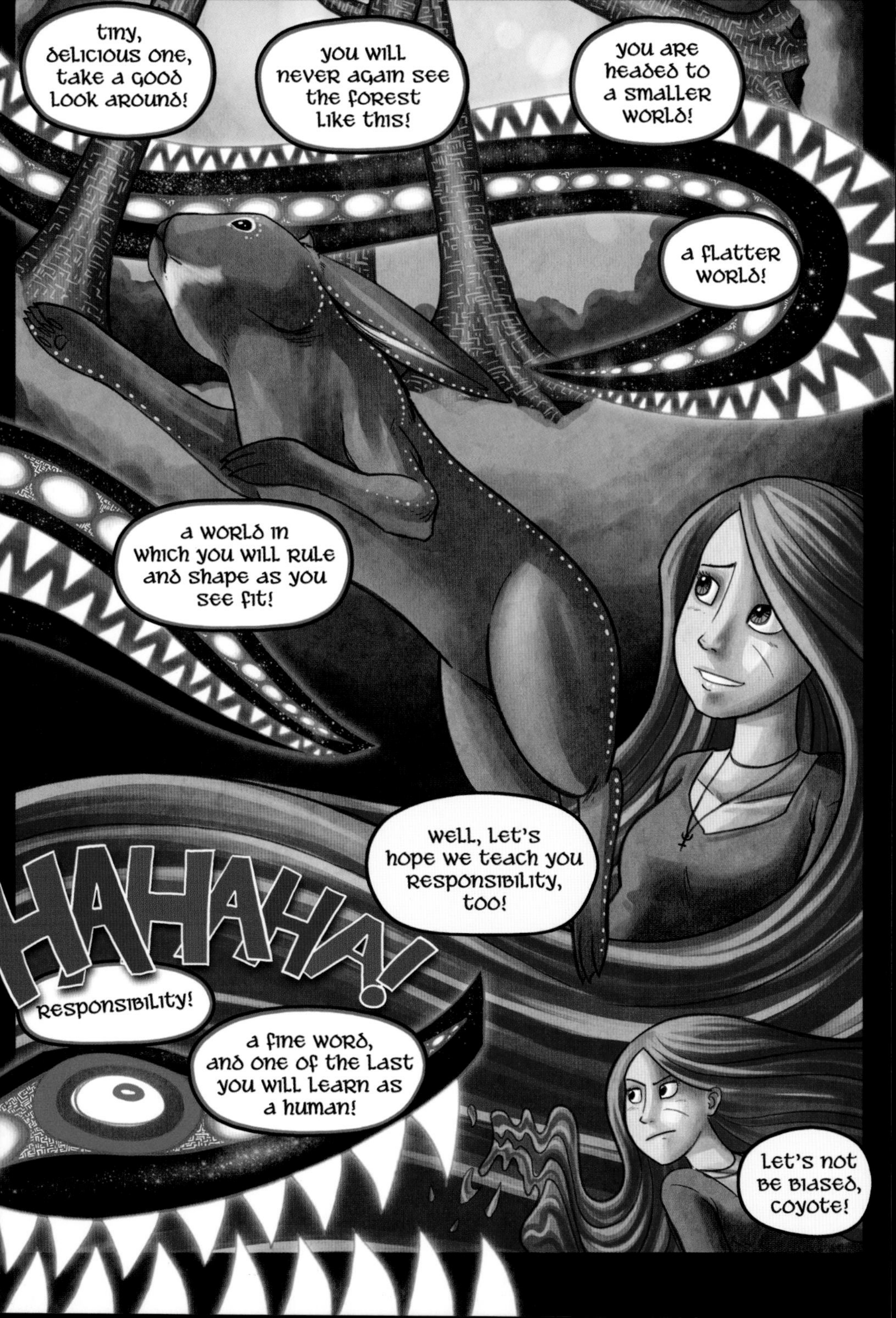
tiny, delicious one, take a good look around!
you will never again see the forest like this!
you are headed to a smaller world!
a flatter world!
a world in which you will rule and shape as you see fit!
well, let's hope we teach you responsibility, too!
HAHAHA!
responsibility!
a fine word, and one of the last you will learn as a human!
let's not be biased, coyote!

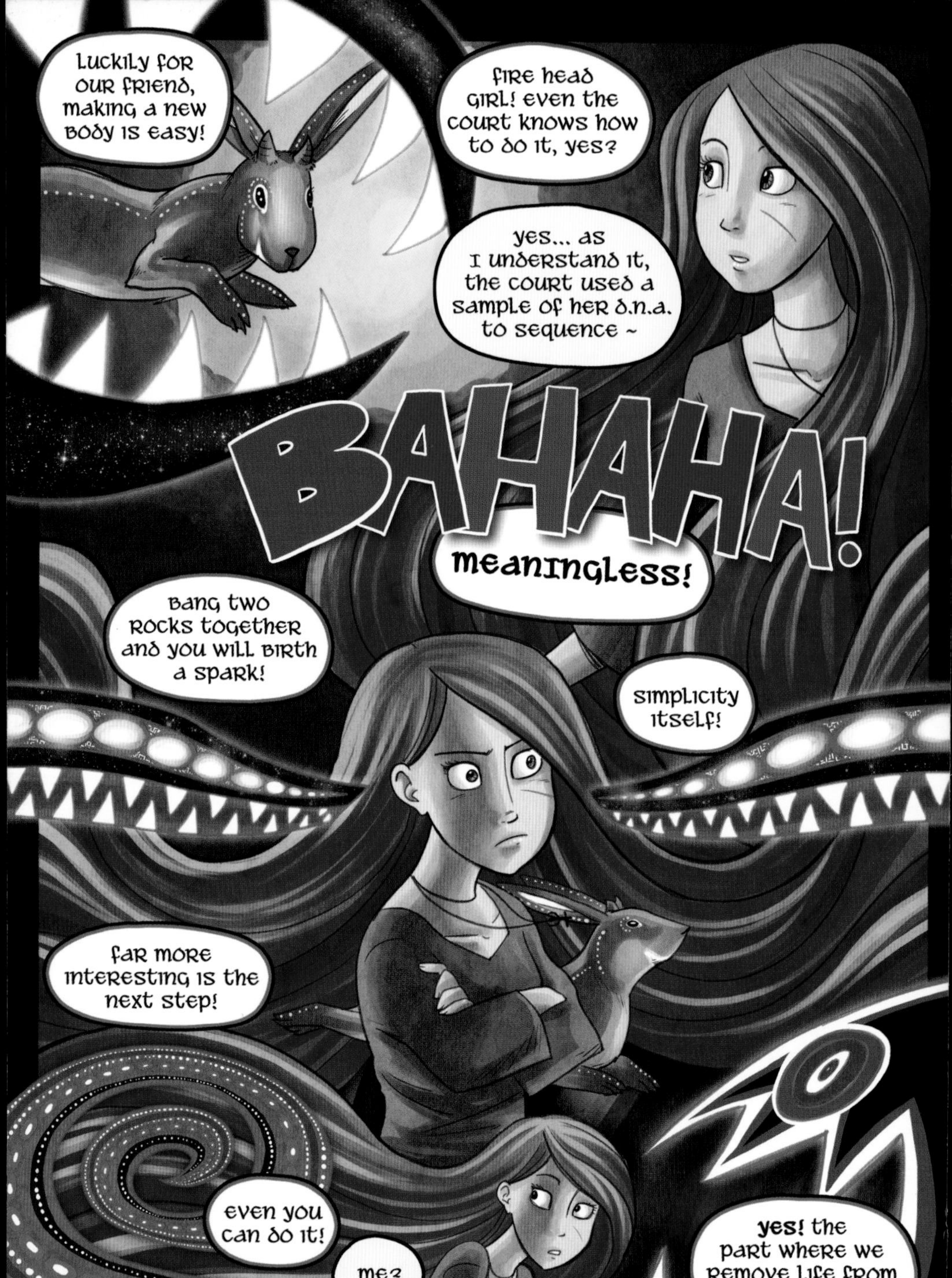
LUCKILY FOR OUR FRIEND, MAKING A NEW BODY IS EASY!
FIRE HEAD GIRL! EVEN THE COURT KNOWS HOW TO DO IT, YES?
YES... AS I UNDERSTAND IT, THE COURT USED A SAMPLE OF HER D.N.A. TO SEQUENCE ~
BAHAHA!
MEANINGLESS!
BANG TWO ROCKS TOGETHER AND YOU WILL BIRTH A SPARK!
SIMPLICITY ITSELF!
FAR MORE INTERESTING IS THE NEXT STEP!
EVEN YOU CAN DO IT!
ME?
YES! THE PART WHERE WE REMOVE LIFE FROM THE RABBIT!

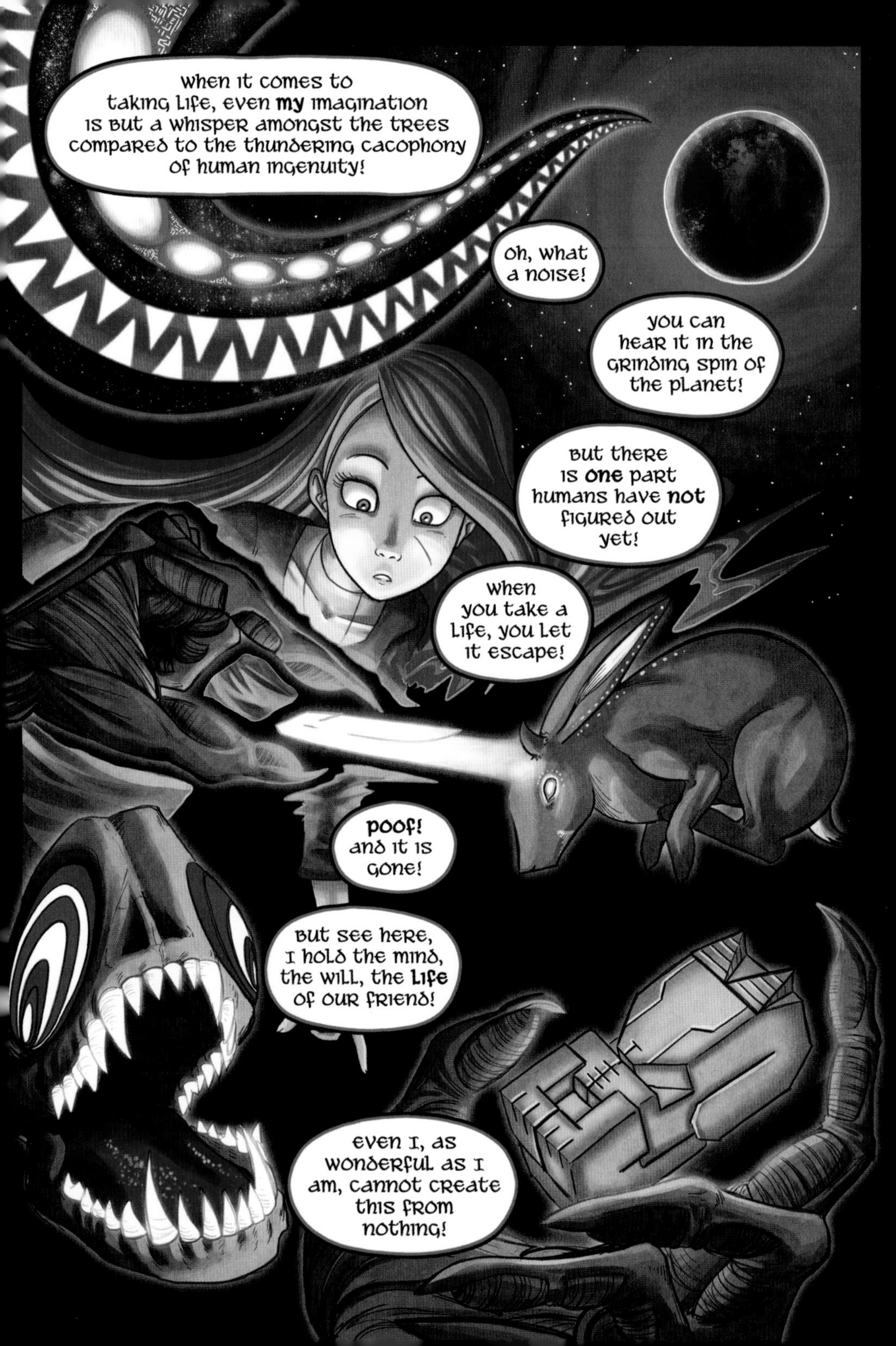
when it comes to taking life, even my imagination is but a whisper amongst the trees compared to the thundering cacophony of human ingenuity!
oh, what a noise!
you can hear it in the grinding spin of the planet!
but there is one part humans have not figured out yet!
when you take a life, you let it escape!
poof! and it is gone!
but see here, I hold the mind, the will, the life of our friend!
even I, as wonderful as I am, cannot create this from nothing!

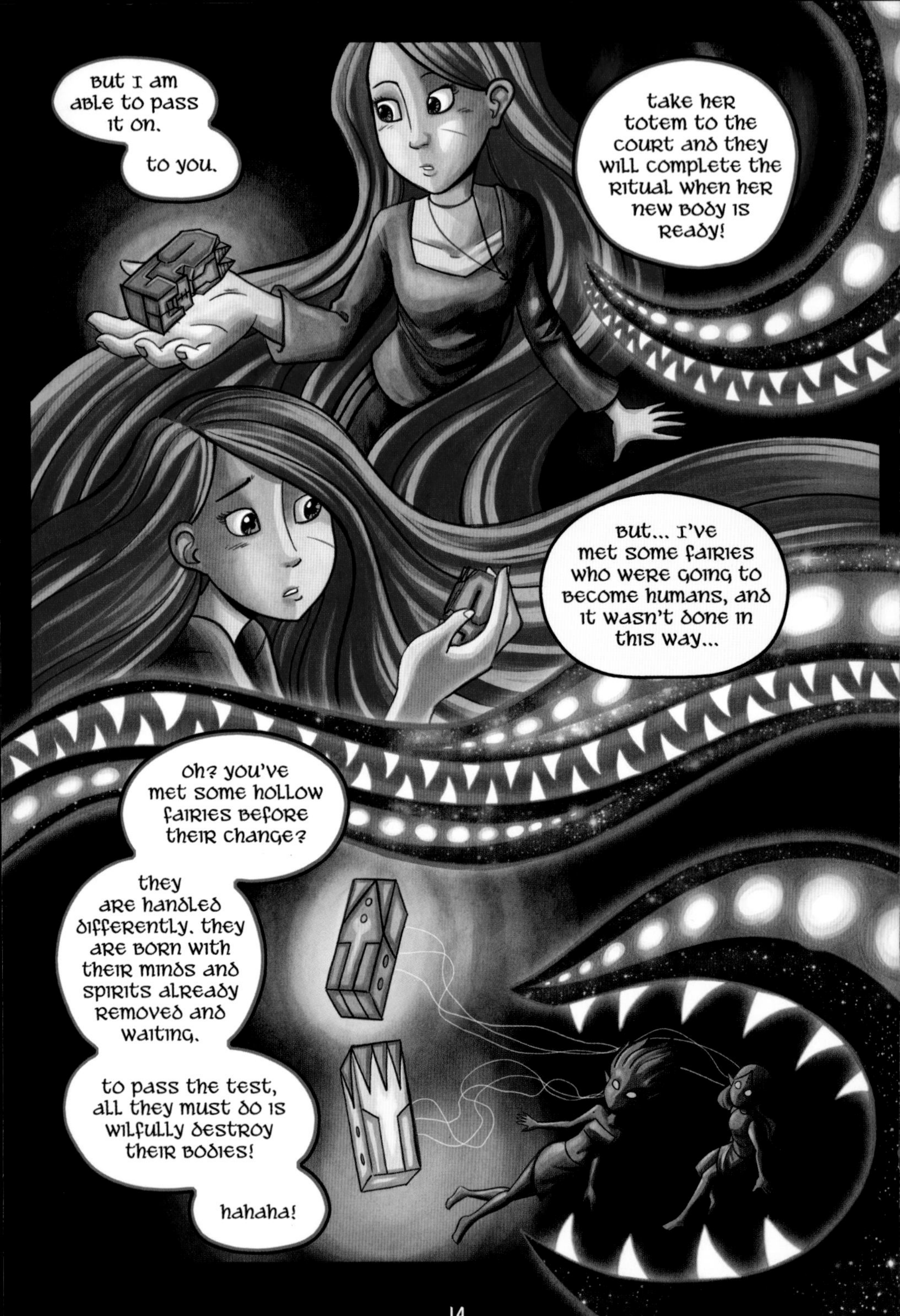
BUT I AM ABLE TO PASS IT ON.
TO YOU.
TAKE HER TOTEM TO THE COURT AND THEY WILL COMPLETE THE RITUAL WHEN HER NEW BODY IS READY!
BUT... I'VE MET SOME FAIRIES WHO WERE GOING TO BECOME HUMANS, AND IT WASN'T DONE IN THIS WAY...
OH? YOU'VE MET SOME HOLLOW FAIRIES BEFORE THEIR CHANGE?
THEY ARE HANDLED DIFFERENTLY. THEY ARE BORN WITH THEIR MINDS AND SPIRITS ALREADY REMOVED AND WAITING.
TO PASS THE TEST, ALL THEY MUST DO IS WILFULLY DESTROY THEIR BODIES!
HAHAHA!

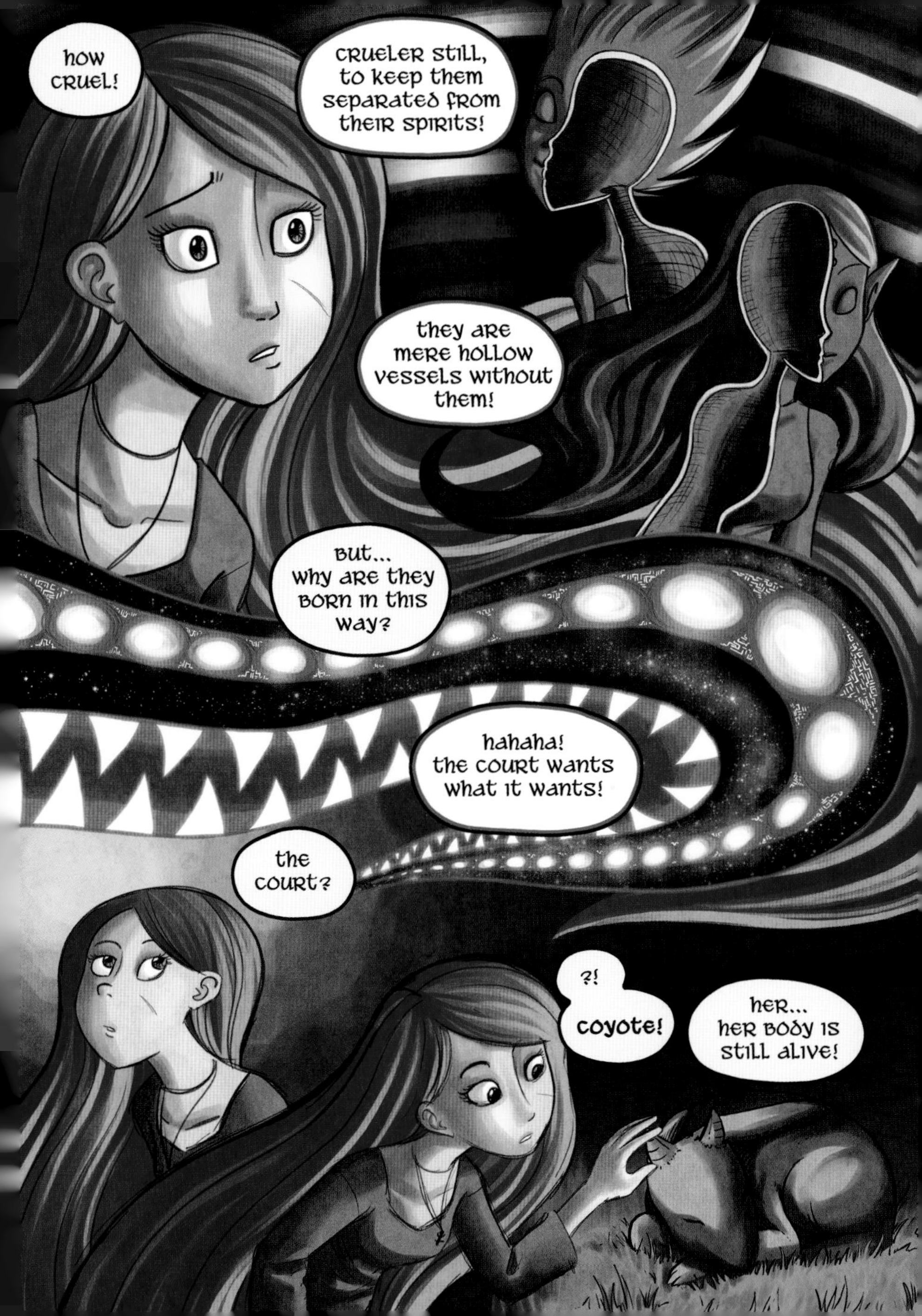
how cruel!
crueler still, to keep them separated from their spirits!
they are mere hollow vessels without them!
but... why are they born in this way?
hahaha! the court wants what it wants!
the court?
?!
coyote!
her... her body is still alive!

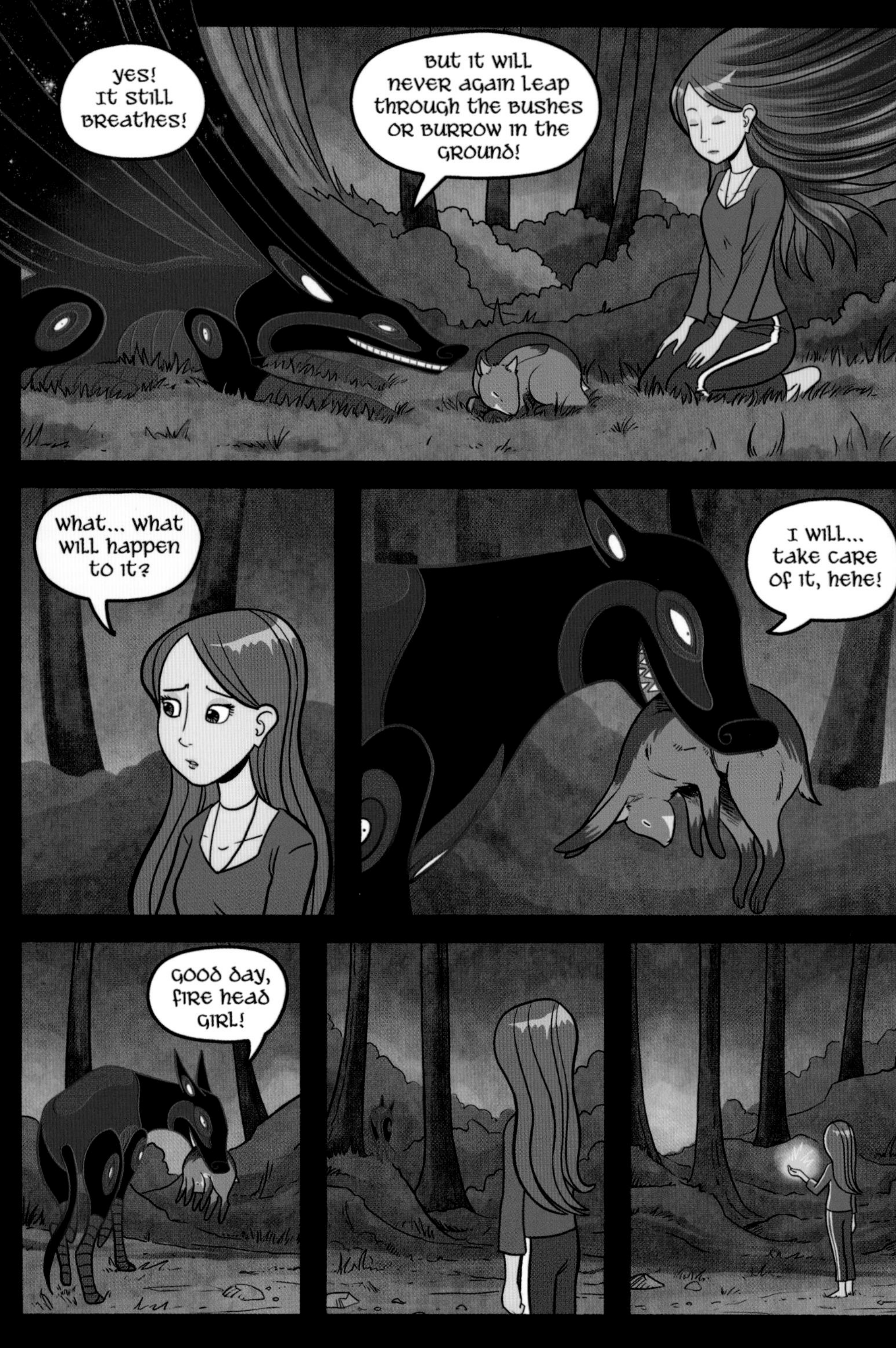
yes! It still breathes!
But it will never again leap through the bushes or burrow in the ground!
What... what will happen to it?
I will... take care of it, hehe!
Good day, fire head girl!

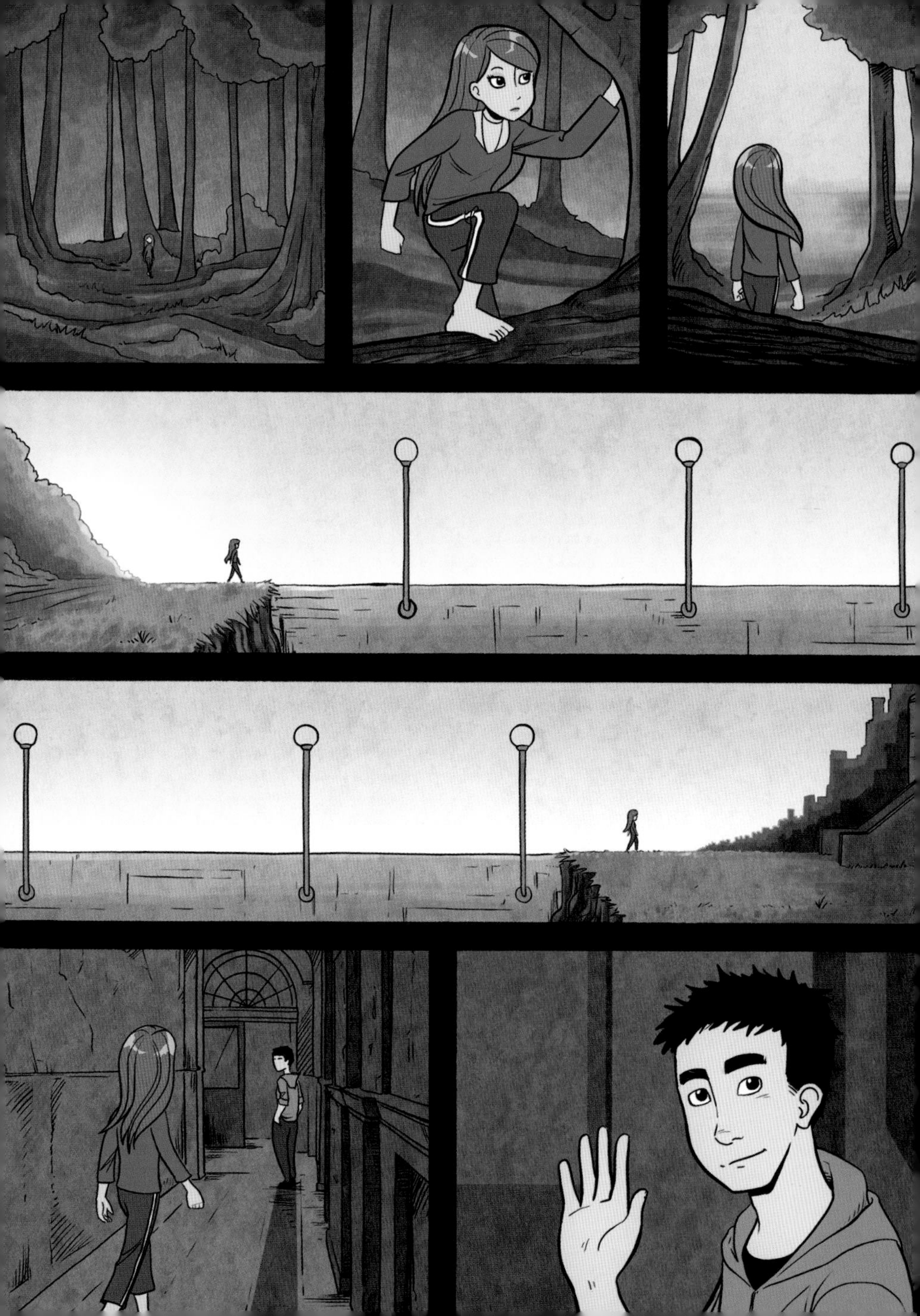

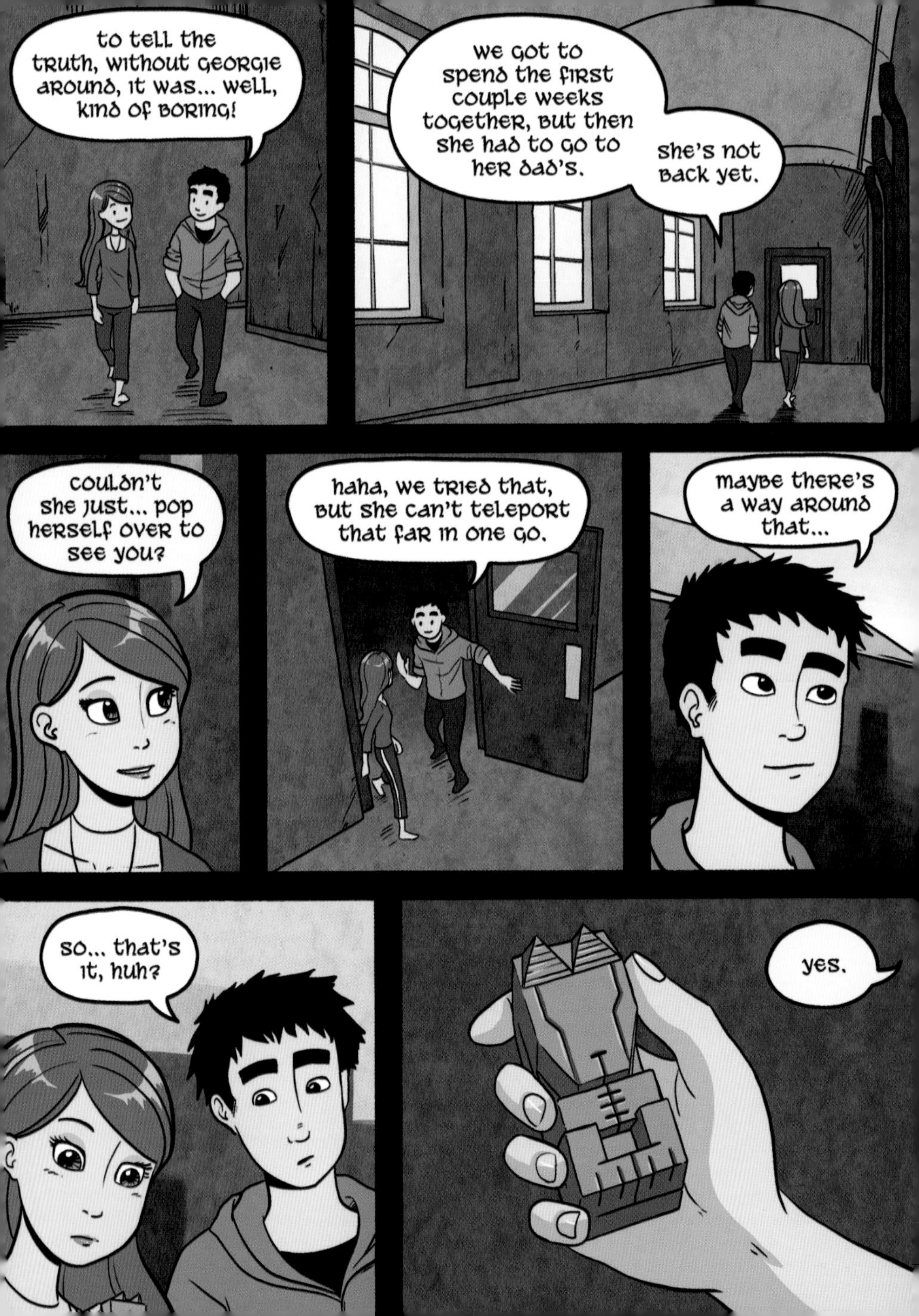
to tell the truth, without georgie around, it was... well, kind of boring!
we got to spend the first couple weeks together, but then she had to go to her dad's.
she's not back yet.
couldn't she just... pop herself over to see you?
haha, we tried that, but she can't teleport that far in one go.
maybe there's a way around that...
so... that's it, huh?
yes.

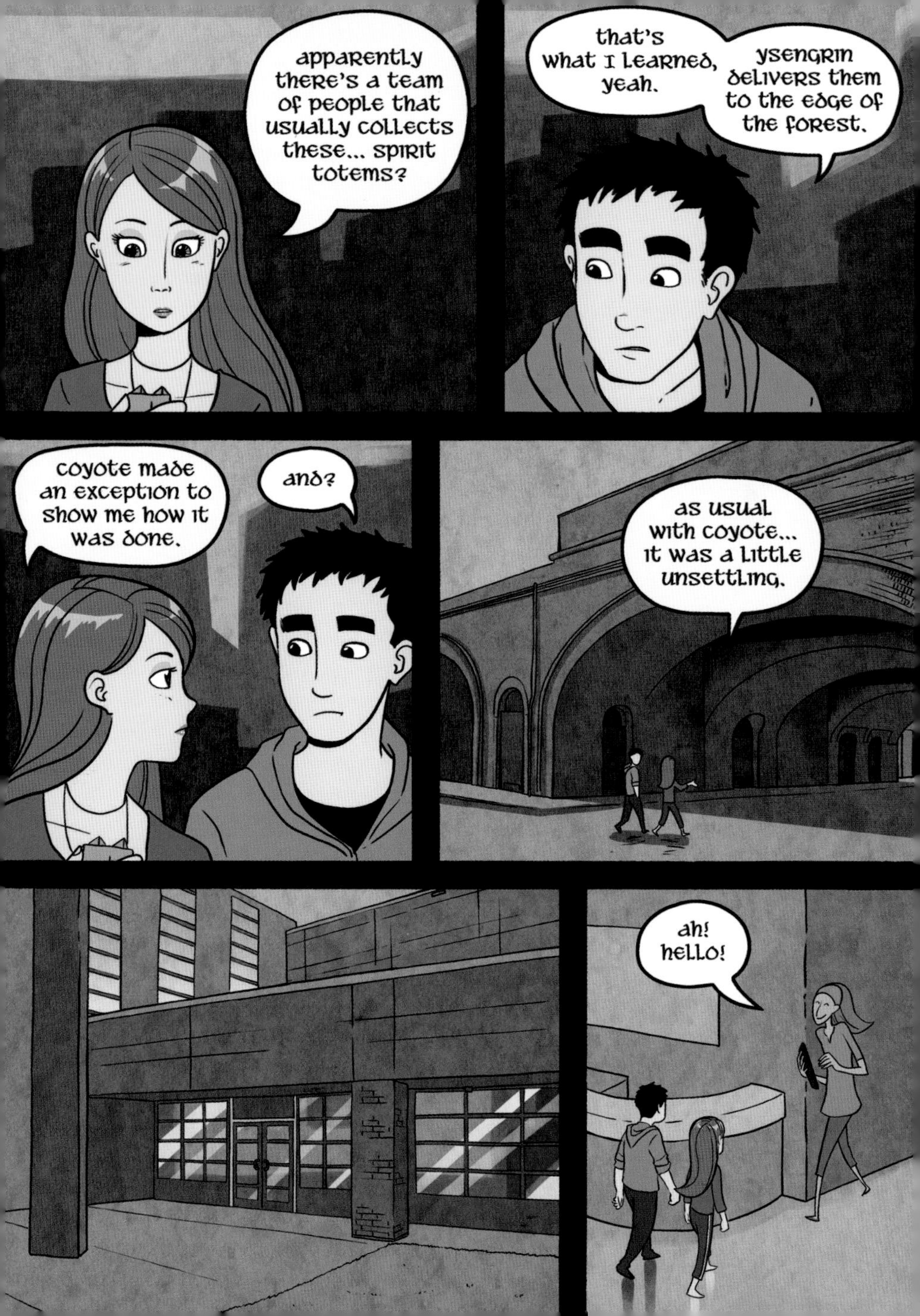
apparently there's a team of people that usually collects these... spirit totems?
that's what I learned, yeah.
ysengrin delivers them to the edge of the forest.
coyote made an exception to show me how it was done.
and?
as usual with coyote... it was a little unsettling.
ah! hello!

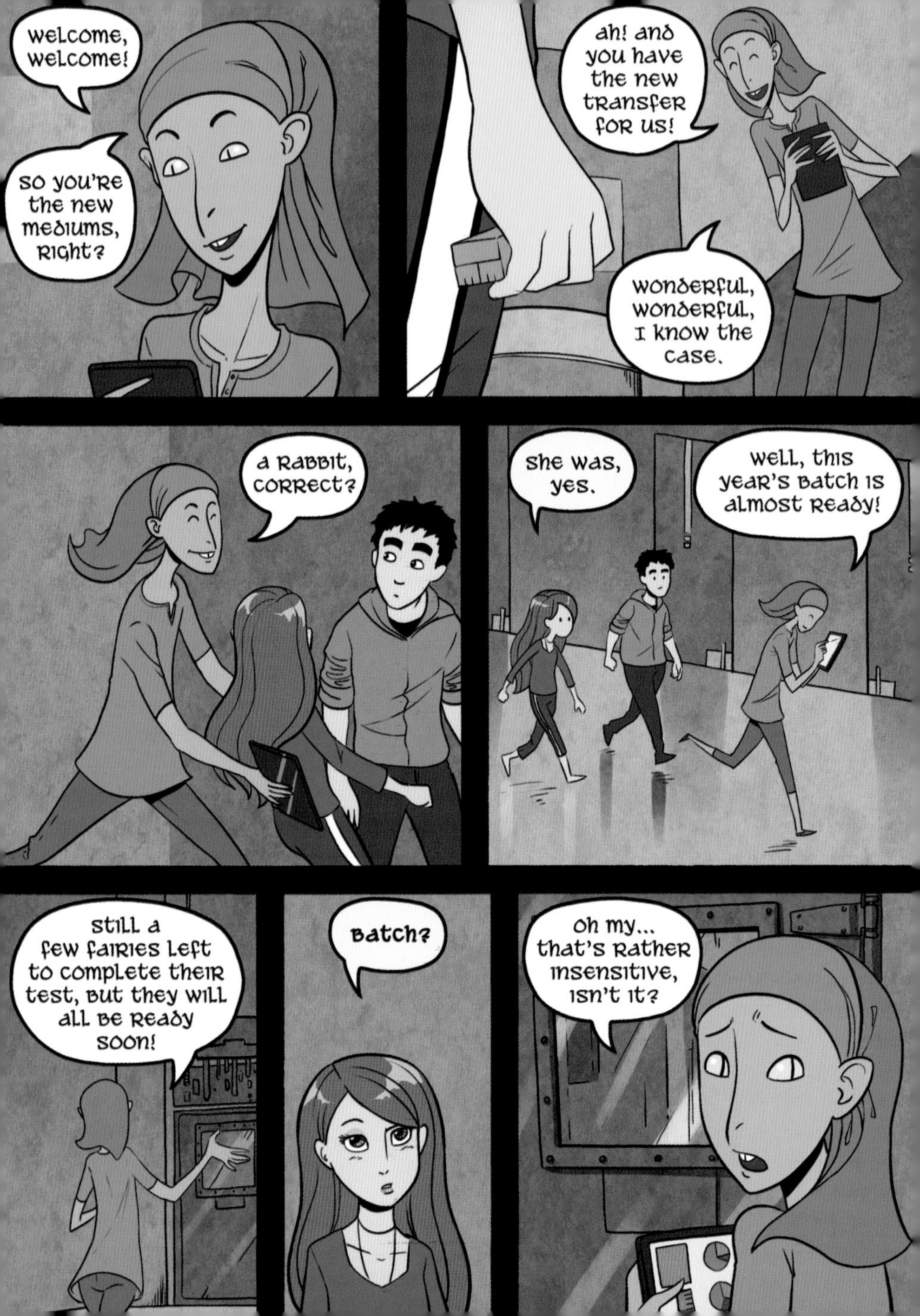
welcome, welcome!
so you're the new mediums, right?
ah! and you have the new transfer for us!
wonderful, wonderful, I know the case.
a rabbit, correct?
she was, yes.
well, this year's batch is almost ready!
still a few fairies left to complete their test, but they will all be ready soon!
batch?
oh my... that's rather insensitive, isn't it?

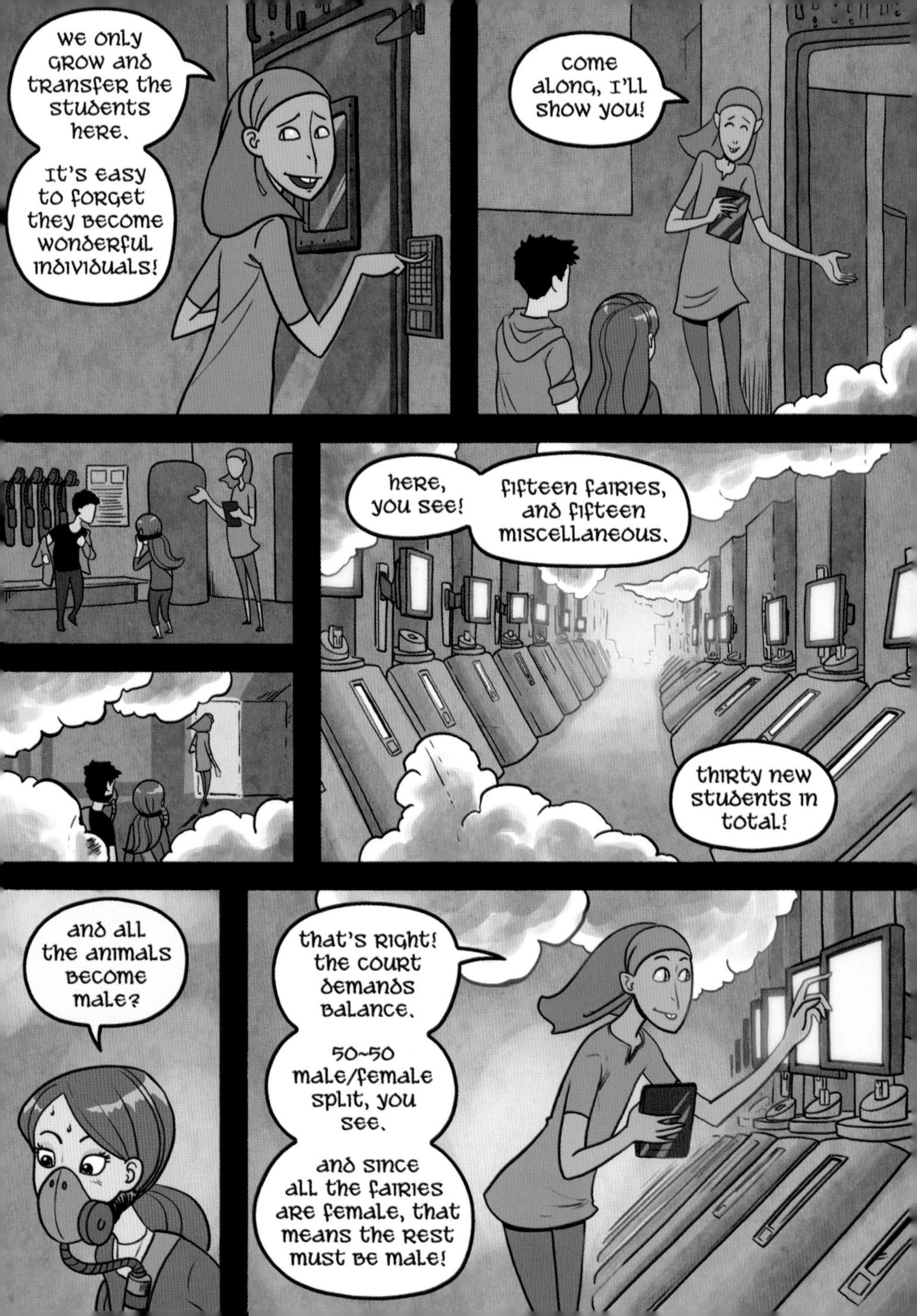
we only grow and transfer the students here.
It's easy to forget they become wonderful individuals!
come along, I'll show you!
here, you see!
fifteen fairies, and fifteen miscellaneous.
thirty new students in total!
and all the animals become male?
that's right! the court demands balance.
50-50 male/female split, you see.
and since all the fairies are female, that means the rest must be male!

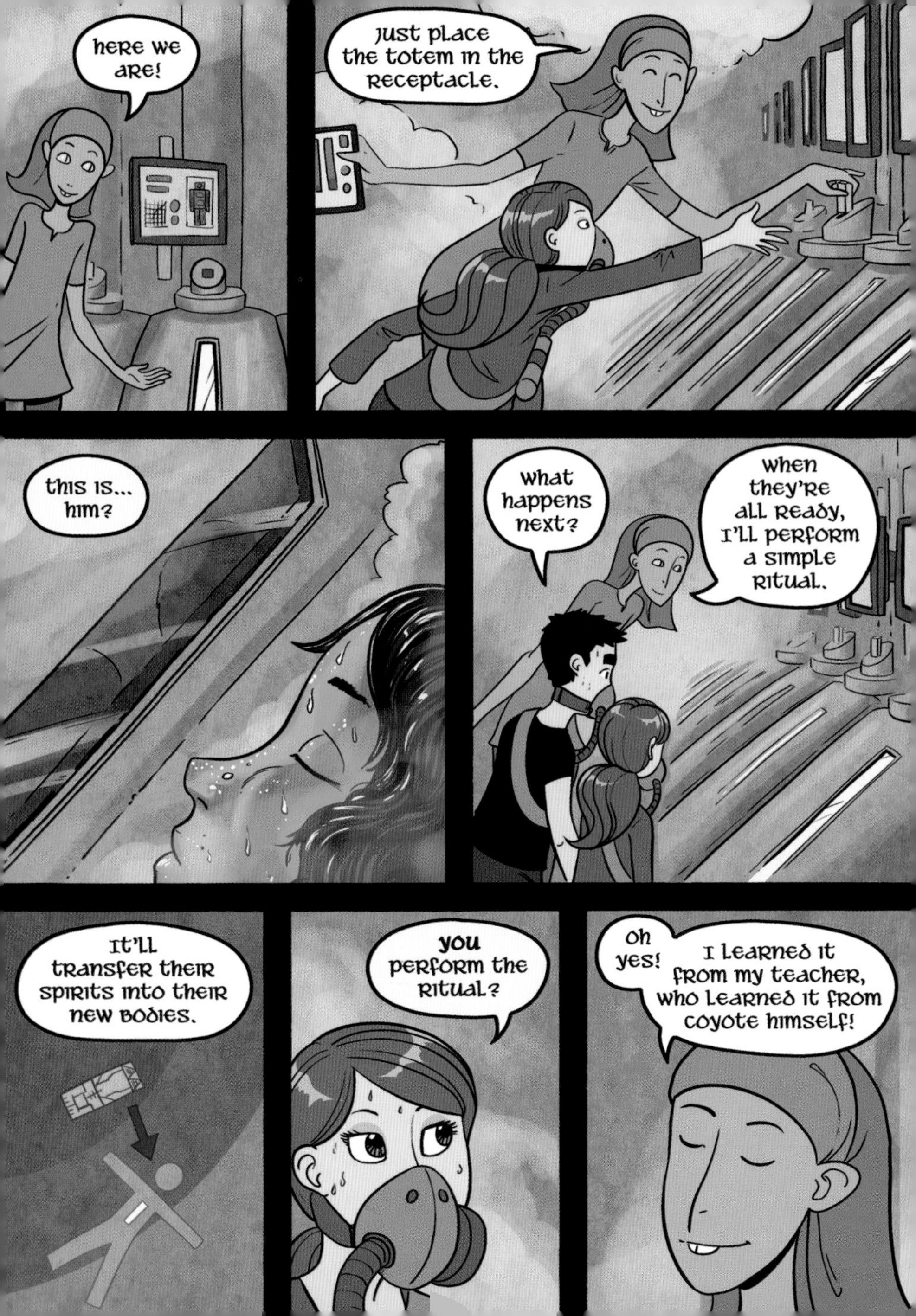
here we are!
just place the totem in the receptacle.
this is... him?
what happens next?
when they're all ready, I'll perform a simple ritual.
It'll transfer their spirits into their new bodies.
you perform the ritual?
oh yes!
I learned it from my teacher, who learned it from coyote himself!

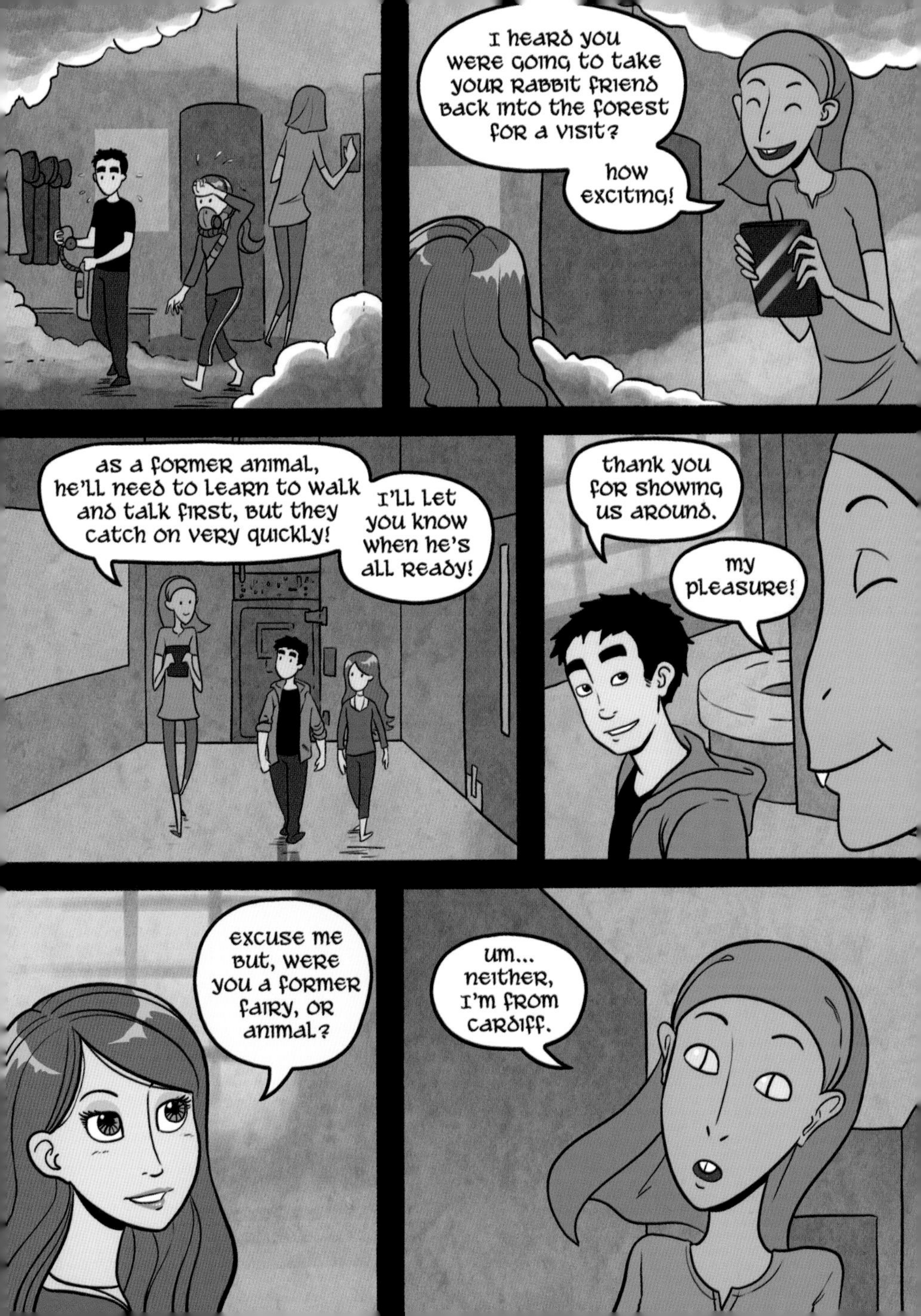
I heard you were going to take your rabbit friend back into the forest for a visit?
how exciting!
as a former animal, he'll need to learn to walk and talk first, but they catch on very quickly!
I'll let you know when he's all ready!
thank you for showing us around.
my pleasure!
excuse me but, were you a former fairy, or animal?
um... neither, I'm from cardiff.

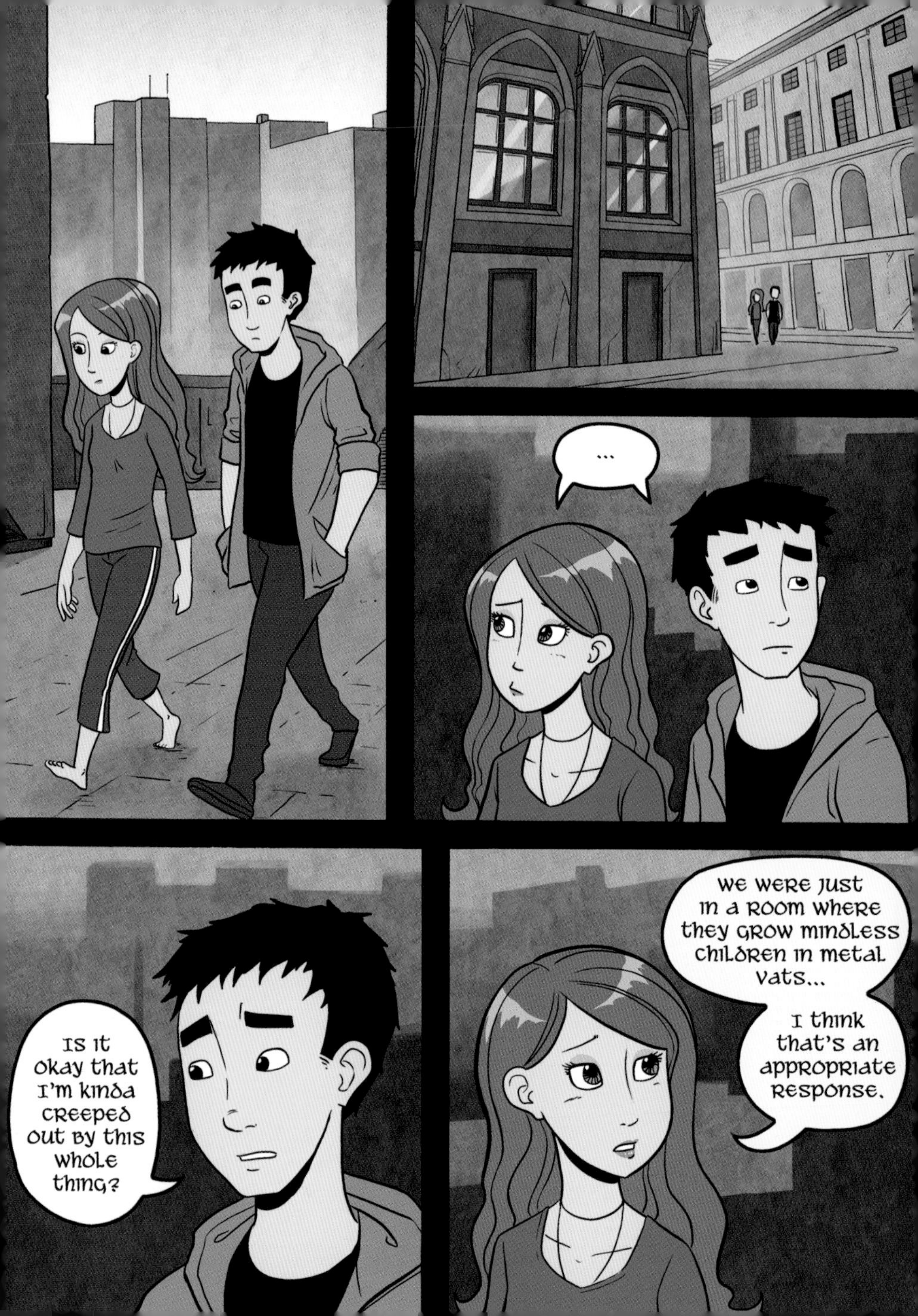
...
Is it okay that I'm kinda creeped out by this whole thing?
We were just in a room where they grow mindless children in metal vats...
I think that's an appropriate response.

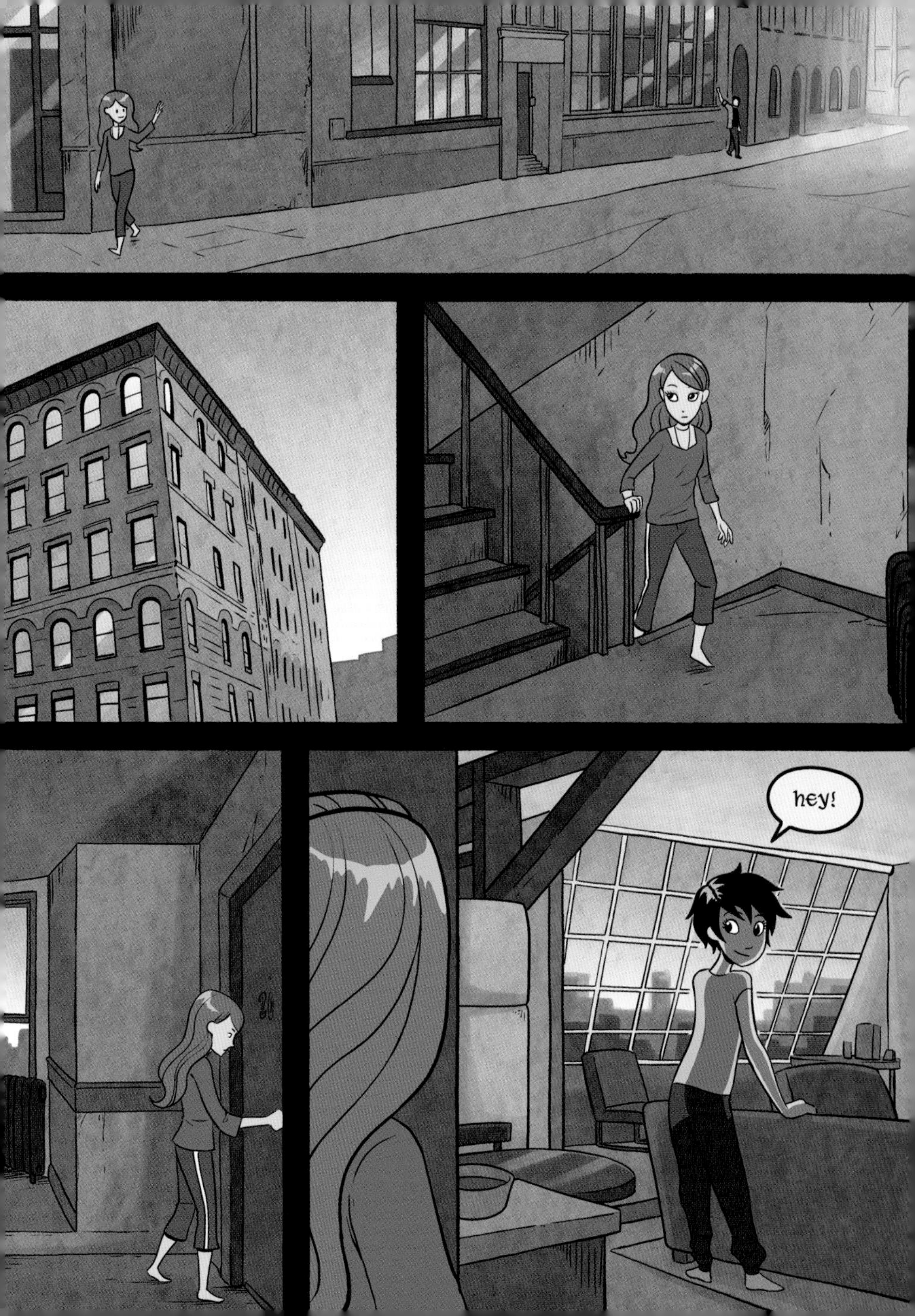
hey!

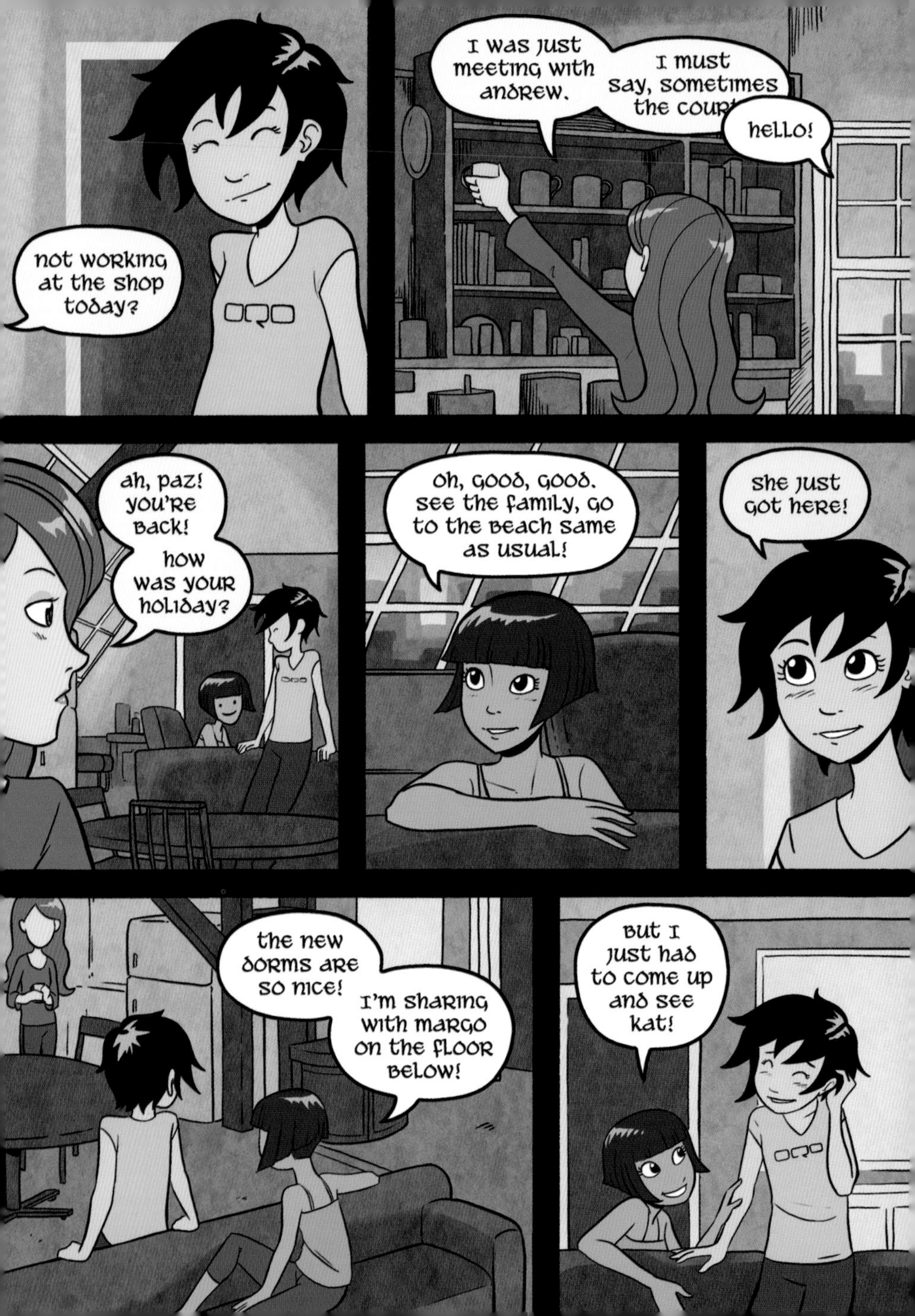
not working at the shop today?
I was just meeting with andrew.
I must say, sometimes the cour
hello!
ah, paz! you're back!
how was your holiday?
oh, good, good. see the family, go to the beach same as usual!
she just got here!
the new dorms are so nice!
I'm sharing with margo on the floor below!
but I just had to come up and see kat!

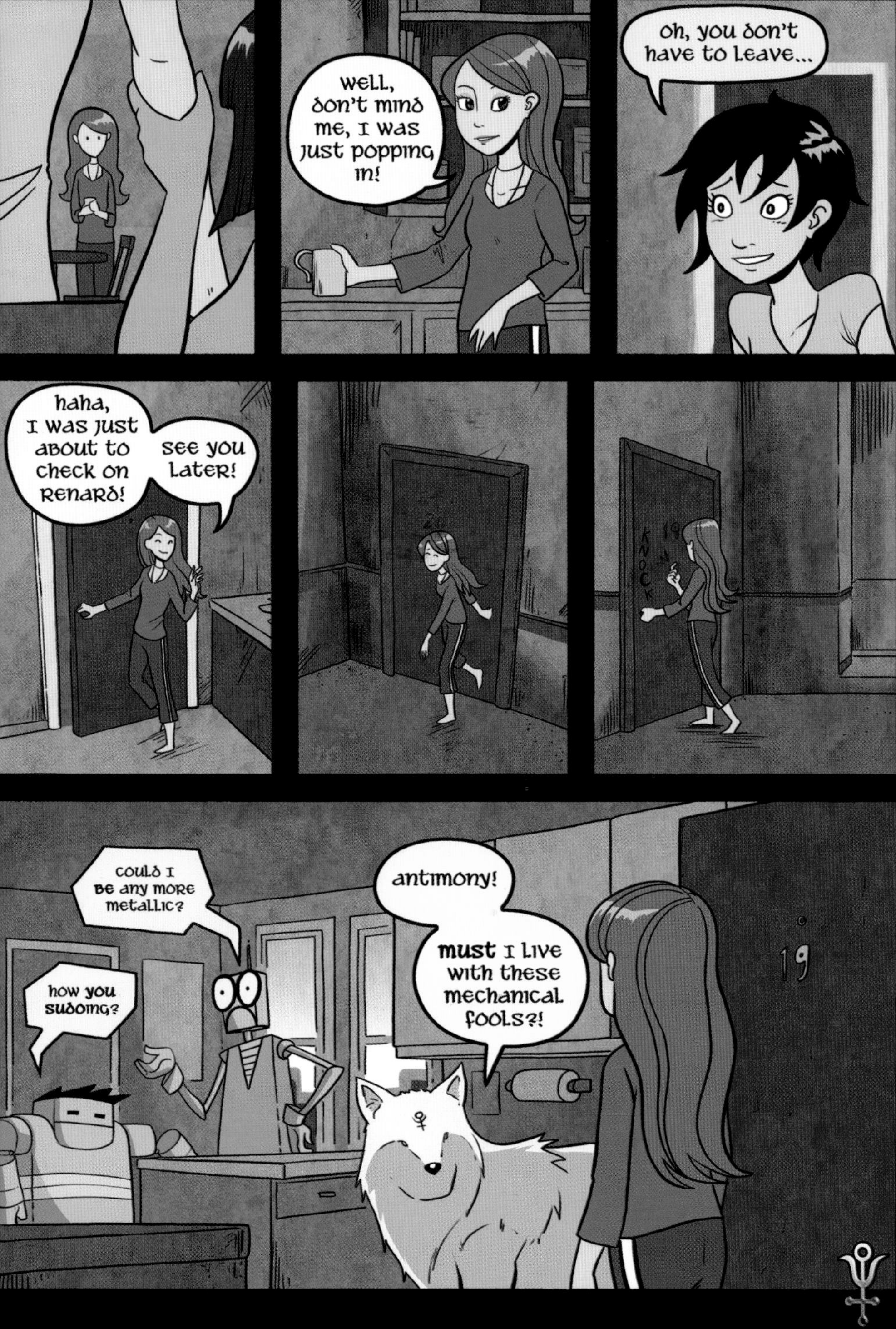
well, don't mind me, I was just popping in!
oh, you don't have to leave...
haha, I was just about to check on Renard!
see you later!
20
19
KNOCK
KNOCK
could I be any more metallic?
how you sudoing?
antimony!
must I live with these mechanical fools?!
19

Welcome to

Y·E·A·R 1·0

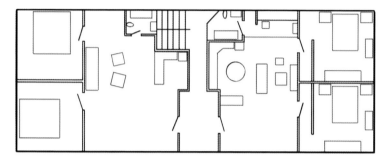

Could I BE any more excited to welcome you all to Year 10? I'm CLANGLER BING, and these are your new dorms! You may notice each floor of the building is identical, and you each get your own room, sharing an apartment style layout with a friend!

Hello! I'm JOEY TRIBBIANOID, and I share my apartment across the hall with Clangler! There is a pair of Clanglers and Joeys on every floor, so if you need anything, WE'LL BE THERE FOR YOU!

Our research has determined that this particular layout is the perfect way to prepare you for life as an adult! Living together like this you will learn cohabitation and cooperation with your roommate, as well as how to deal with the many amusing situations you might face as young adults! I bet YOU didn't think life would be this way!

Did You Know?

The boys' dorms are set up just as yours are, but OPPOSITE! They live across the hall from two robots called MONO-CAN and RACHEL GREEN!

Gunnerkrigg Court

Chapter 51:

The Tree

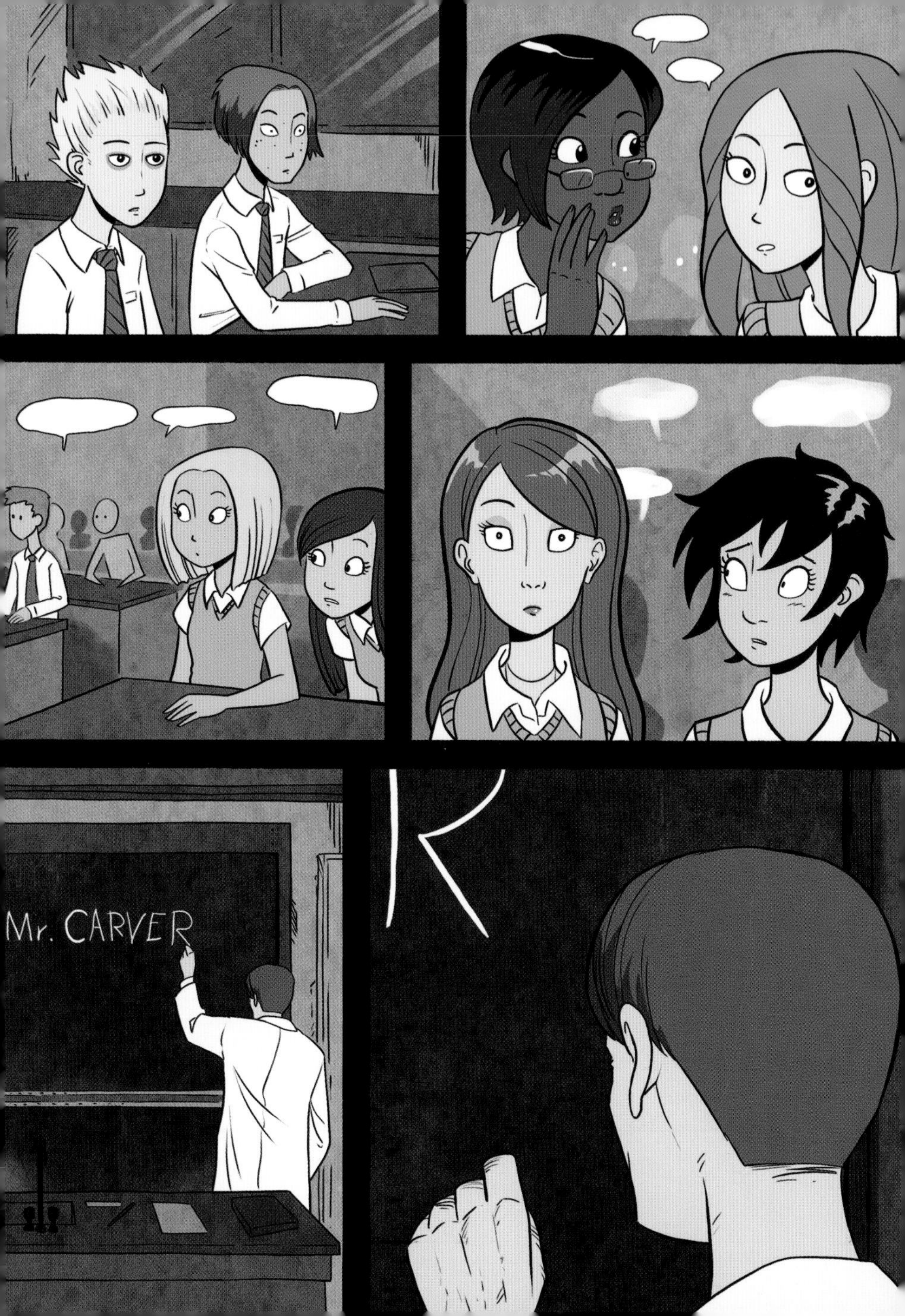
Mr. CARVER

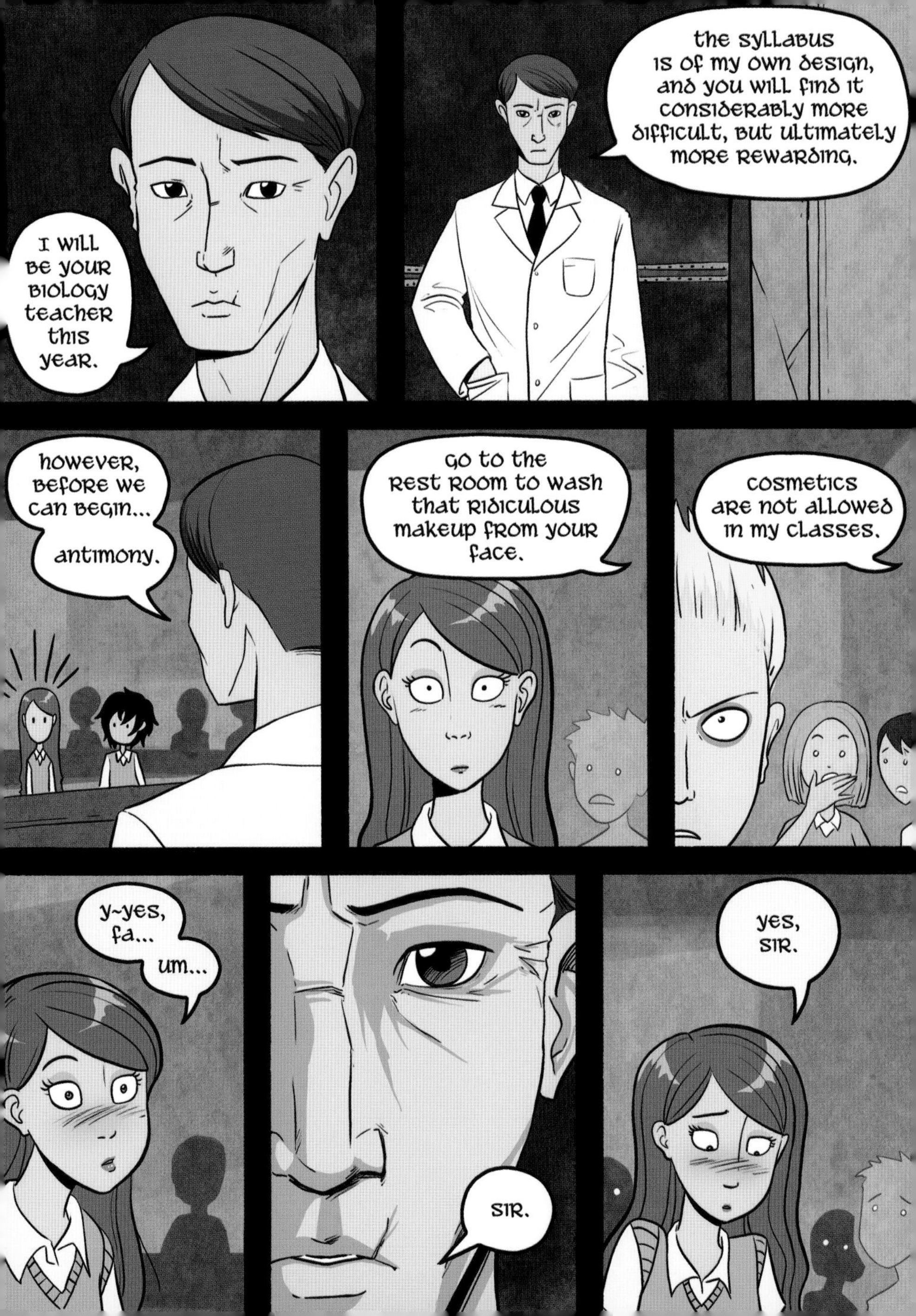
I WILL BE YOUR BIOLOGY teacher this year.
the syllabus is of my own design, and you will find it considerably more difficult, but ultimately more rewarding.
however, before we can begin...
antimony.
go to the rest room to wash that ridiculous makeup from your face.
cosmetics are not allowed in my classes.
y-yes, fa...
um...
sir.
yes, sir.

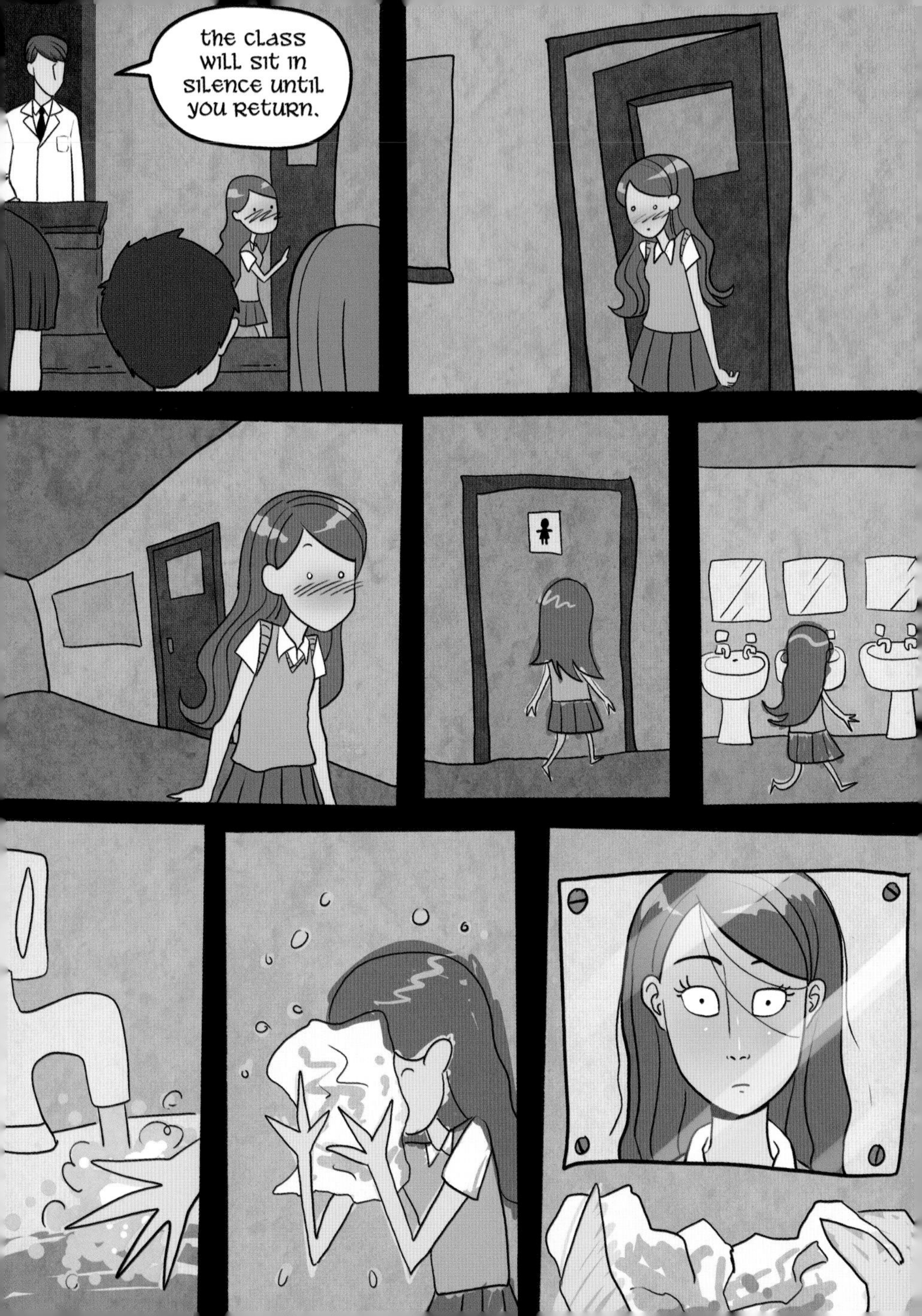
the class will sit in silence until you return.

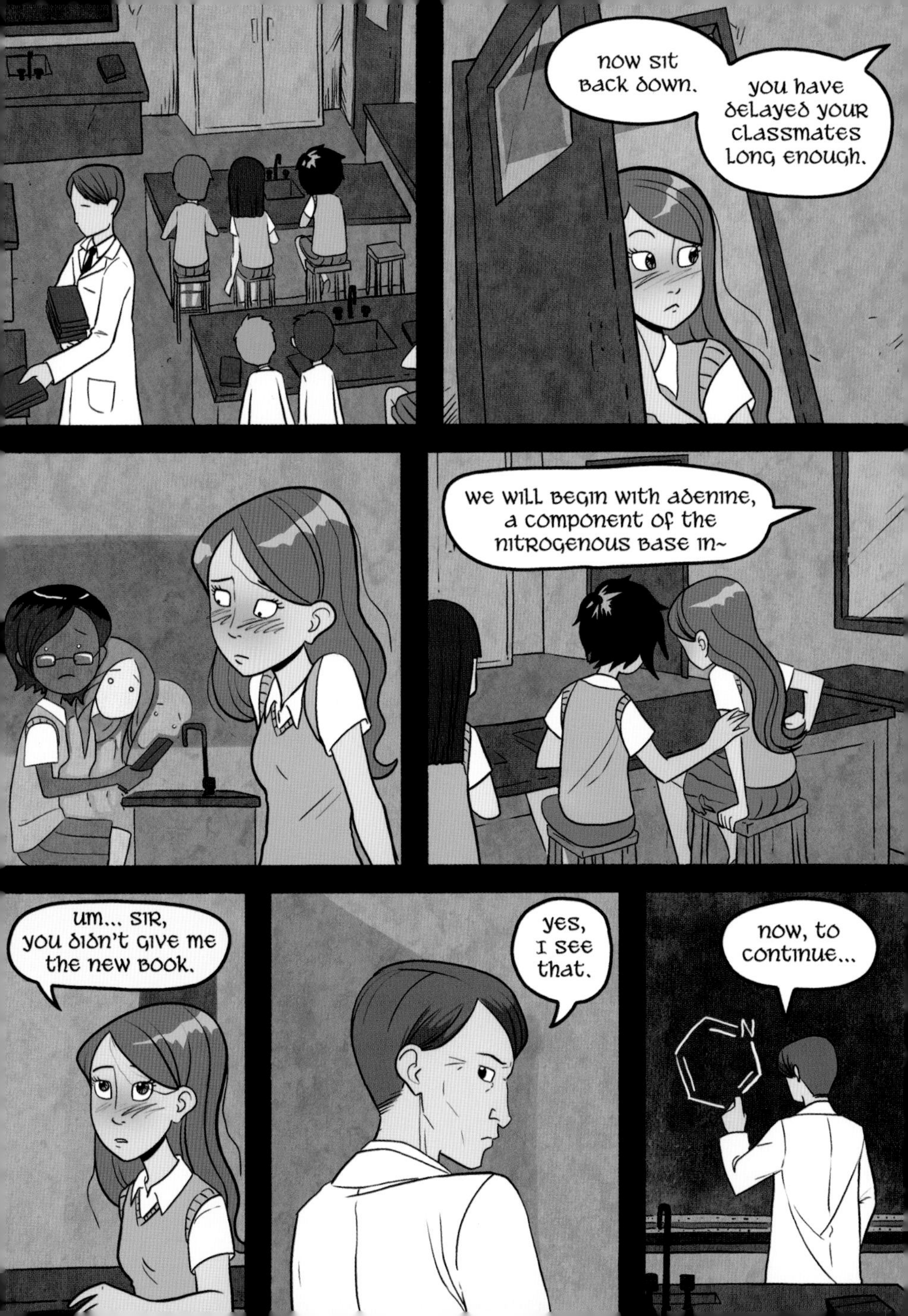
now sit back down.
you have delayed your classmates long enough.
we will begin with adenine, a component of the nitrogenous base in~
um... sir, you didn't give me the new book.
yes, I see that.
now, to continue...
N

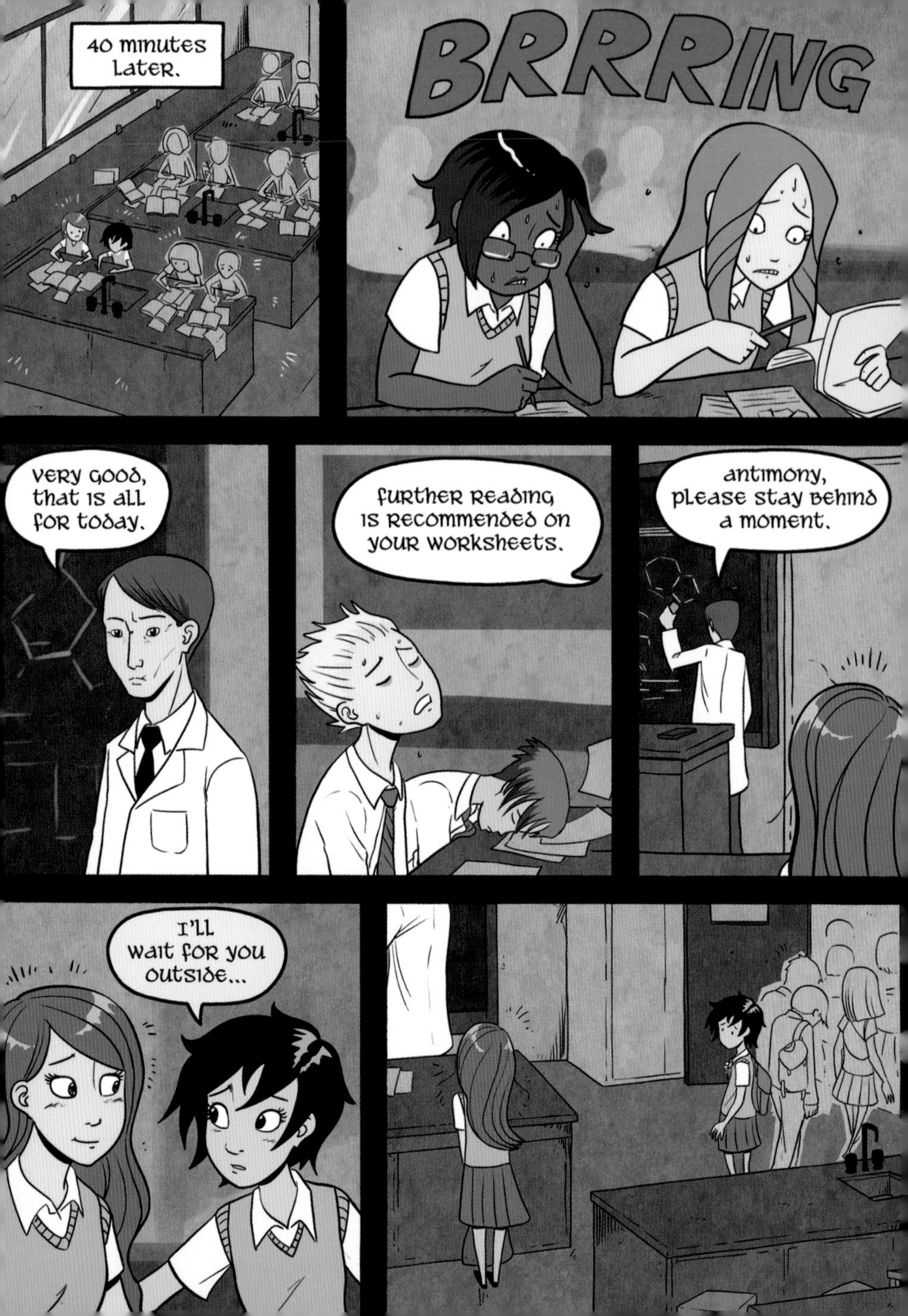
40 minutes later.
BRRRING
very good, that is all for today.
further reading is recommended on your worksheets.
antimony, please stay behind a moment.
I'll wait for you outside...

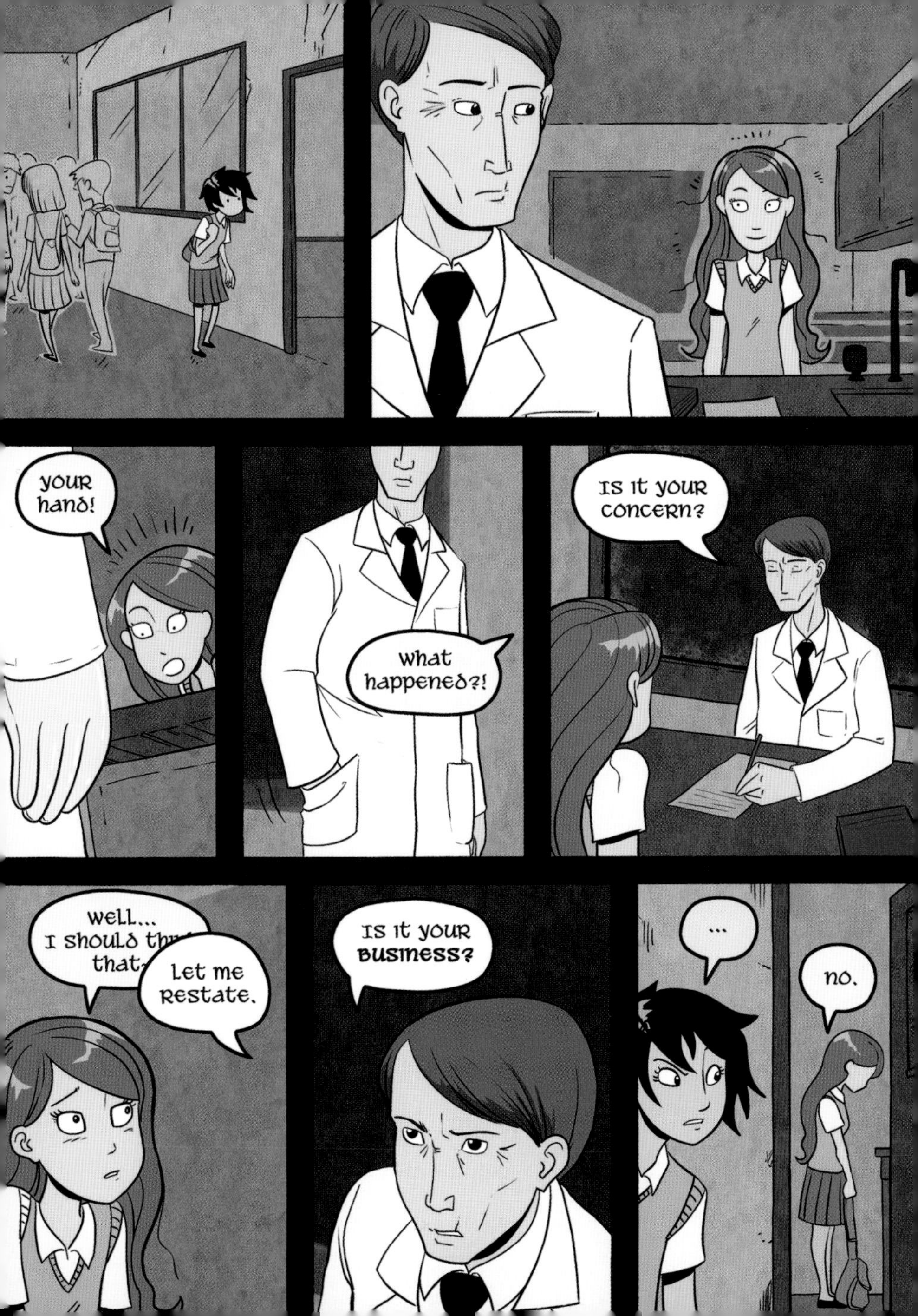
your hand!
what happened?!
Is it your concern?
well... I should th
that
Let me Restate.
Is it your BUSINESS?
...
no.

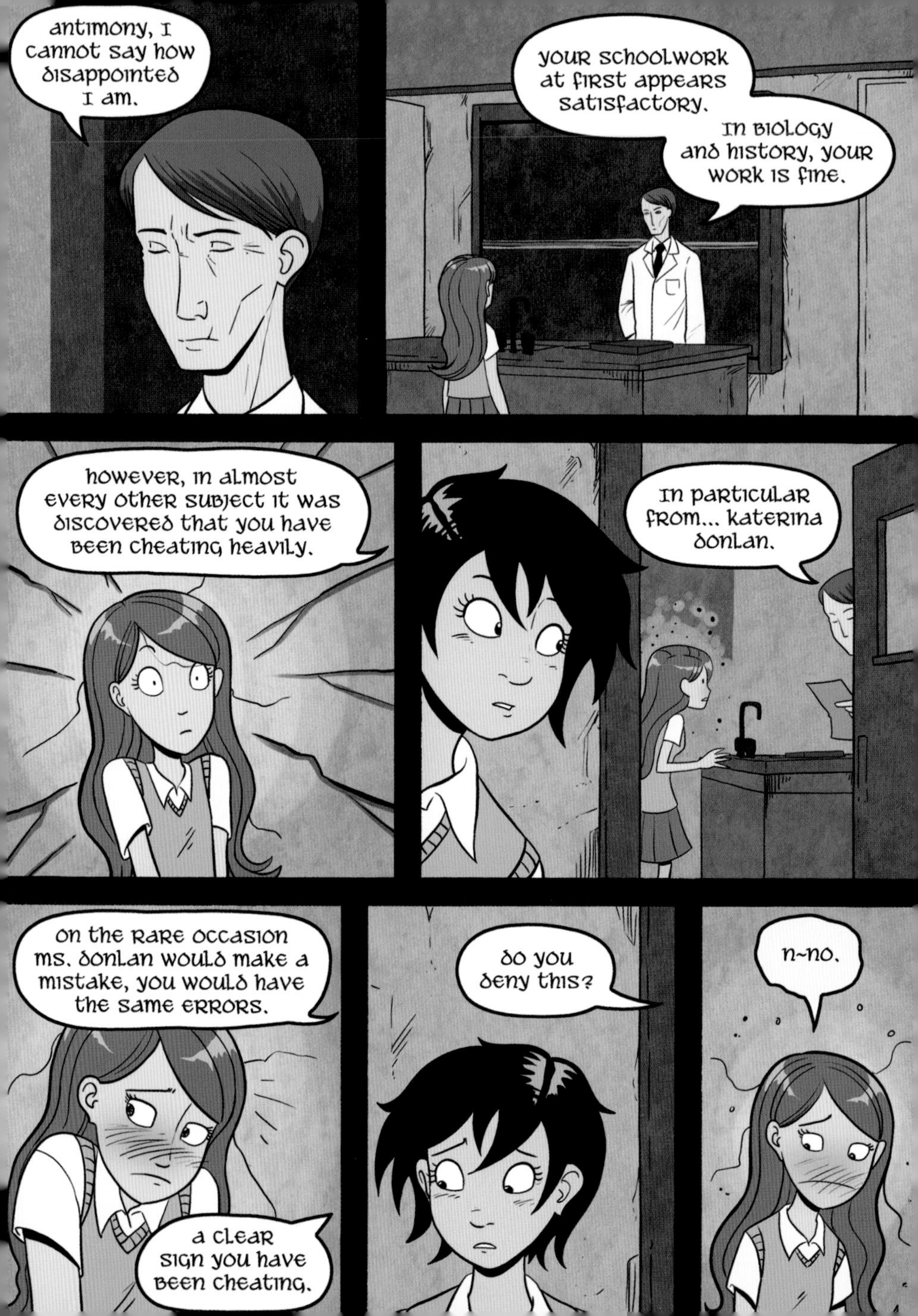
antimony, I cannot say how disappointed I am.
your schoolwork at first appears satisfactory.
In biology and history, your work is fine.
however, in almost every other subject it was discovered that you have been cheating heavily.
In particular from... katerina donlan.
on the rare occasion ms. donlan would make a mistake, you would have the same errors.
a clear sign you have been cheating.
do you deny this?
n-no.

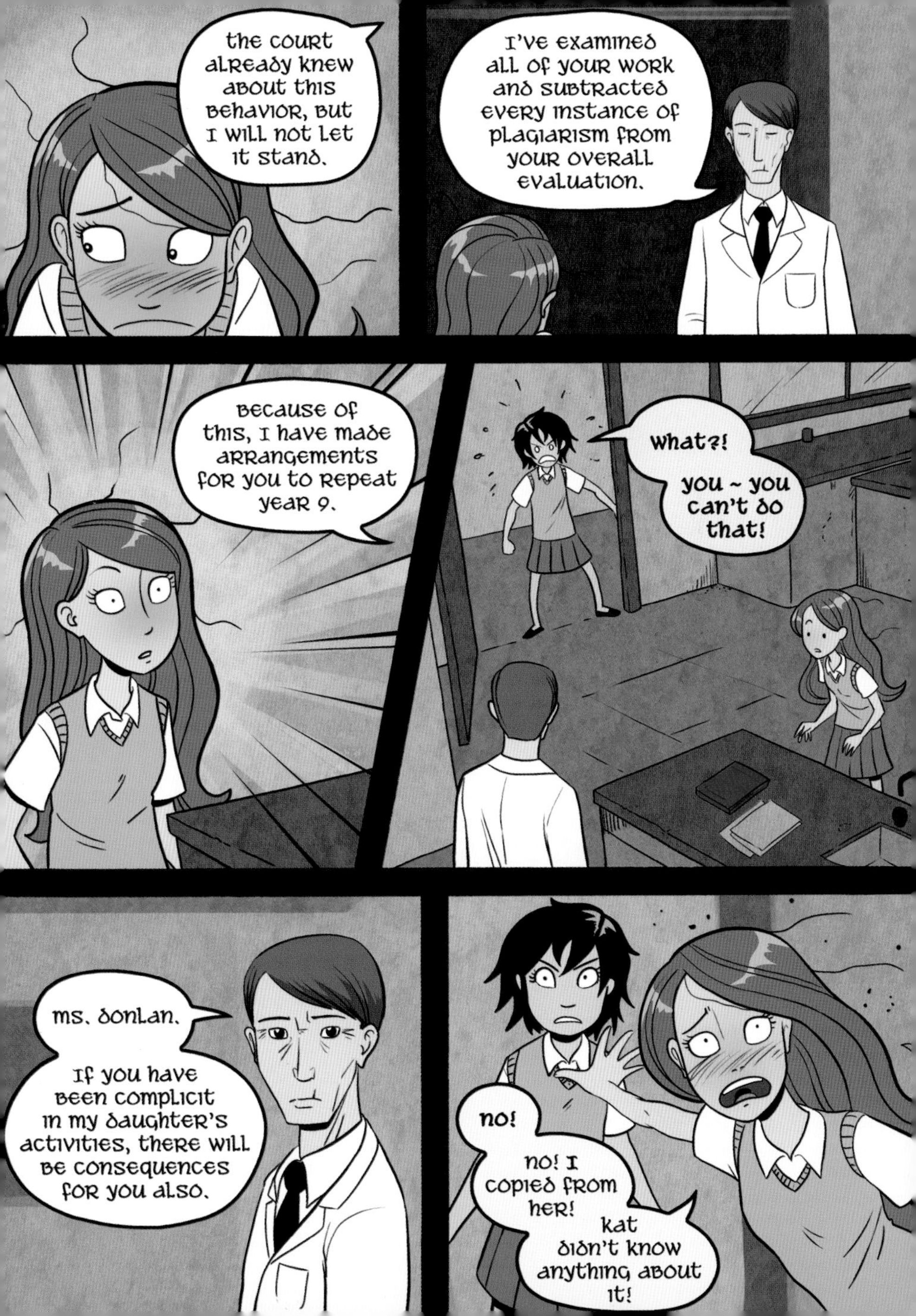
the court already knew about this behavior, but I will not let it stand.
I've examined all of your work and subtracted every instance of plagiarism from your overall evaluation.
Because of this, I have made arrangements for you to repeat year 9.
what?!
you ~ you can't do that!
ms. donlan.
If you have been complicit in my daughter's activities, there will be consequences for you also.
no!
no! I copied from her!
kat didn't know anything about it!

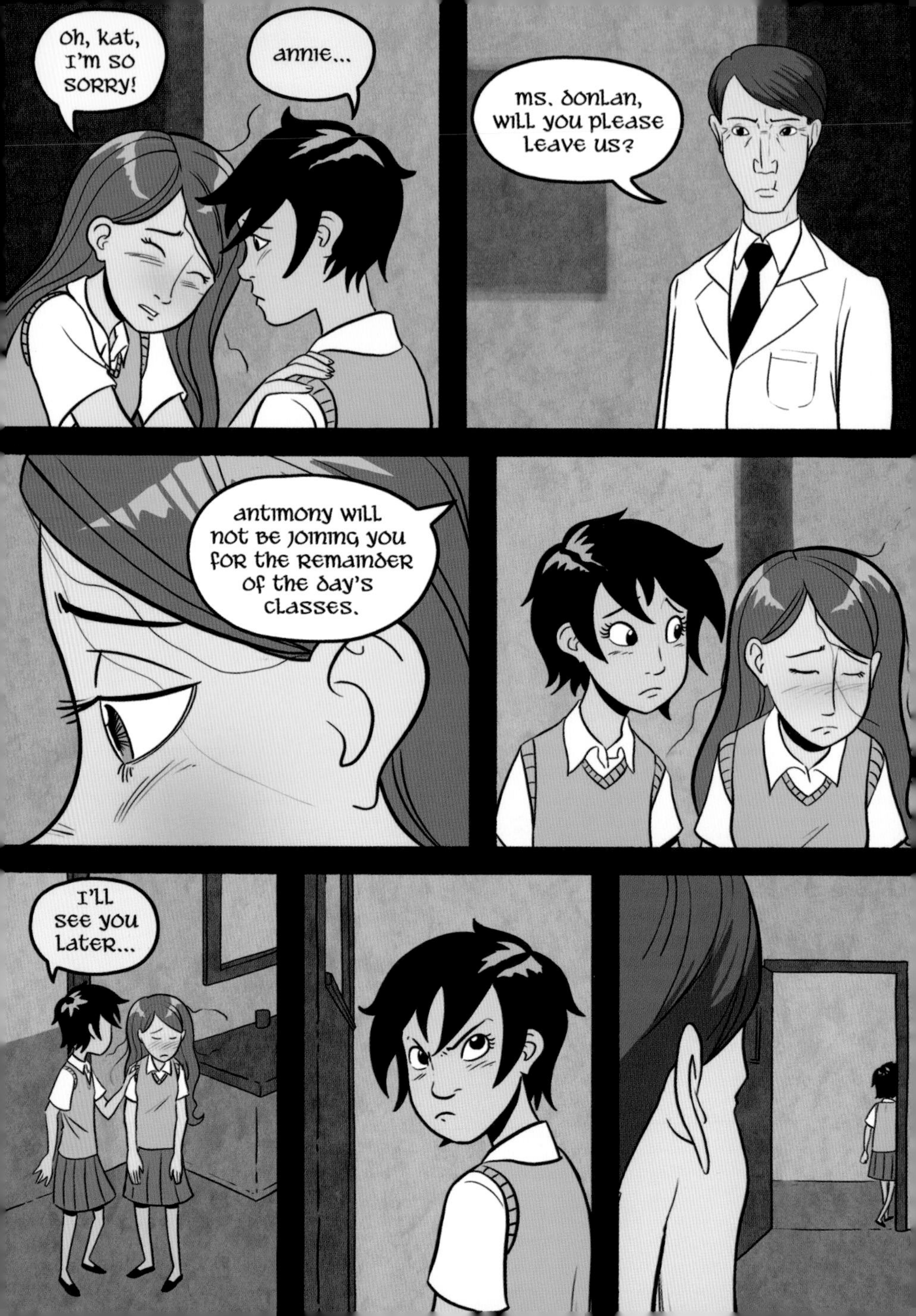
Oh, kat, I'm so sorry!
annie...
ms. donlan, will you please leave us?
antimony will not be joining you for the remainder of the day's classes.
I'll see you later...

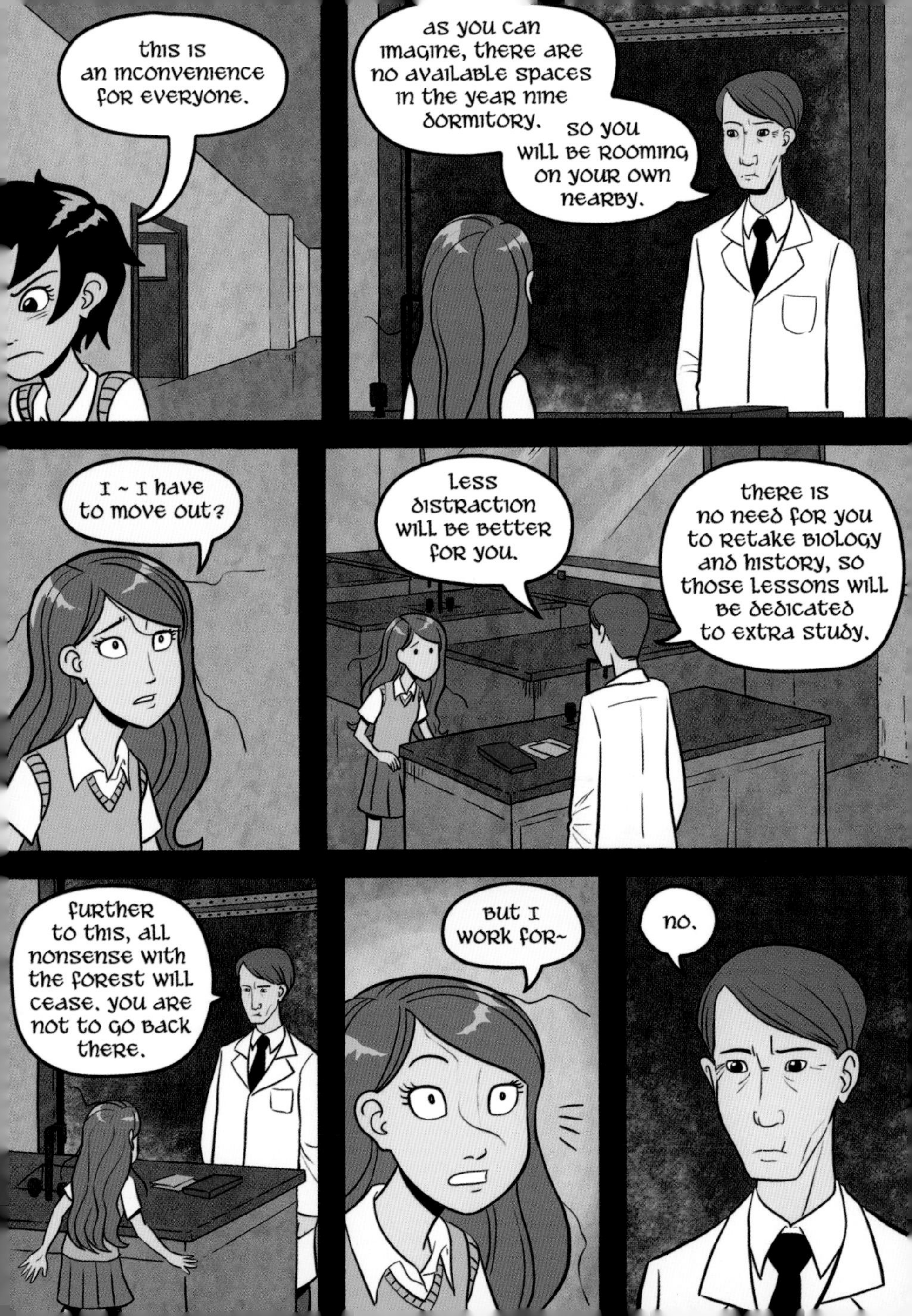
this is an inconvenience for everyone.
as you can imagine, there are no available spaces in the year nine dormitory.
so you will be rooming on your own nearby.
I ~ I have to move out?
less distraction will be better for you.
there is no need for you to retake biology and history, so those lessons will be dedicated to extra study.
further to this, all nonsense with the forest will cease. you are not to go back there.
but I work for~
no.

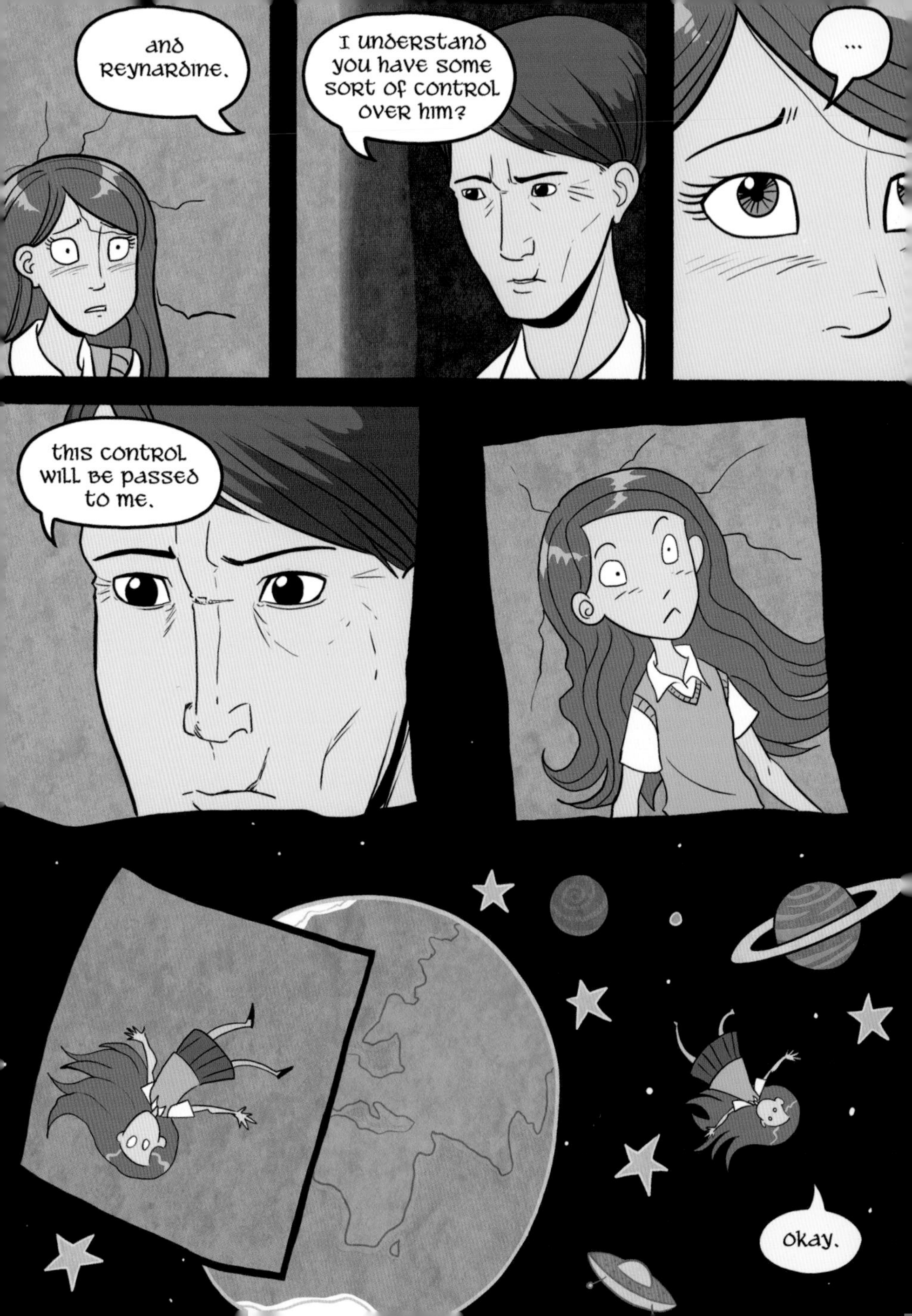
and Reynardine.
I understand you have some sort of control over him?
...
this control will be passed to me.
Okay.

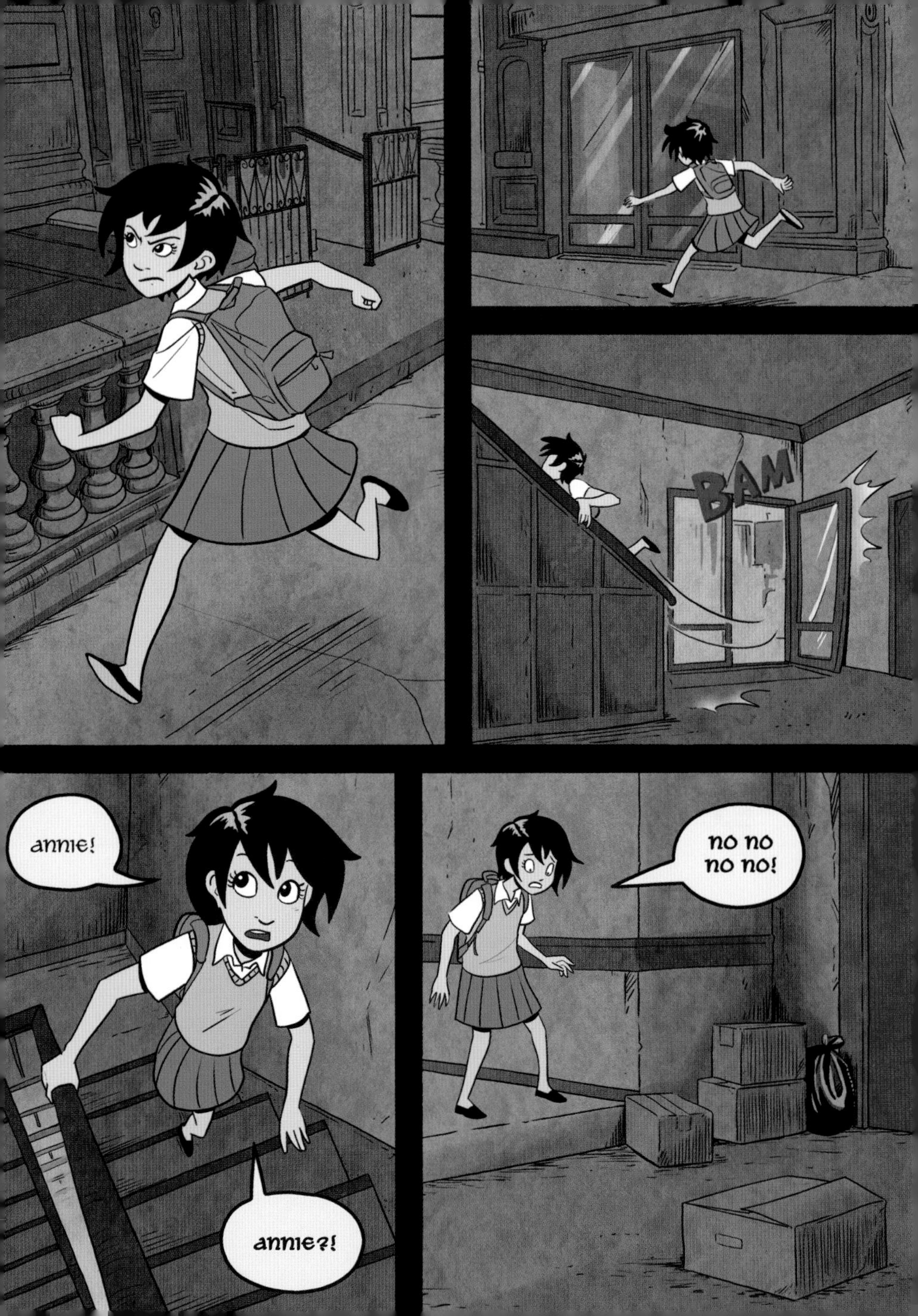
BAM
annie!
annie?!
no no no no!

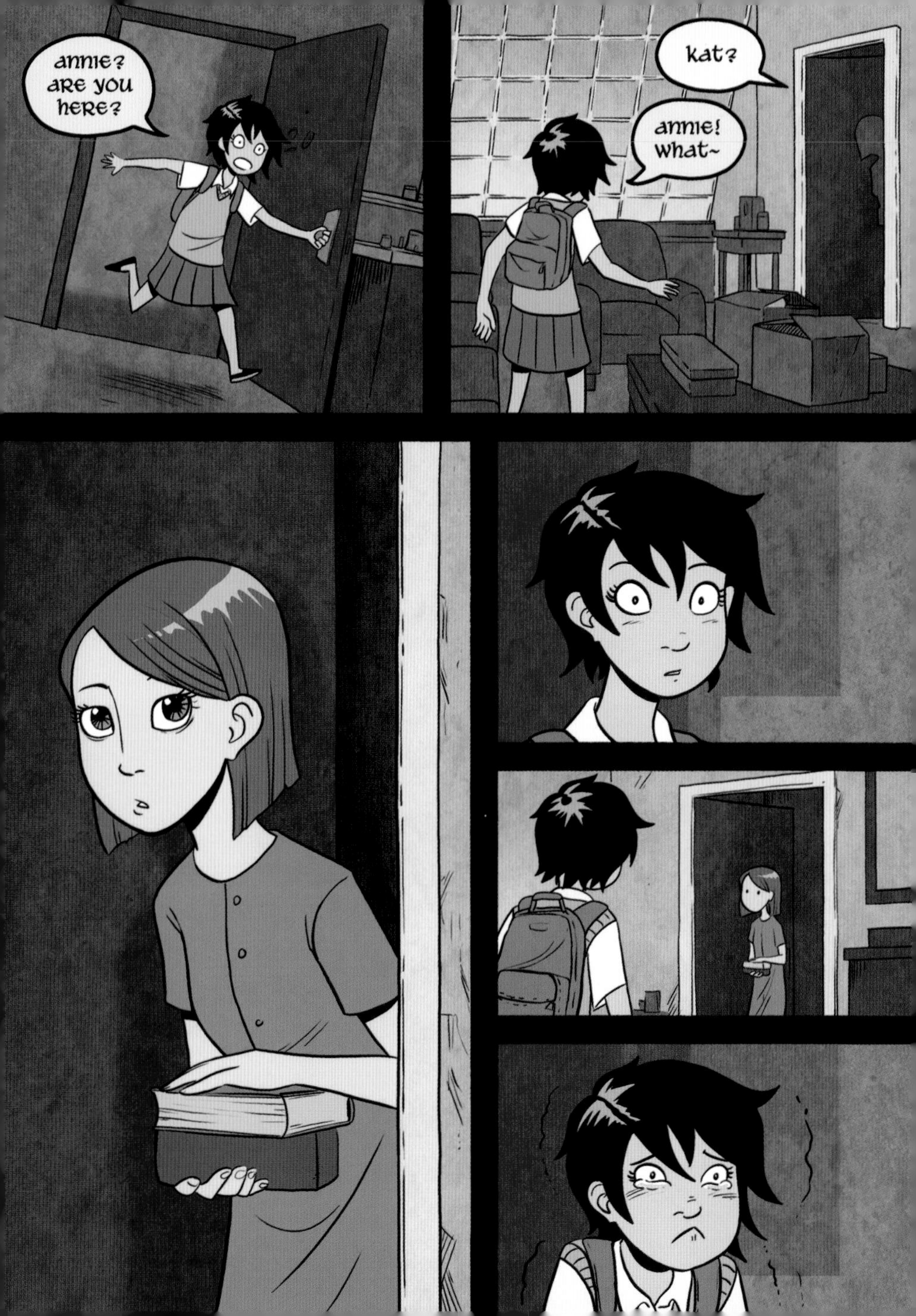
annie? are you here?
kat?
annie! what~

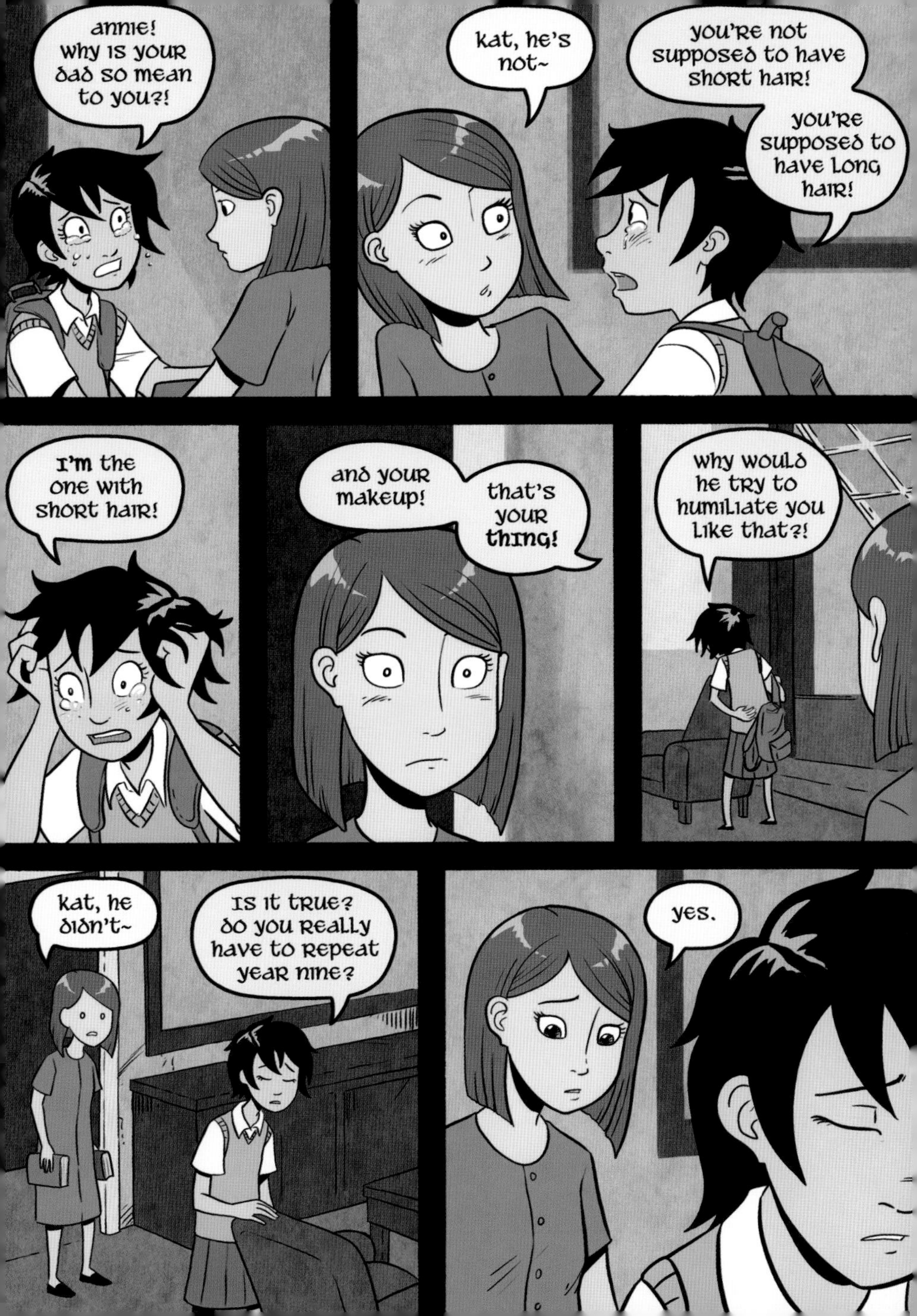
annie! why is your dad so mean to you?!
kat, he's not~
you're not supposed to have short hair!
you're supposed to have long hair!
I'm the one with short hair!
and your makeup!
that's your thing!
why would he try to humiliate you like that?!
kat, he didn't~
is it true? do you really have to repeat year nine?
yes.

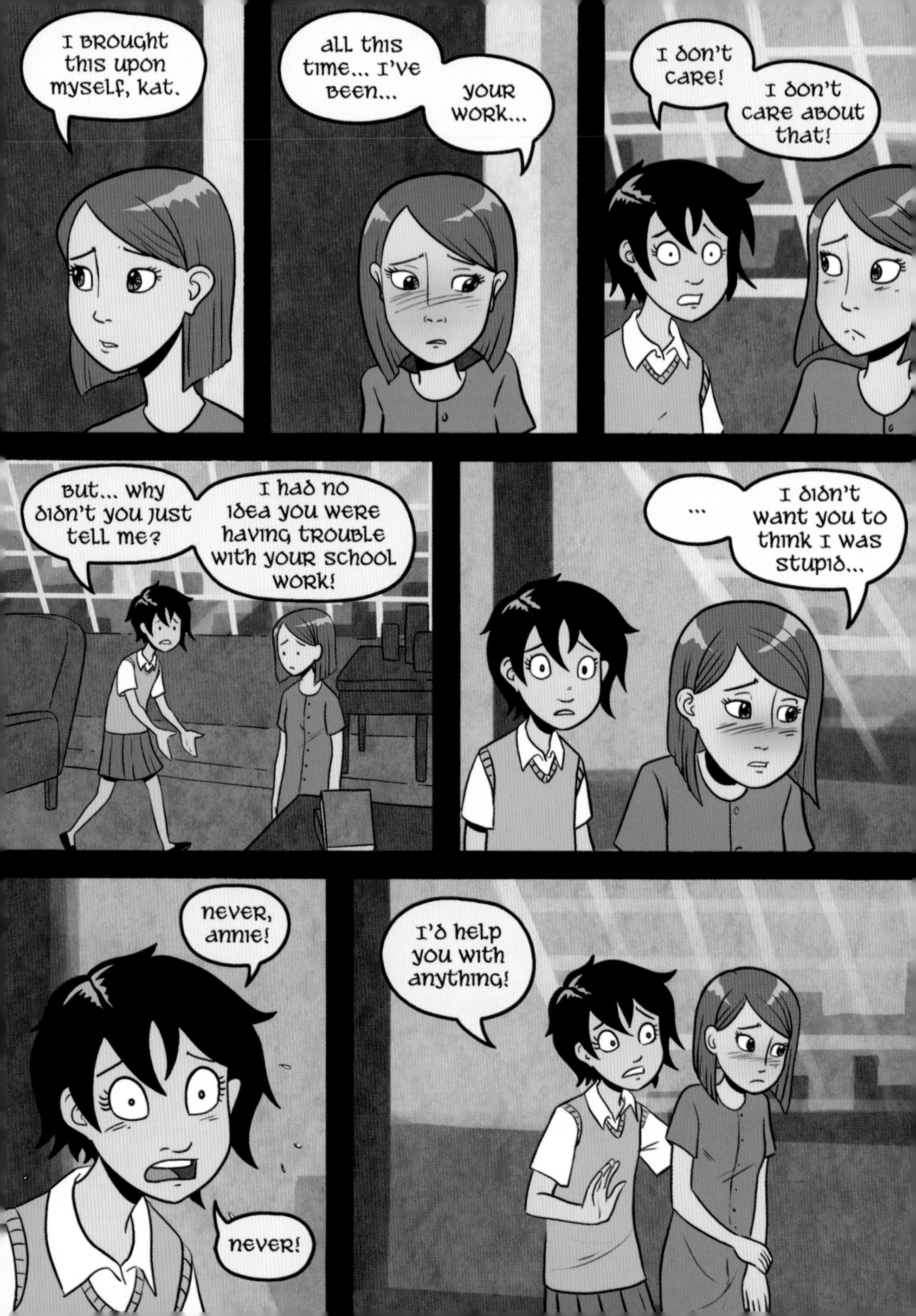
I BROUGHT this upon myself, kat.
all this time... I've been...
your work...
I don't care!
I don't care about that!
But... why didn't you just tell me?
I had no idea you were having trouble with your school work!
...
I didn't want you to think I was stupid...
never, annie!
never!
I'd help you with anything!

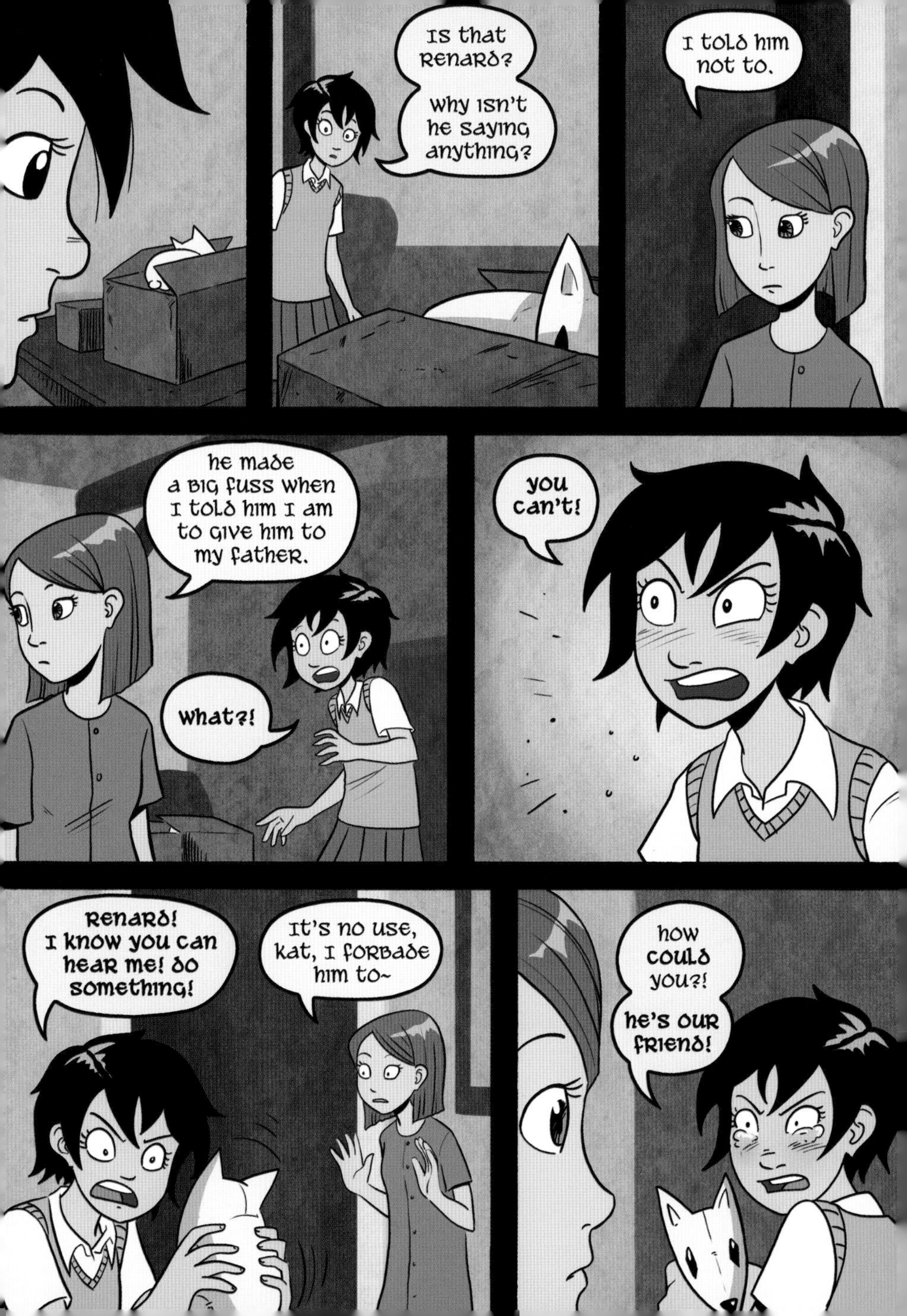

Is that Renard?
Why isn't he saying anything?
I told him not to.
He made a big fuss when I told him I am to give him to my father.
What?!
You can't!
Renard! I know you can hear me! Do something!
It's no use, Kat, I forbade him to~
How could you?!
He's our friend!

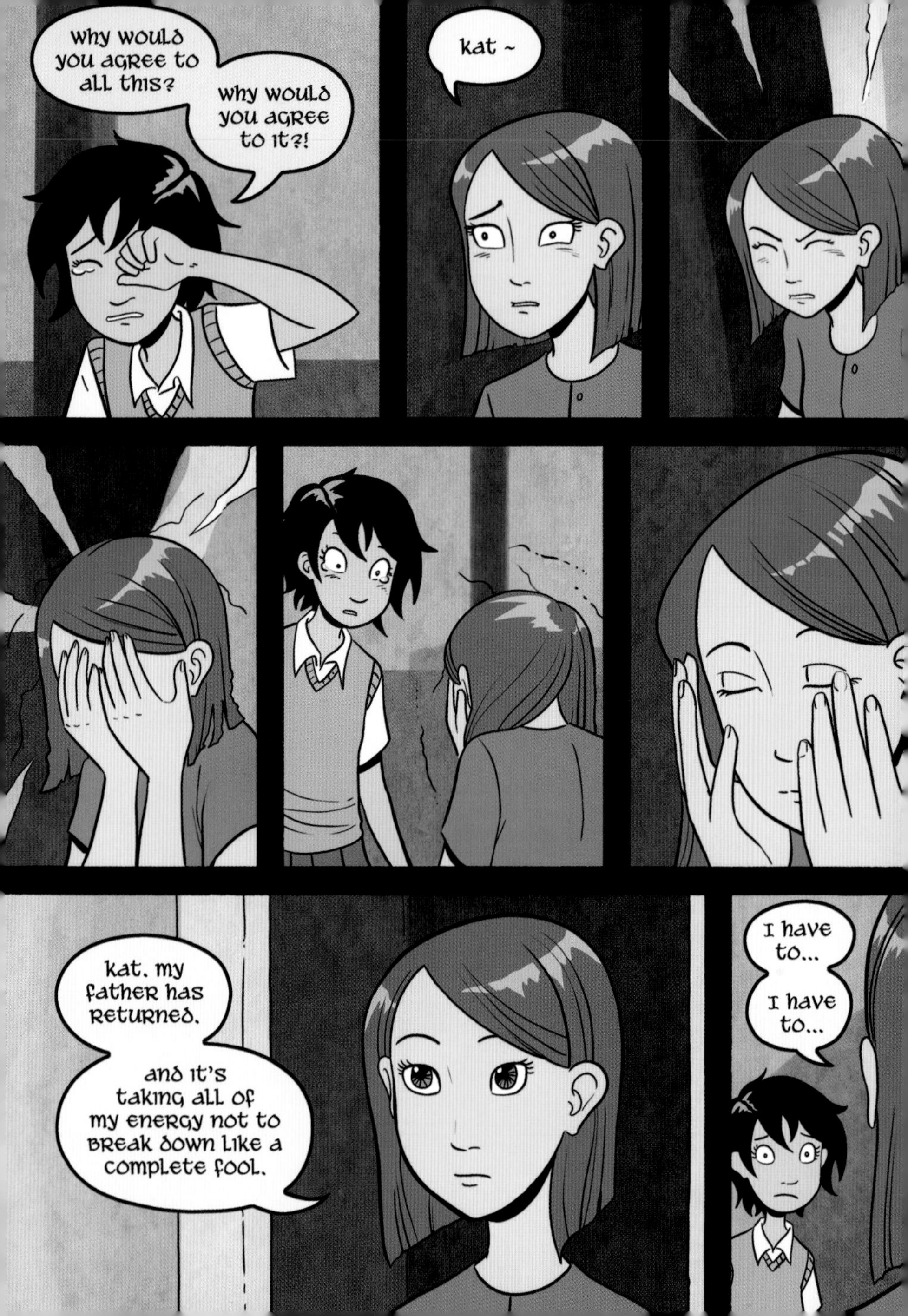
why would you agree to all this?
why would you agree to it?!
kat ~
kat. my father has returned.
and it's taking all of my energy not to break down like a complete fool.
I have to...
I have to...

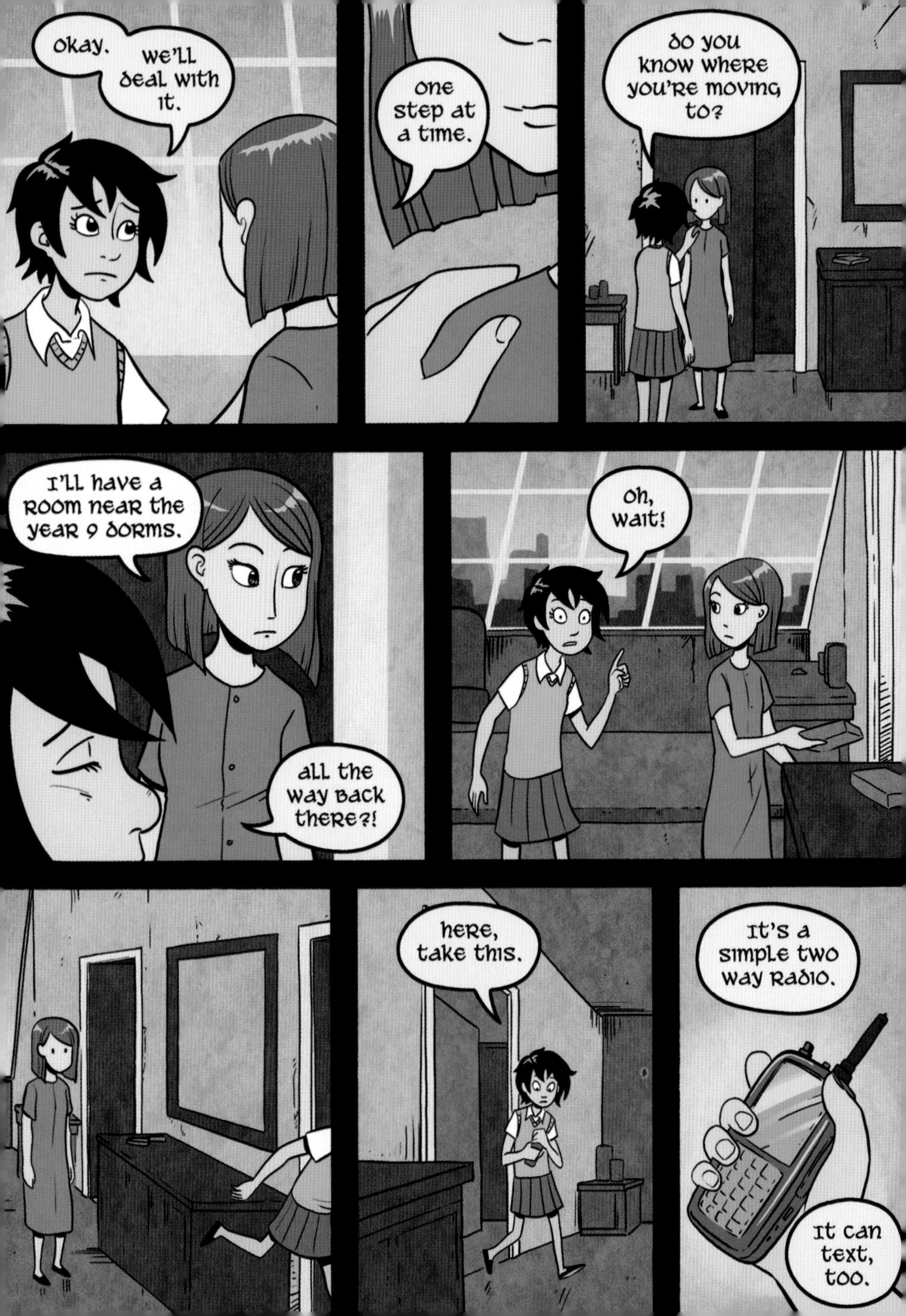

Okay.
We'll deal with it.
One step at a time.
Do you know where you're moving to?
I'll have a room near the year 9 dorms.
All the way back there?!
Oh, wait!
Here, take this.
It's a simple two way radio.
It can text, too.

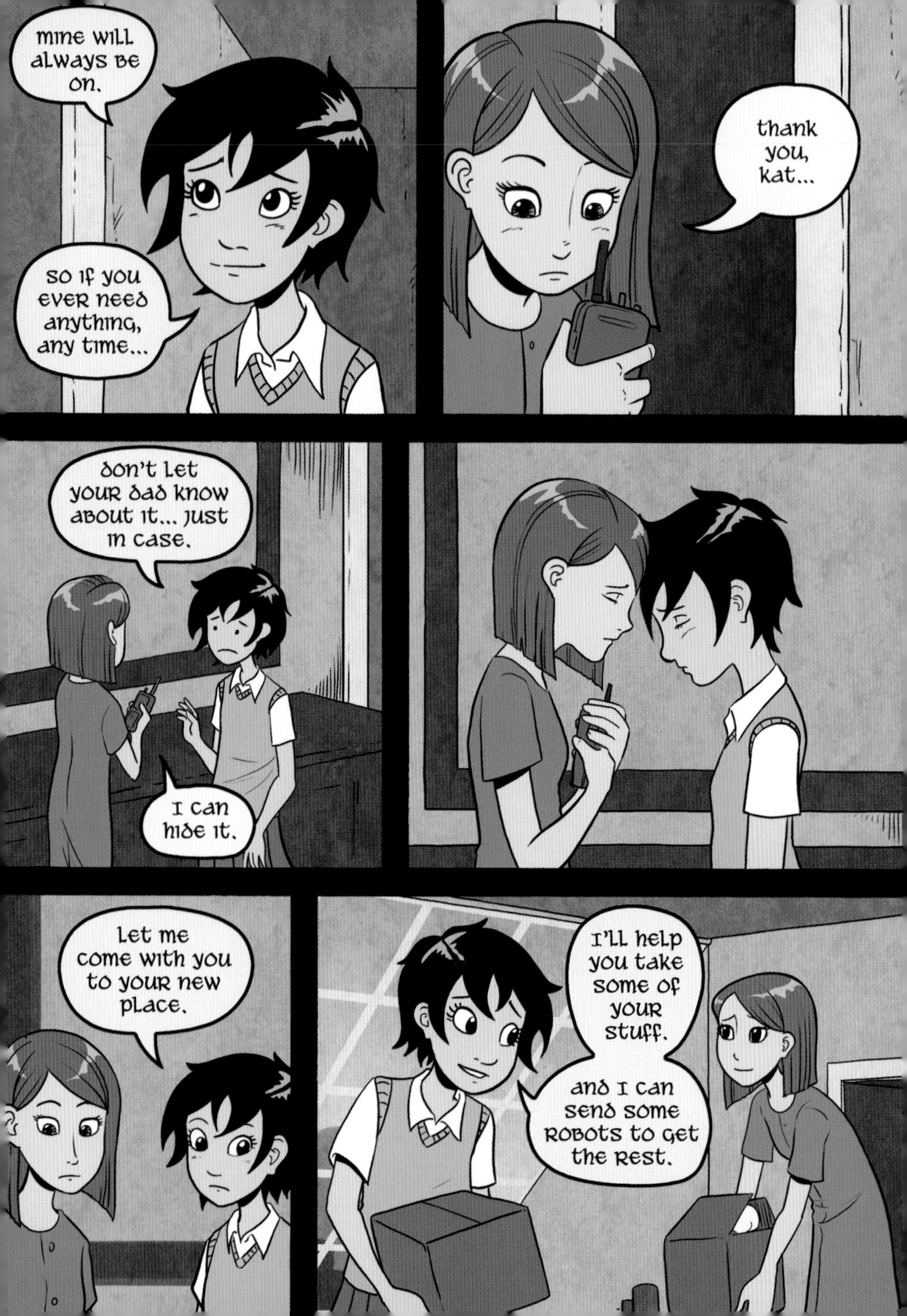
mine will always be on.
so if you ever need anything, any time...
thank you, kat...
don't let your dad know about it... just in case.
I can hide it.
Let me come with you to your new place.
I'll help you take some of your stuff.
and I can send some robots to get the rest.

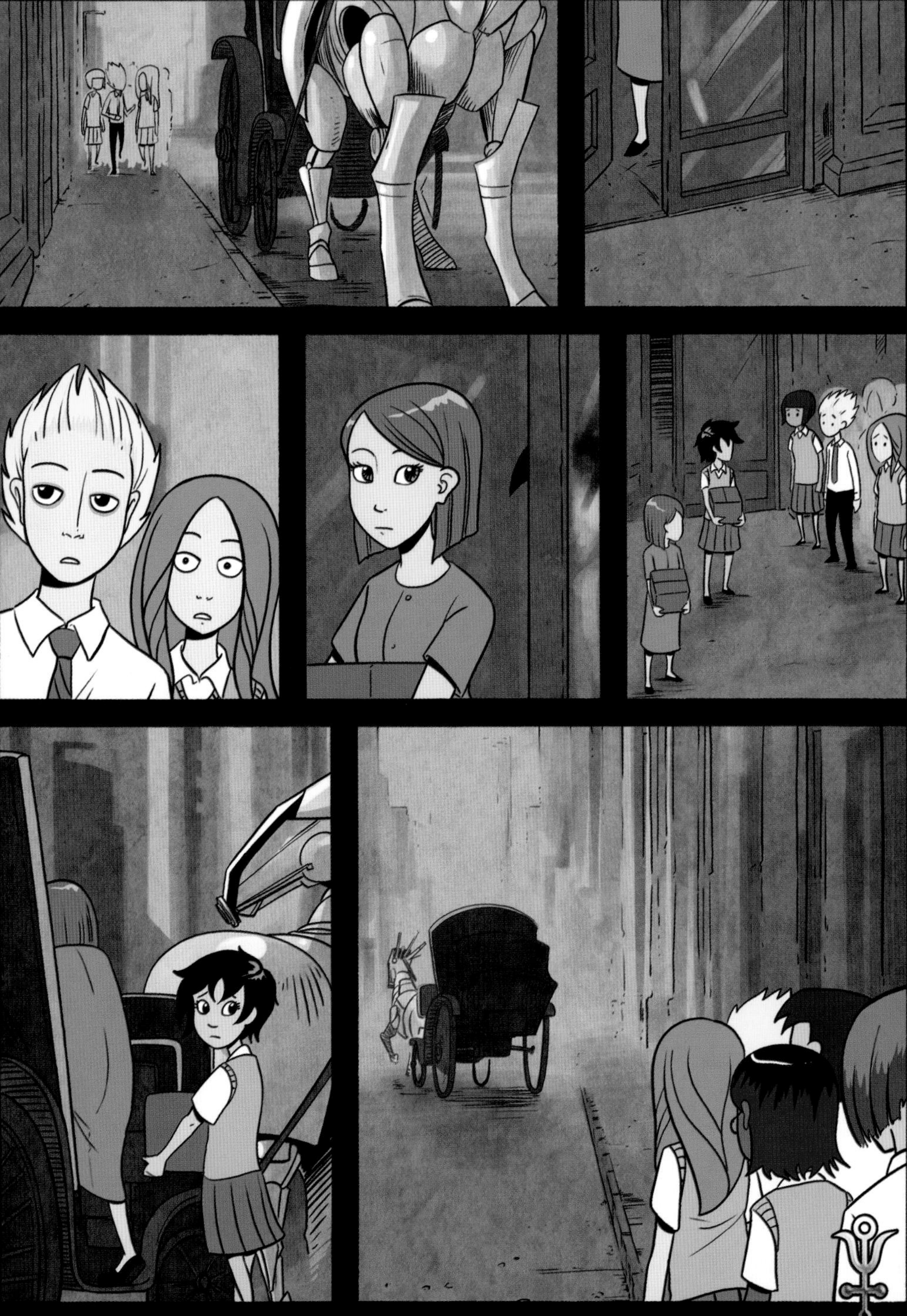

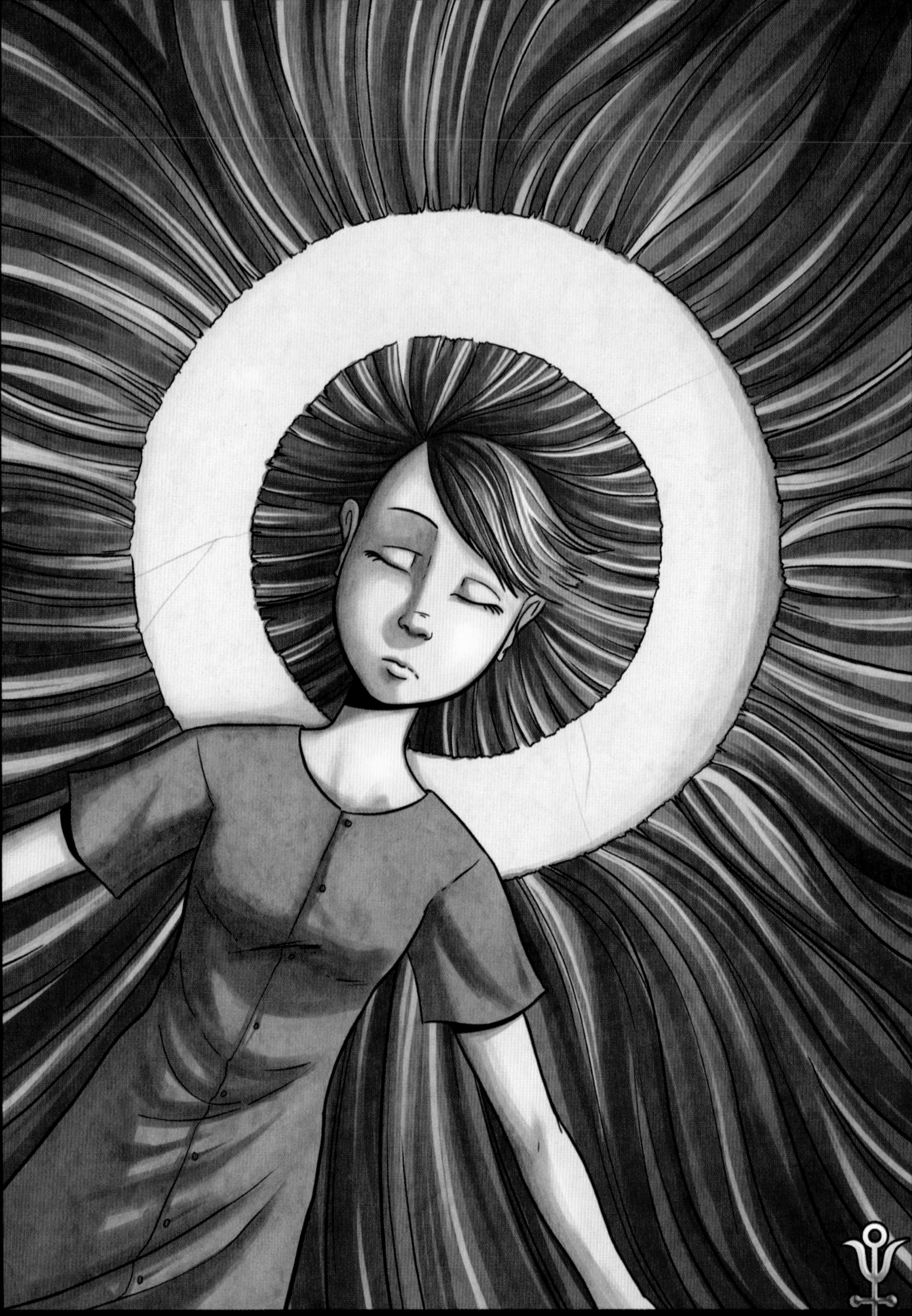

Gunnerkrigg Court

Chapter 52:

Sneak

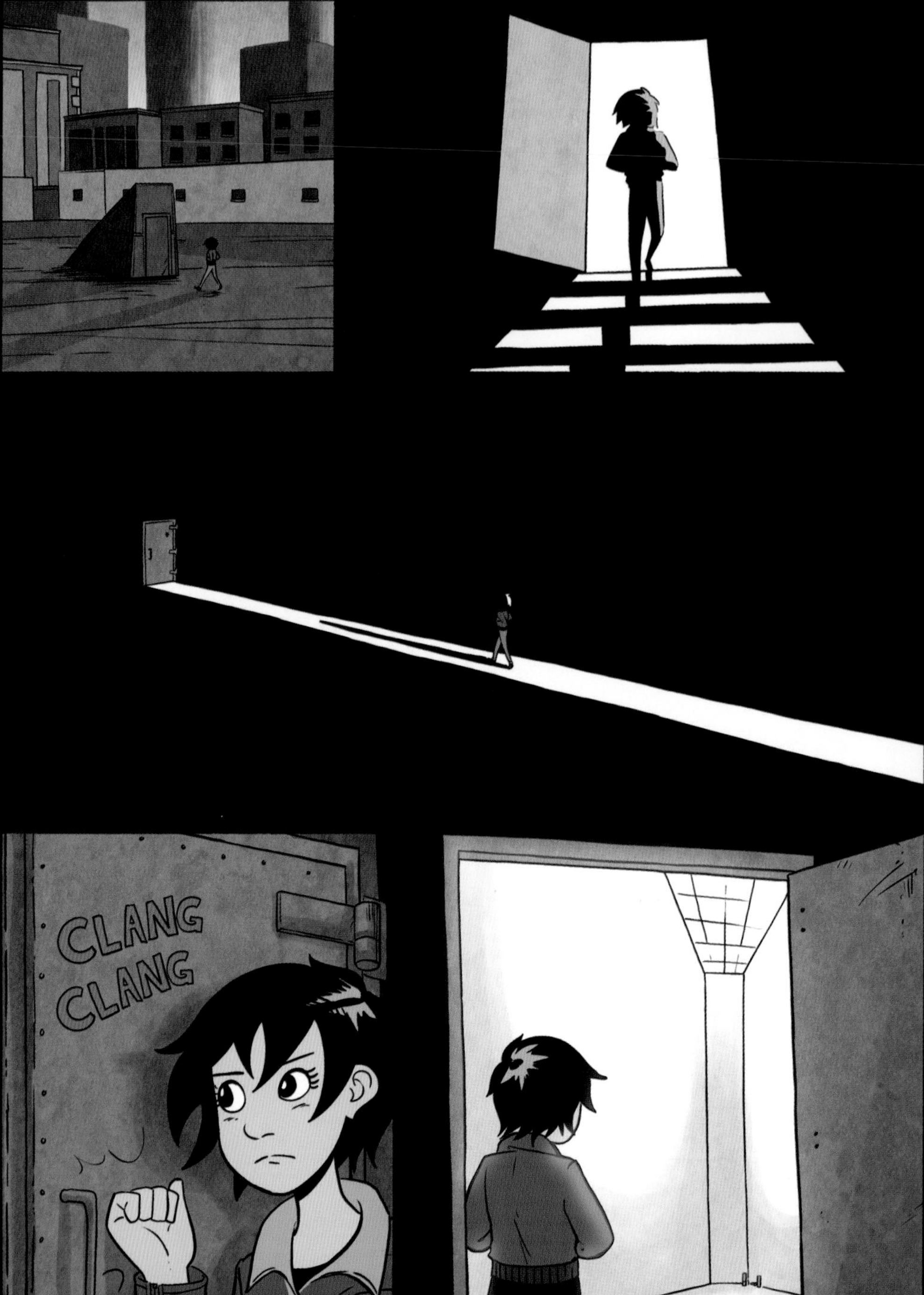
CLANG
CLANG

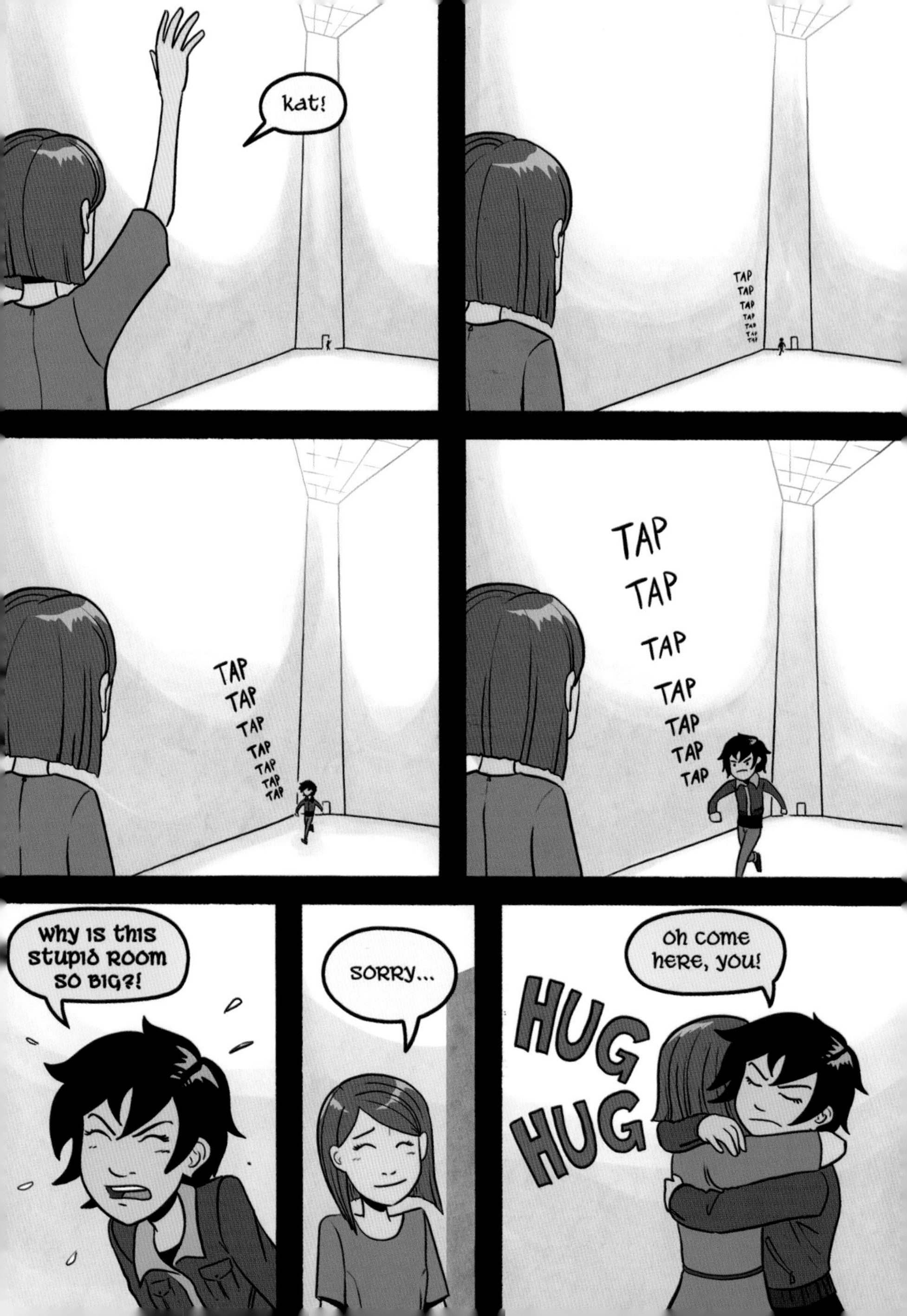
kat!
TAP TAP TAP TAP TAP TAP TAP
TAP TAP TAP TAP TAP TAP TAP
TAP TAP TAP TAP TAP TAP TAP
Why is this stupid room so big?!
SORRY...
Oh come here, you!
HUG HUG

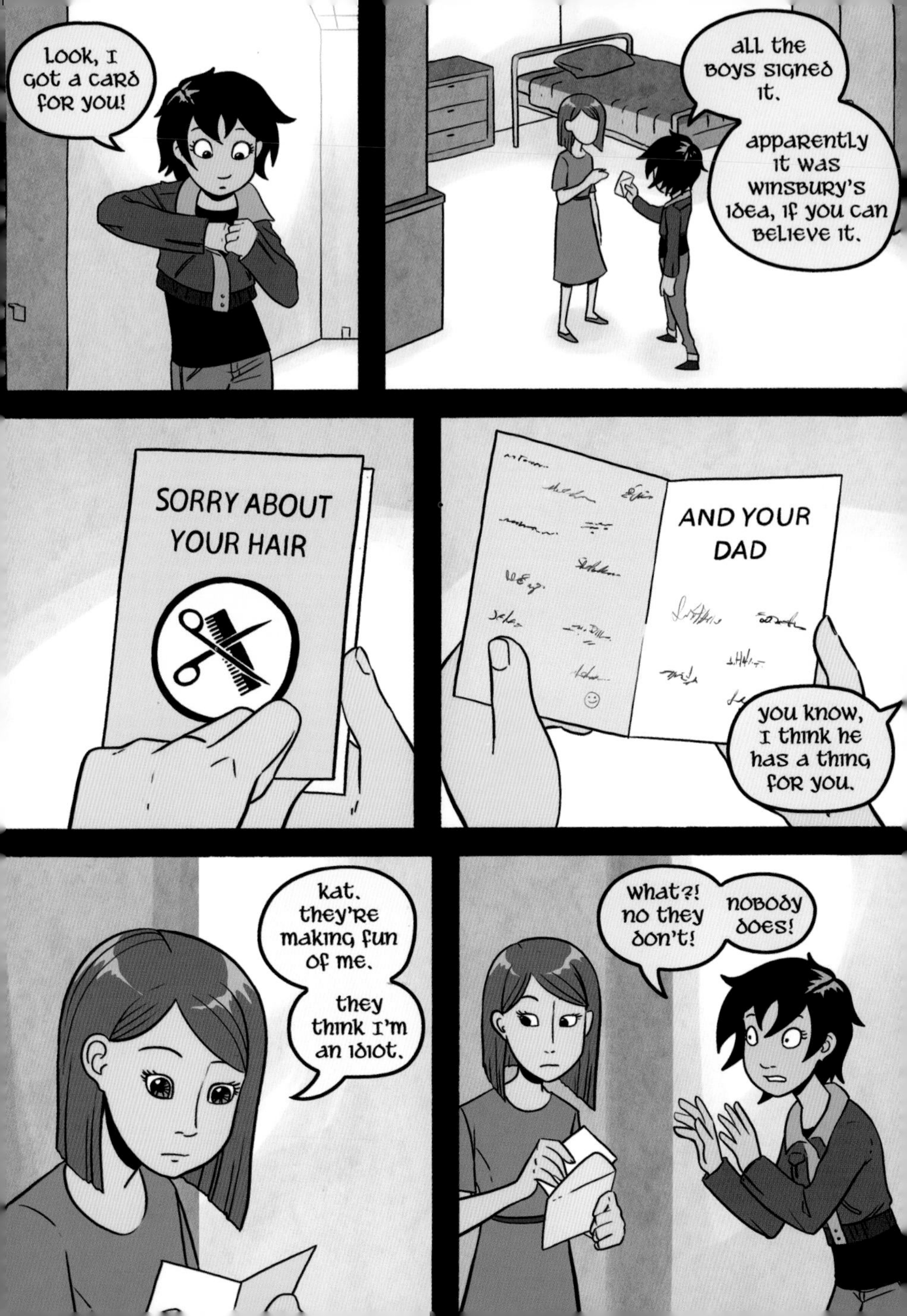

look, I got a card for you!
all the boys signed it.
apparently it was Winsbury's idea, if you can believe it.
SORRY ABOUT YOUR HAIR
AND YOUR DAD
you know, I think he has a thing for you.
kat. they're making fun of me.
they think I'm an idiot.
what?! no they don't!
nobody does!

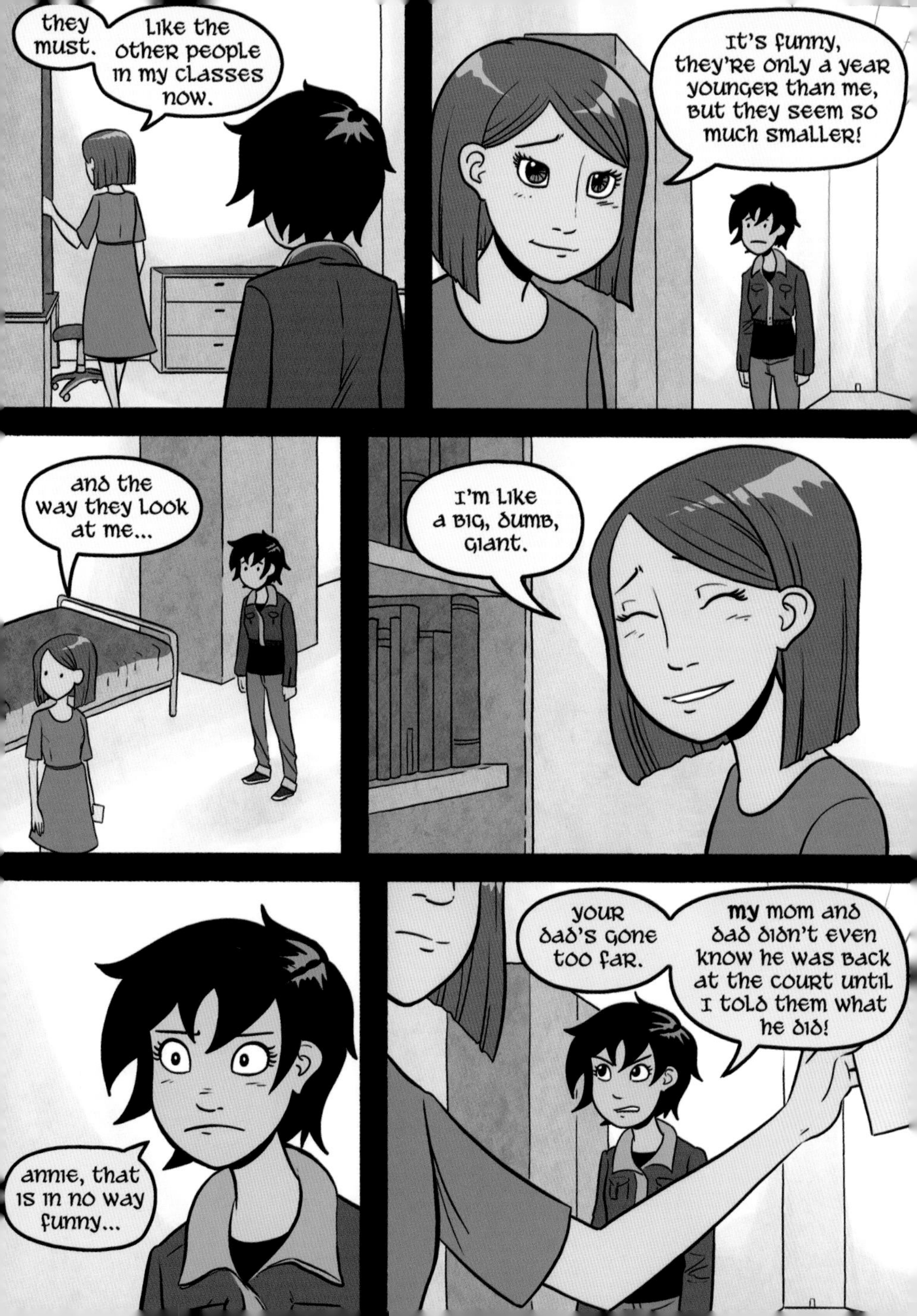
they must.
Like the other people in my classes now.
It's funny, they're only a year younger than me, but they seem so much smaller!
and the way they look at me...
I'm like a big, dumb, giant.
annie, that is in no way funny...
your dad's gone too far.
my mom and dad didn't even know he was back at the court until I told them what he did!

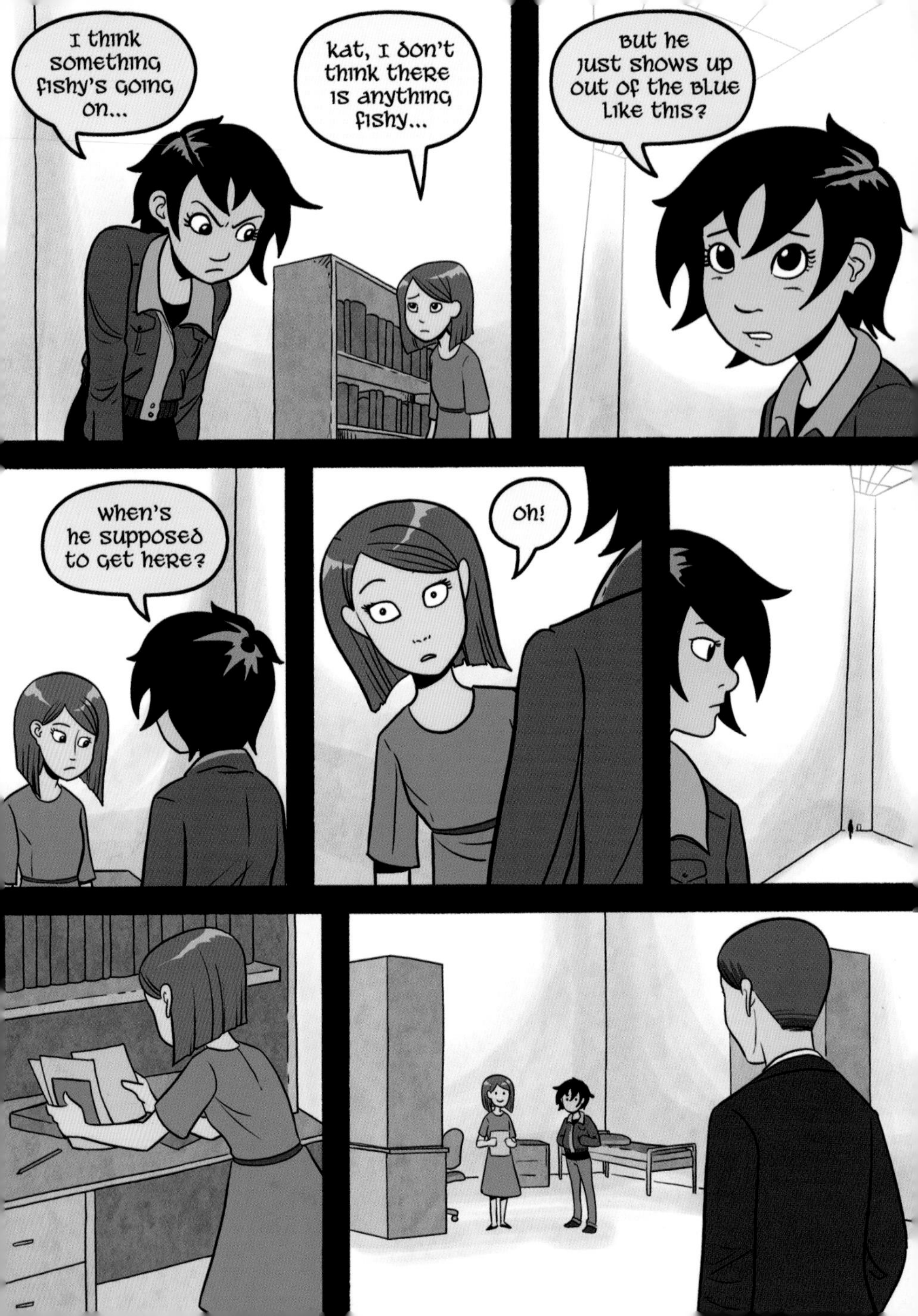
I think something fishy's going on...
Kat, I don't think there is anything fishy...
But he just shows up out of the blue like this?
When's he supposed to get here?
Oh!

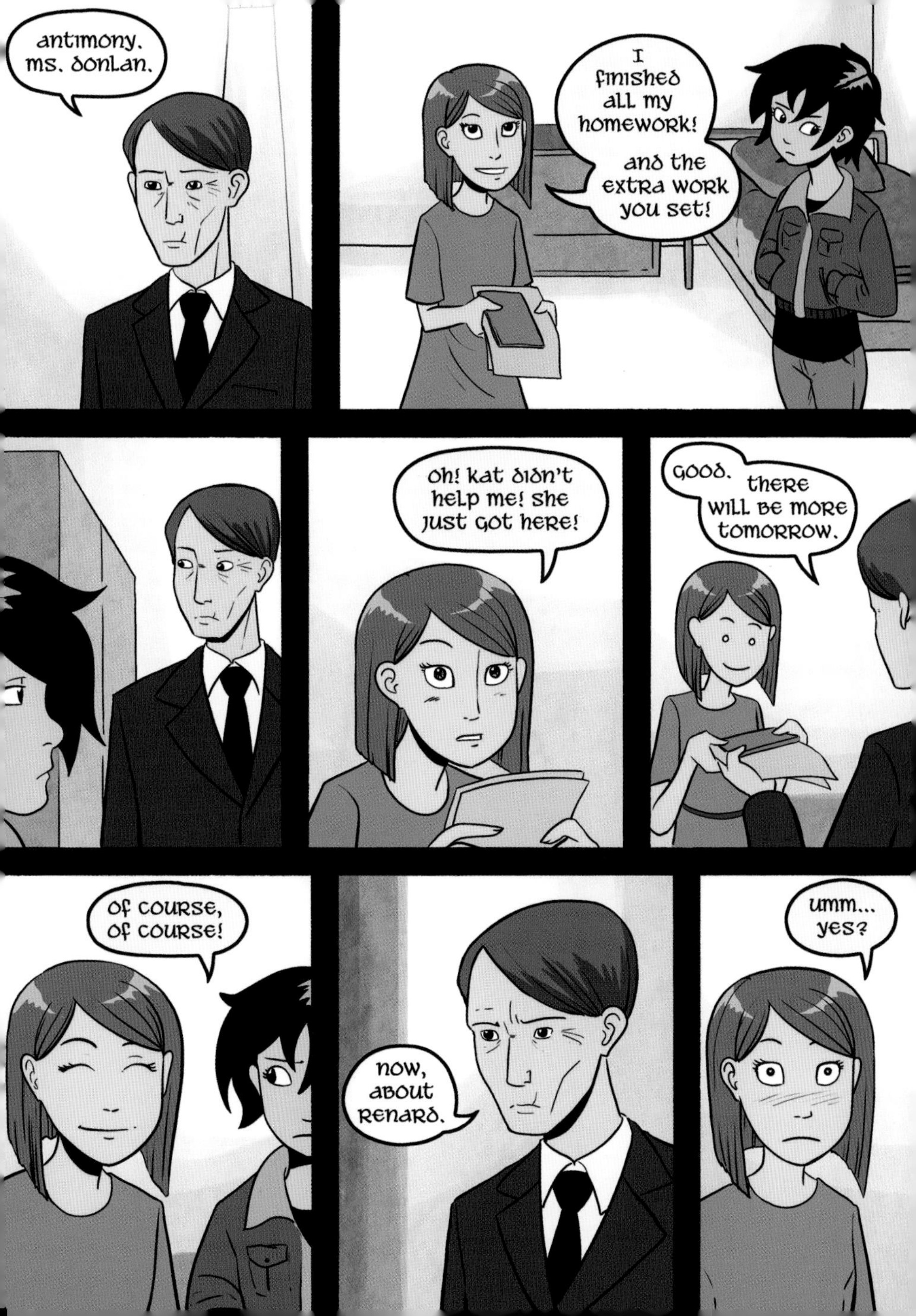
antimony. ms. donlan.
I finished all my homework!
and the extra work you set!
oh! kat didn't help me! she just got here!
good.
there will be more tomorrow.
of course, of course!
now, about renard.
umm... yes?

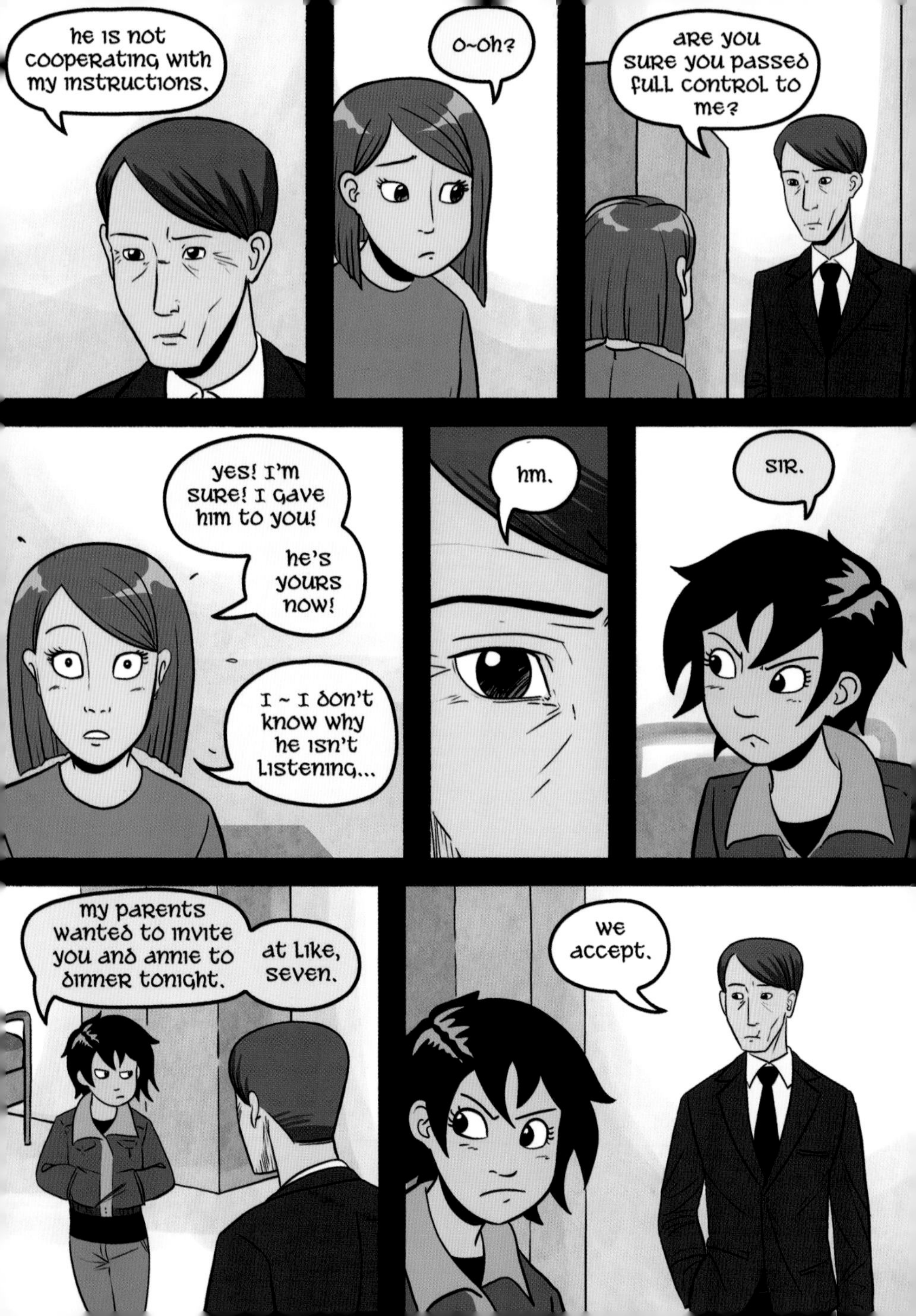
he is not cooperating with my instructions.
o-oh?
are you sure you passed full control to me?
yes! I'm sure! I gave him to you!
he's yours now!
I ~ I don't know why he isn't listening...
hm.
sir.
my parents wanted to invite you and annie to dinner tonight.
at like, seven.
we accept.

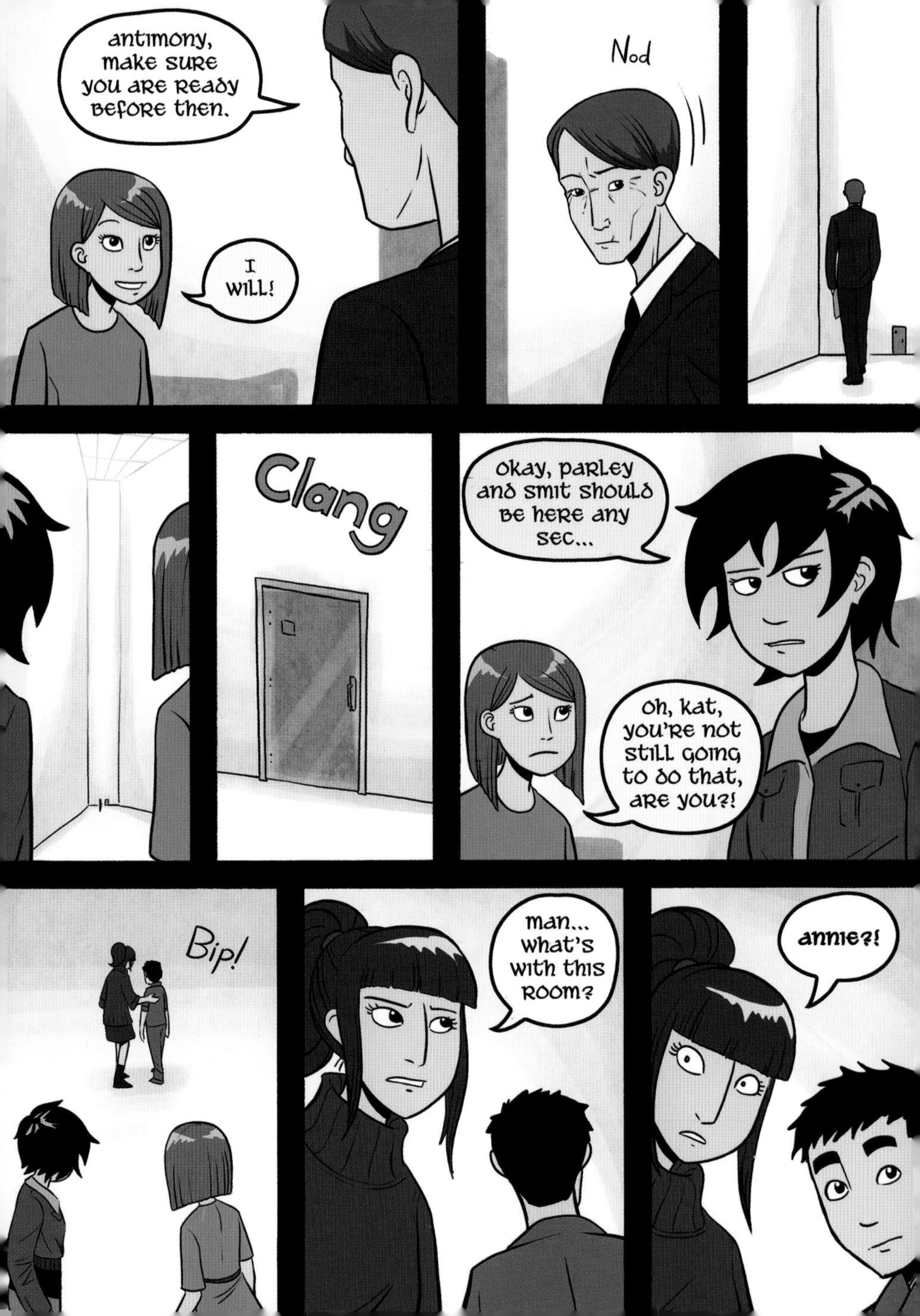
antimony, make sure you are ready before then.
I will!
Nod
Clang
Okay, parley and smit should be here any sec...
Oh, kat, you're not still going to do that, are you?!
Bip!
man... what's with this room?
annie?!

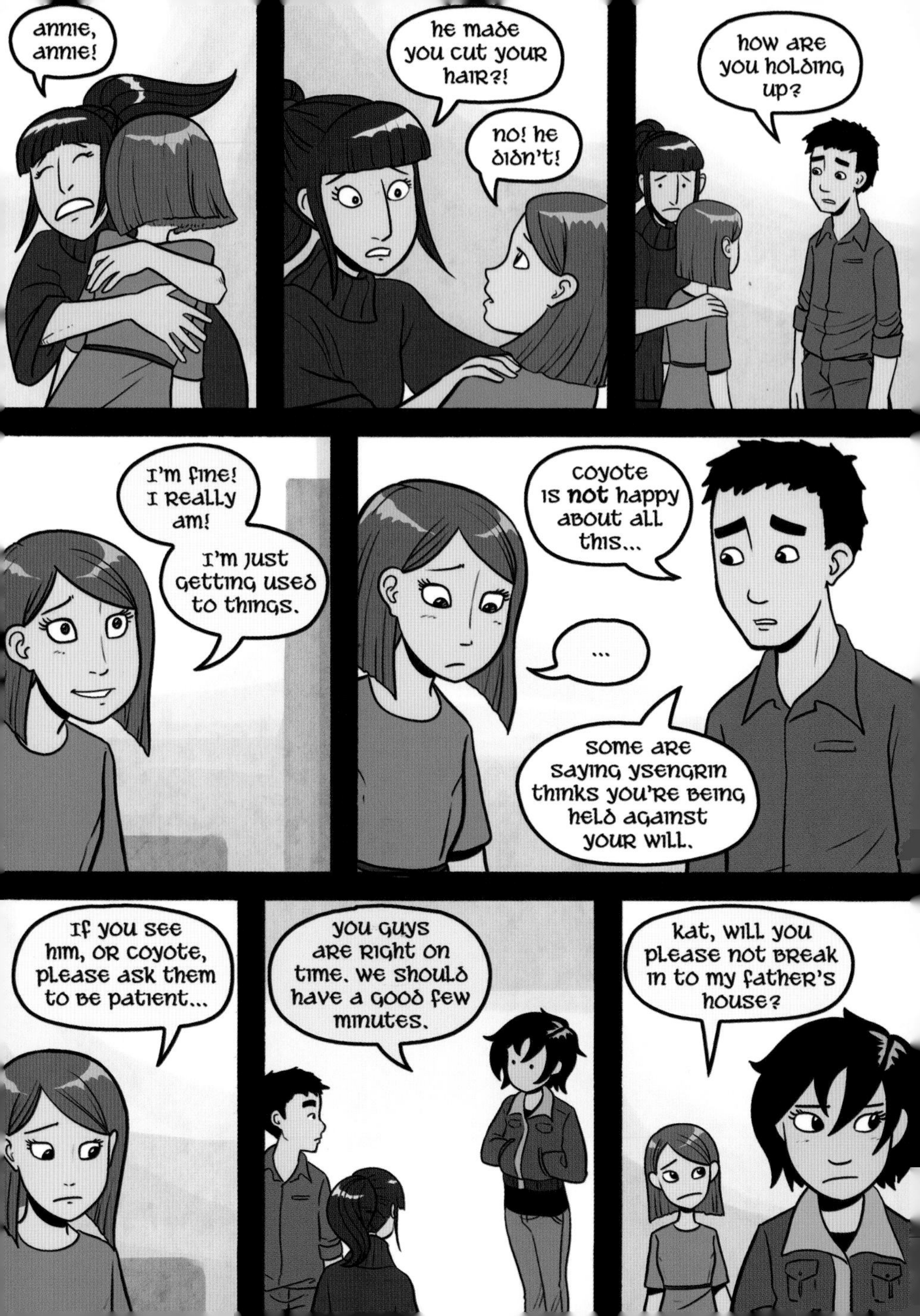
annie, annie!
he made you cut your hair?!
no! he didn't!
how are you holding up?
I'm fine! I really am!
I'm just getting used to things.
coyote is **not** happy about all this...
...
some are saying ysengrin thinks you're being held against your will.
If you see him, or coyote, please ask them to be patient...
you guys are right on time. we should have a good few minutes.
kat, will you please not break in to my father's house?

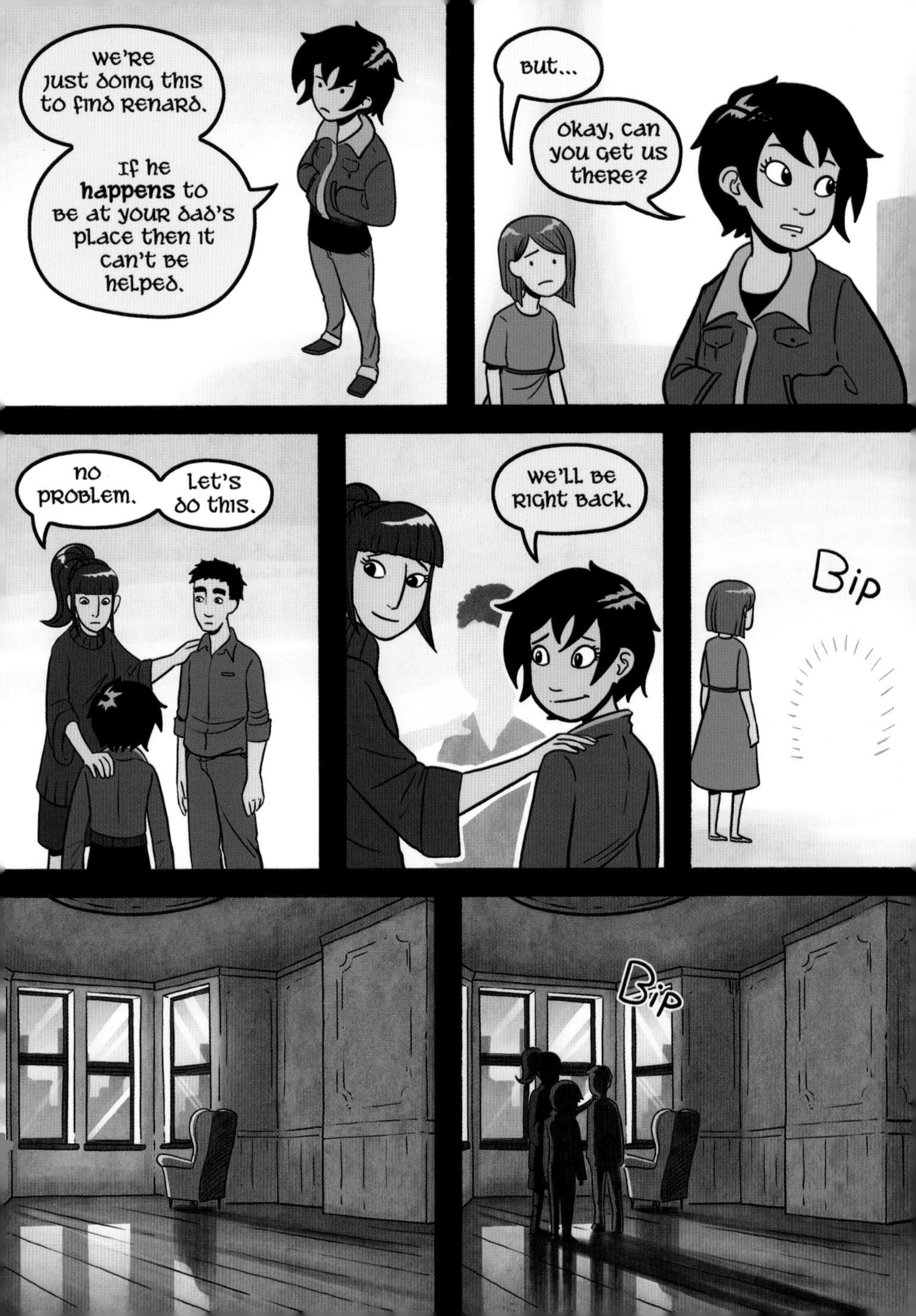
We're just doing this to find Renard.
If he **happens** to be at your dad's place then it can't be helped.
But...
Okay, can you get us there?
No problem.
Let's do this.
We'll be right back.
Bip
Bip

HERE!

REY, ARE YOU OKAY?

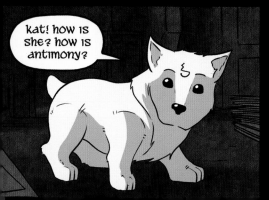

KAT! HOW IS SHE? HOW IS ANTIMONY?

SHE'S A MESS. IT'S LIKE SHE'S BARELY HOLDING IT TOGETHER.

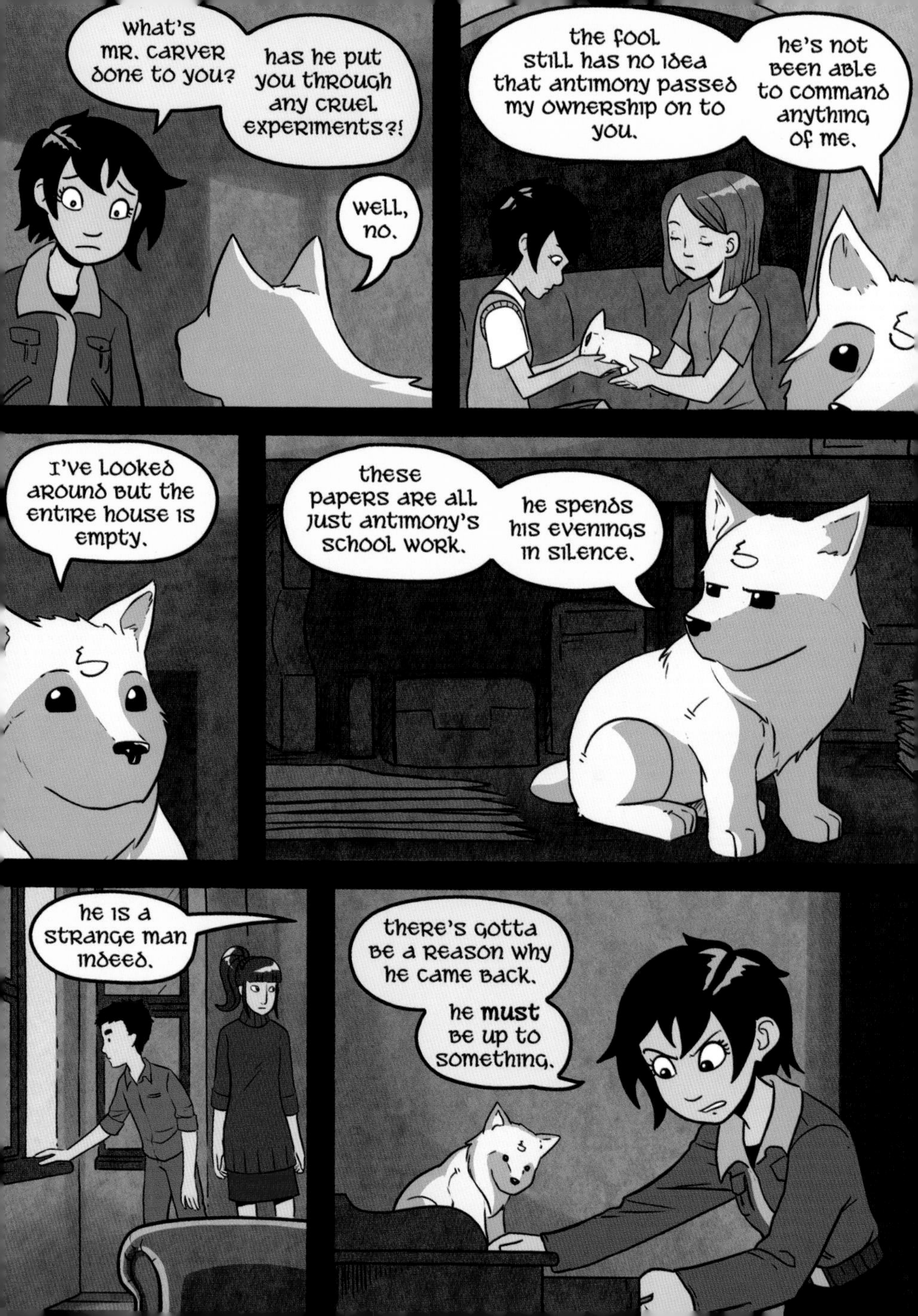
What's mr. carver done to you?
has he put you through any cruel experiments?!
well, no.
the fool still has no idea that antimony passed my ownership on to you.
he's not been able to command anything of me.
I've looked around but the entire house is empty.
these papers are all just antimony's school work.
he spends his evenings in silence.
he is a strange man indeed.
there's gotta be a reason why he came back.
he **must** be up to something.

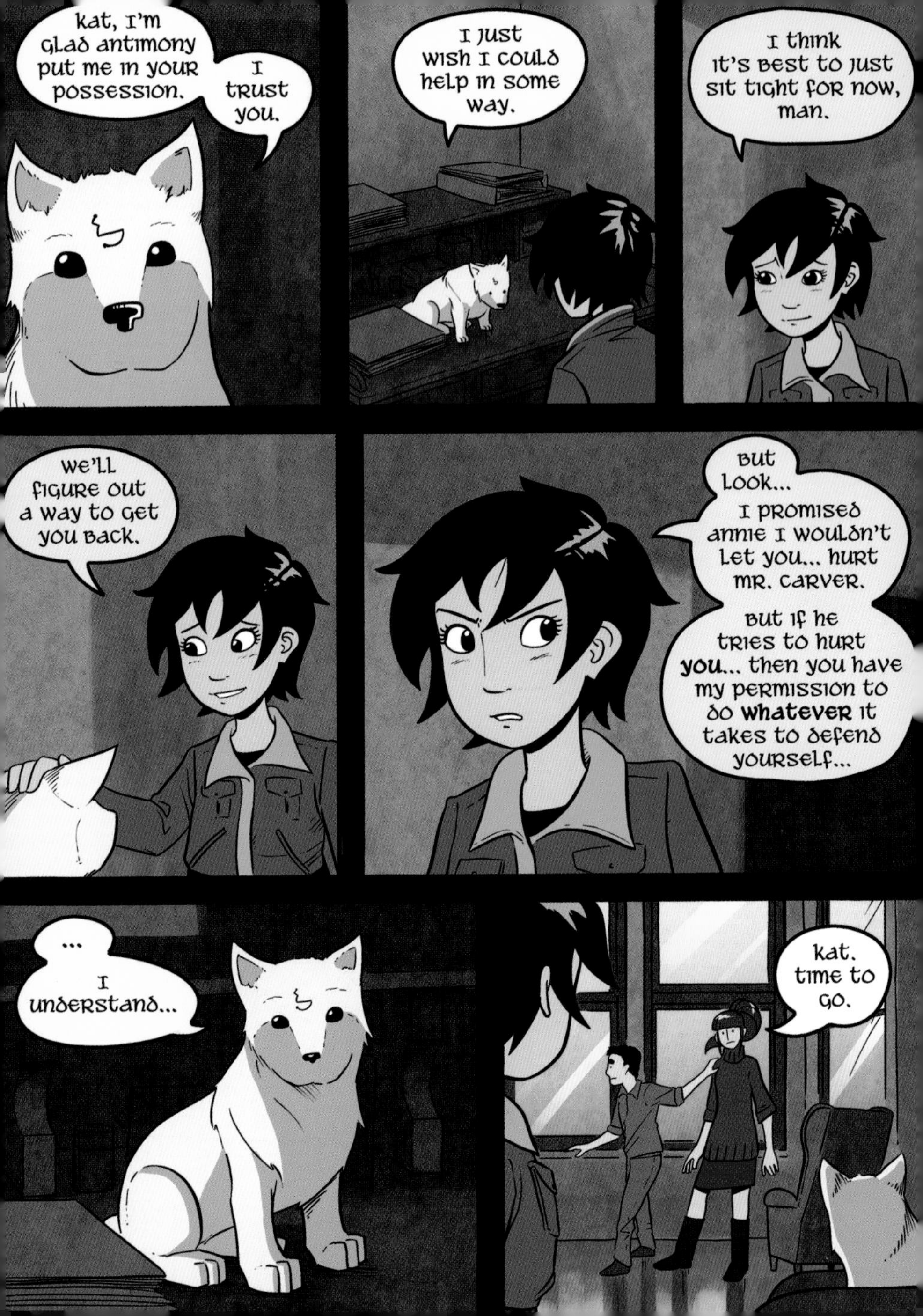
kat, I'm GLad antimony put me in your possession.
I trust you.
I just wish I could help in some way.
I think it's best to just sit tight for now, man.
we'll figure out a way to get you back.
But look...
I promised annie I wouldn't let you... hurt mr. carver.
But if he tries to hurt **you**... then you have my permission to do **whatever** it takes to defend yourself...
...
I understand...
kat. time to go.

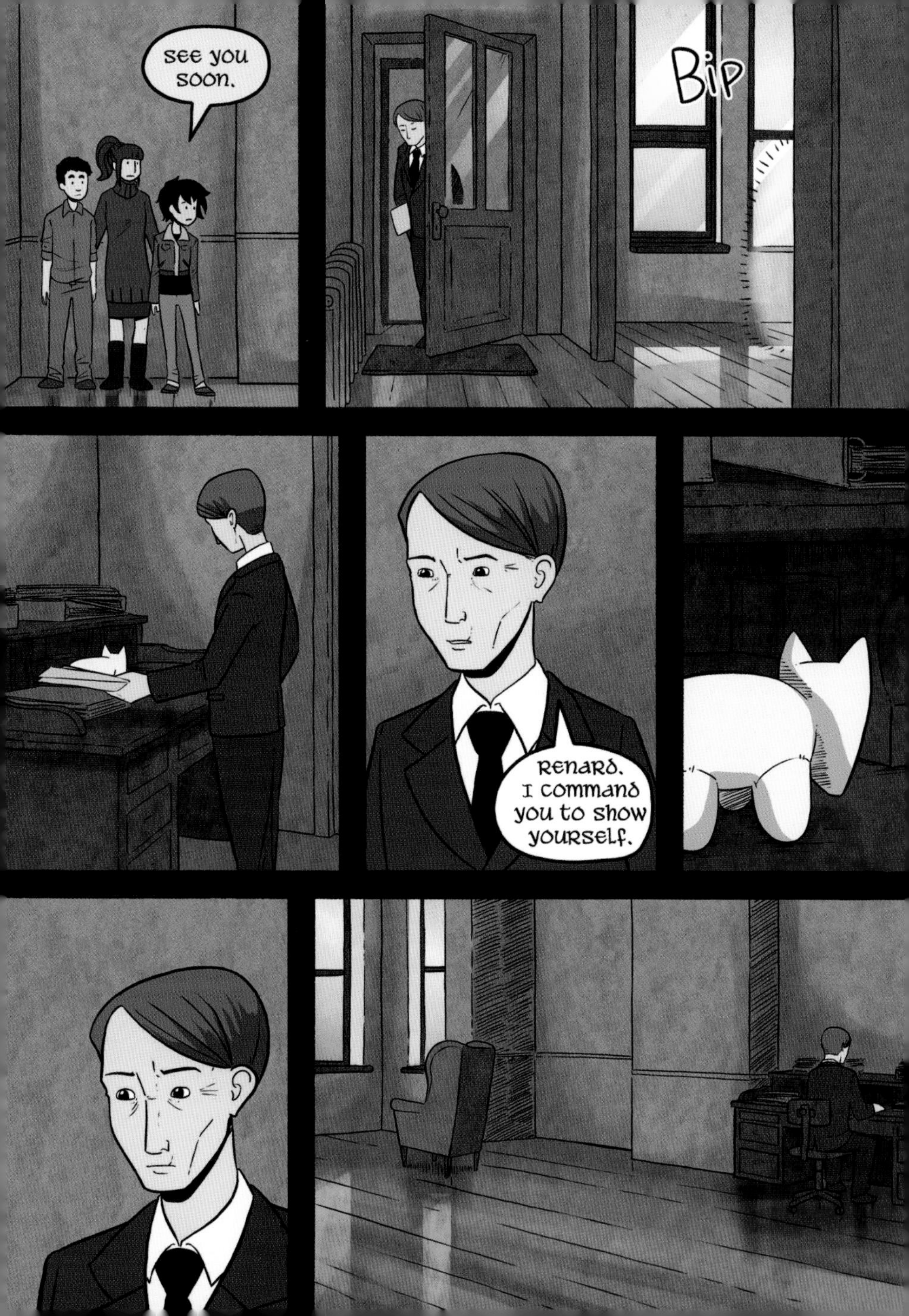
see you soon.
Bip
Renard. I command you to show yourself.

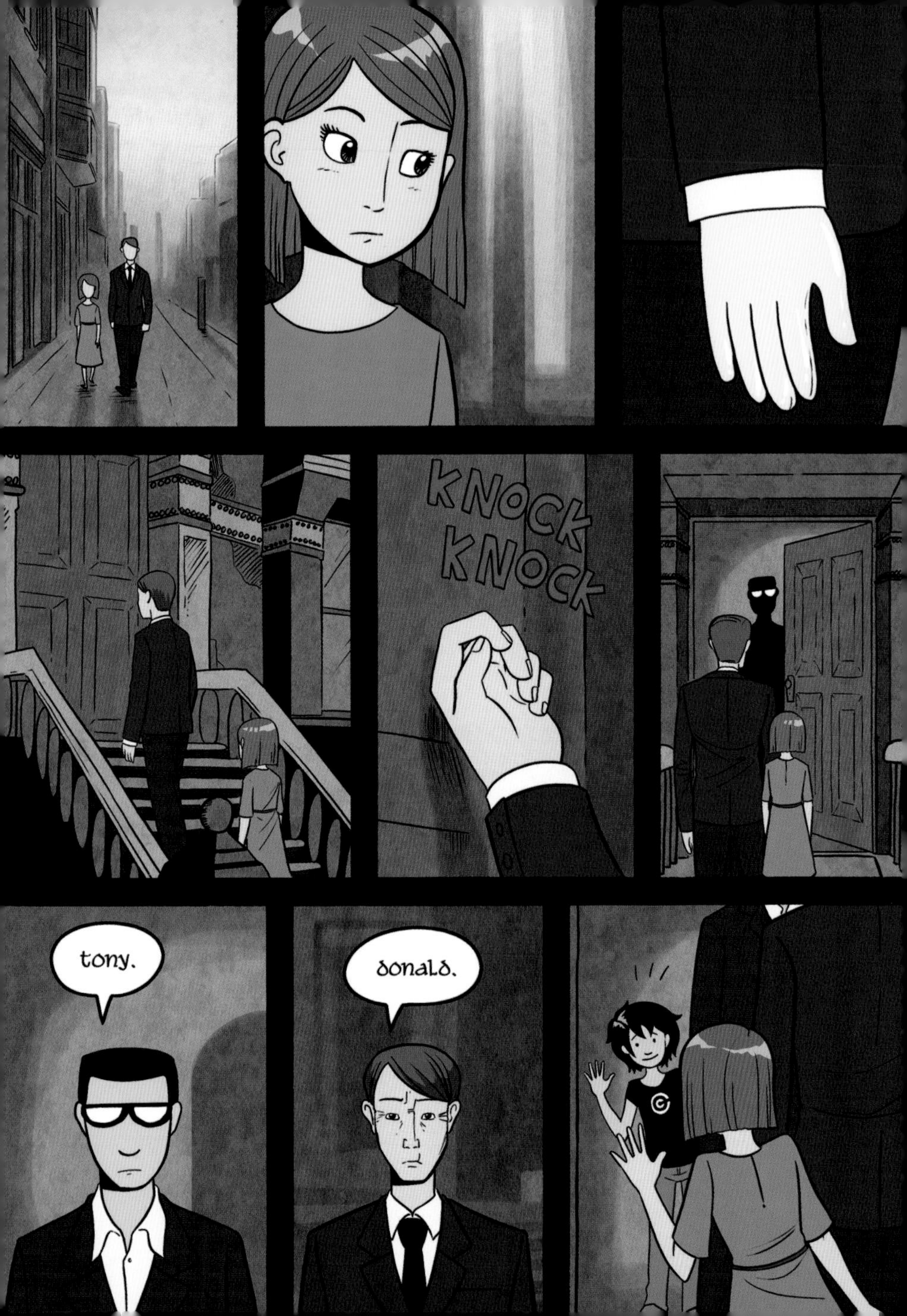
KNOCK
KNOCK
tony.
donald.

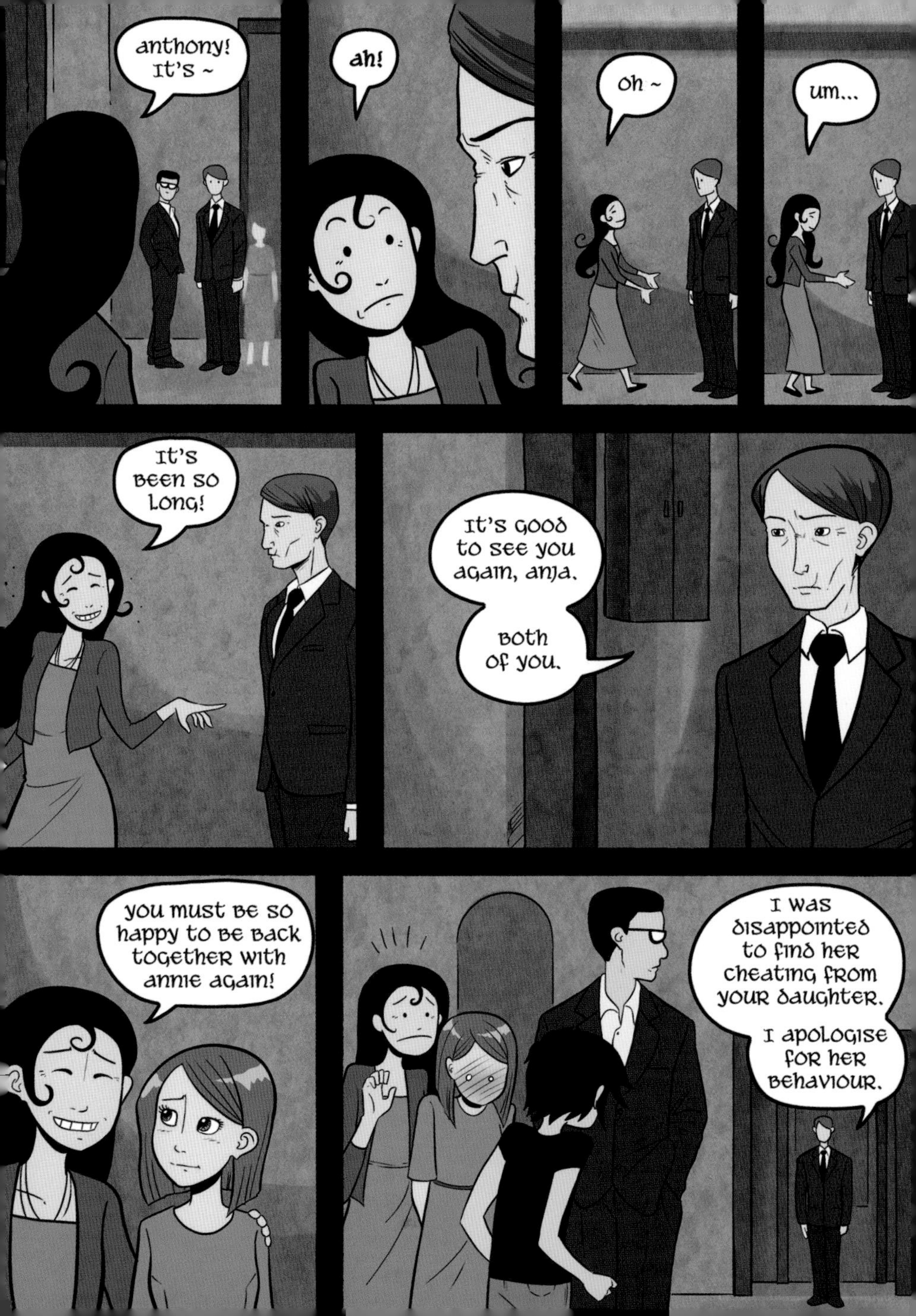
anthony! It's ~
ah!
oh ~
um...
It's been so long!
It's good to see you again, anja.
Both of you.
you must be so happy to be back together with annie again!
I was disappointed to find her cheating from your daughter.
I apologise for her behaviour.

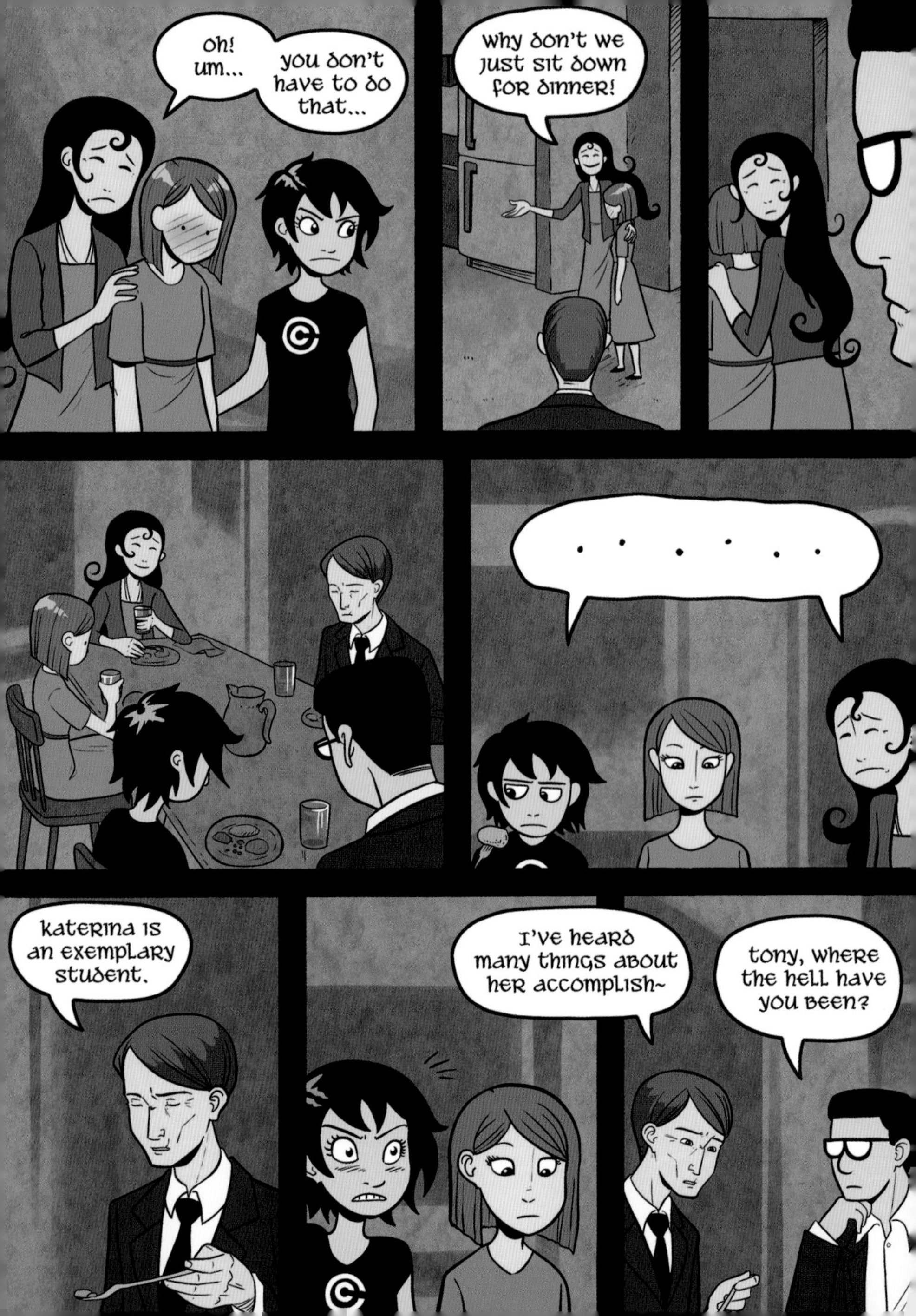
oh! um...
you don't have to do that...
why don't we just sit down for dinner!
. . . . . .
katerina is an exemplary student.
I've heard many things about her accomplish~
tony, where the hell have you been?

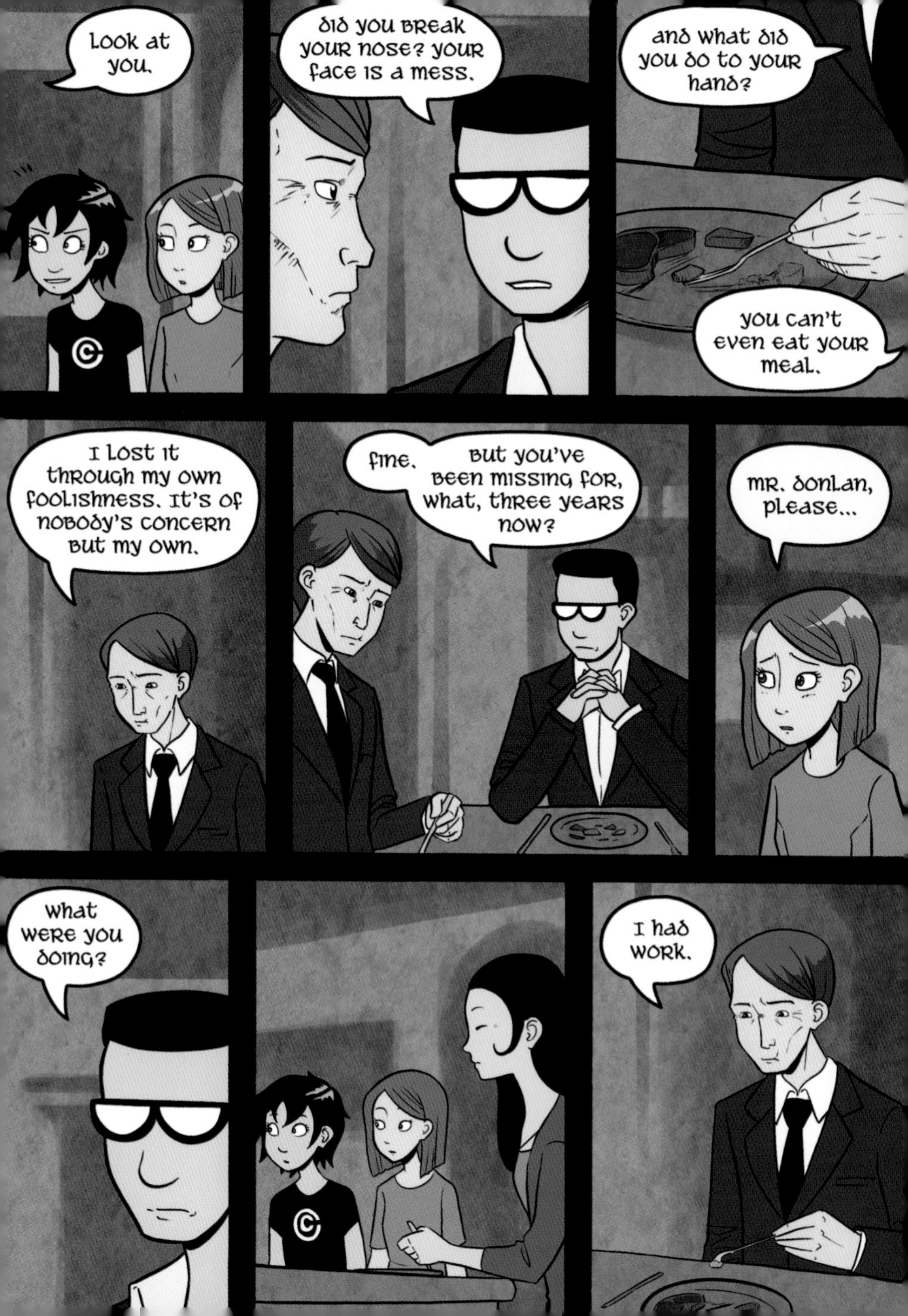
LOOK AT YOU.
DID YOU BREAK YOUR NOSE? YOUR FACE IS A MESS.
AND WHAT DID YOU DO TO YOUR HAND?
YOU CAN'T EVEN EAT YOUR MEAL.
I LOST IT THROUGH MY OWN FOOLISHNESS. IT'S OF NOBODY'S CONCERN BUT MY OWN.
FINE.
BUT YOU'VE BEEN MISSING FOR, WHAT, THREE YEARS NOW?
MR. DONLAN, PLEASE...
WHAT WERE YOU DOING?
I HAD WORK.

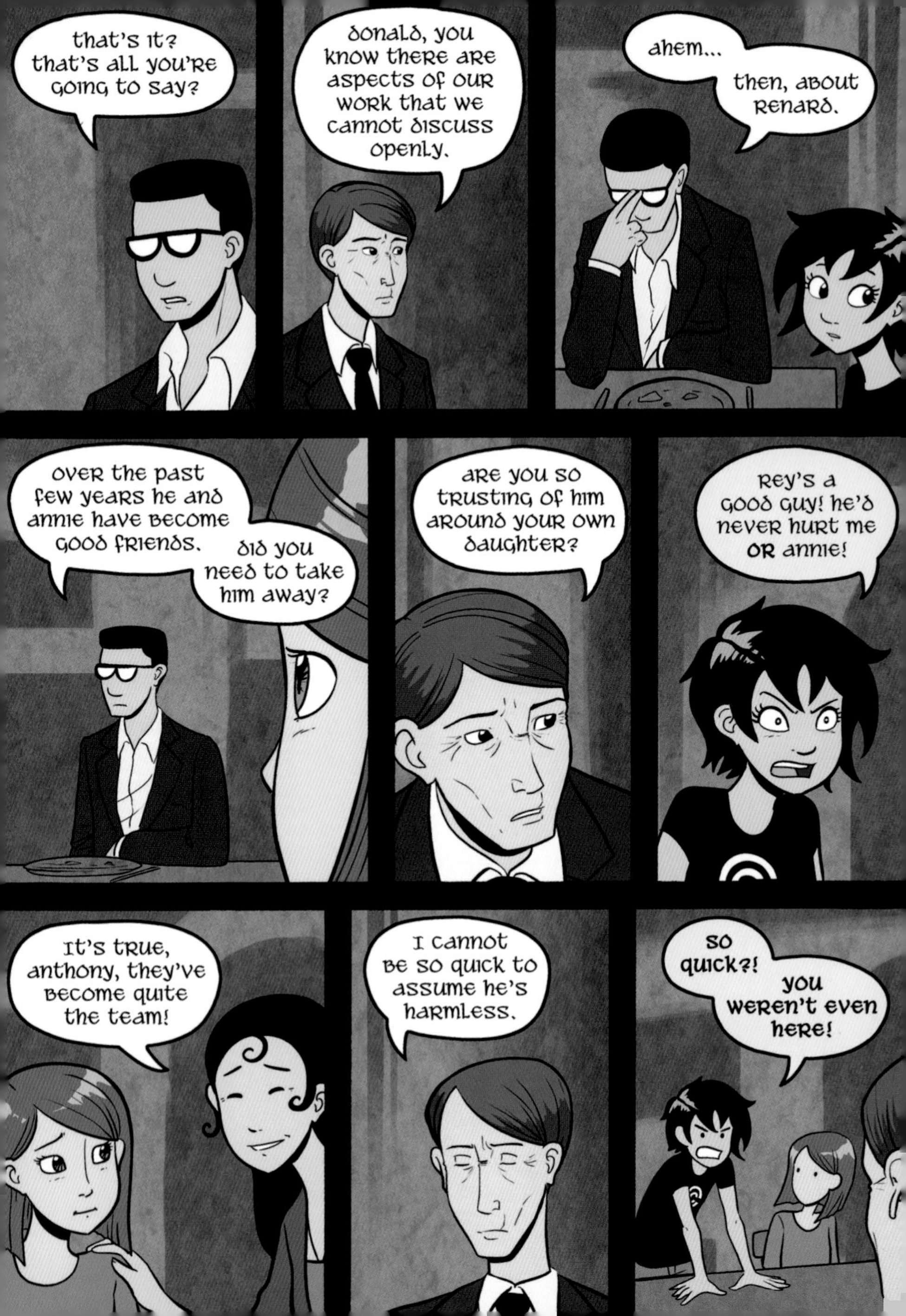
that's it? that's all you're going to say?
donald, you know there are aspects of our work that we cannot discuss openly.
ahem...
then, about renard.
over the past few years he and annie have become good friends.
did you need to take him away?
are you so trusting of him around your own daughter?
rey's a good guy! he'd never hurt me OR annie!
it's true, anthony, they've become quite the team!
I cannot be so quick to assume he's harmless.
so quick?!
you weren't even here!

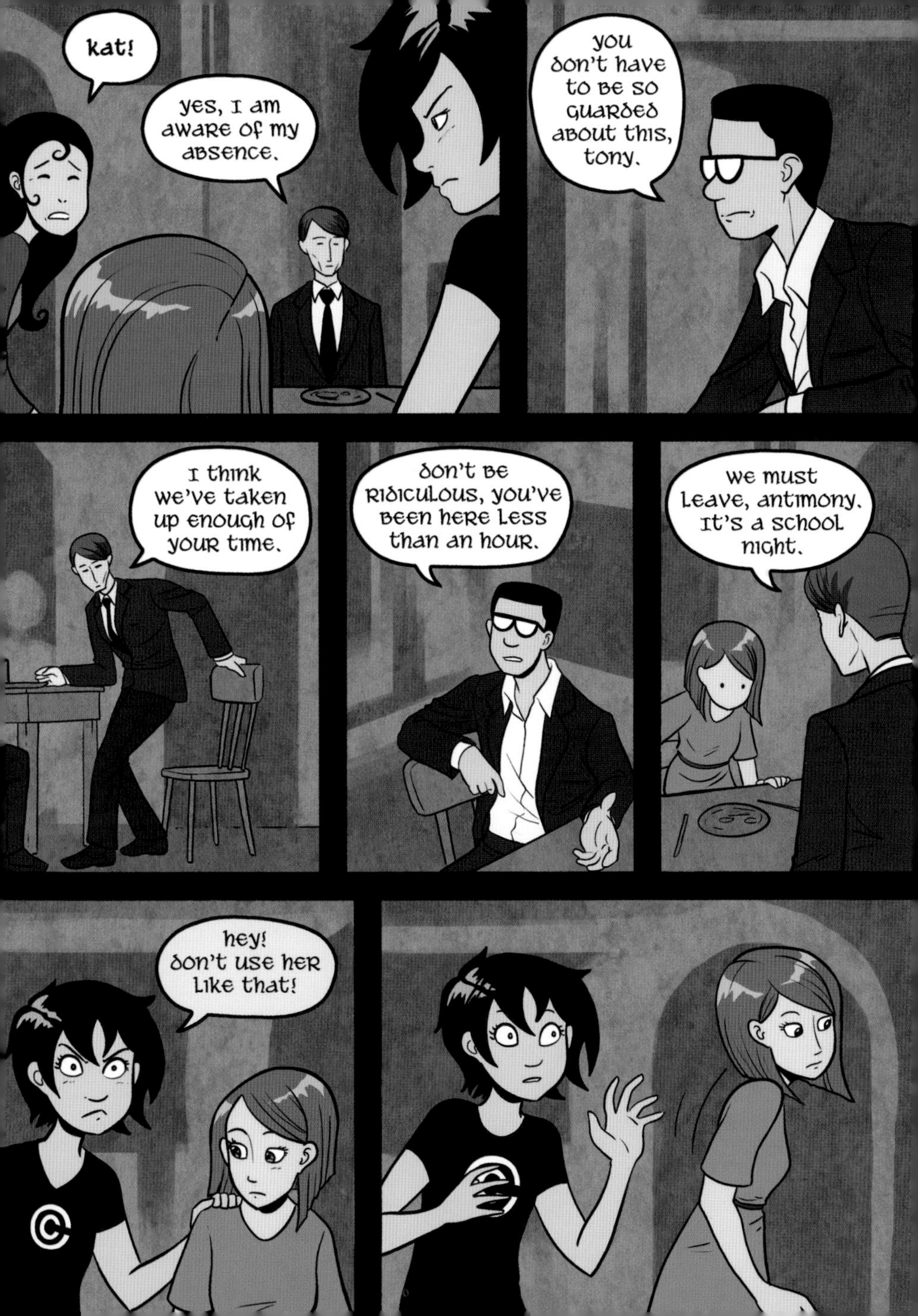
kat!
yes, I am aware of my absence.
you don't have to be so guarded about this, tony.
I think we've taken up enough of your time.
don't be ridiculous, you've been here less than an hour.
we must leave, antimony. It's a school night.
hey! don't use her like that!

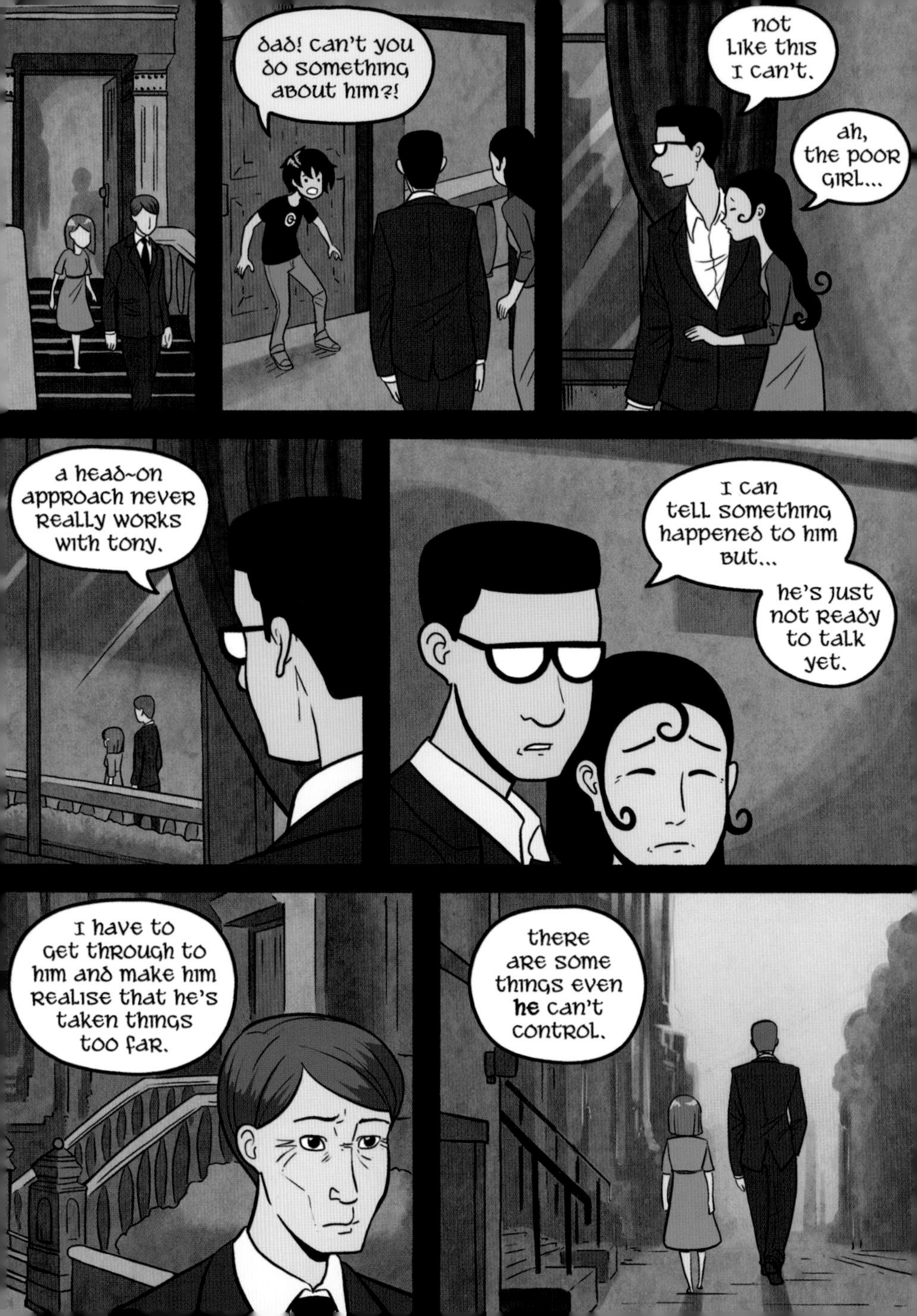
dad! can't you do something about him?!
not like this I can't.
ah, the poor girl...
a head~on approach never really works with tony.
I can tell something happened to him but...
he's just not ready to talk yet.
I have to get through to him and make him realise that he's taken things too far.
there are some things even **he** can't control.

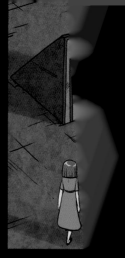

Goodnight, antimony.

Goodnight!

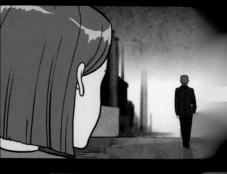

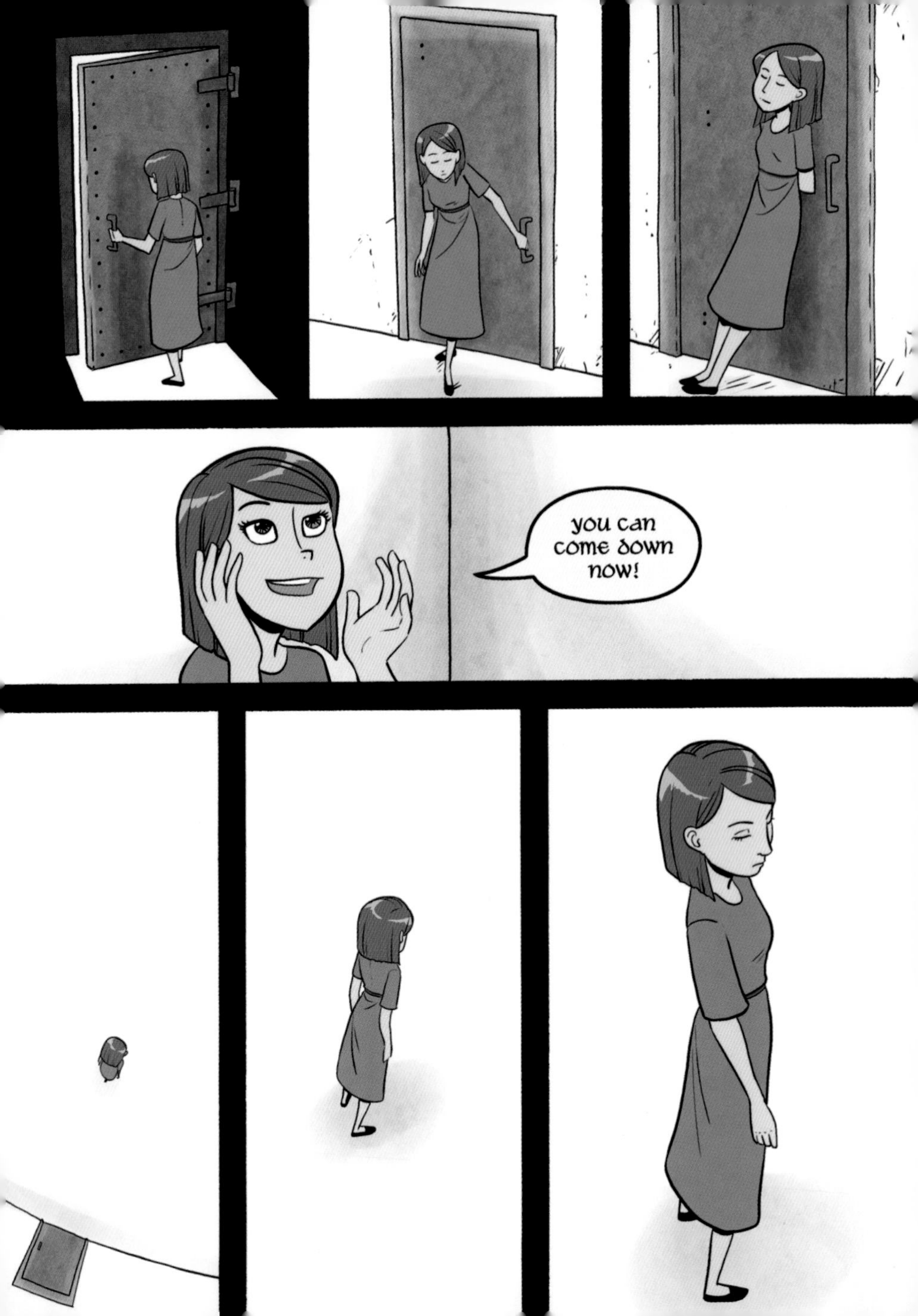
you can come down now!

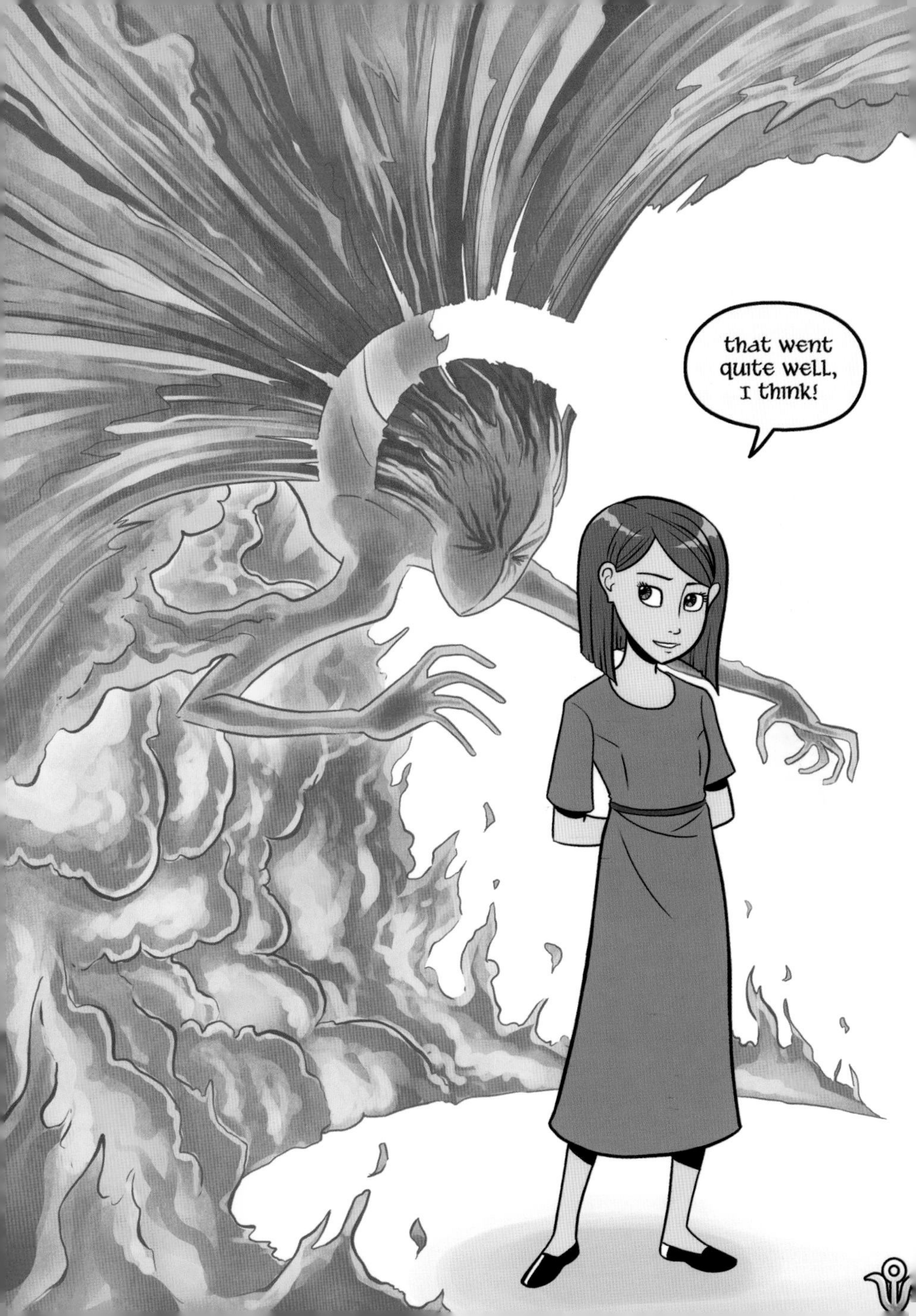
that went quite well, I think!

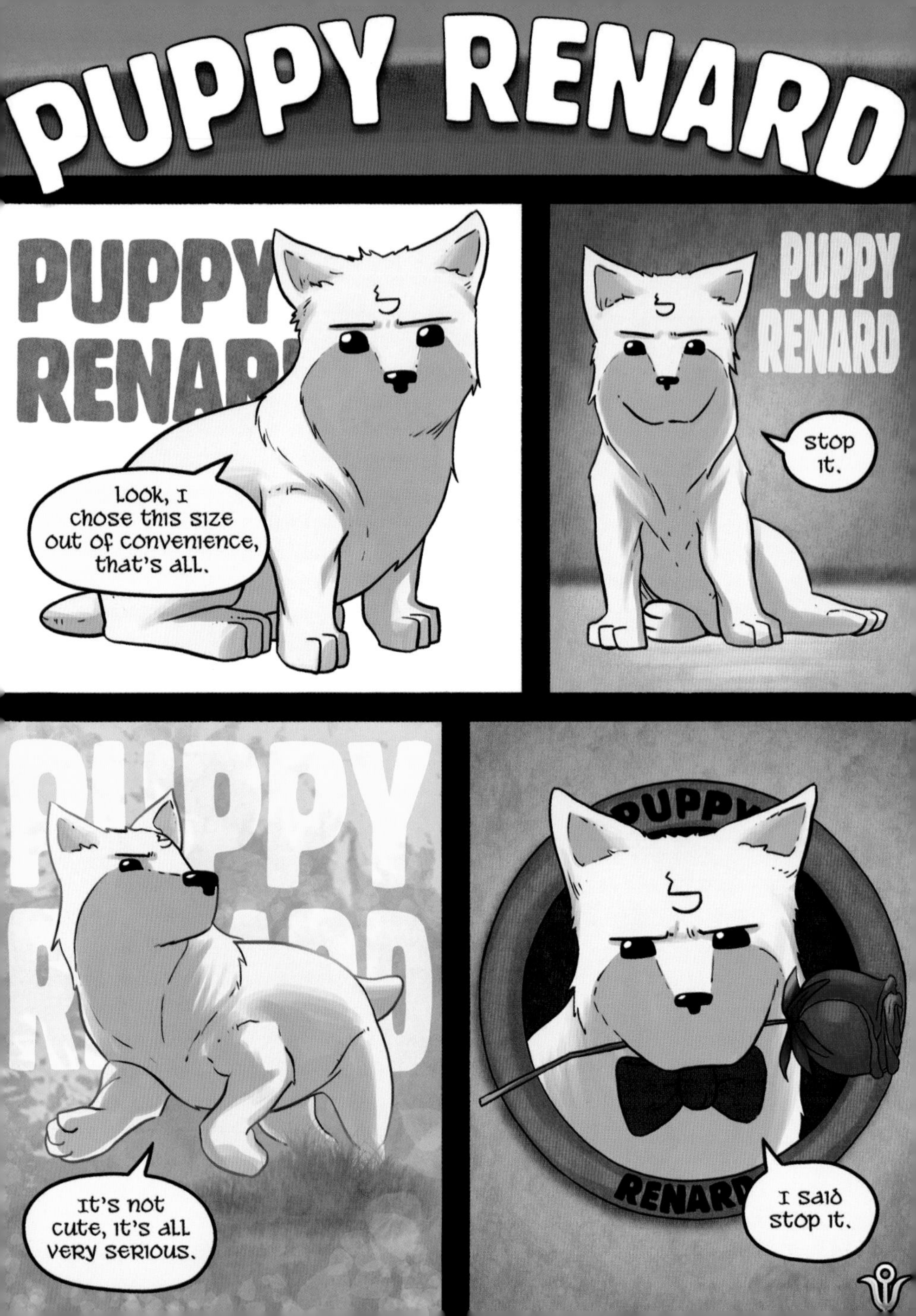
PUPPY RENARD
PUPPY RENARD
Look, I chose this size out of convenience, that's all.
PUPPY RENARD
stop it.
PUPPY
It's not cute, it's all very serious.
RENARD
I said stop it.

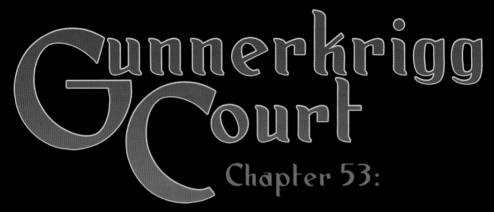

Gunnerkrigg Court

Chapter 53:

Annie and the Fire

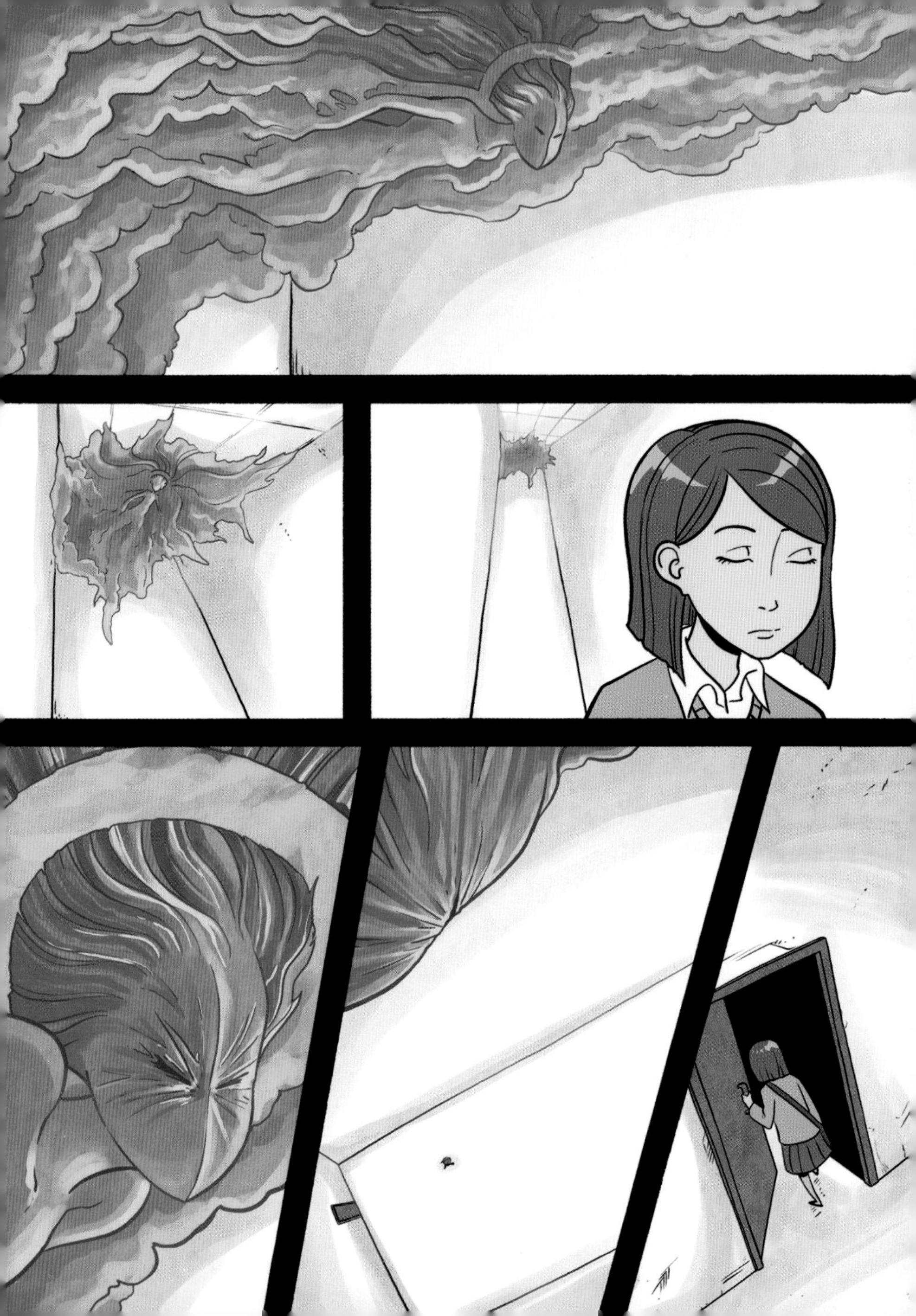

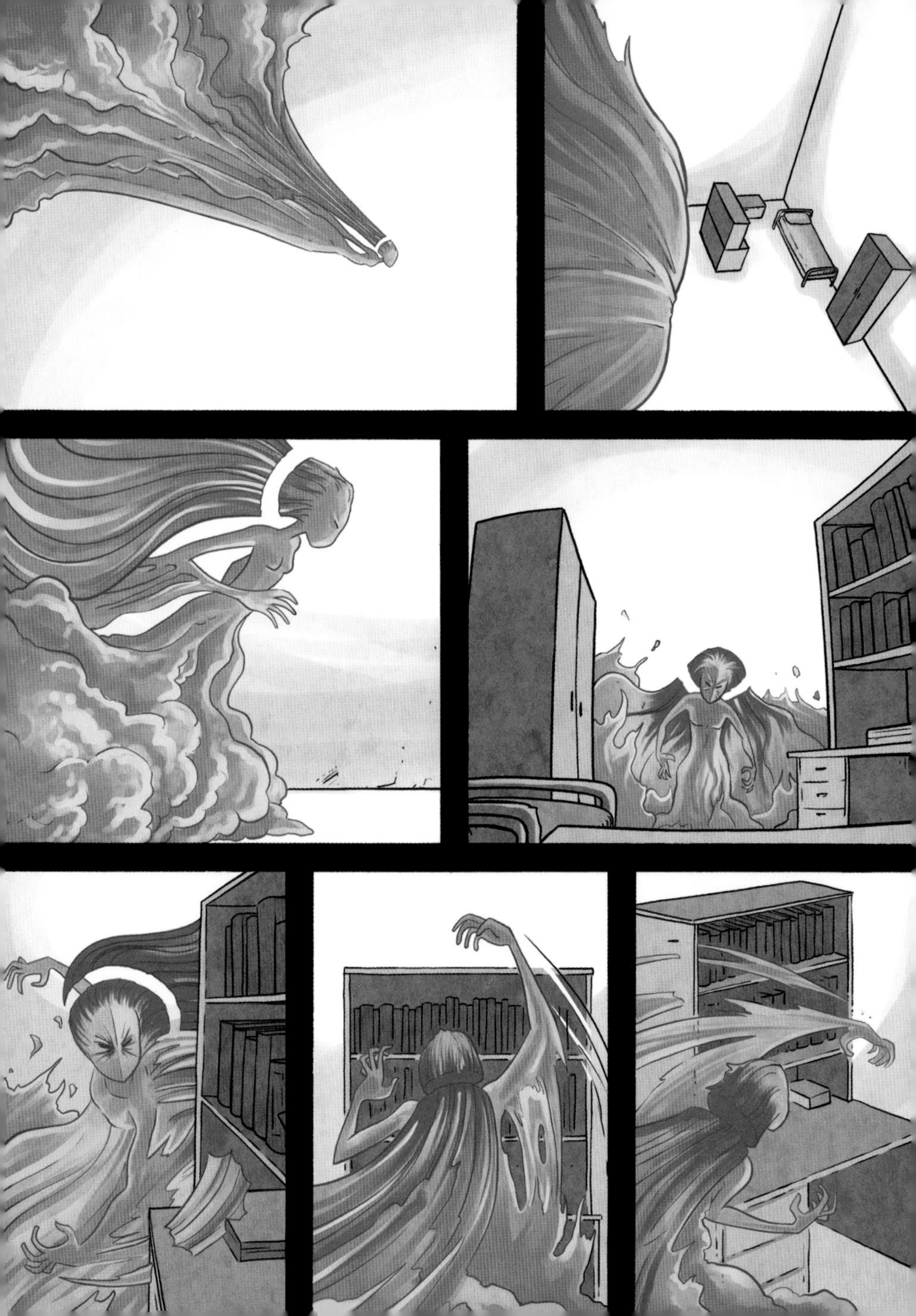

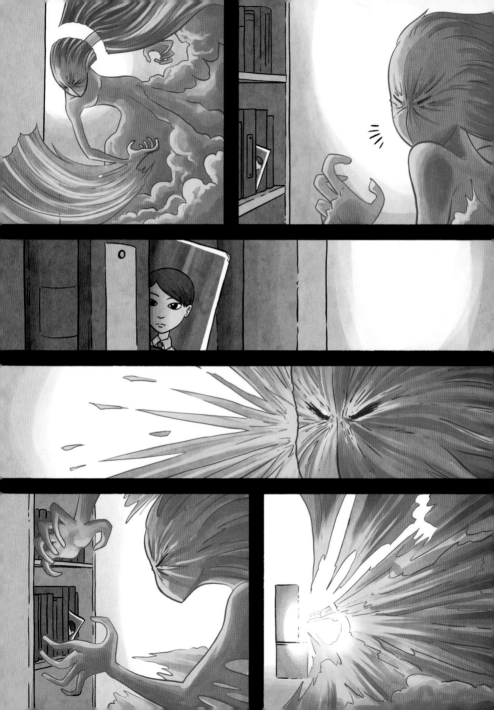

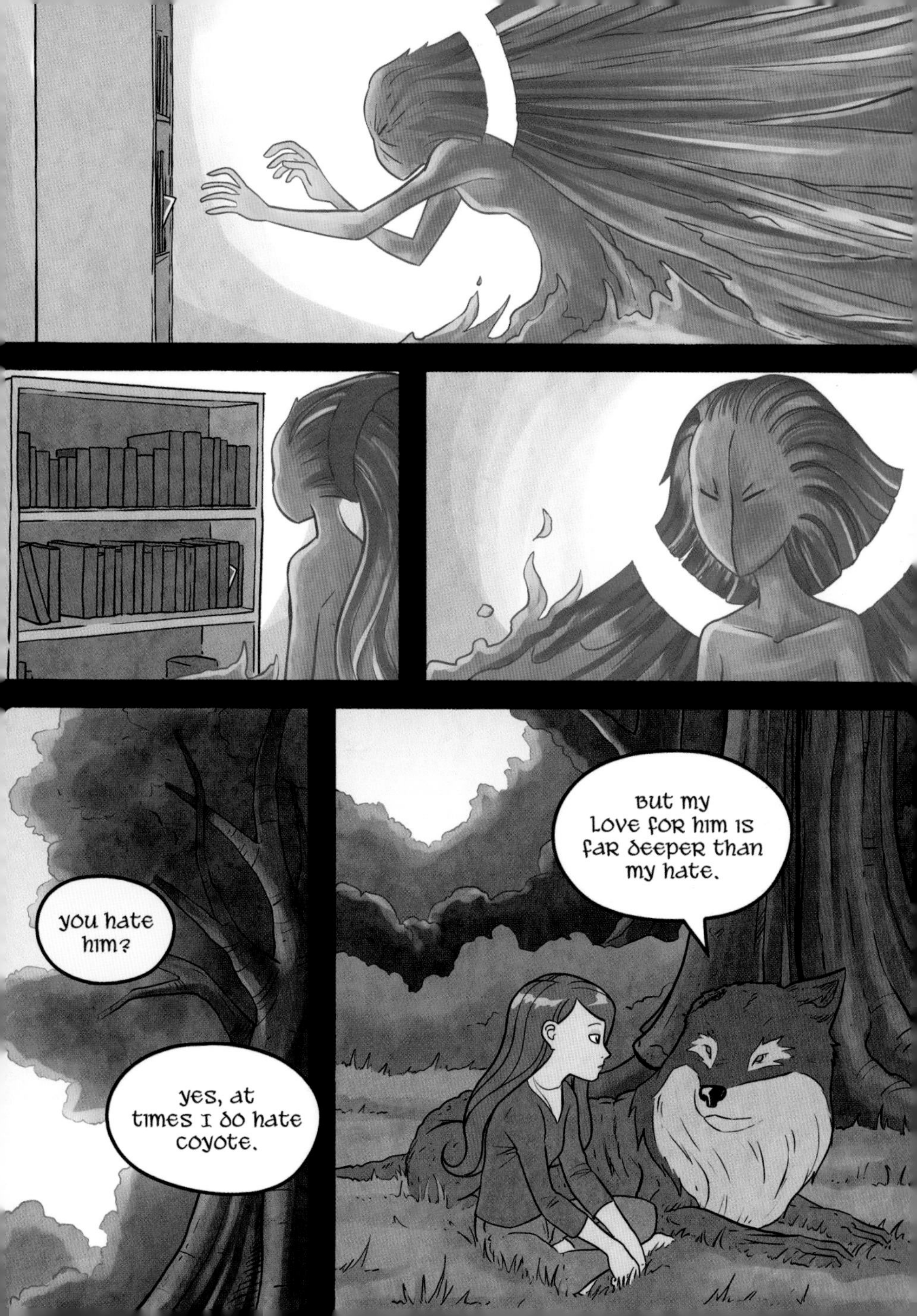
you hate him?
yes, at times I do hate coyote.
But my love for him is far deeper than my hate.

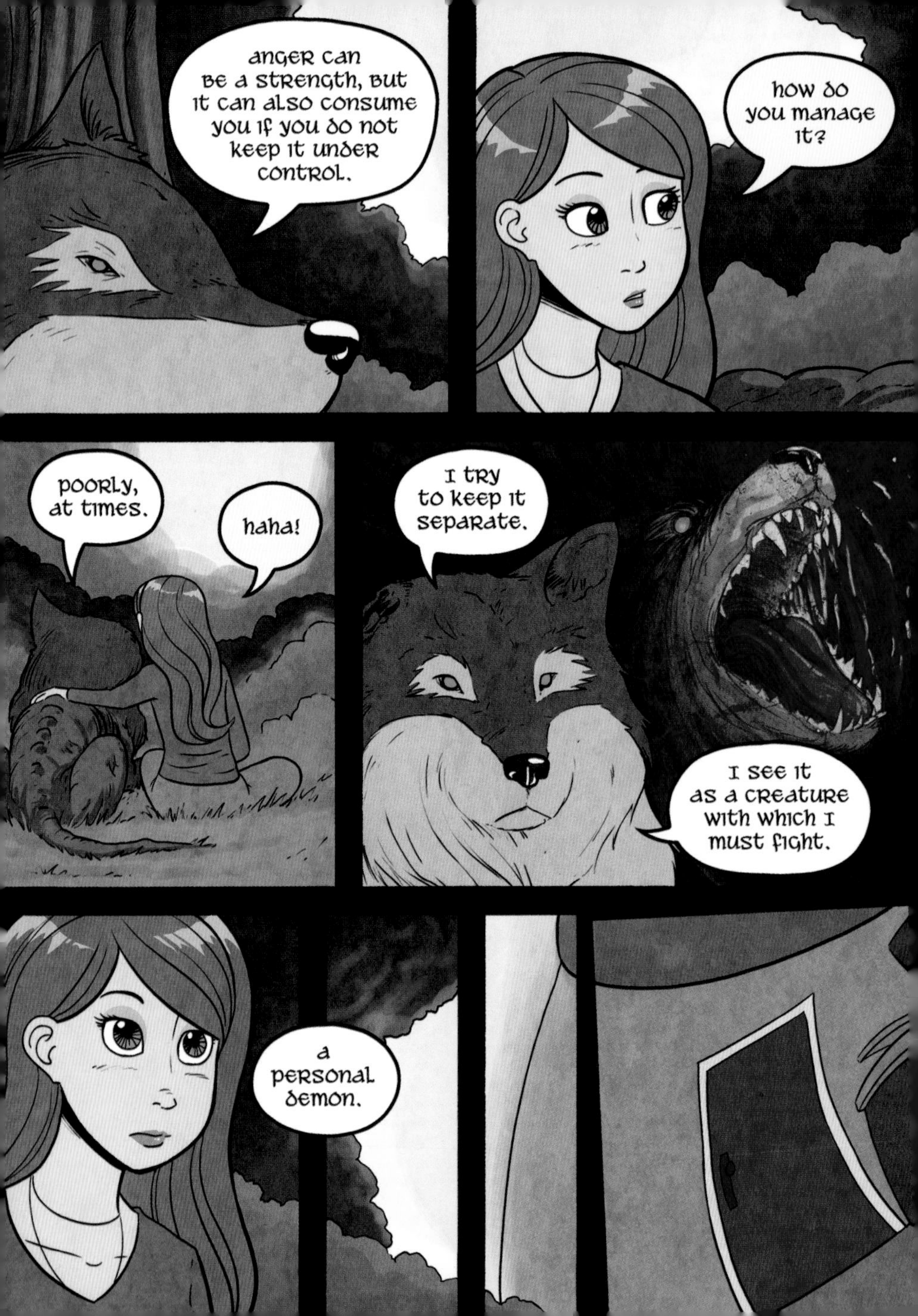
anger can be a strength, but it can also consume you if you do not keep it under control.
how do you manage it?
poorly, at times.
haha!
I try to keep it separate.
I see it as a creature with which I must fight.
a personal demon.

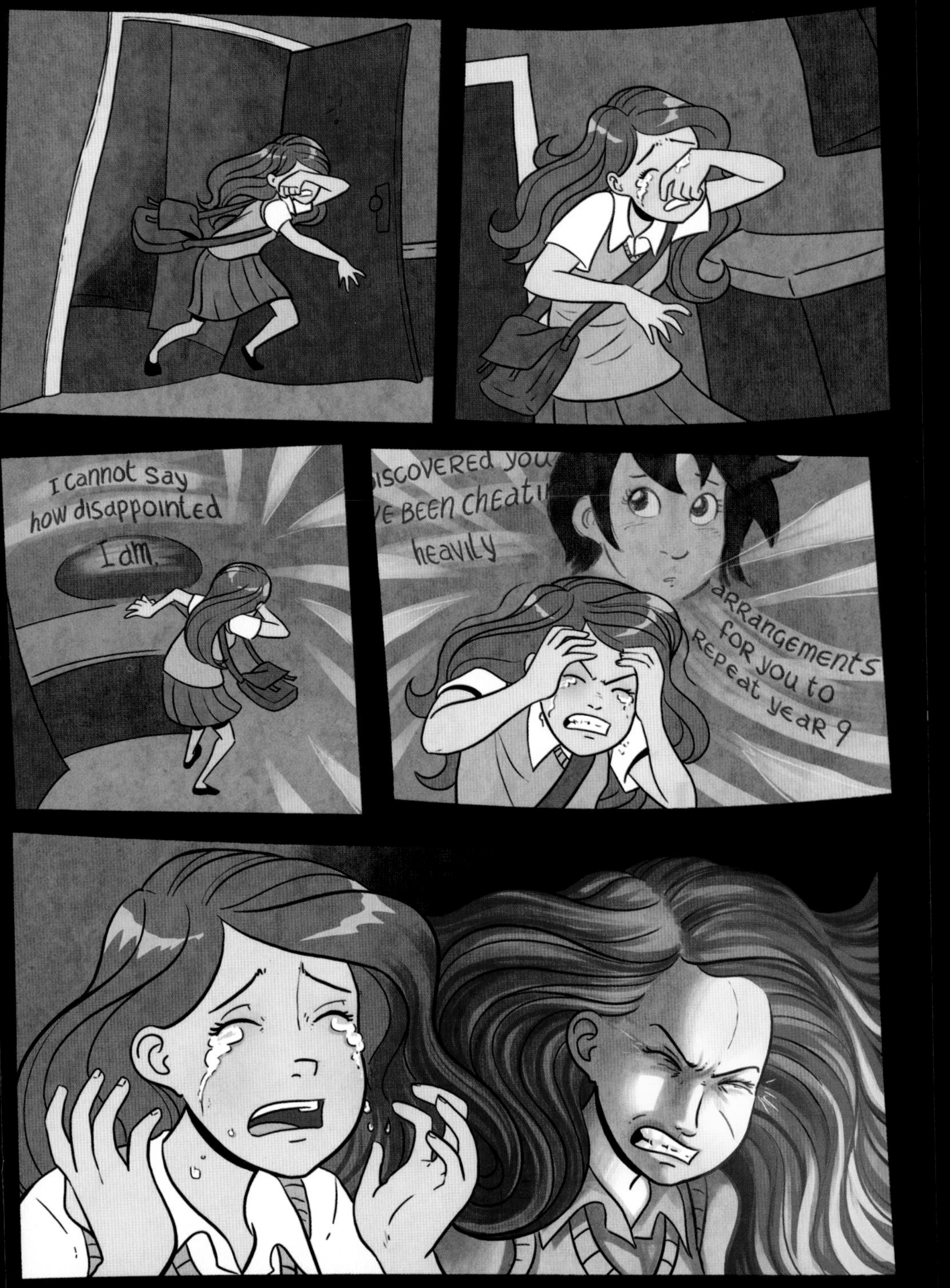
I cannot say how disappointed I am.
ISCOVERED YOU
VE BEEN CHEATI
heavily
arrangements for you to repeat year 9

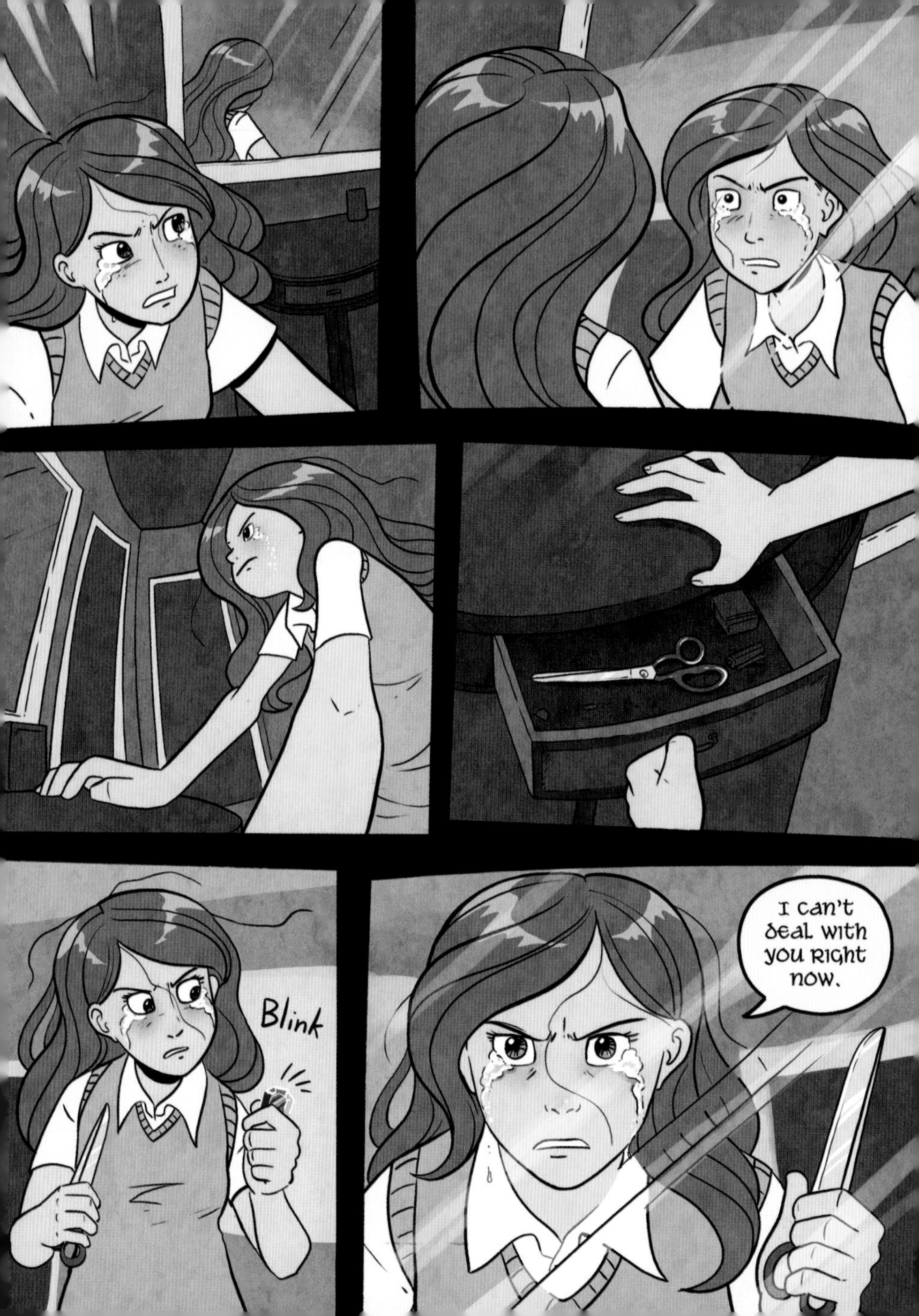
Blink
I can't deal with you right now.

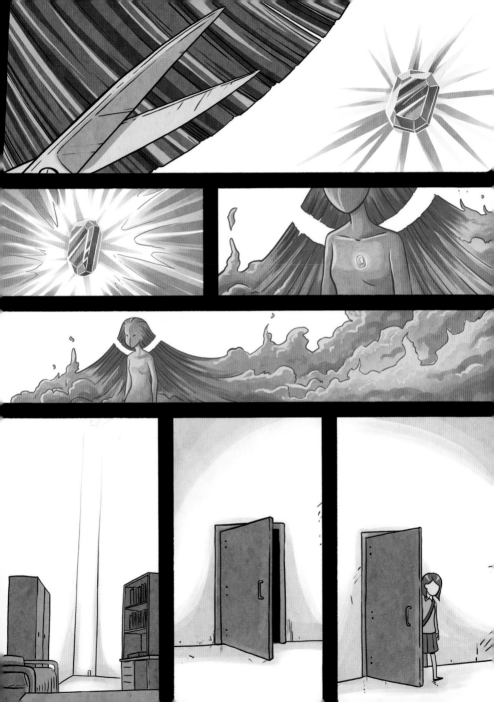

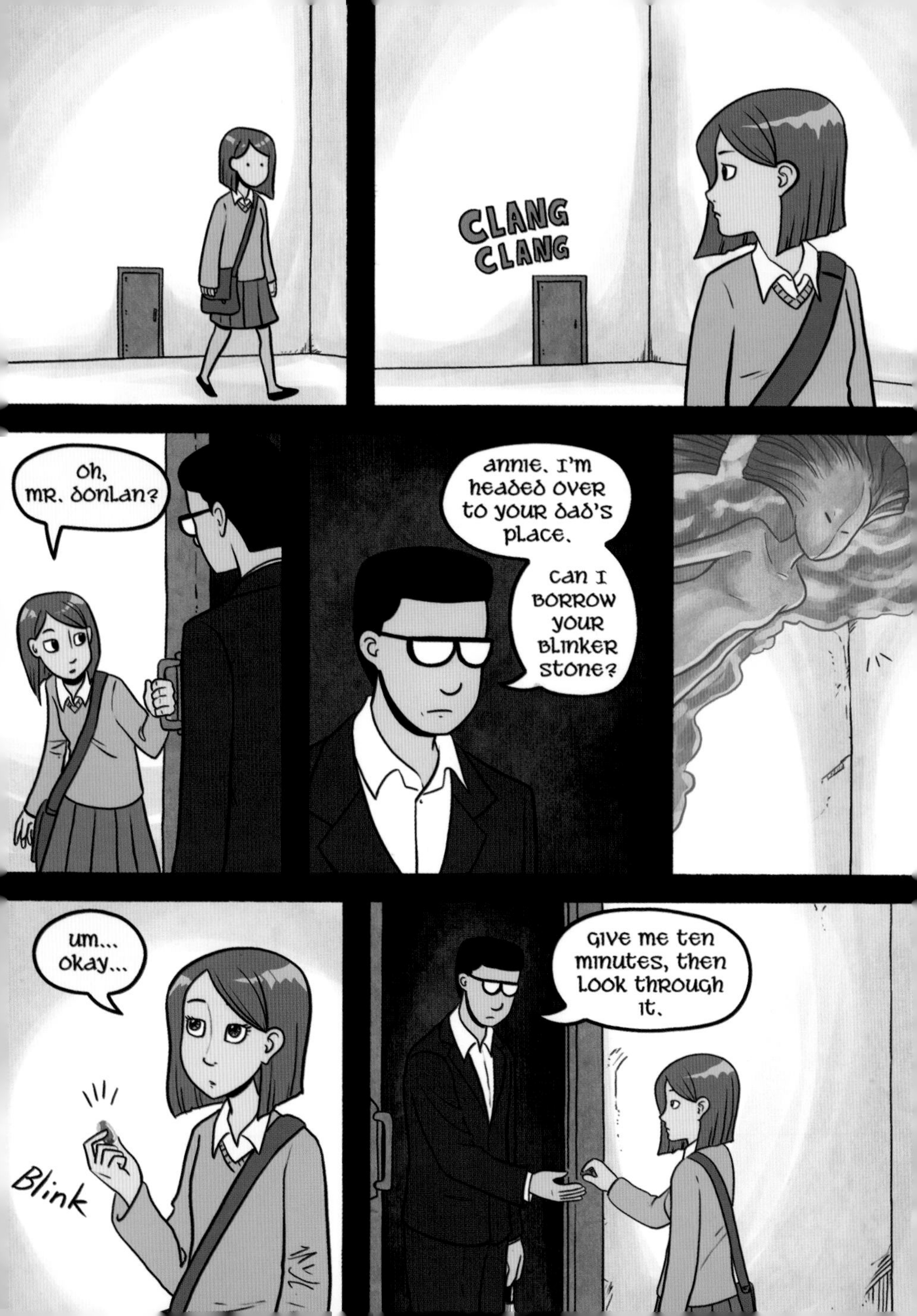
CLANG
CLANG
Oh, mr. donlan?
annie. I'm headed over to your dad's place.
can I borrow your blinker stone?
um... okay...
Blink
give me ten minutes, then look through it.

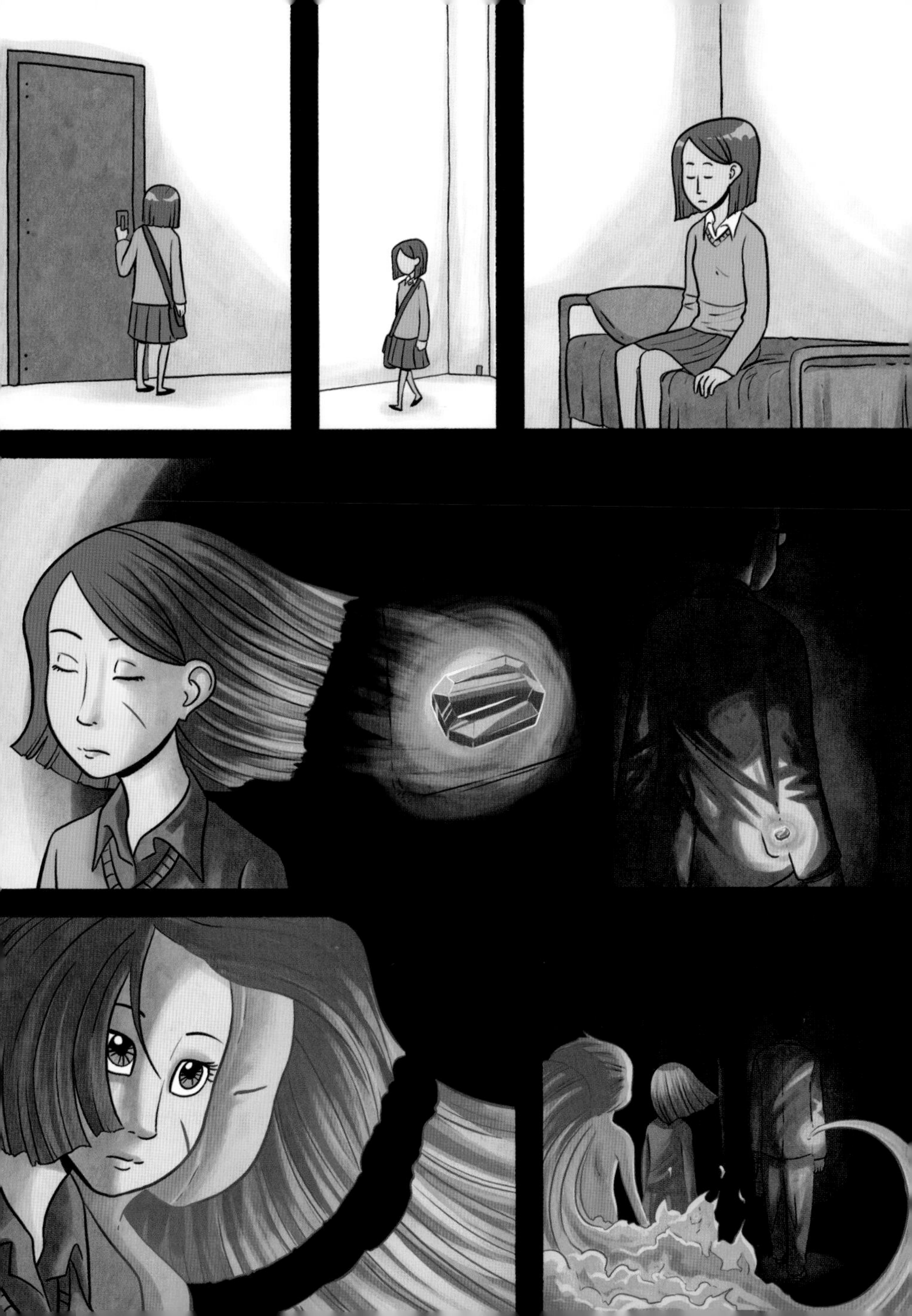

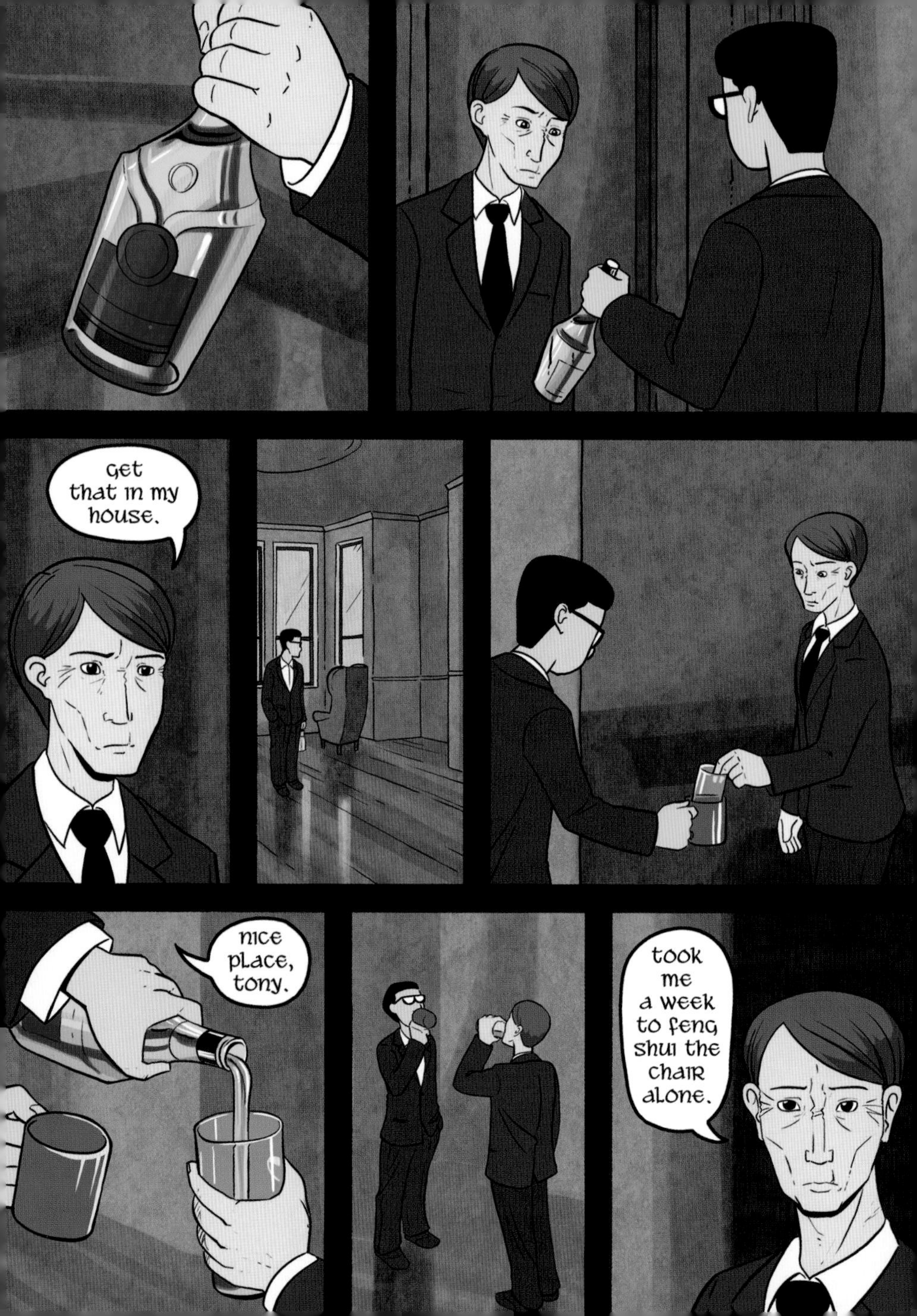
get that in my house.
nice place, tony.
took me a week to feng shui the chair alone.

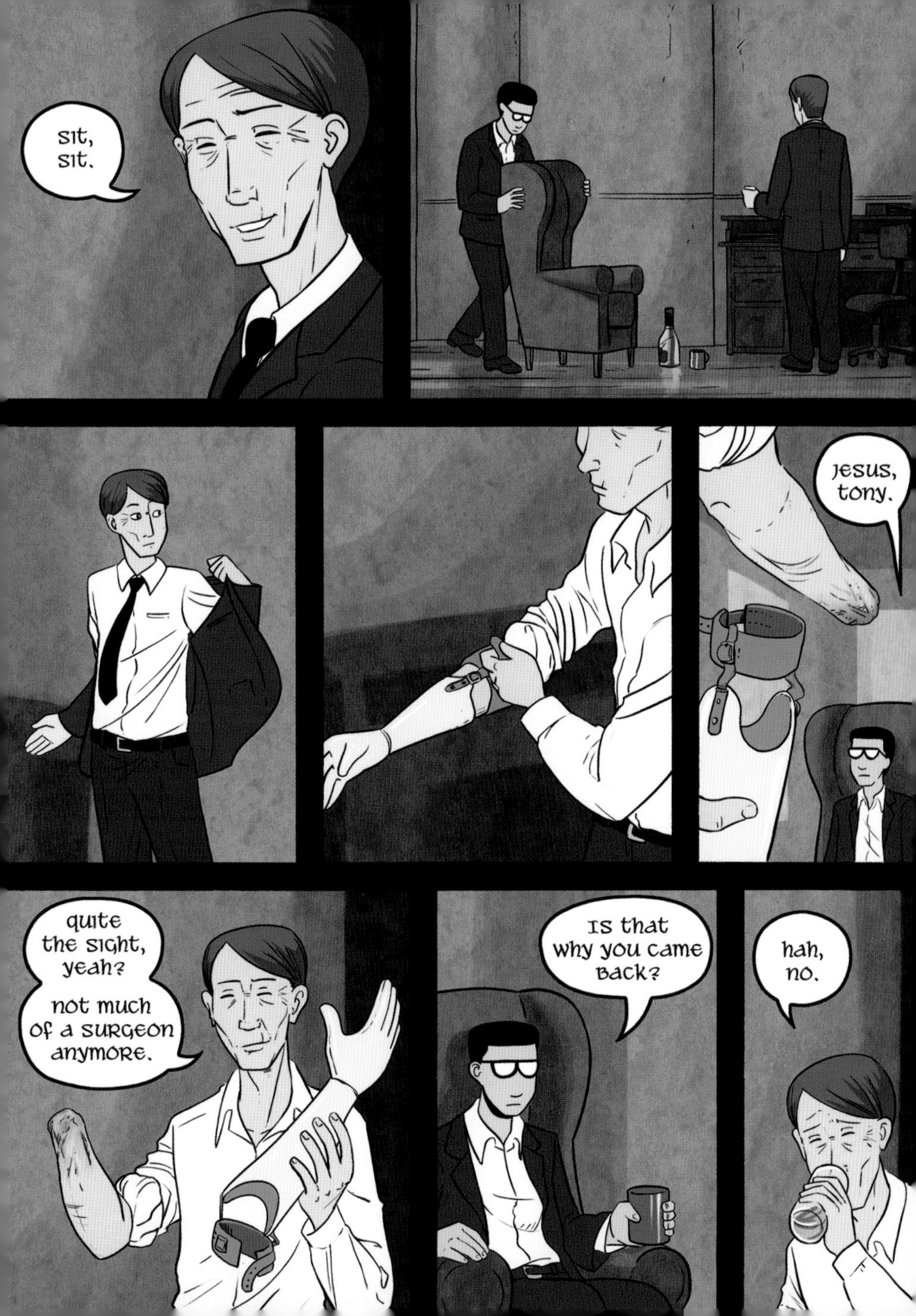
sit,
sit.
Jesus,
tony.
quite the sight, yeah?
not much of a surgeon anymore.
is that why you came back?
hah,
no.

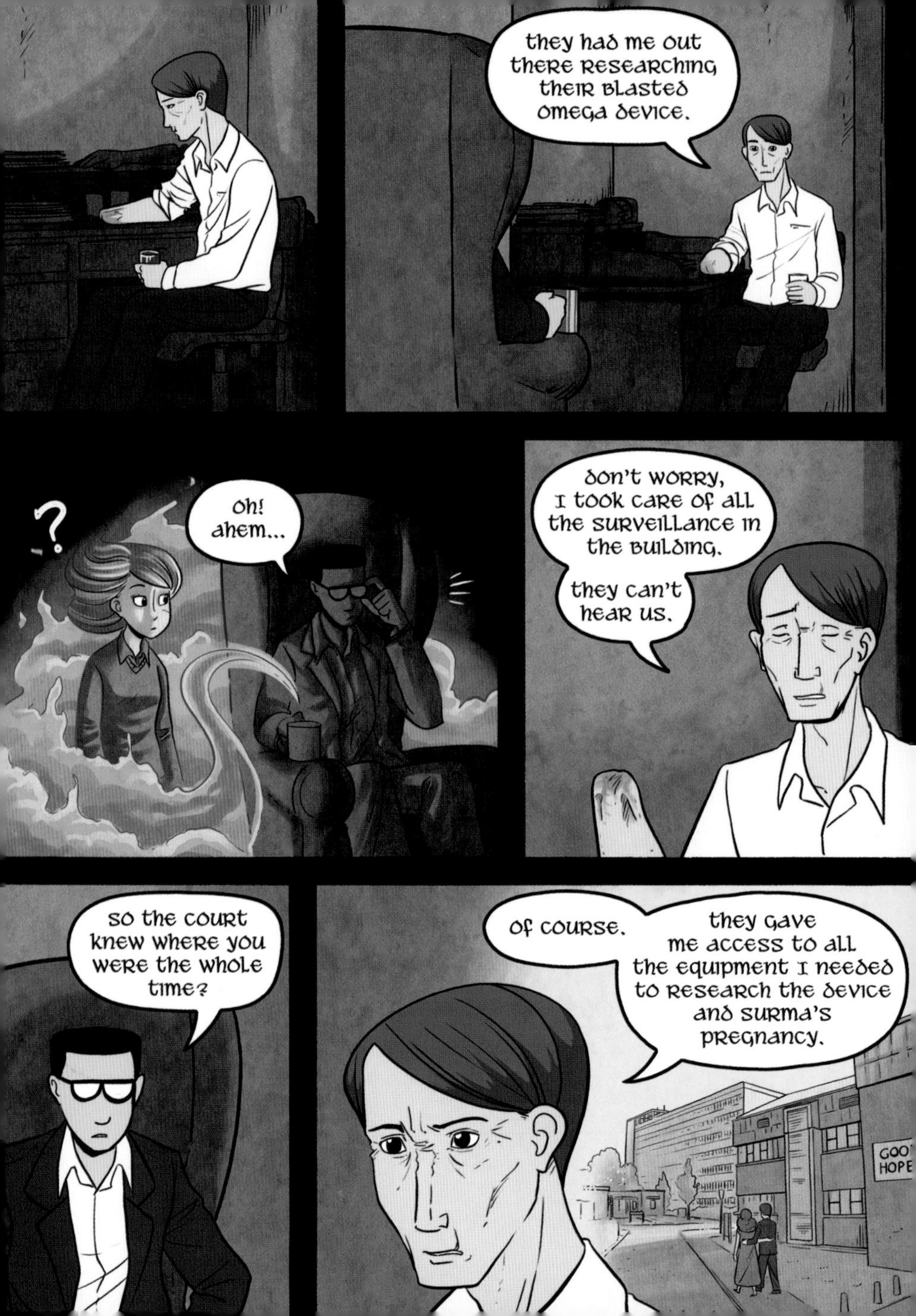
they had me out there researching their blasted omega device.
oh! ahem...
don't worry, I took care of all the surveillance in the building.
they can't hear us.
so the court knew where you were the whole time?
of course.
they gave me access to all the equipment I needed to research the device and surma's pregnancy.
GOO HOPE

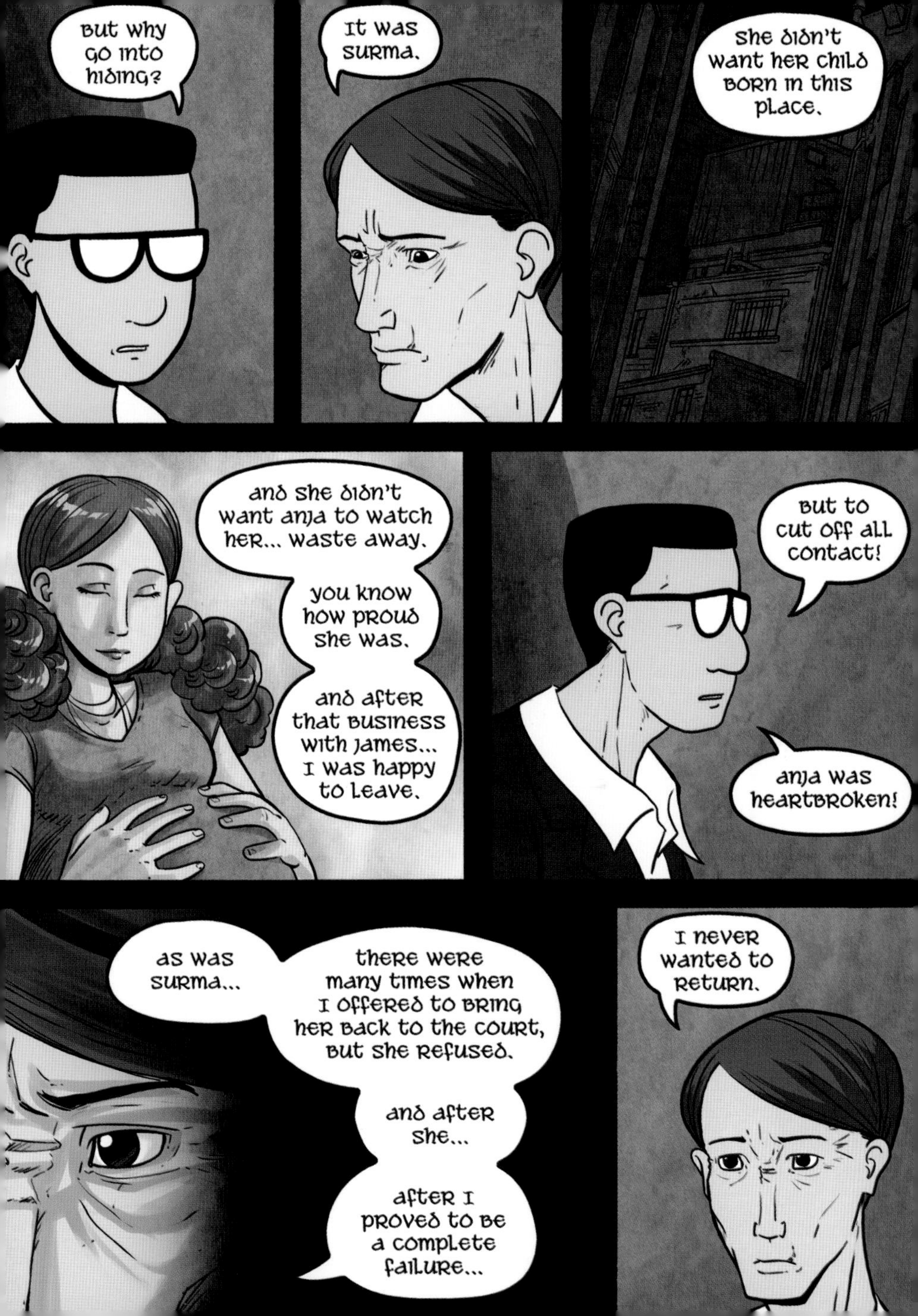
But why go into hiding?
It was Surma.
She didn't want her child born in this place.
And she didn't want Anja to watch her... waste away.
You know how proud she was.
And after that business with James... I was happy to leave.
But to cut off all contact!
Anja was heartbroken!
As was Surma...
There were many times when I offered to bring her back to the court, but she refused.
And after she...
After I proved to be a complete failure...
I never wanted to return.

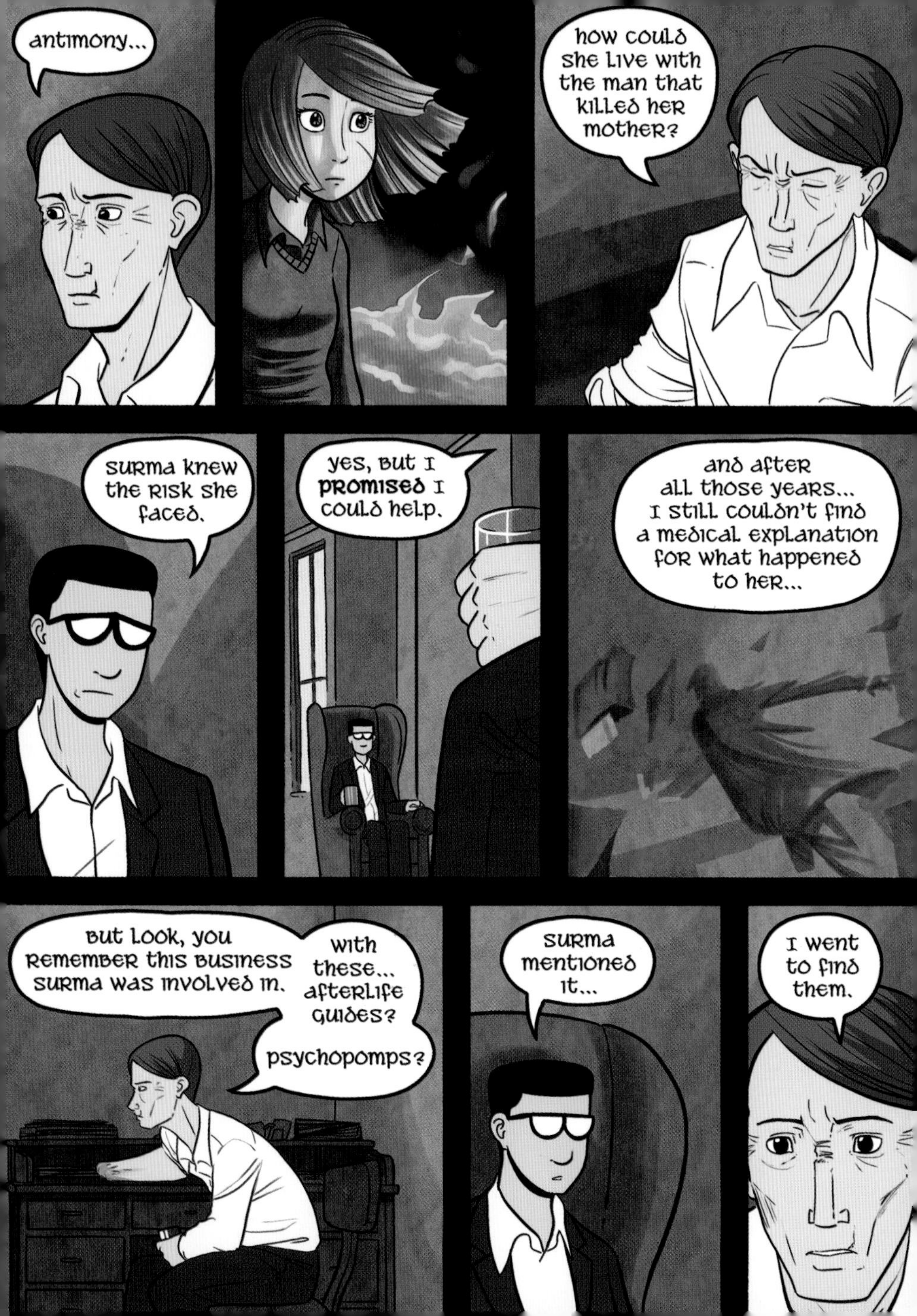
antimony...
how could she live with the man that killed her mother?
surma knew the risk she faced.
yes, but I **promised** I could help.
and after all those years... I still couldn't find a medical explanation for what happened to her...
but look, you remember this business surma was involved in.
with these... afterlife guides?
psychopomps?
surma mentioned it...
I went to find them.

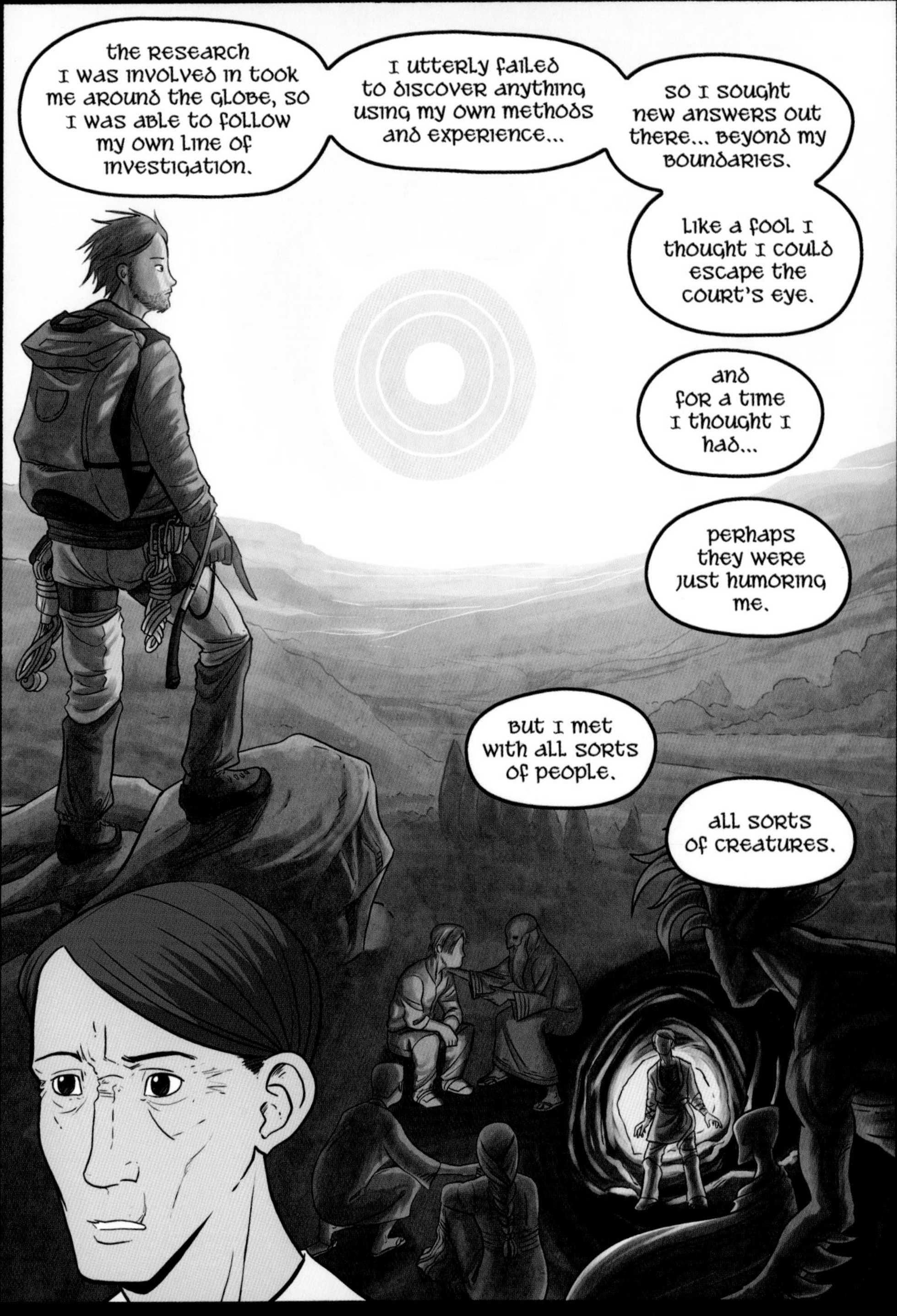
the research I was involved in took me around the globe, so I was able to follow my own line of investigation.
I utterly failed to discover anything using my own methods and experience...
so I sought new answers out there... beyond my boundaries.
like a fool I thought I could escape the court's eye.
and for a time I thought I had...
perhaps they were just humoring me.
but I met with all sorts of people.
all sorts of creatures.

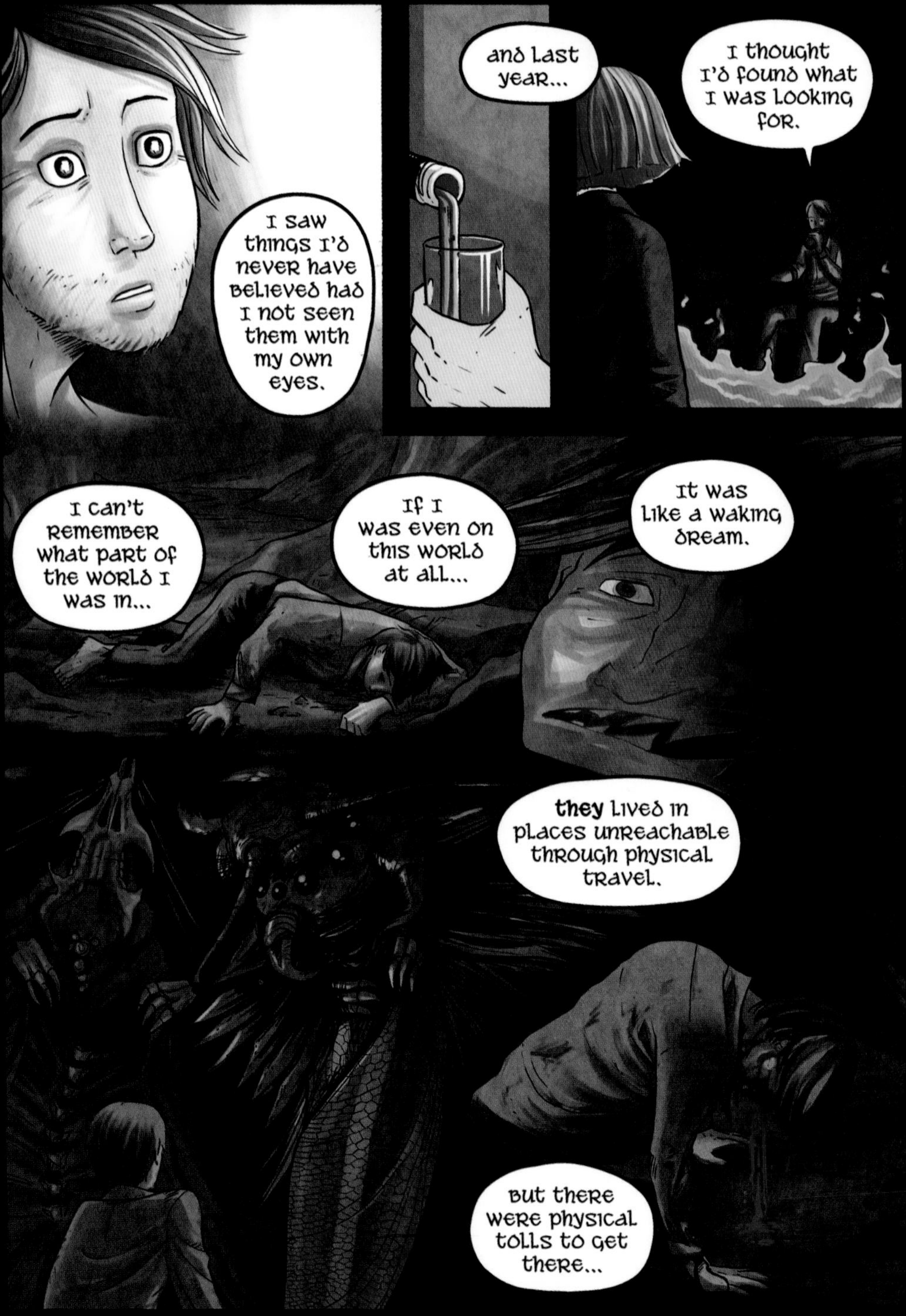
I saw things I'd never have believed had I not seen them with my own eyes.
and last year...
I thought I'd found what I was looking for.
I can't remember what part of the world I was in...
If I was even on this world at all...
It was like a waking dream.
they lived in places unreachable through physical travel.
But there were physical tolls to get there...

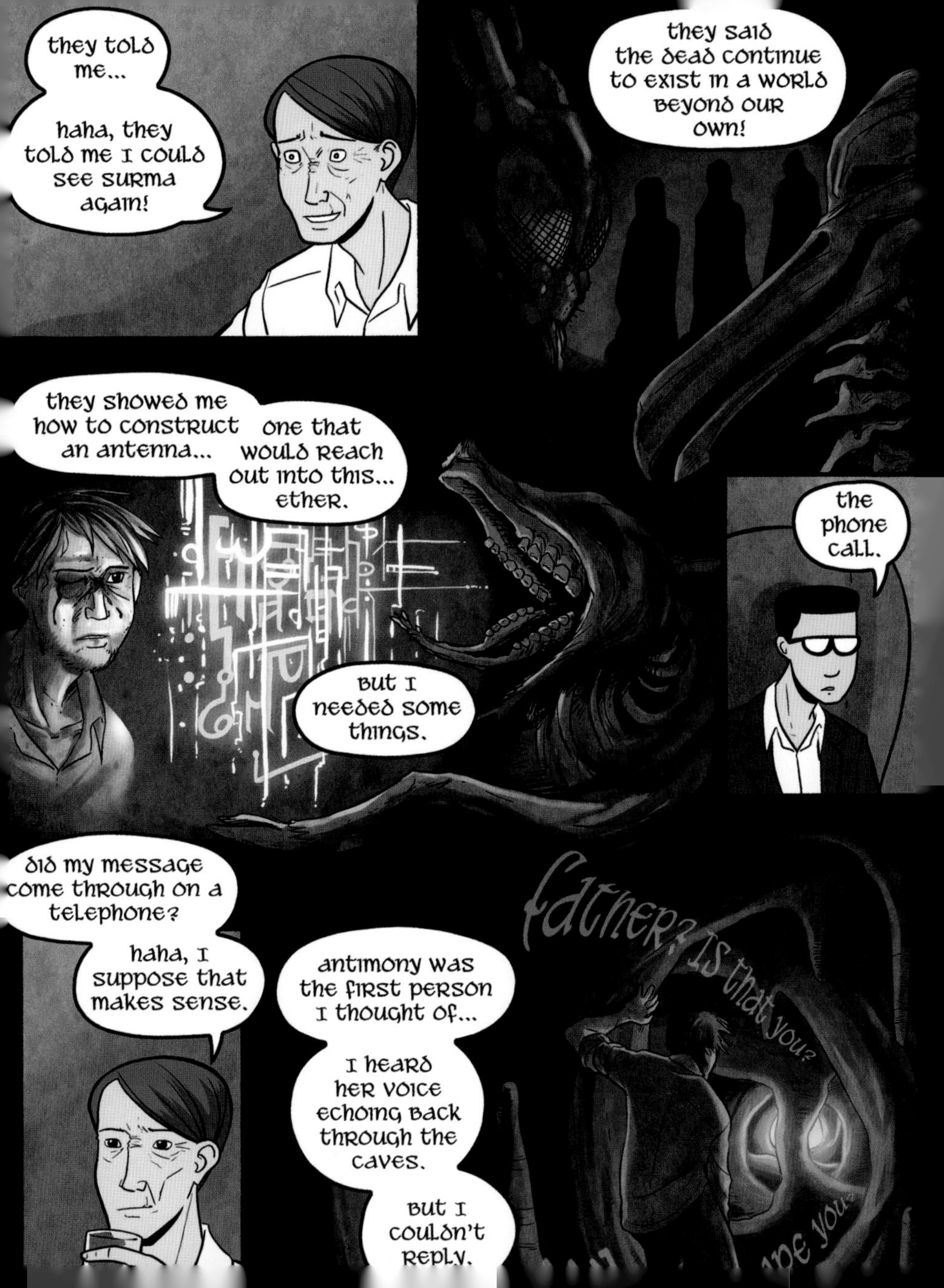
they told me...
haha, they told me I could see surma again!
they said the dead continue to exist in a world beyond our own!
they showed me how to construct an antenna...
one that would reach out into this... ether.
but I needed some things.
the phone call.
did my message come through on a telephone?
haha, I suppose that makes sense.
antimony was the first person I thought of...
I heard her voice echoing back through the caves.
but I couldn't reply.
father? is that you?

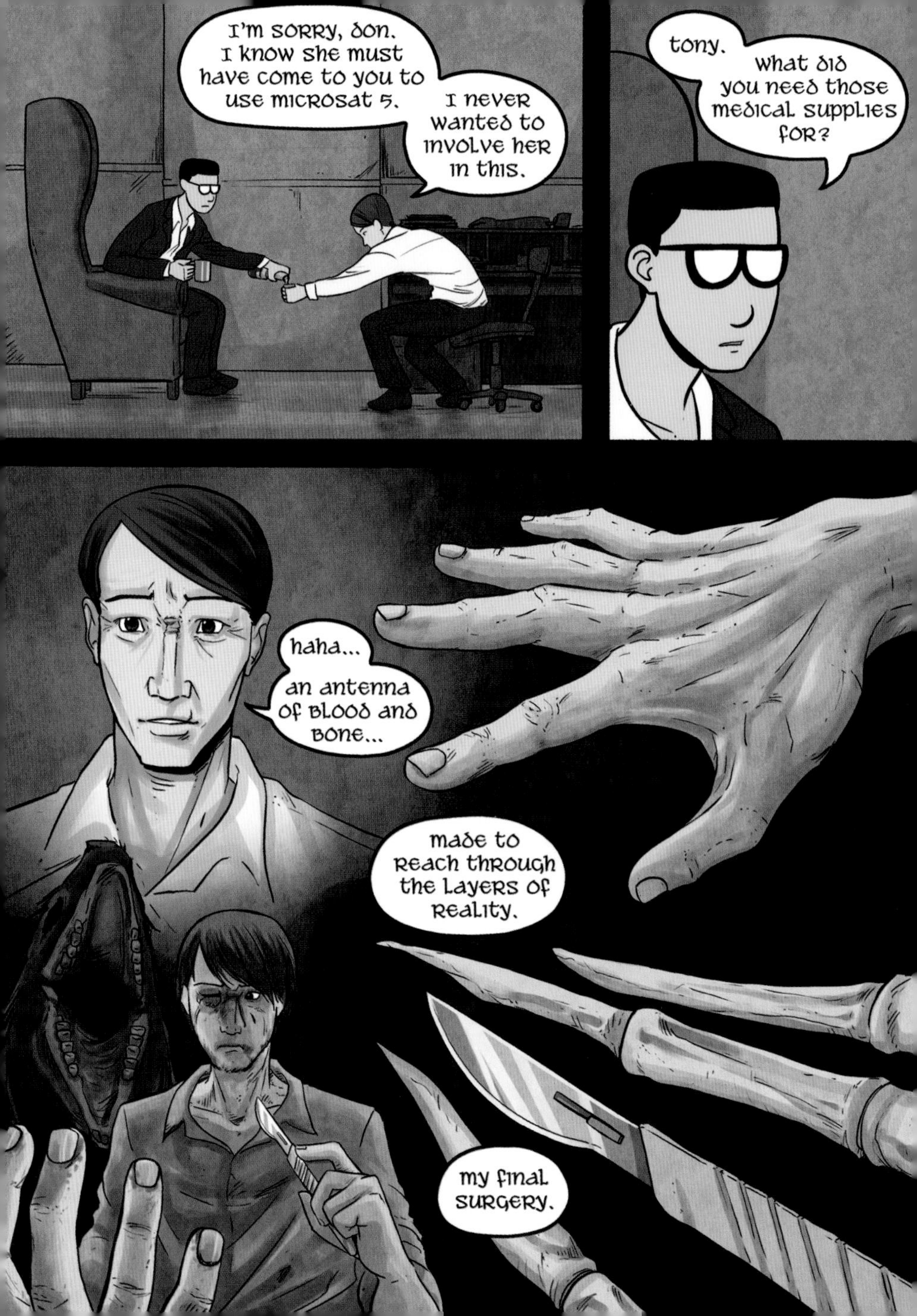
I'm SORRY, don.
I know she must
have come to you to
use microsat 5.
I never
wanted to
involve her
in this.
tony.
what did
you need those
medical supplies
for?
haha...
an antenna
of blood and
bone...
made to
reach through
the layers of
reality.
my final
surgery.

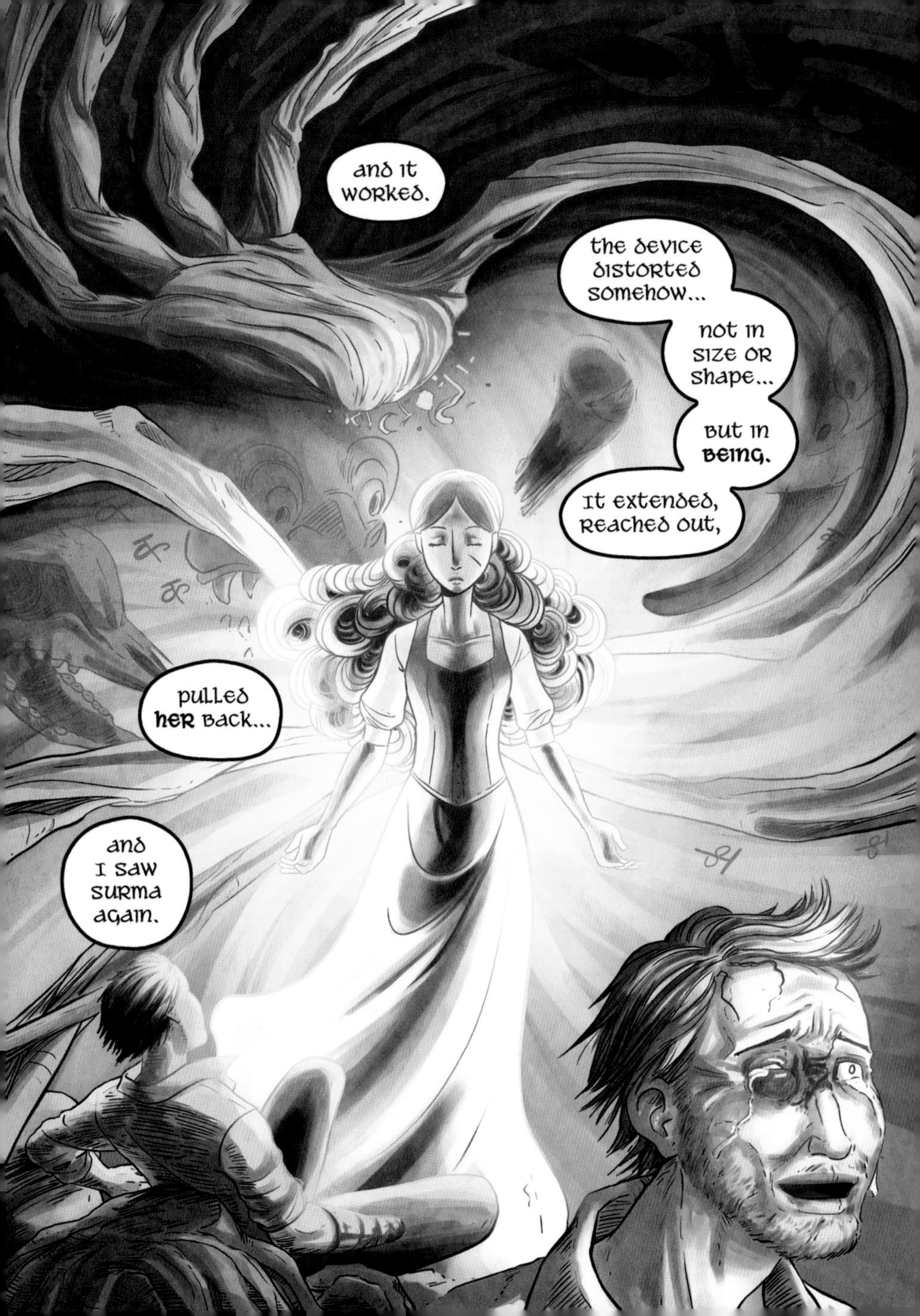
and it worked.
the device distorted somehow...
not in size or shape...
but in **being.**
it extended, reached out,
pulled **her** back...
and I saw surma again.

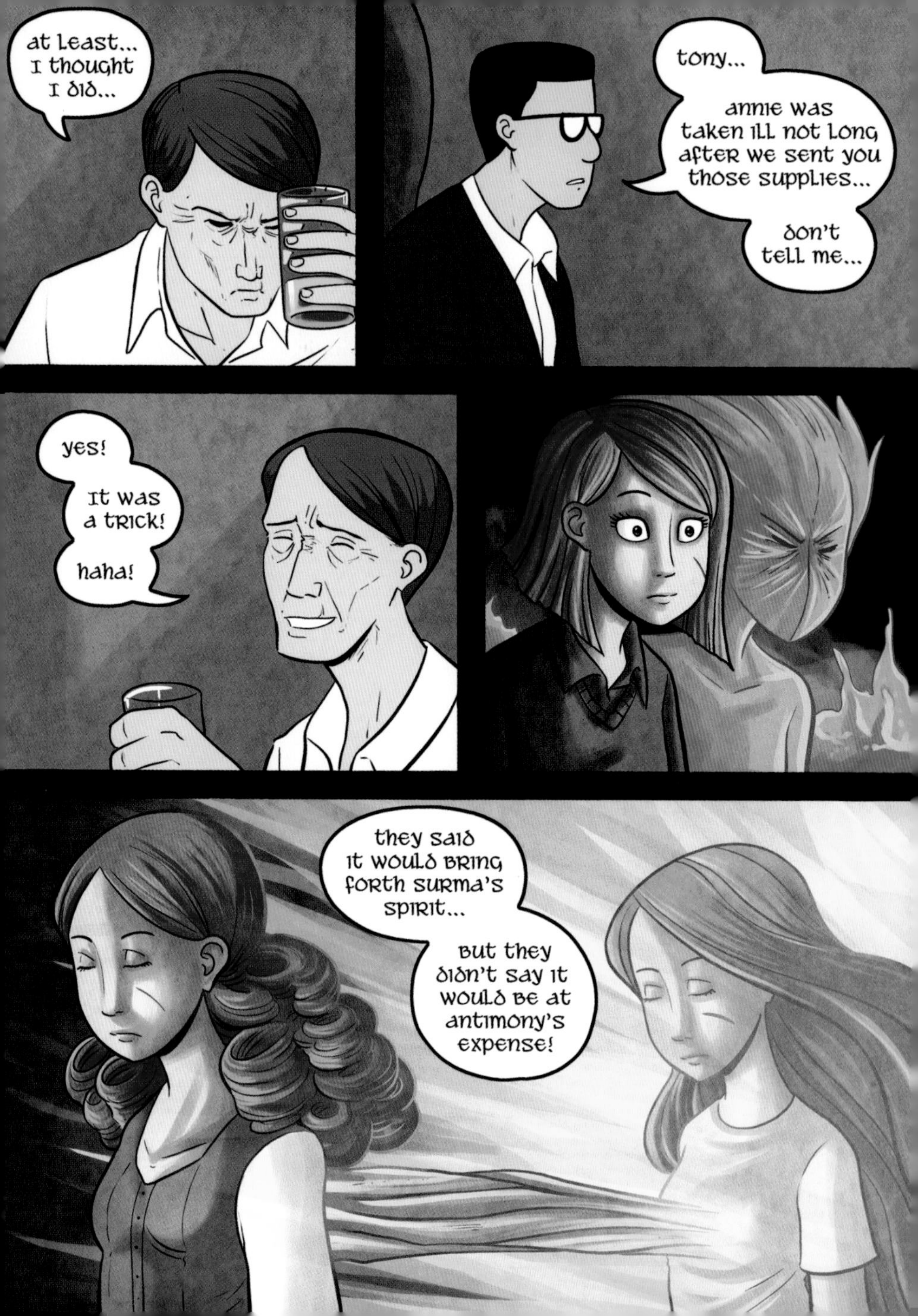
at least... I thought I did...
tony...
annie was taken ill not long after we sent you those supplies...
don't tell me...
yes!
it was a trick!
haha!
they said it would bring forth surma's spirit...
but they didn't say it would be at antimony's expense!

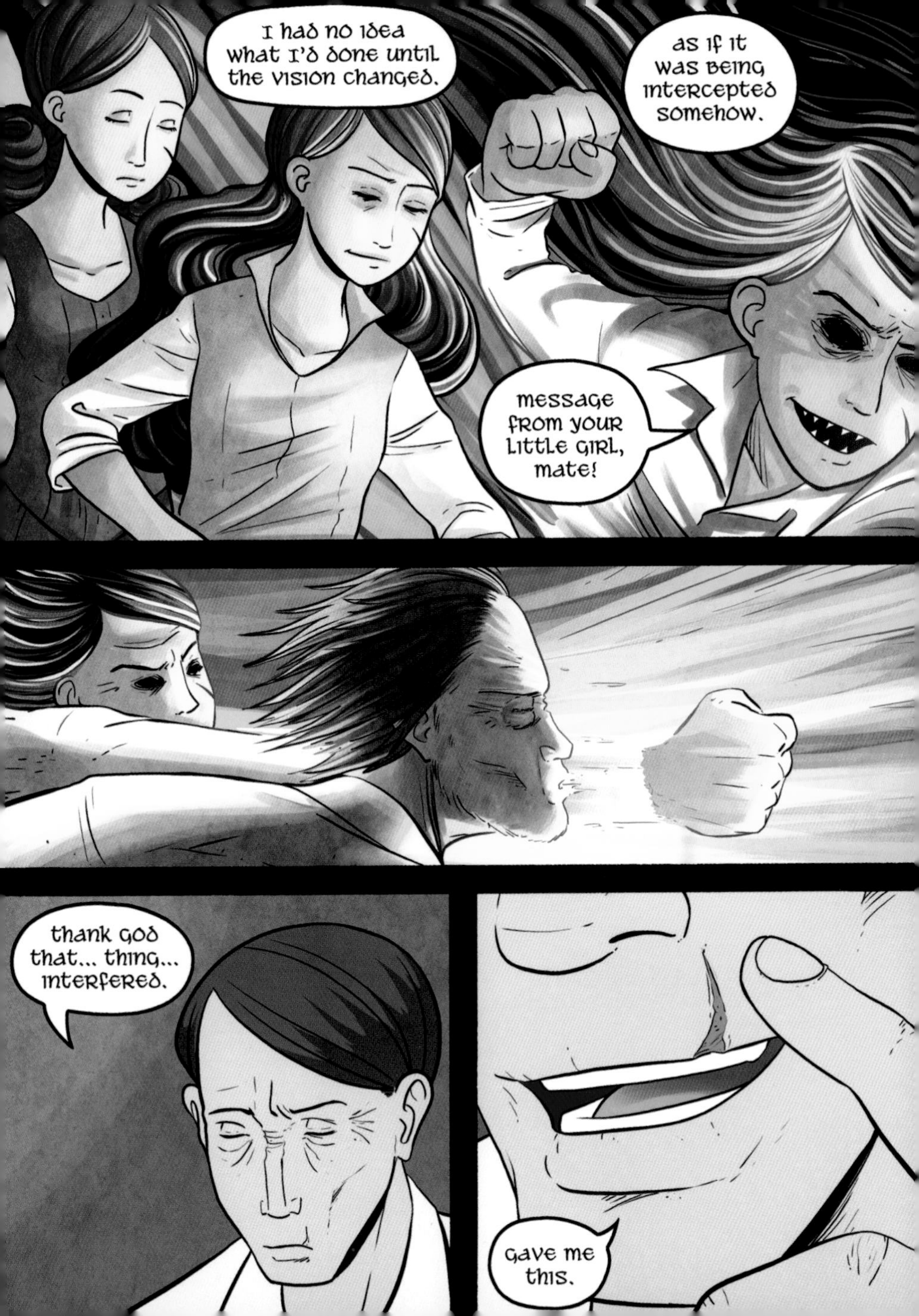
I had no idea what I'd done until the vision changed.
as if it was being intercepted somehow.
message from your little girl, mate!
thank God that... thing... interfered.
gave me this.

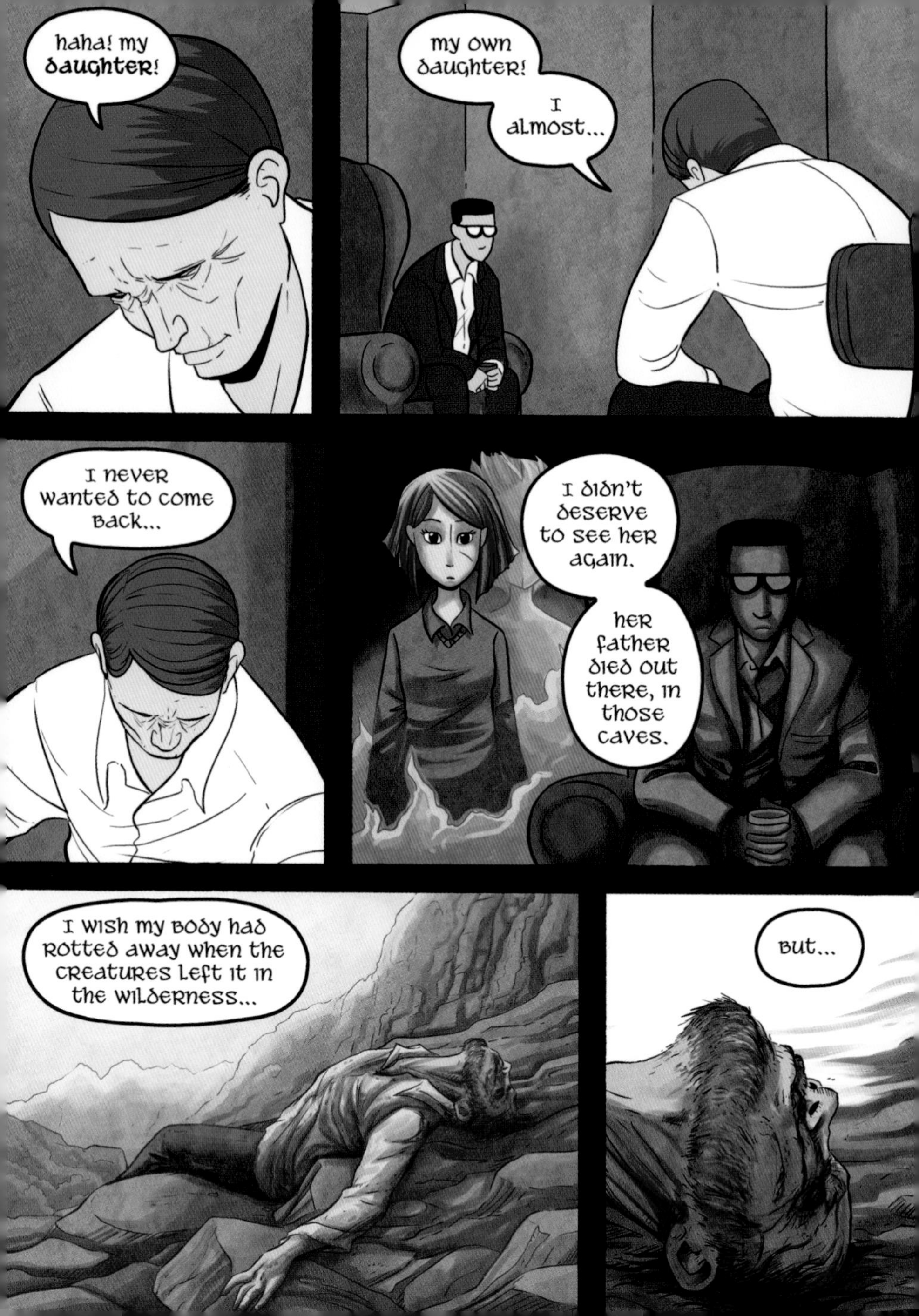
haha! my daughter!
my own daughter!
I almost...
I never wanted to come back...
I didn't deserve to see her again.
her father died out there, in those caves.
I wish my body had rotted away when the creatures left it in the wilderness...
but...

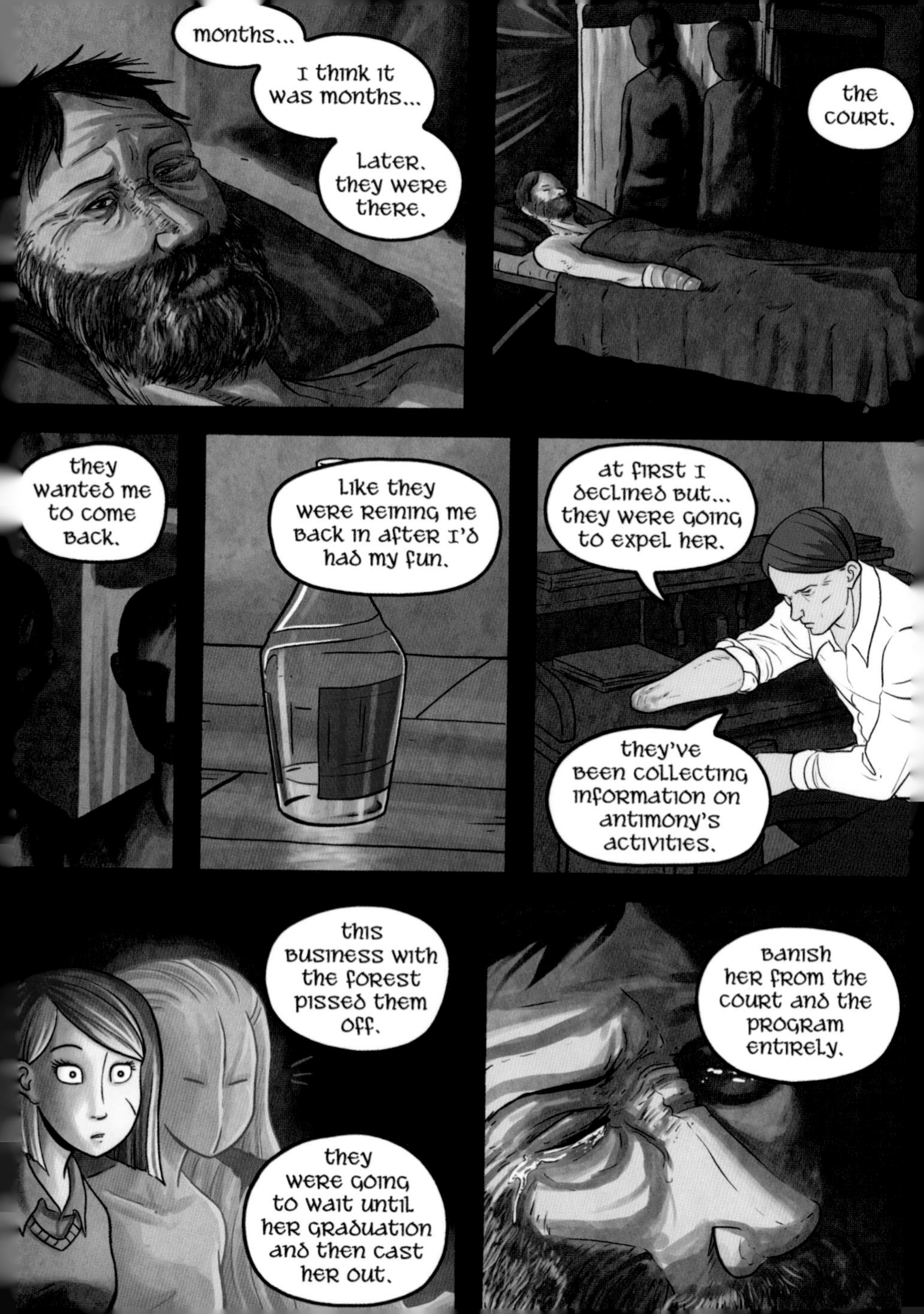

months...
I think it was months...
later. they were there.
the court.
they wanted me to come back.
like they were reining me back in after I'd had my fun.
at first I declined but... they were going to expel her.
they've been collecting information on antimony's activities.
this business with the forest pissed them off.
they were going to wait until her graduation and then cast her out.
banish her from the court and the program entirely.

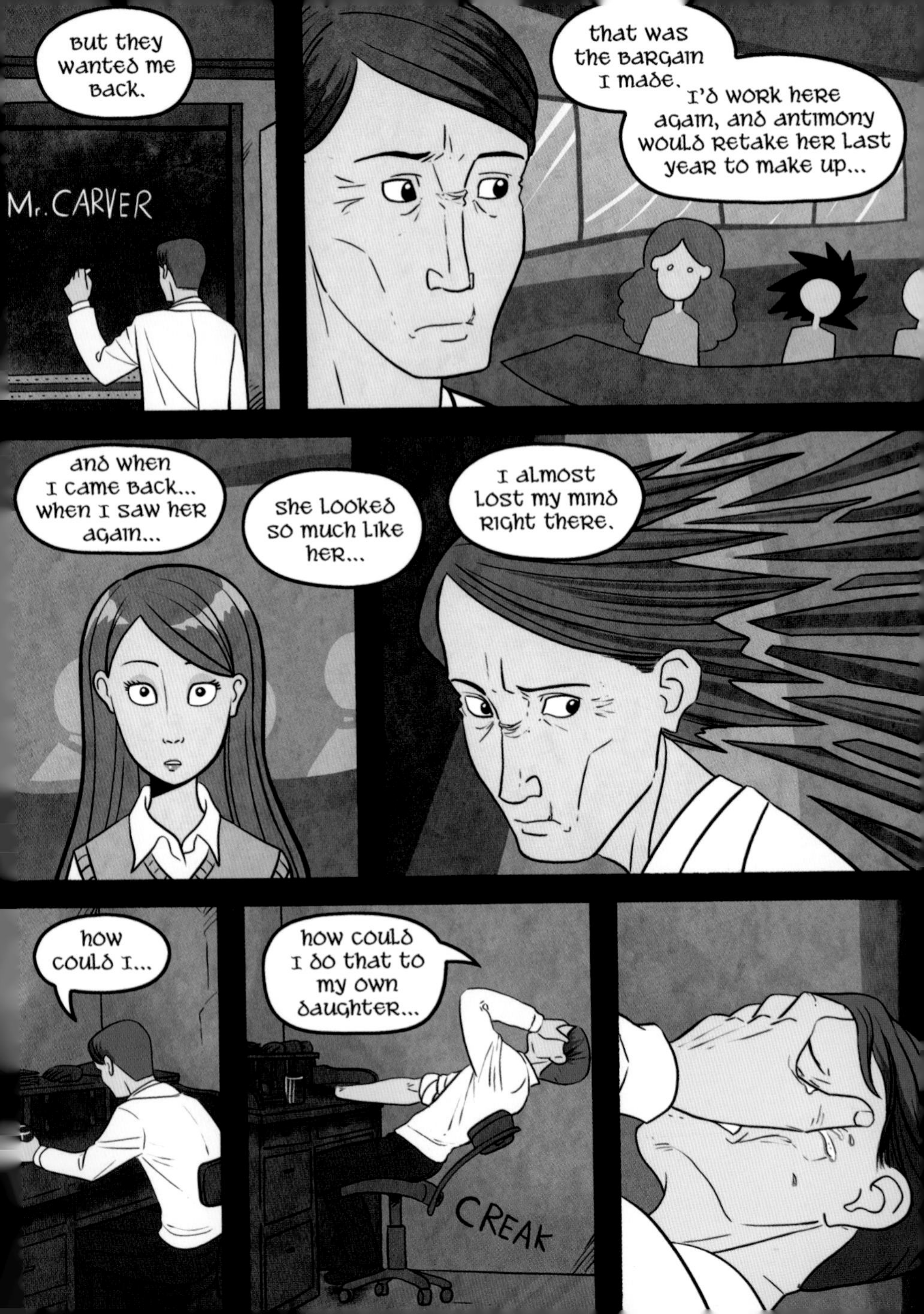
But they wanted me back.
M r. CARVER
that was the bargain I made.
I'd work here again, and antimony would retake her last year to make up...
and when I came back... when I saw her again...
she looked so much like her...
I almost lost my mind right there.
how could I...
how could I do that to my own daughter...
CREAK

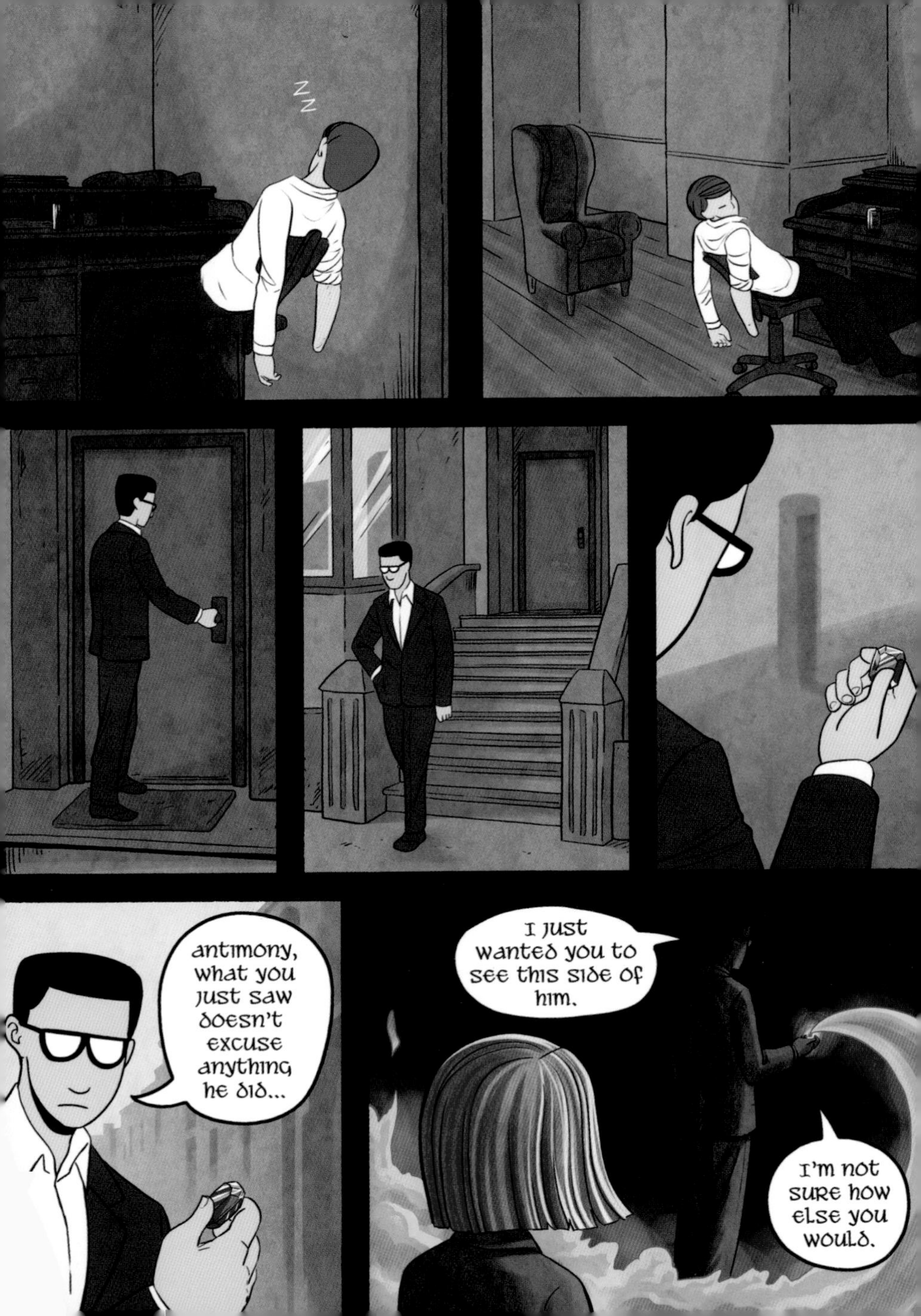
Z
Z
antimony, what you just saw doesn't excuse anything he did...
I just wanted you to see this side of him.
I'm not sure how else you would.

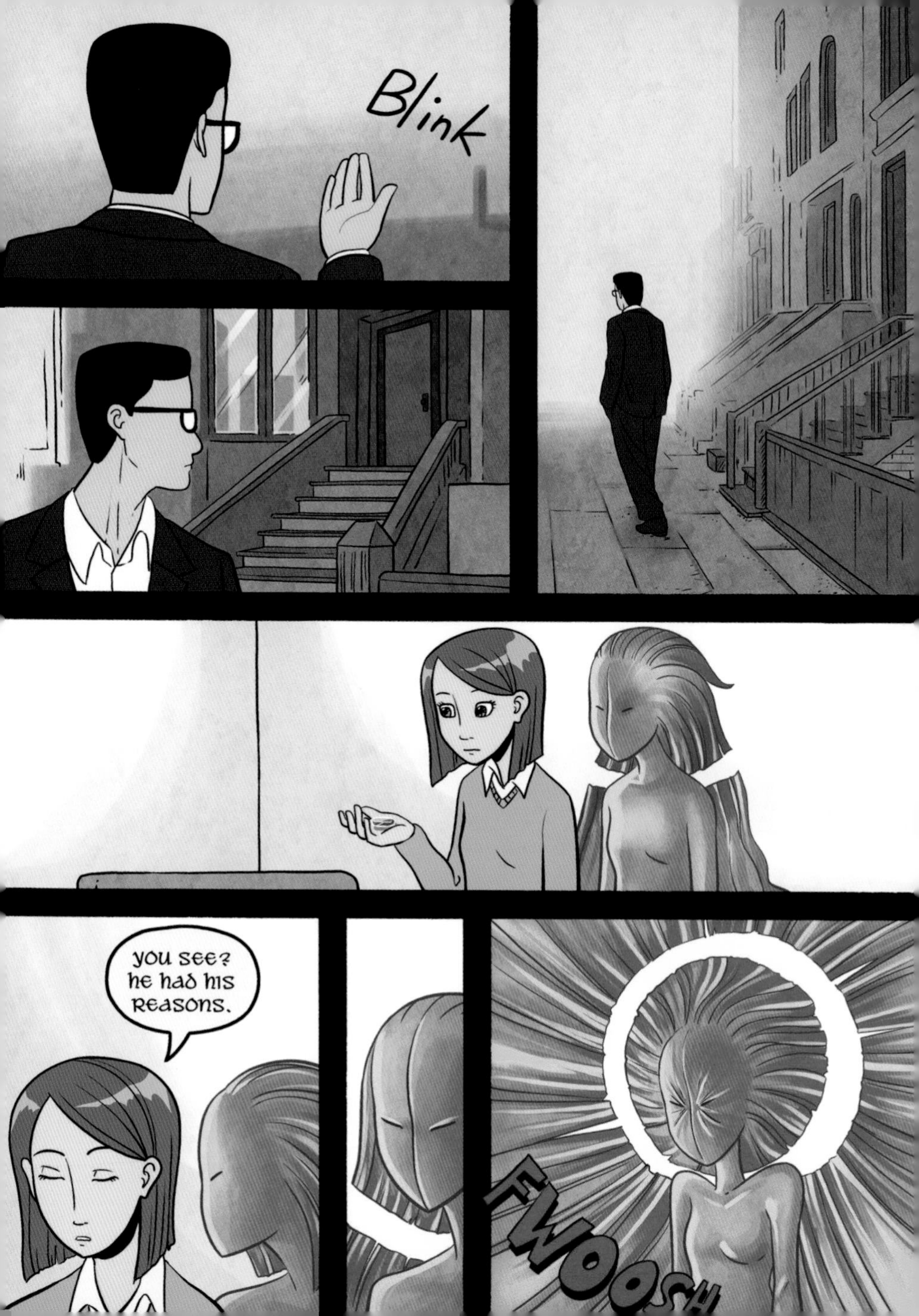
Blink
you see? he had his reasons.
FWOOSH

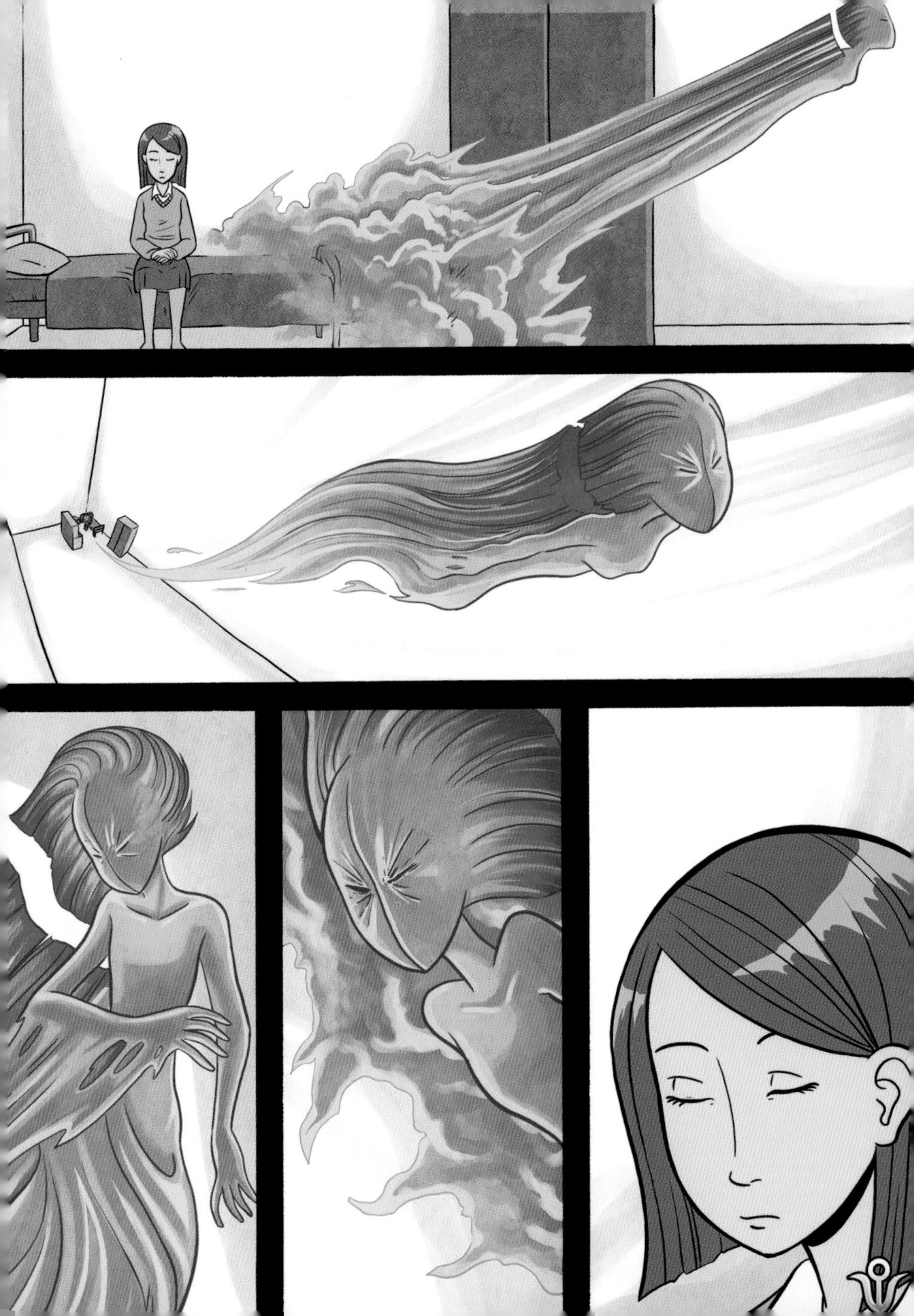

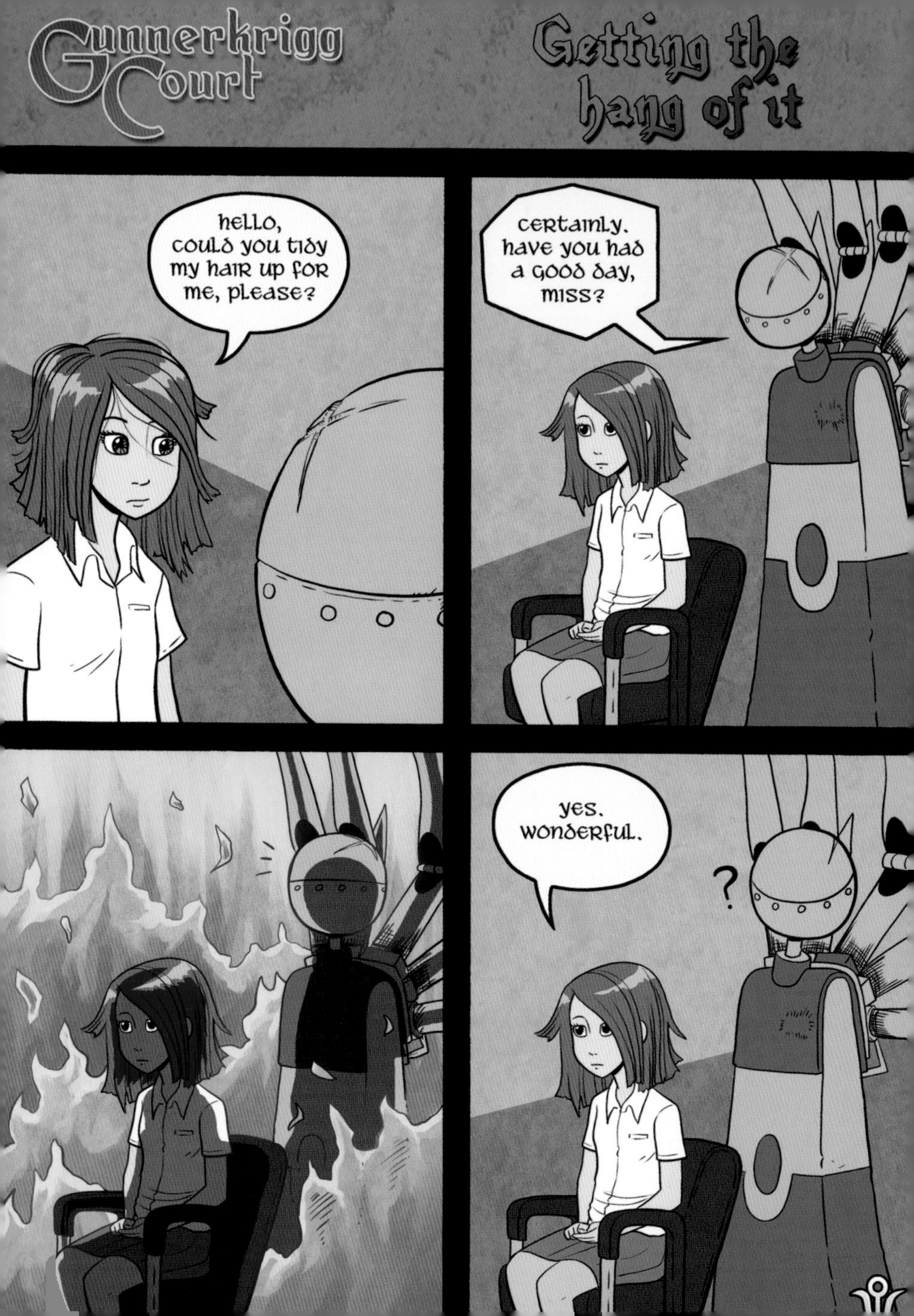
Gunnerkrigg Court
Getting the hang of it
hello, could you tidy my hair up for me, please?
certainly. have you had a good day, miss?
yes. wonderful.
?

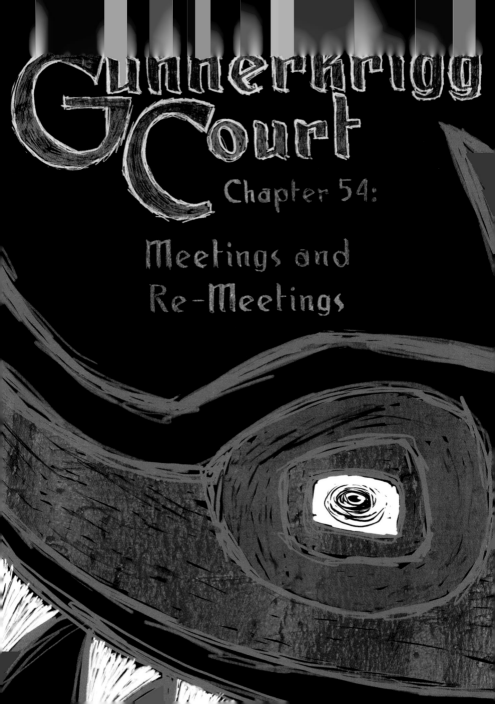

Gunnerkrigg Court

Chapter 54:

Meetings and Re-Meetings

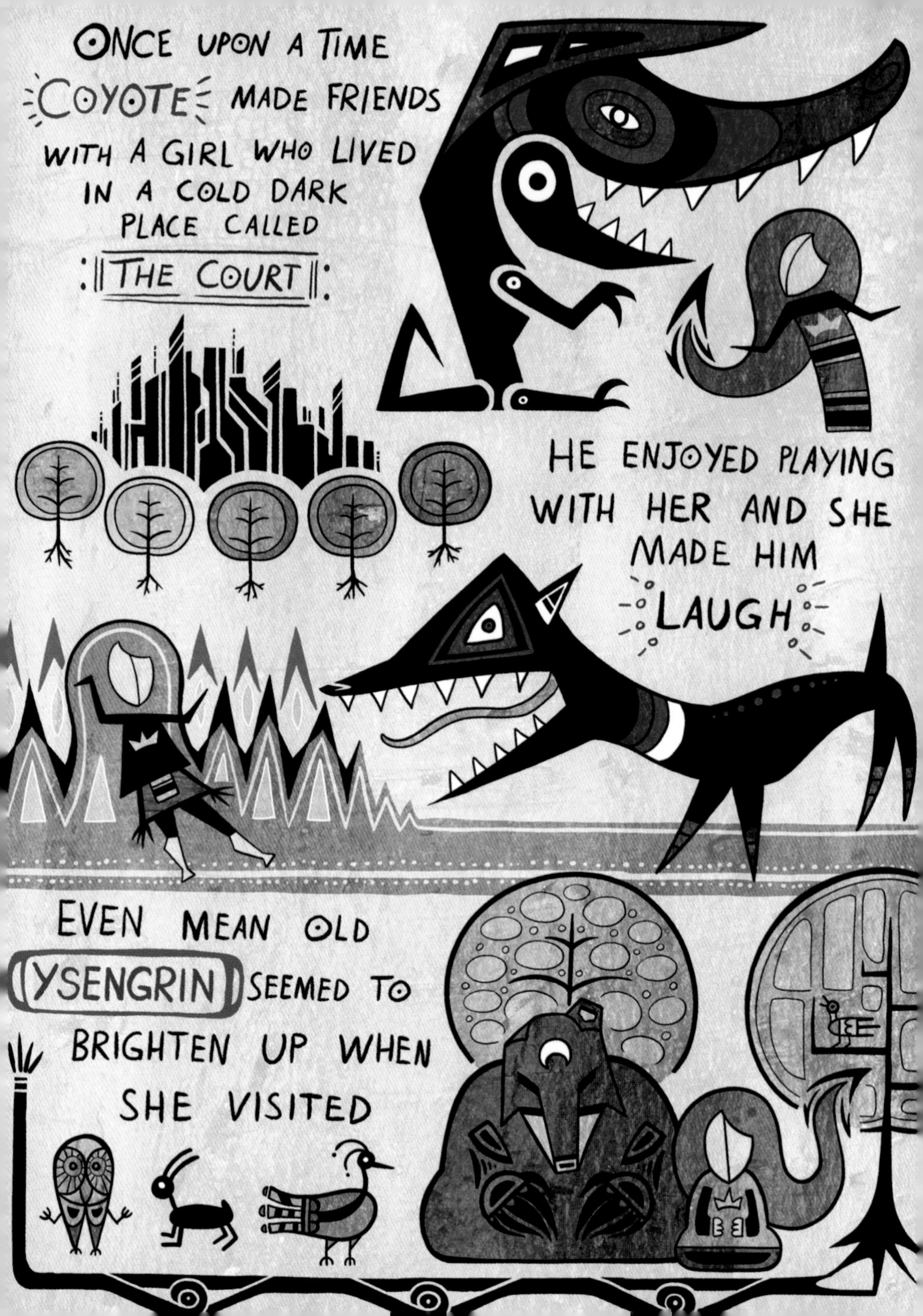
ONCE UPON A TIME COYOTE MADE FRIENDS WITH A GIRL WHO LIVED IN A COLD DARK PLACE CALLED THE COURT
HE ENJOYED PLAYING WITH HER AND SHE MADE HIM LAUGH
EVEN MEAN OLD YSENGRIN SEEMED TO BRIGHTEN UP WHEN SHE VISITED

BUT ONE DAY THE GIRL STOPPED VISITING
=COYOTE= IN HIS FOREST

SHE WAS BEING KEPT IN :‖THE COURT‖:
AND =COYOTE= DIDN'T LIKE THIS AT ALL

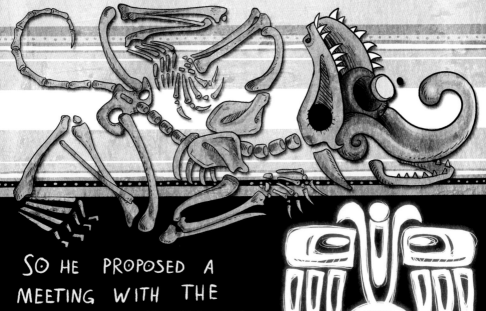

SO HE PROPOSED A
MEETING WITH THE
LORDS OF :‖THE COURT‖:

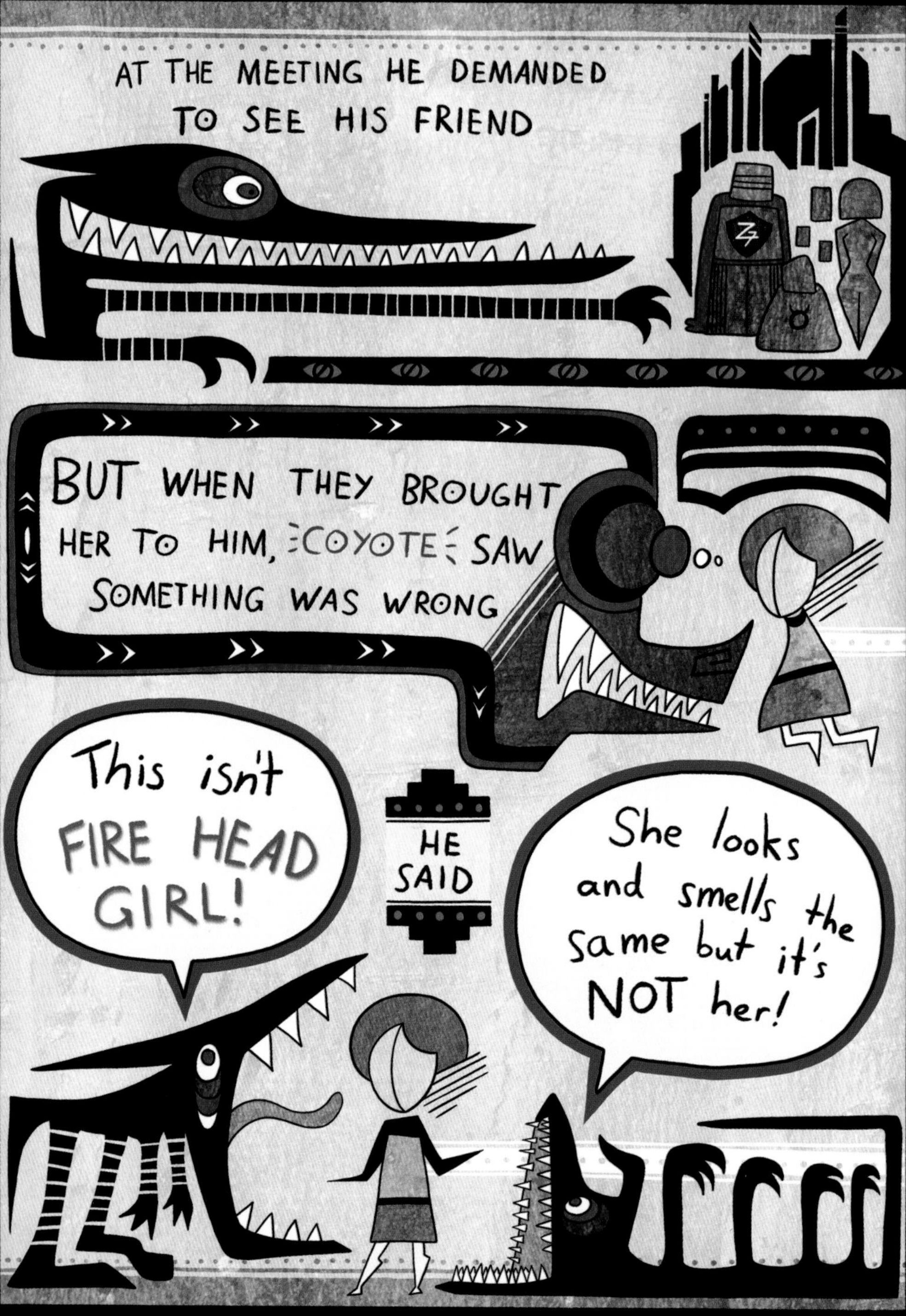
AT THE MEETING HE DEMANDED TO SEE HIS FRIEND
BUT WHEN THEY BROUGHT HER TO HIM, COYOTE SAW SOMETHING WAS WRONG
This isn't FIRE HEAD GIRL!
HE SAID
She looks and smells the same but it's NOT her!

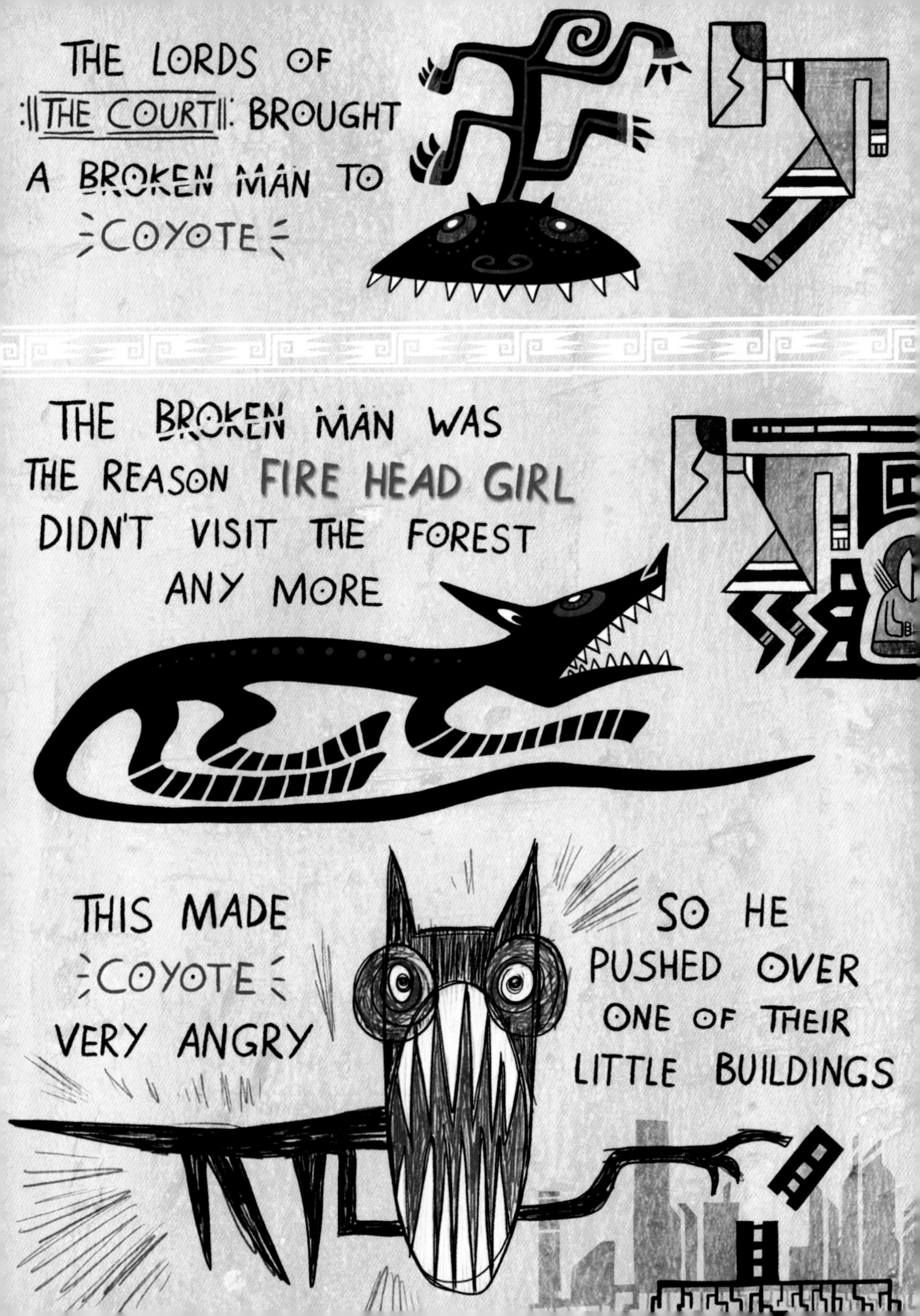
THE LORDS OF THE COURT BROUGHT A BROKEN MAN TO COYOTE
THE BROKEN MAN WAS THE REASON FIRE HEAD GIRL DIDN'T VISIT THE FOREST ANY MORE
THIS MADE COYOTE VERY ANGRY
SO HE PUSHED OVER ONE OF THEIR LITTLE BUILDINGS

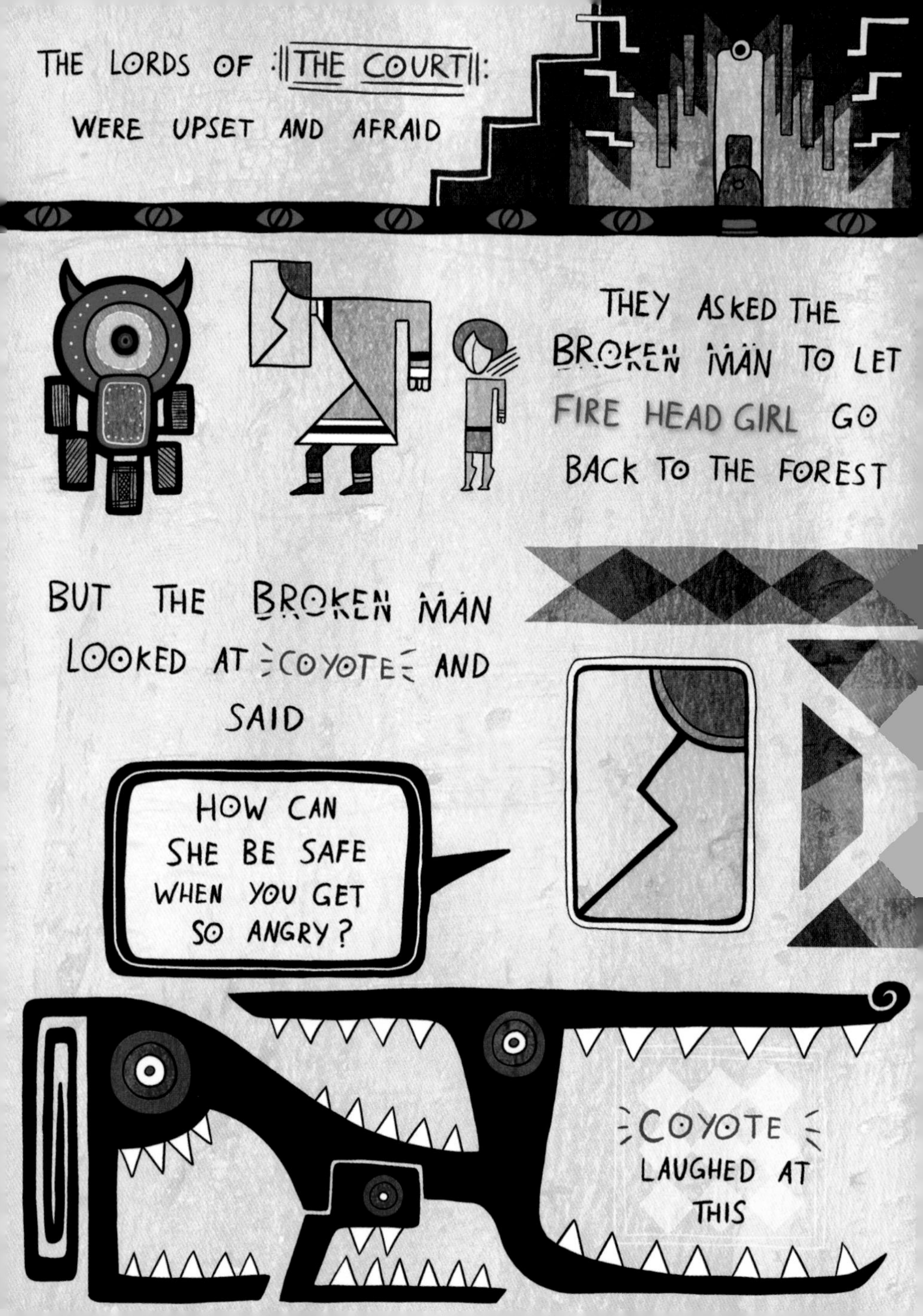
THE LORDS OF THE COURT
WERE UPSET AND AFRAID
THEY ASKED THE BROKEN MAN TO LET FIRE HEAD GIRL GO BACK TO THE FOREST
BUT THE BROKEN MAN LOOKED AT COYOTE AND SAID
HOW CAN SHE BE SAFE WHEN YOU GET SO ANGRY?
COYOTE
COYOTE LAUGHED AT THIS

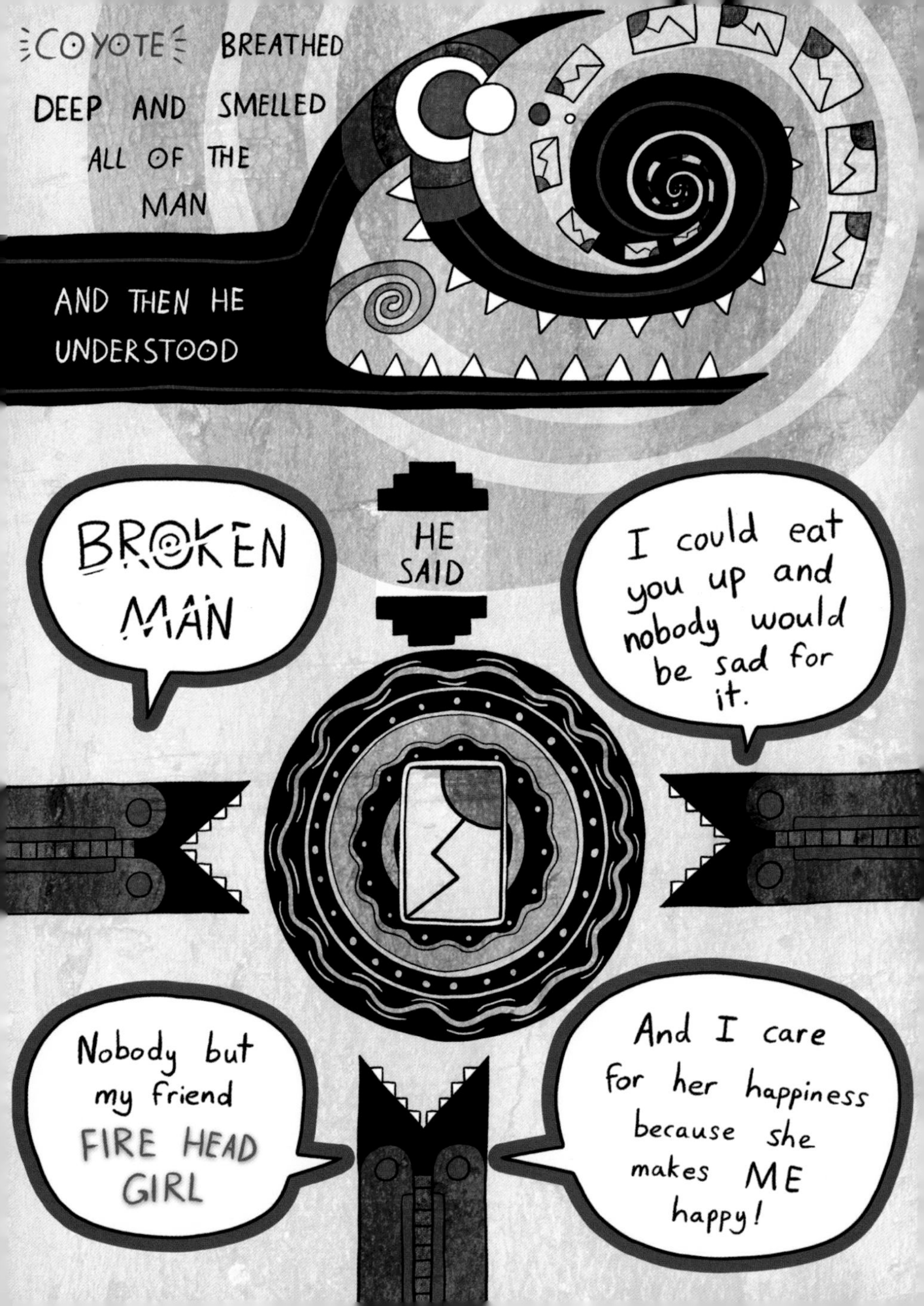
COYOTE BREATHED DEEP AND SMELLED ALL OF THE MAN
AND THEN HE UNDERSTOOD
BROKEN MAN
HE SAID
I could eat you up and nobody would be sad for it.
Nobody but my friend FIRE HEAD GIRL
And I care for her happiness because she makes ME happy!

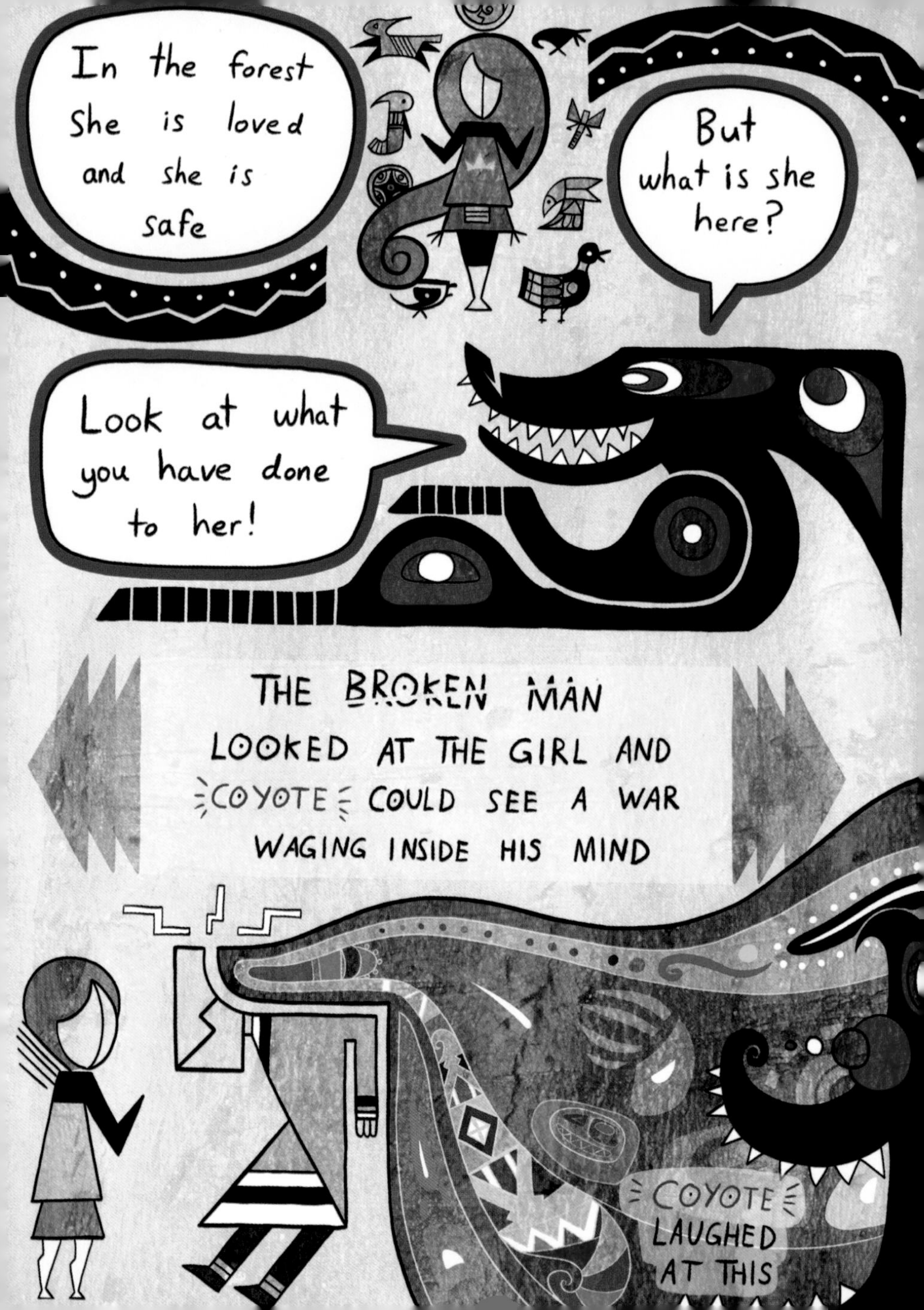
In the forest She is loved and she is safe
But what is she here?
Look at what you have done to her!
THE BROKEN MAN LOOKED AT THE GIRL AND COYOTE COULD SEE A WAR WAGING INSIDE HIS MIND
COYOTE LAUGHED AT THIS

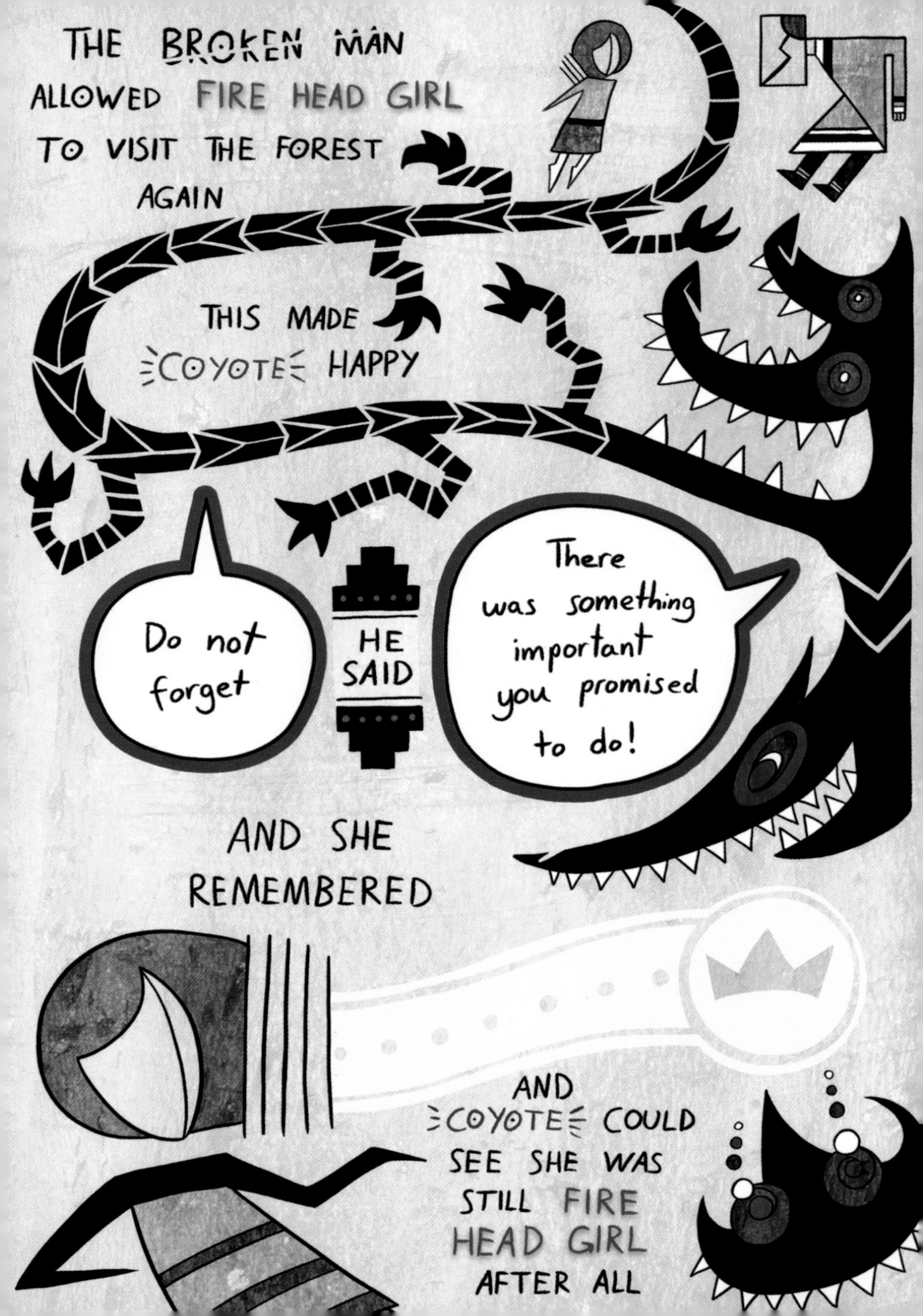
THE BROKEN MAN ALLOWED FIRE HEAD GIRL TO VISIT THE FOREST AGAIN
THIS MADE COYOTE HAPPY
Do not forget
HE SAID
There was something important you promised to do!
AND SHE REMEMBERED
AND COYOTE COULD SEE SHE WAS STILL FIRE HEAD GIRL AFTER ALL

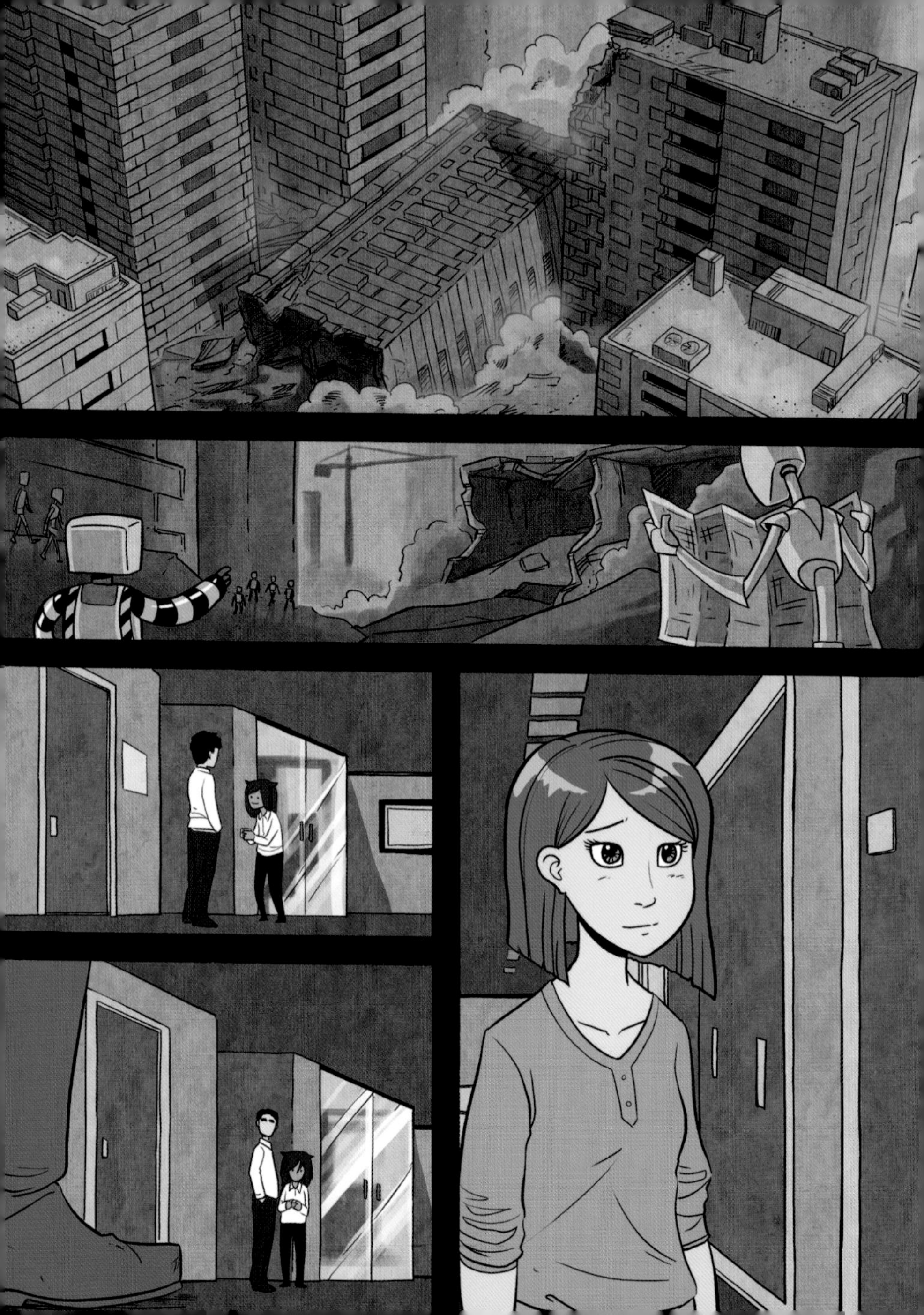

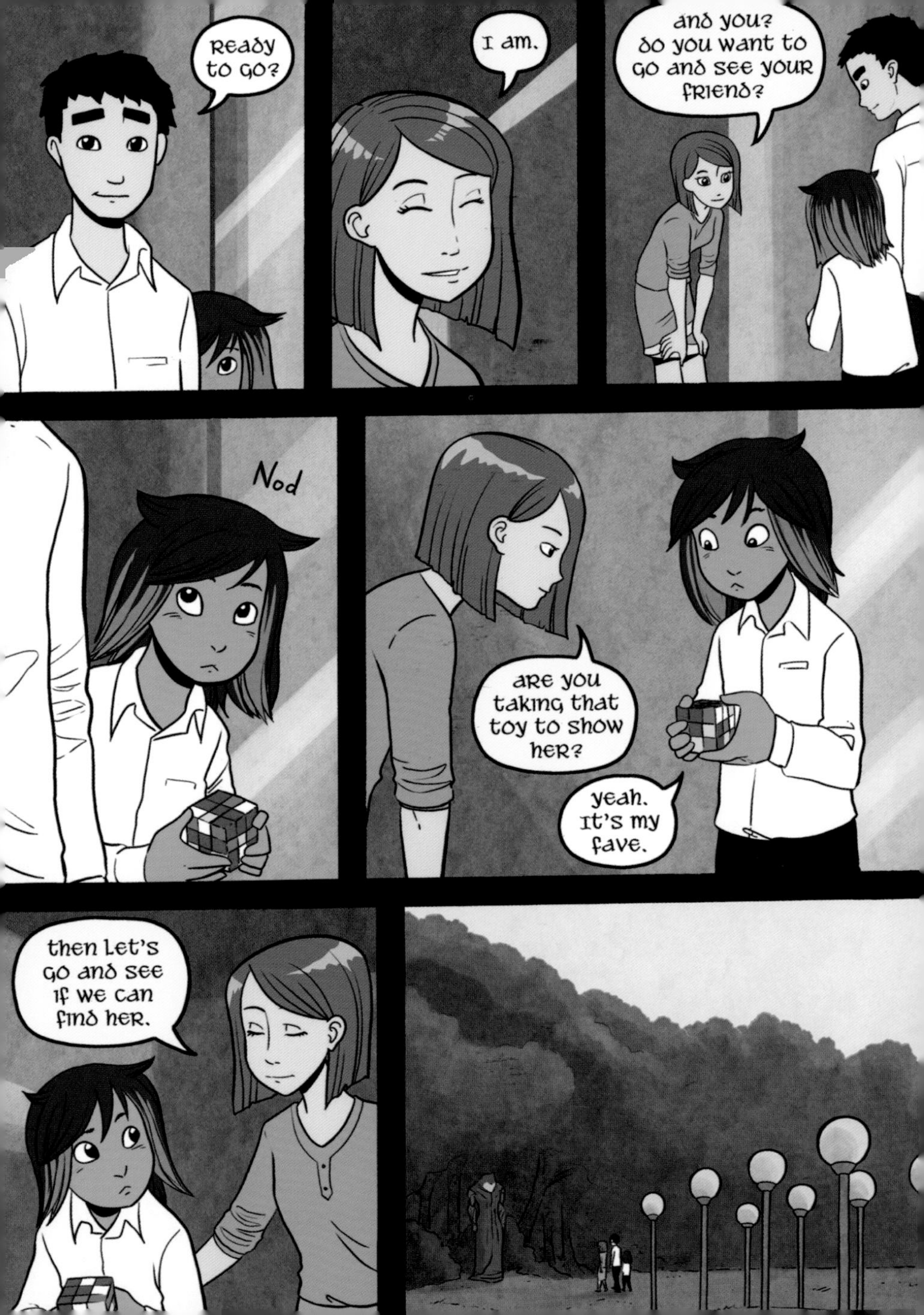
Ready to go?
I am.
and you? do you want to go and see your friend?
Nod
are you taking that toy to show her?
yeah. It's my fave.
then Let's go and see if we can find her.

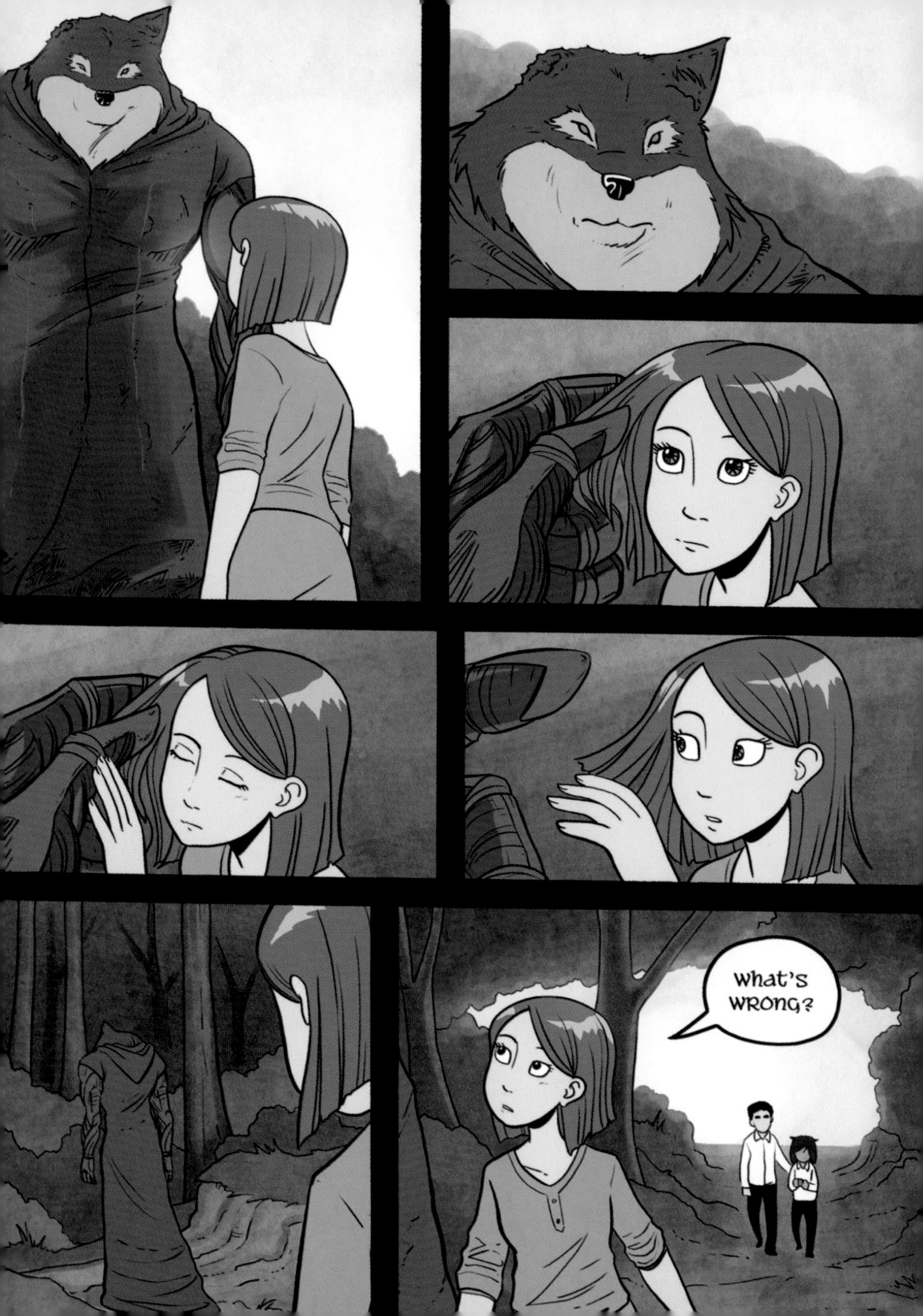
What's WRONG?

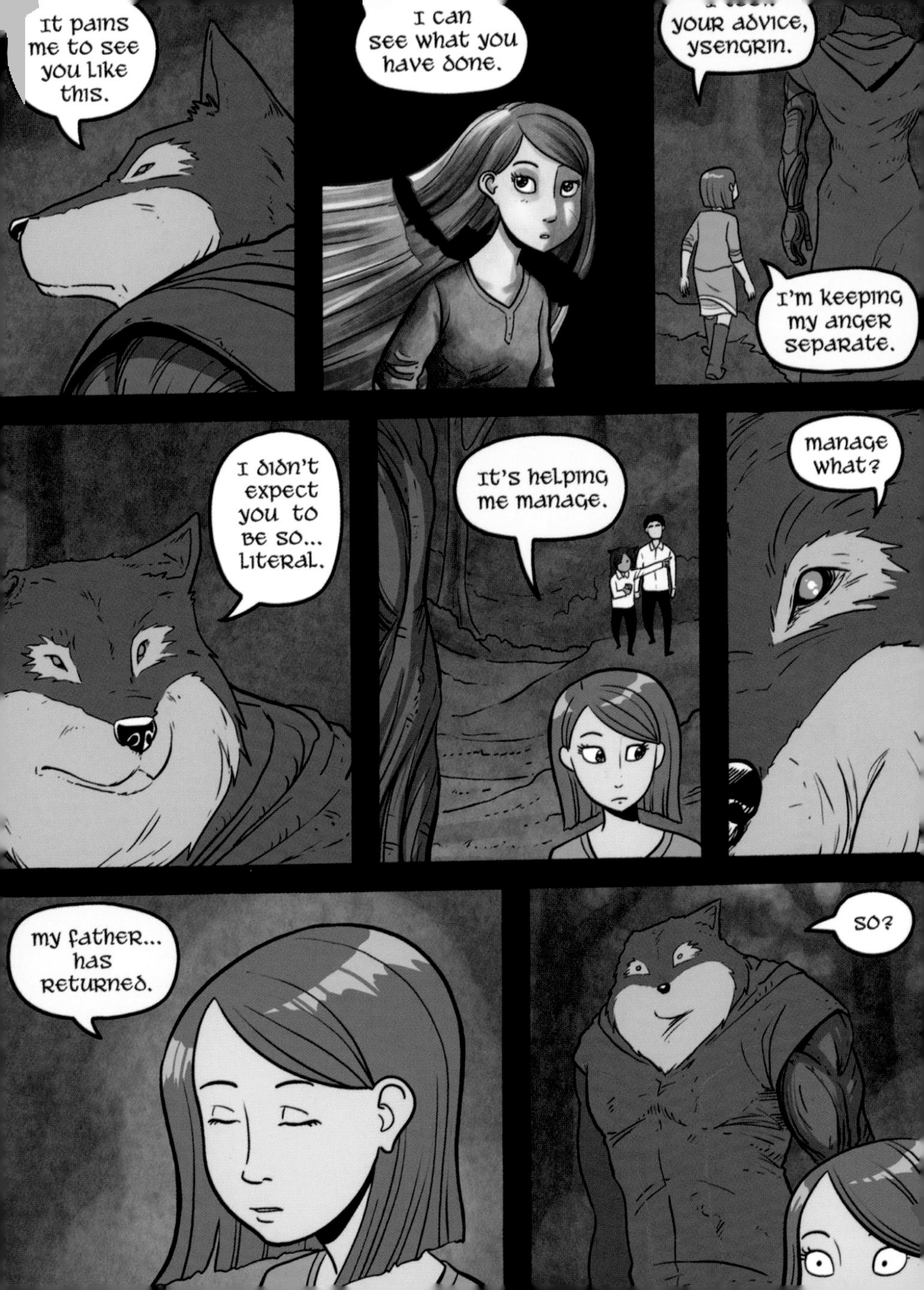
It pains me to see you like this.
I can see what you have done.
your advice, ysengrin.
I'm keeping my anger separate.
I didn't expect you to be so... literal.
It's helping me manage.
manage what?
my father... has returned.
so?

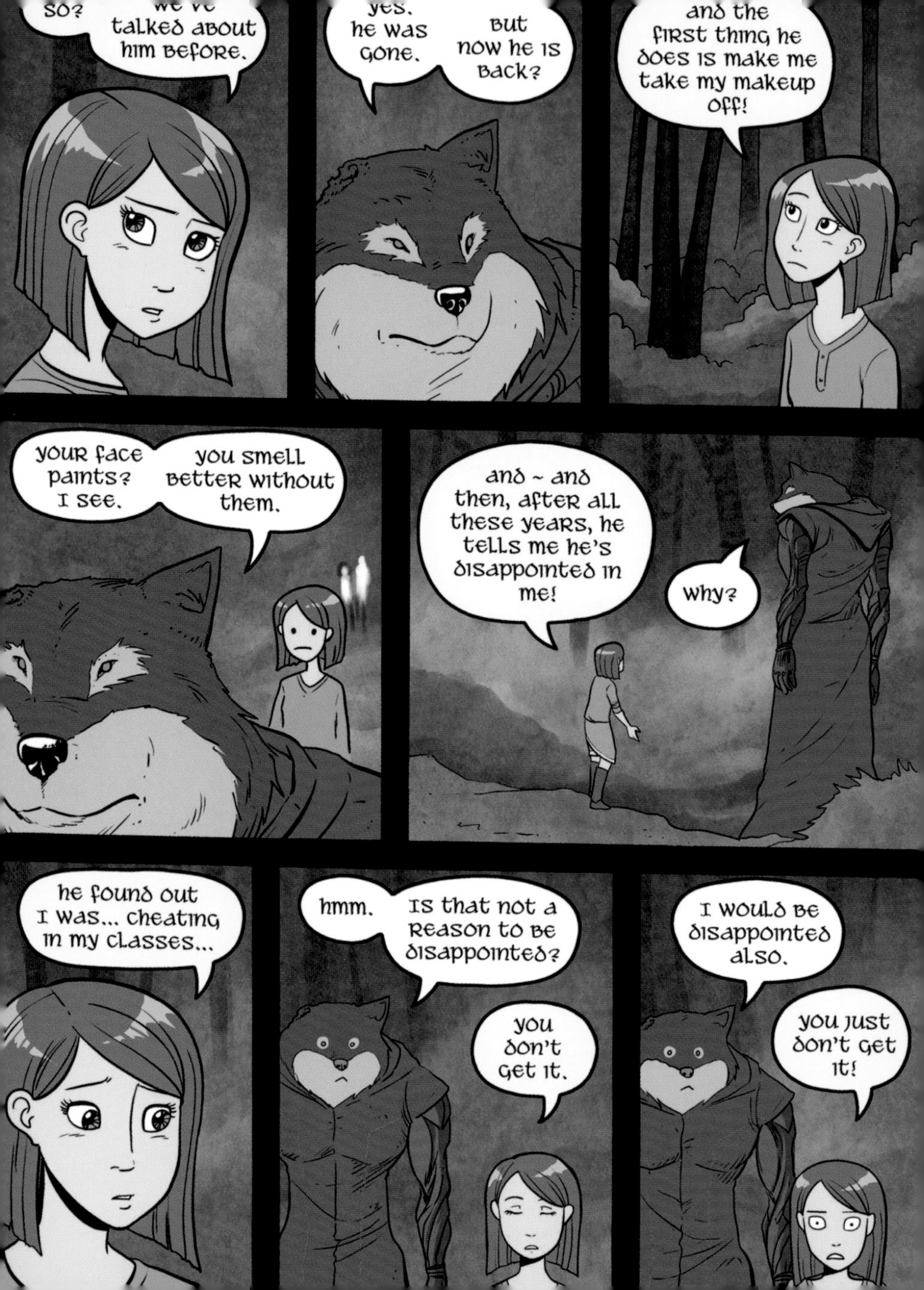
so?
talked about him before.
yes. he was gone.
but now he is back?
and the first thing he does is make me take my makeup off!
your face paints? I see.
you smell better without them.
and ~ and then, after all these years, he tells me he's disappointed in me!
why?
he found out I was... cheating in my classes...
hmm.
is that not a reason to be disappointed?
you don't get it.
I would be disappointed also.
you just don't get it!

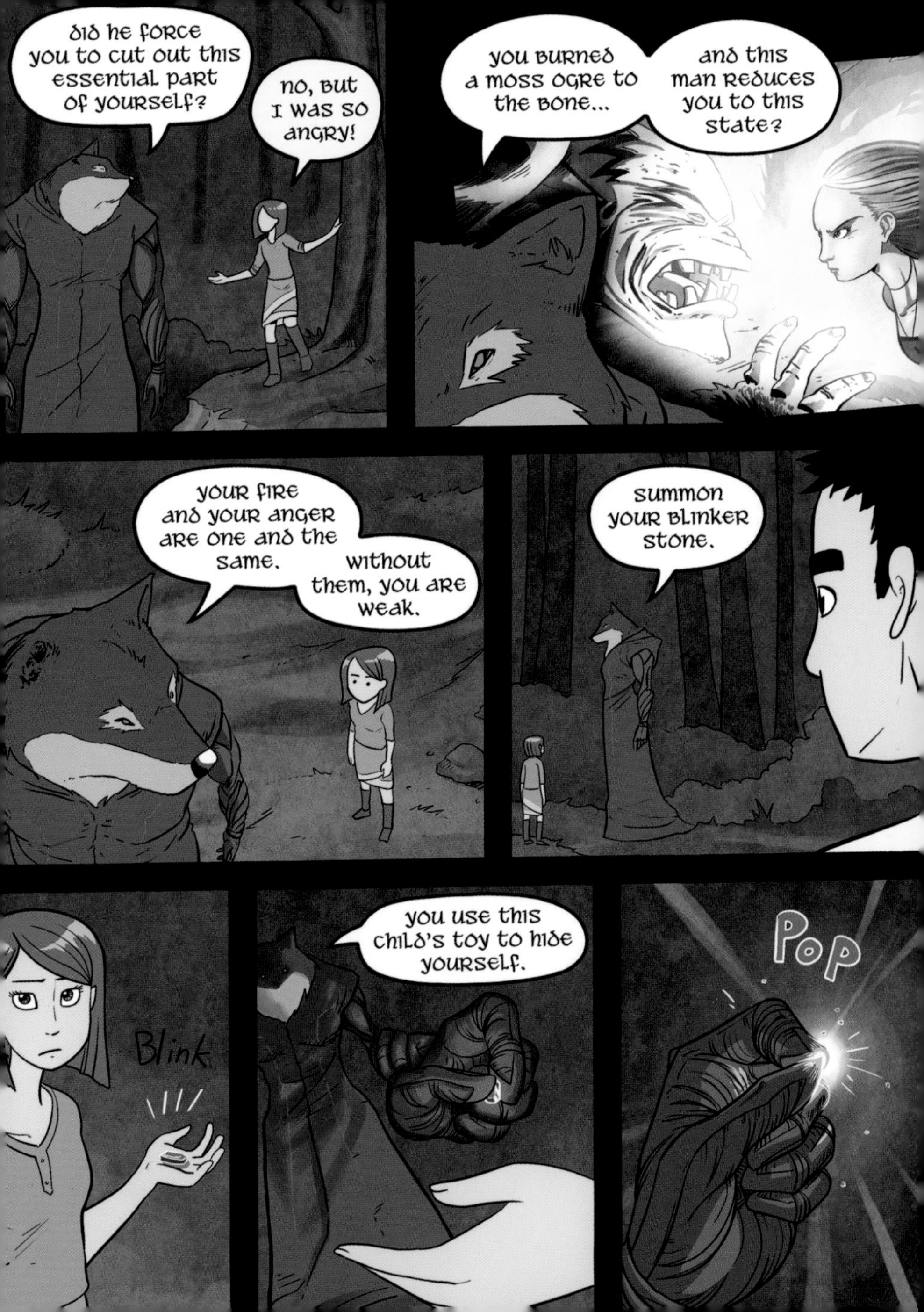

did he force you to cut out this essential part of yourself?
no, but I was so angry!
you burned a moss ogre to the bone...
and this man reduces you to this state?
your fire and your anger are one and the same.
without them, you are weak.
summon your blinker stone.
Blink
you use this child's toy to hide yourself.
Pop

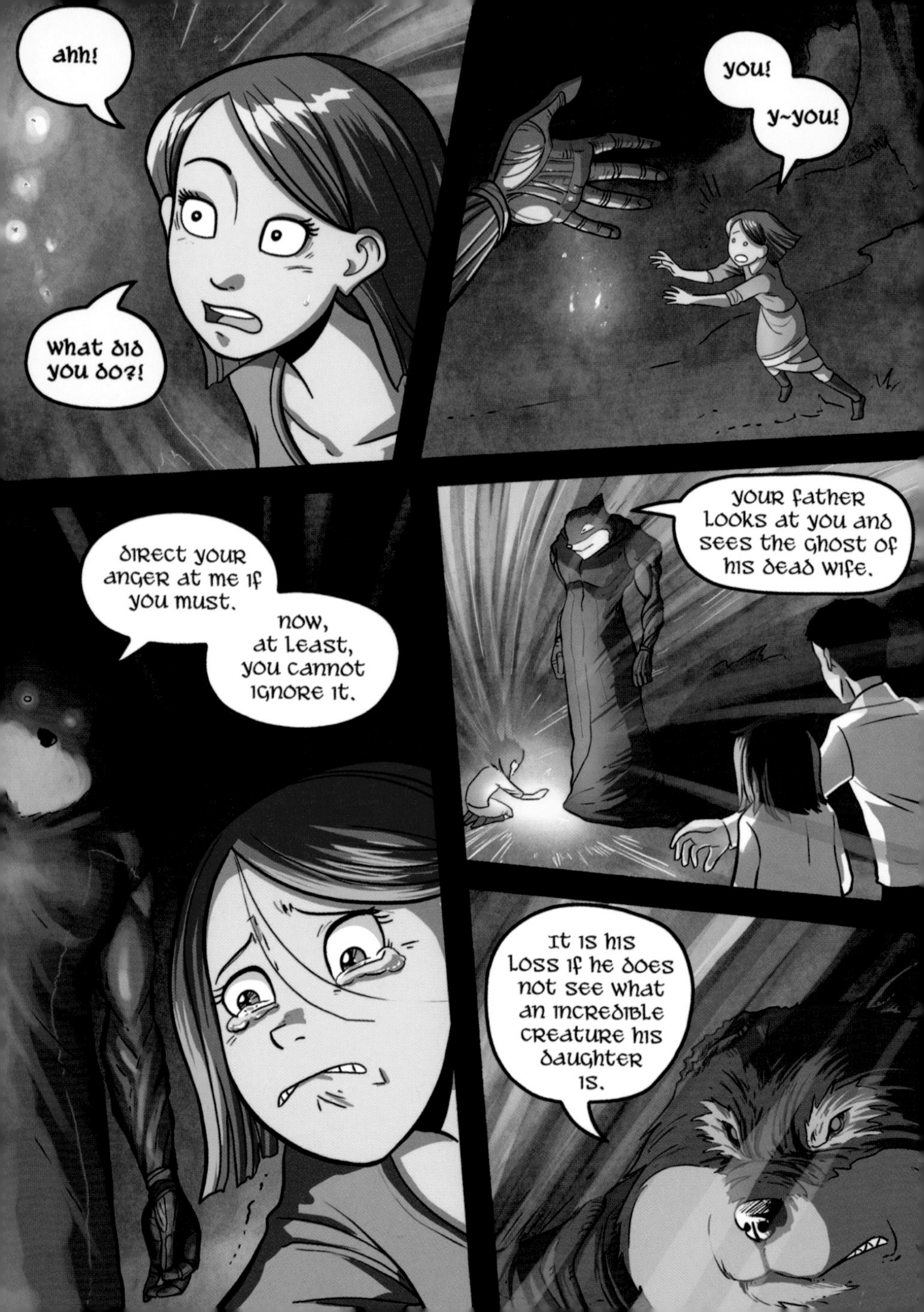
ahh!
what did you do?!
you!
y~you!
direct your anger at me if you must.
now, at least, you cannot ignore it.
your father looks at you and sees the ghost of his dead wife.
It is his loss if he does not see what an incredible creature his daughter is.

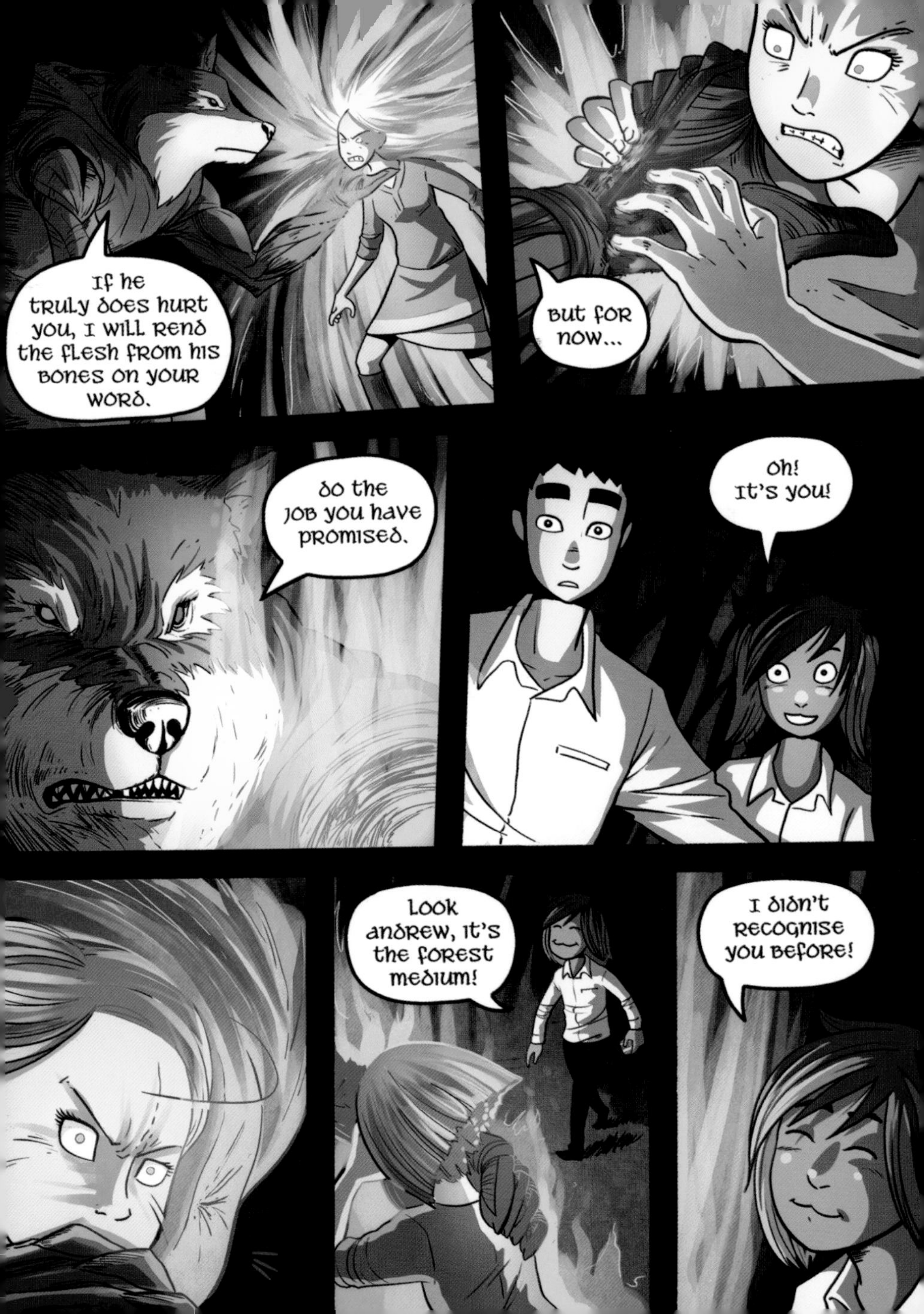
If he truly does hurt you, I will rend the flesh from his bones on your word.
But for now...
Do the job you have promised.
Oh! It's you!
Look Andrew, it's the forest medium!
I didn't recognise you before!

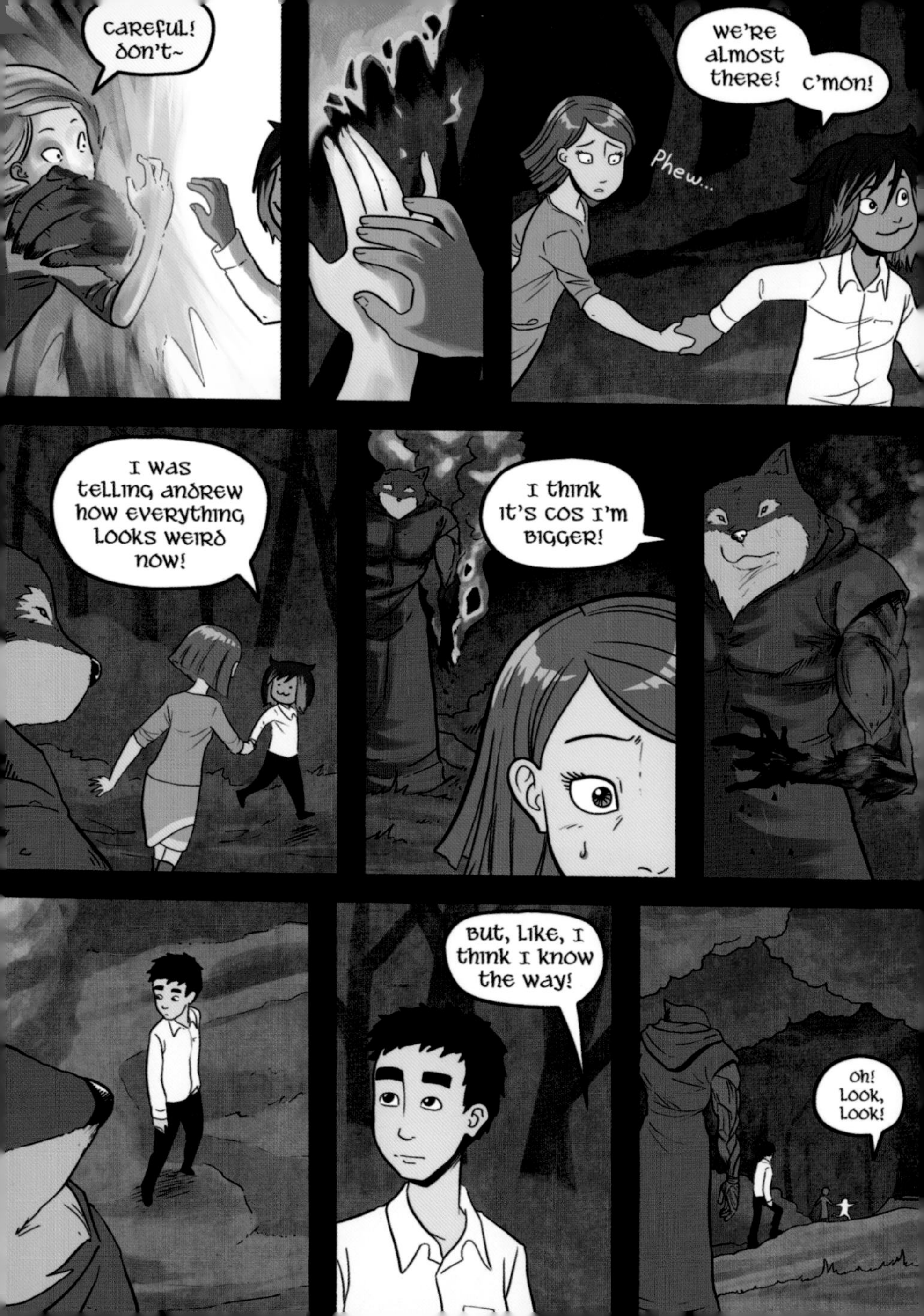
careful! don't~
We're almost there!
c'mon!
Phew...
I was telling andrew how everything looks weird now!
I think it's cos I'm BIGGER!
But, like, I think I know the way!
Oh! Look, look!

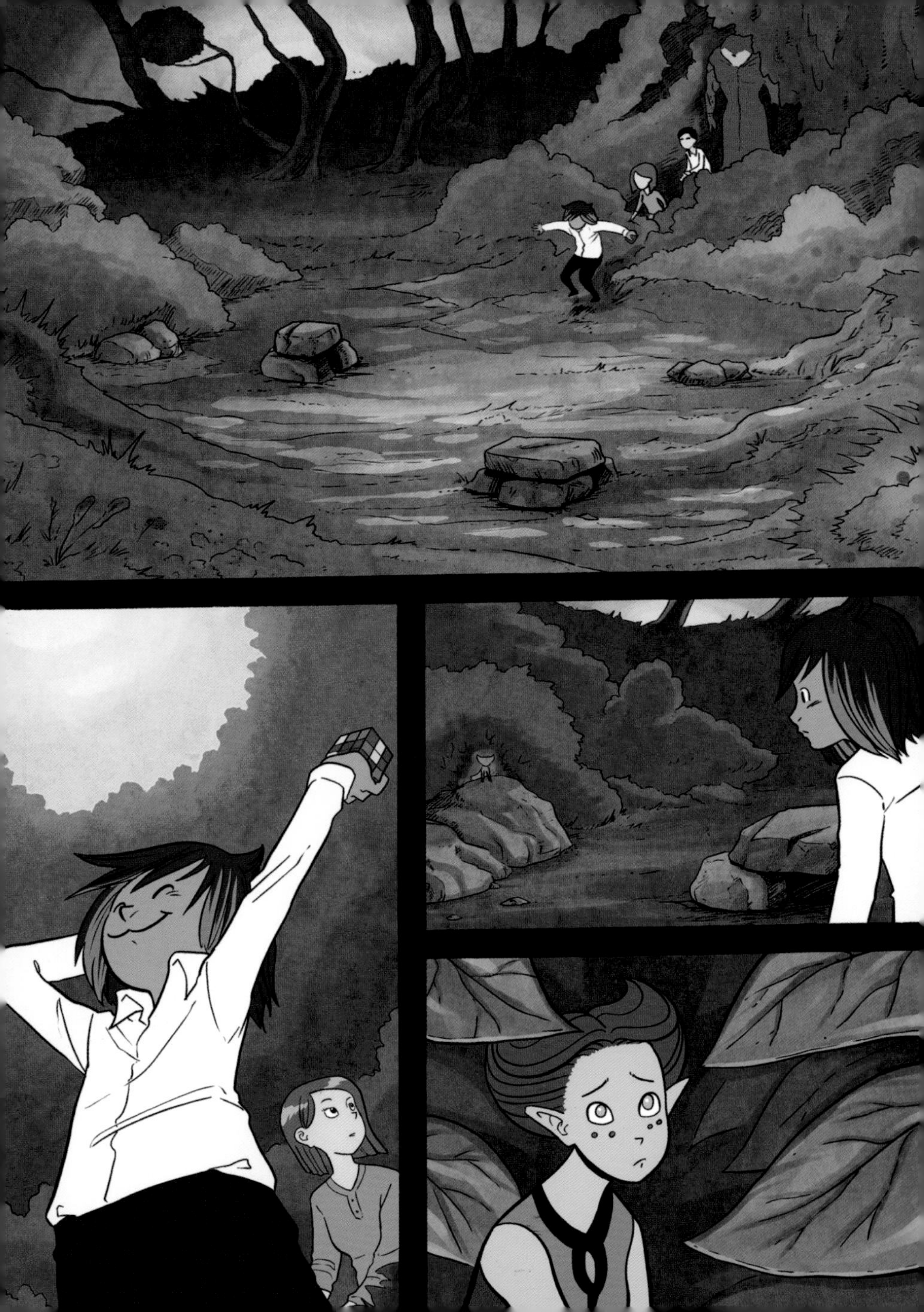

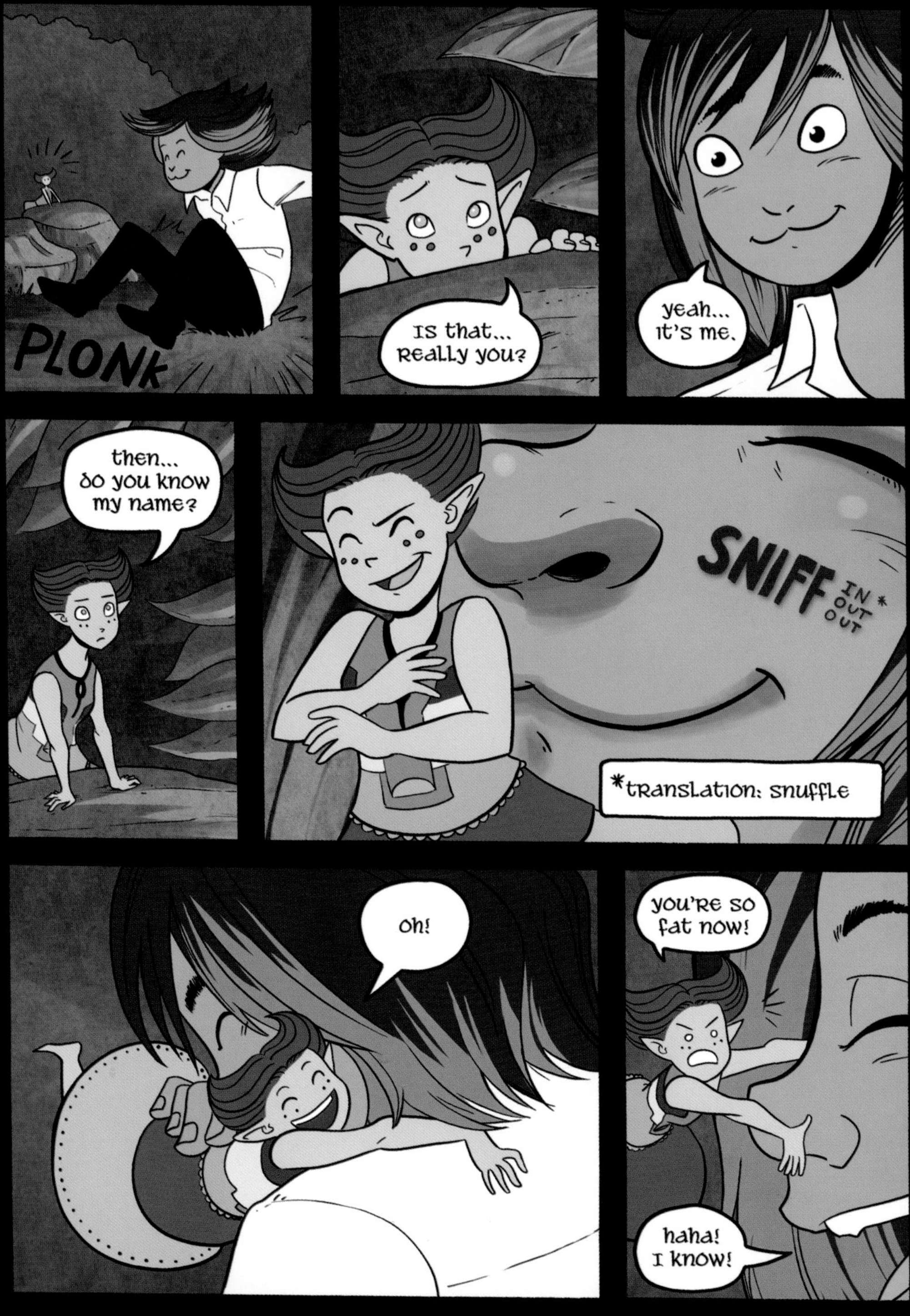
PLONK
Is that... Really you?
yeah... it's me.
then... do you know my name?
SNIFF IN* OUT OUT
*translation: snuffle
oh!
you're so fat now!
haha! I know!

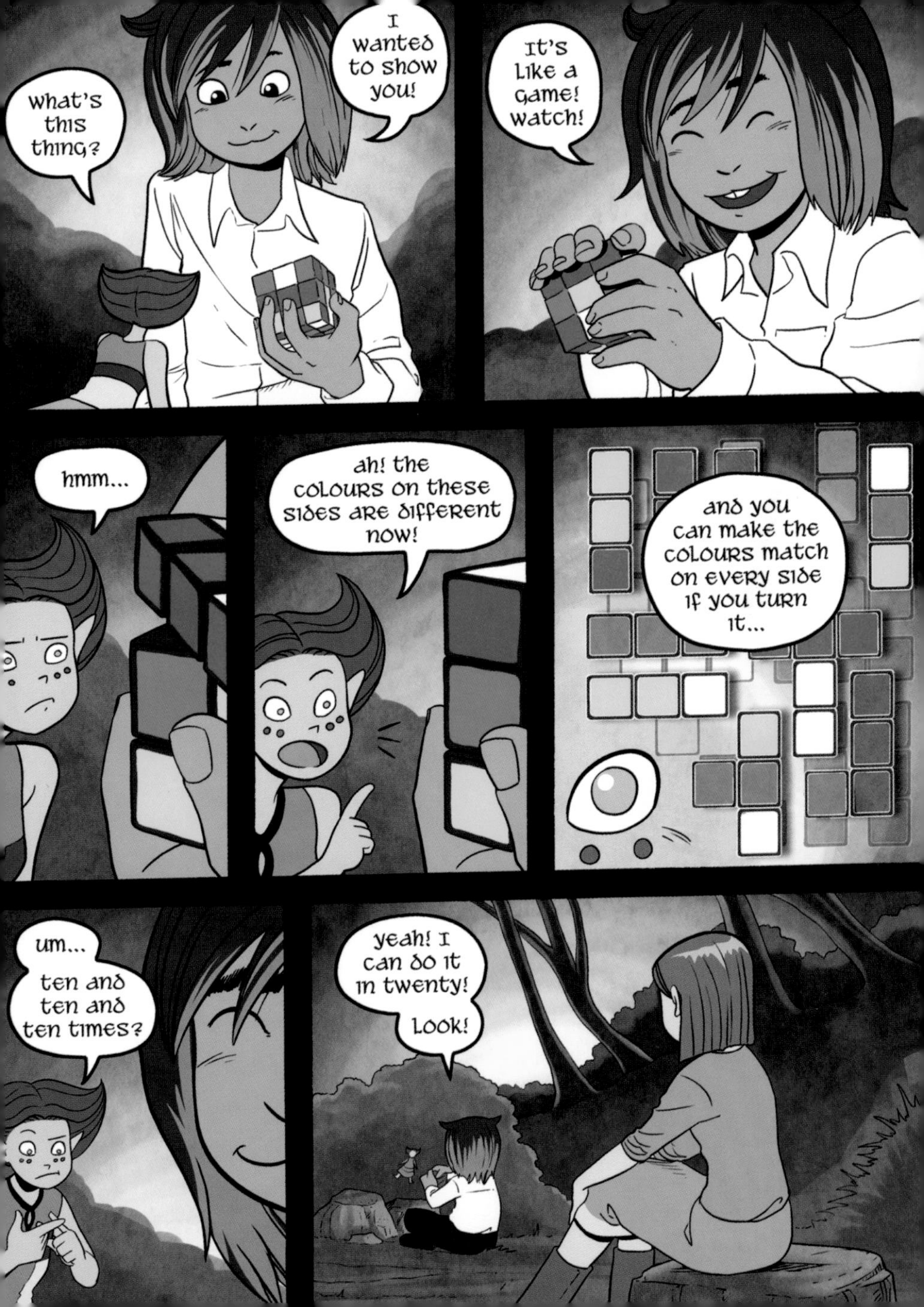

what's this thing?
I wanted to show you!
It's like a game! watch!
hmm...
ah! the colours on these sides are different now!
and you can make the colours match on every side if you turn it...
um...
ten and ten and ten times?
yeah! I can do it in twenty!
look!

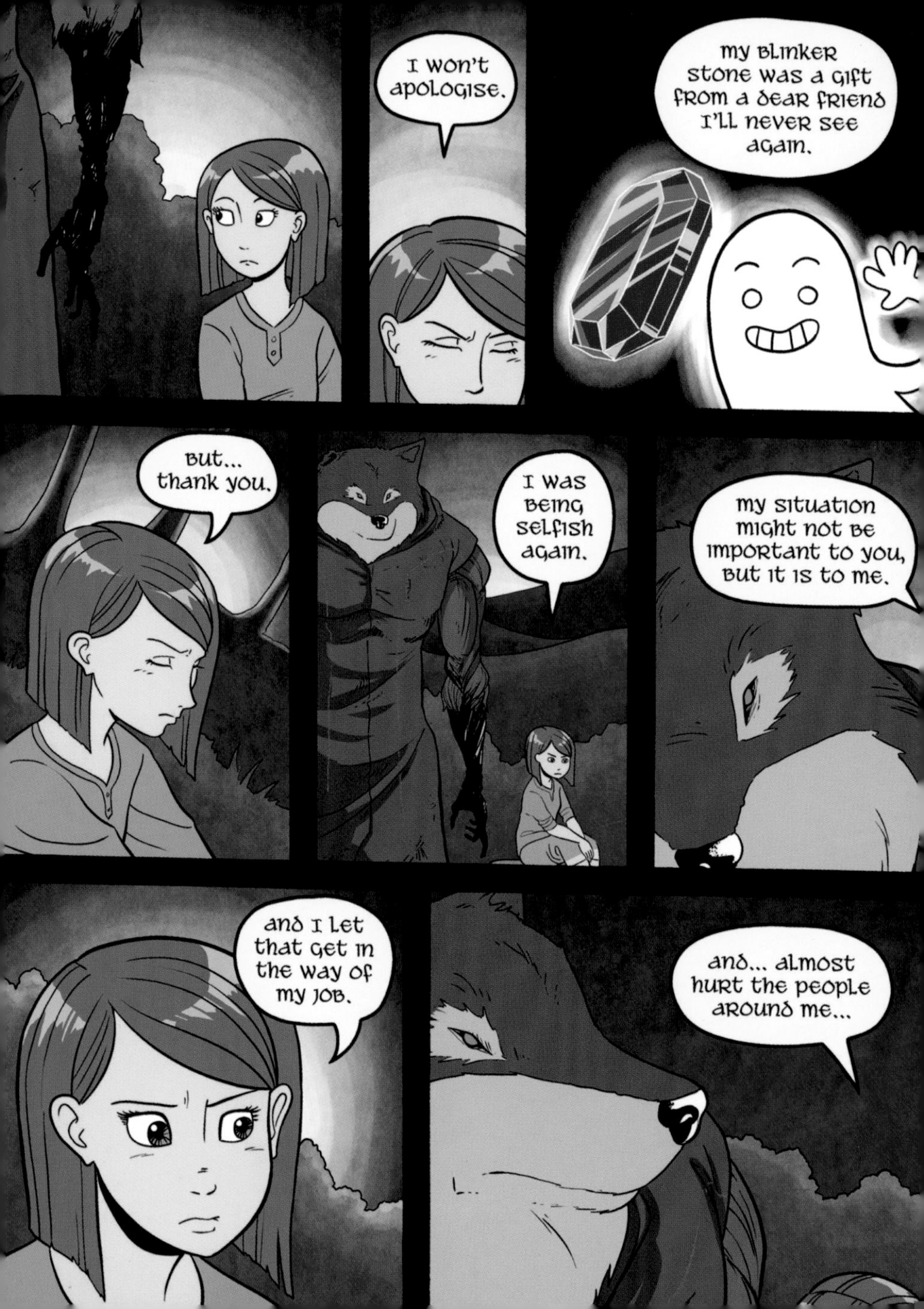
I won't apologise.
my blinker stone was a gift from a dear friend I'll never see again.
but... thank you.
I was being selfish again.
my situation might not be important to you, but it is to me.
and I let that get in the way of my job.
and... almost hurt the people around me...

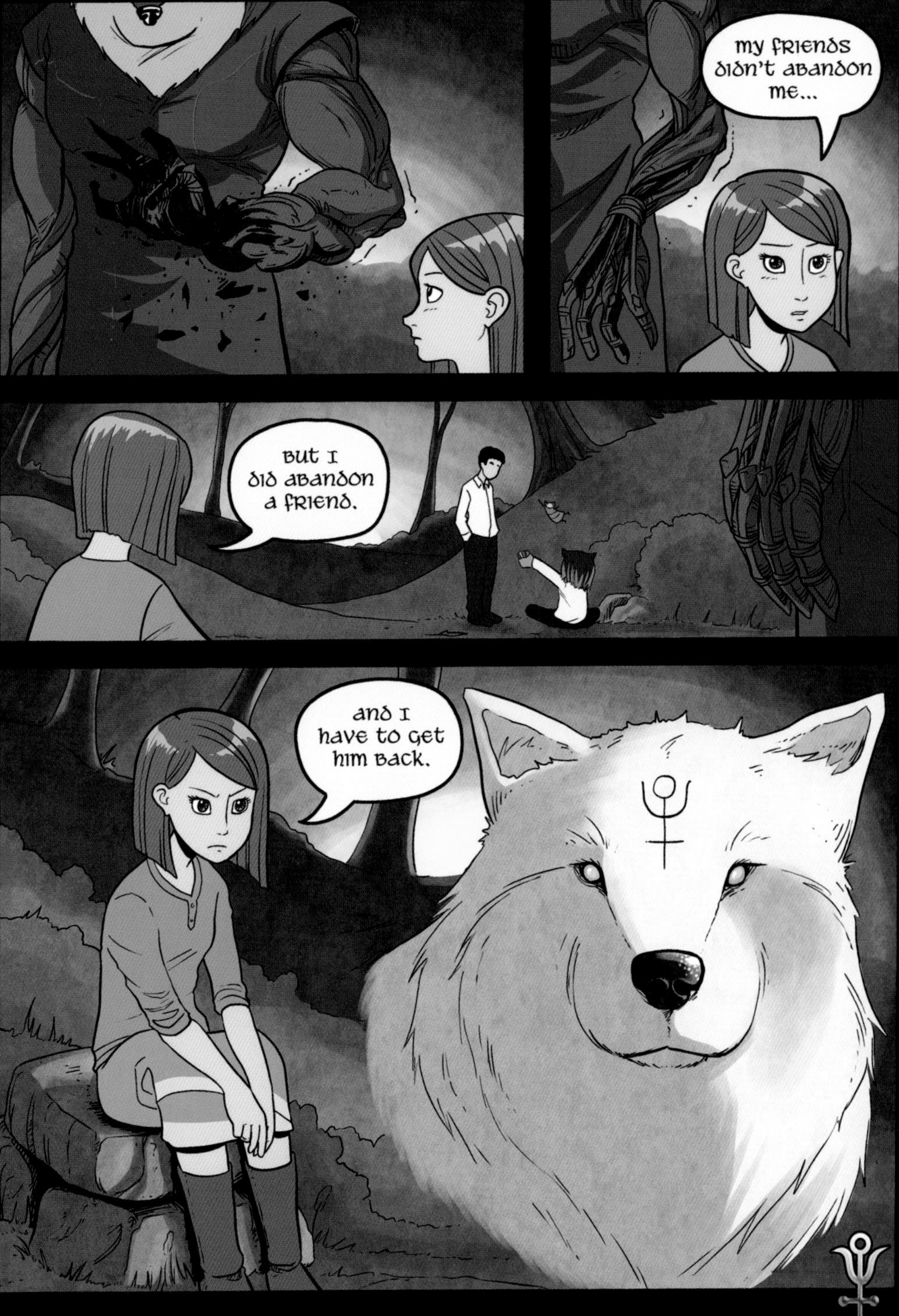
my friends didn't abandon me...
but I did abandon a friend.
and I have to get him back.

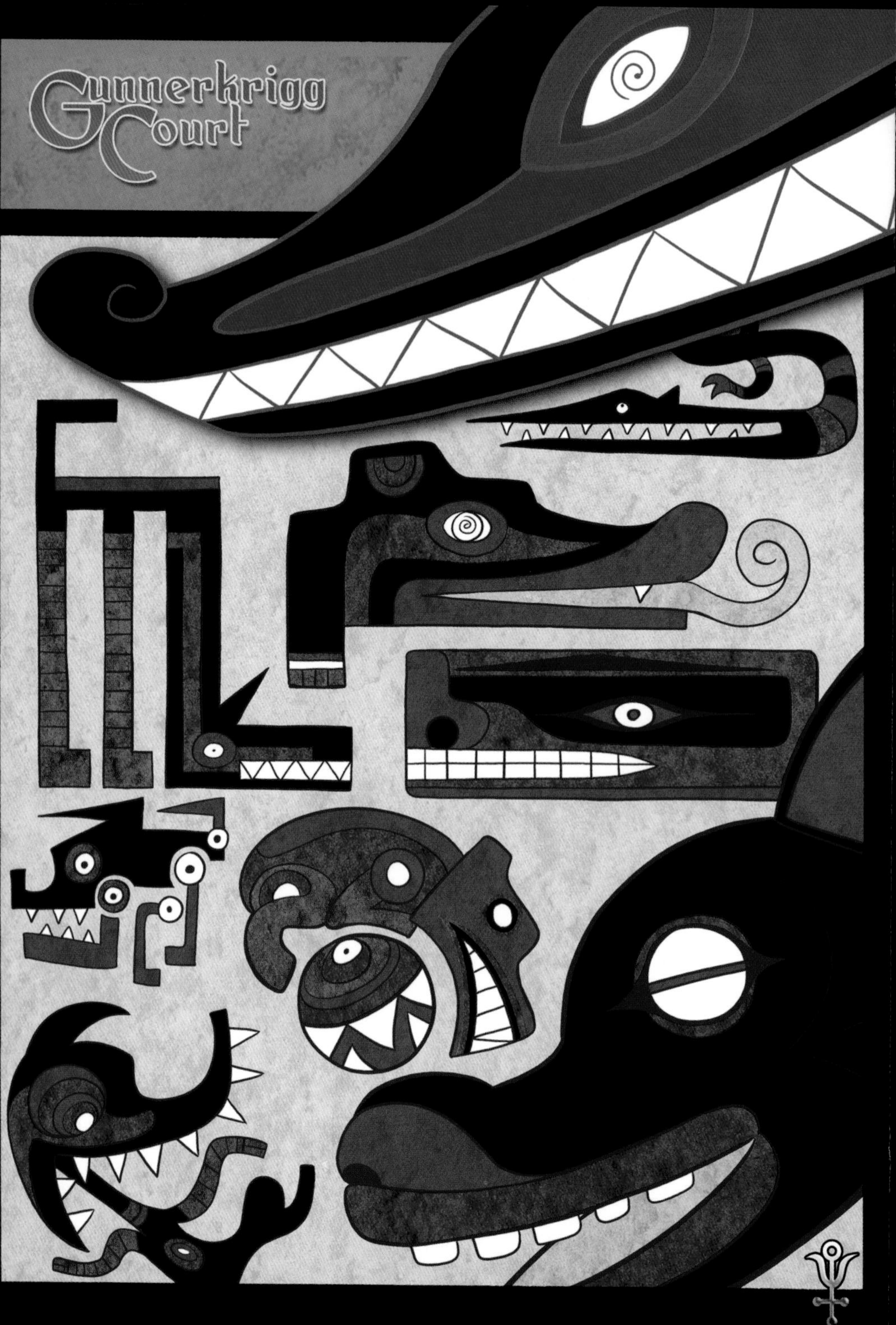
Gunnerkrigg
Court

Gunnerkrigg Court

Chapter 55:

The Break Out

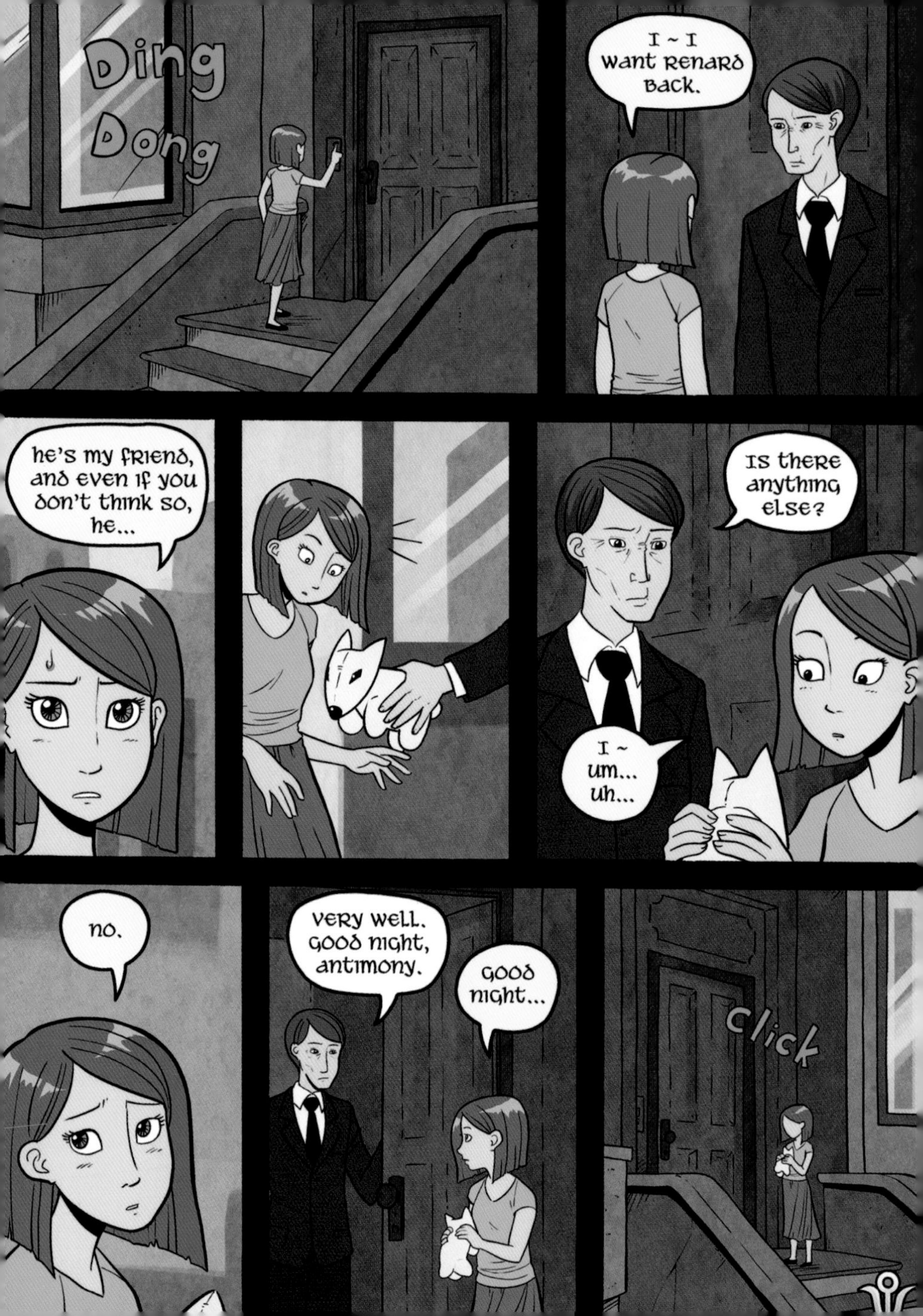
Ding Dong
I ~ I want Renard back.
he's my friend, and even if you don't think so, he...
Is there anything else?
I ~ um... uh...
no.
very well. good night, antimony.
good night...
Click

Hehe!

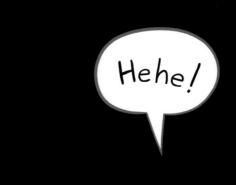

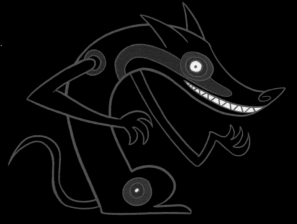

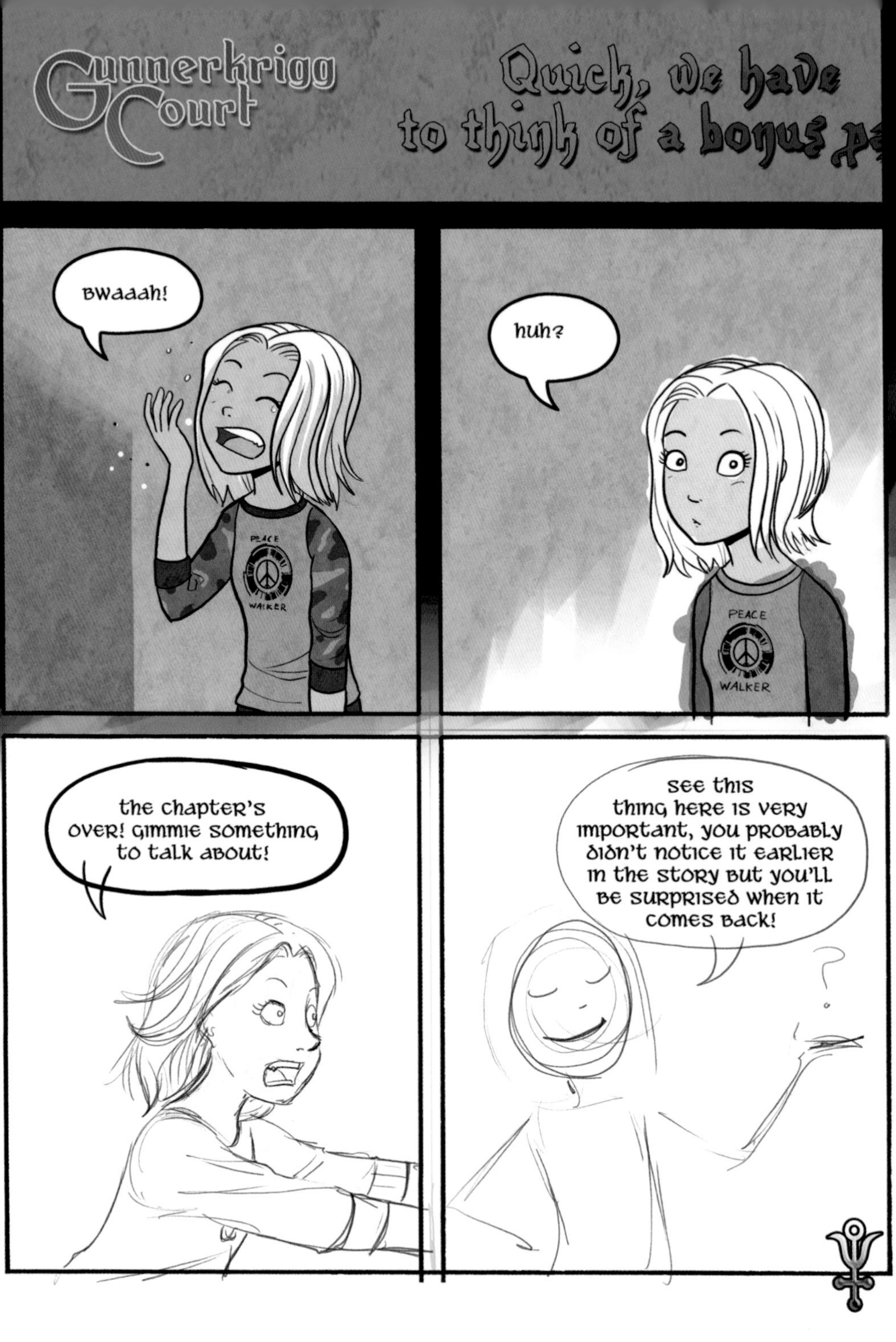
Gunnerkrigg Court
Quick, we have to think of a bonus pa
BWaaah!
huh?
PEACE WALKER
the chapter's over! Gimmie something to talk about!
see this thing here is very important, you probably didn't notice it earlier in the story but you'll be surprised when it comes back!
?

Gunnerkrigg Court

Chapter 56:

New Data

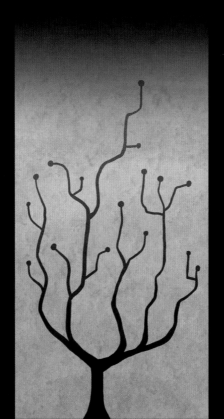

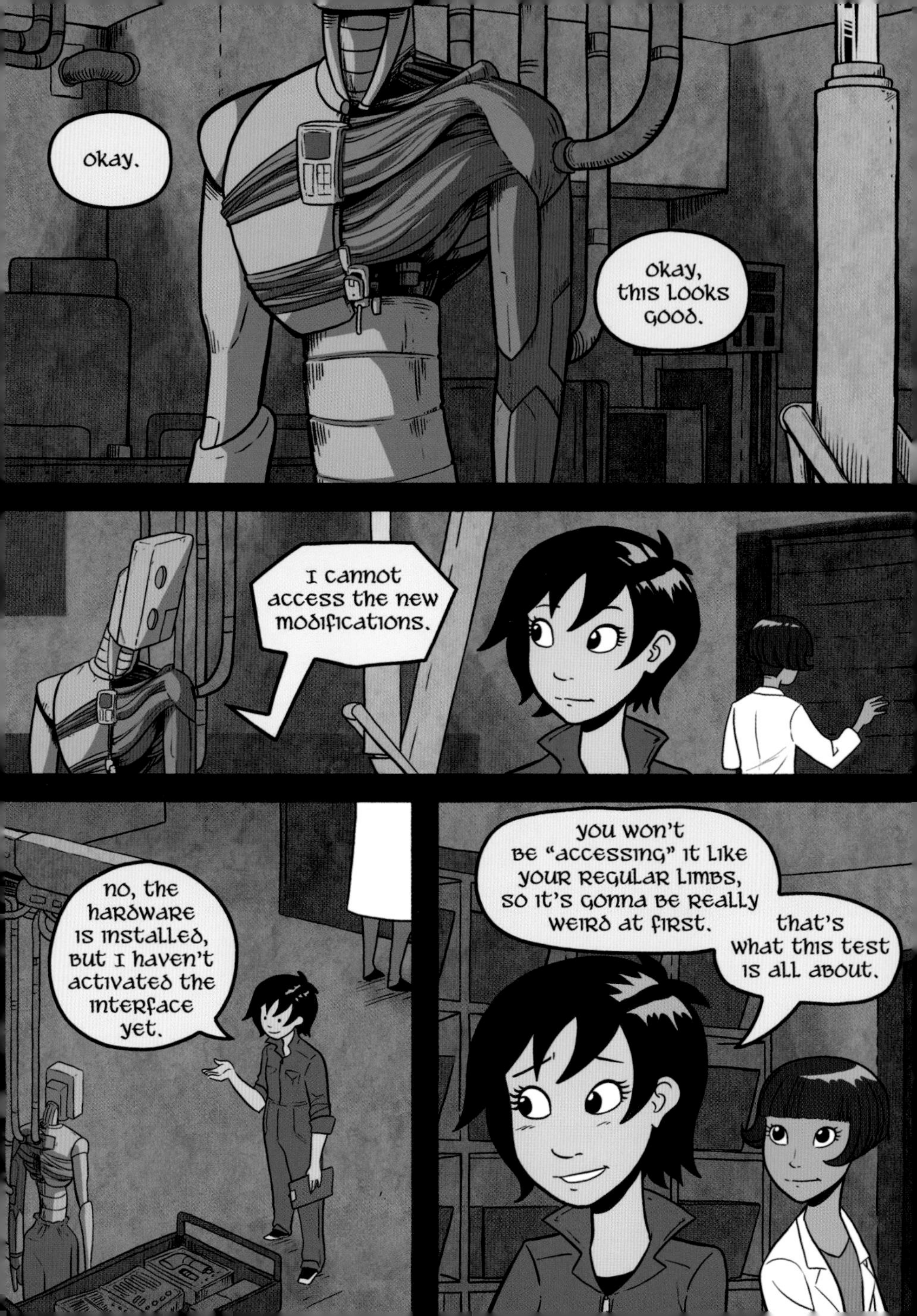
Okay.
Okay, this looks good.
I cannot access the new modifications.
No, the hardware is installed, but I haven't activated the interface yet.
You won't be "accessing" it like your regular limbs, so it's gonna be really weird at first.
That's what this test is all about.

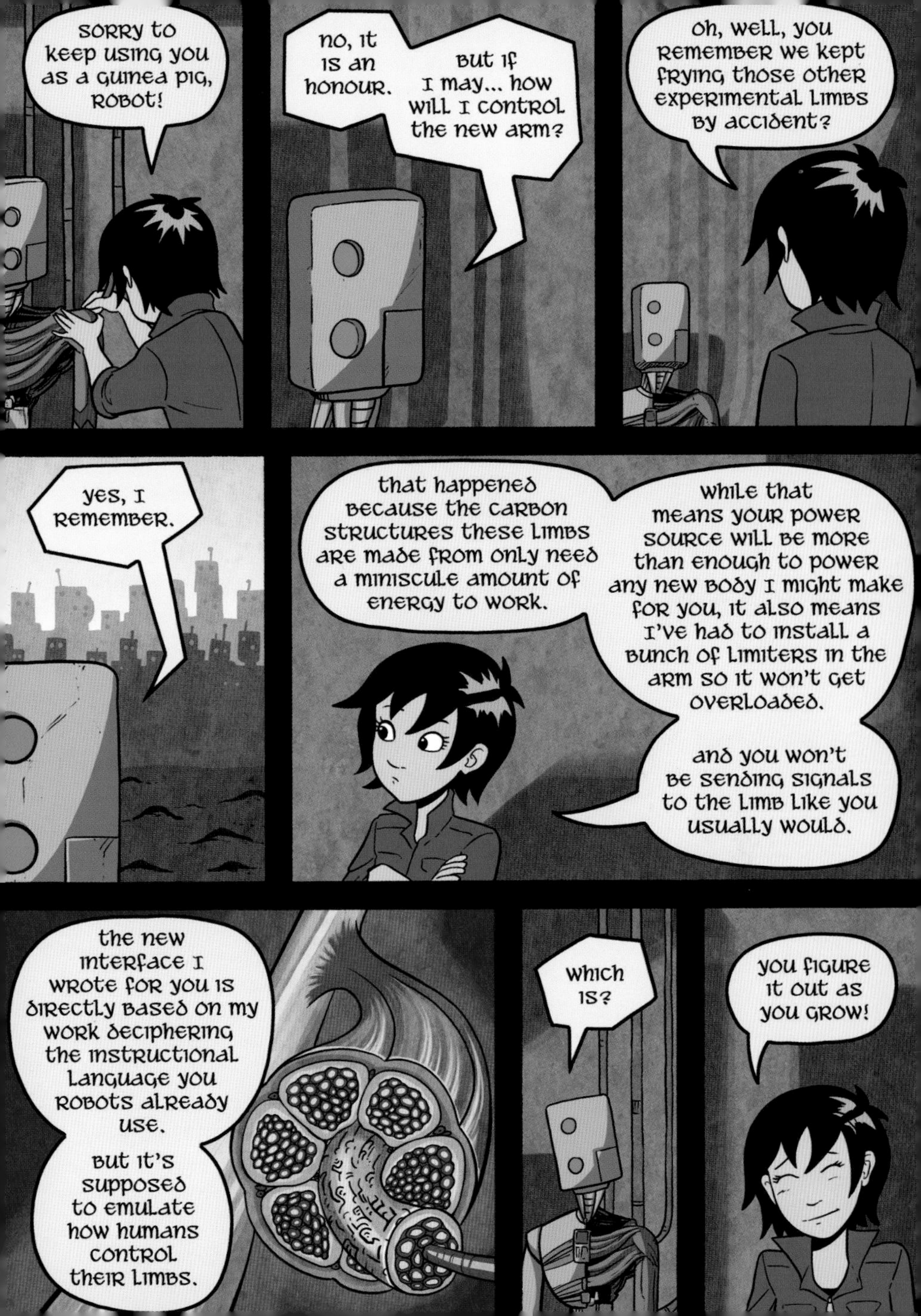
SORRY to keep using you as a guinea pig, ROBOT!
no, it is an honour.
But if I may... how will I control the new arm?
oh, well, you remember we kept frying those other experimental limbs by accident?
yes, I remember.
that happened because the carbon structures these limbs are made from only need a miniscule amount of energy to work.
while that means your power source will be more than enough to power any new body I might make for you, it also means I've had to install a bunch of limiters in the arm so it won't get overloaded.
and you won't be sending signals to the limb like you usually would.
the new interface I wrote for you is directly based on my work deciphering the instructional language you robots already use.
But it's supposed to emulate how humans control their limbs.
which is?
you figure it out as you grow!

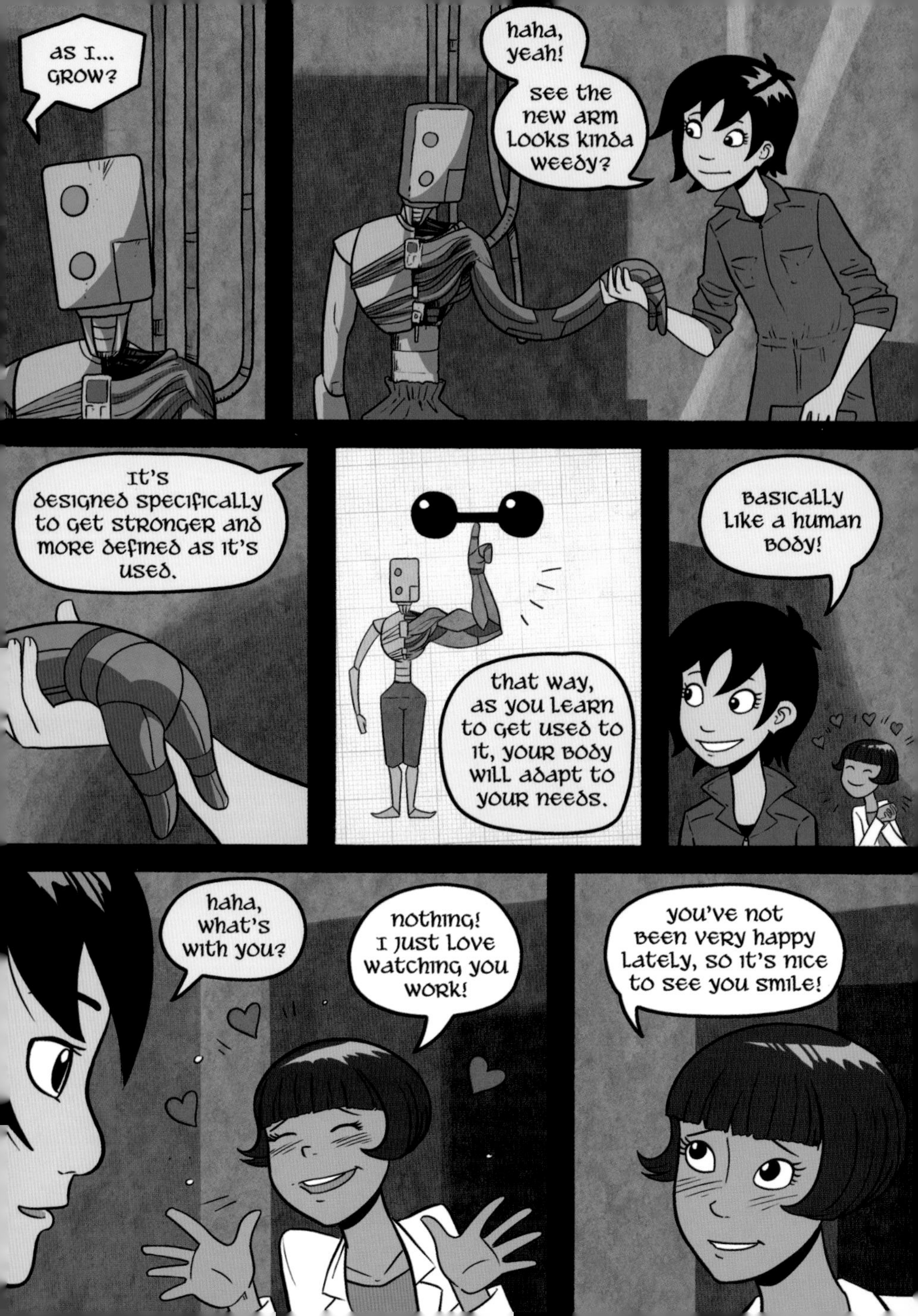
as I... GROW?
haha, yeah!
see the new arm looks kinda weedy?
It's designed specifically to get stronger and more defined as it's used.
that way, as you learn to get used to it, your body will adapt to your needs.
Basically like a human body!
haha, what's with you?
nothing! I just love watching you work!
you've not been very happy lately, so it's nice to see you smile!

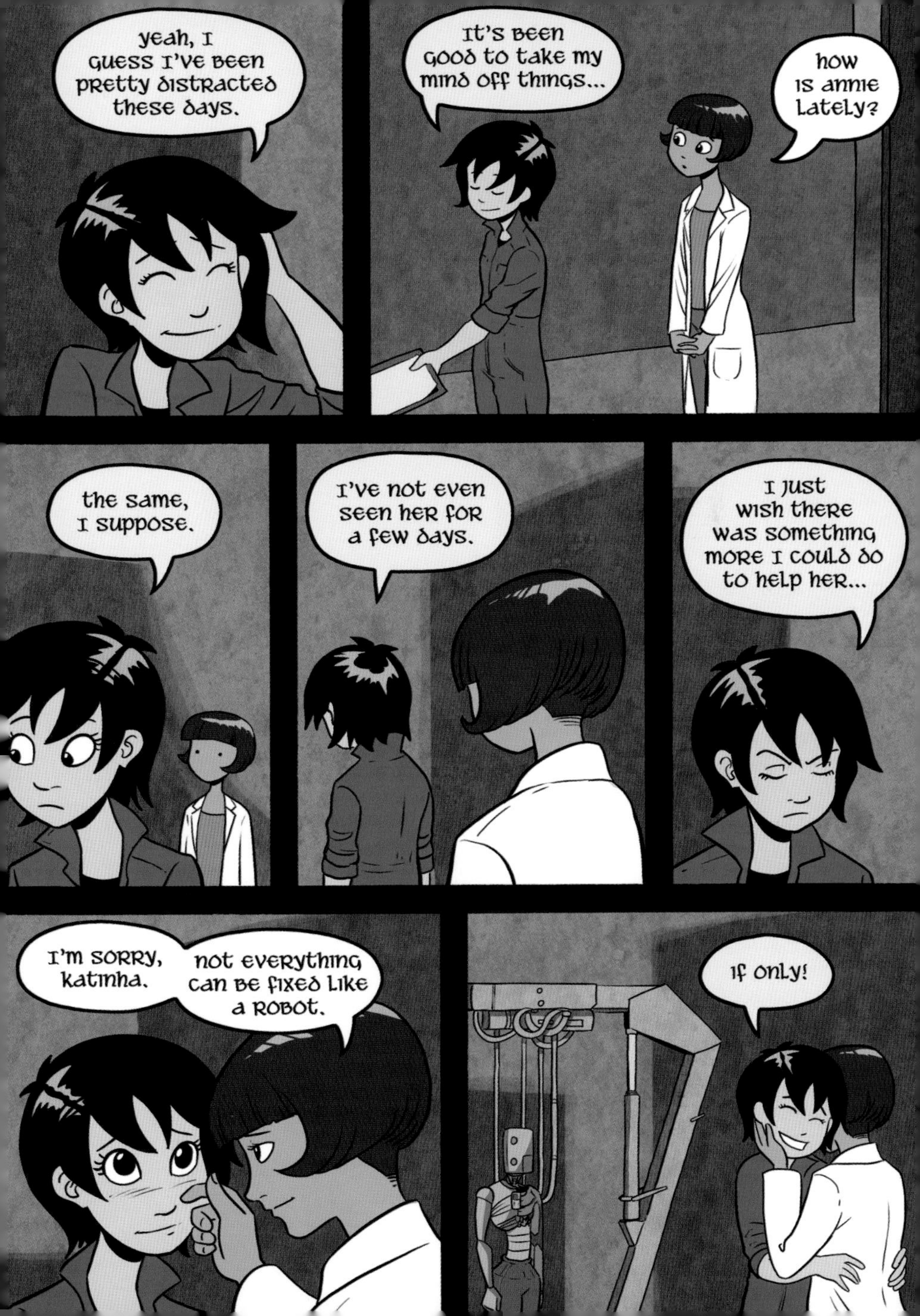
yeah, I guess I've been pretty distracted these days.
It's been good to take my mind off things...
how is annie lately?
the same, I suppose.
I've not even seen her for a few days.
I just wish there was something more I could do to help her...
I'm sorry, katinha.
not everything can be fixed like a robot.
if only!

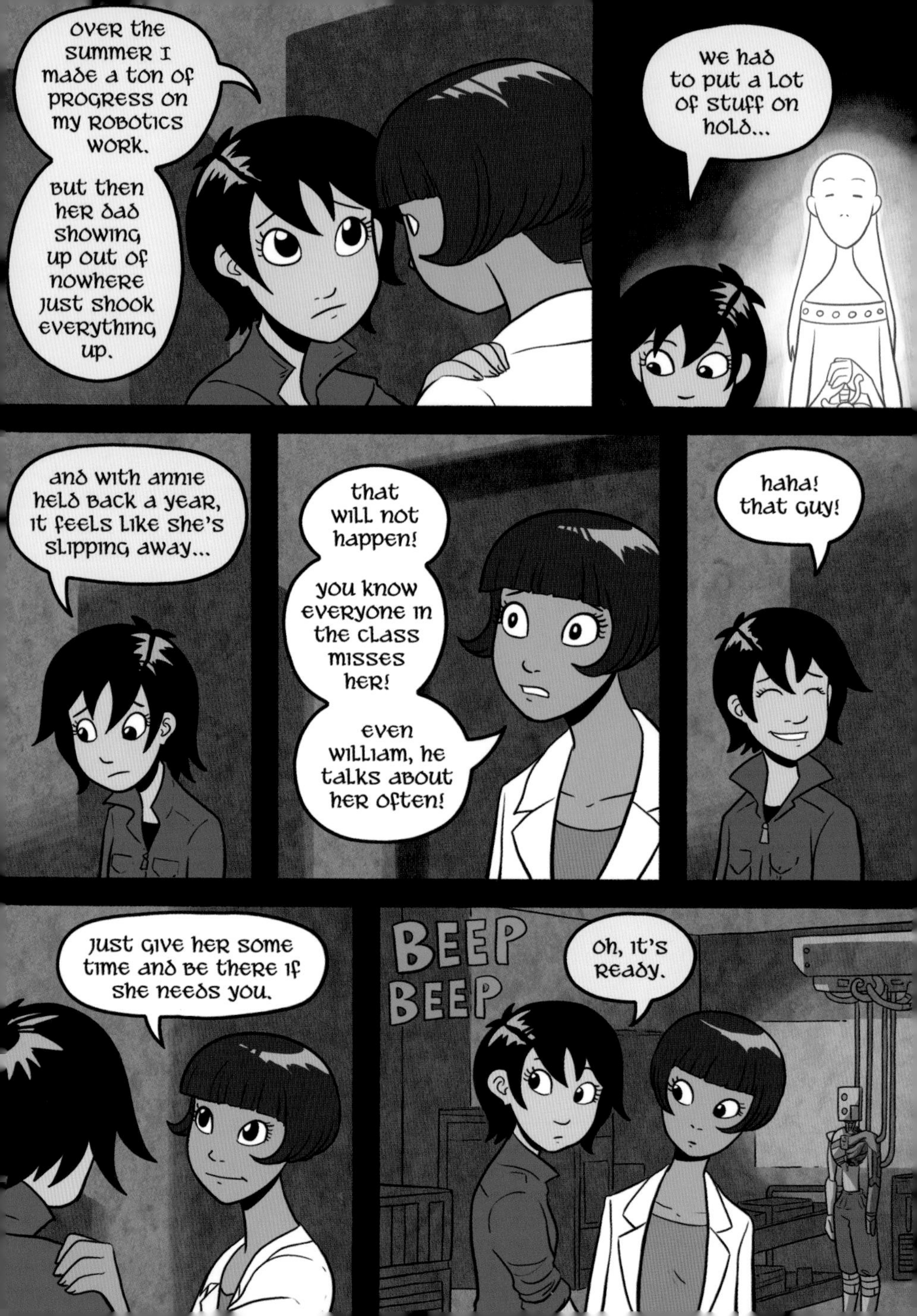
over the summer I made a ton of progress on my robotics work.
but then her dad showing up out of nowhere just shook everything up.
we had to put a lot of stuff on hold...
and with annie held back a year, it feels like she's slipping away...
that will not happen!
you know everyone in the class misses her!
even william, he talks about her often!
haha! that guy!
just give her some time and be there if she needs you.
BEEP BEEP
oh, it's ready.

Okay, I'm sending you the new code.

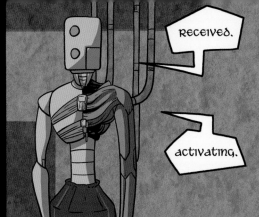

RECEIVED.

activating.

Oh.

Oh.

REBOOTING.

...

you there?

I apologise for my outburst. that was a strange experience.

can you describe it?

I WILL TRY.

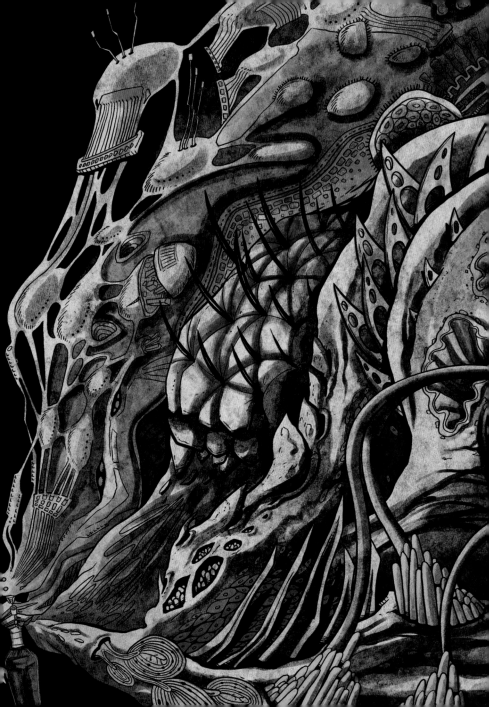

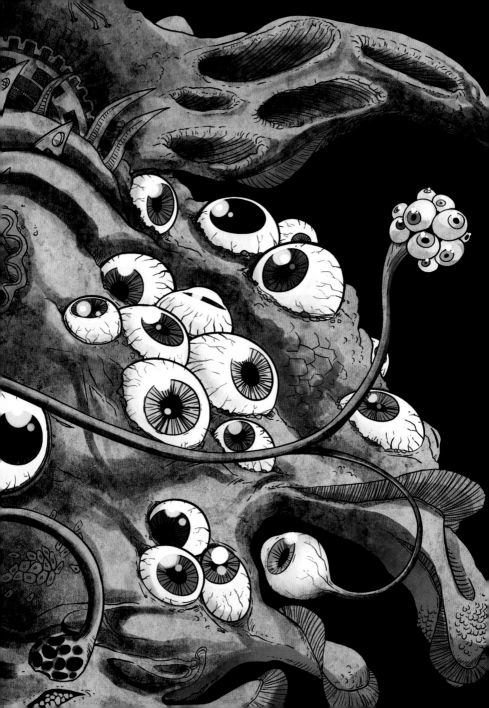

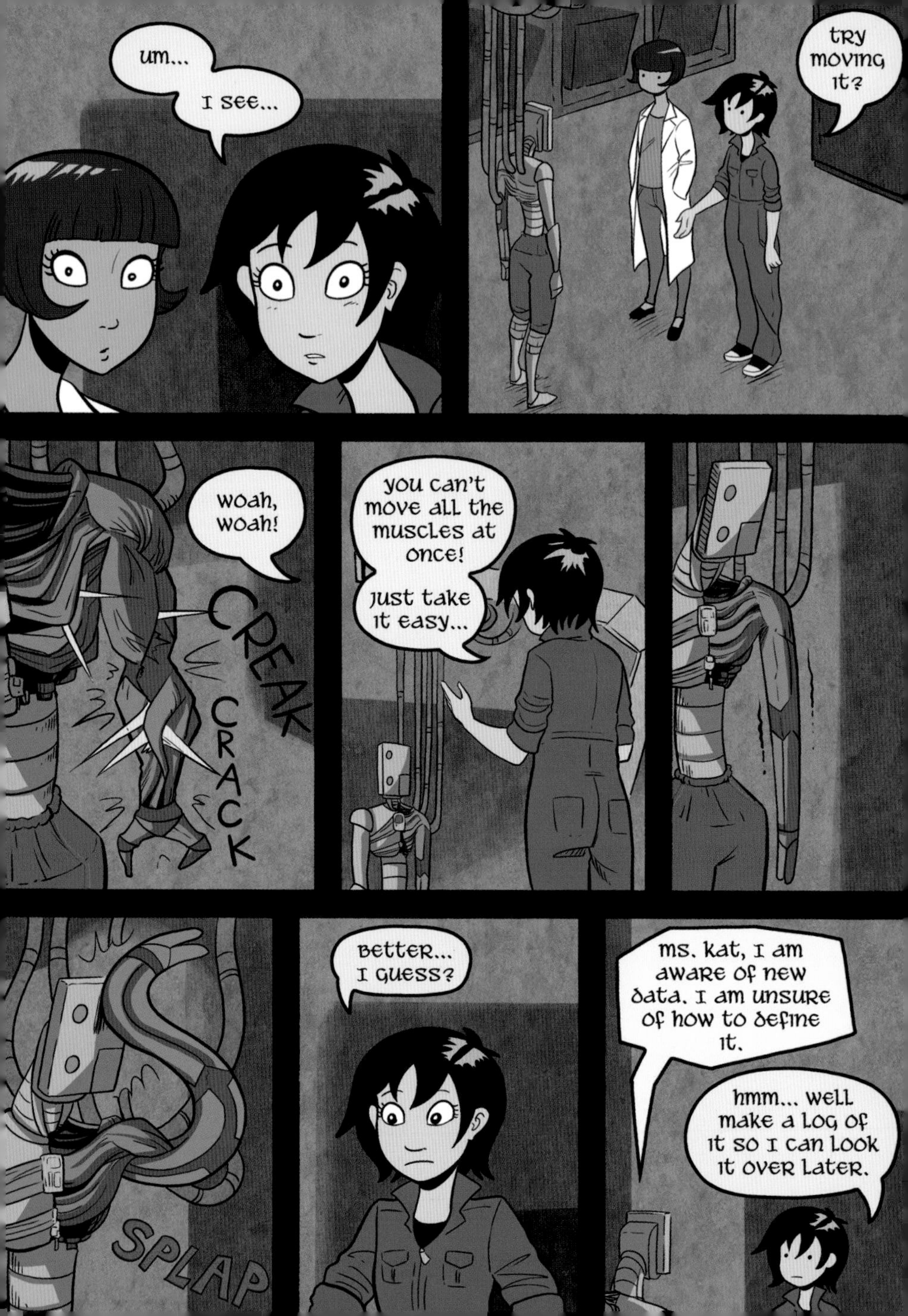
um...
I see...
try moving it?
woah, woah!
CREAK
CRACK
you can't move all the muscles at once!
just take it easy...
SPLAP
better... I guess?
ms. kat, I am aware of new data. I am unsure of how to define it.
hmm... well make a log of it so I can look it over later.

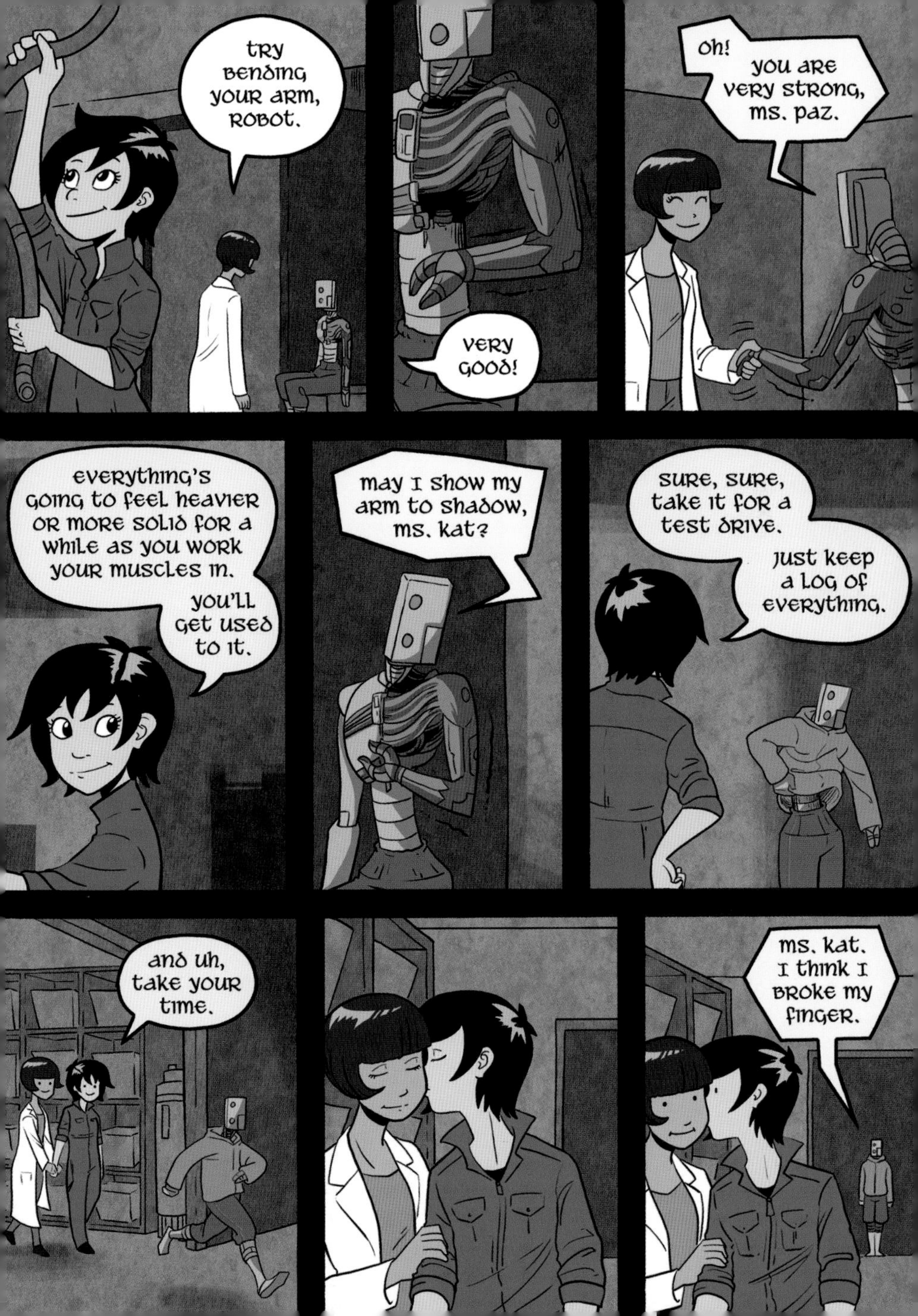
try bending your arm, robot.
very good!
oh!
you are very strong, ms. paz.
everything's going to feel heavier or more solid for a while as you work your muscles in.
you'll get used to it.
may I show my arm to shadow, ms. kat?
sure, sure, take it for a test drive.
just keep a log of everything.
and uh, take your time.
ms. kat. I think I broke my finger.

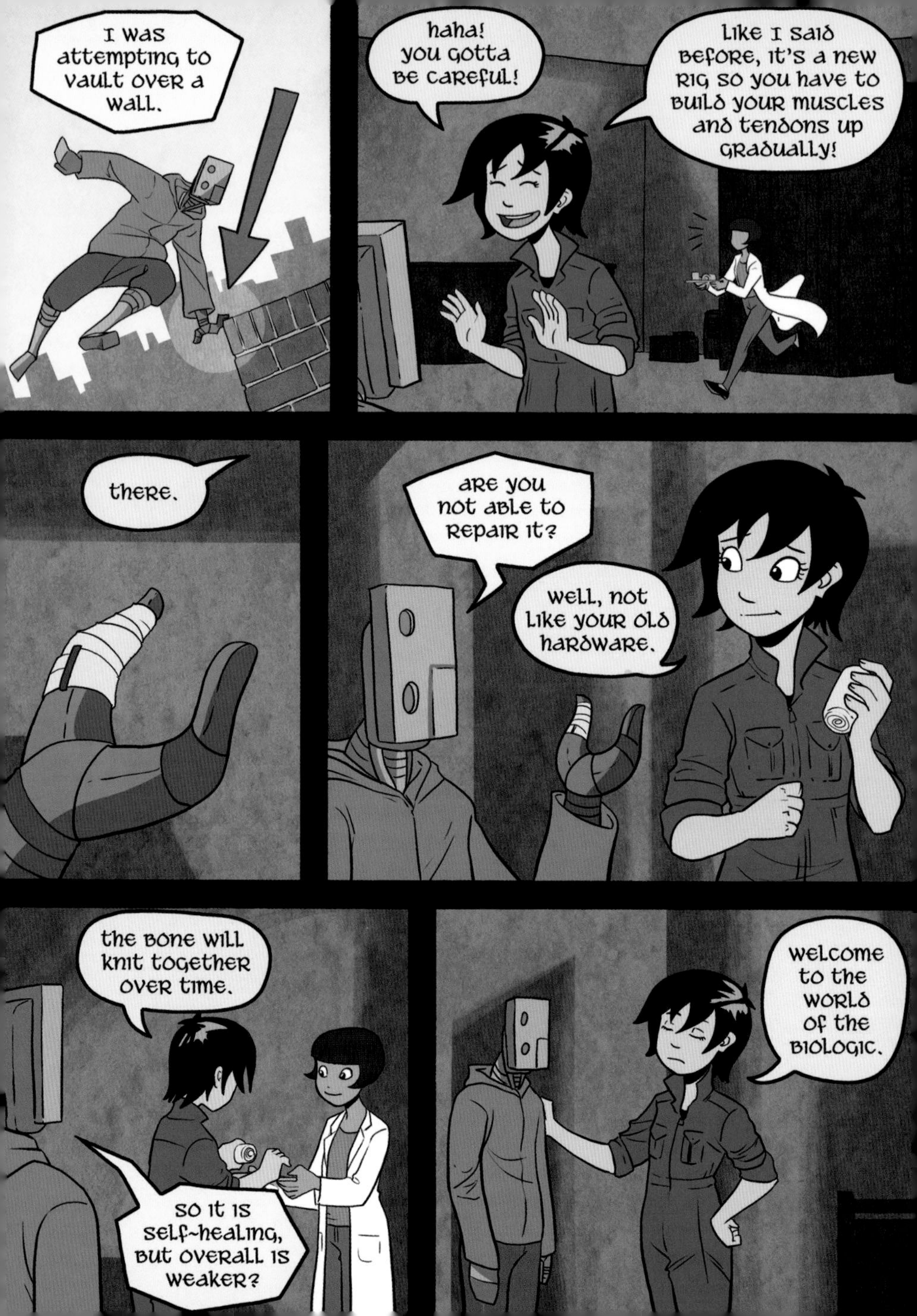
I was attempting to vault over a wall.
haha! you gotta be careful!
Like I said before, it's a new rig so you have to build your muscles and tendons up gradually!
there.
are you not able to repair it?
well, not like your old hardware.
the bone will knit together over time.
so it is self-healing, but overall is weaker?
welcome to the world of the biologic.

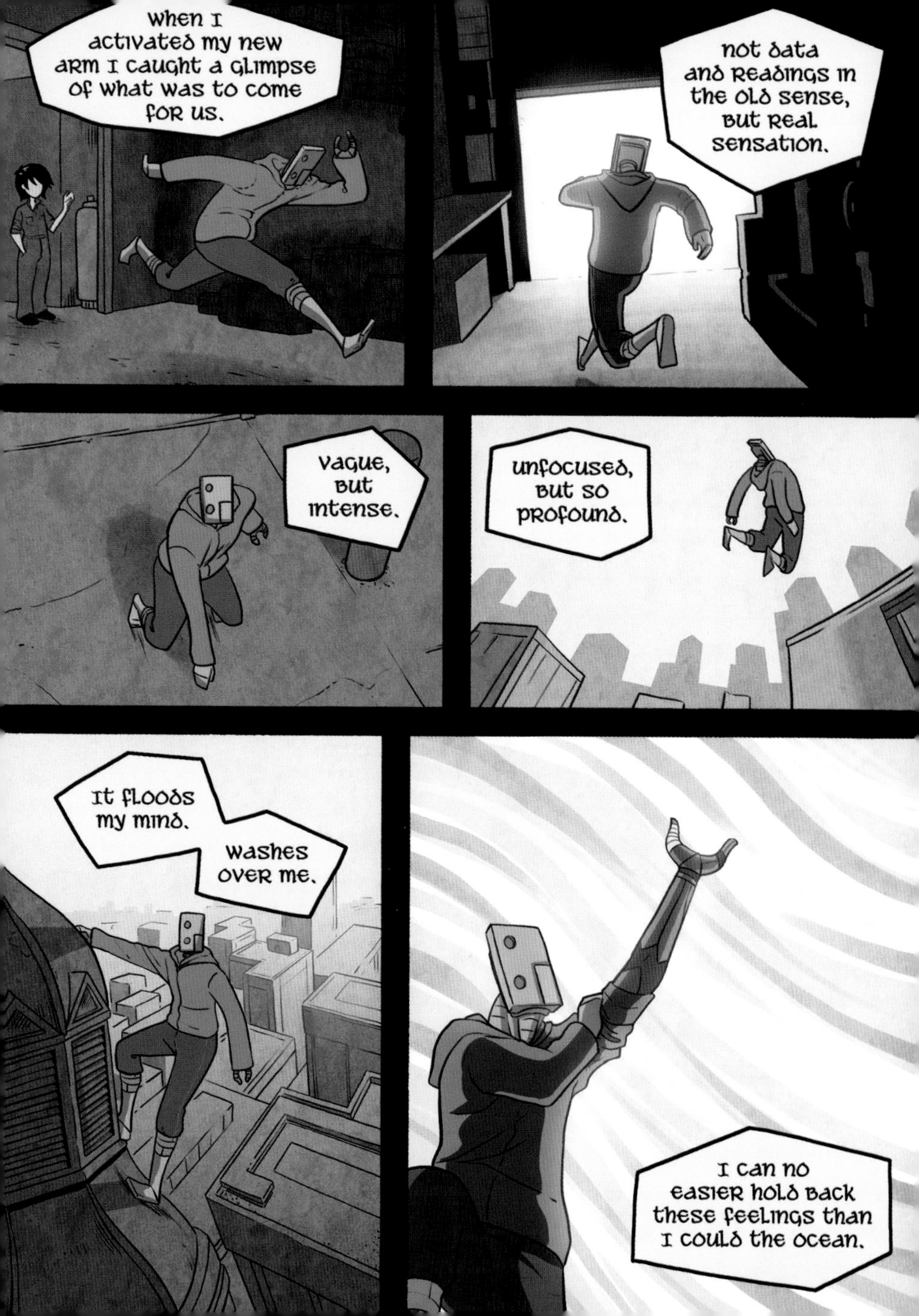

When I activated my new arm I caught a glimpse of what was to come for us.
not data and readings in the old sense, but real sensation.
vague, but intense.
unfocused, but so profound.
It floods my mind.
washes over me.
I can no easier hold back these feelings than I could the ocean.

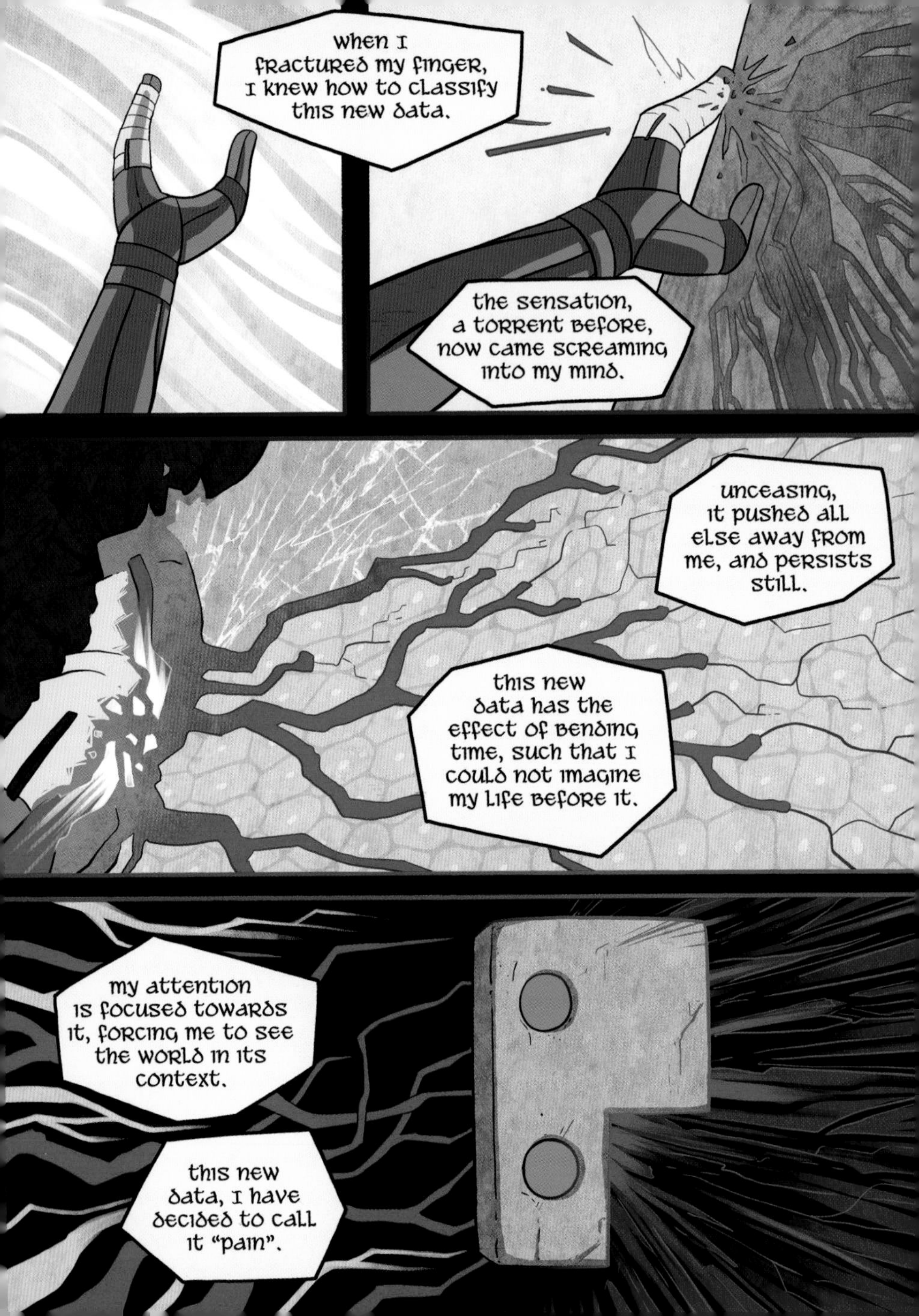
when I fractured my finger, I knew how to classify this new data.
the sensation, a torrent before, now came screaming into my mind.
unceasing, it pushed all else away from me, and persists still.
this new data has the effect of bending time, such that I could not imagine my life before it.
my attention is focused towards it, forcing me to see the world in its context.
this new data, I have decided to call it "pain".

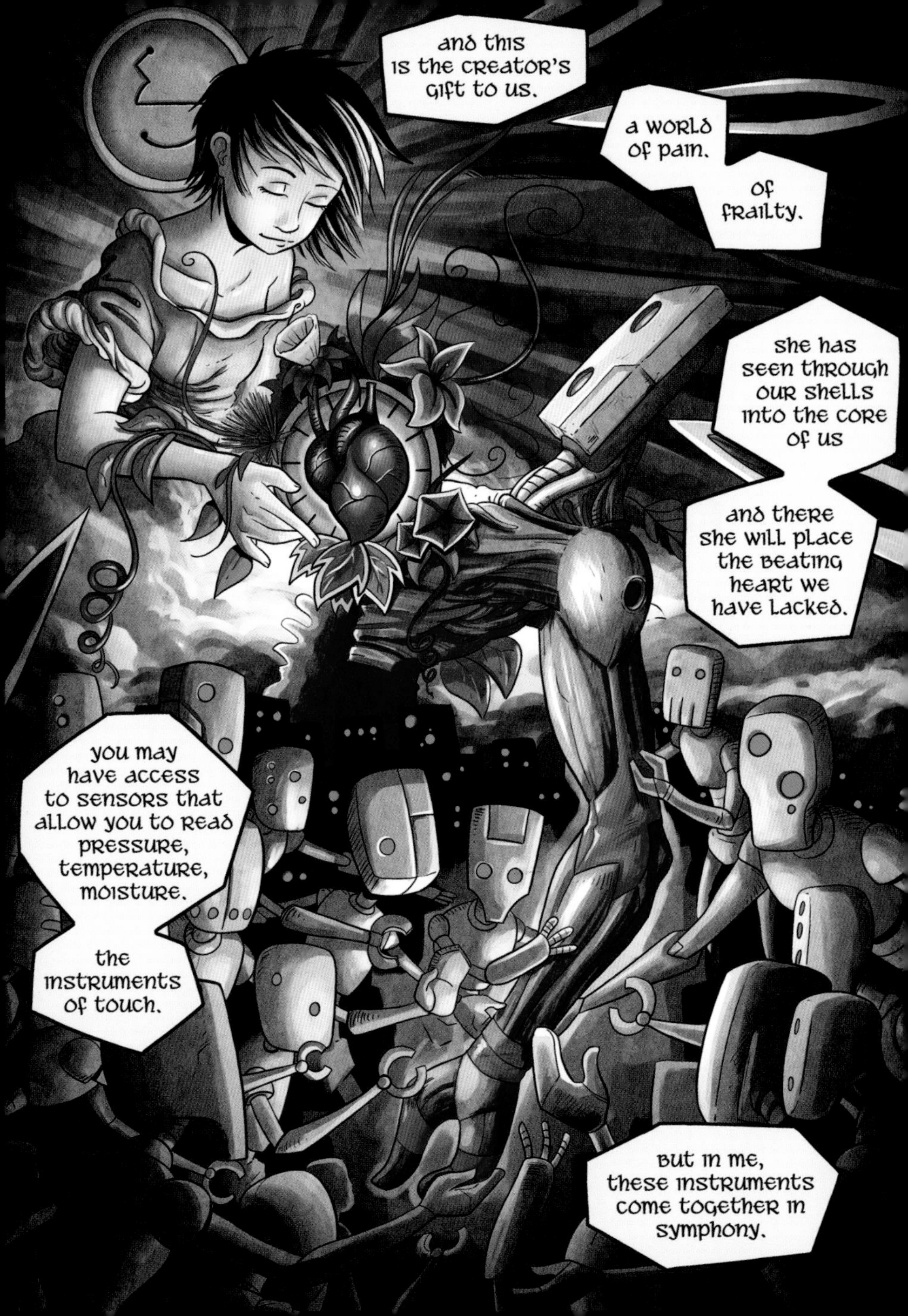
and this is the creator's gift to us.
a world of pain.
of frailty.
she has seen through our shells into the core of us
and there she will place the beating heart we have lacked.
you may have access to sensors that allow you to read pressure, temperature, moisture.
the instruments of touch.
but in me, these instruments come together in symphony.

but why should we want frailty?
and it is my understanding that humans go to great lengths to avoid pain...
yes, and consider those lengths.
not just here in the court, but how they have shaped the world to meet their needs.
they overcome their physical weakness with the power of their minds.
our bodies are strong, but we do not create.
we are content to act as mere tools.
but I enjoy using my strength to help humans!
me too!

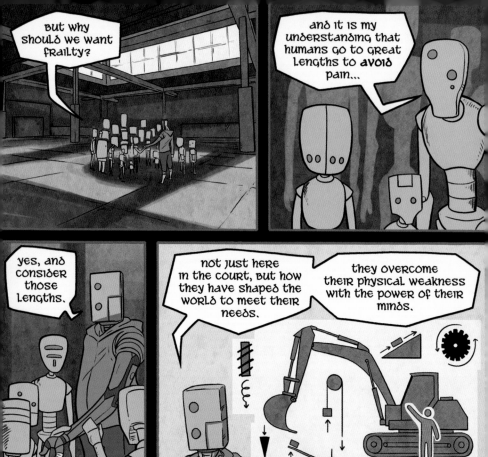

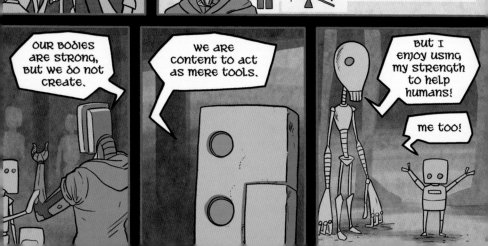

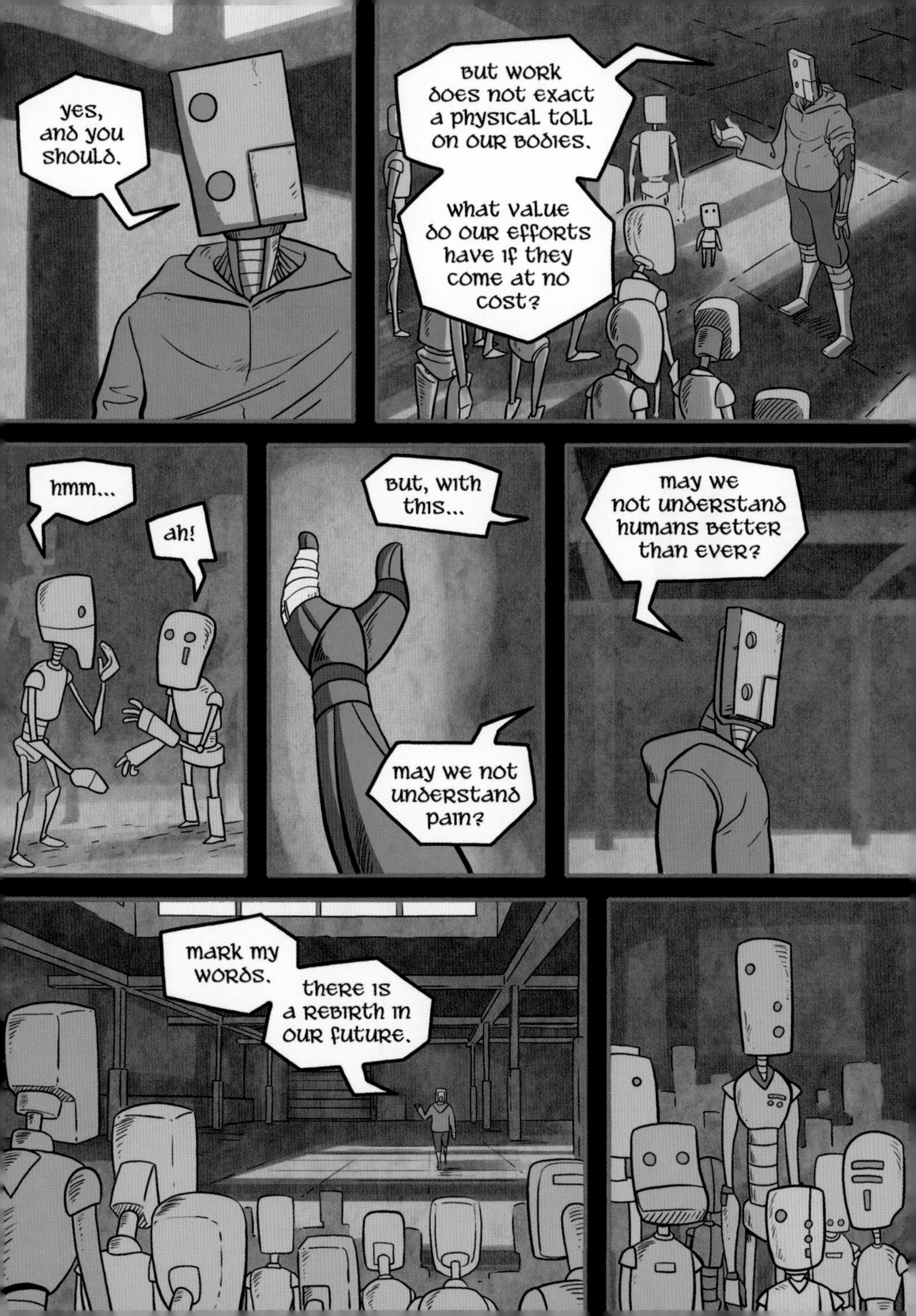
yes, and you should.
But work does not exact a physical toll on our bodies.
what value do our efforts have if they come at no cost?
hmm...
ah!
But, with this...
may we not understand pain?
may we not understand humans better than ever?
mark my words.
there is a rebirth in our future.

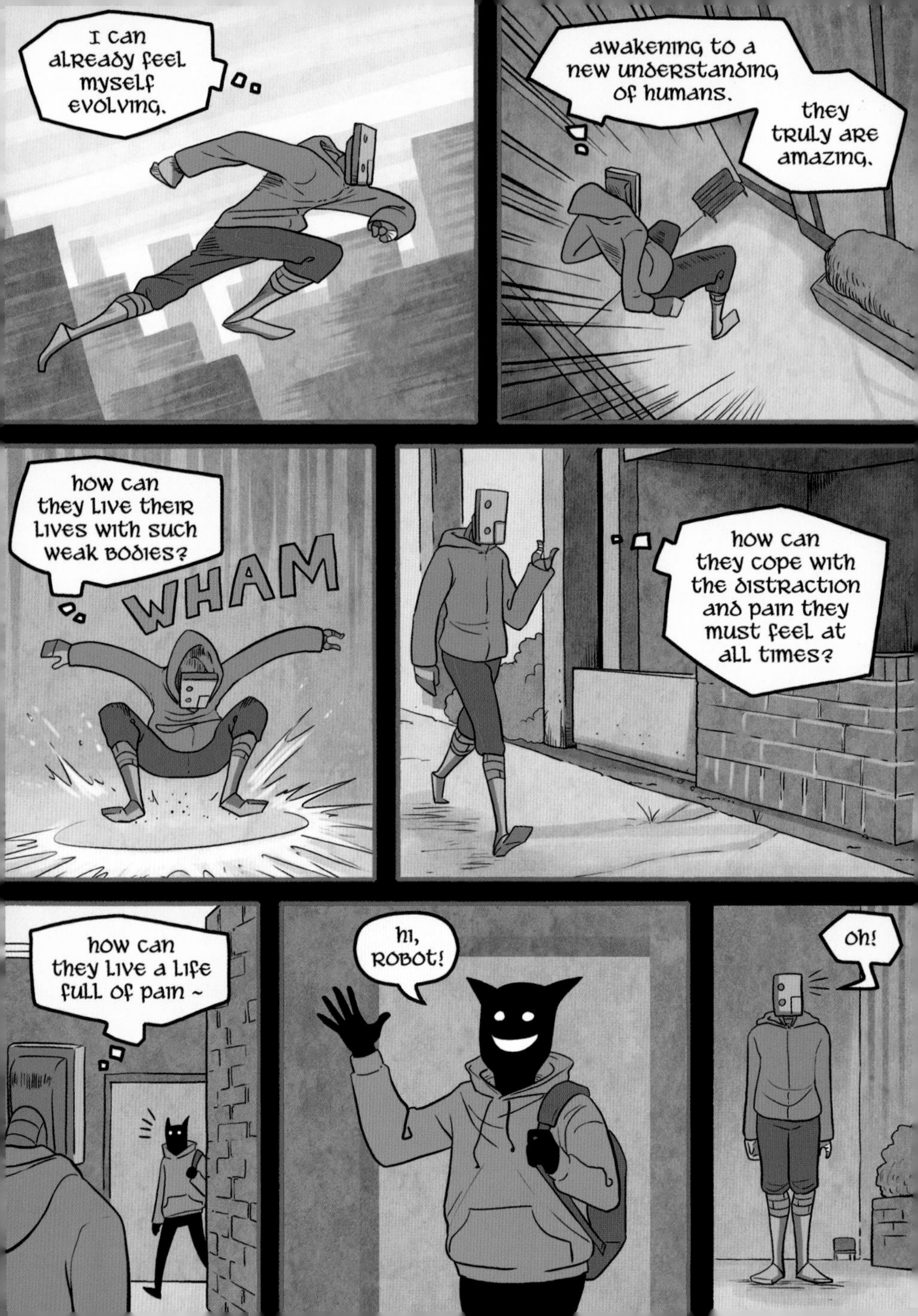

I can already feel myself evolving.
awakening to a new understanding of humans.
they truly are amazing.
how can they live their lives with such weak bodies?
WHAM
how can they cope with the distraction and pain they must feel at all times?
how can they live a life full of pain ~
hi, ROBOT!
oh!

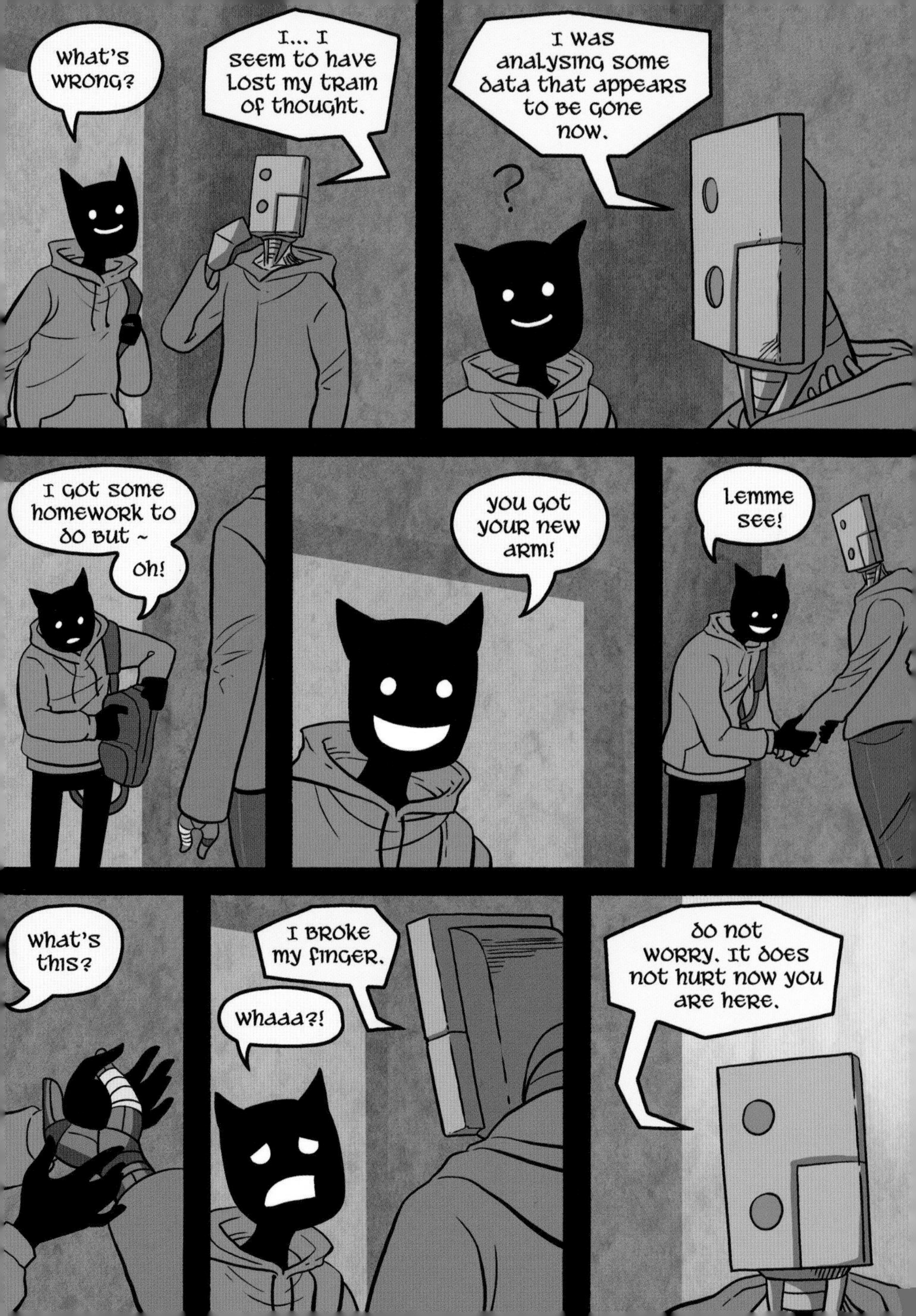
What's WRONG?
I... I seem to have lost my train of thought.
I was analysing some data that appears to be gone now.
?
I got some homework to do but ~
oh!
you got your new arm!
Lemme see!
What's this?
I BROKE my finger.
Whaaa?!
do not worry. It does not hurt now you are here.

WOWW!

kat REALLY is incREDIBLE, ISN'T SHE?

She is.

It's totally DIFFERENT TO YOUR OTHER ARM!

It's soft!

Prod

Squeeze

hehe!

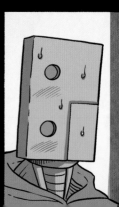

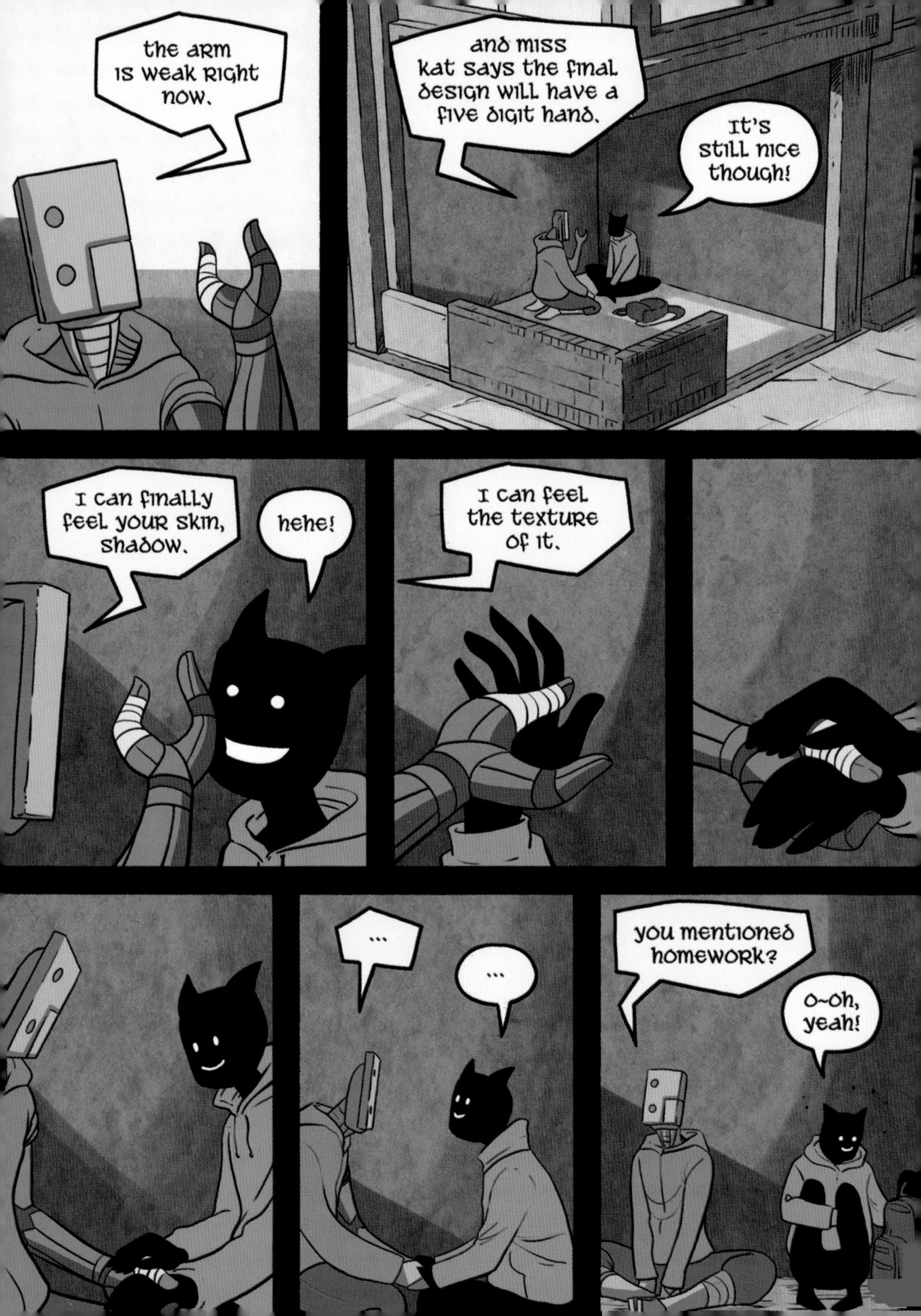
the arm is weak right now.
and miss kat says the final design will have a five digit hand.
It's still nice though!
I can finally feel your skin, shadow.
hehe!
I can feel the texture of it.
...
...
you mentioned homework?
O-Oh, yeah!

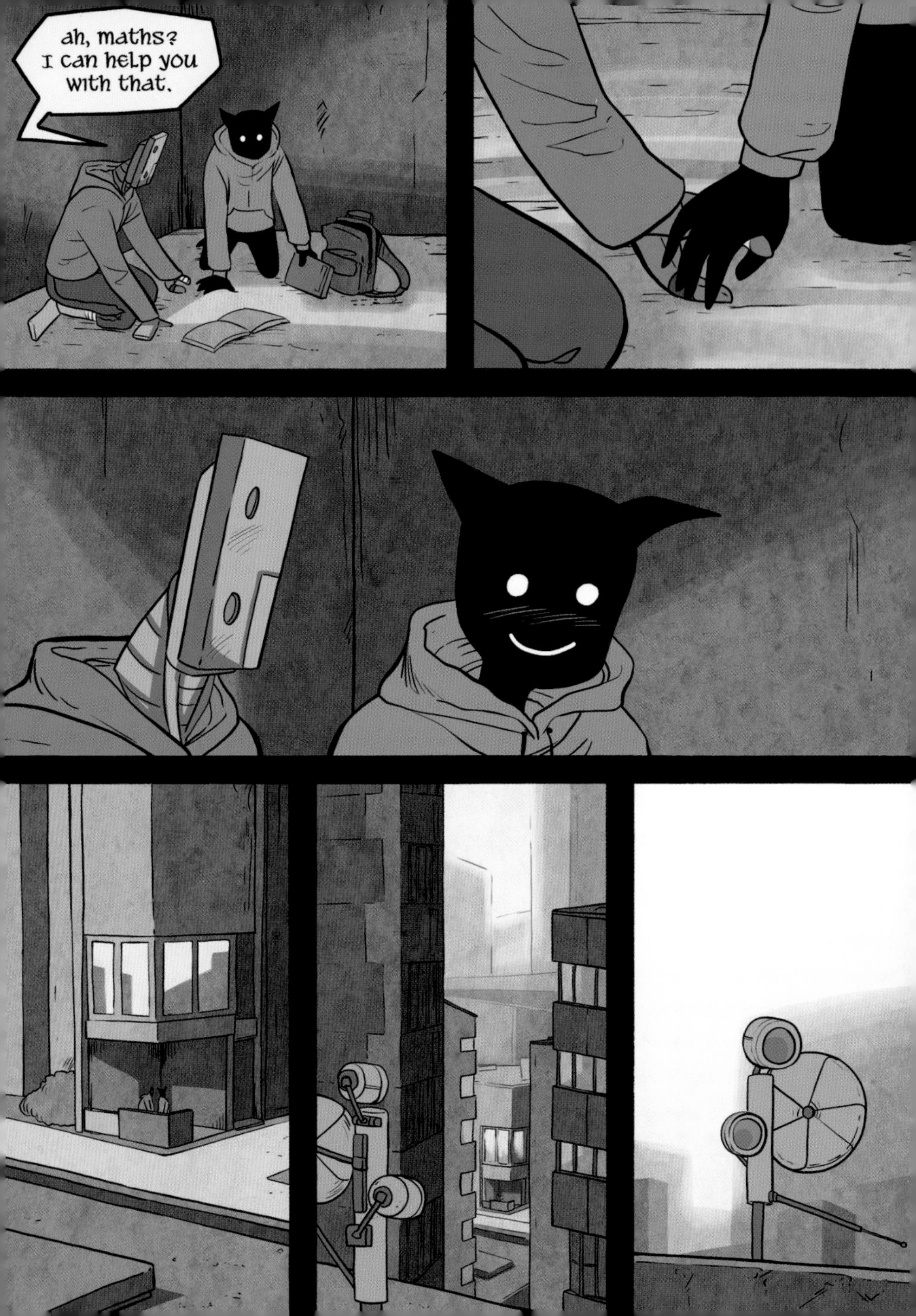
ah, maths?
I can help you
with that.

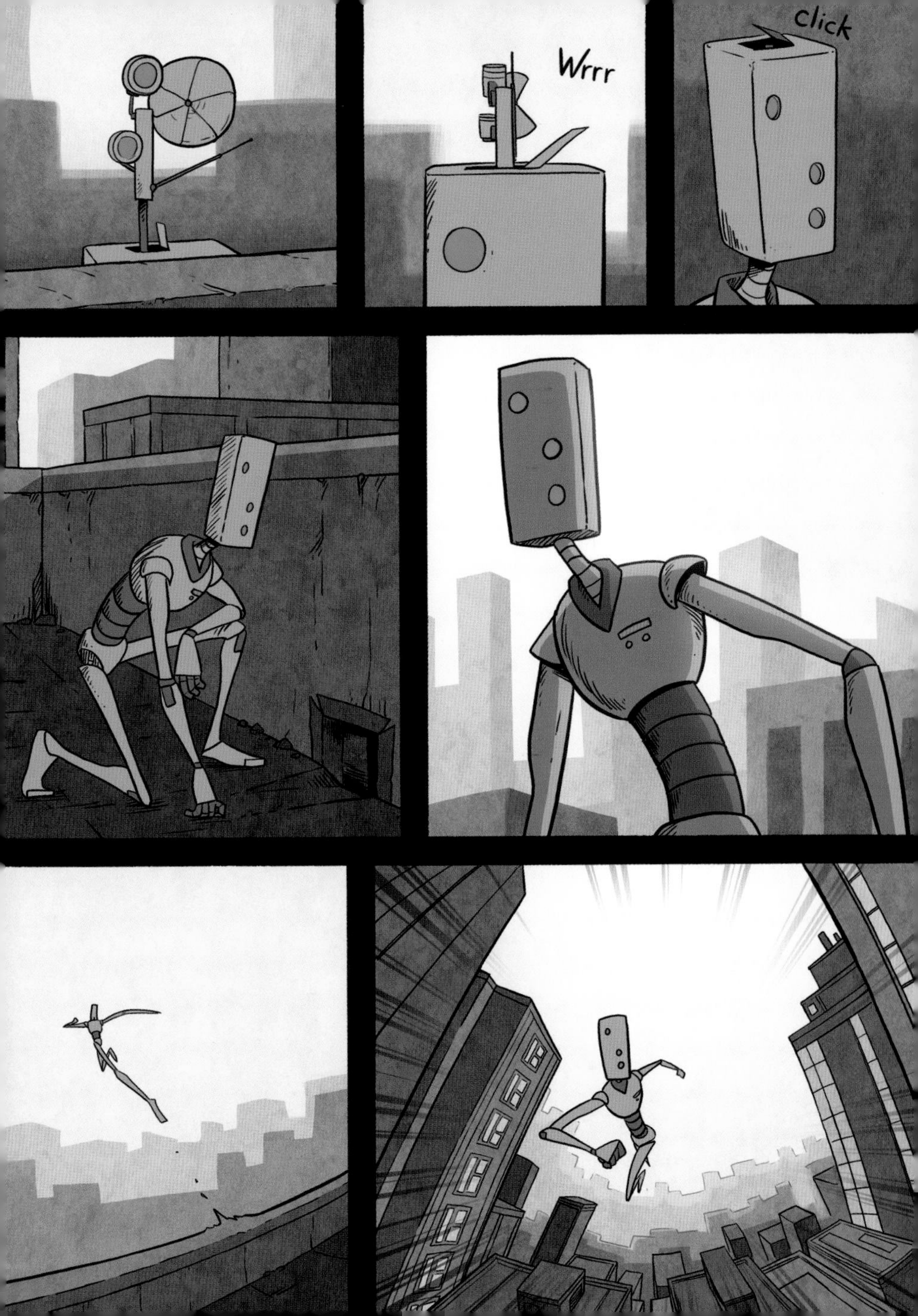
Wrrr
click

THE RUMORS ARE TRUE.

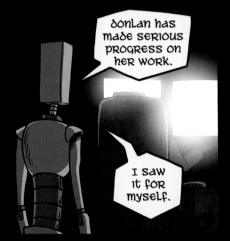

DONLAN HAS MADE SERIOUS PROGRESS ON HER WORK.

I SAW IT FOR MYSELF.

BUT THERE WAS SOMETHING ELSE.

I saw a creature posing as a student.

I think it was a shadow man.

a shadow man, here in the court?

yes, but it looked different. It was able to take the shape of a human.

there is nothing on record of such a creature.

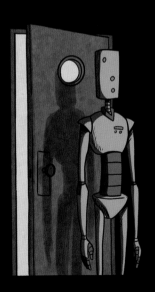

We'll have to monitor this more closely.

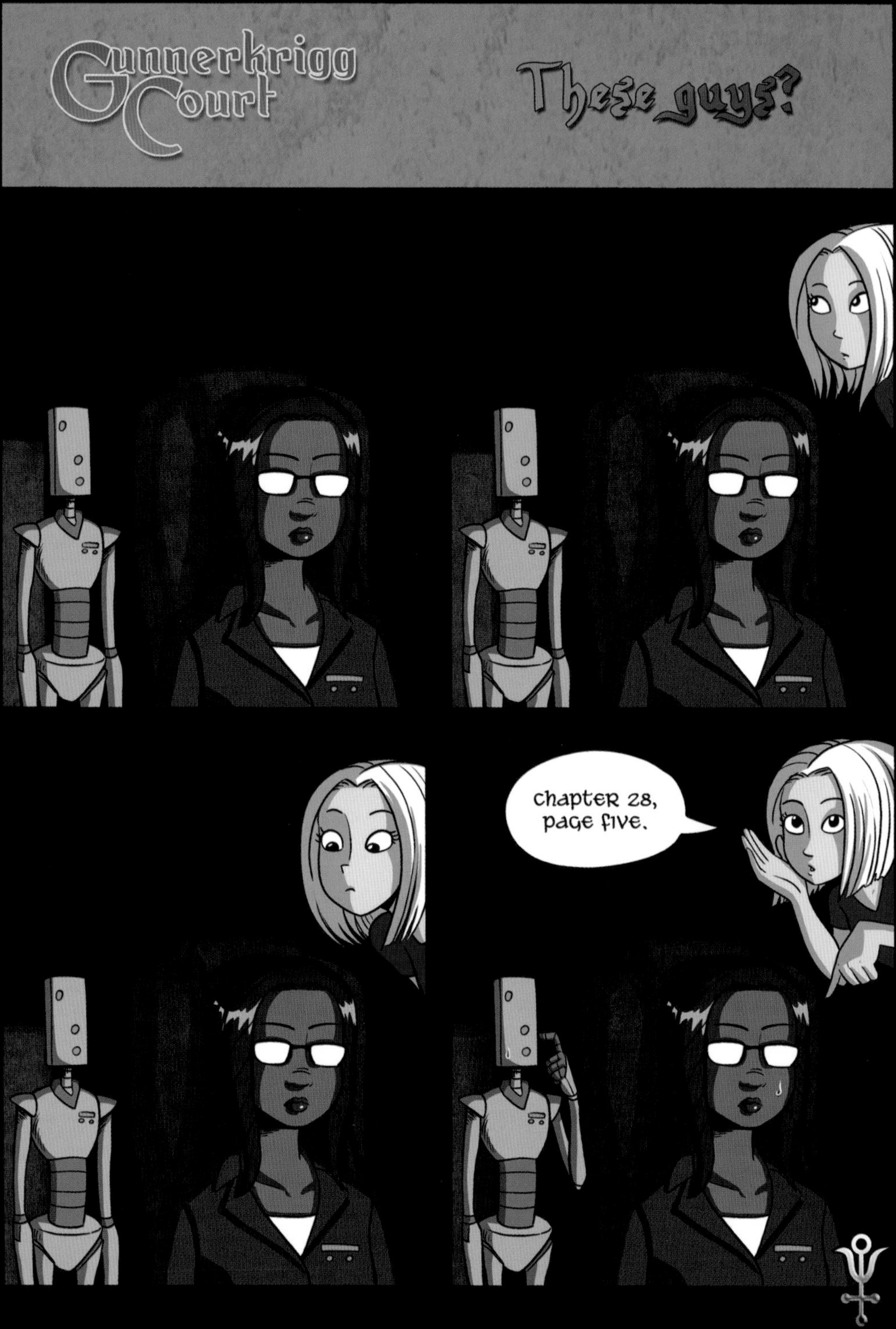
Gunnerkrigg Court
These guys?
chapter 28, page five.

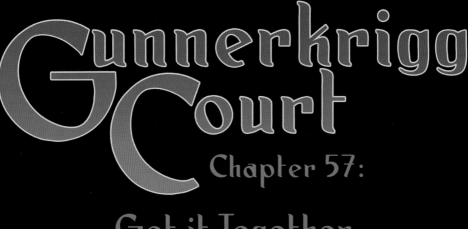

Gunnerkrigg Court

Chapter 57:

Get it Together

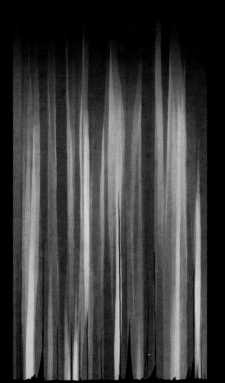

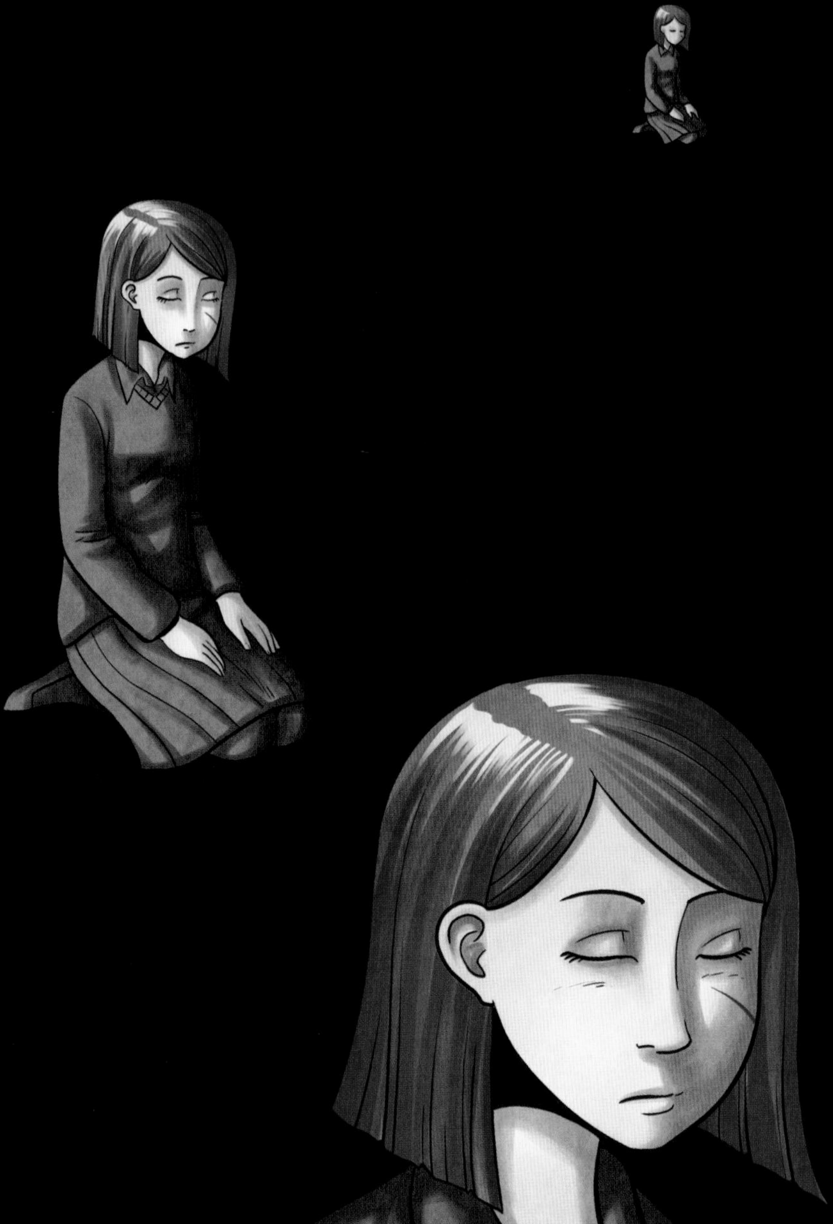

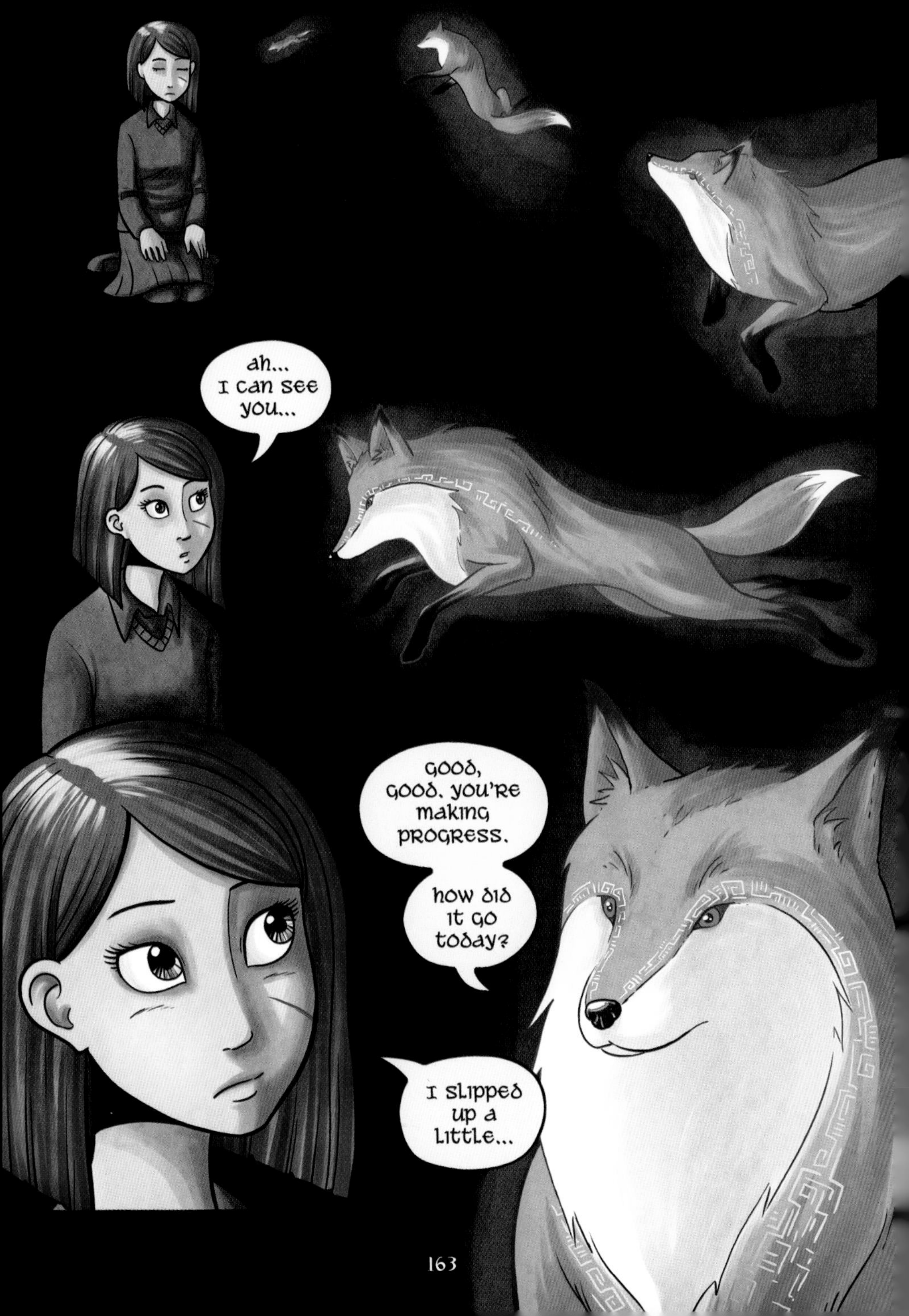
ah...
I can see you...
good, good. you're making progress.
how did it go today?
I slipped up a little...

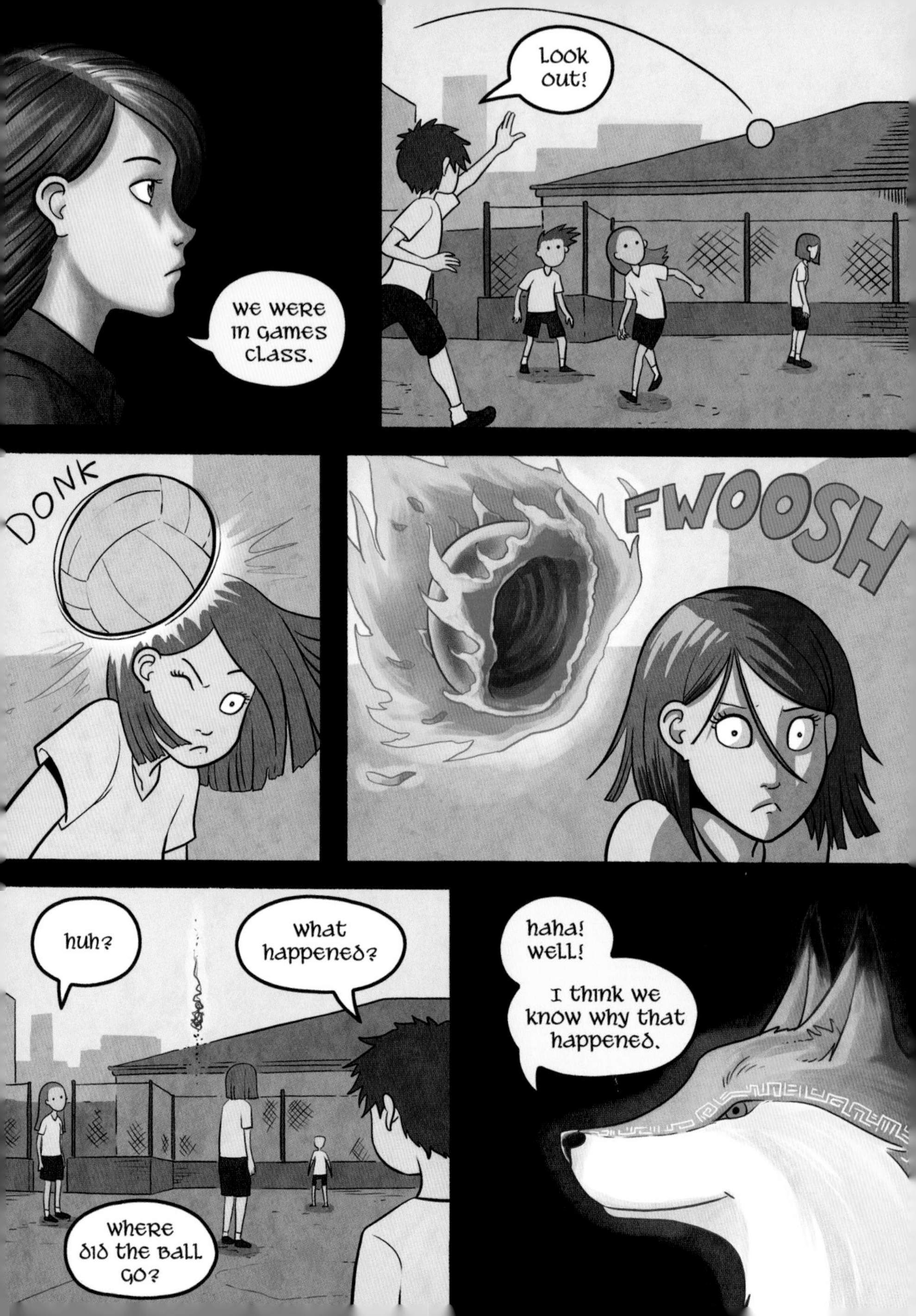
WE WERE IN GAMES CLASS.
LOOK OUT!
DONK
FWOOSH
HUH?
WHAT HAPPENED?
WHERE DID THE BALL GO?
HAHA! WELL!
I THINK WE KNOW WHY THAT HAPPENED.

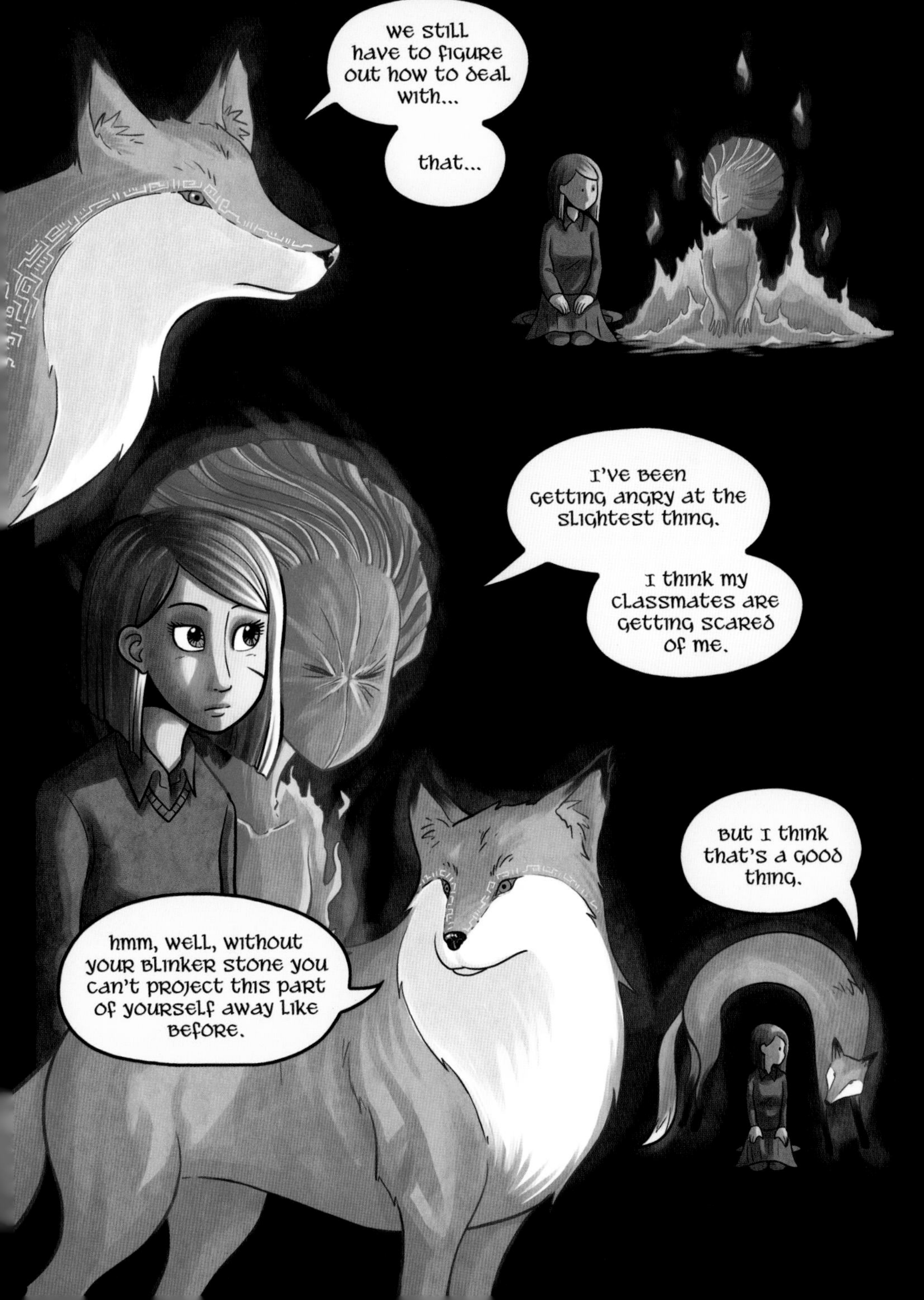
we still have to figure out how to deal with...
that...
I've been getting angry at the slightest thing.
I think my classmates are getting scared of me.
But I think that's a good thing.
hmm, well, without your blinker stone you can't project this part of yourself away like before.

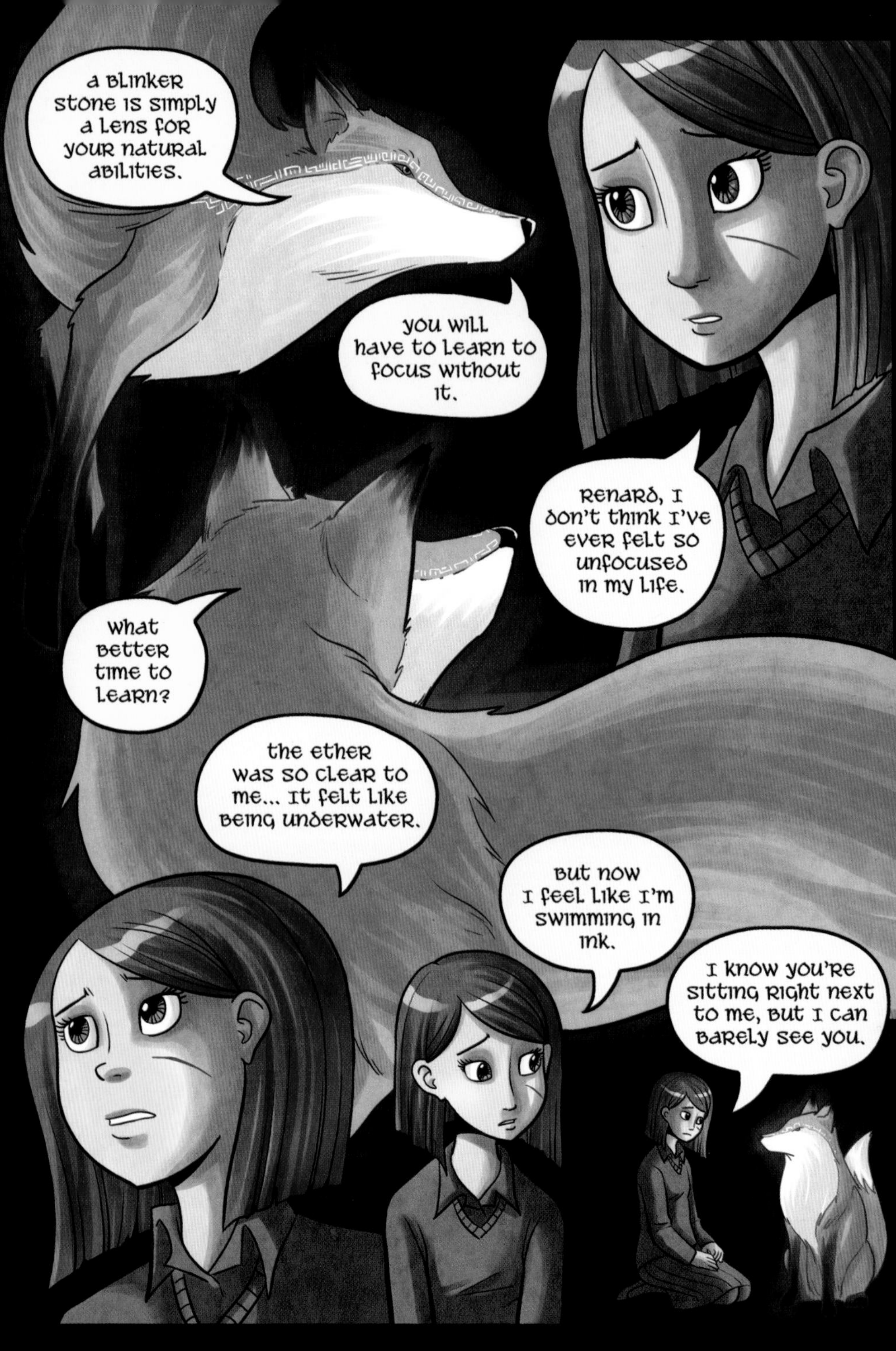
a BLINKER stone is simply a Lens for your natural abilities.
you will have to Learn to focus without it.
Renard, I don't think I've ever felt so unfocused in my Life.
What Better time to Learn?
the ether was so clear to me... it felt Like Being underwater.
But now I feel Like I'm swimming in ink.
I know you're sitting right next to me, But I can Barely see you.

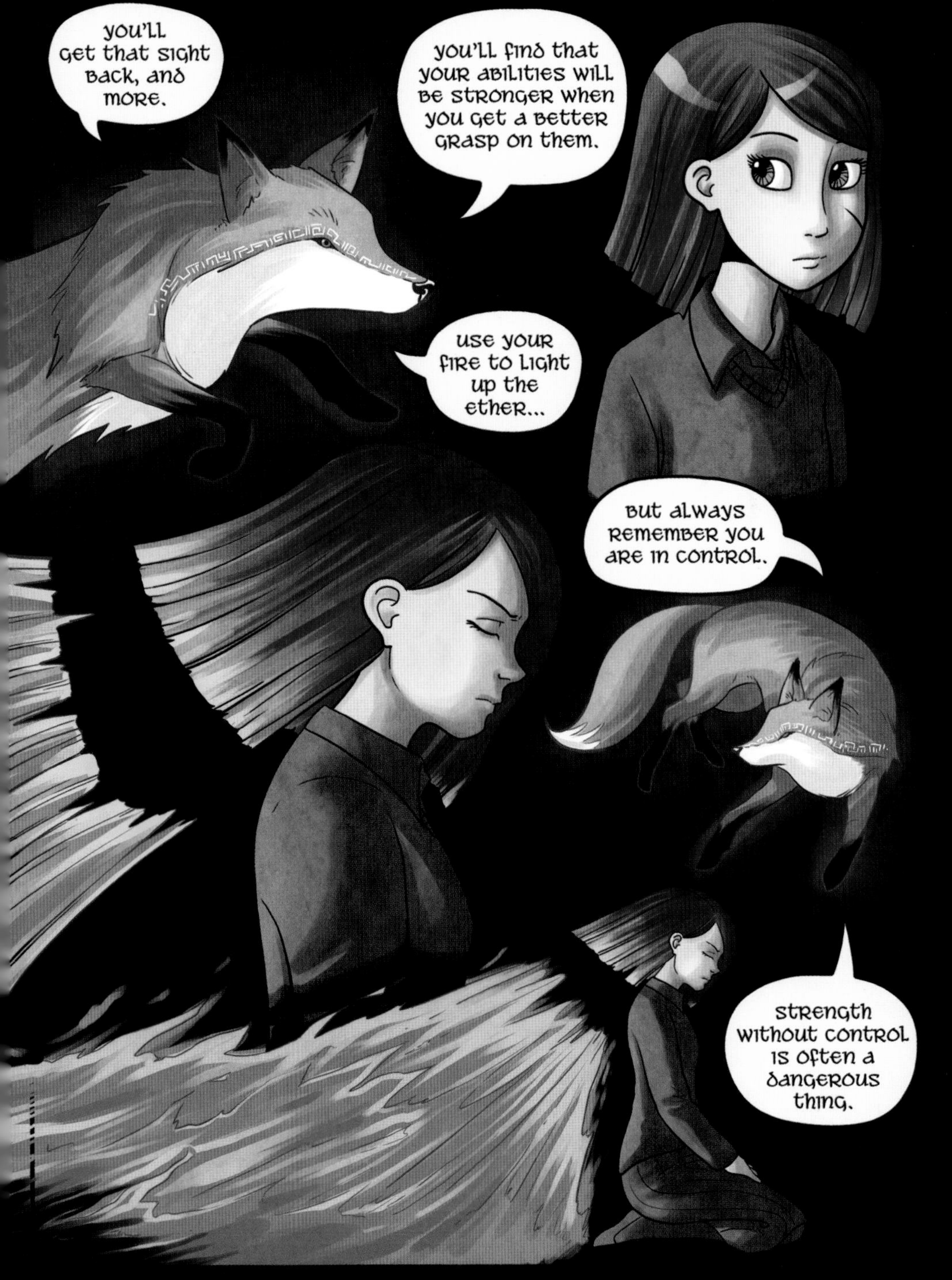
you'll get that sight back, and more.
you'll find that your abilities will be stronger when you get a better grasp on them.
use your fire to light up the ether...
but always remember you are in control.
strength without control is often a dangerous thing.

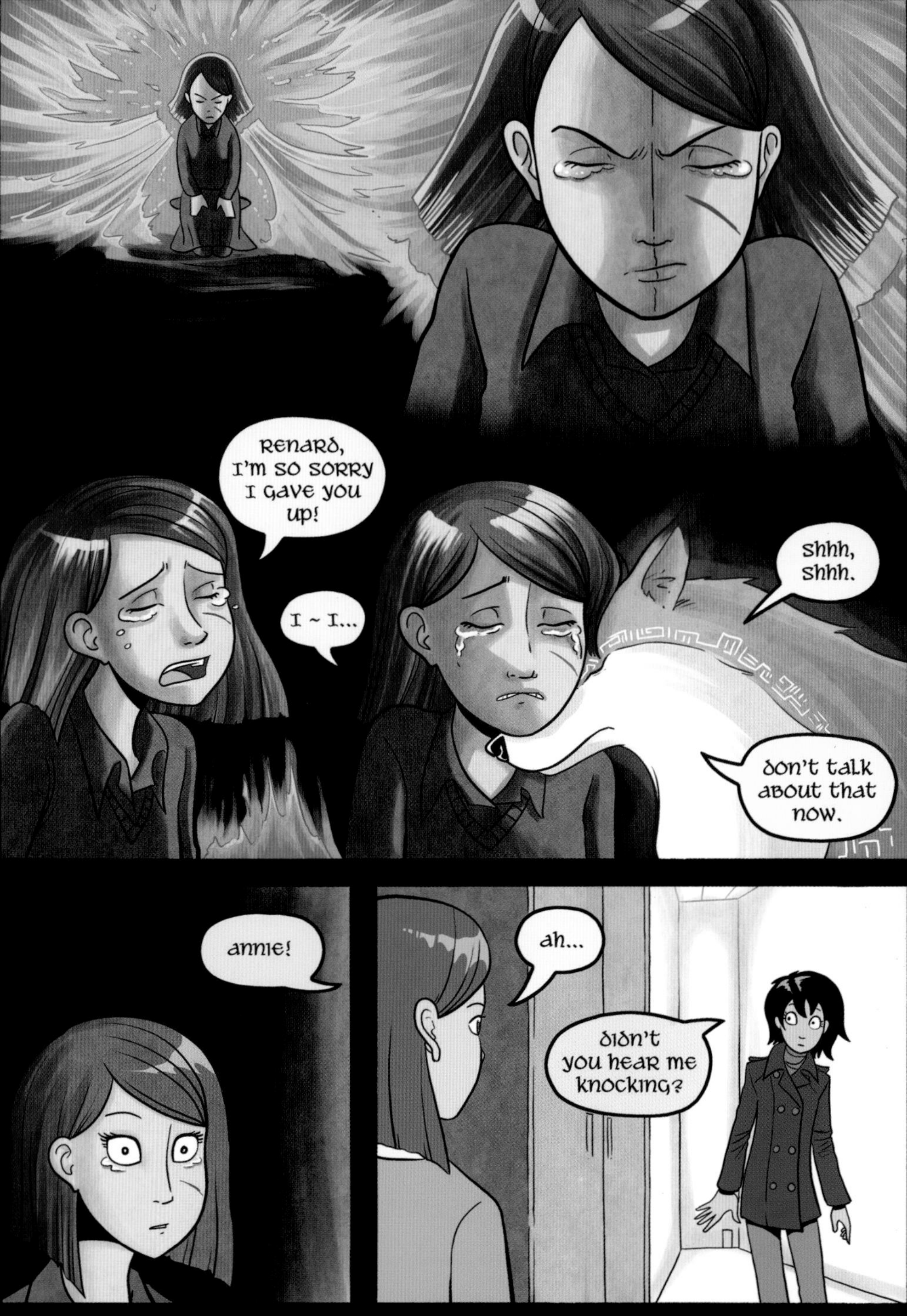
Renard, I'm so sorry I gave you up!
I ~ I...
Shhh, shhh.
Don't talk about that now.
Annie!
Ah...
Didn't you hear me knocking?

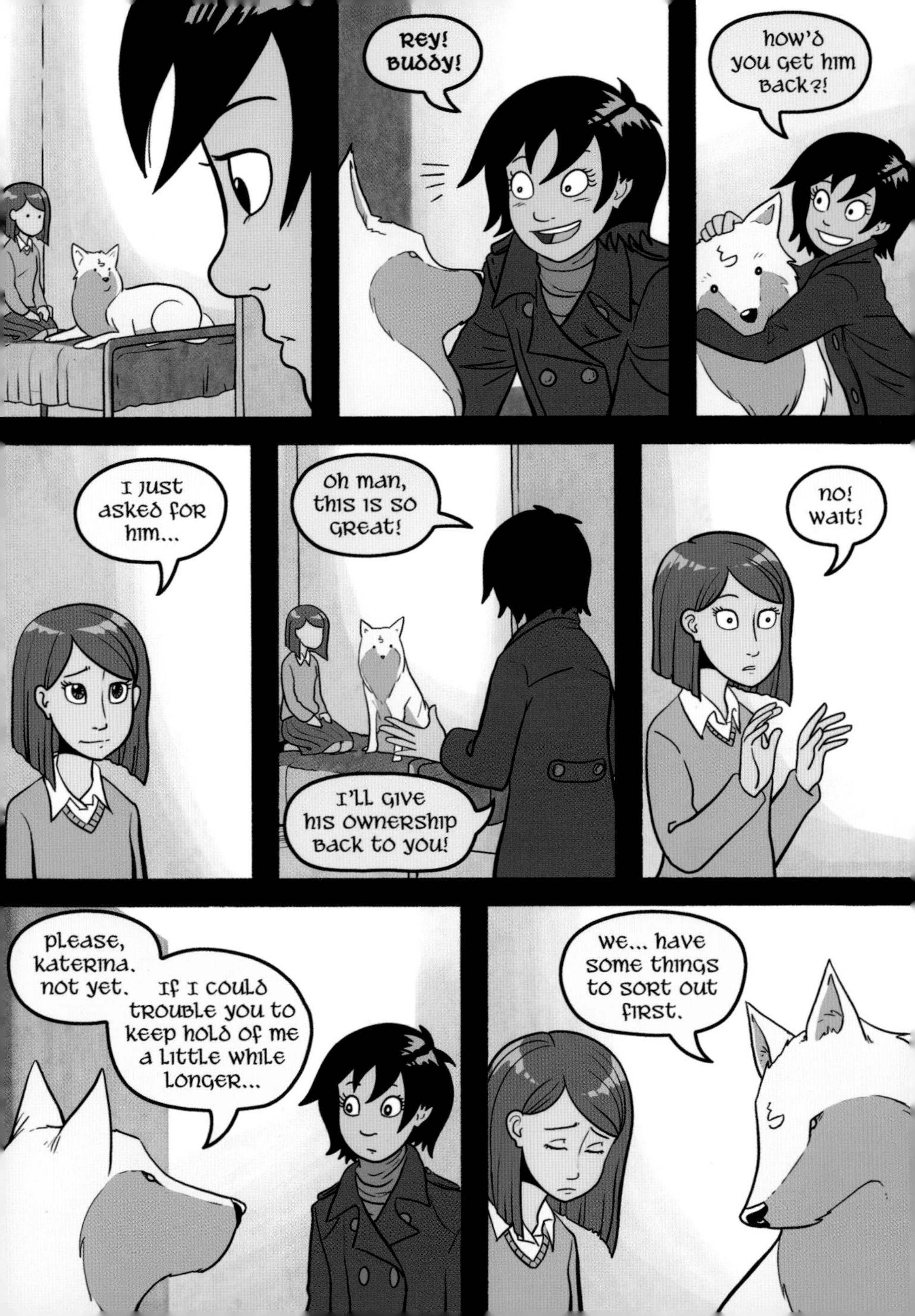
Rey! Buddy!
how'd you get him back?!
I just asked for him...
Oh man, this is so great!
I'll give his ownership back to you!
no! wait!
please, katerina. not yet.
If I could trouble you to keep hold of me a little while longer...
we... have some things to sort out first.

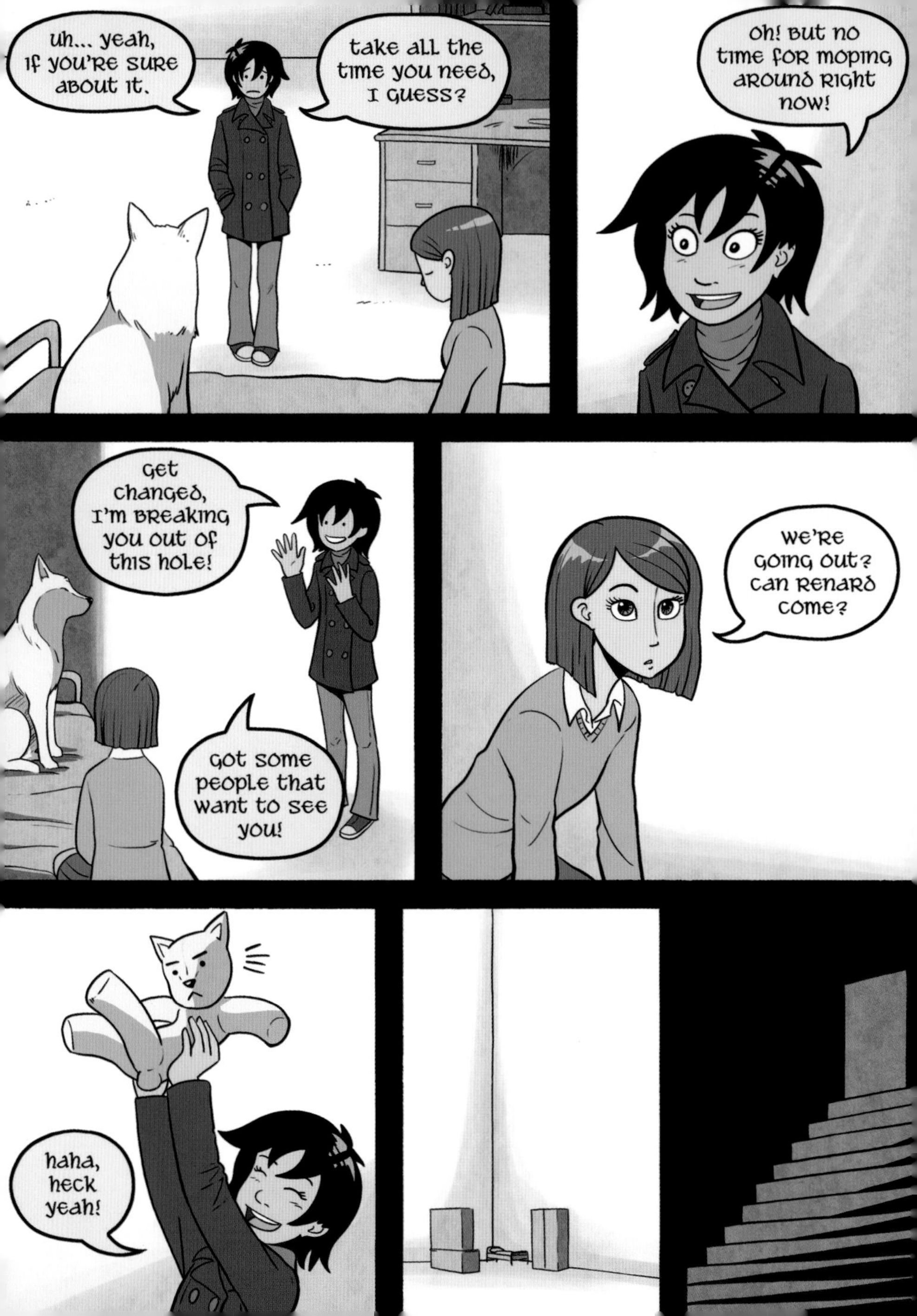
uh... yeah, if you're sure about it.
take all the time you need, I guess?
oh! but no time for moping around right now!
get changed, I'm breaking you out of this hole!
got some people that want to see you!
we're going out? can Renard come?
haha, heck yeah!

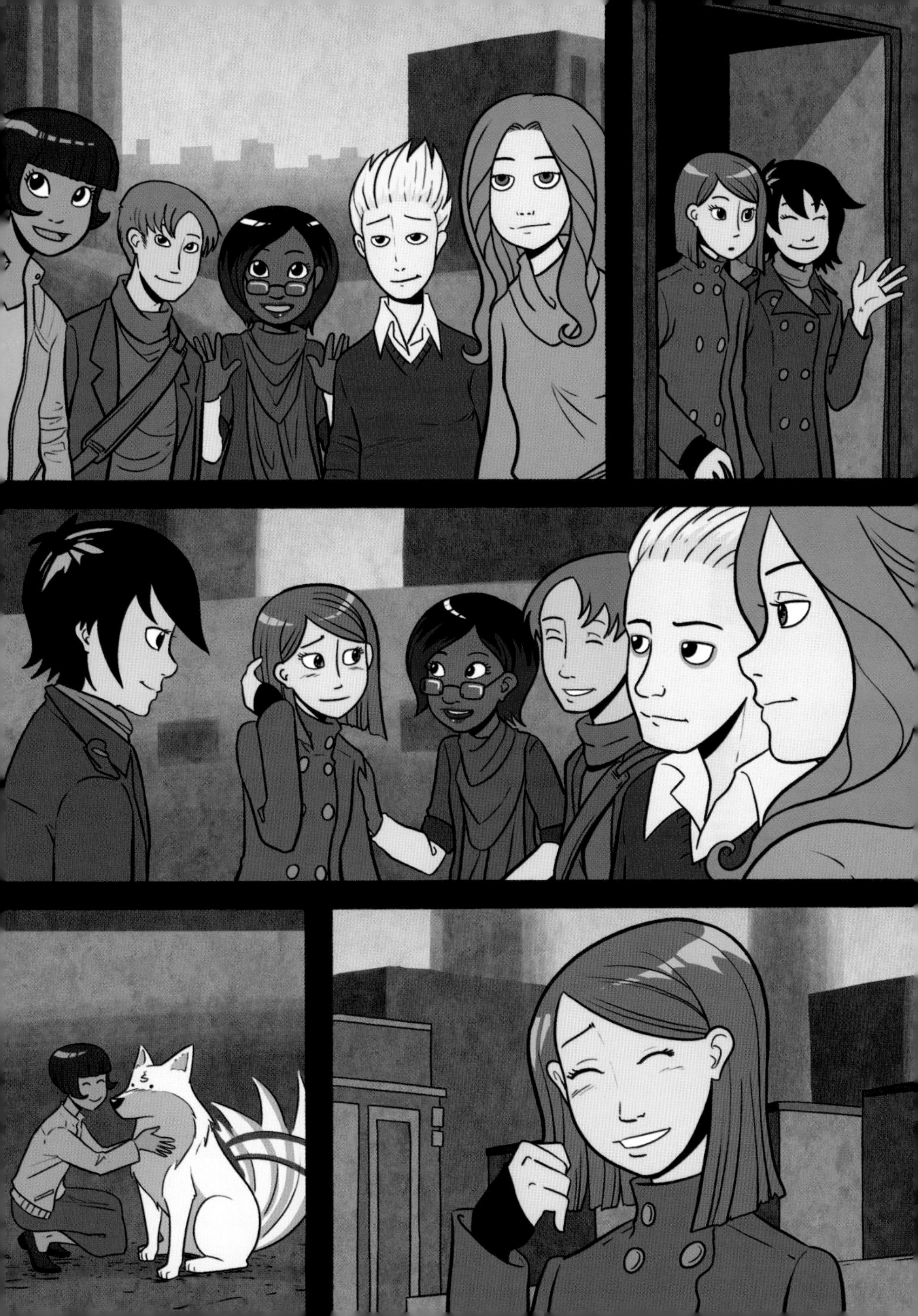

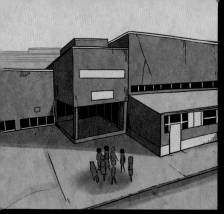

BOWLING?
I'VE NEVER DONE
THIS BEFORE...

IT'S
EASY!

YEAH,
YOU'LL
SEE!

KATERINA, I THINK
THIS WAS A GOOD IDEA
TO GET ANTIMONY OUT
AMONGST FRIENDS.

HEHE... WELL,
THERE WAS
AN ULTERIOR
MOTIVE!

OH?

WINSBURY'S
GOING TO ASK
ANNIE TO BE HIS
GIRLFRIEND!

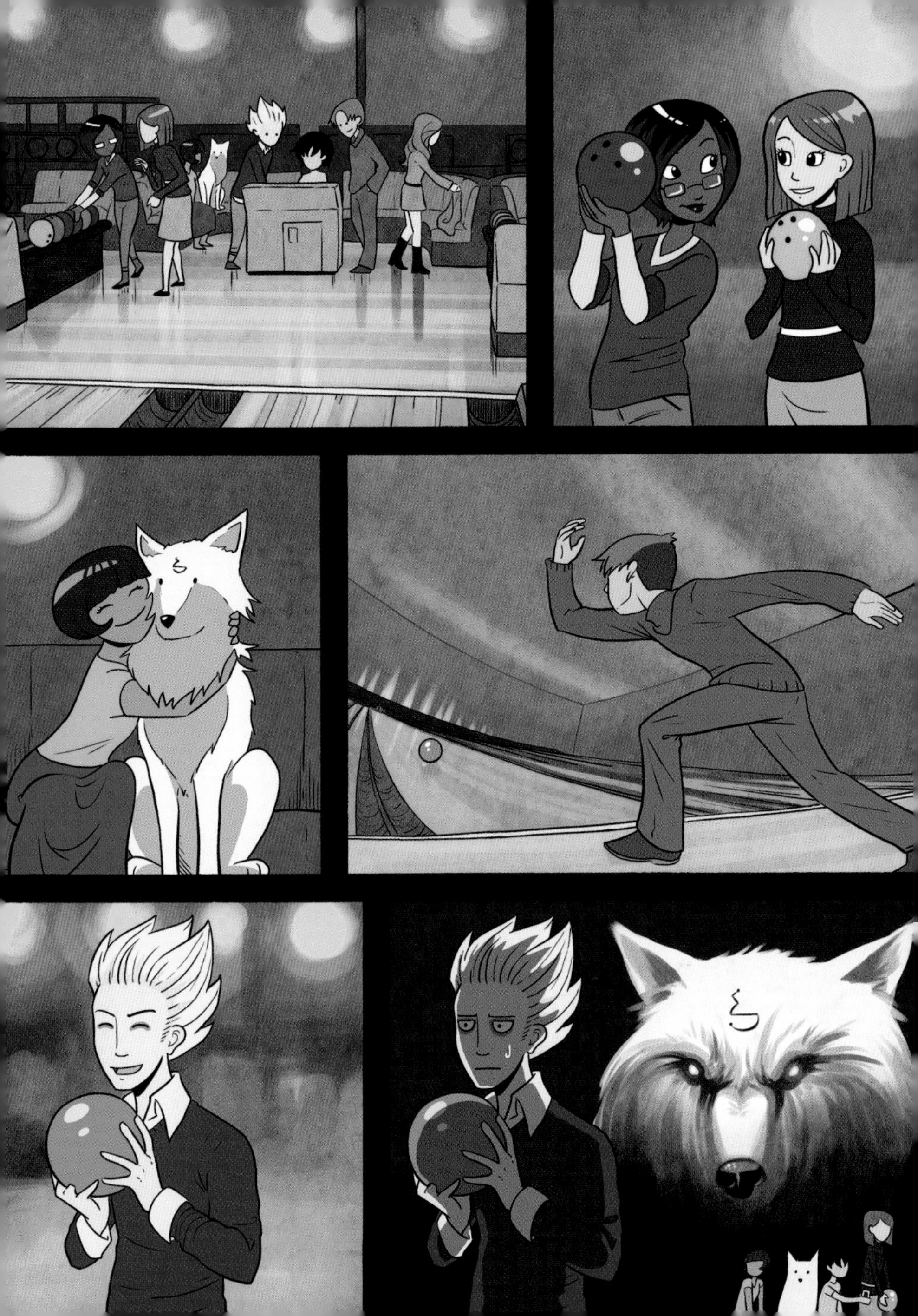

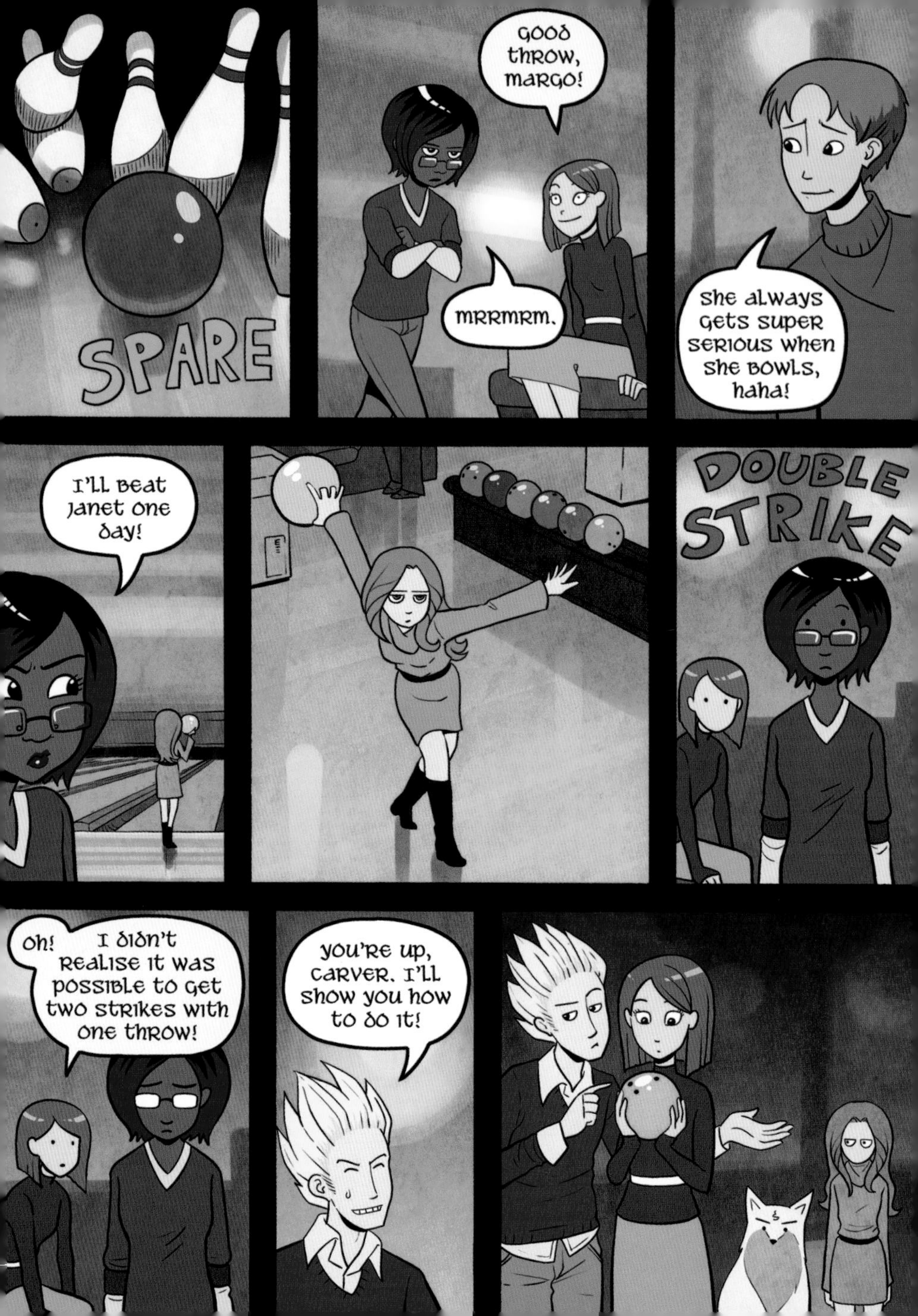
SPARE
GOOD THROW, MARGO!
MRRMRM.
SHE ALWAYS GETS SUPER SERIOUS WHEN SHE BOWLS, HAHA!
I'LL BEAT JANET ONE DAY!
DOUBLE STRIKE
OH! I DIDN'T REALISE IT WAS POSSIBLE TO GET TWO STRIKES WITH ONE THROW!
YOU'RE UP, CARVER. I'LL SHOW YOU HOW TO DO IT!

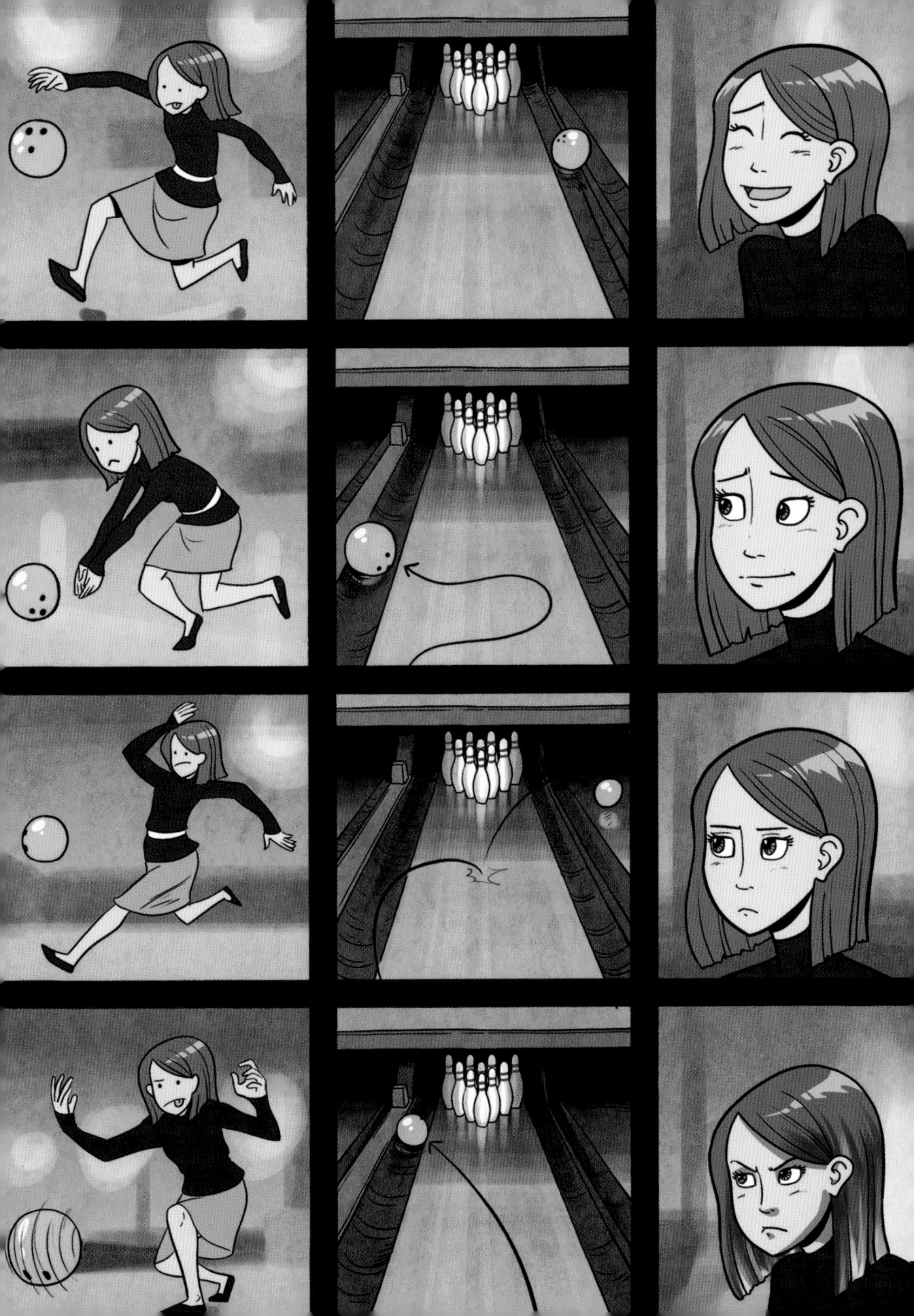

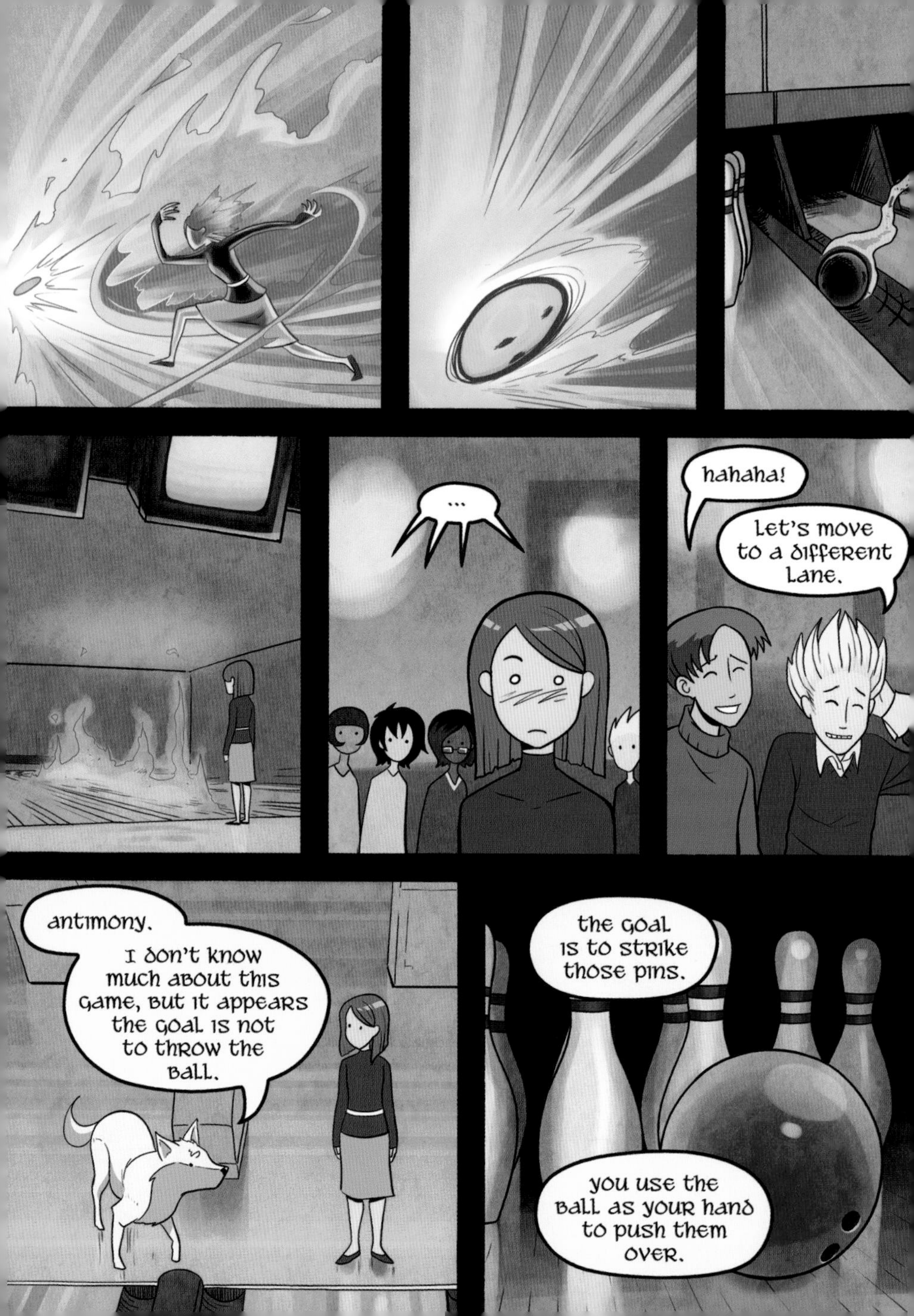
...
hahaha!
Let's move to a different lane.
antimony.
I don't know much about this game, but it appears the goal is not to throw the ball.
the goal is to strike those pins.
you use the ball as your hand to push them over.

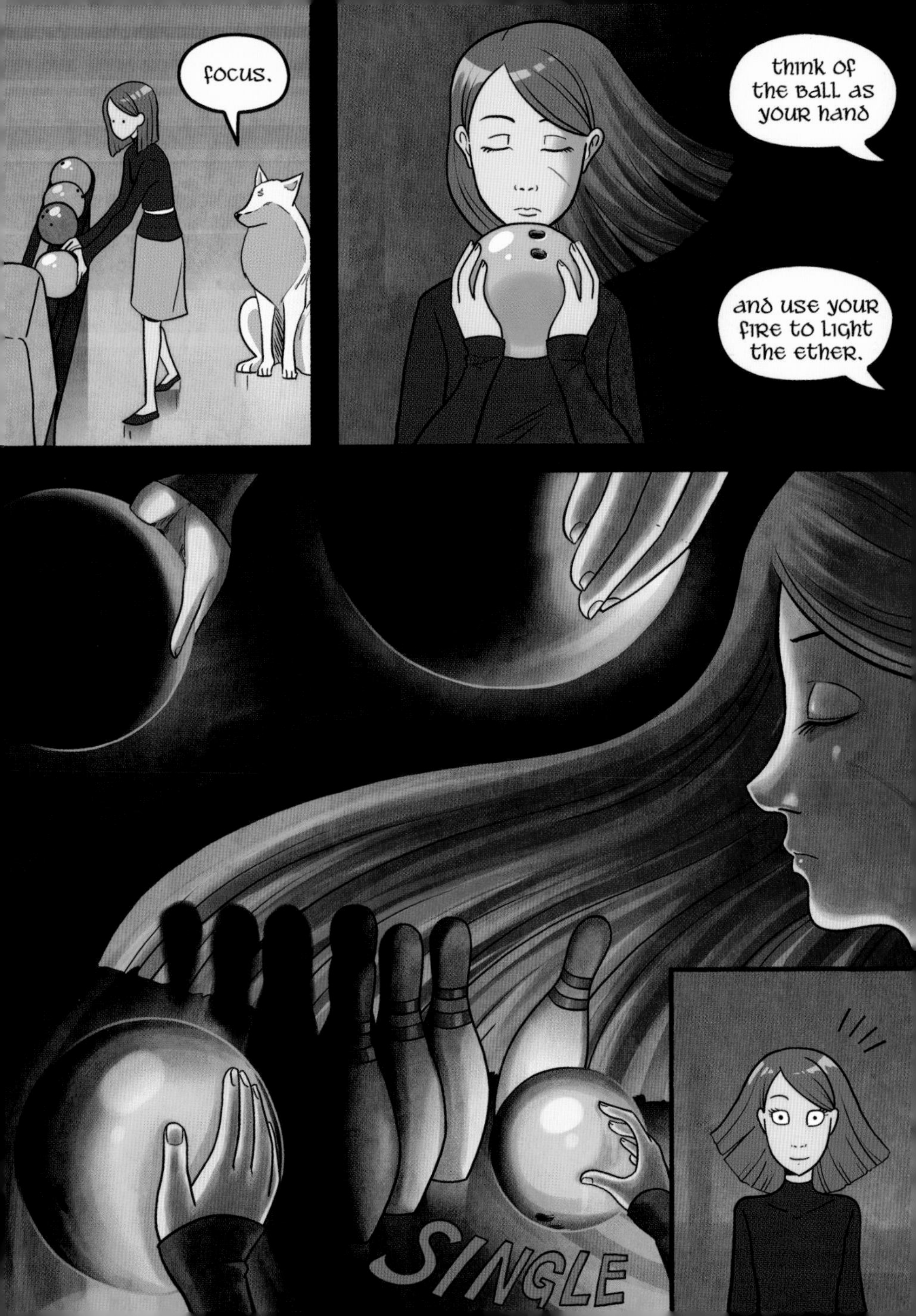
focus.
think of the ball as your hand
and use your fire to light the ether.
SINGLE

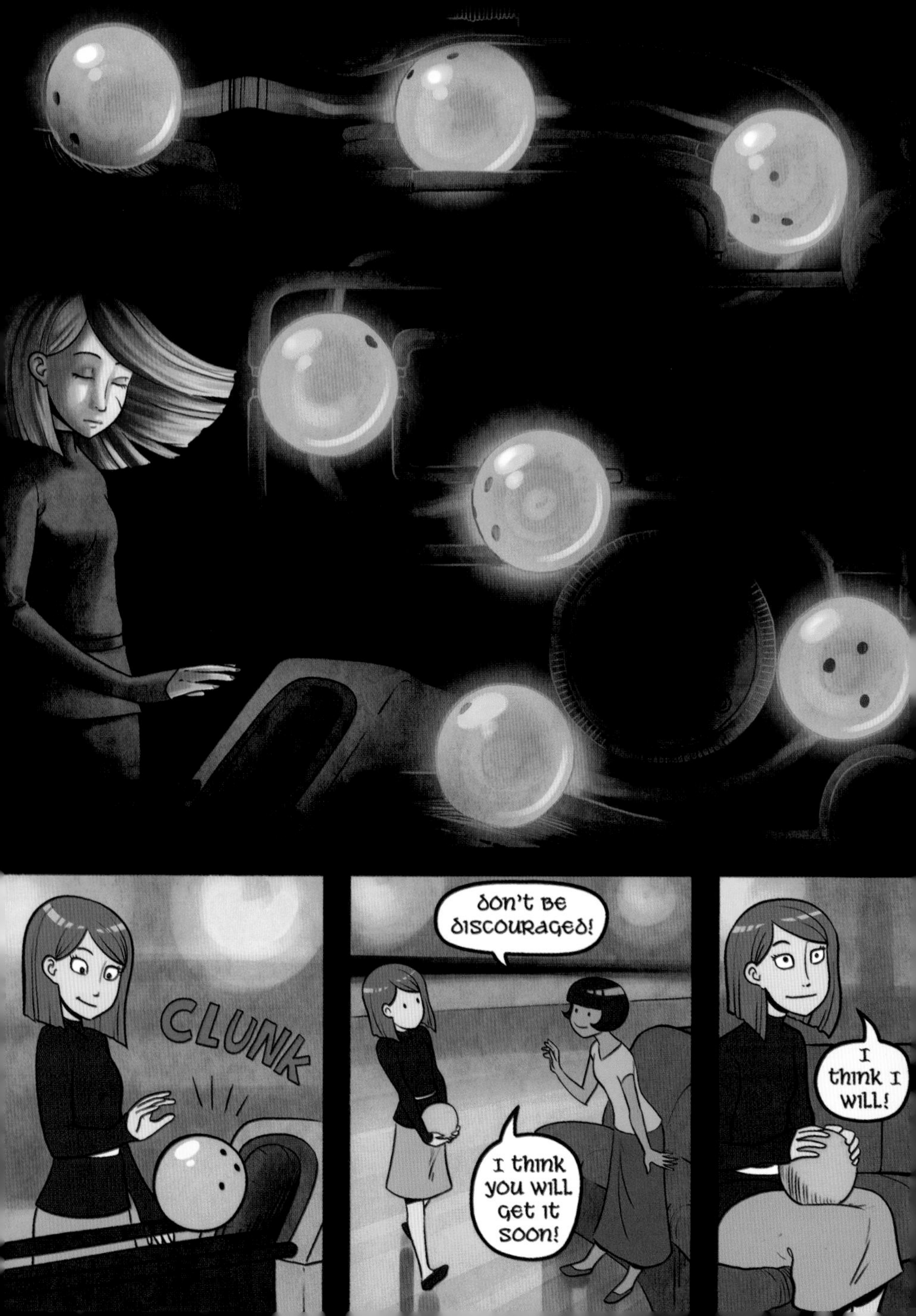
CLUNK
DON'T BE DISCOURAGED!
I THINK YOU WILL GET IT SOON!
I THINK I WILL!

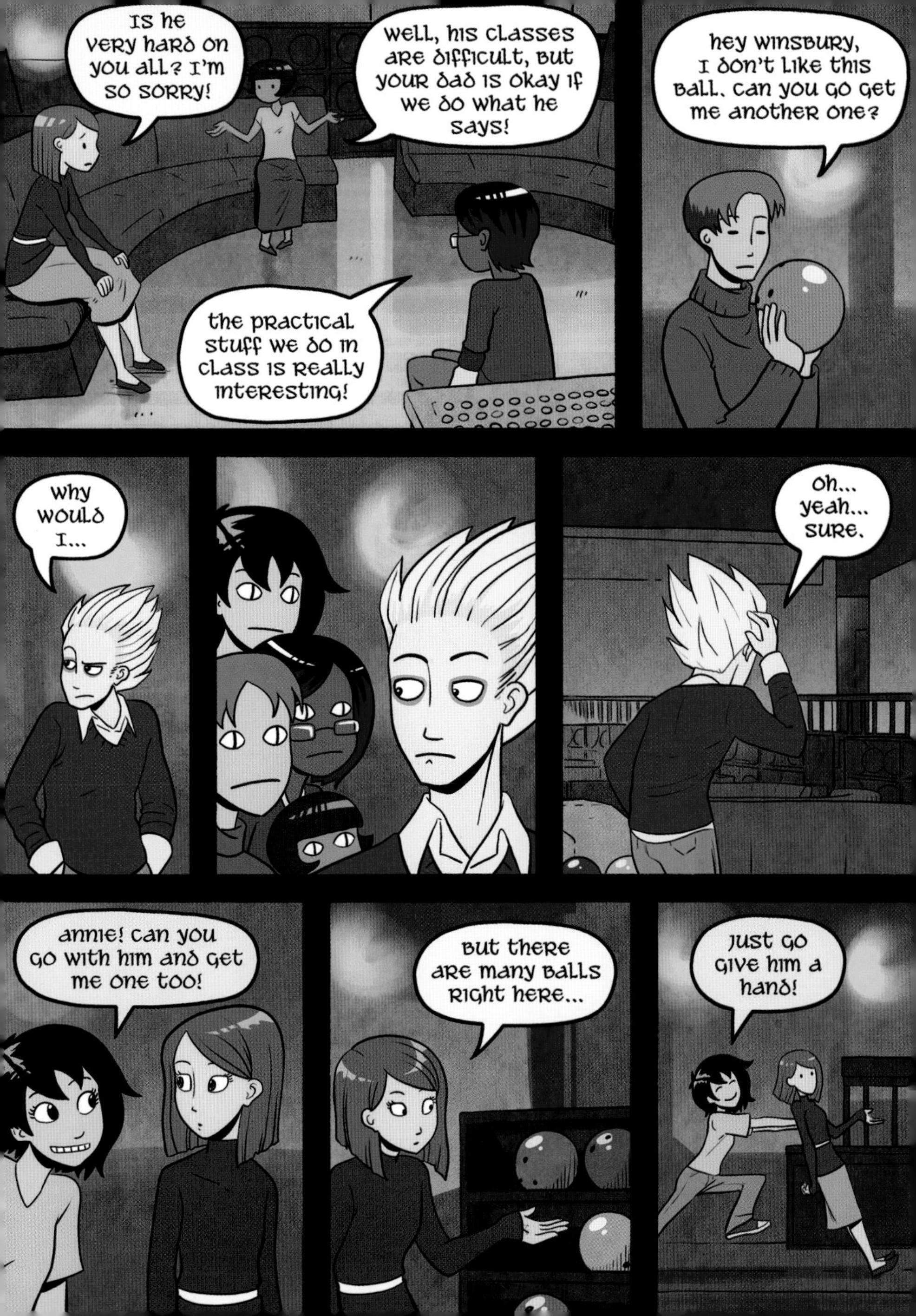
Is he very hard on you all? I'm so sorry!
Well, his classes are difficult, but your dad is okay if we do what he says!
the practical stuff we do in class is really interesting!
hey Winsbury, I don't like this ball. can you go get me another one?
Why would I...
Oh... yeah... sure.
Annie! can you go with him and get me one too!
But there are many balls right here...
Just go give him a hand!

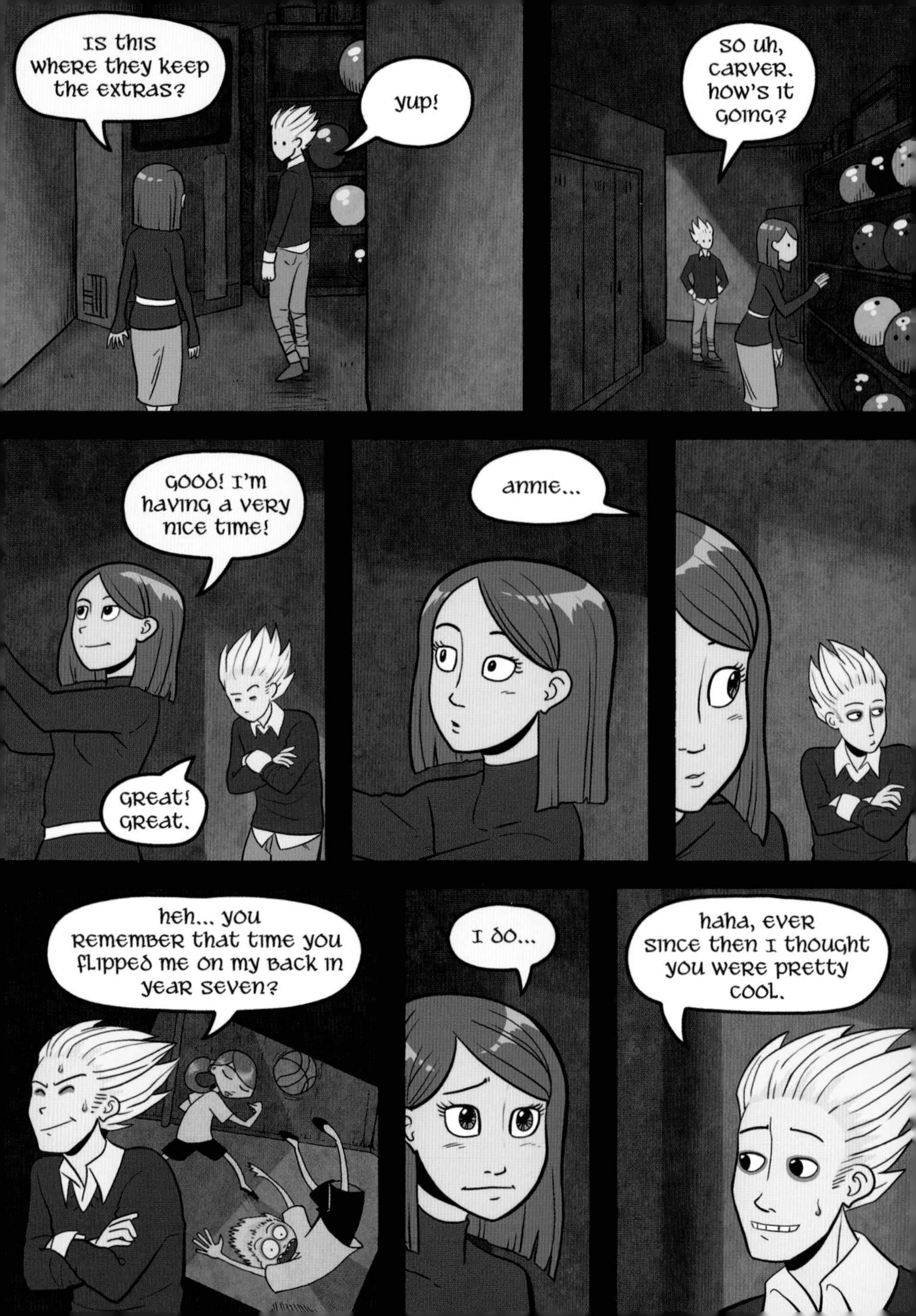
Is this where they keep the extras?
yup!
So uh, Carver. How's it going?
Good! I'm having a very nice time!
Great! Great.
Annie...
Heh... you remember that time you flipped me on my back in year seven?
I do...
Haha, ever since then I thought you were pretty cool.

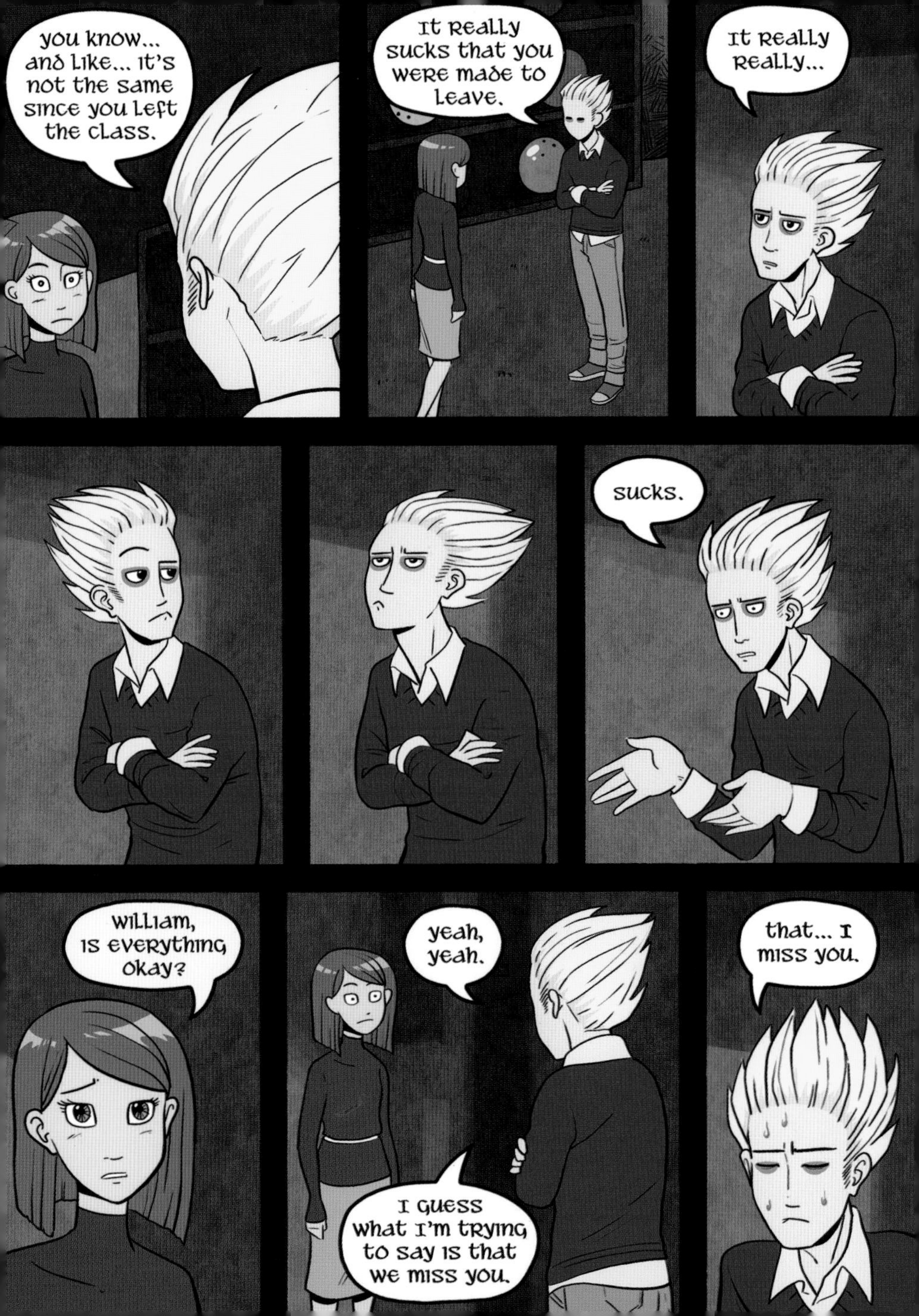
you know... and like... it's not the same since you left the class.
It really sucks that you were made to leave.
It really really...
sucks.
William, is everything okay?
yeah, yeah.
I guess what I'm trying to say is that we miss you.
that... I miss you.

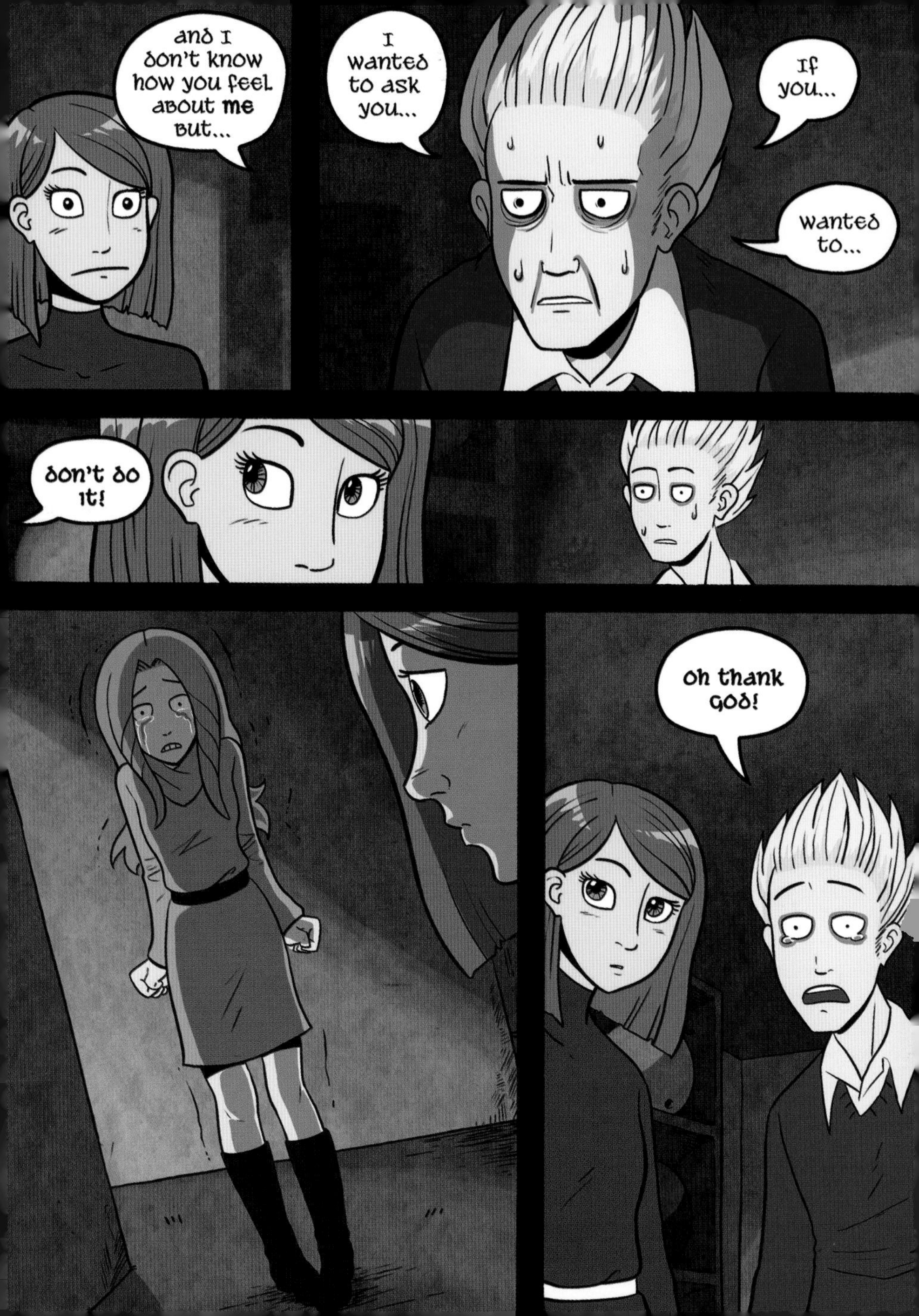
and I don't know how you feel about me but...
I wanted to ask you...
If you...
wanted to...
don't do it!
Oh thank GOD!

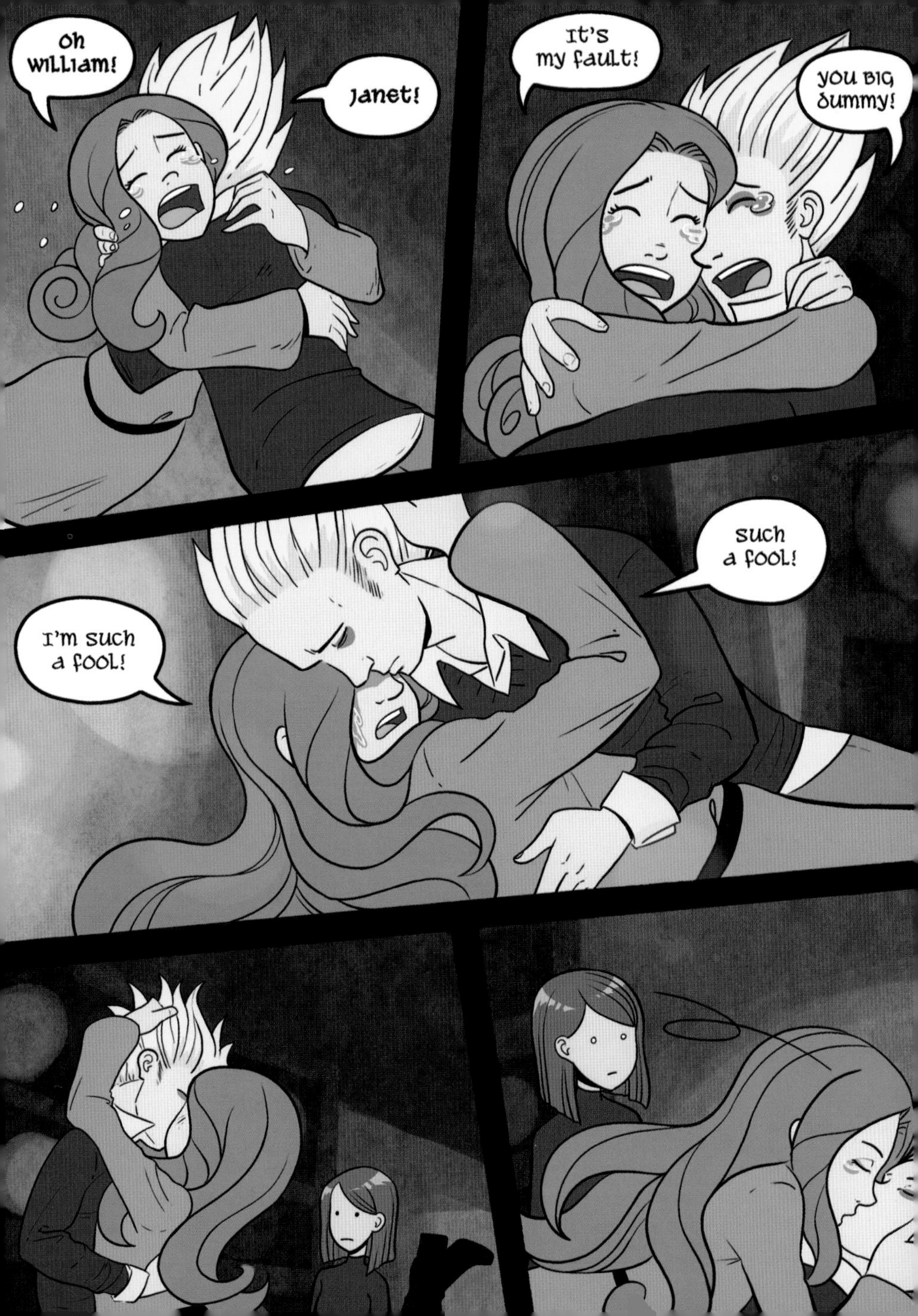
Oh William!
Janet!
It's my fault!
You big dummy!
Such a fool!
I'm such a fool!

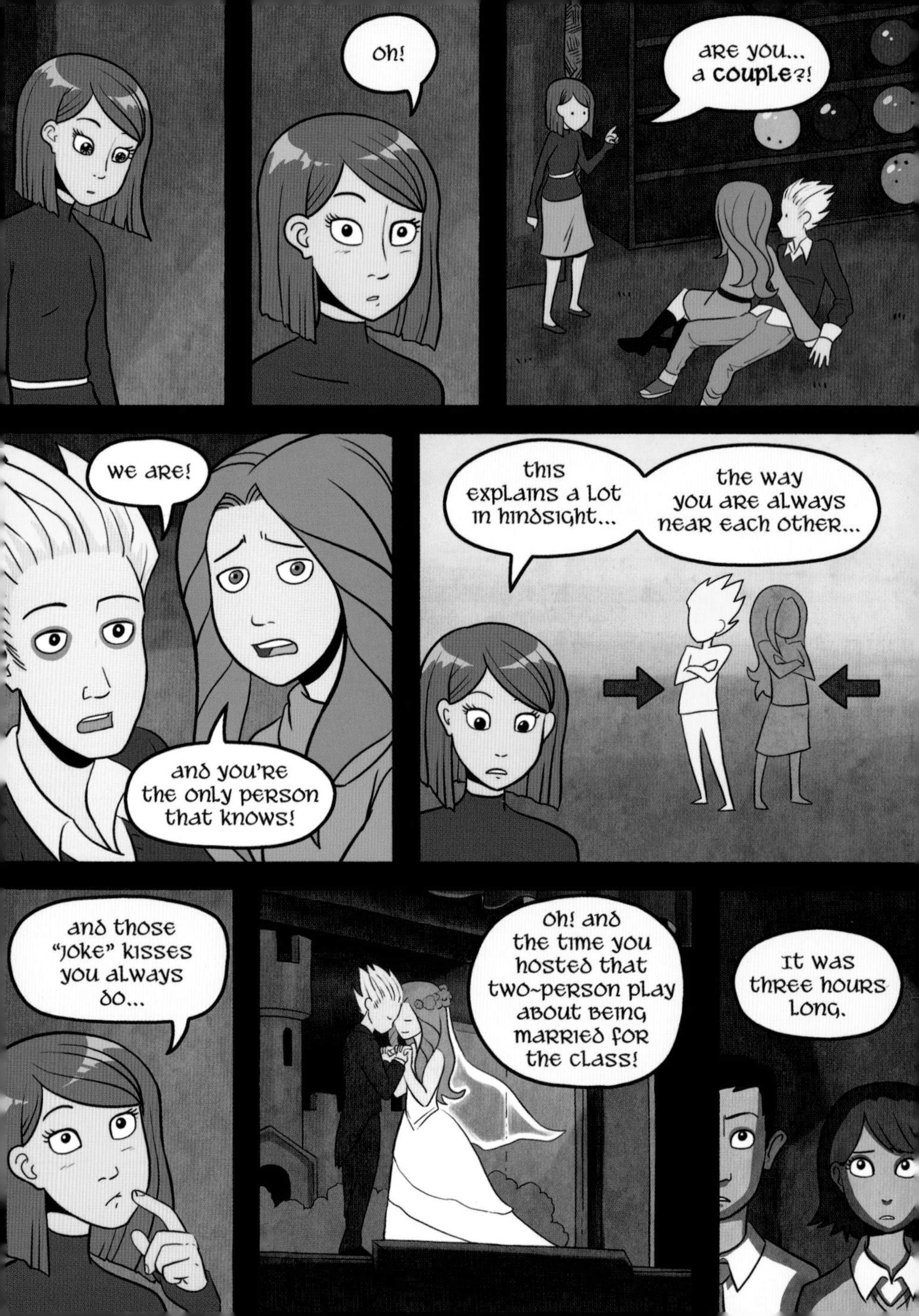
Oh!
are you... a couple?!
We are!
and you're the only person that knows!
this explains a lot in hindsight...
the way you are always near each other...
and those "joke" kisses you always do...
Oh! and the time you hosted that two-person play about being married for the class!
It was three hours long.

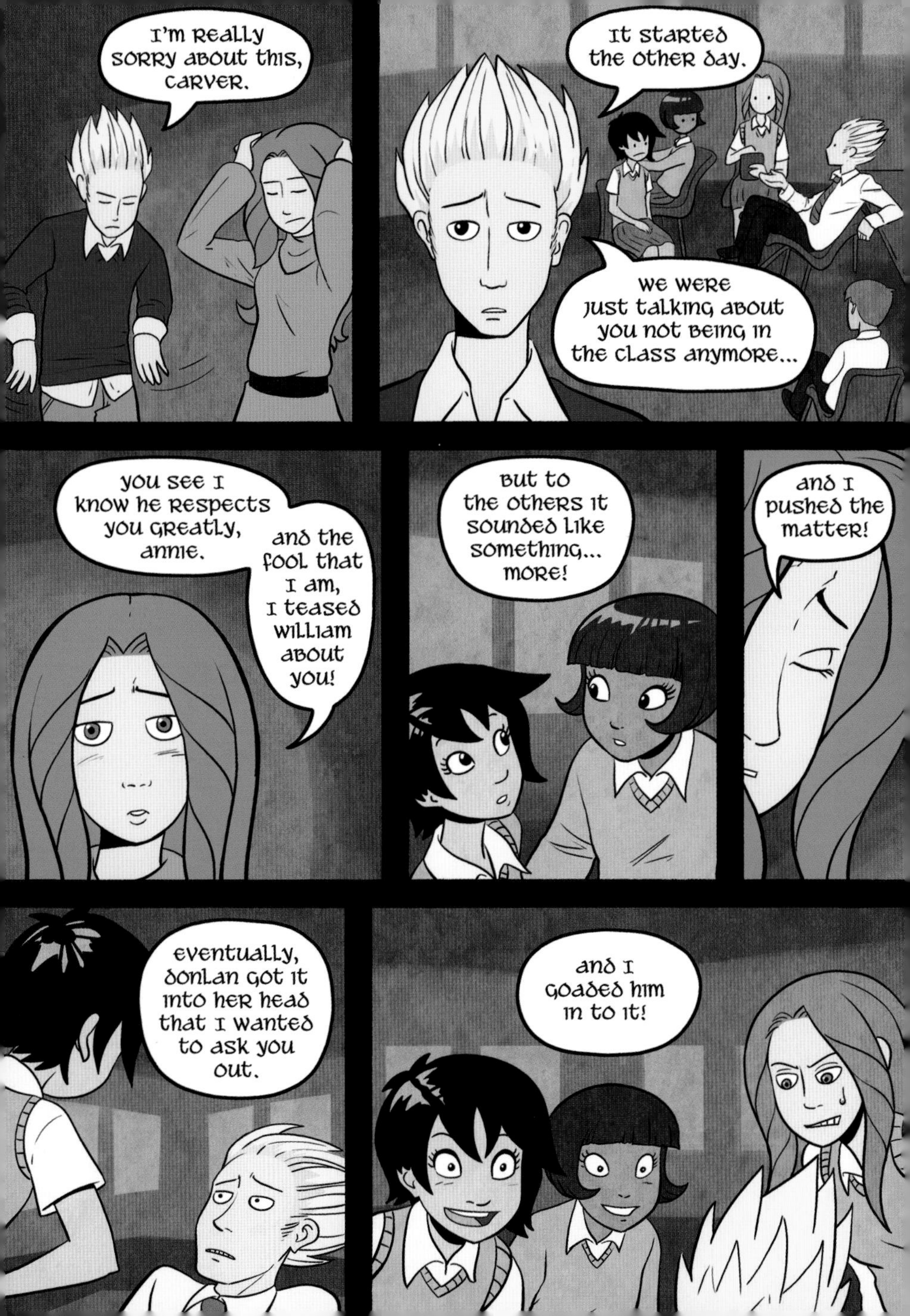
I'm really sorry about this, Carver.
It started the other day.
We were just talking about you not being in the class anymore...
You see I know he respects you greatly, Annie.
And the fool that I am, I teased William about you!
But to the others it sounded like something... more!
And I pushed the matter!
Eventually, Donlan got it into her head that I wanted to ask you out.
And I goaded him in to it!

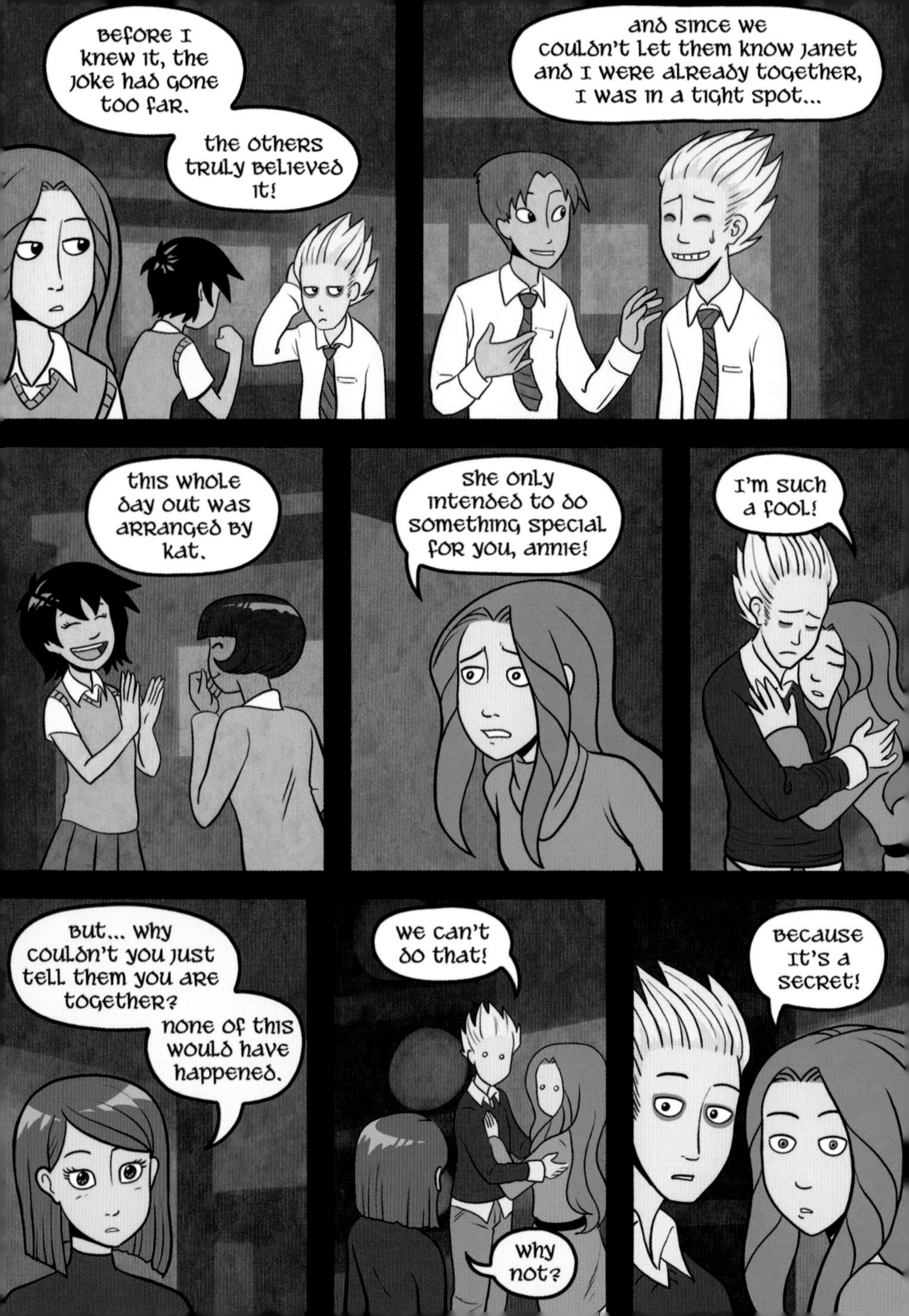
Before I knew it, the joke had gone too far.
the others truly believed it!
and since we couldn't let them know janet and I were already together, I was in a tight spot...
this whole day out was arranged by kat.
she only intended to do something special for you, annie!
I'm such a fool!
But... why couldn't you just tell them you are together?
none of this would have happened.
we can't do that!
why not?
Because it's a secret!

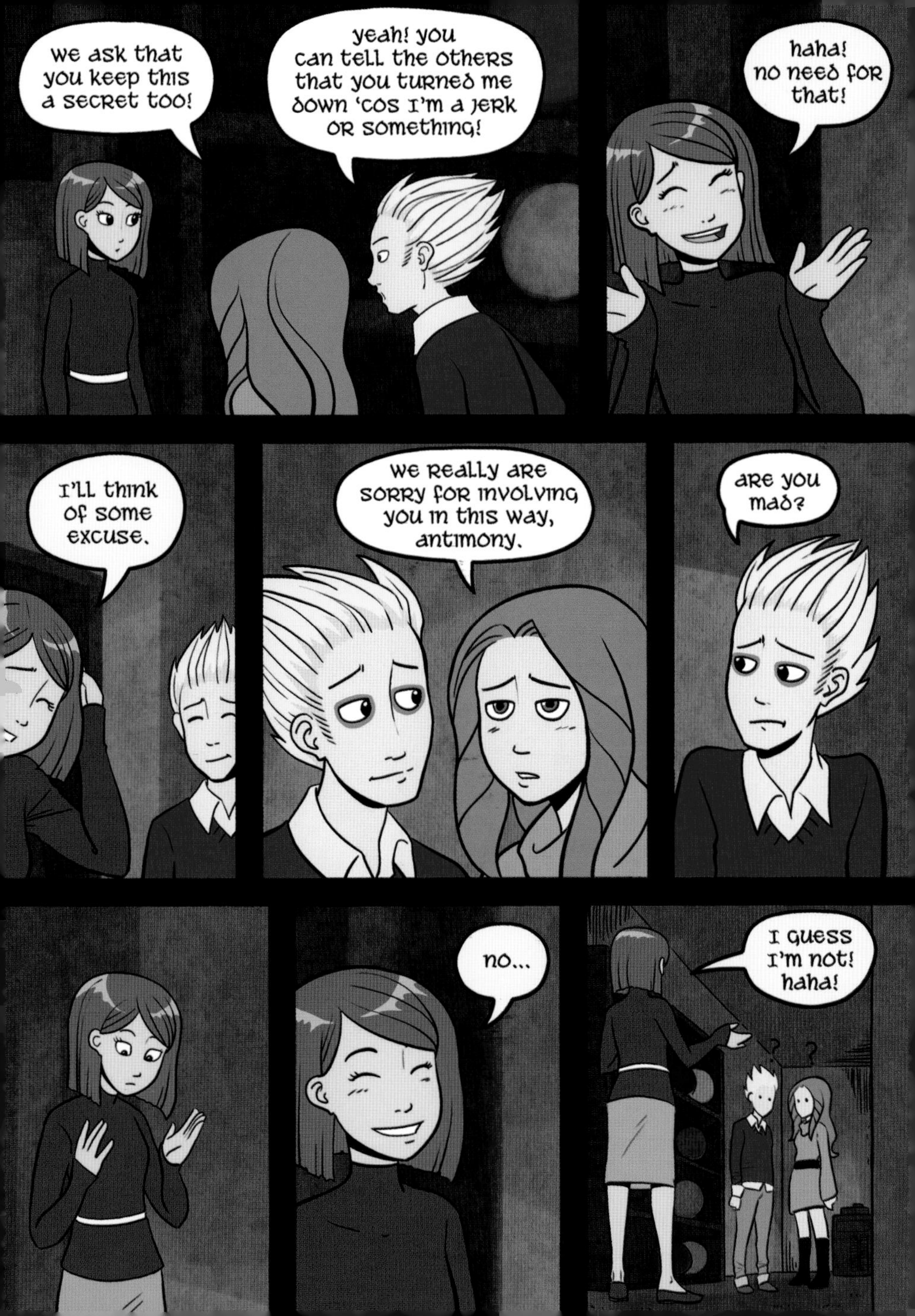
we ask that you keep this a secret too!
yeah! you can tell the others that you turned me down 'cos I'm a jerk or something!
haha! no need for that!
I'll think of some excuse.
we really are sorry for involving you in this way, antimony.
are you mad?
no...
I guess I'm not! haha!

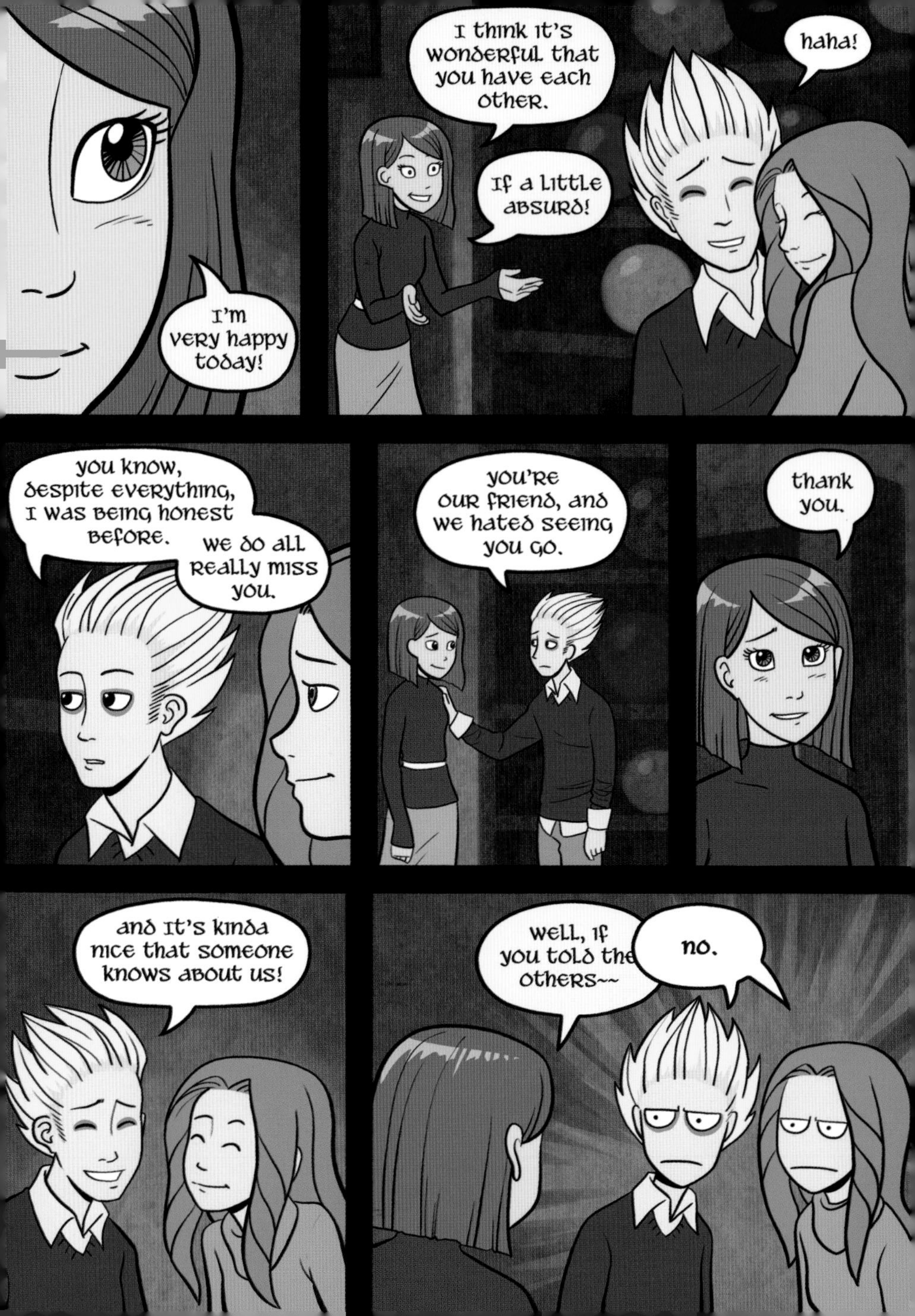
I'm very happy today!
I think it's wonderful that you have each other.
If a little absurd!
haha!
you know, despite everything, I was being honest before.
we do all really miss you.
you're our friend, and we hated seeing you go.
thank you.
and it's kinda nice that someone knows about us!
well, if you told the others~~
no.

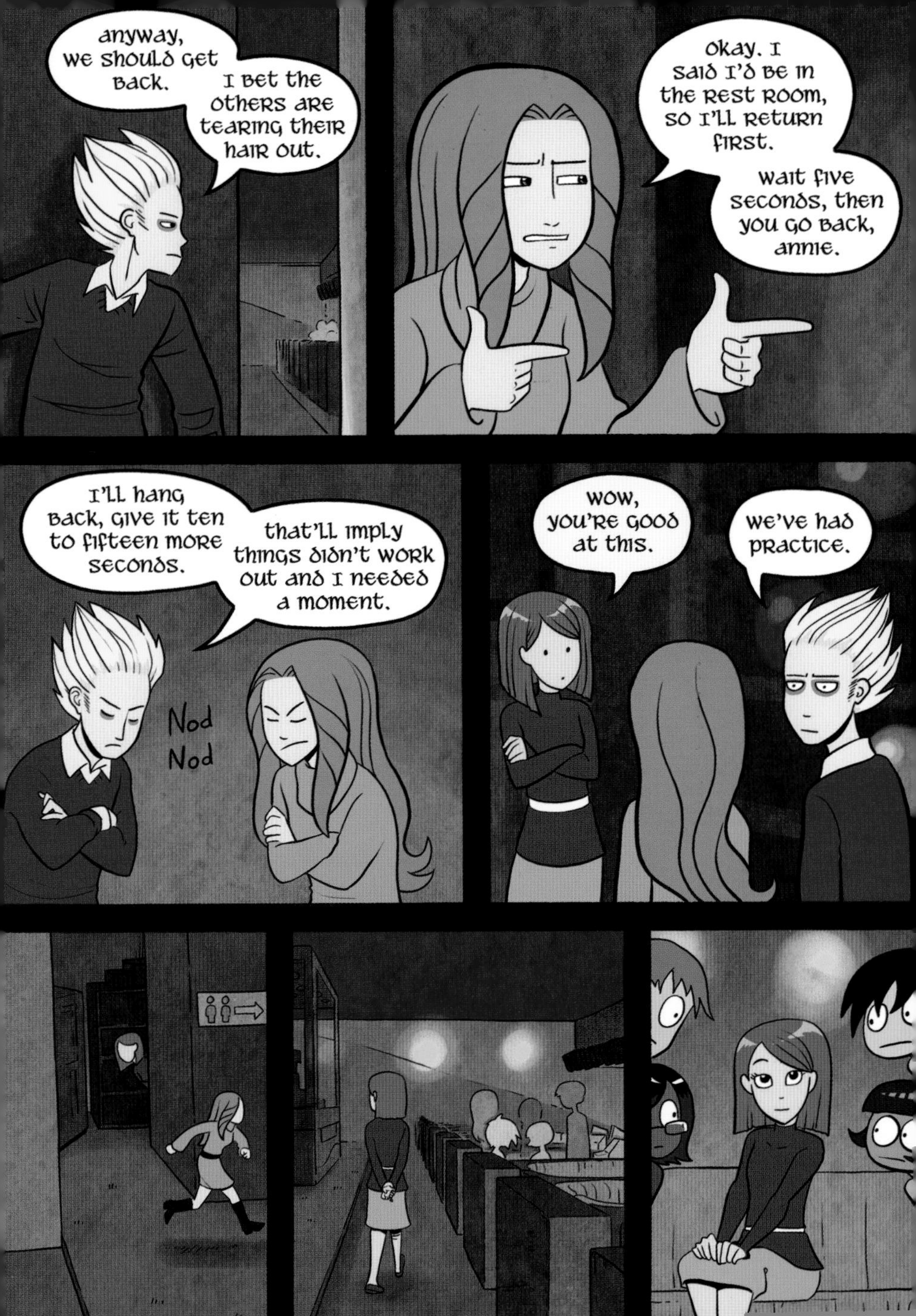
anyway, we should get back.
I bet the others are tearing their hair out.
Okay. I said I'd be in the rest room, so I'll return first.
Wait five seconds, then you go back, Annie.
I'll hang back, give it ten to fifteen more seconds.
That'll imply things didn't work out and I needed a moment.
Nod
Nod
Wow, you're good at this.
We've had practice.

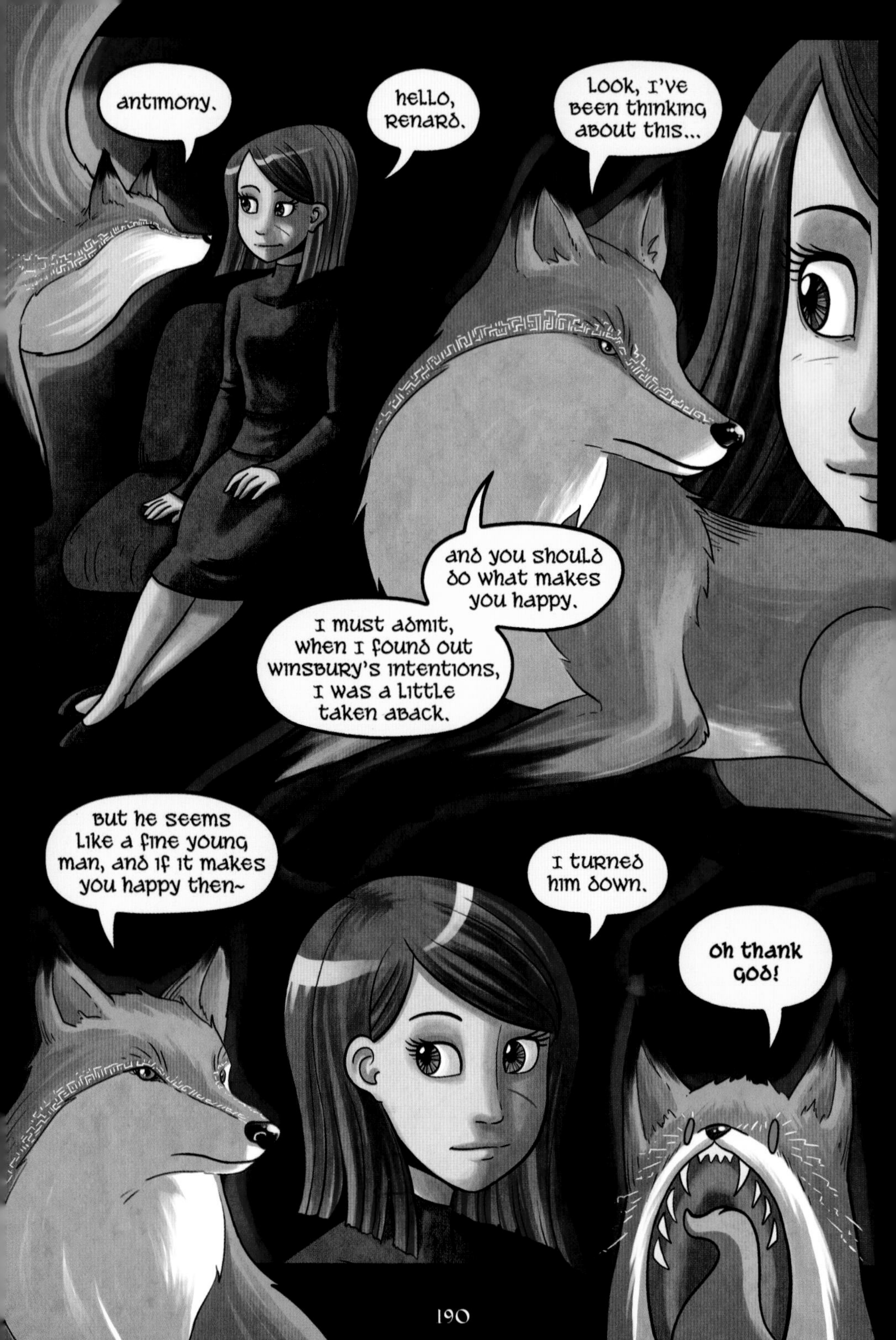
antimony.
hello, Renard.
Look, I've been thinking about this...
I must admit, when I found out Winsbury's intentions, I was a little taken aback.
and you should do what makes you happy.
But he seems like a fine young man, and if it makes you happy then~
I turned him down.
Oh thank God!

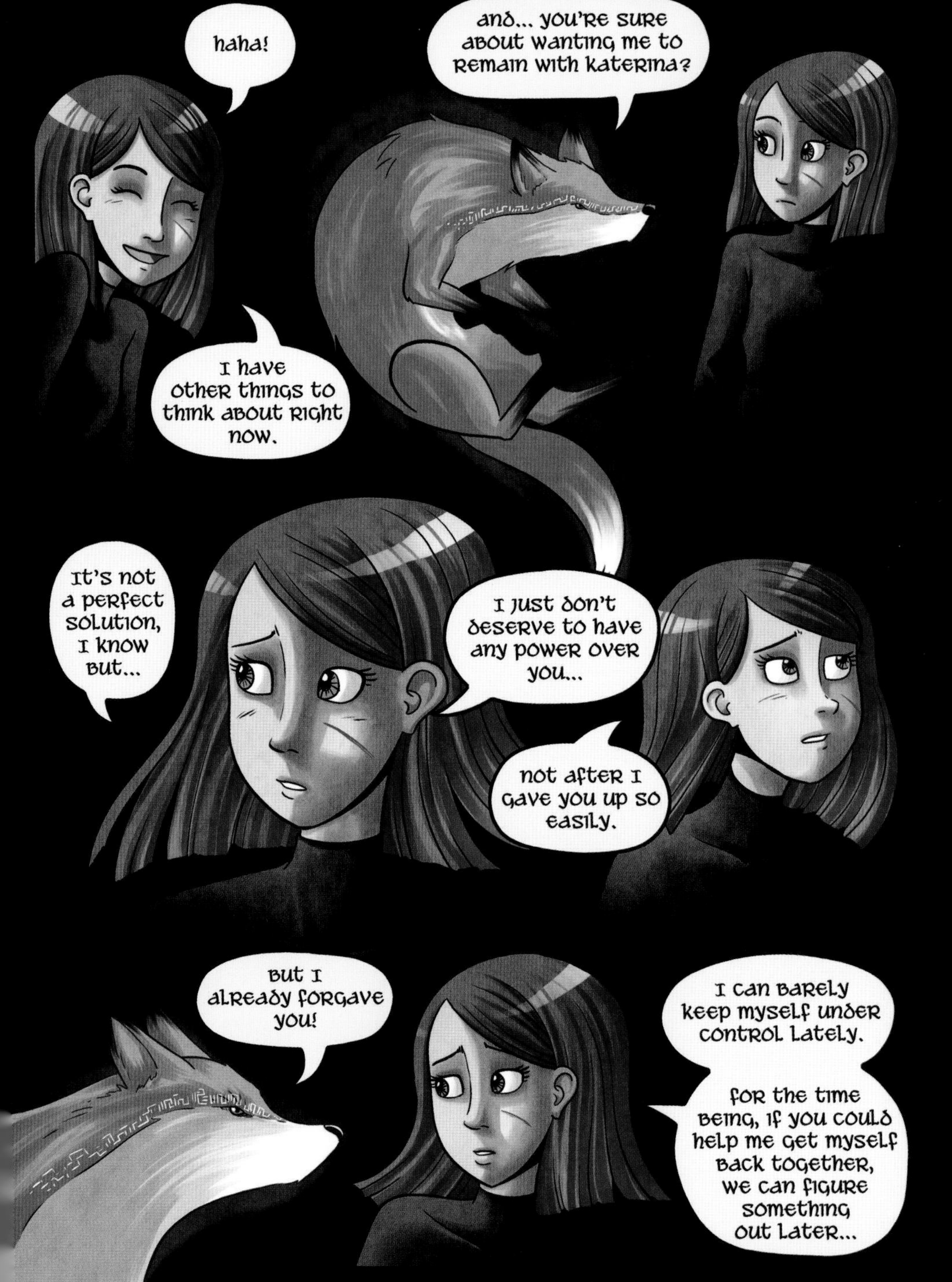
haha!
and... you're sure about wanting me to remain with katerina?
I have other things to think about right now.
It's not a perfect solution, I know but...
I just don't deserve to have any power over you...
not after I gave you up so easily.
But I already forgave you!
I can barely keep myself under control lately.
for the time being, if you could help me get myself back together, we can figure something out later...

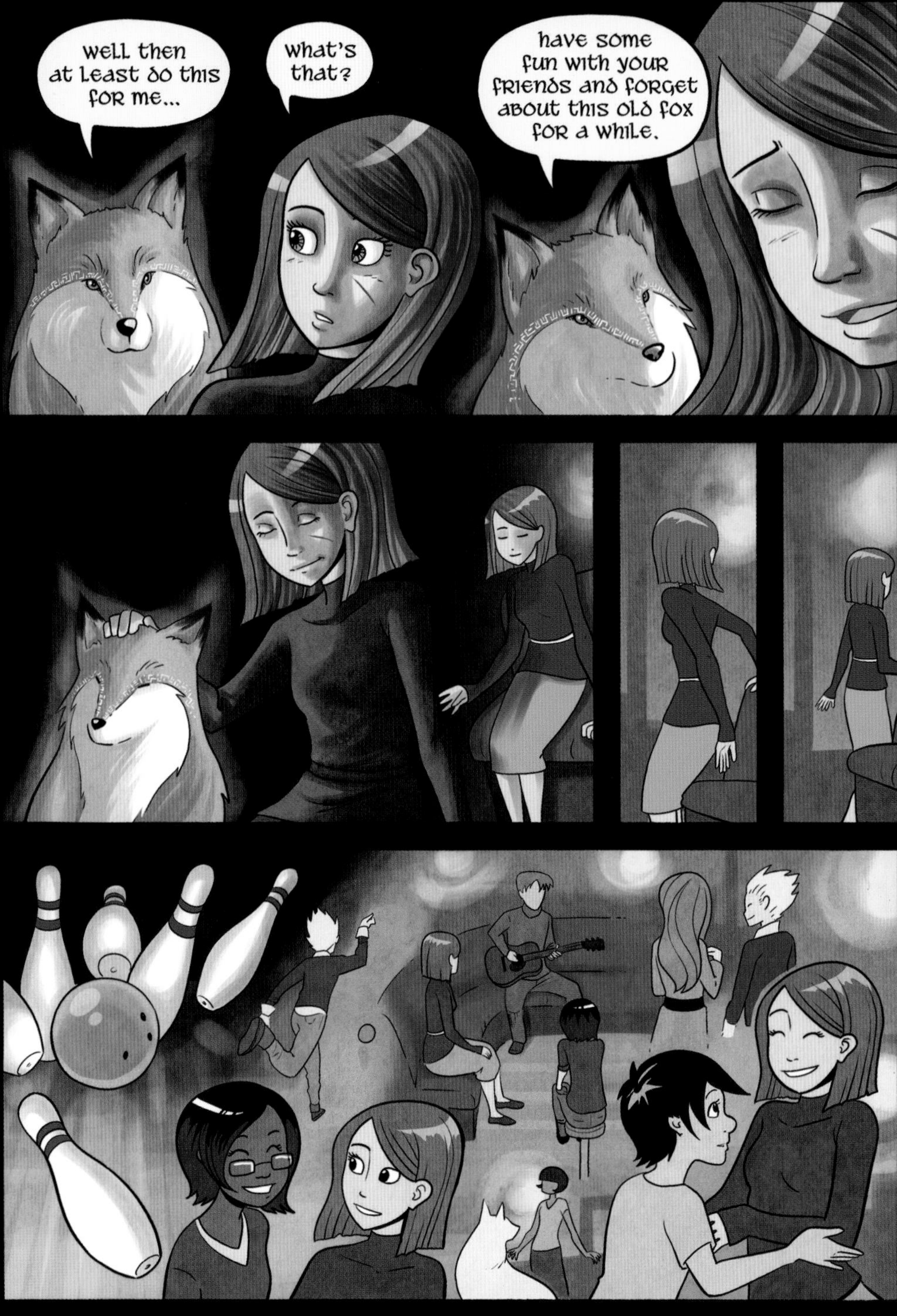
Well then at least do this for me...
What's that?
Have some fun with your friends and forget about this old fox for a while.

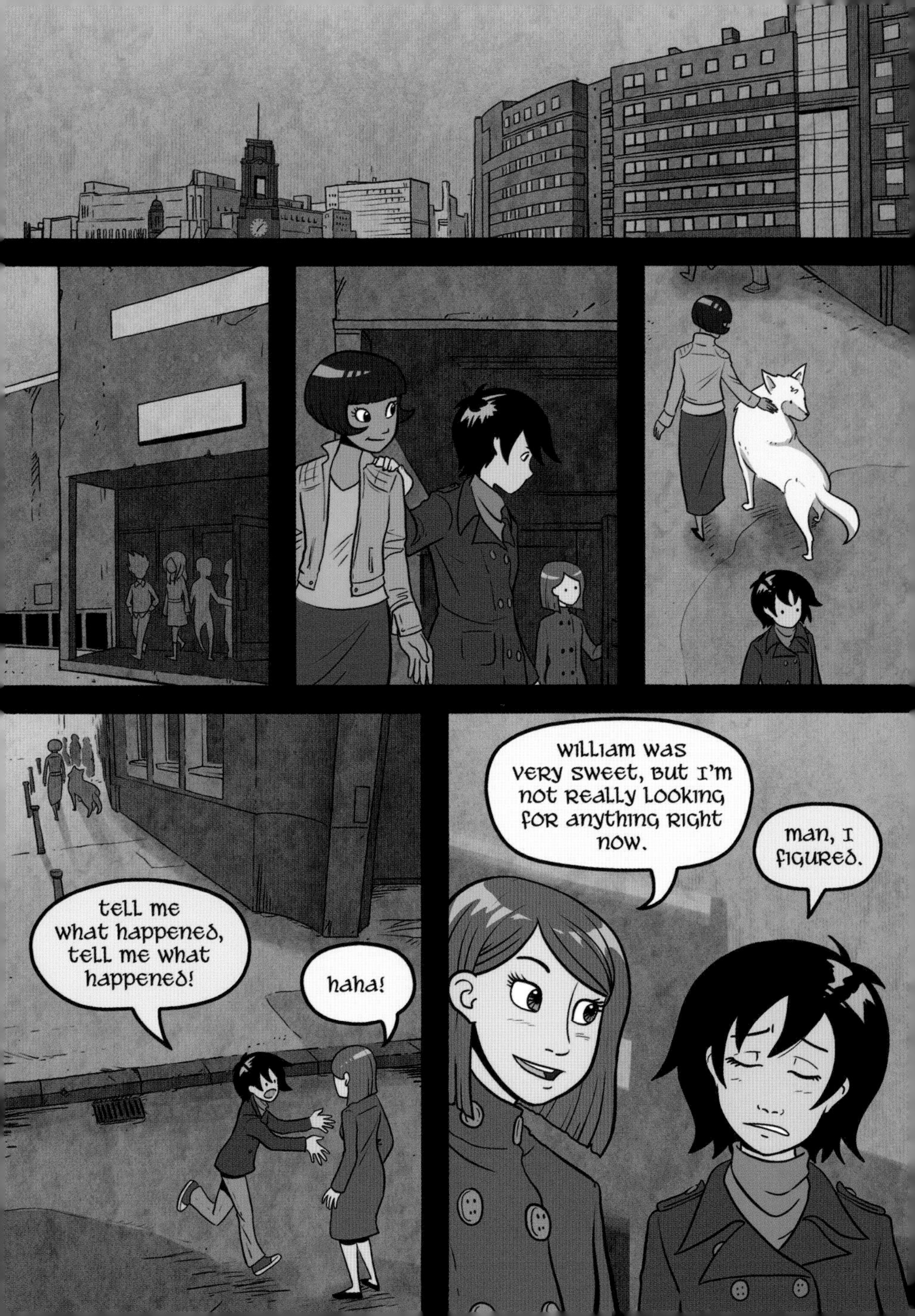
tell me what happened, tell me what happened!
haha!
William was very sweet, but I'm not really looking for anything right now.
man, I figured.

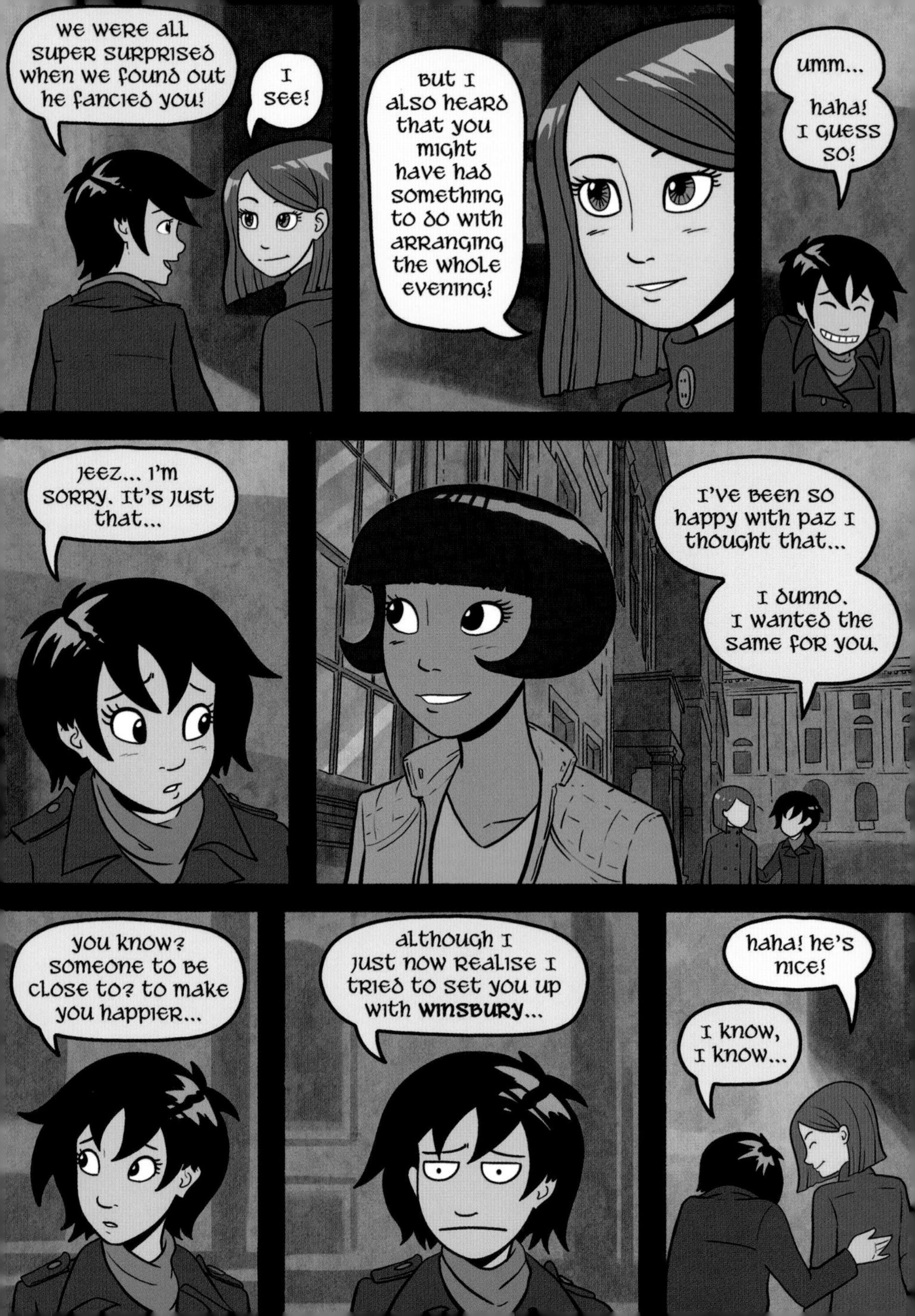

We were all super surprised when we found out he fancied you!
I see!
But I also heard that you might have had something to do with arranging the whole evening!
Umm...
Haha! I guess so!
Jeez... I'm sorry. It's just that...
I've been so happy with Paz I thought that...
I dunno. I wanted the same for you.
You know? Someone to be close to? To make you happier...
Although I just now realise I tried to set you up with **Winsbury**...
Haha! He's nice!
I know, I know...

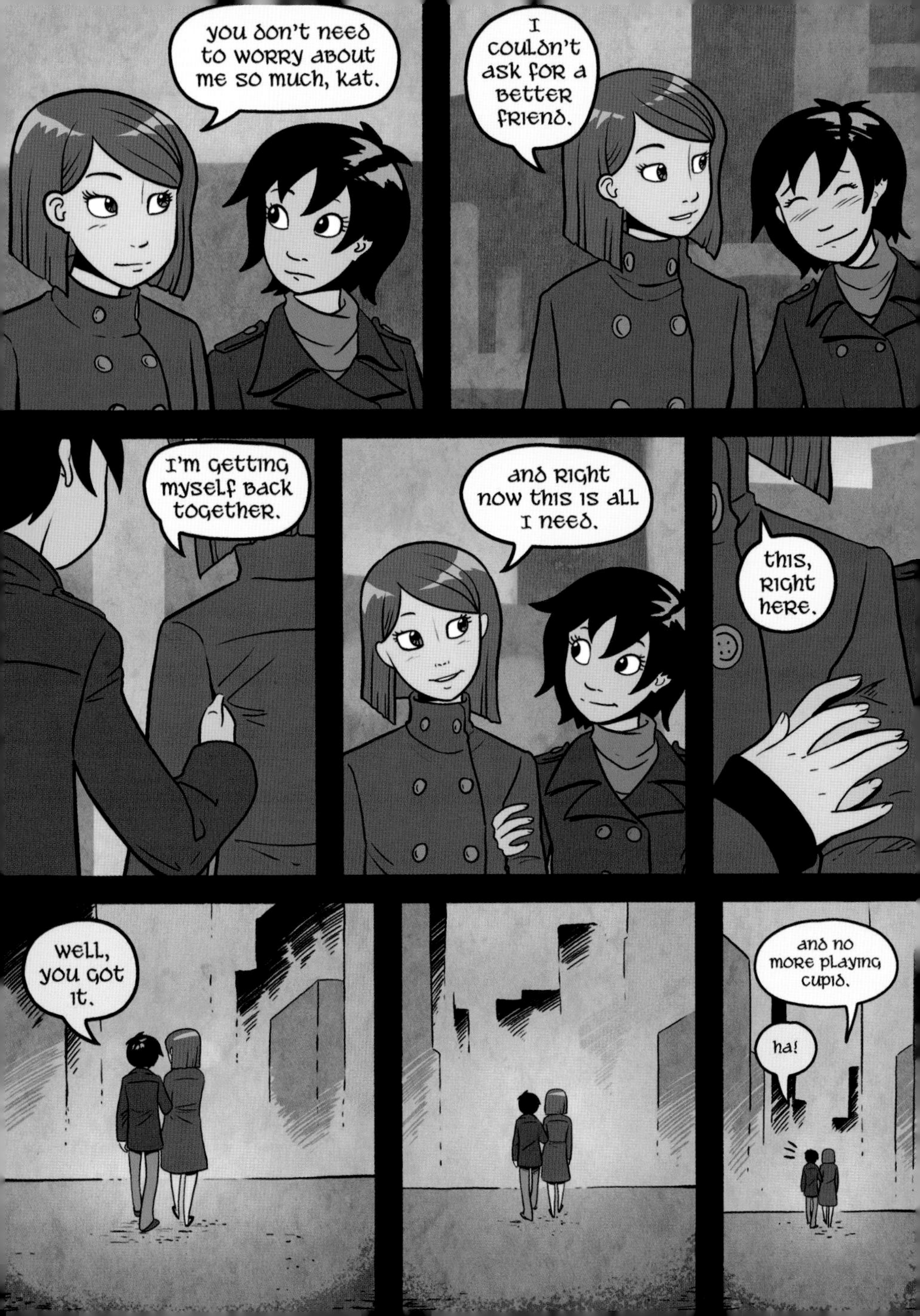
you don't need to worry about me so much, kat.
I couldn't ask for a better friend.
I'm getting myself back together.
and right now this is all I need.
this, right here.
well, you got it.
and no more playing cupid.
ha!

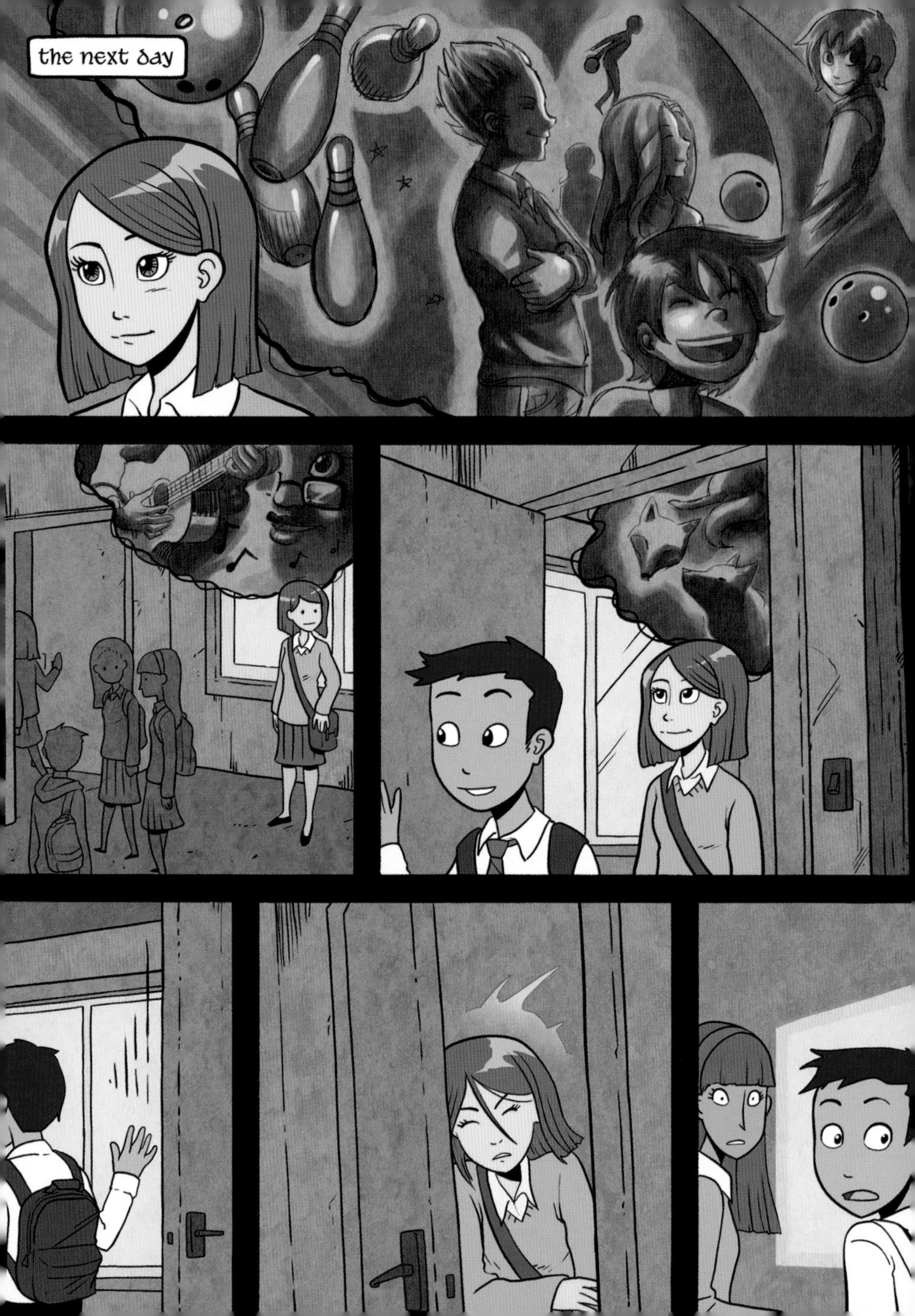
the next day

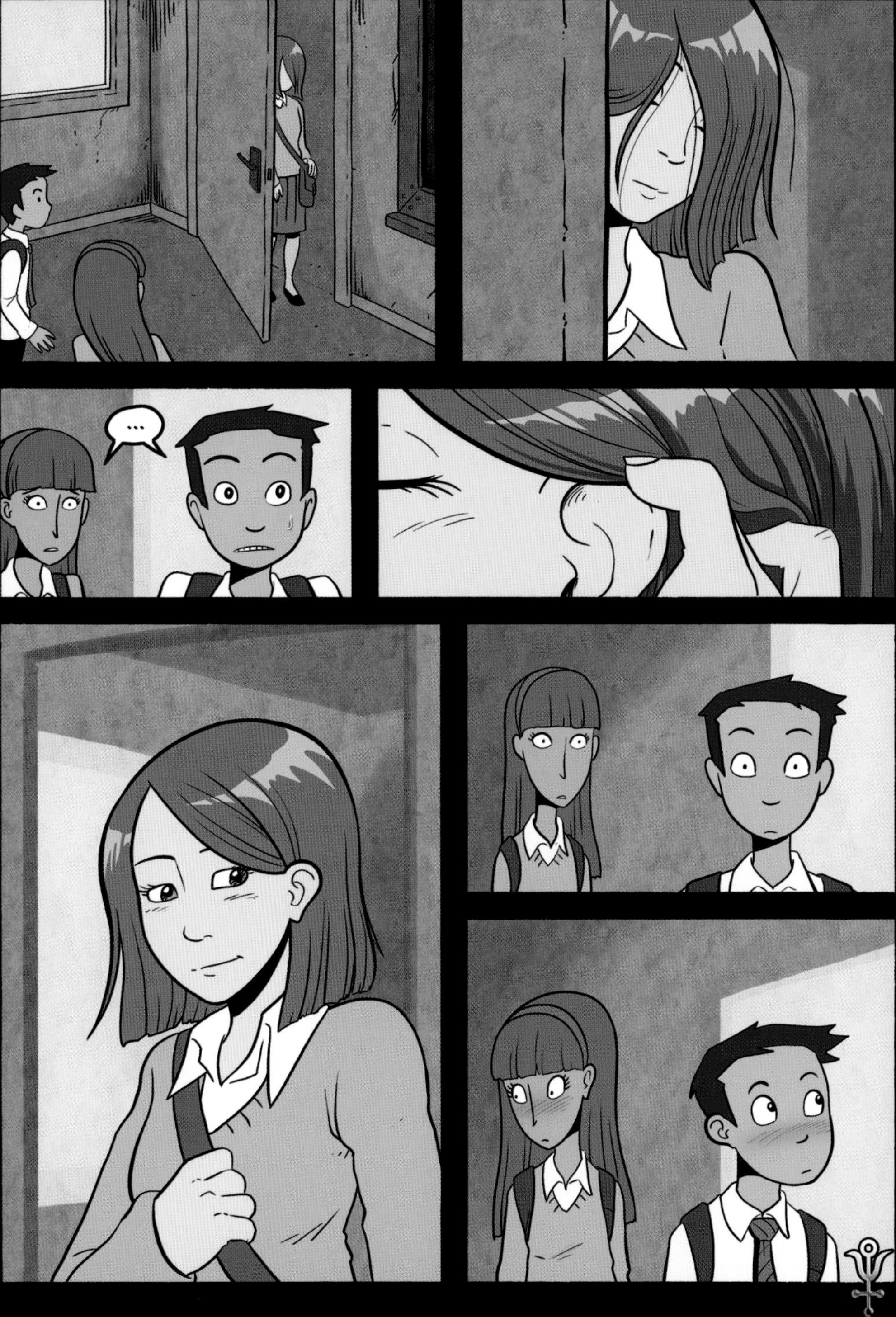
...

Gunnerkrigg Court

Cleared Up

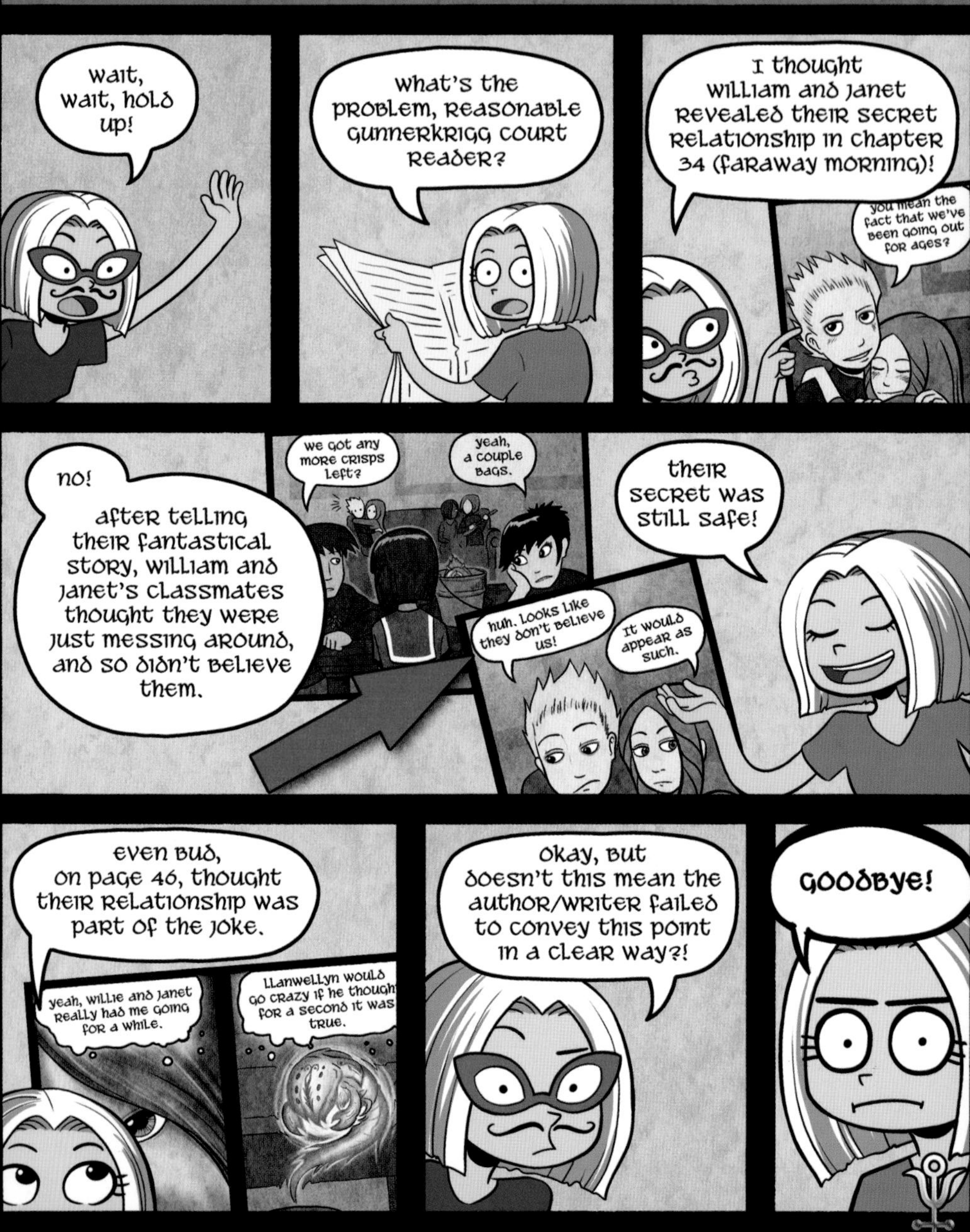

Wait, wait, hold up!
What's the problem, reasonable Gunnerkrigg Court reader?
I thought William and Janet revealed their secret relationship in chapter 34 (Faraway Morning)!
You mean the fact that we've been going out for ages?
No!
After telling their fantastical story, William and Janet's classmates thought they were just messing around, and so didn't believe them.
We got any more crisps left?
Yeah, a couple bags.
Huh. Looks like they don't believe us!
It would appear as such.
Their secret was still safe!
Even Bud, on page 46, thought their relationship was part of the joke.
Yeah, Willie and Janet really had me going for a while.
Llanwellyn would go crazy if he though for a second it was true.
Okay, but doesn't this mean the author/writer failed to convey this point in a clear way?!
GOODBYE!

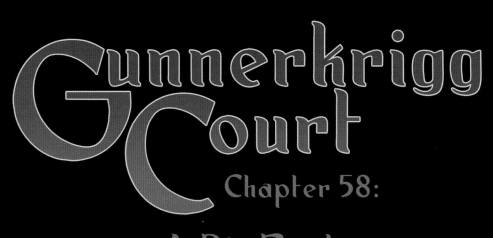

Gunnerkrigg Court

Chapter 58:

A Big Day!

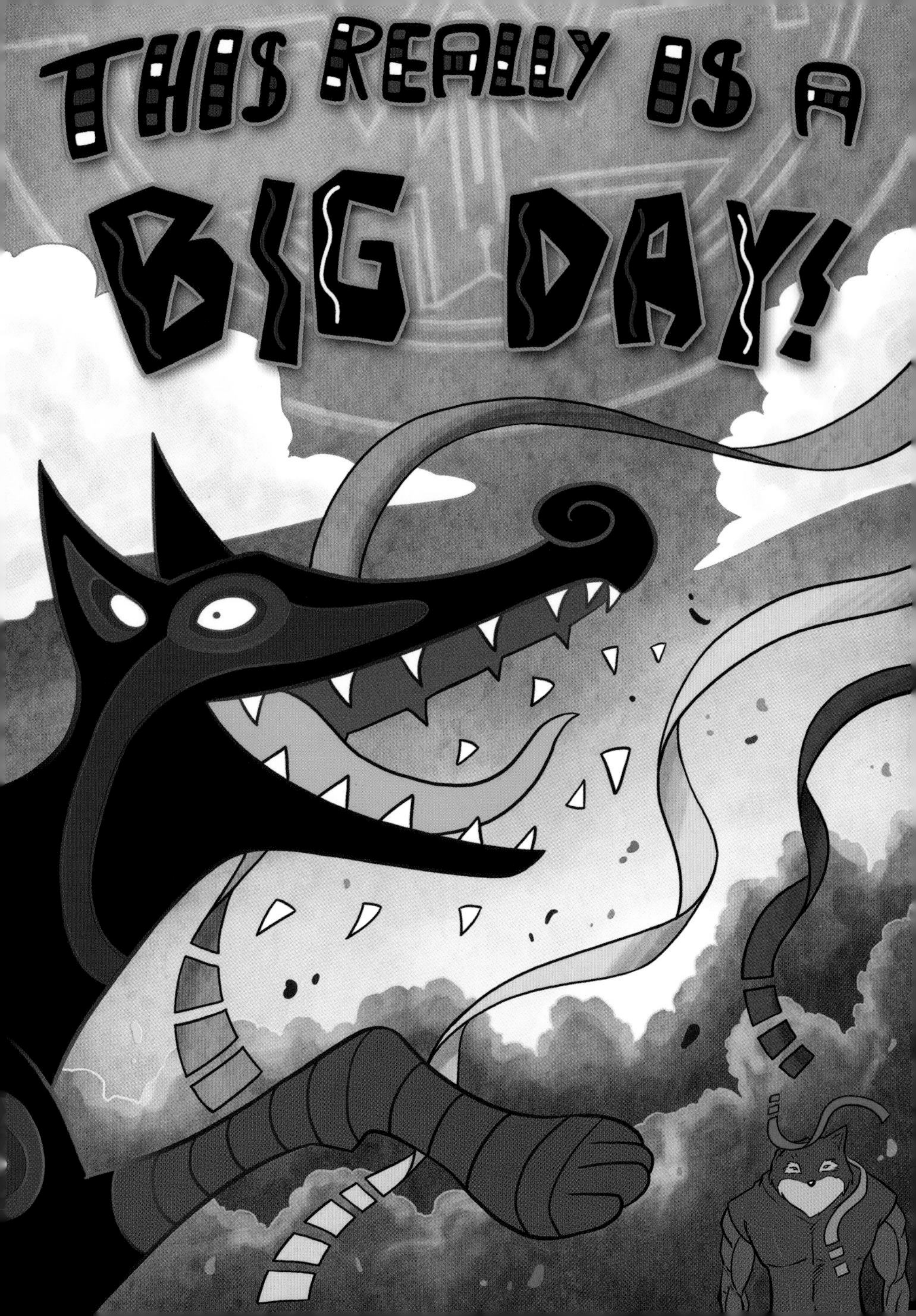
THIS REALLY IS A
BIG DAY!

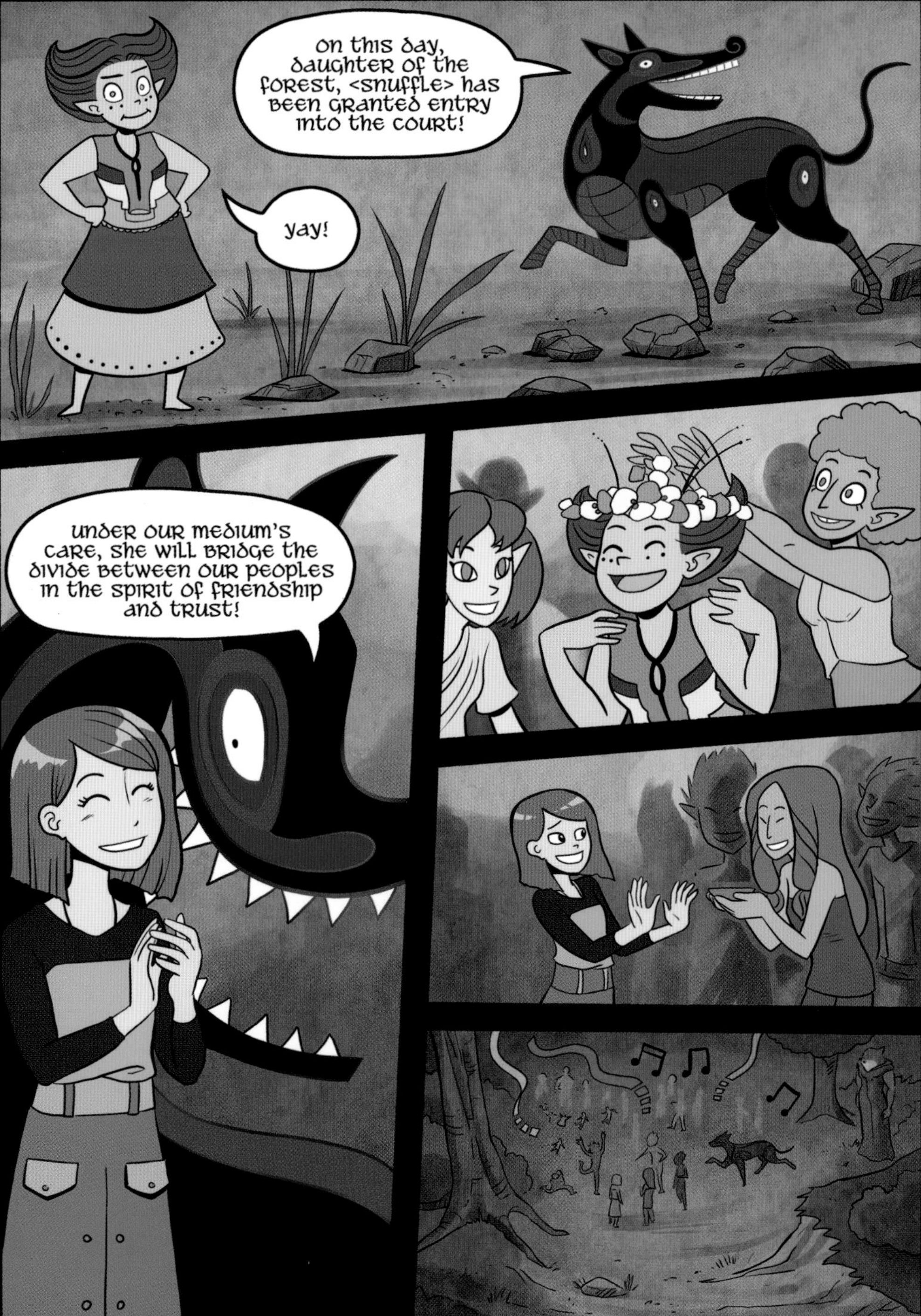
on this day, daughter of the forest, <snuffle> has been granted entry into the court!
yay!
under our medium's care, she will bridge the divide between our peoples in the spirit of friendship and trust!

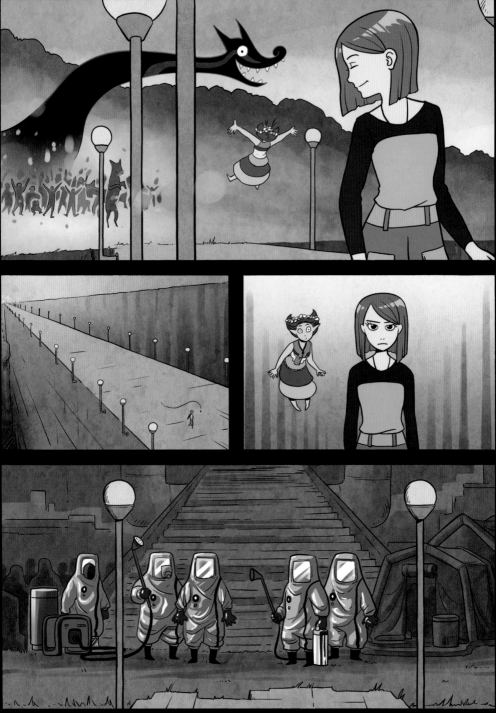

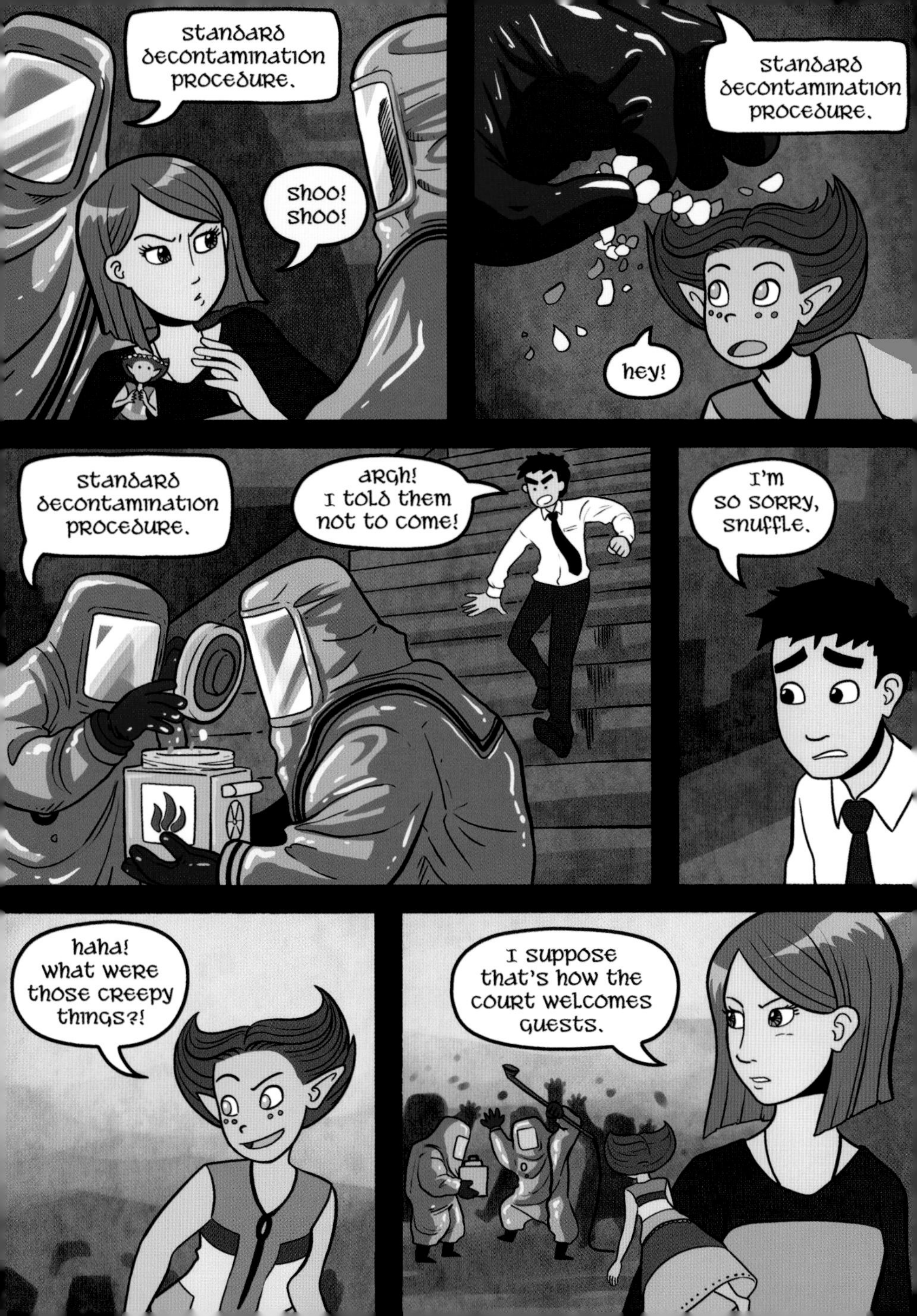
standard decontamination procedure.
shoo! shoo!
standard decontamination procedure.
hey!
standard decontamination procedure.
argh! I told them not to come!
I'm so sorry, snuffle.
haha! what were those creepy things?!
I suppose that's how the court welcomes guests.

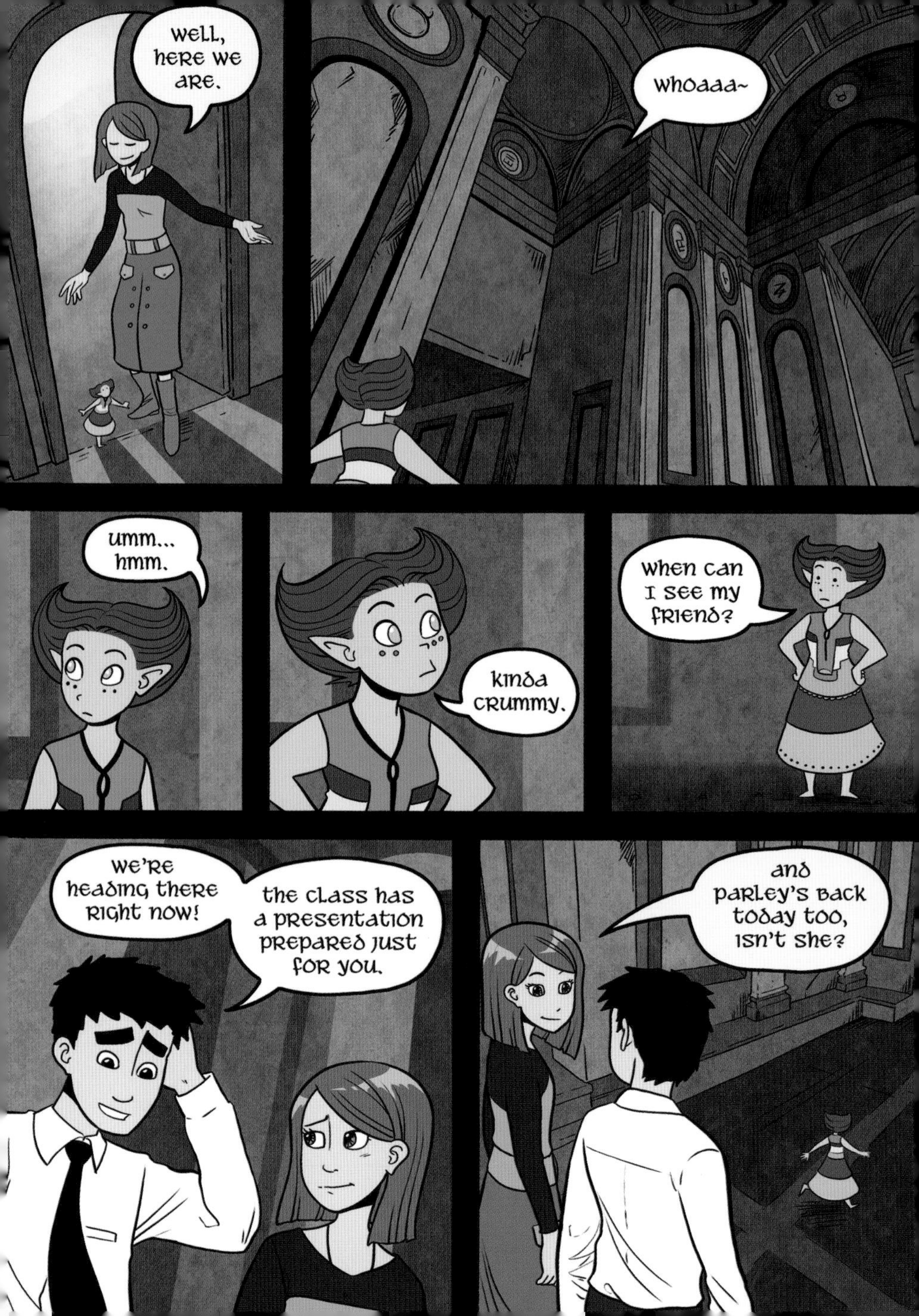
WELL, HERE WE ARE.
WHOAAA~
UMM... HMM.
KINDA CRUMMY.
WHEN CAN I SEE MY FRIEND?
WE'RE HEADING THERE RIGHT NOW!
THE CLASS HAS A PRESENTATION PREPARED JUST FOR YOU.
AND PARLEY'S BACK TODAY TOO, ISN'T SHE?

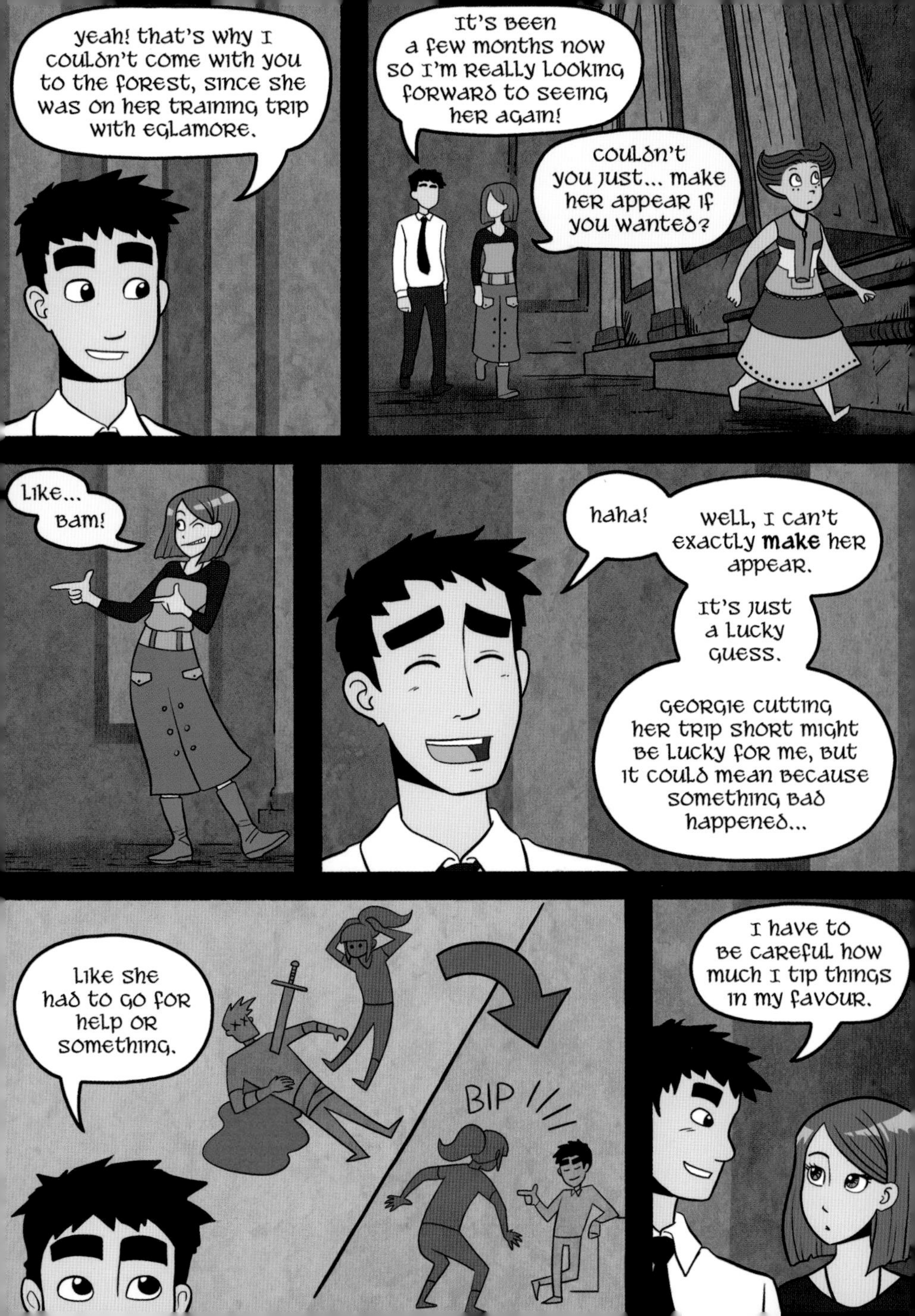
yeah! that's why I couldn't come with you to the forest, since she was on her training trip with Eglamore.
It's been a few months now so I'm really looking forward to seeing her again!
couldn't you just... make her appear if you wanted?
Like... Bam!
haha!
Well, I can't exactly **make** her appear.
It's just a lucky guess.
Georgie cutting her trip short might be lucky for me, but it could mean because something bad happened...
Like she had to go for help or something.
BIP
I have to be careful how much I tip things in my favour.

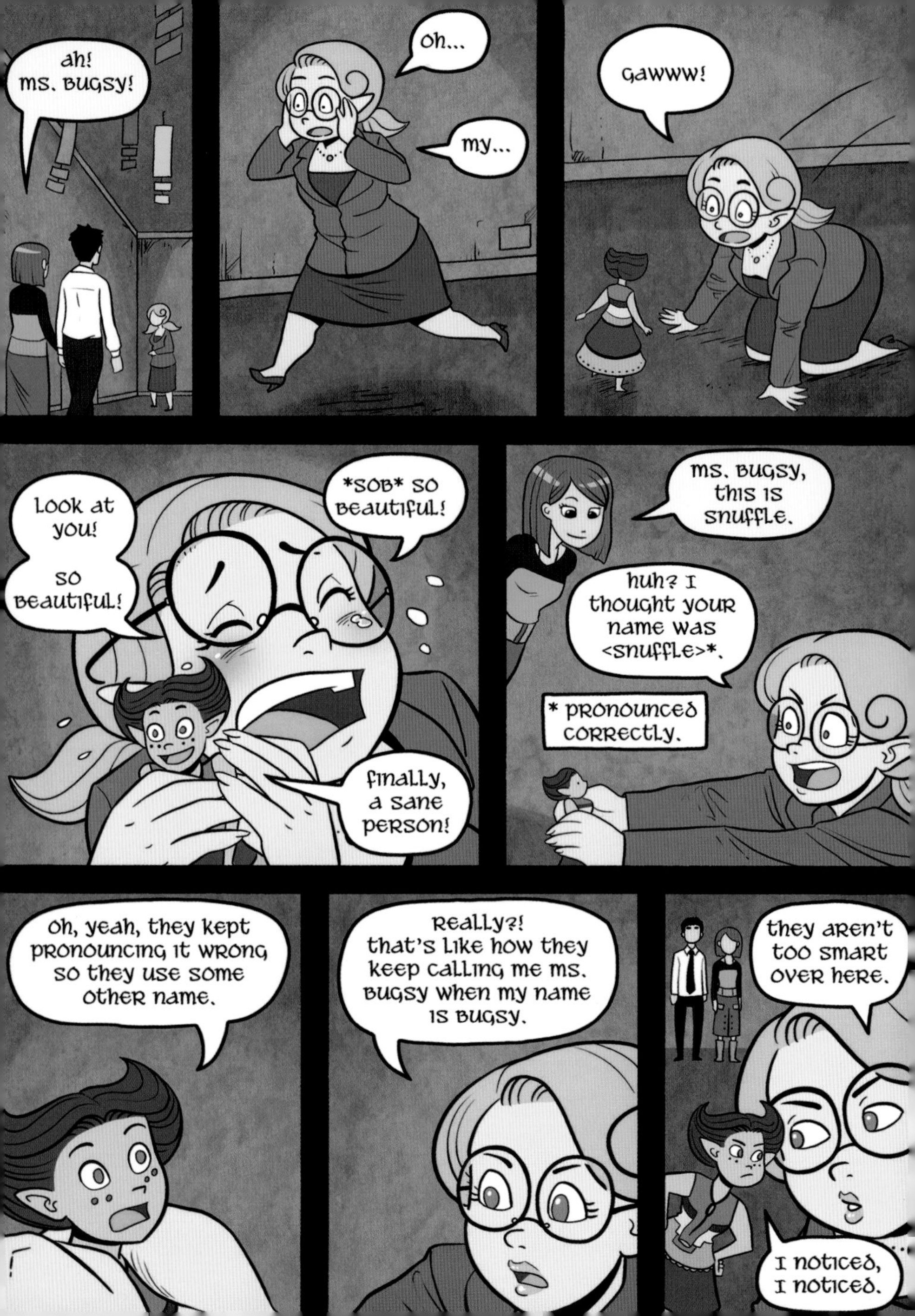

ah! ms. BUGSY!
Oh...
my...
GAWWW!
LOOK at you!
SO BEAUTIFUL!
SOB SO BEAUTIFUL!
finally, a sane person!
ms. BUGSY, this is snuffle.
huh? I thought your name was <snuffle>*.
* pronounced correctly.
Oh, yeah, they kept pronouncing it wrong so they use some other name.
Really?! that's like how they keep calling me ms. BUGSY when my name is BUGSY.
they aren't too smart over here.
I noticed, I noticed.

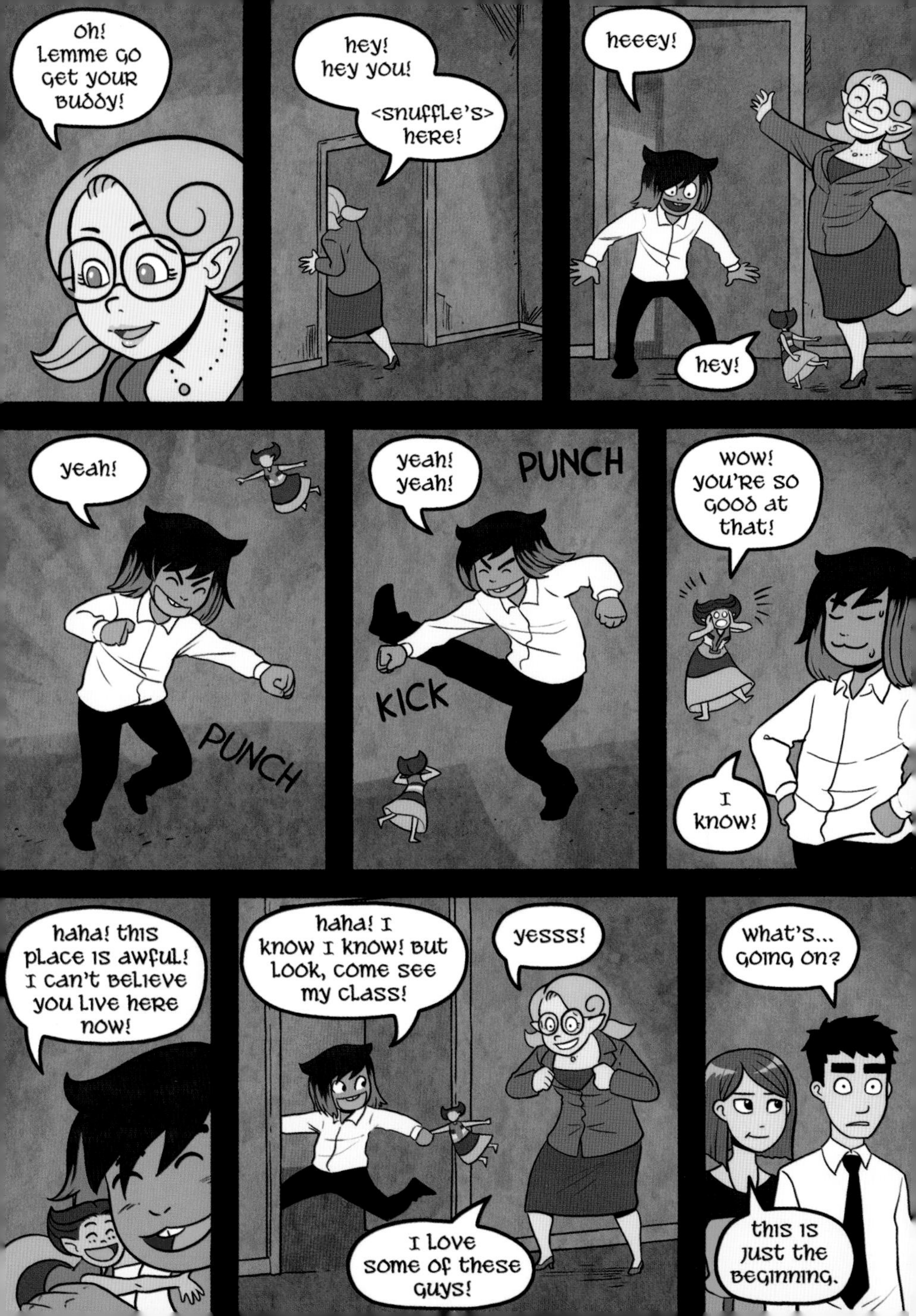
oh! Lemme go get your buddy!
hey! hey you!
<snuffle's> here!
heeey!
hey!
yeah!
yeah! yeah!
PUNCH
KICK
PUNCH
wow! you're so good at that!
I know!
haha! this place is awful! I can't believe you live here now!
haha! I know I know! but look, come see my class!
I love some of these guys!
yesss!
what's... going on?
this is just the beginning.

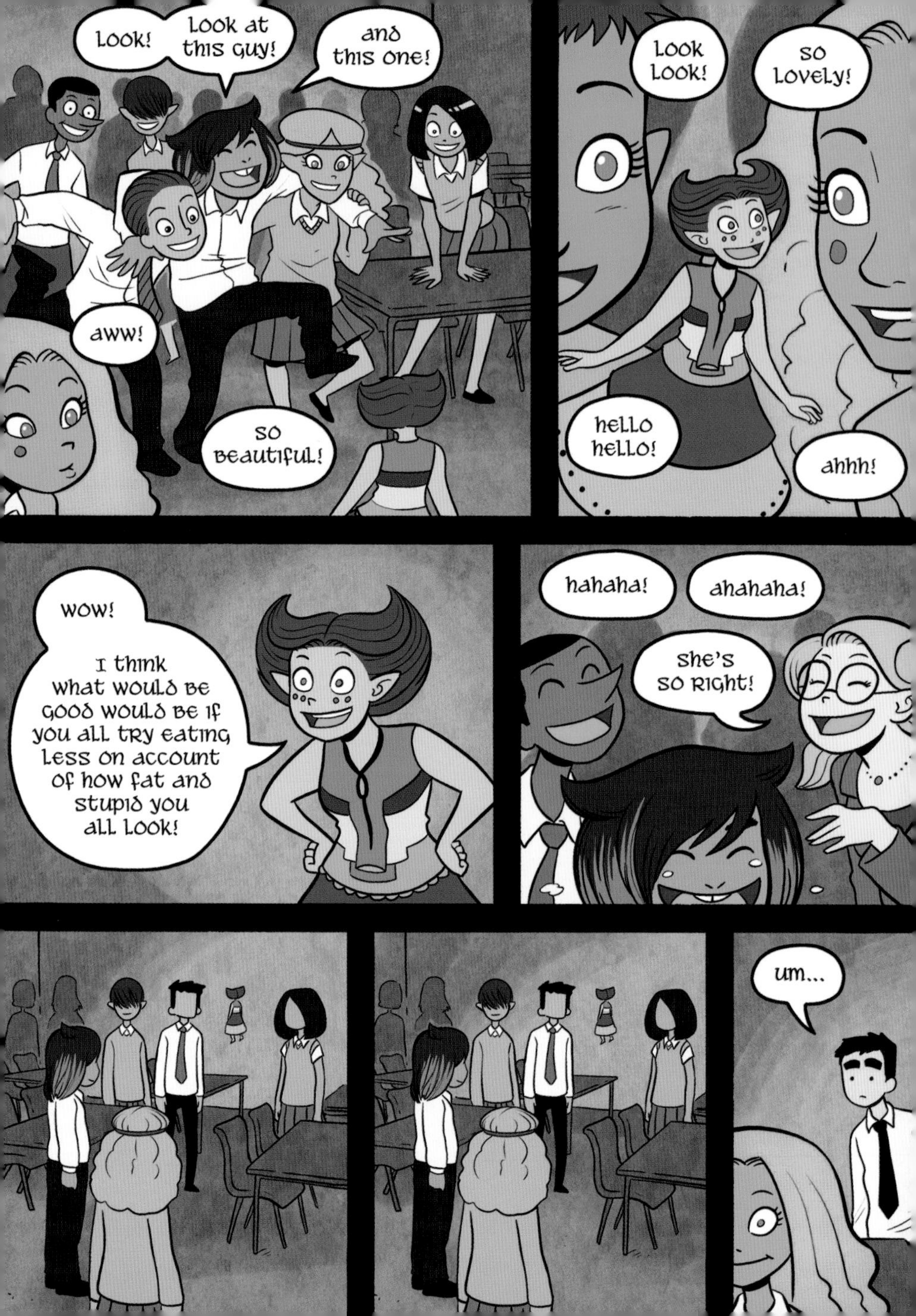
LOOK!
LOOK at this guy!
and this one!
aww!
SO BEAUTIFUL!
LOOK LOOK!
SO LOVELY!
hELLO hELLO!
ahhh!
WOW!
I think what would be good would be if you all try eating less on account of how fat and stupid you all look!
hahaha!
ahahaha!
she's so right!
um...

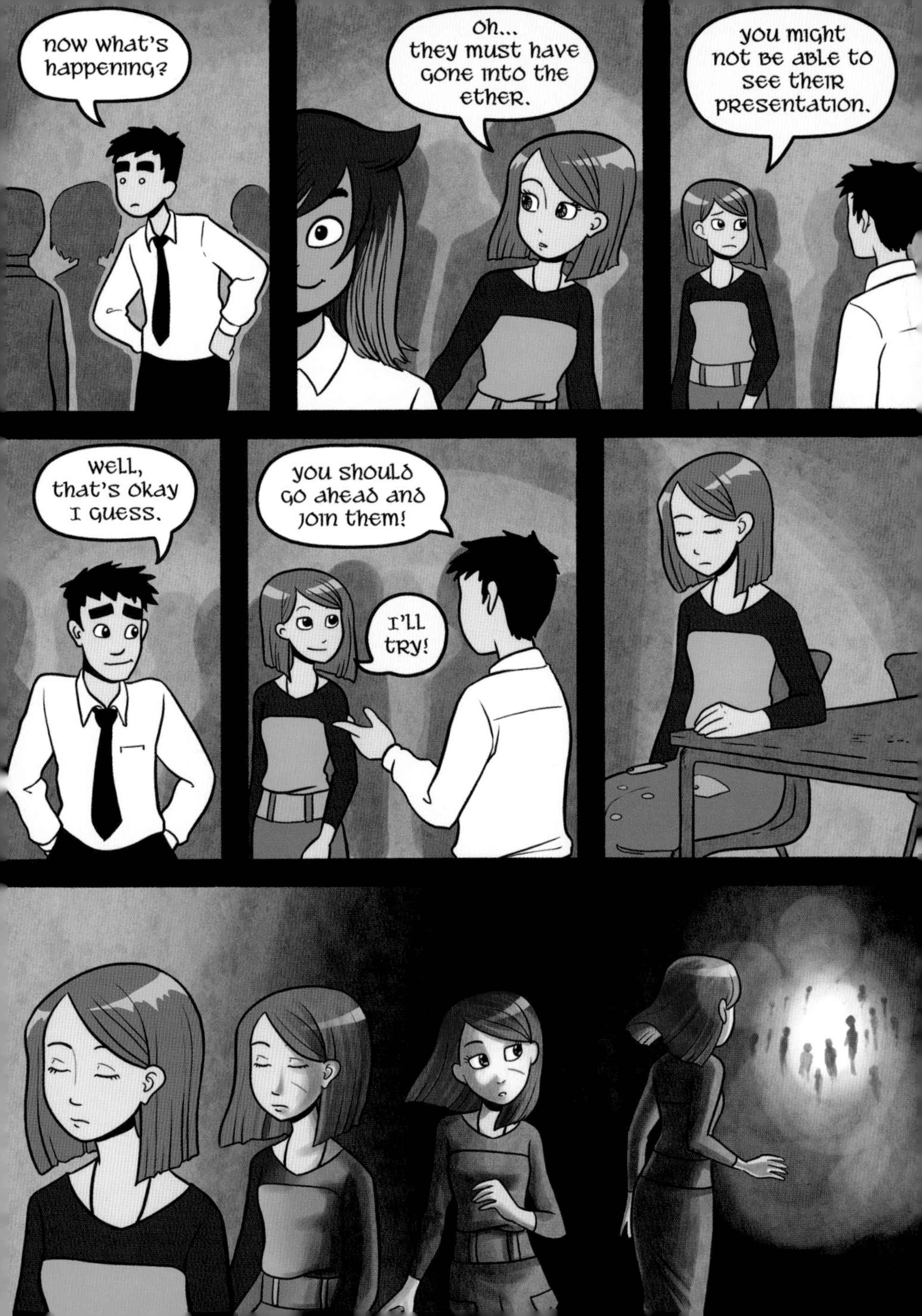
now what's happening?
oh... they must have gone into the ether.
you might not be able to see their presentation.
well, that's okay I guess.
you should go ahead and join them!
I'll try!

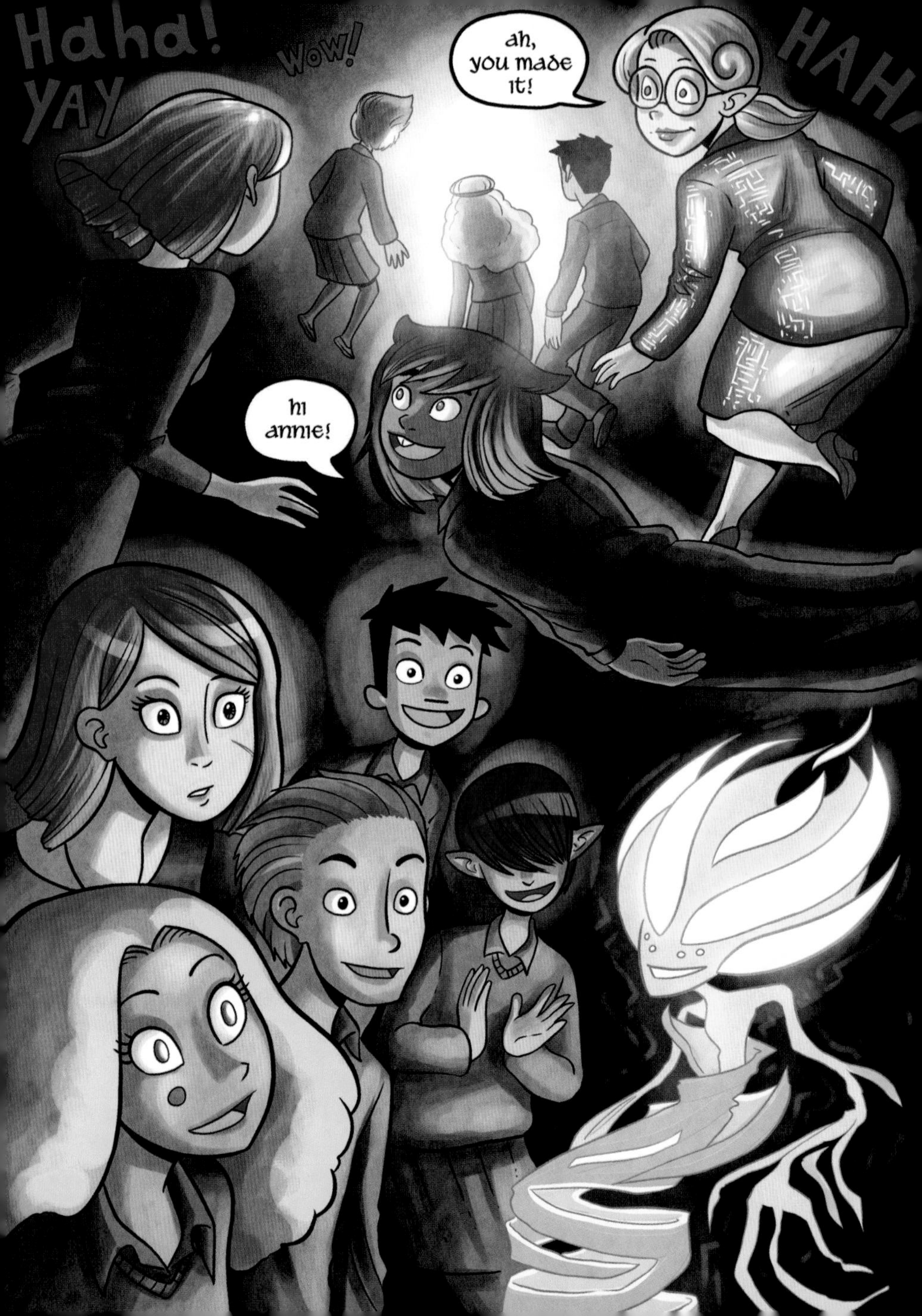
Haha!
YAY
WOW!
ah, you made it!
HAHA
hi annie!

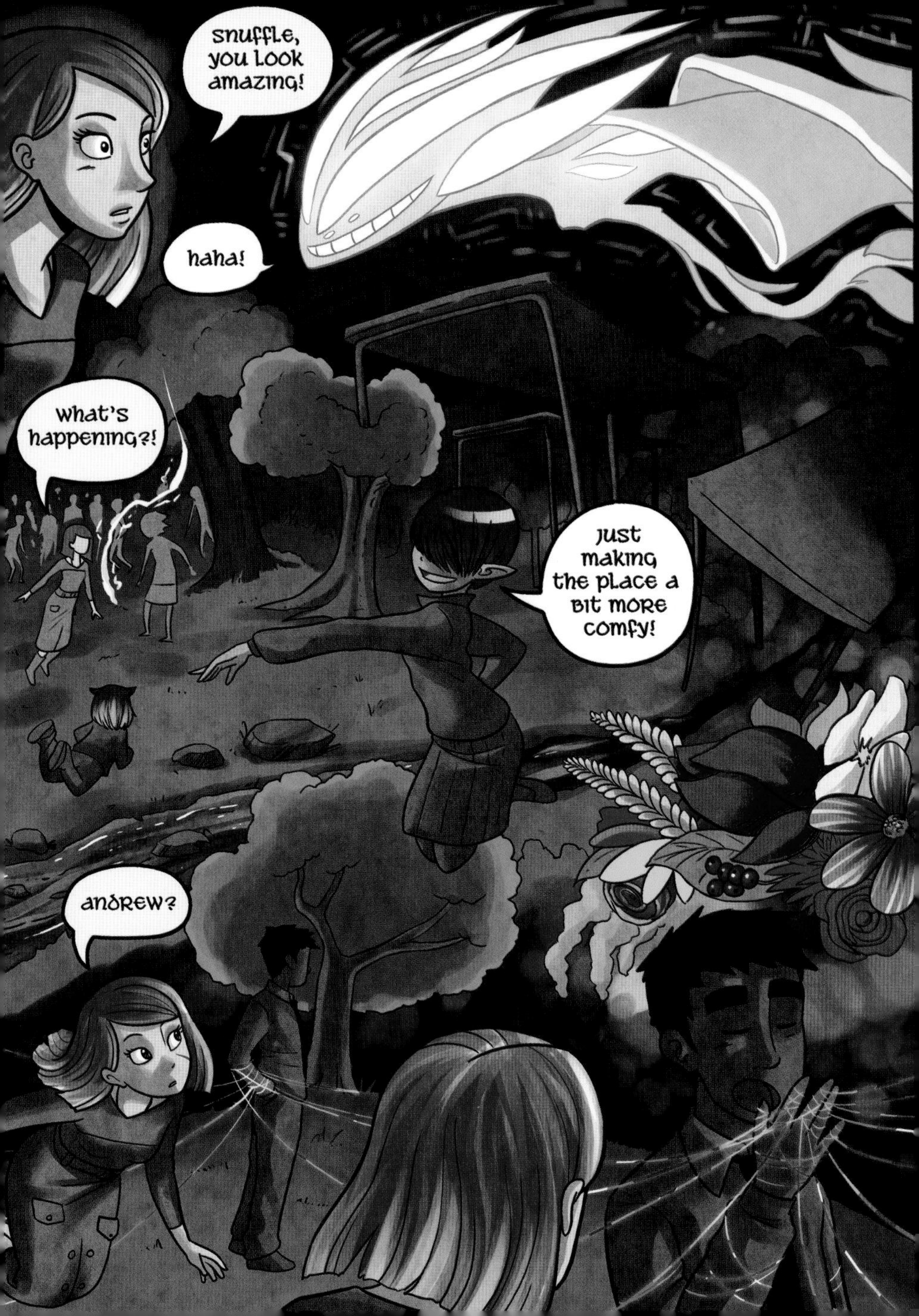
Snuffle, you look amazing!
haha!
What's happening?!
Just making the place a bit more comfy!
Andrew?

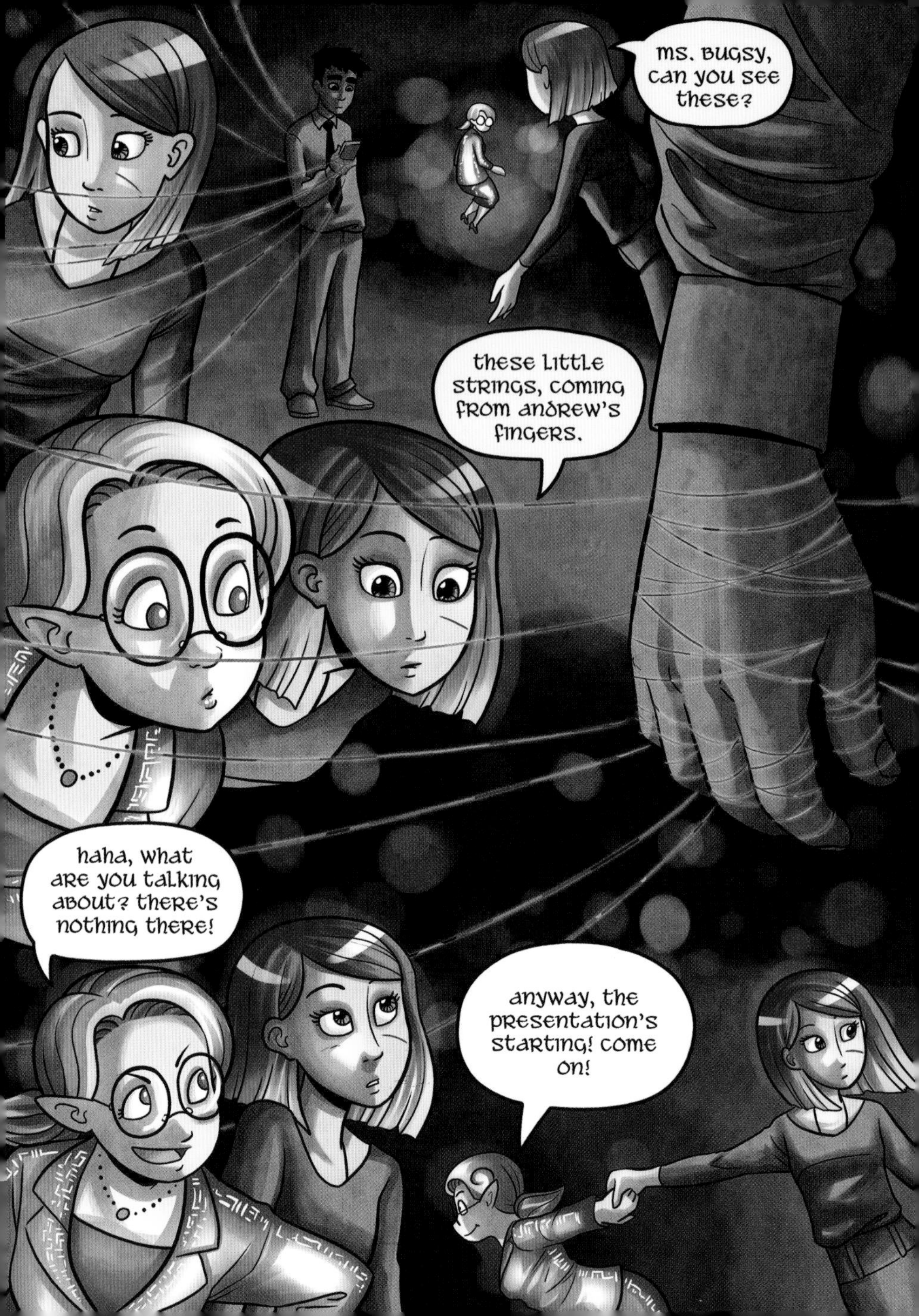
ms. bugsy, can you see these?
these little strings, coming from andrew's fingers.
haha, what are you talking about? there's nothing there!
anyway, the presentation's starting! come on!

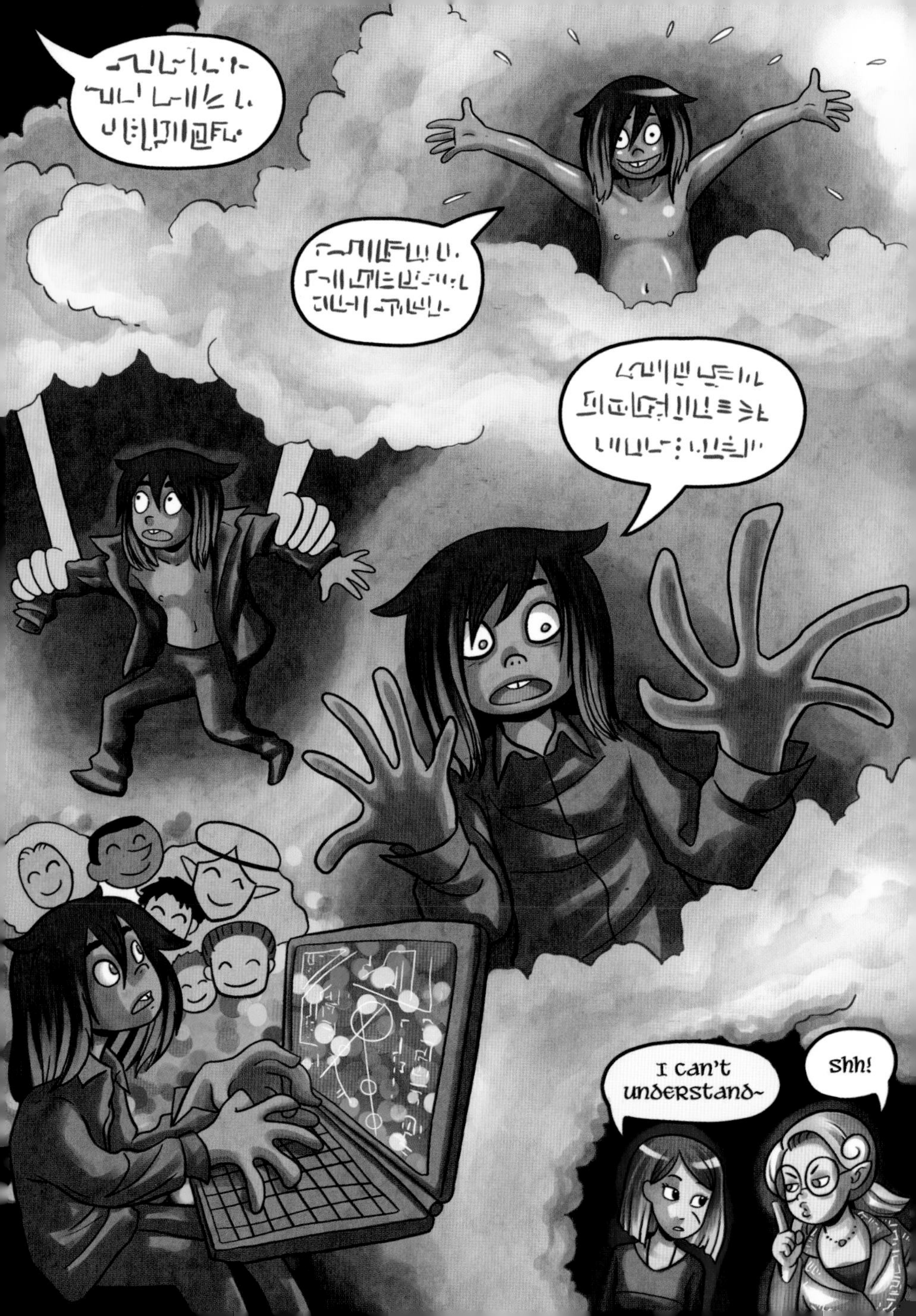
I can't understand~
Shh!

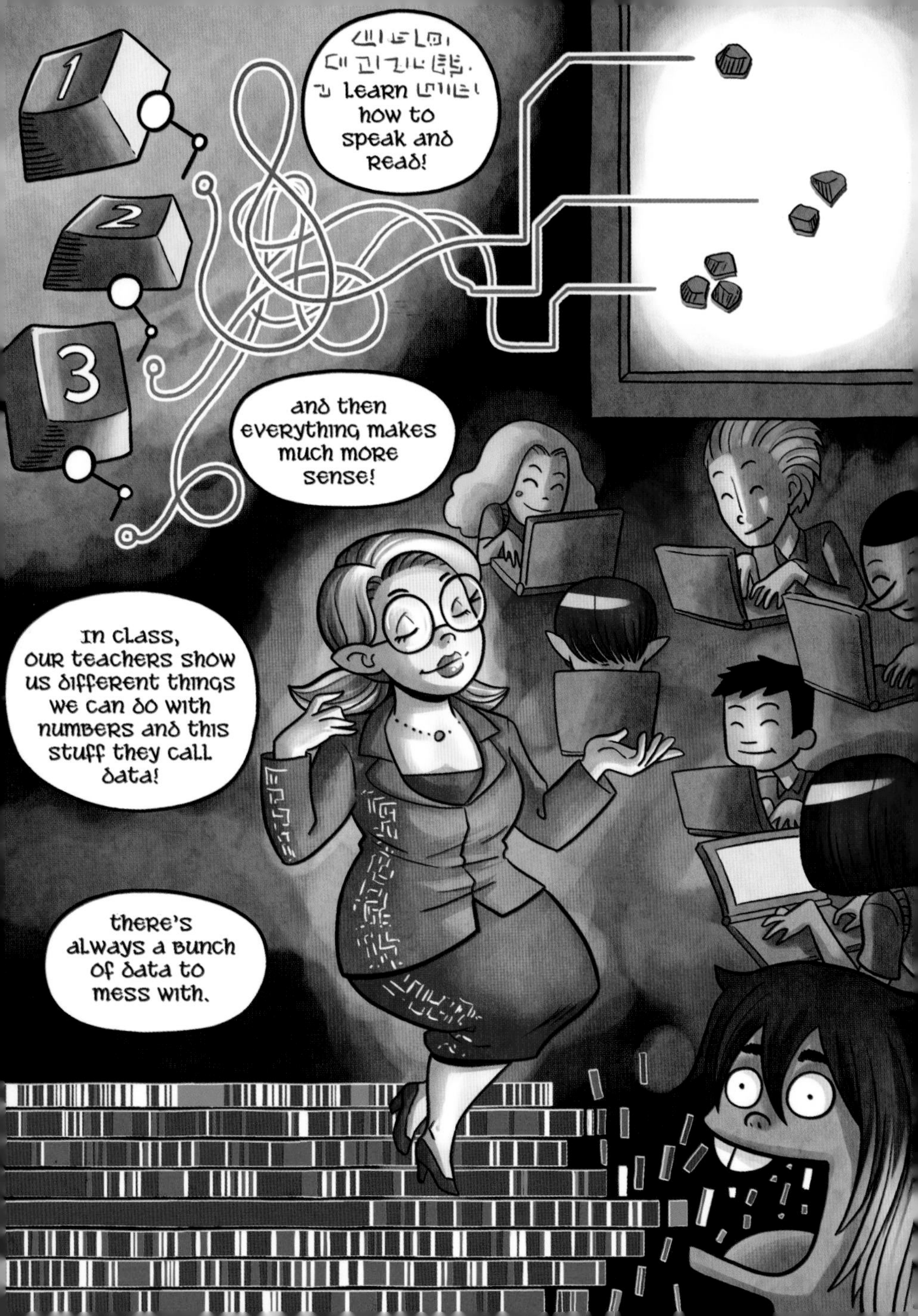
learn
how to
speak and
read!
and then everything makes much more sense!
In class, our teachers show us different things we can do with numbers and this stuff they call data!
there's always a bunch of data to mess with.

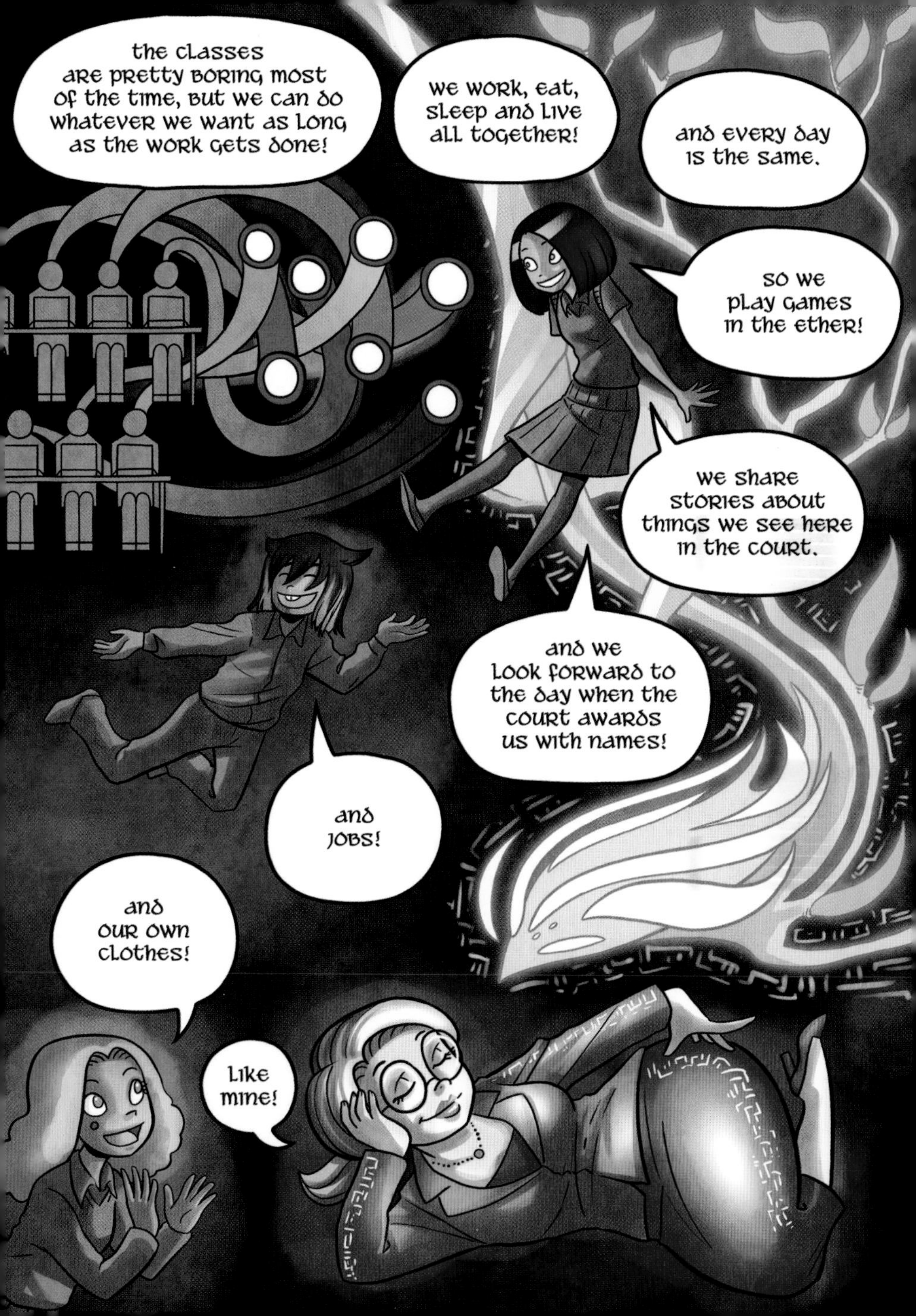
the classes are pretty boring most of the time, but we can do whatever we want as long as the work gets done!
we work, eat, sleep and live all together!
and every day is the same.
so we play games in the ether!
we share stories about things we see here in the court.
and we look forward to the day when the court awards us with names!
and jobs!
and our own clothes!
like mine!

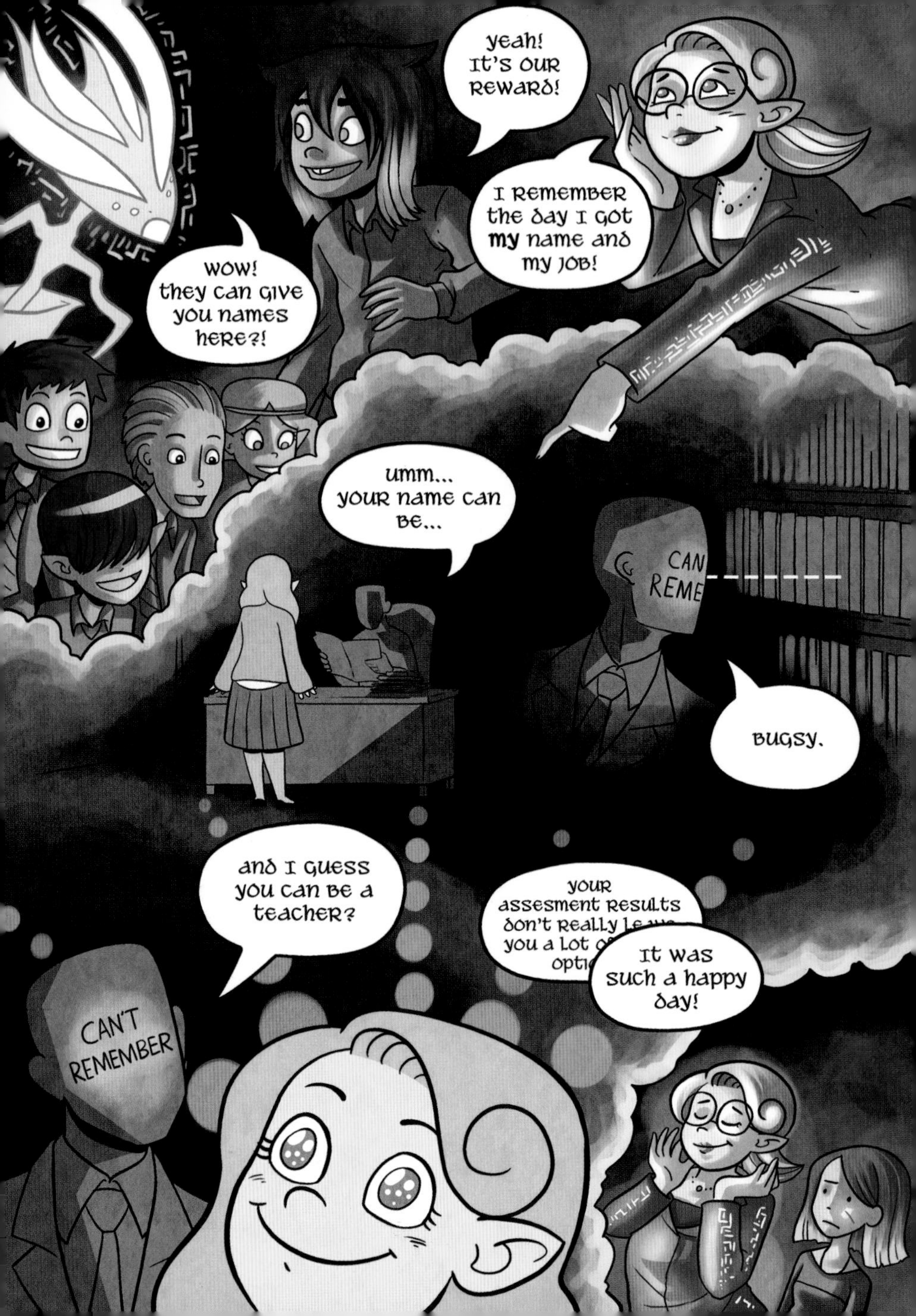
yeah! It's our reward!
I remember the day I got **my** name and my job!
wow! they can give you names here?!
umm... your name can be...
CAN
Bugsy.
and I guess you can be a teacher?
your assesment results don't really
you a lot
It was such a happy day!
CAN'T REMEMBER

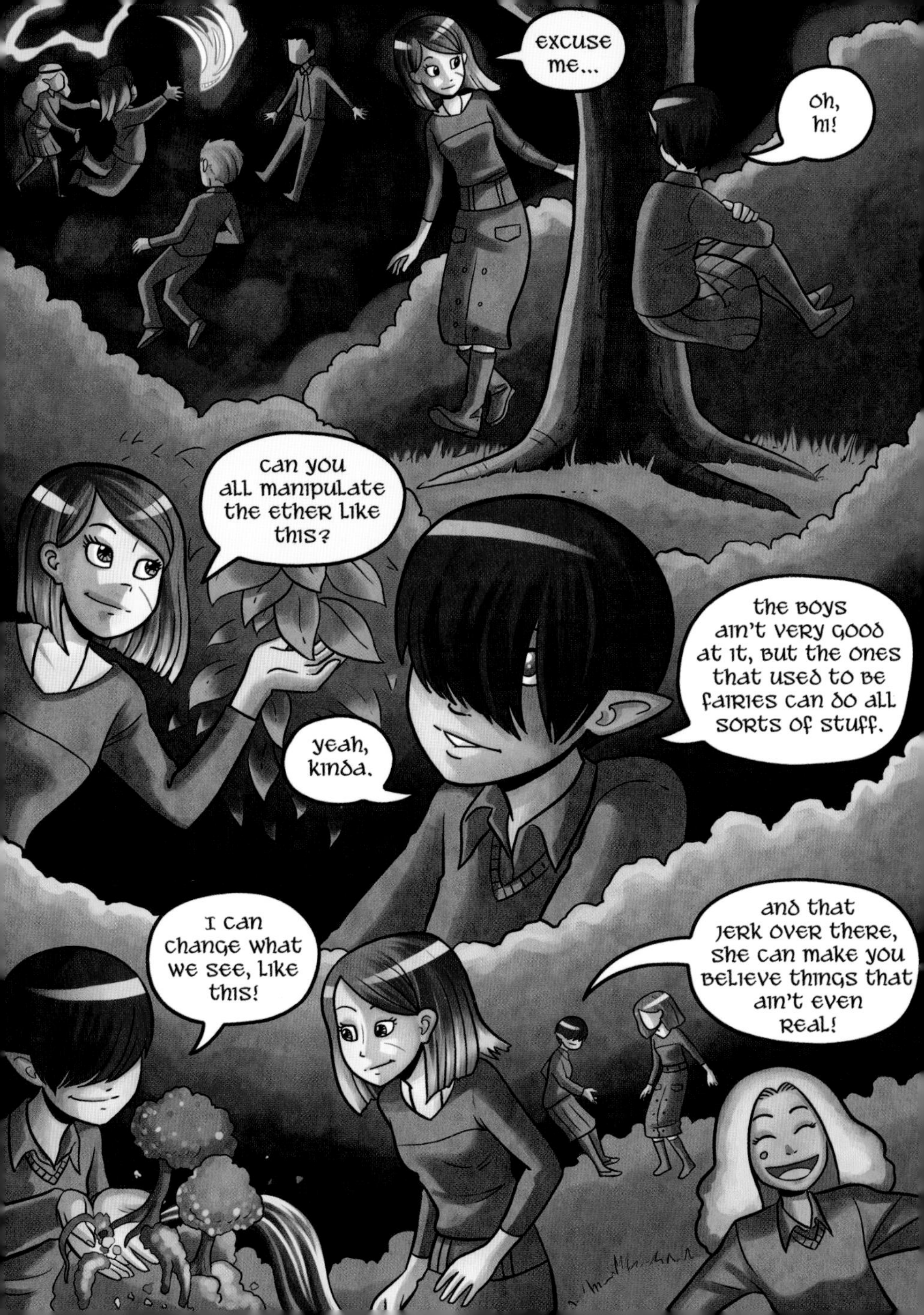
EXCUSE ME...
OH, HI!
CAN YOU ALL MANIPULATE THE ETHER LIKE THIS?
YEAH, KINDA.
THE BOYS AIN'T VERY GOOD AT IT, BUT THE ONES THAT USED TO BE FAIRIES CAN DO ALL SORTS OF STUFF.
I CAN CHANGE WHAT WE SEE, LIKE THIS!
AND THAT JERK OVER THERE, SHE CAN MAKE YOU BELIEVE THINGS THAT AIN'T EVEN REAL!

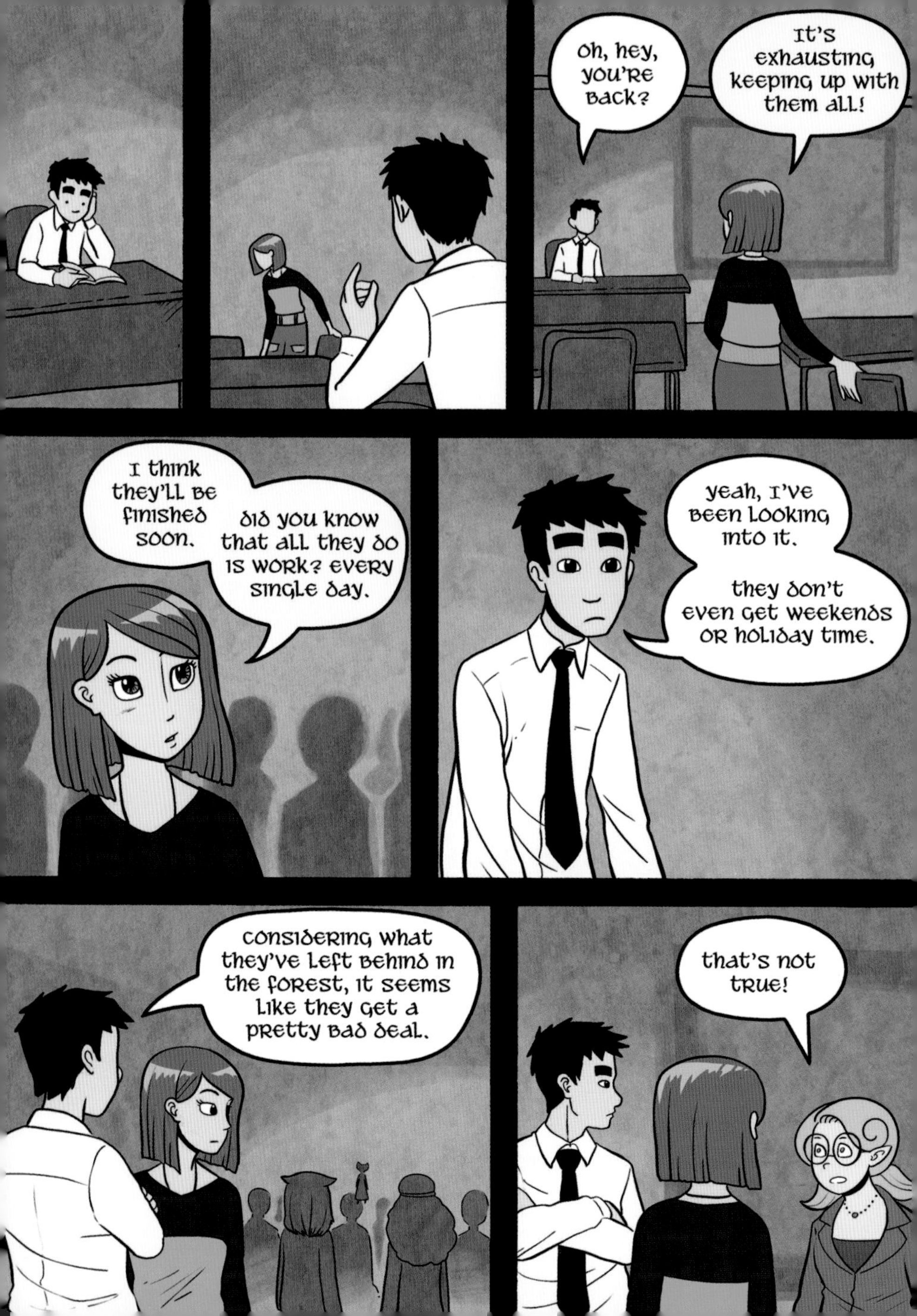
Oh, hey, you're back?
It's exhausting keeping up with them all!
I think they'll be finished soon.
Did you know that all they do is work? Every single day.
Yeah, I've been looking into it.
They don't even get weekends or holiday time.
Considering what they've left behind in the forest, it seems like they get a pretty bad deal.
That's not true!

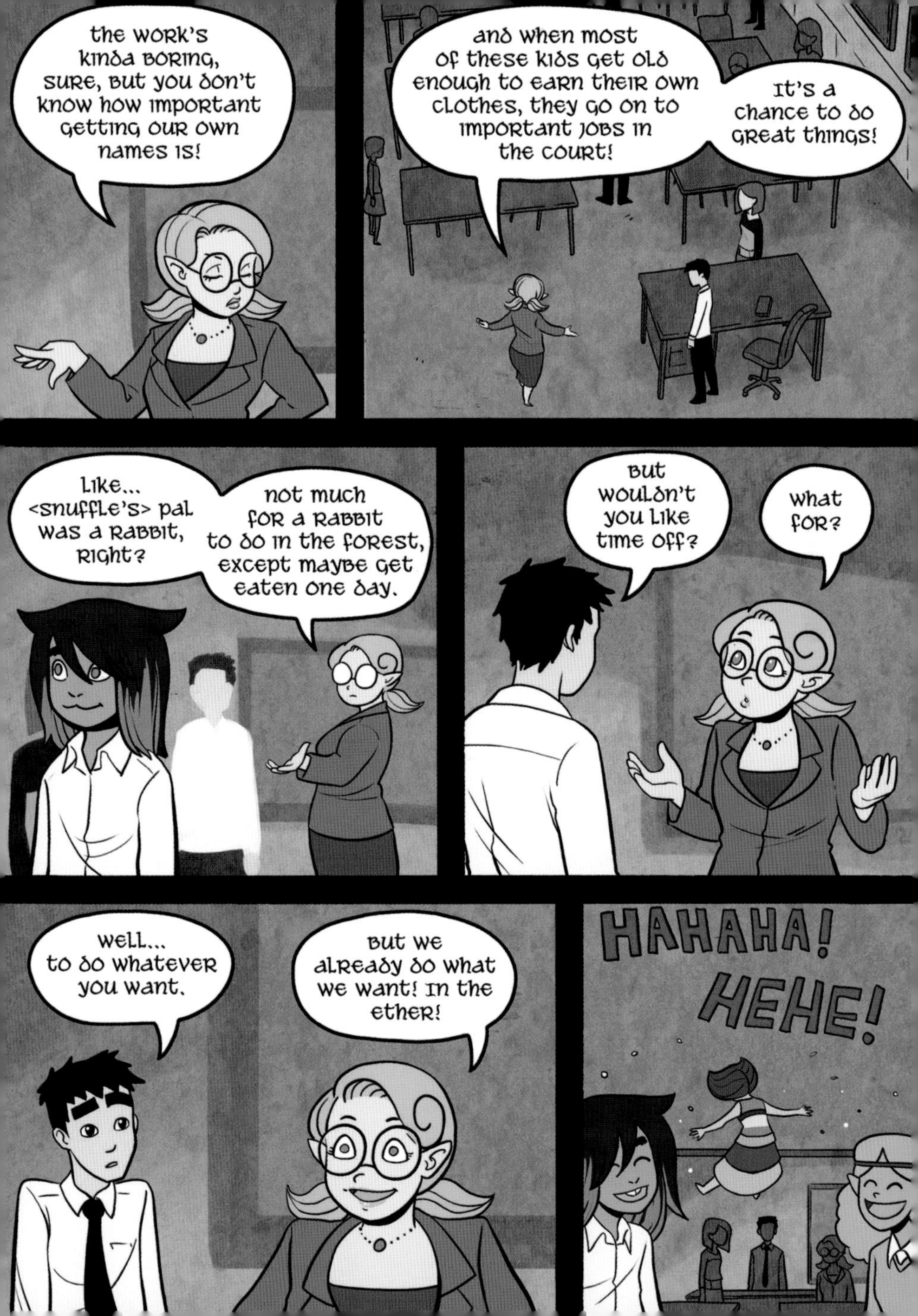
the work's kinda boring, sure, but you don't know how important getting our own names is!
and when most of these kids get old enough to earn their own clothes, they go on to important jobs in the court!
It's a chance to do great things!
Like... <snuffle's> pal was a rabbit, right?
not much for a rabbit to do in the forest, except maybe get eaten one day.
But wouldn't you like time off?
What for?
well... to do whatever you want.
But we already do what we want! In the ether!
HAHAHA!
HEHE!

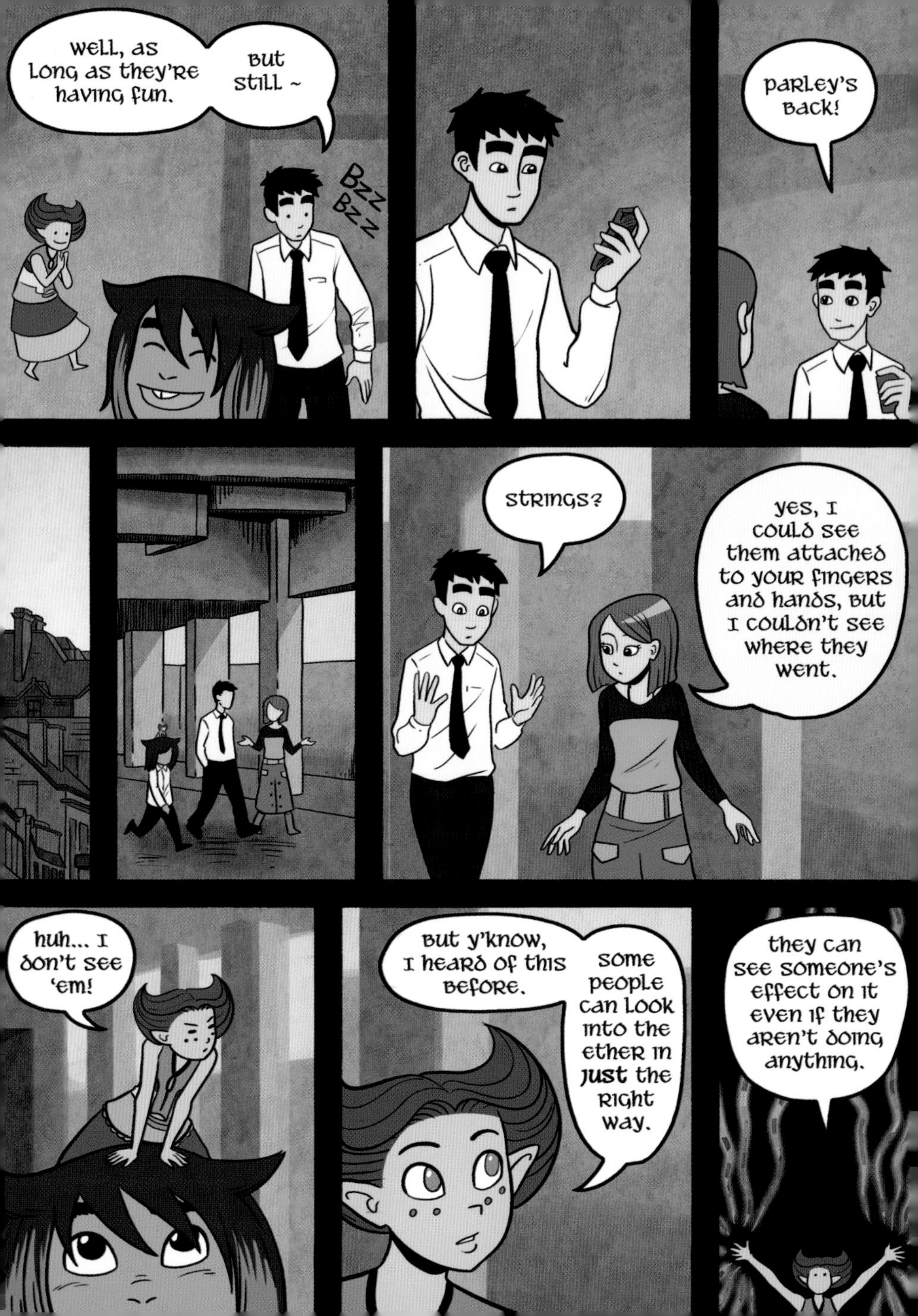
well, as long as they're having fun.
but still ~
Bzz Bzz
parley's back!
strings?
yes, I could see them attached to your fingers and hands, but I couldn't see where they went.
huh... I don't see 'em!
but y'know, I heard of this before.
some people can look into the ether in **just** the right way.
they can see someone's effect on it even if they aren't doing anything.

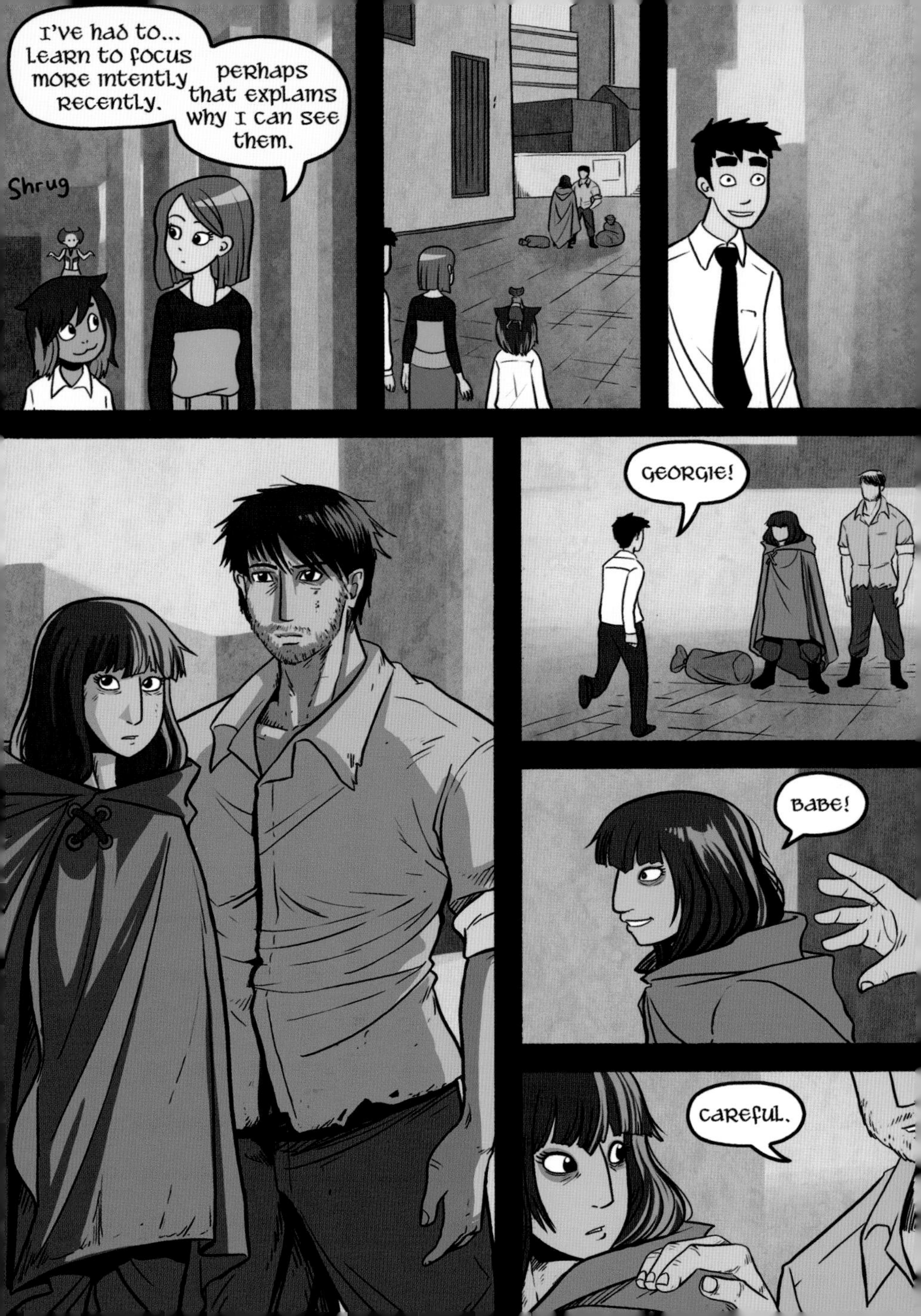
I've had to... learn to focus more intently recently.
perhaps that explains why I can see them.
Shrug
GEORGIE!
BABE!
careful.

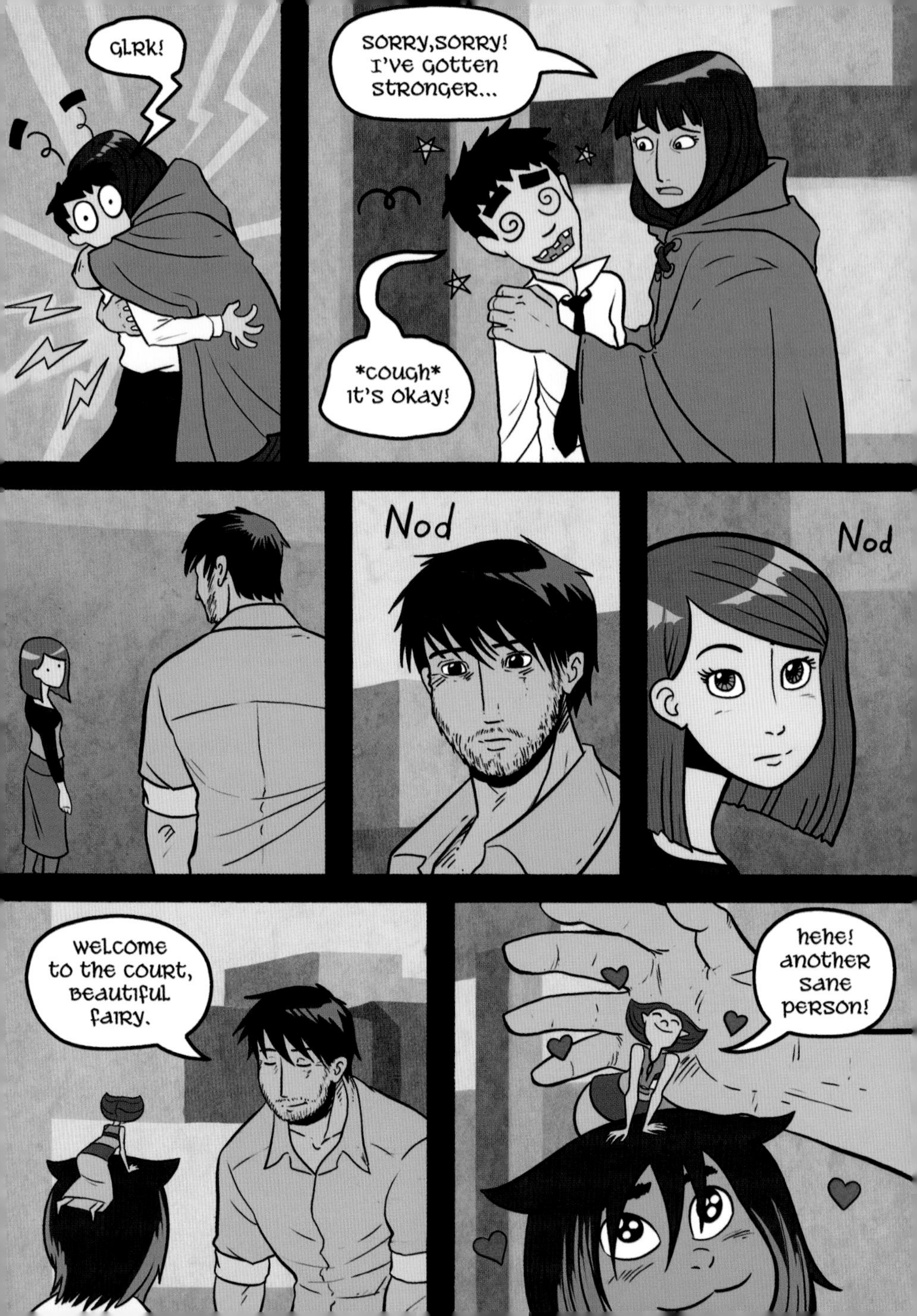
GLRK!
SORRY,SORRY! I'VE GOTTEN STRONGER...
COUGH IT'S OKAY!
Nod
Nod
WELCOME TO THE COURT, BEAUTIFUL FAIRY.
HEHE! ANOTHER SANE PERSON!

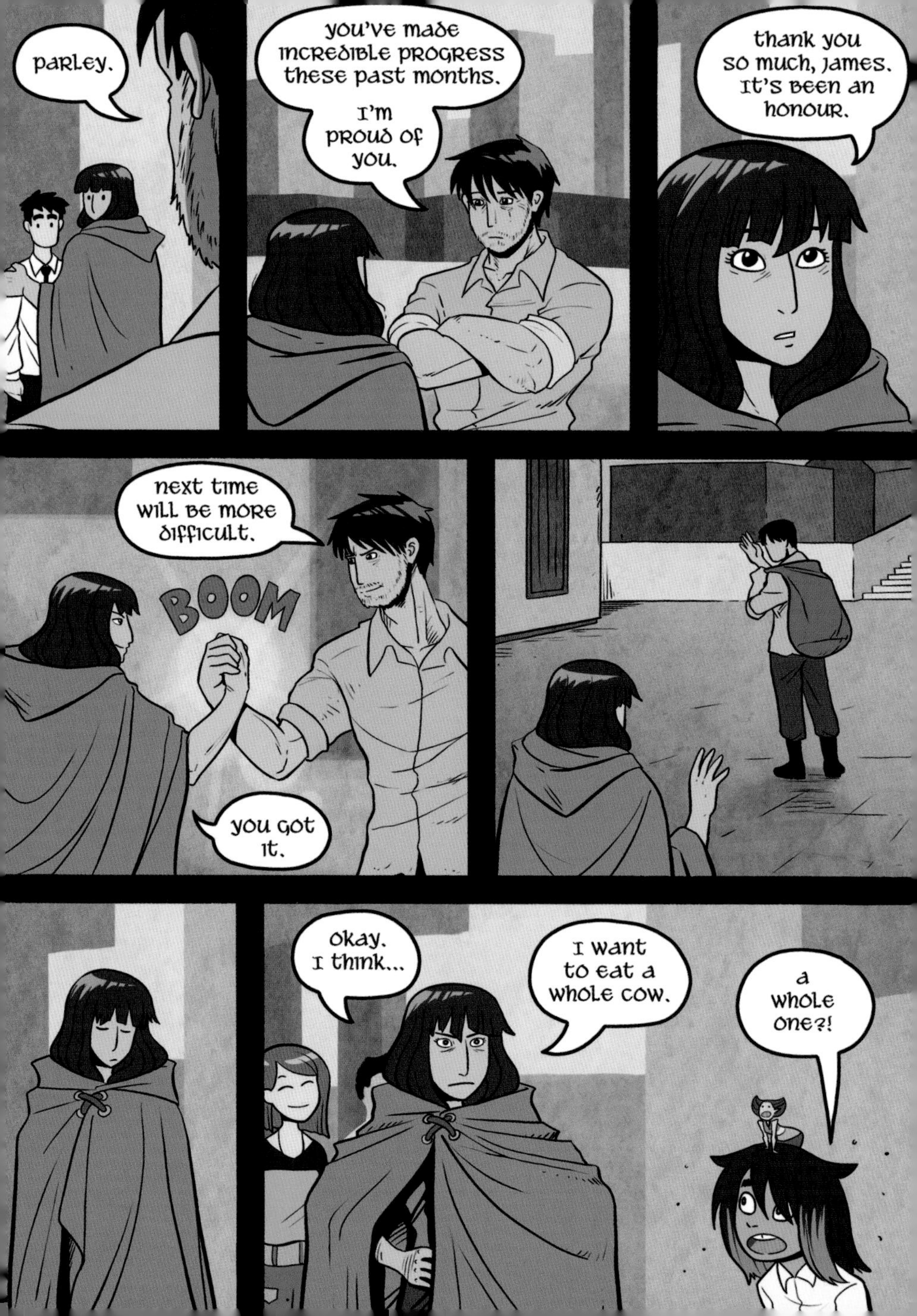
parley.
you've made incredible progress these past months.
I'm proud of you.
thank you so much, james. It's been an honour.
next time will be more difficult.
BOOM
you got it.
Okay. I think...
I want to eat a whole cow.
a whole one?!

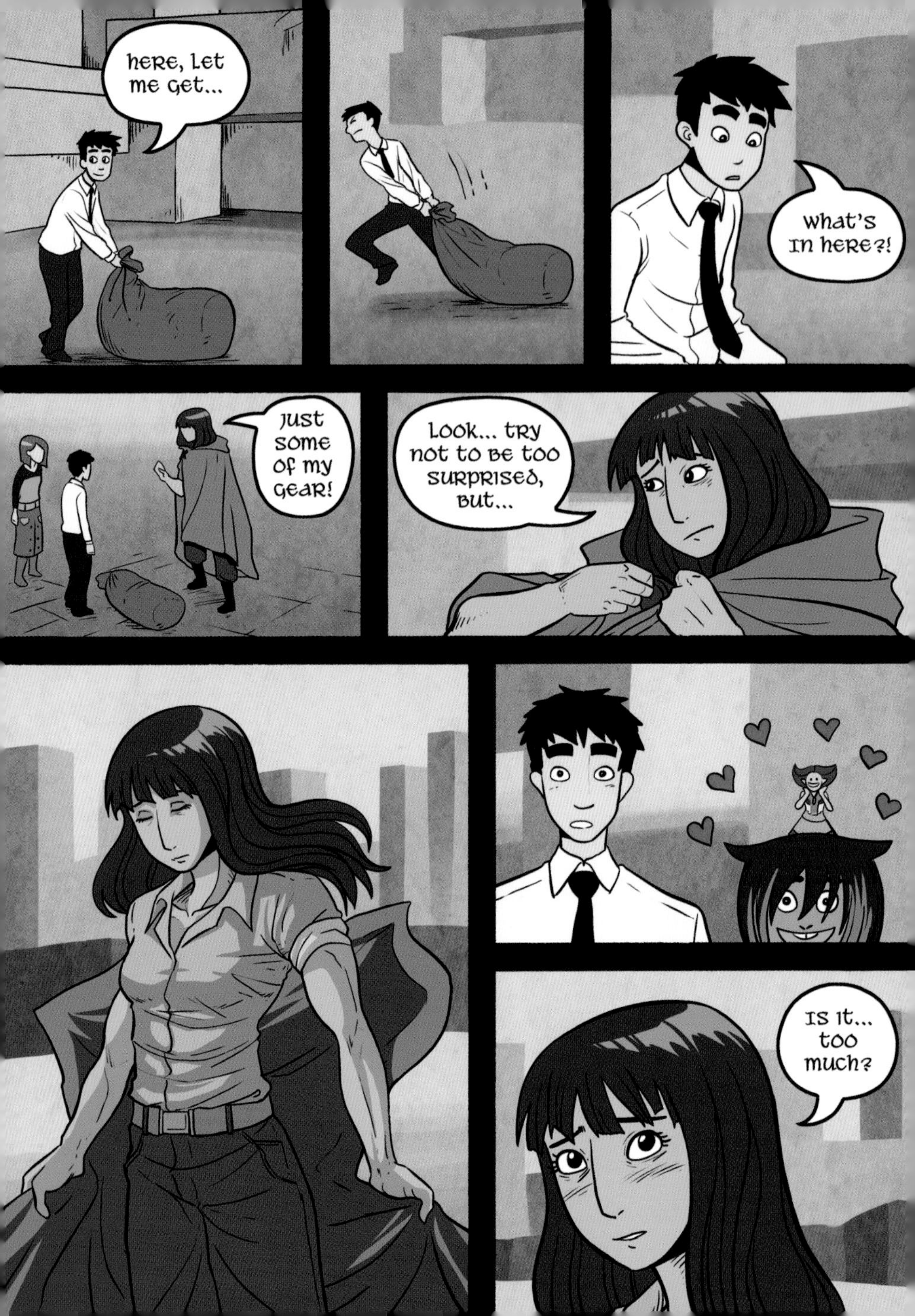
here, let me get...
what's in here?!
just some of my gear!
look... try not to be too surprised, but...
is it... too much?

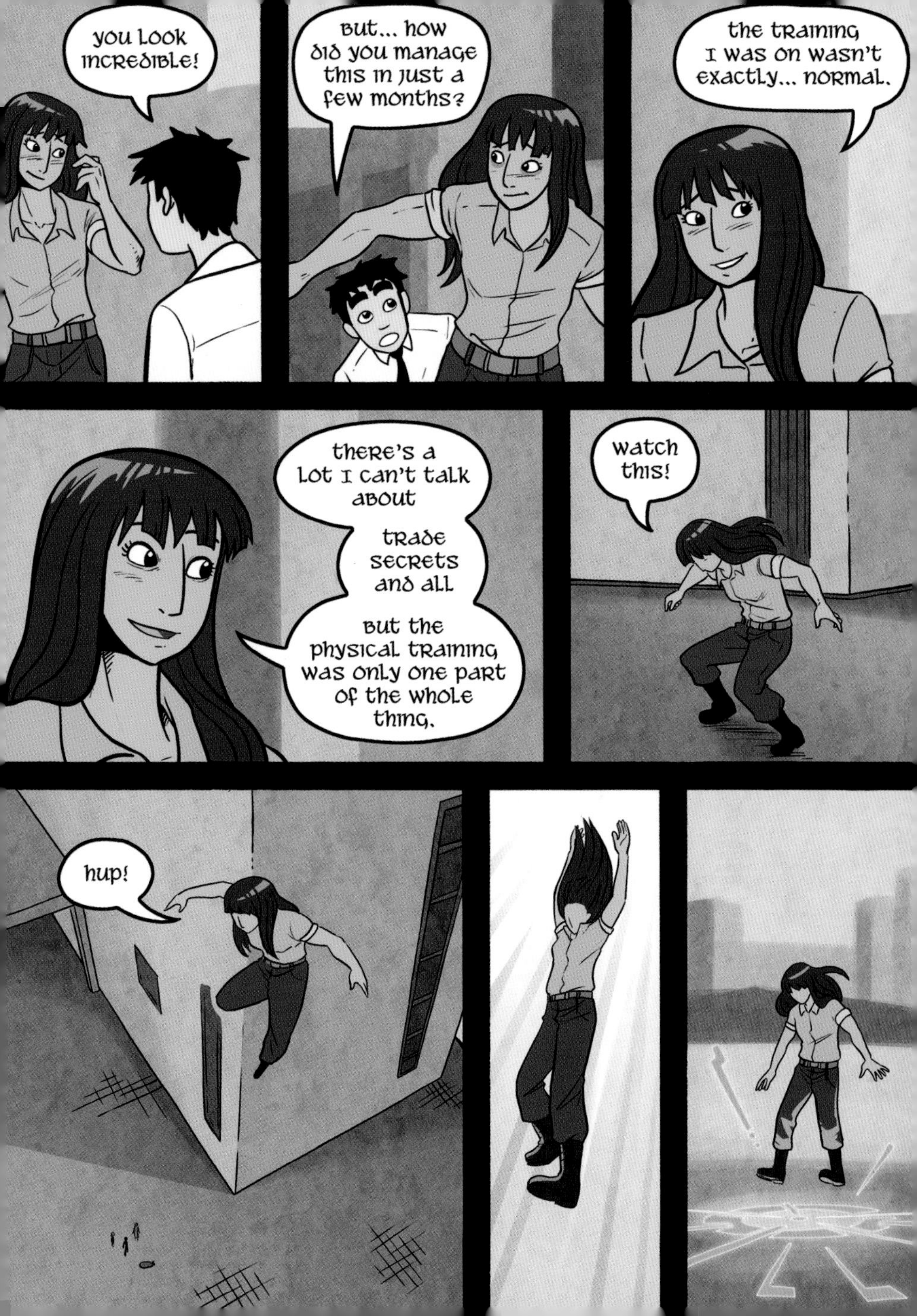
you look incredible!
but... how did you manage this in just a few months?
the training I was on wasn't exactly... normal.
there's a lot I can't talk about
trade secrets and all
but the physical training was only one part of the whole thing.
watch this!
hup!

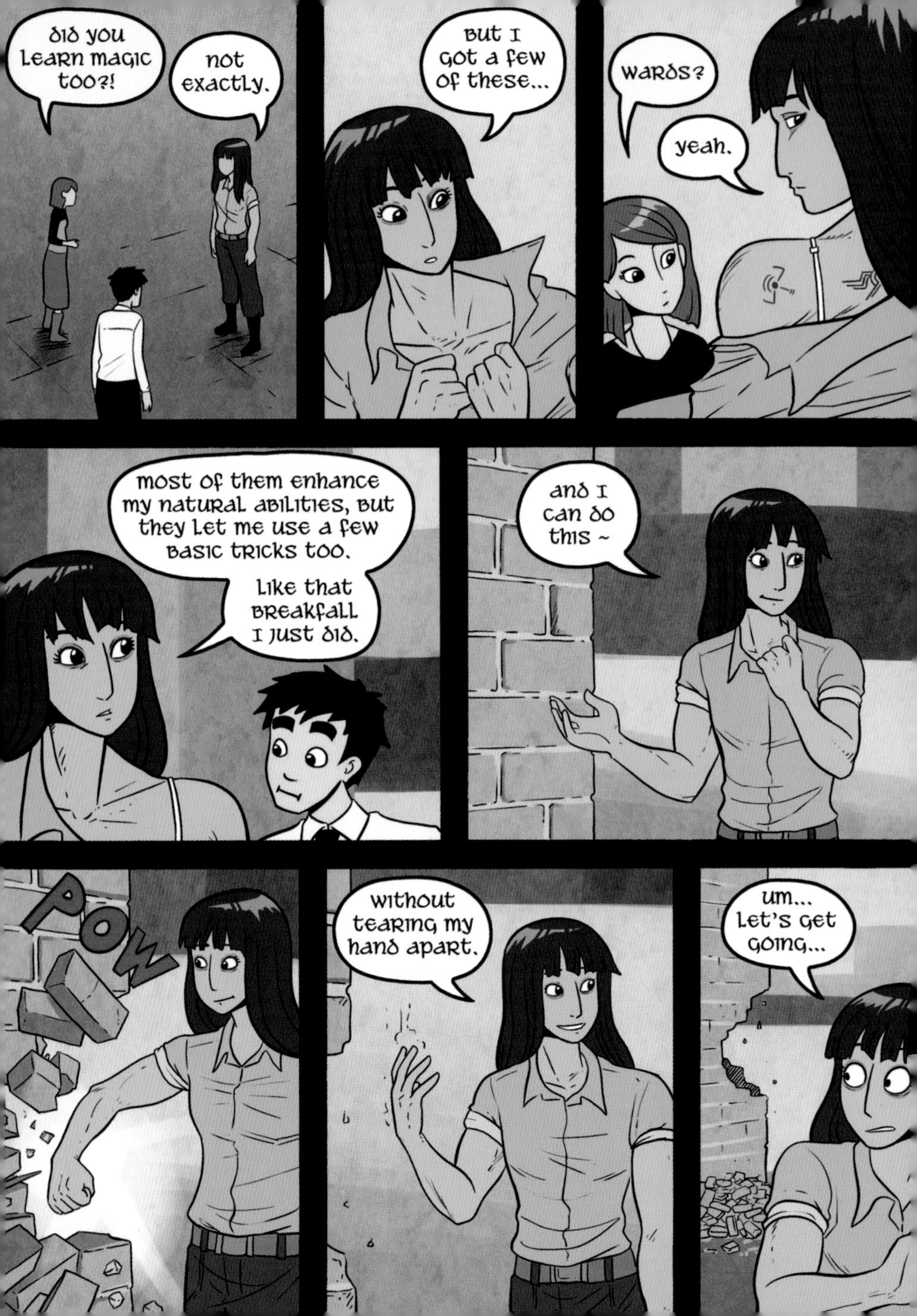
did you learn magic too?!
not exactly.
But I got a few of these...
wards?
yeah.
most of them enhance my natural abilities, but they let me use a few basic tricks too.
like that breakfall I just did.
and I can do this ~
POW
without tearing my hand apart.
um... let's get going...

we spent most of our time out in the mountains.

I'm not even sure what country we were in.

the only other people we saw were teachers like eglamore.

apparently there aren't many left.

teachers I mean.

one of the first things I learned was how to open channels in my body.

I wouldn't make it through the training otherwise.

channels?

yeah like pathways I guess? anybody can do it.

lets you control your body in ways you couldn't before.

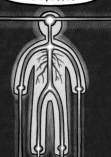

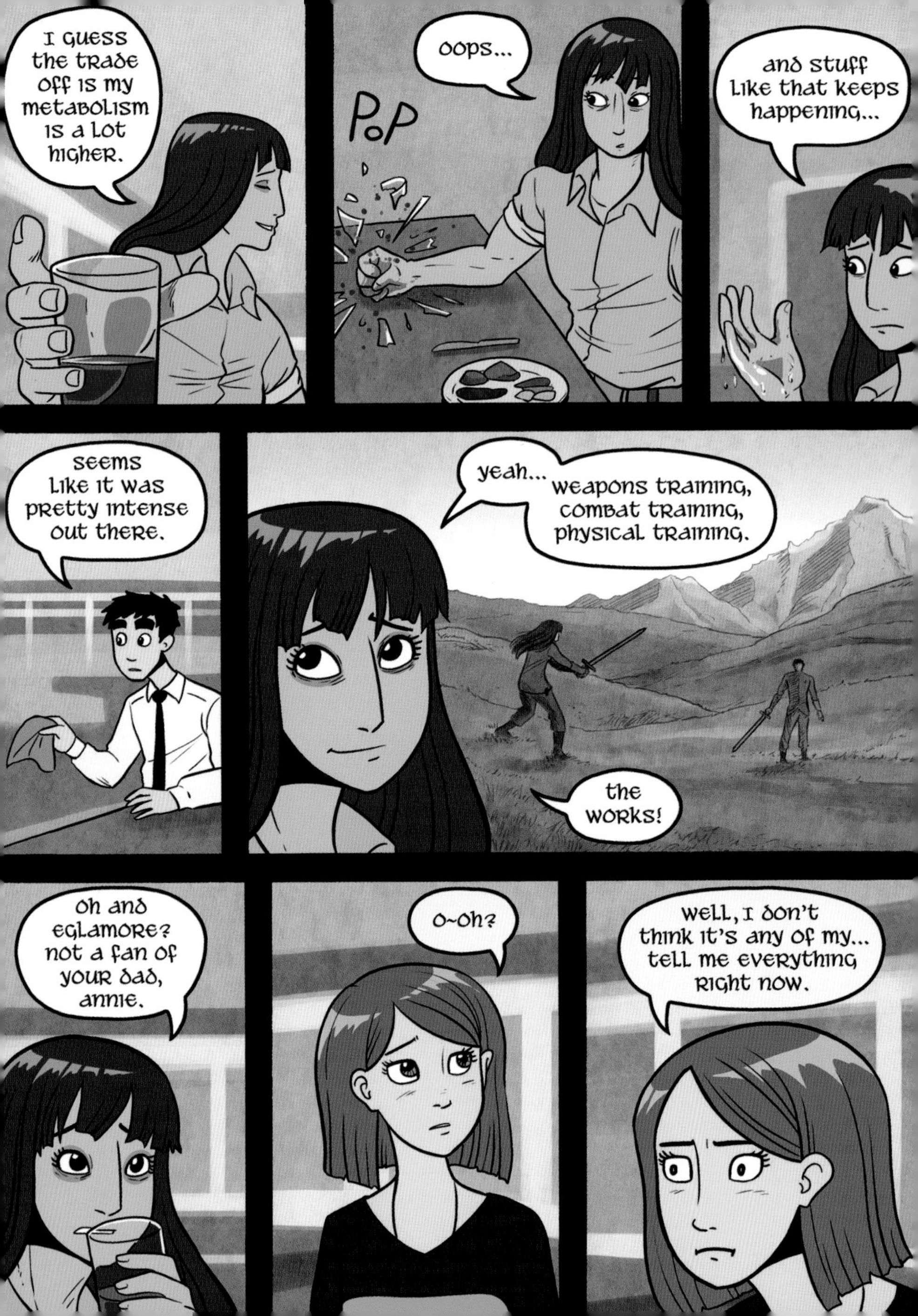
I GUESS the trade off is my metabolism is a lot higher.
oops...
PoP
and stuff like that keeps happening...
seems like it was pretty intense out there.
yeah...
weapons training, combat training, physical training.
the works!
oh and eglamore? not a fan of your dad, annie.
o-oh?
well, I don't think it's any of my... tell me everything right now.

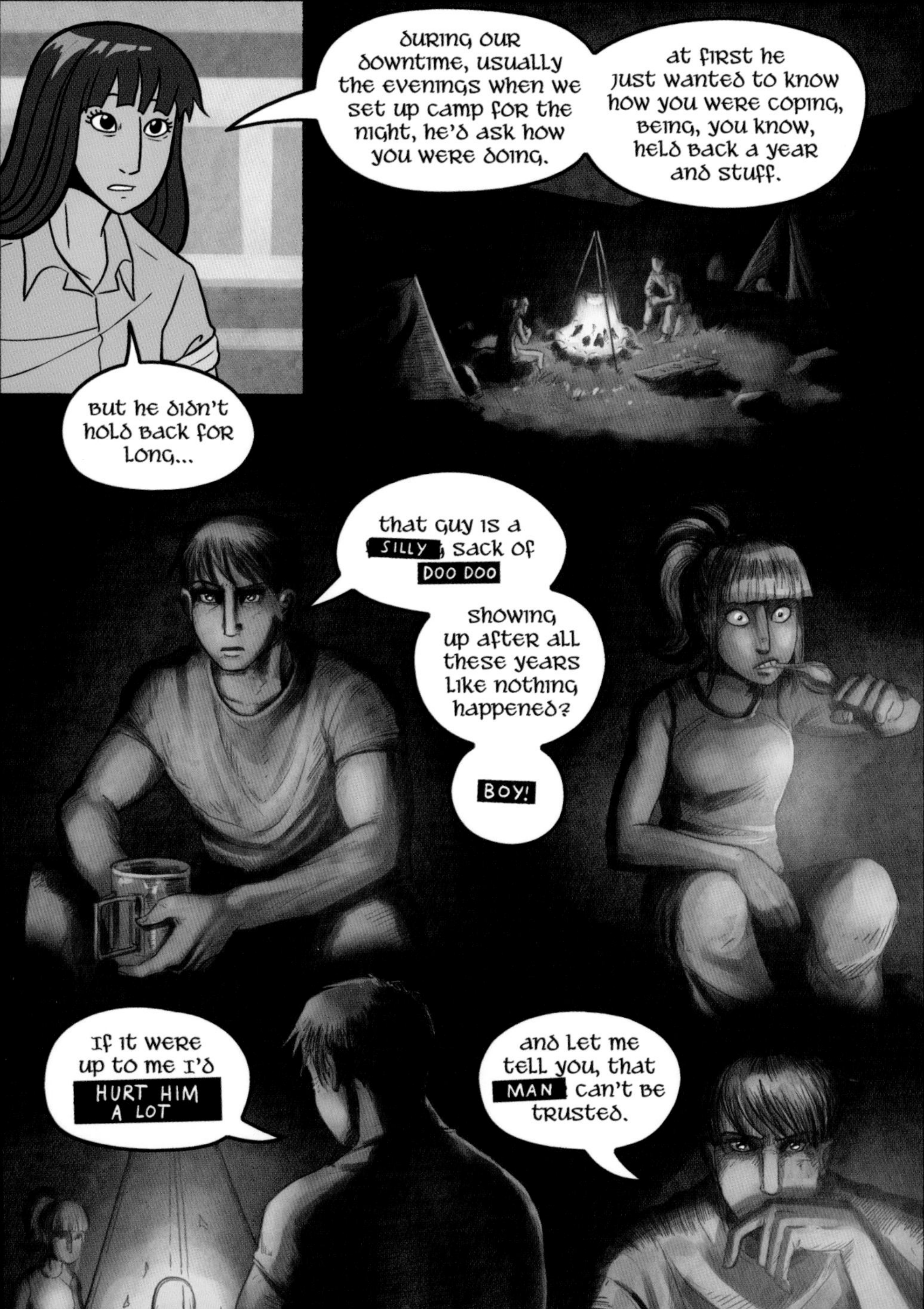
during our downtime, usually the evenings when we set up camp for the night, he'd ask how you were doing.
at first he just wanted to know how you were coping, being, you know, held back a year and stuff.
but he didn't hold back for long...
that guy is a SILLY, sack of DOO DOO
showing up after all these years like nothing happened?
BOY!
if it were up to me I'd HURT HIM A LOT
and let me tell you, that MAN can't be trusted.

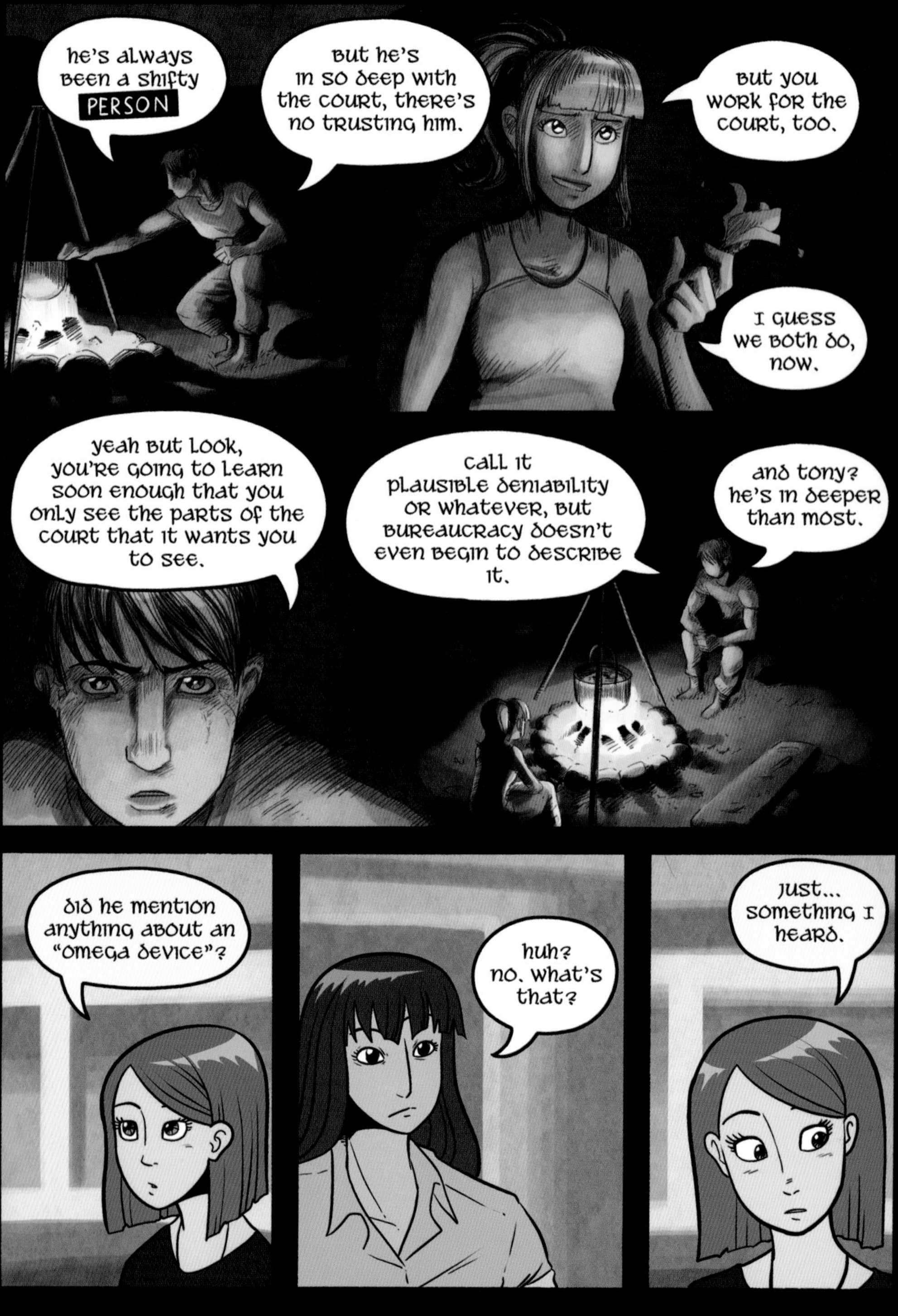
he's always been a shifty PERSON
but he's in so deep with the court, there's no trusting him.
but you work for the court, too.
I guess we both do, now.
yeah but look, you're going to learn soon enough that you only see the parts of the court that it wants you to see.
call it plausible deniability or whatever, but bureaucracy doesn't even begin to describe it.
and tony? he's in deeper than most.
did he mention anything about an "omega device"?
huh? no. what's that?
just... something I heard.

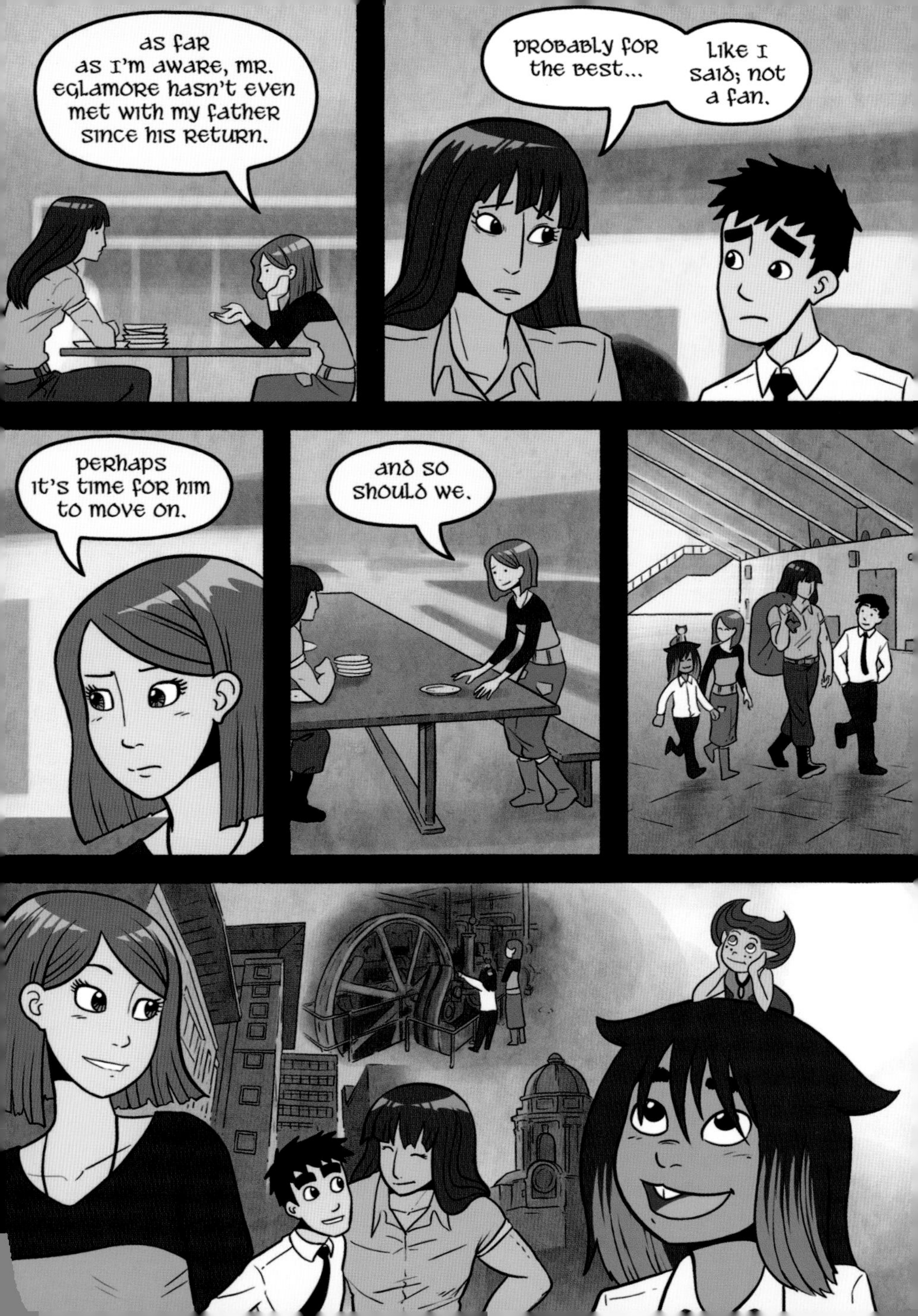
as far as I'm aware, mr. eglamore hasn't even met with my father since his return.
probably for the best...
like I said; not a fan.
perhaps it's time for him to move on.
and so should we.

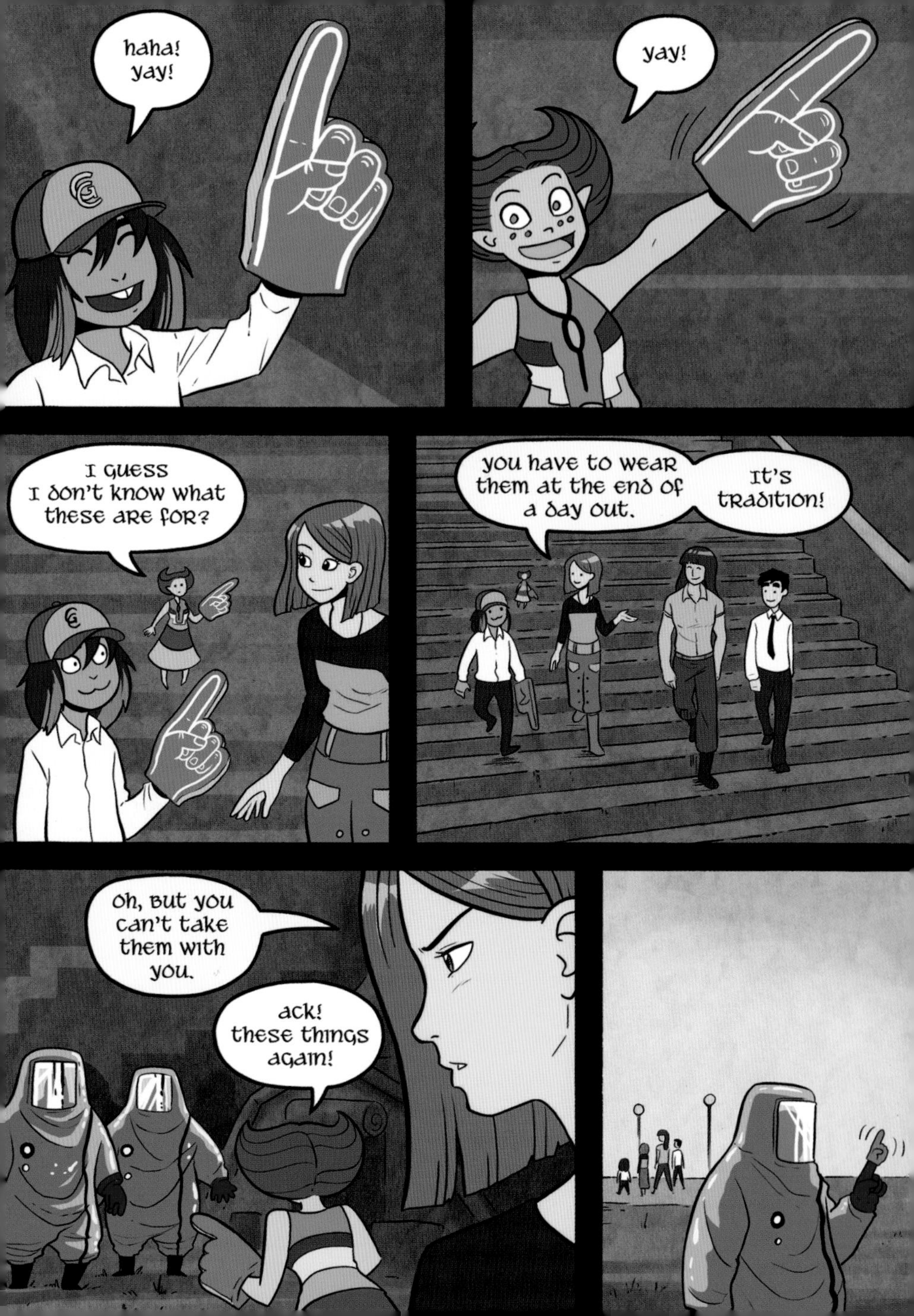
haha! yay!
yay!
I guess I don't know what these are for?
you have to wear them at the end of a day out.
It's tradition!
Oh, but you can't take them with you.
ack! these things again!

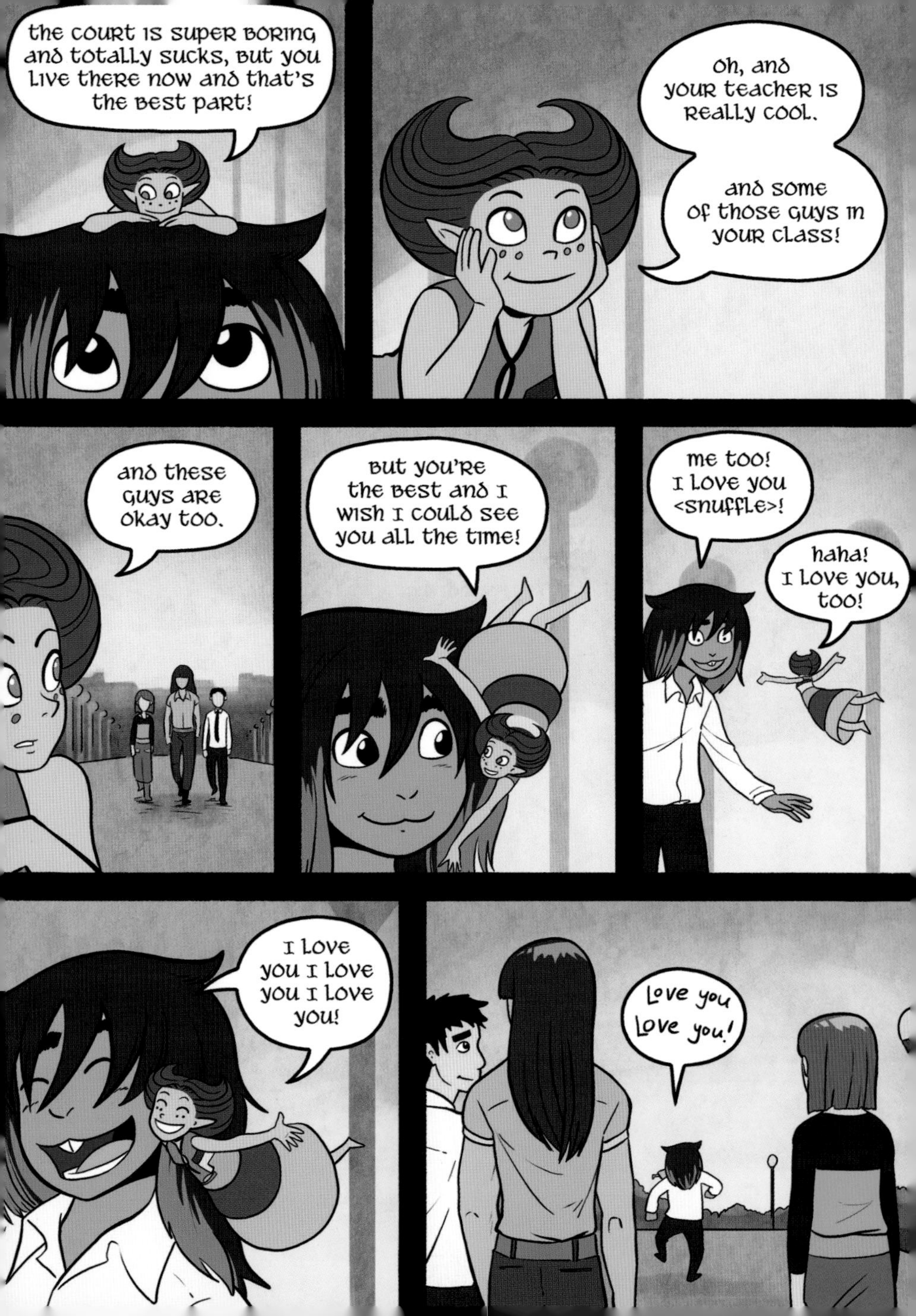
the court is super boring and totally sucks, but you live there now and that's the best part!
Oh, and your teacher is really cool.
and some of those guys in your class!
and these guys are okay too.
But you're the best and I wish I could see you all the time!
me too! I love you <snuffle>!
haha! I love you, too!
I love you I love you I love you!
Love you Love you!

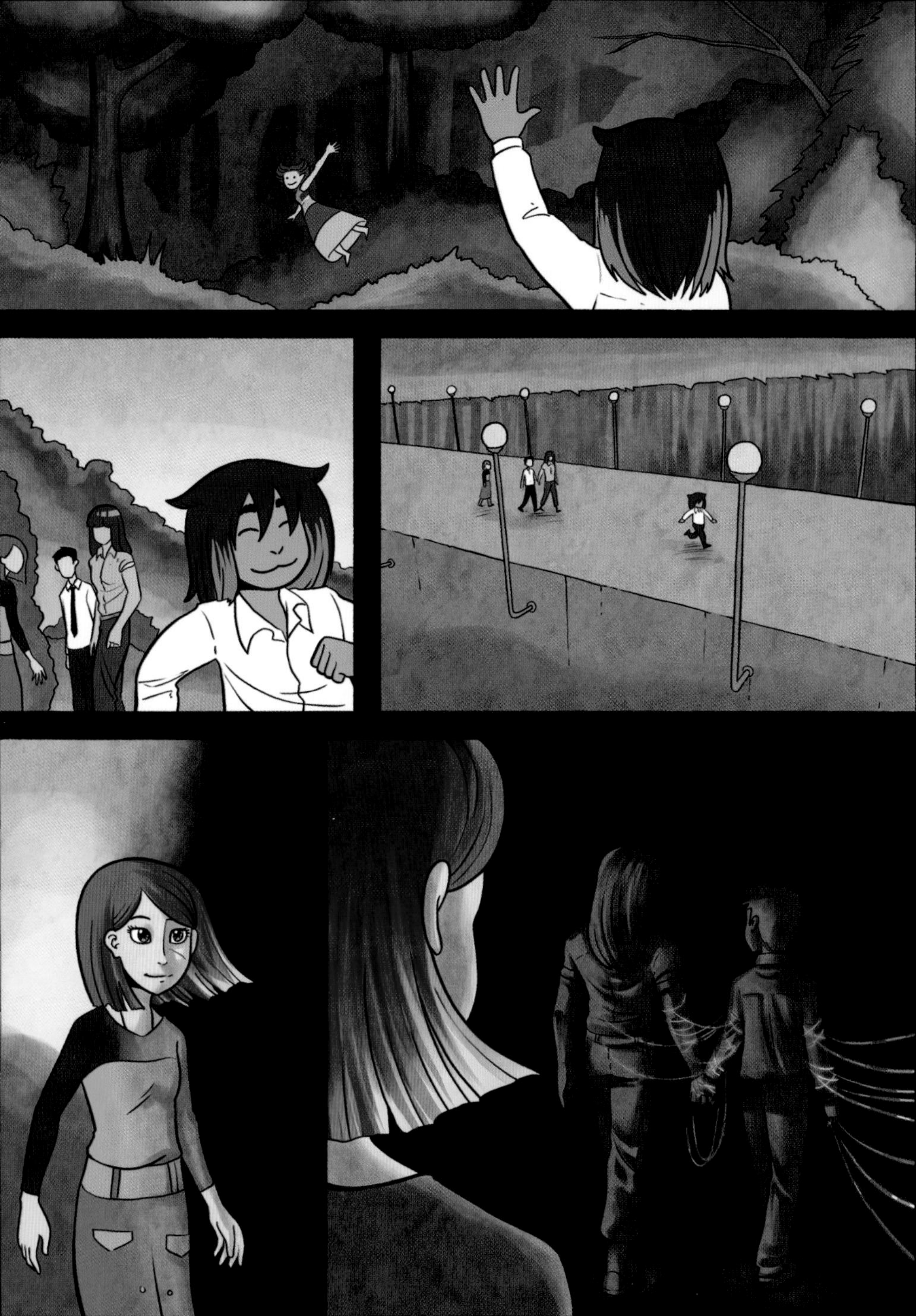

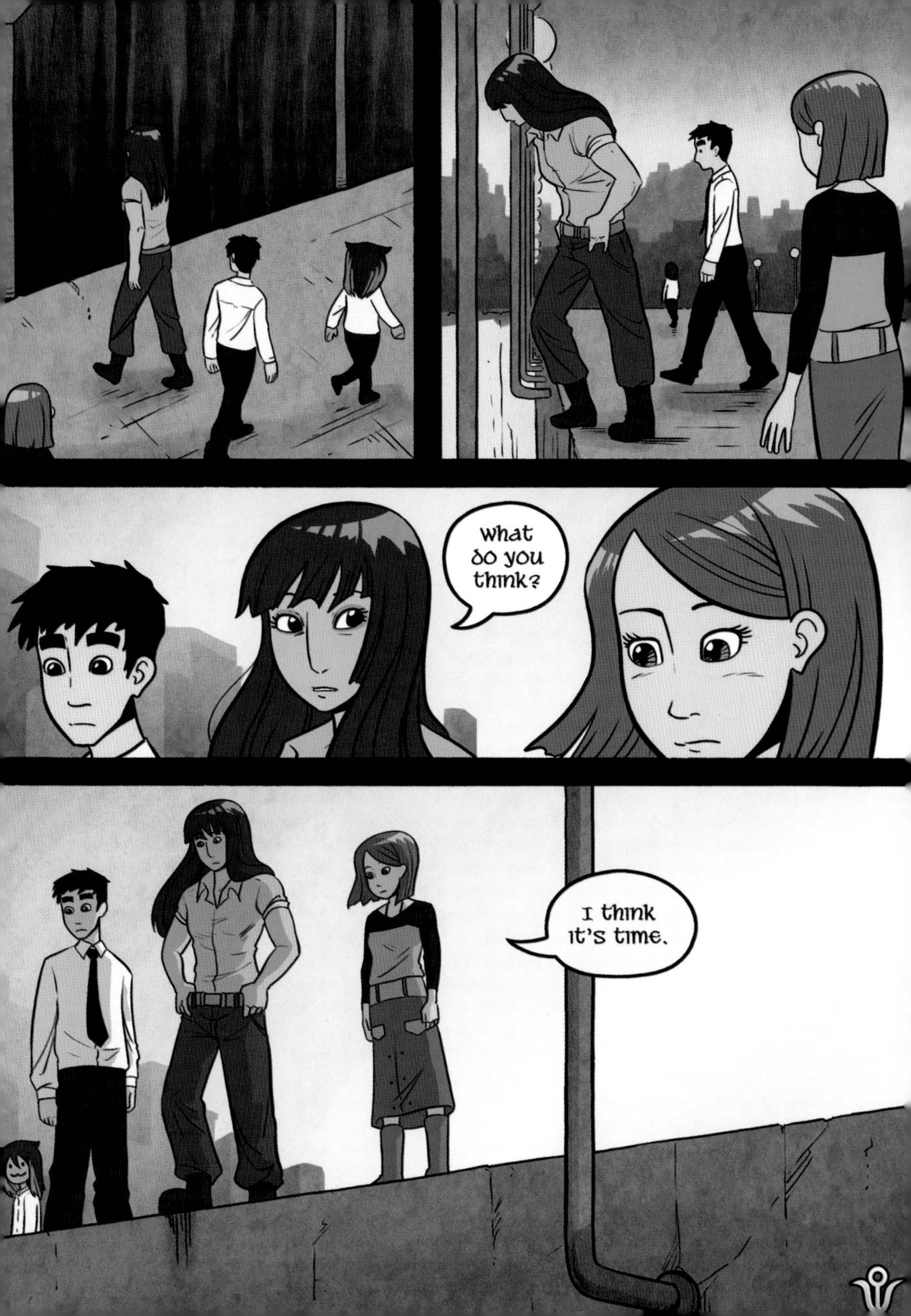
what do you think?
I think it's time.

Oh look it's more of these guys
(chapter 58 character guide)

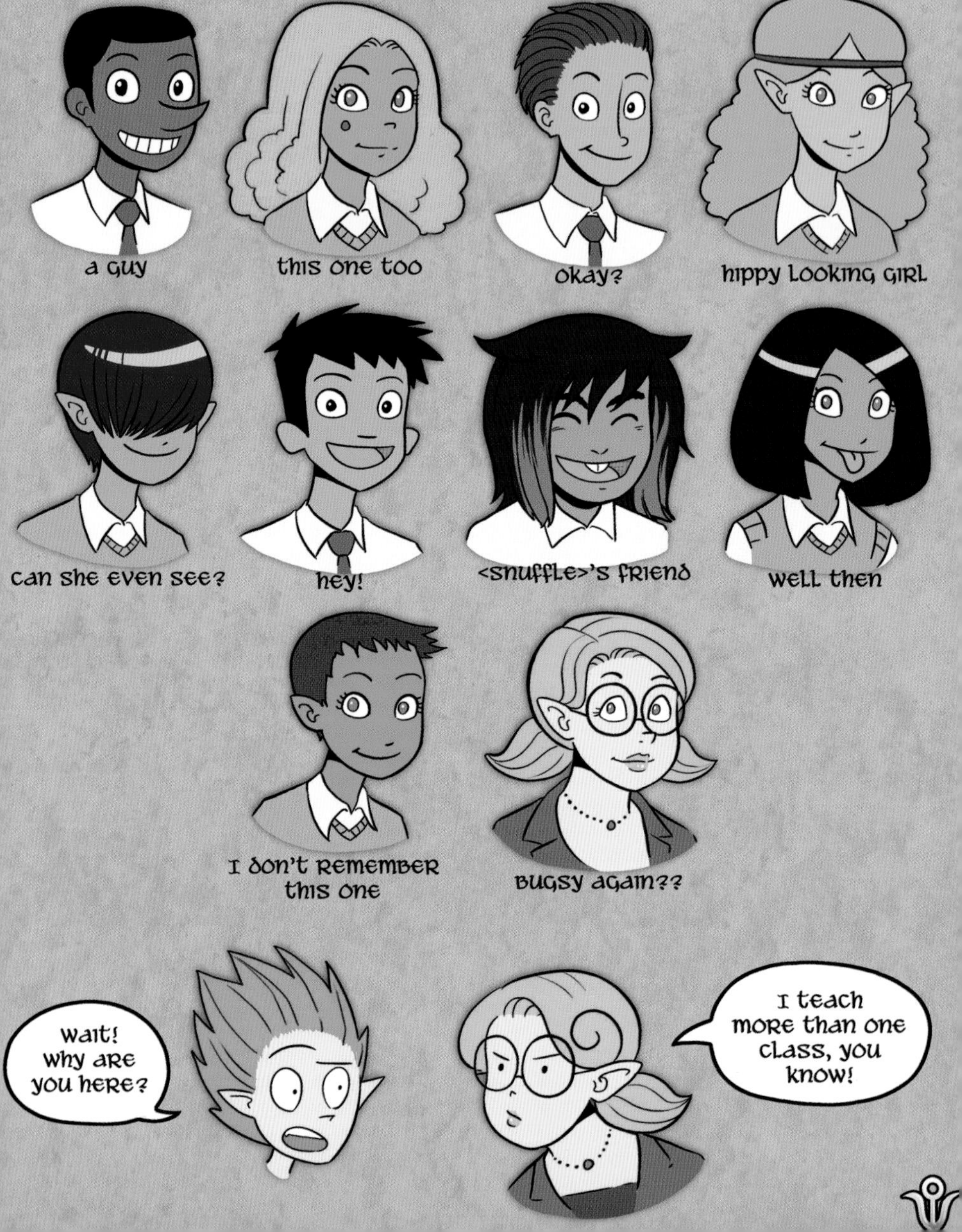
a guy
this one too
okay?
hippy looking girl
can she even see?
hey!
<snuffle>'s friend
well then
I don't remember this one
Bugsy again??
Wait! Why are you here?
I teach more than one class, you know!

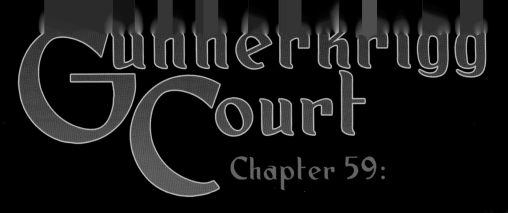

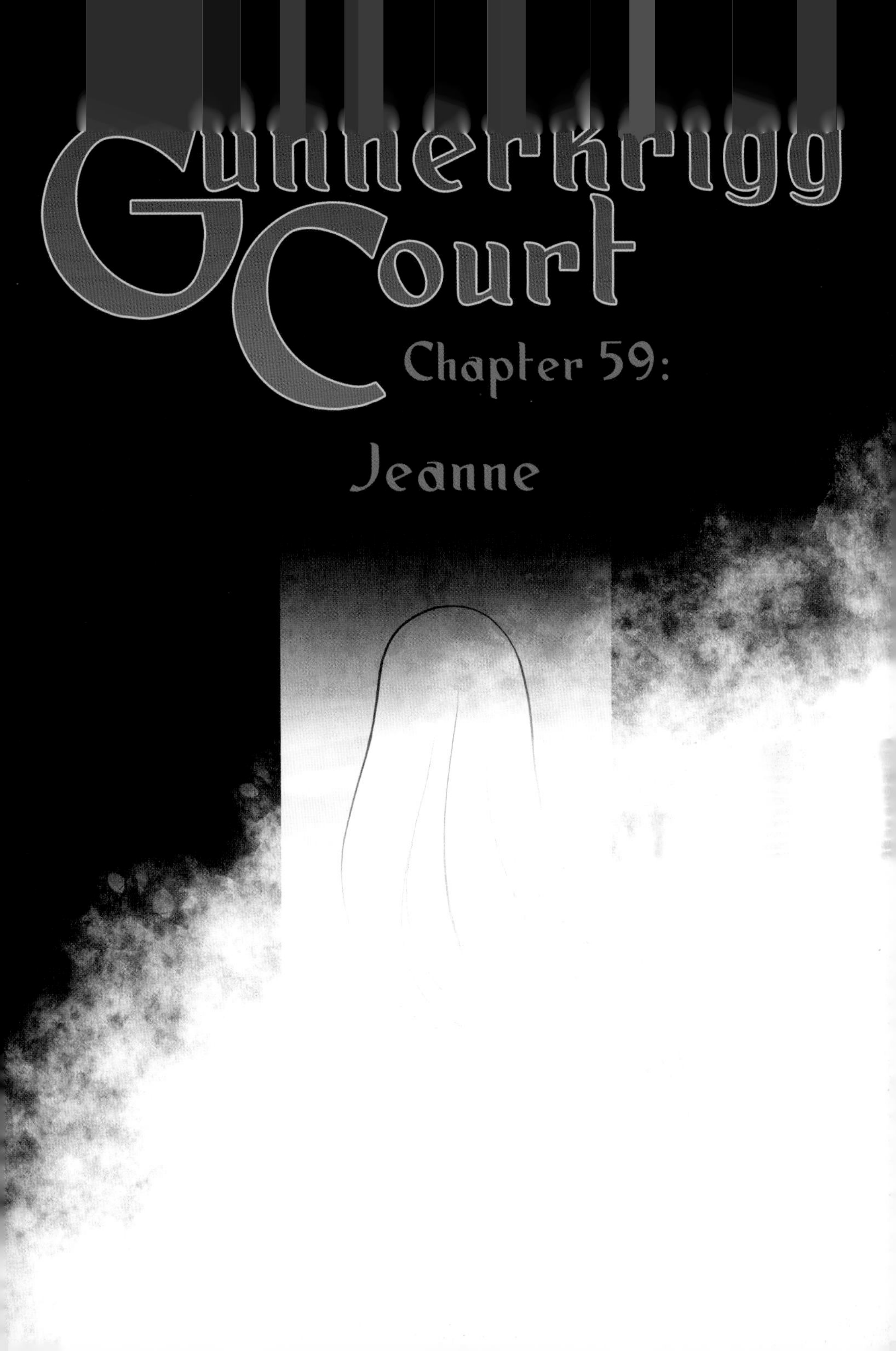

Gunnerkrigg Court

Chapter 59:

Jeanne

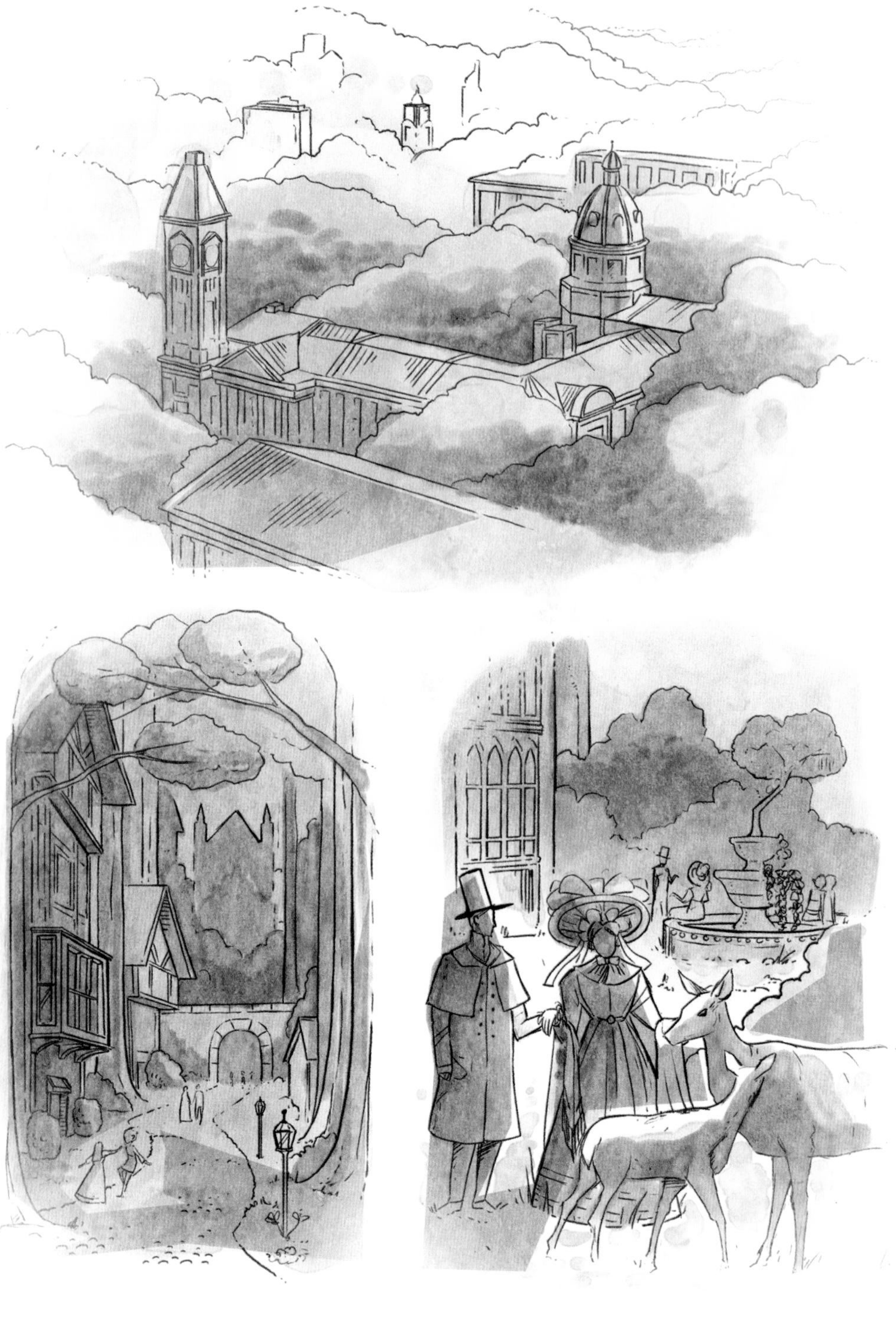

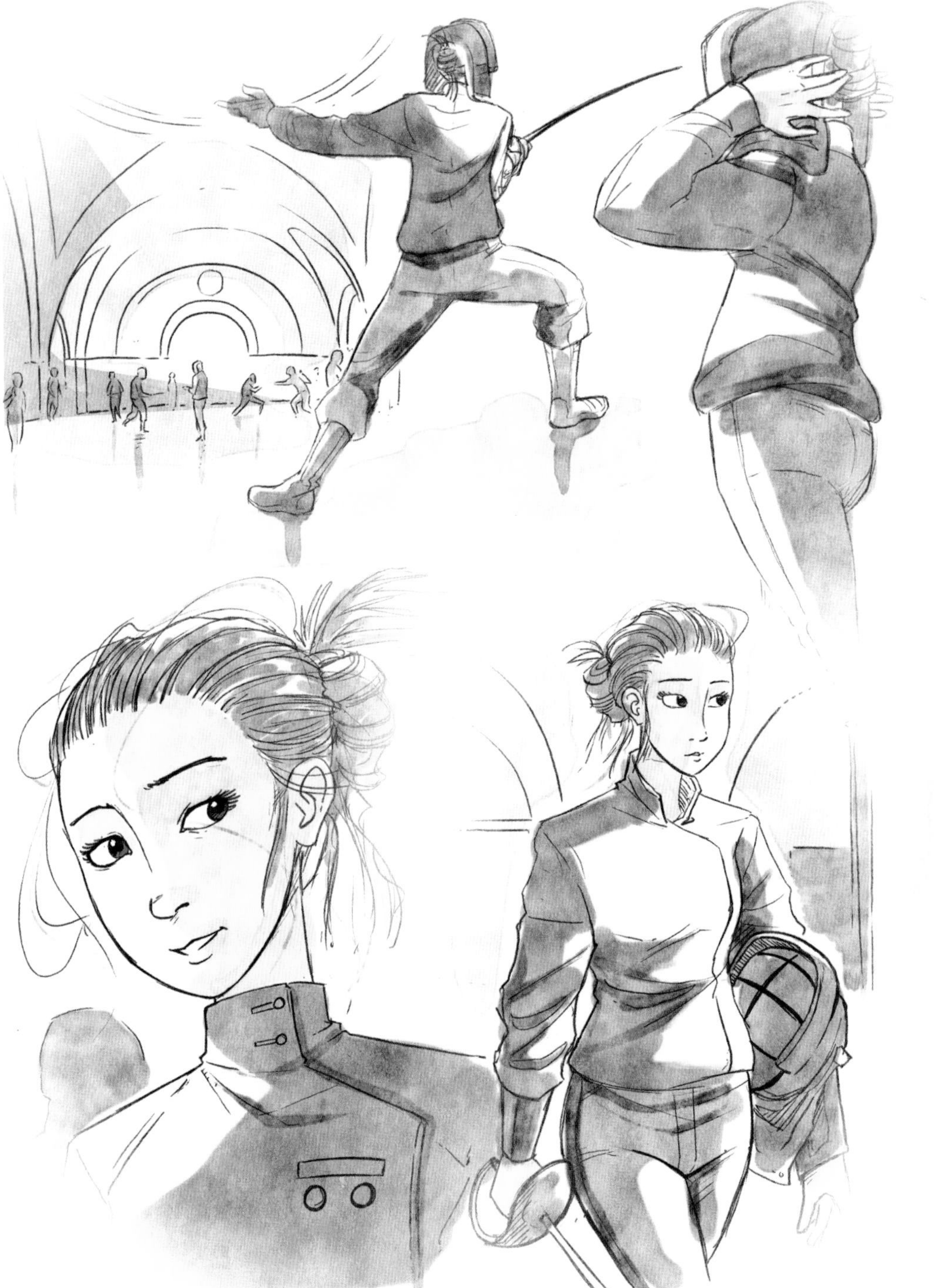

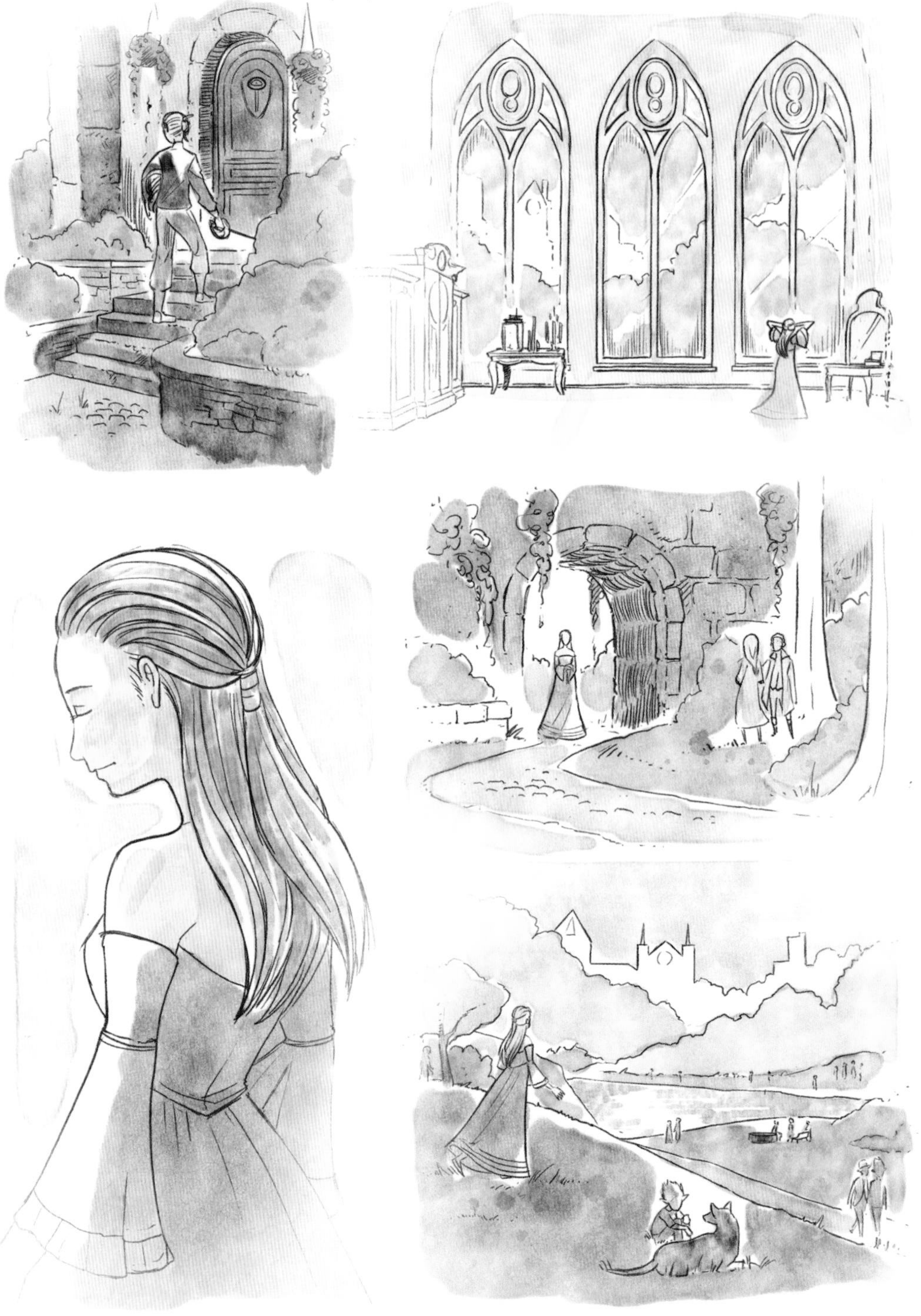

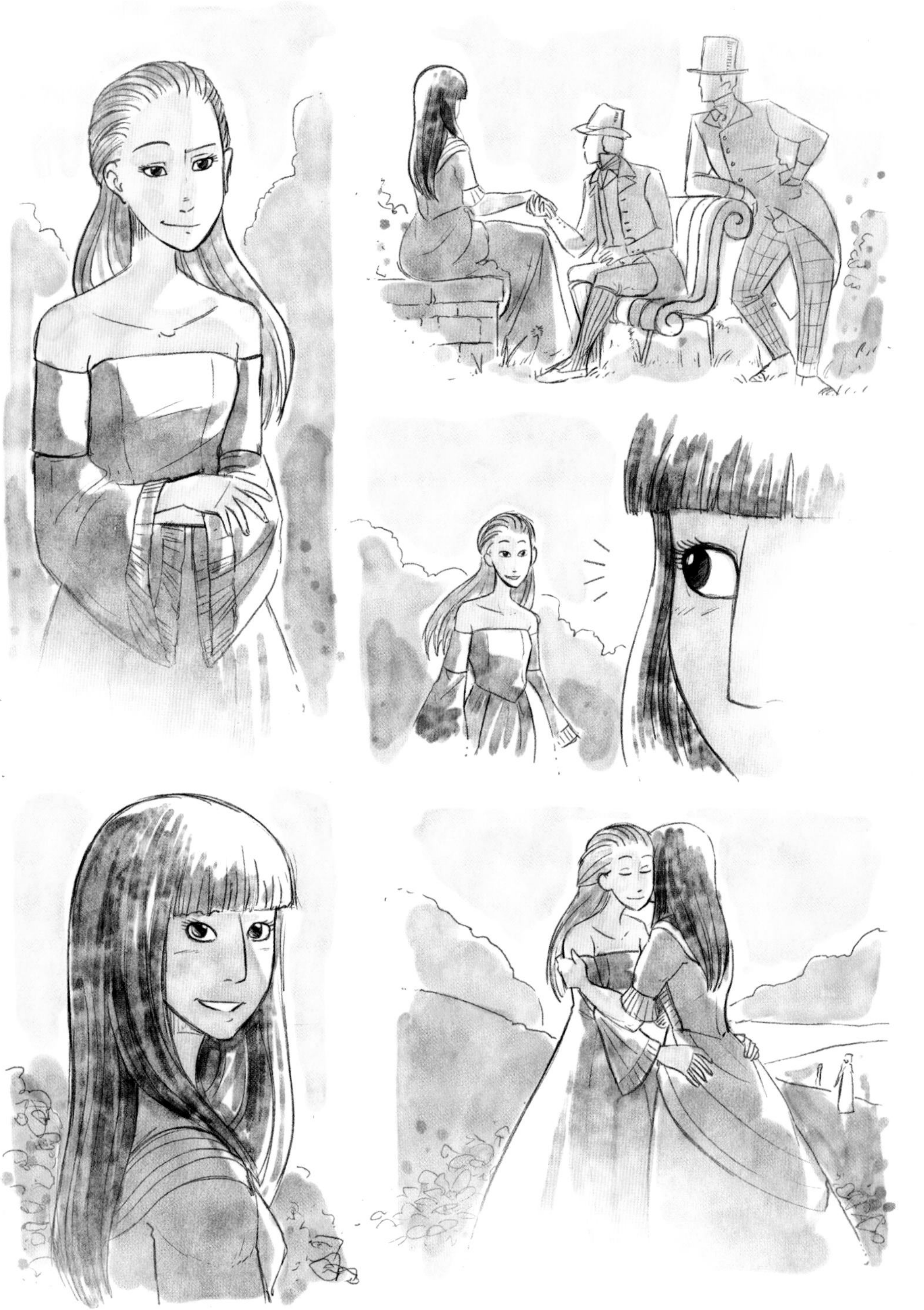

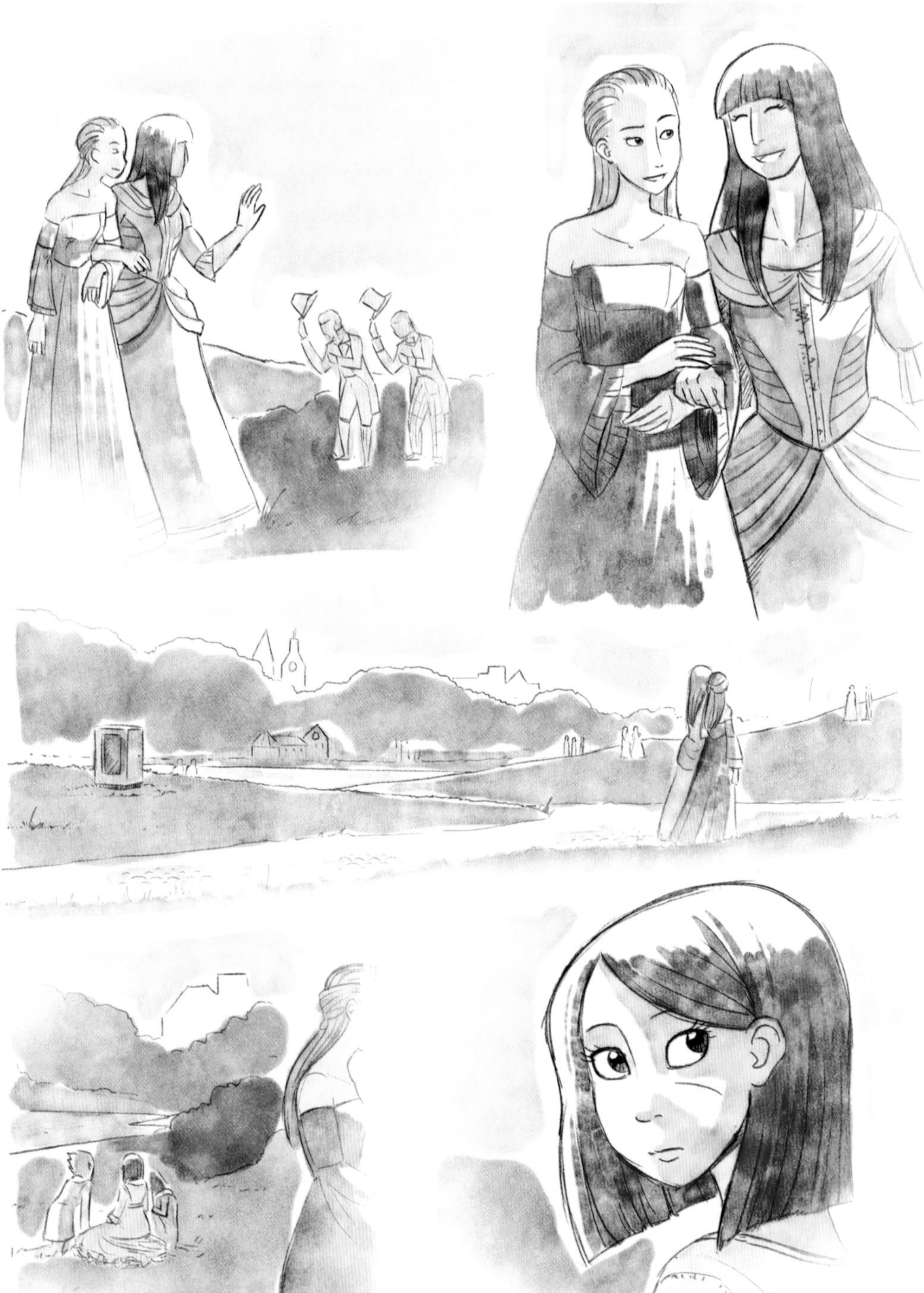

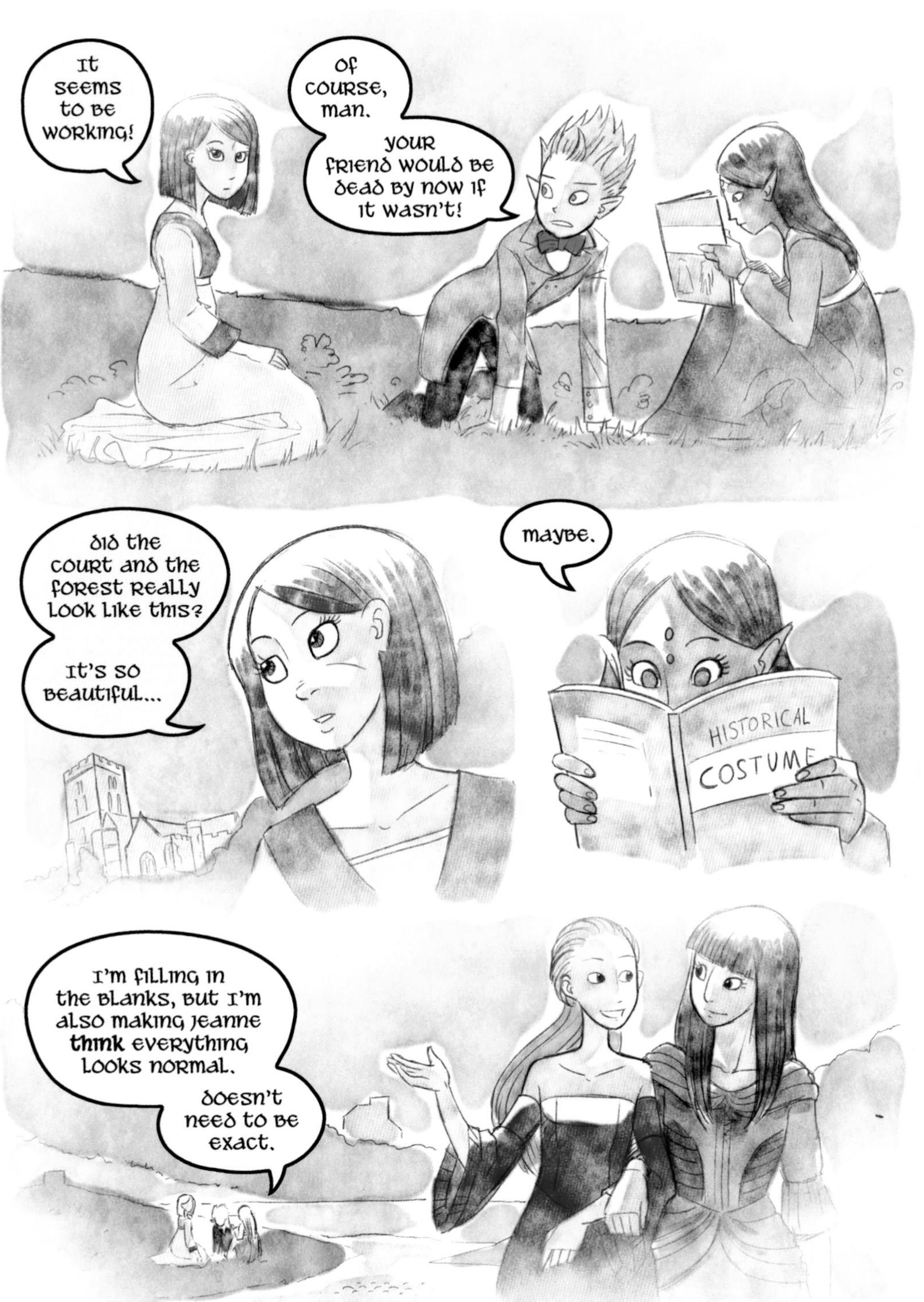

It seems to be working!
Of course, man.
Your friend would be dead by now if it wasn't!
Did the court and the forest really look like this?
It's so beautiful...
Maybe.
HISTORICAL COSTUME
I'm filling in the blanks, but I'm also making Jeanne **think** everything looks normal.
Doesn't need to be exact.

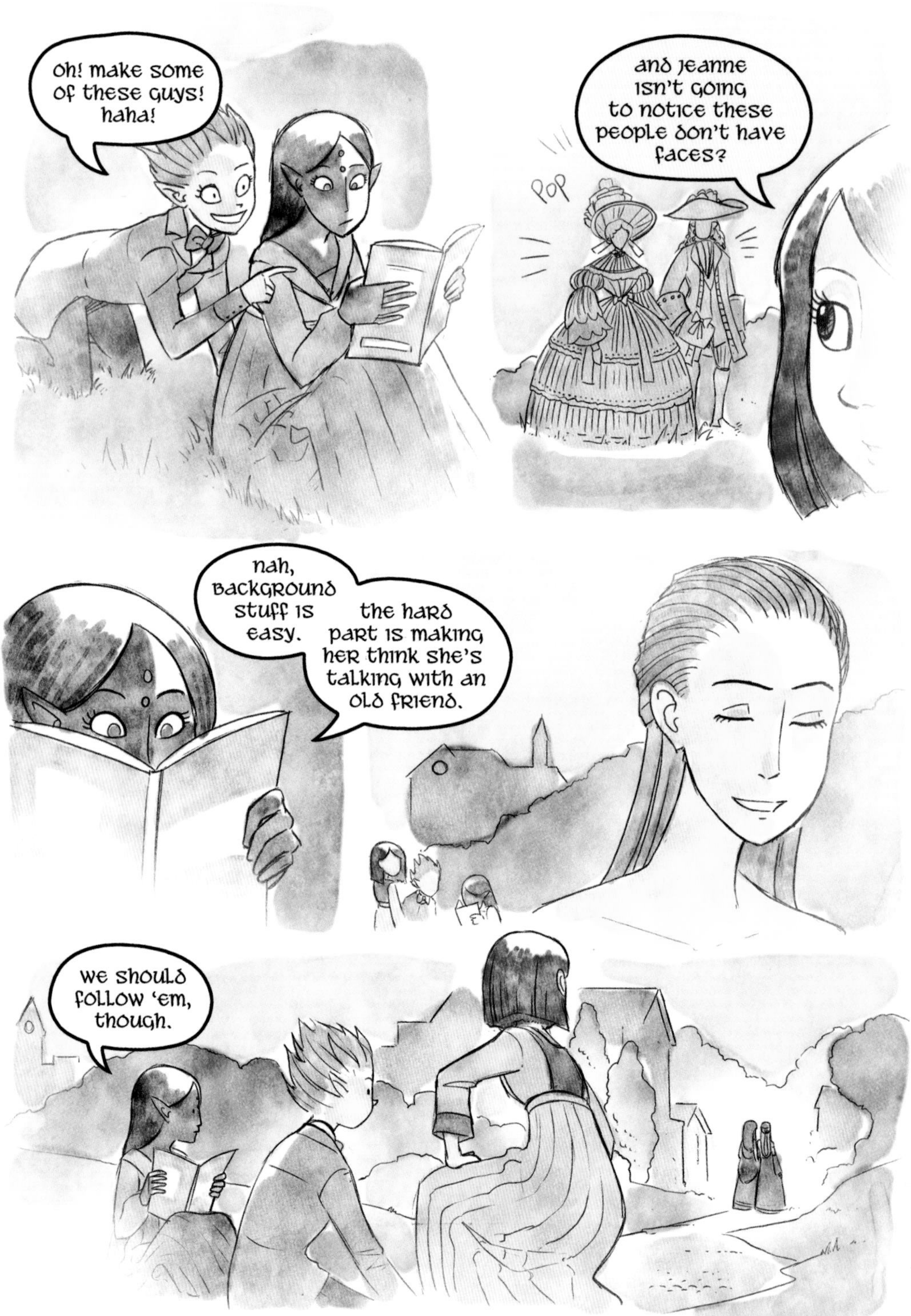
oh! make some of these guys! haha!
and jeanne isn't going to notice these people don't have faces?
pop
nah, background stuff is easy.
the hard part is making her think she's talking with an old friend.
we should follow 'em, though.

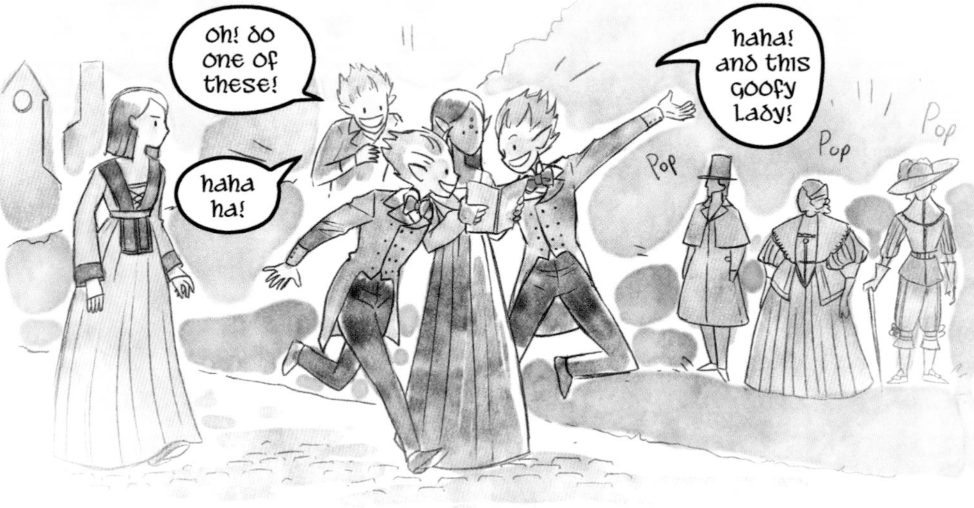
Oh! do one of these!
haha ha!
haha! and this goofy lady!
Pop
Pop
Pop

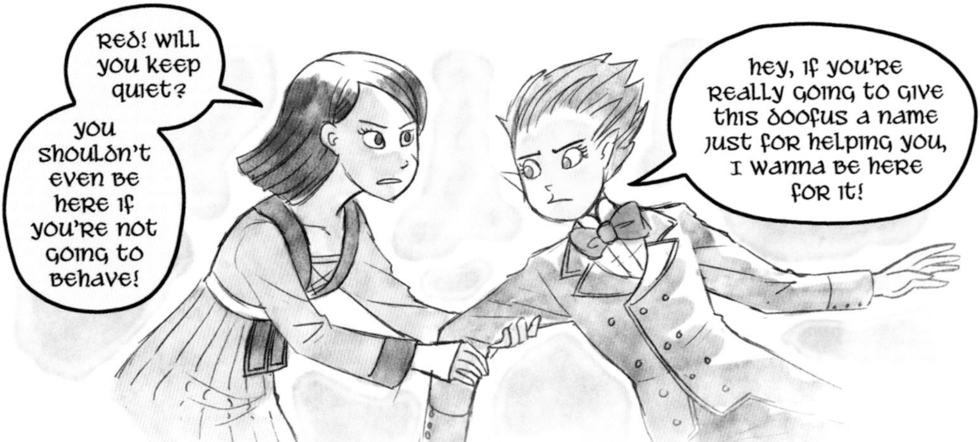
Red! Will you keep quiet?
You shouldn't even be here if you're not going to behave!
Hey, if you're really going to give this doofus a name just for helping you, I wanna be here for it!

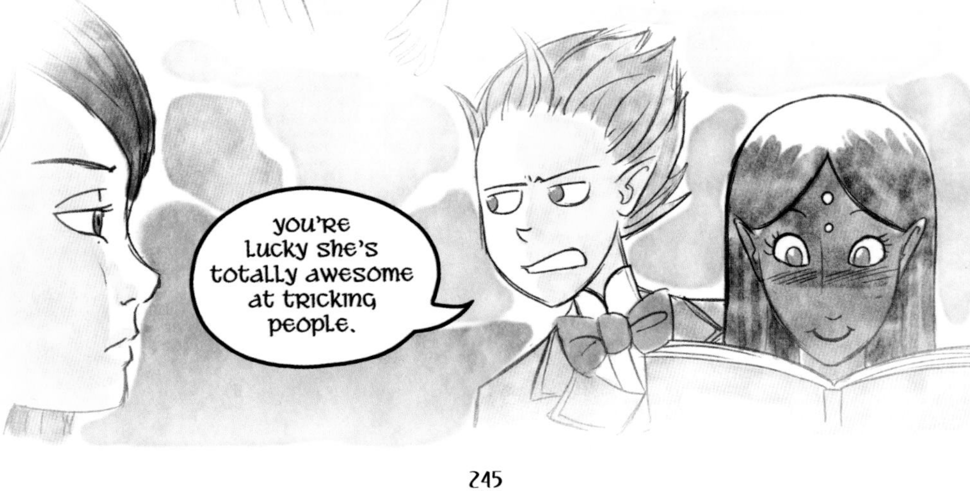
You're lucky she's totally awesome at tricking people.

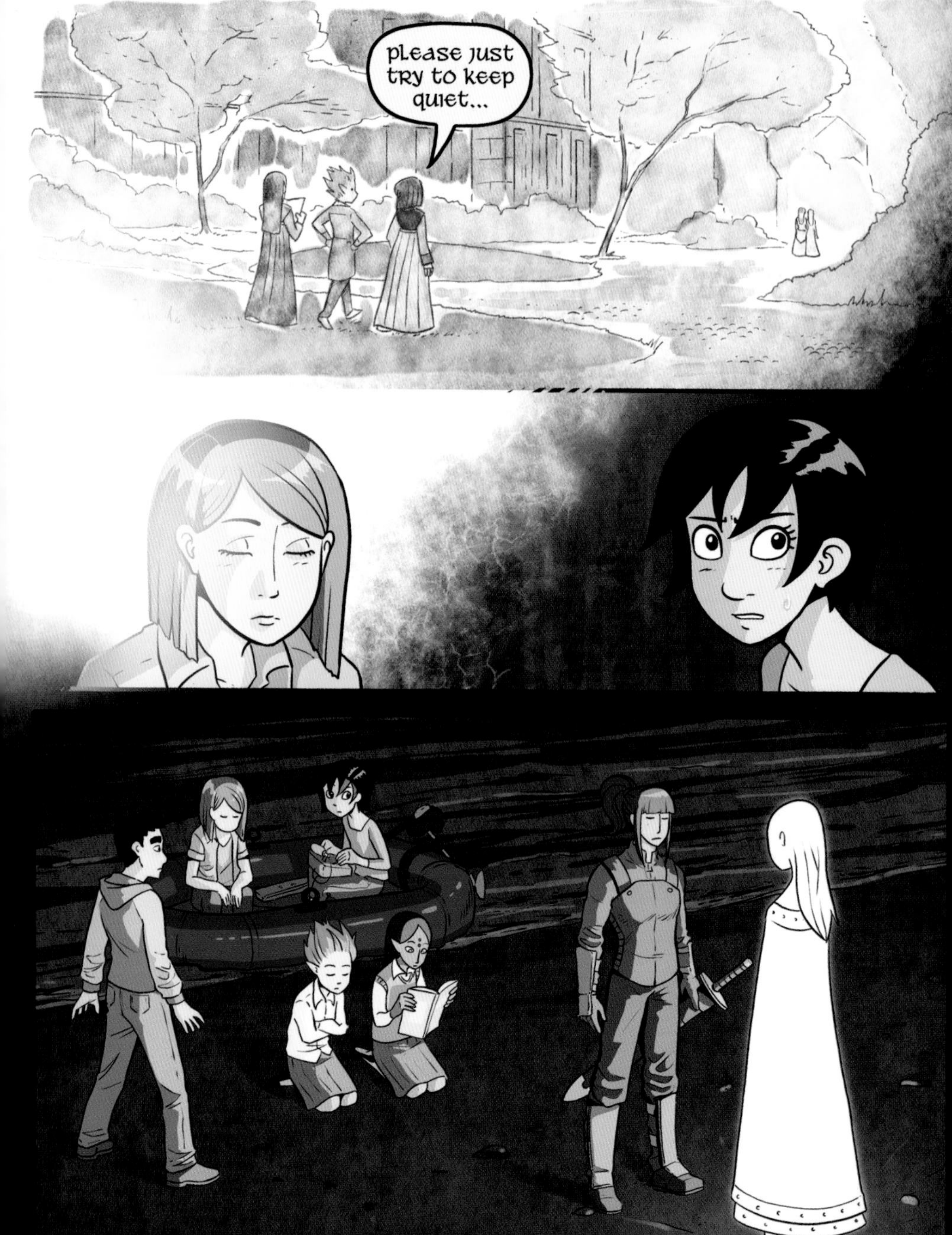
please just try to keep quiet...

IT... WORKED?

I ~ LOOKS LIKE IT...

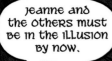

JEANNE AND THE OTHERS MUST BE IN THE ILLUSION BY NOW.

GOOD THING YOU'RE HERE... PARLEY TELEPORTED EVERYONE TO EXACTLY THE RIGHT PLACE.

THAT'S THE PLAN, BUT WE DON'T HAVE MUCH TIME.

DOES YOUR MACHINE WORK?

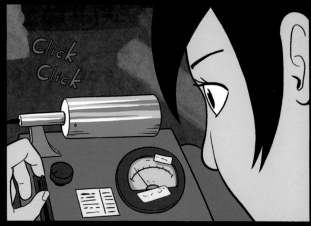

Click
Click

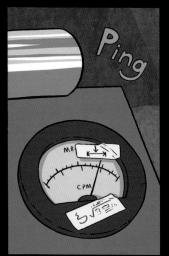

Ping

MR
C.P.M.

phew...

IT'S
GETTING
SOMETHING...

WE'RE
OFF.

ARE YOU
GOING TO BE
OKAY?

WE'LL
SEE.

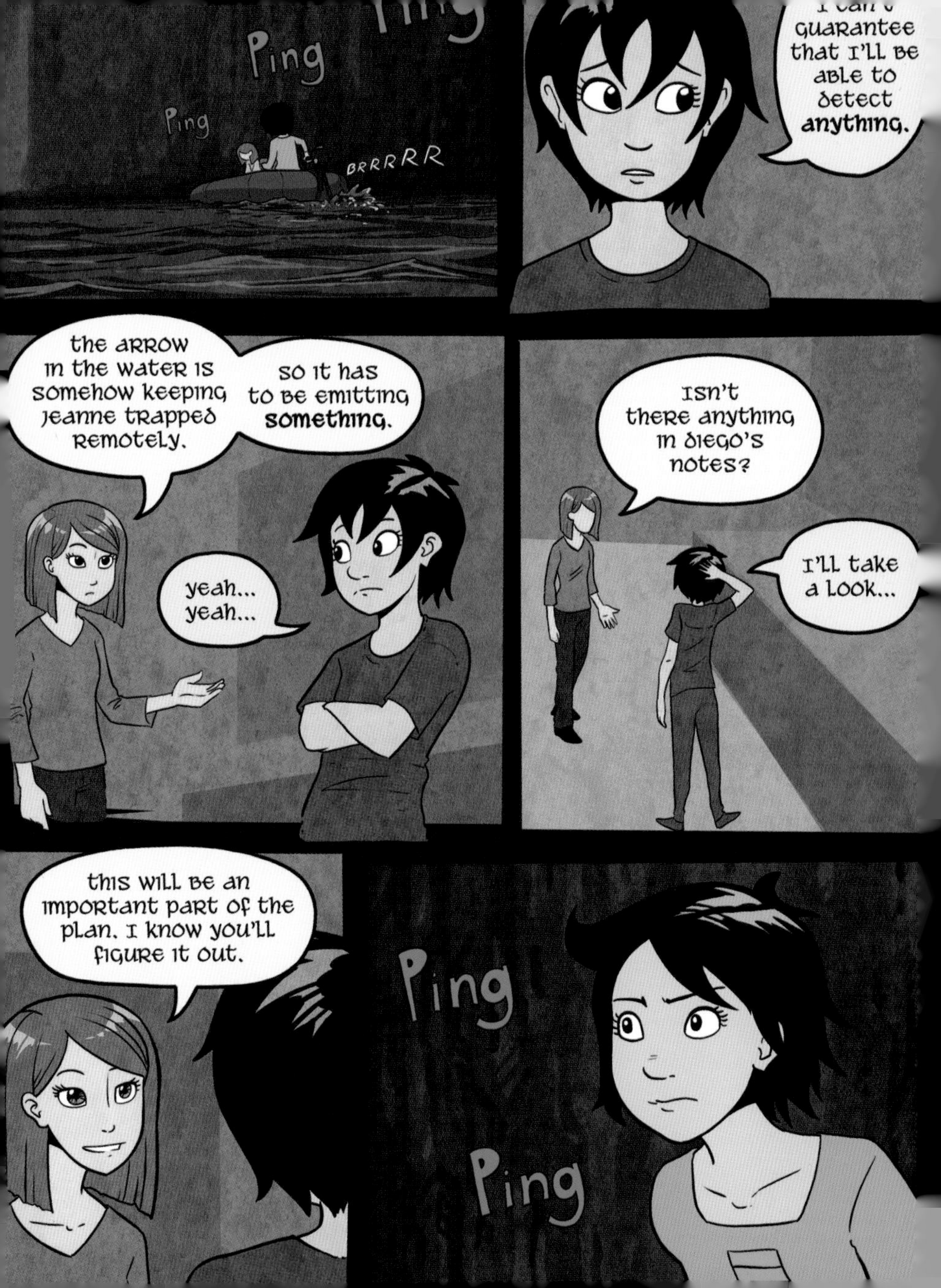
Ping
Ping
BRRRRR
guarantee that I'll be able to detect anything.
the arrow in the water is somehow keeping Jeanne trapped remotely.
so it has to be emitting something.
yeah... yeah...
Isn't there anything in Diego's notes?
I'll take a look...
this will be an important part of the plan. I know you'll figure it out.
Ping
Ping

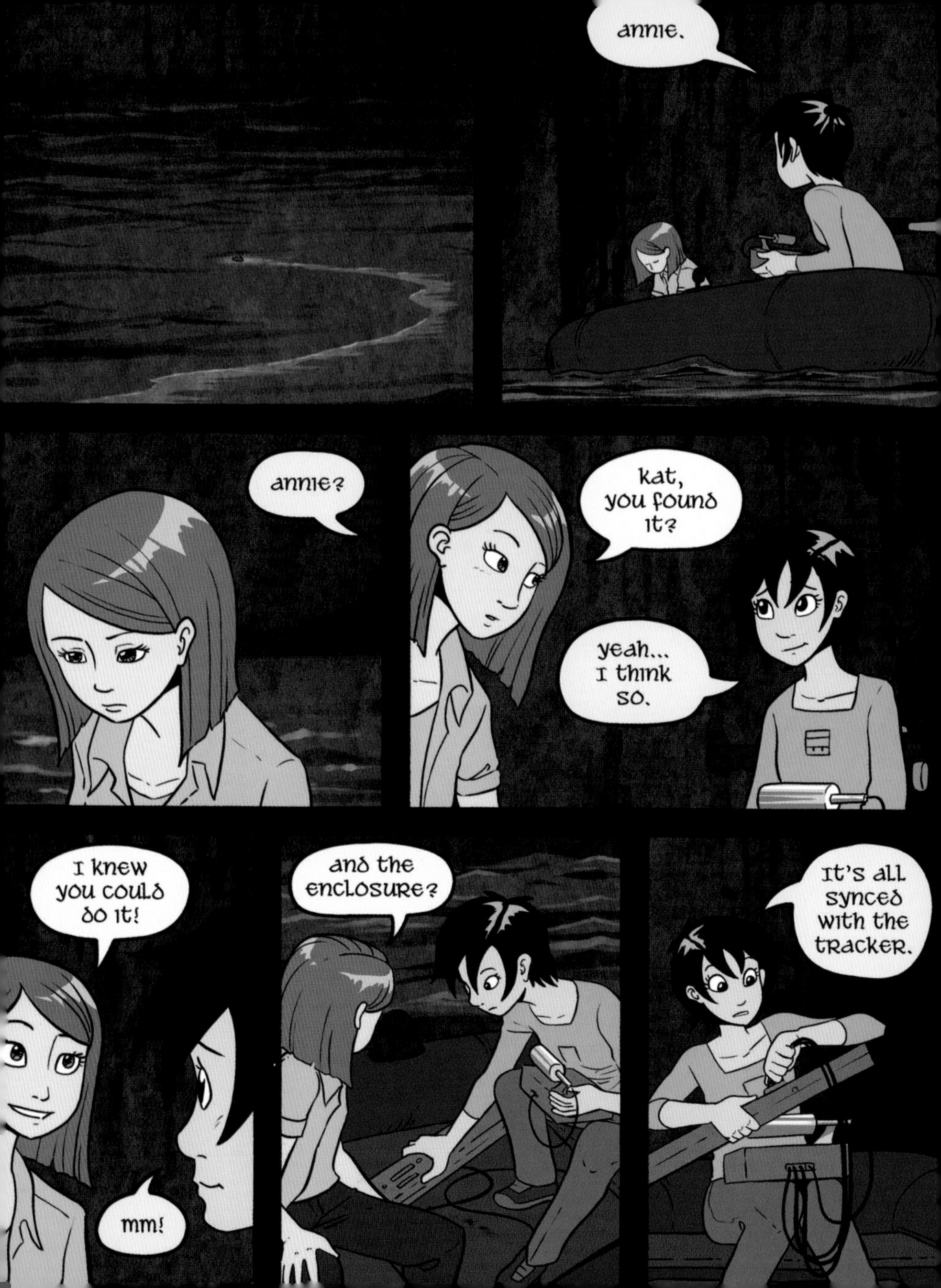
annie.
annie?
kat, you found it?
yeah... I think so.
I knew you could do it!
mm!
and the enclosure?
It's all synced with the tracker.

WELL THEN, DOWN I GO!

ANNIE...

Squeeze

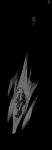

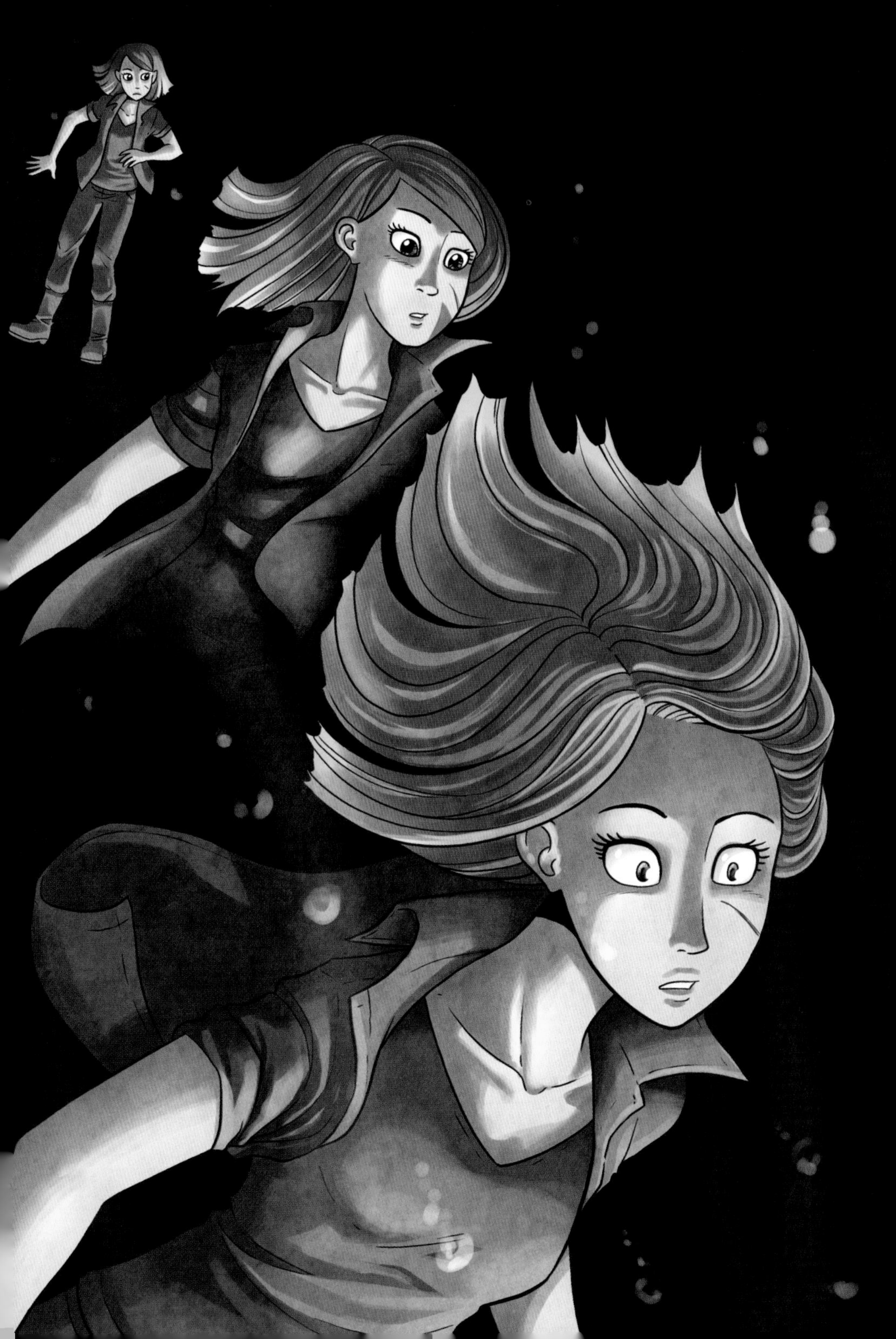

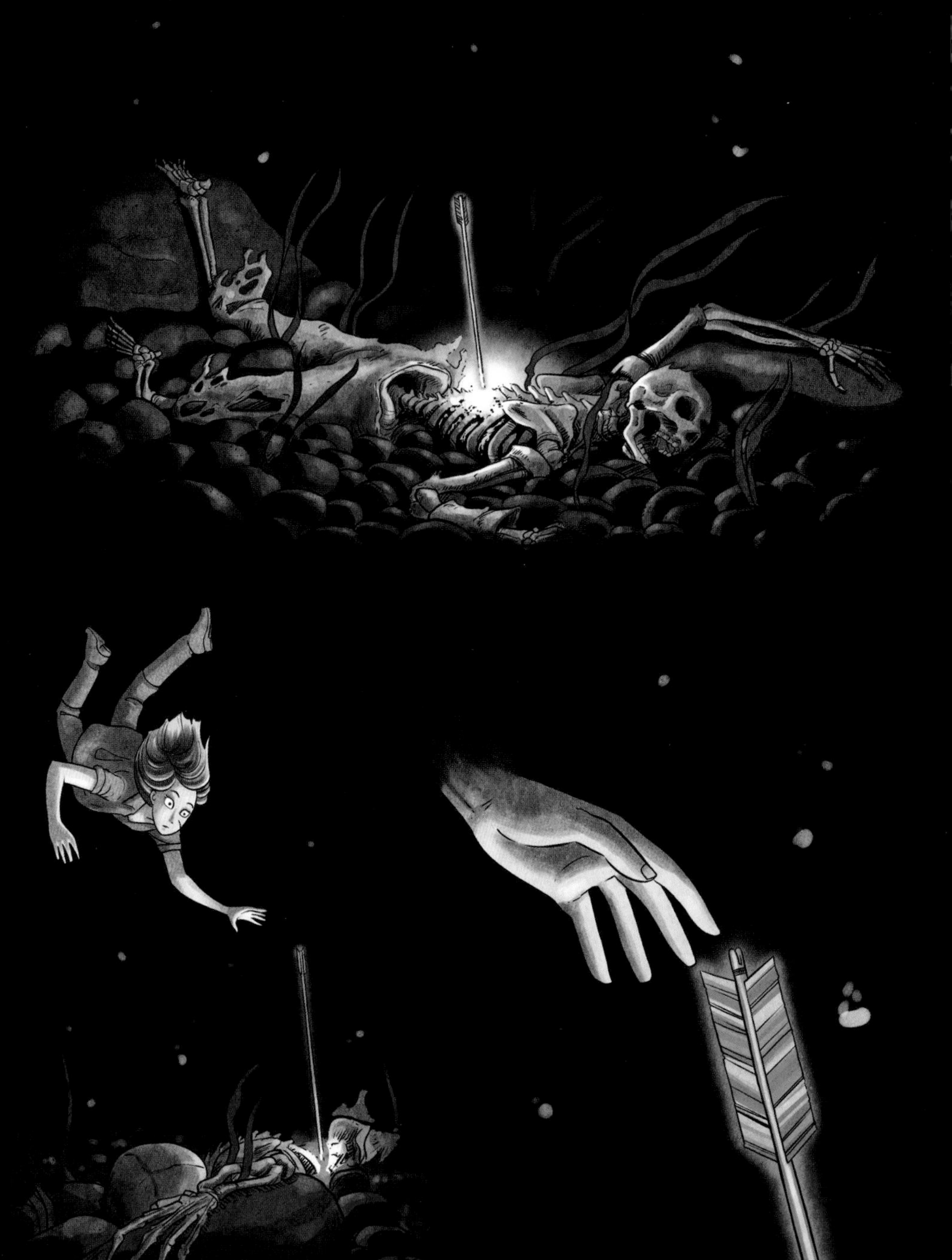

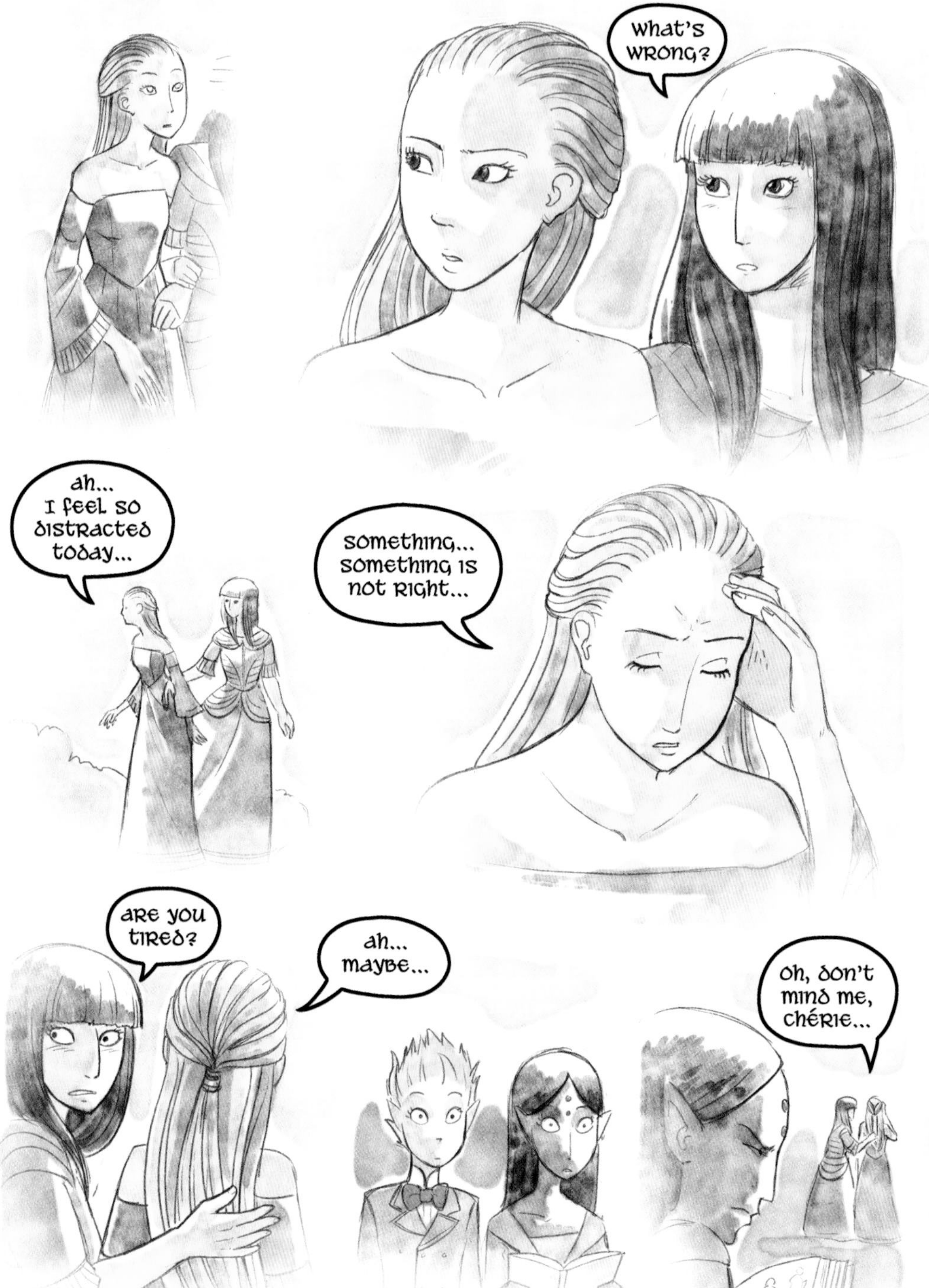
What's wrong?
ah... I feel so distracted today...
something... something is not right...
are you tired?
ah... maybe...
Oh, don't mind me, chérie...

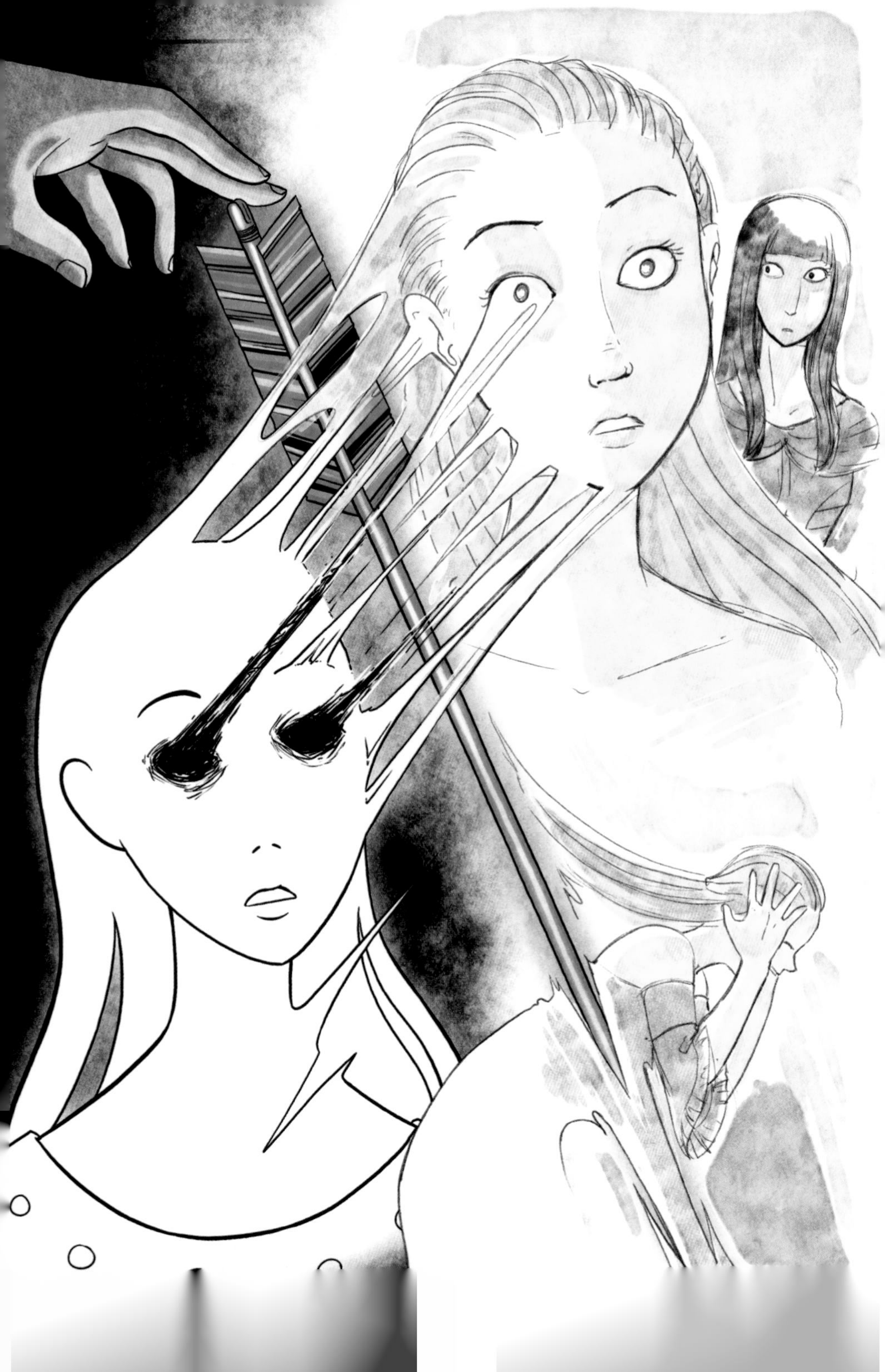

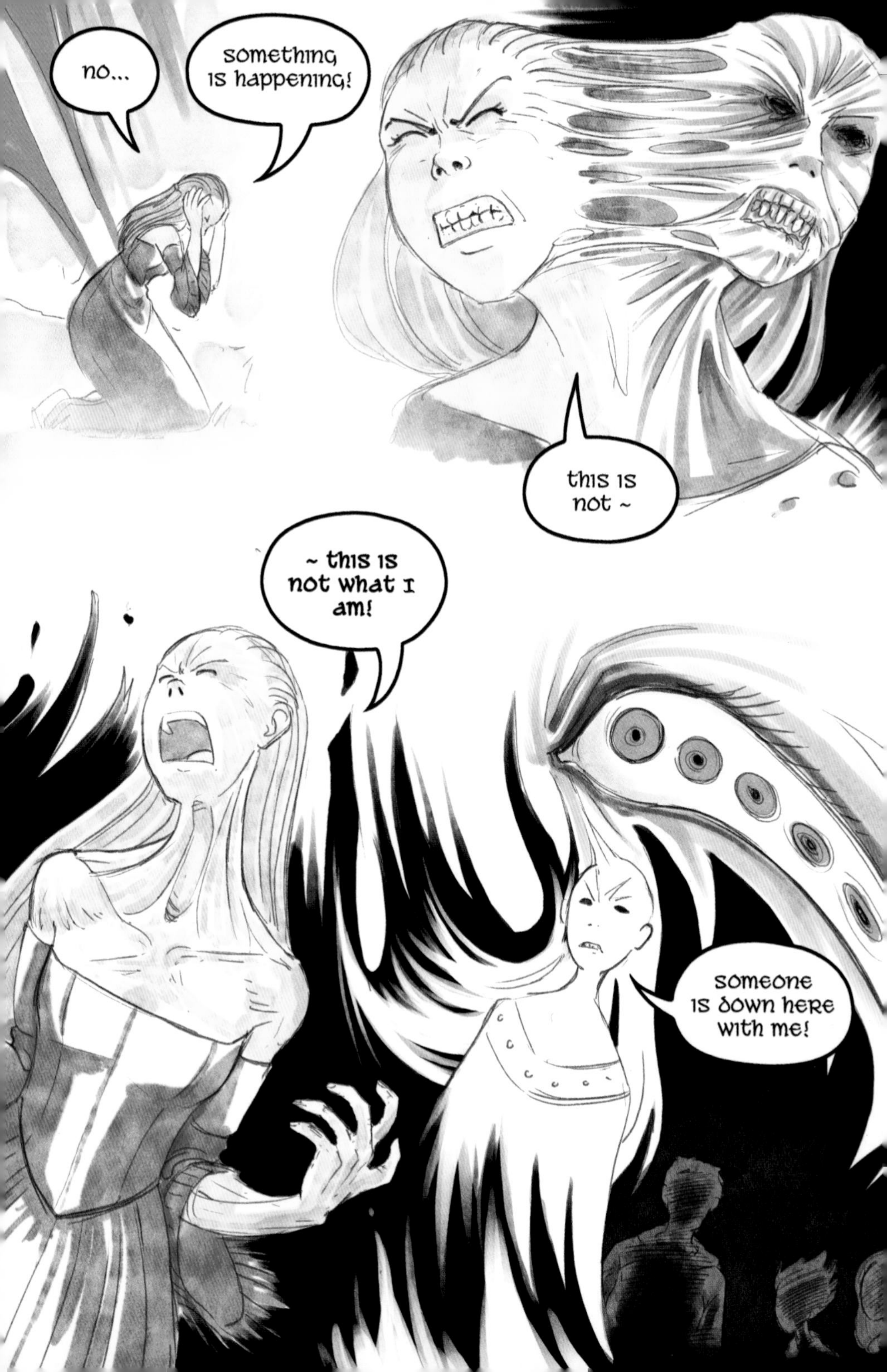
no...
something is happening!
this is not ~
~ this is not what I am!
someone is down here with me!

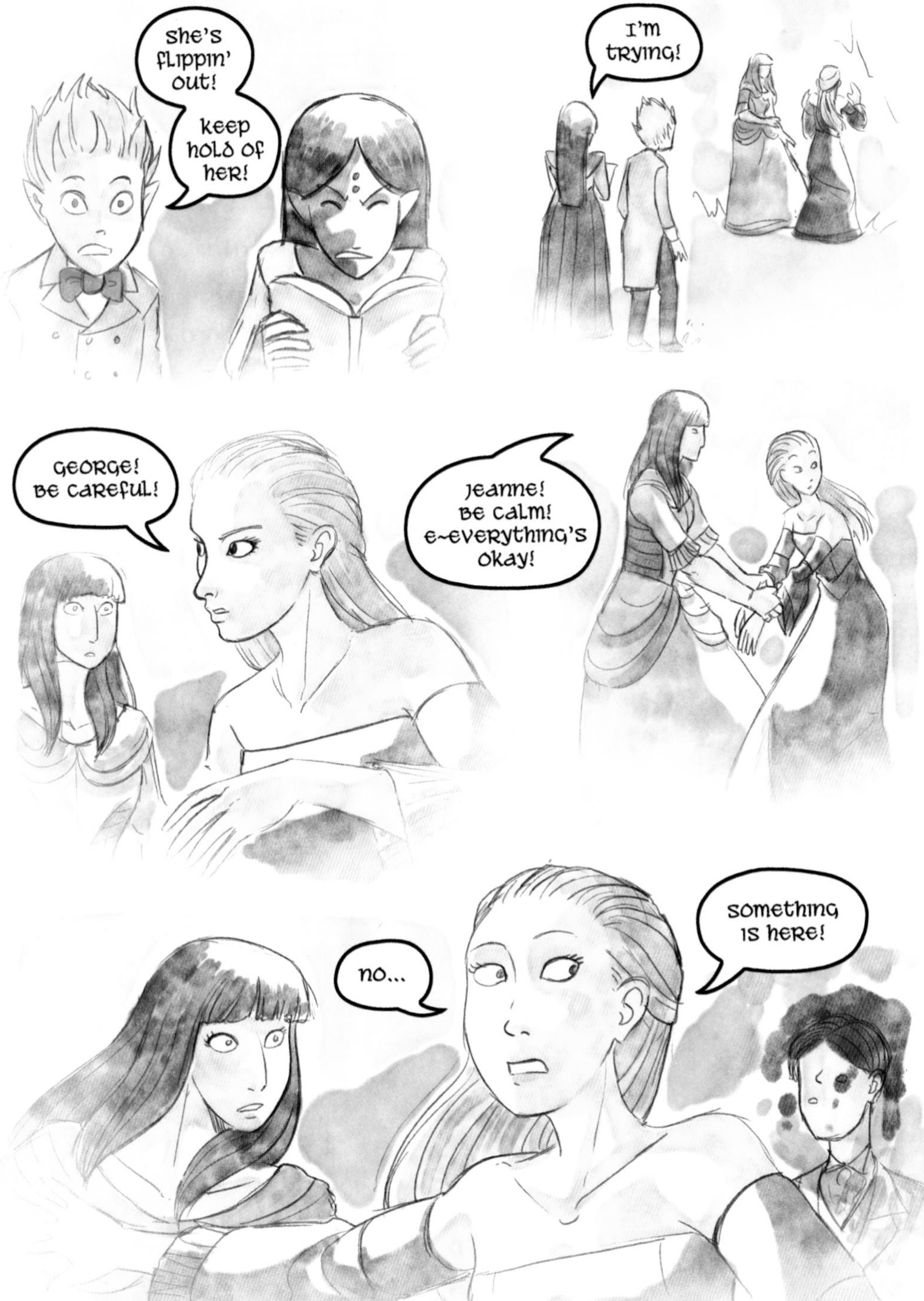
She's flippin' out!
Keep hold of her!
I'm trying!
George! Be careful!
Jeanne! Be calm! E-everything's okay!
No...
Something is here!

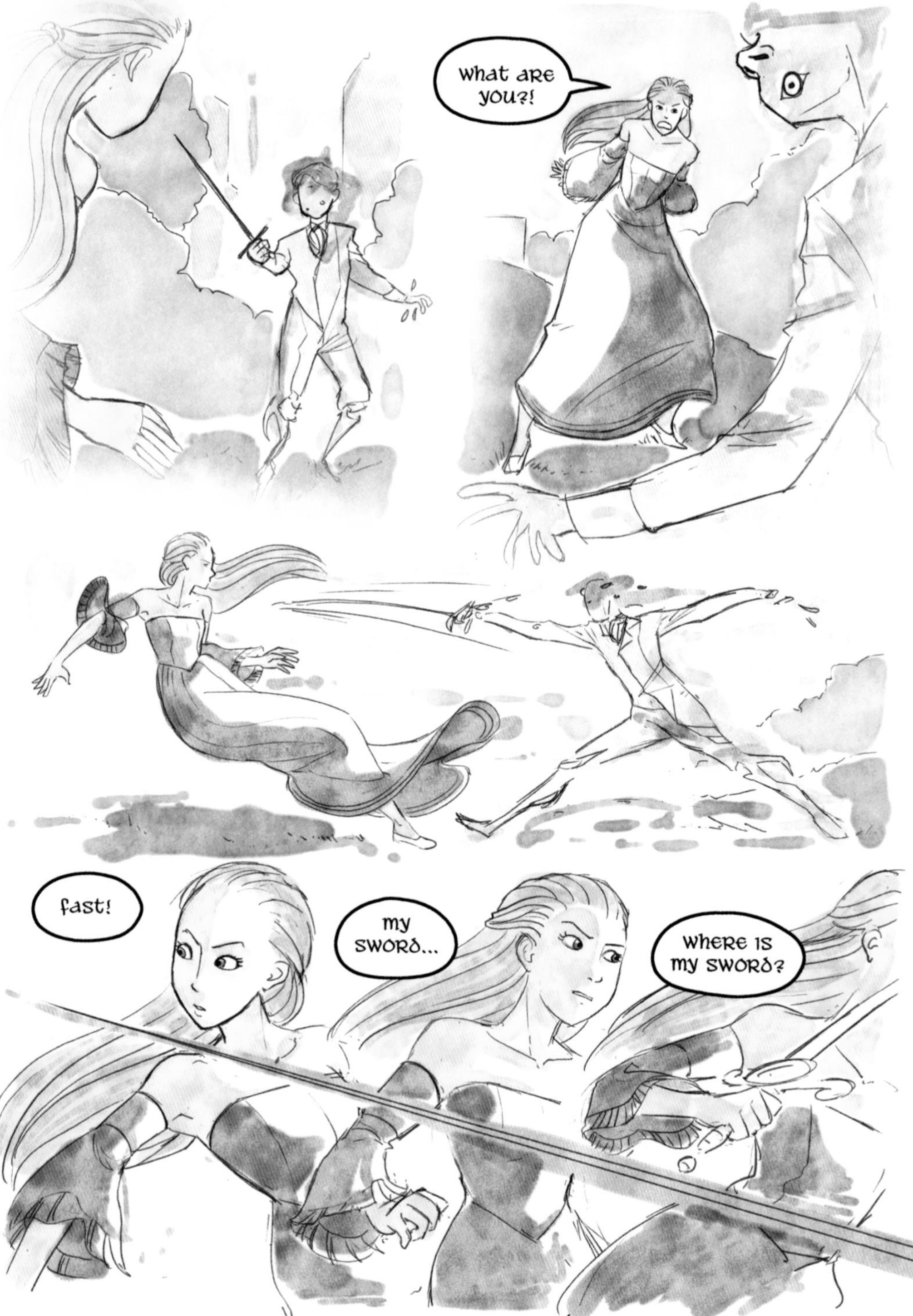
what are you?!
fast!
my sword...
where is my sword?

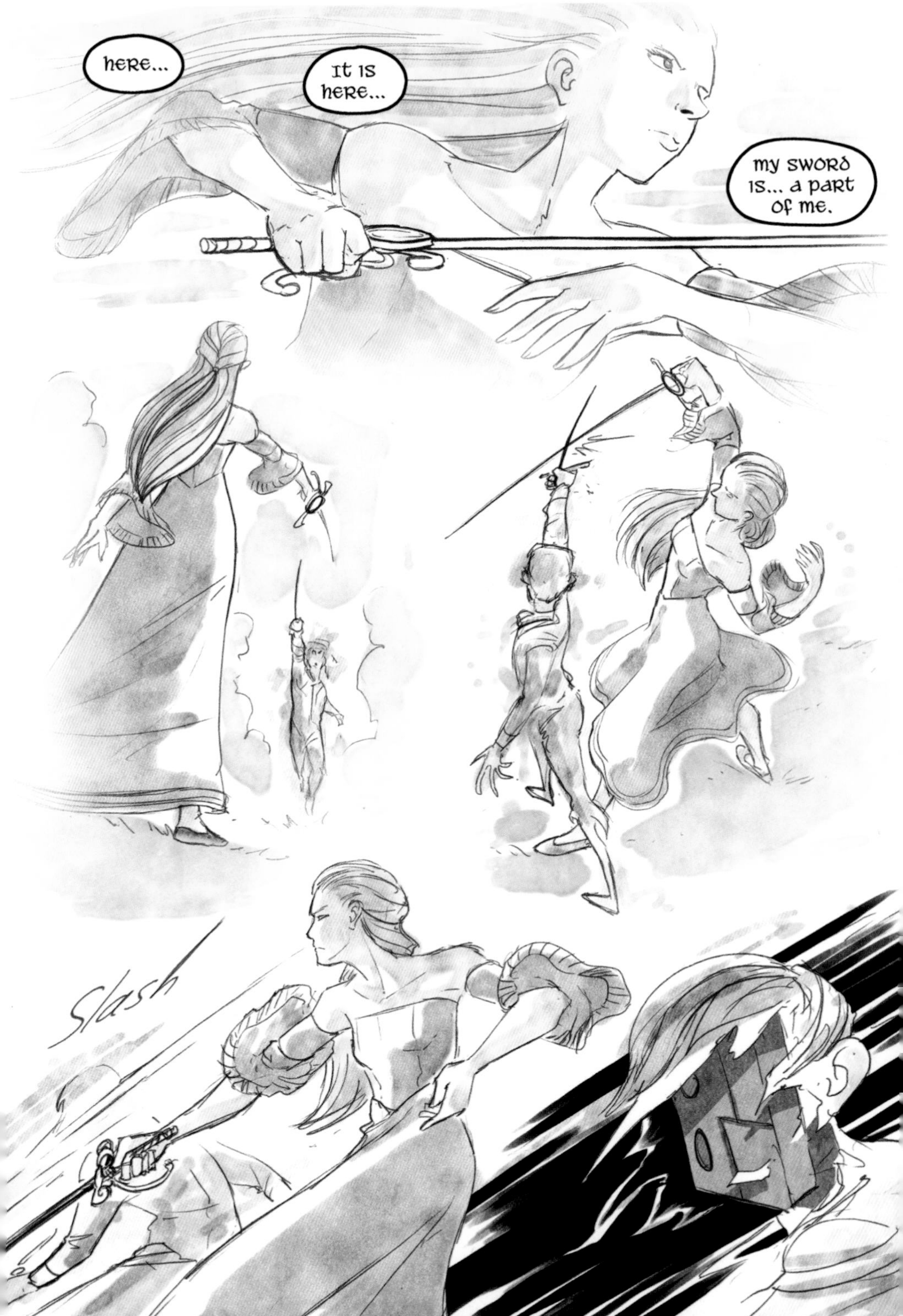
here...
It is here...
my sword is... a part of me.
Slash

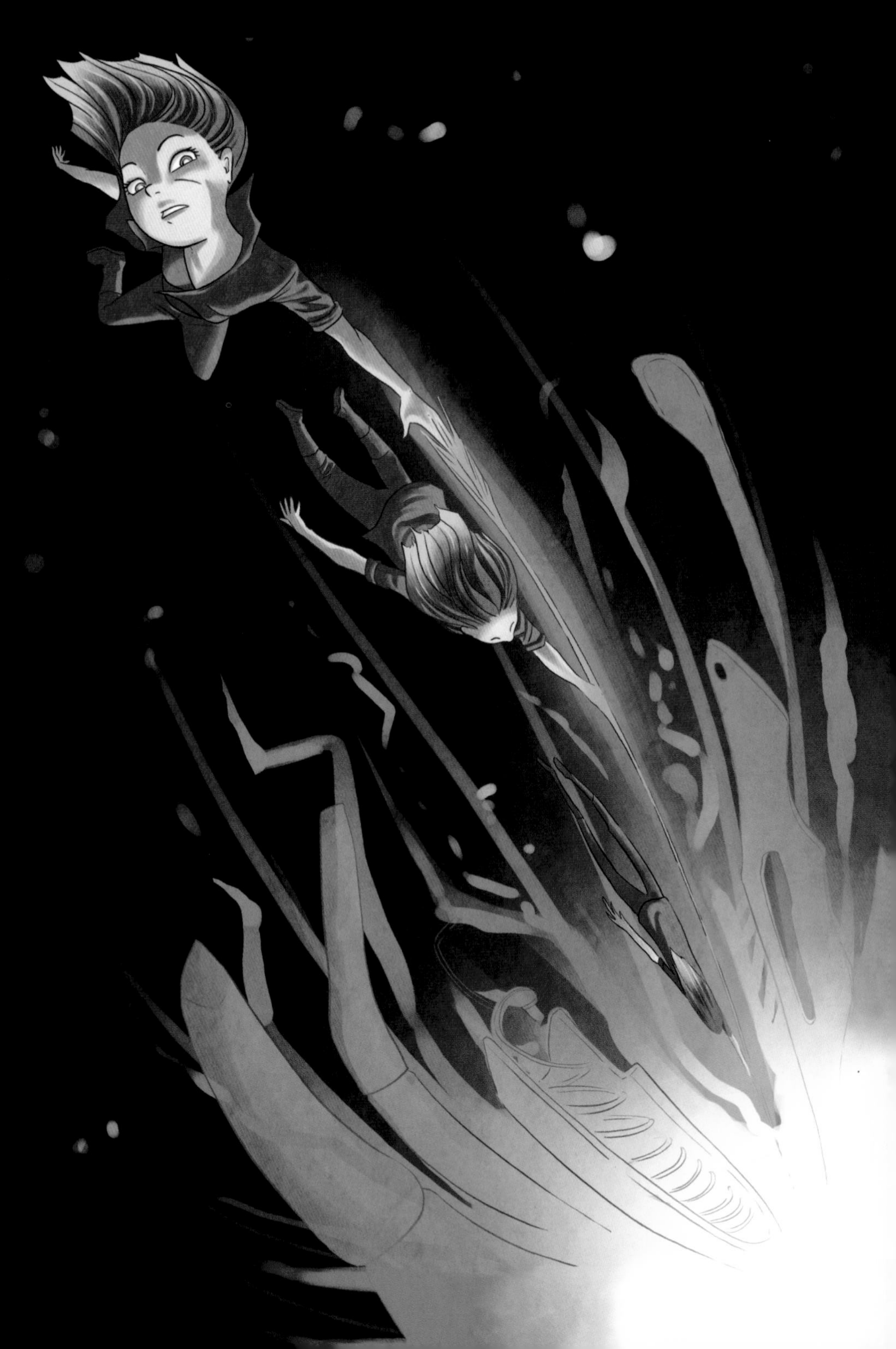

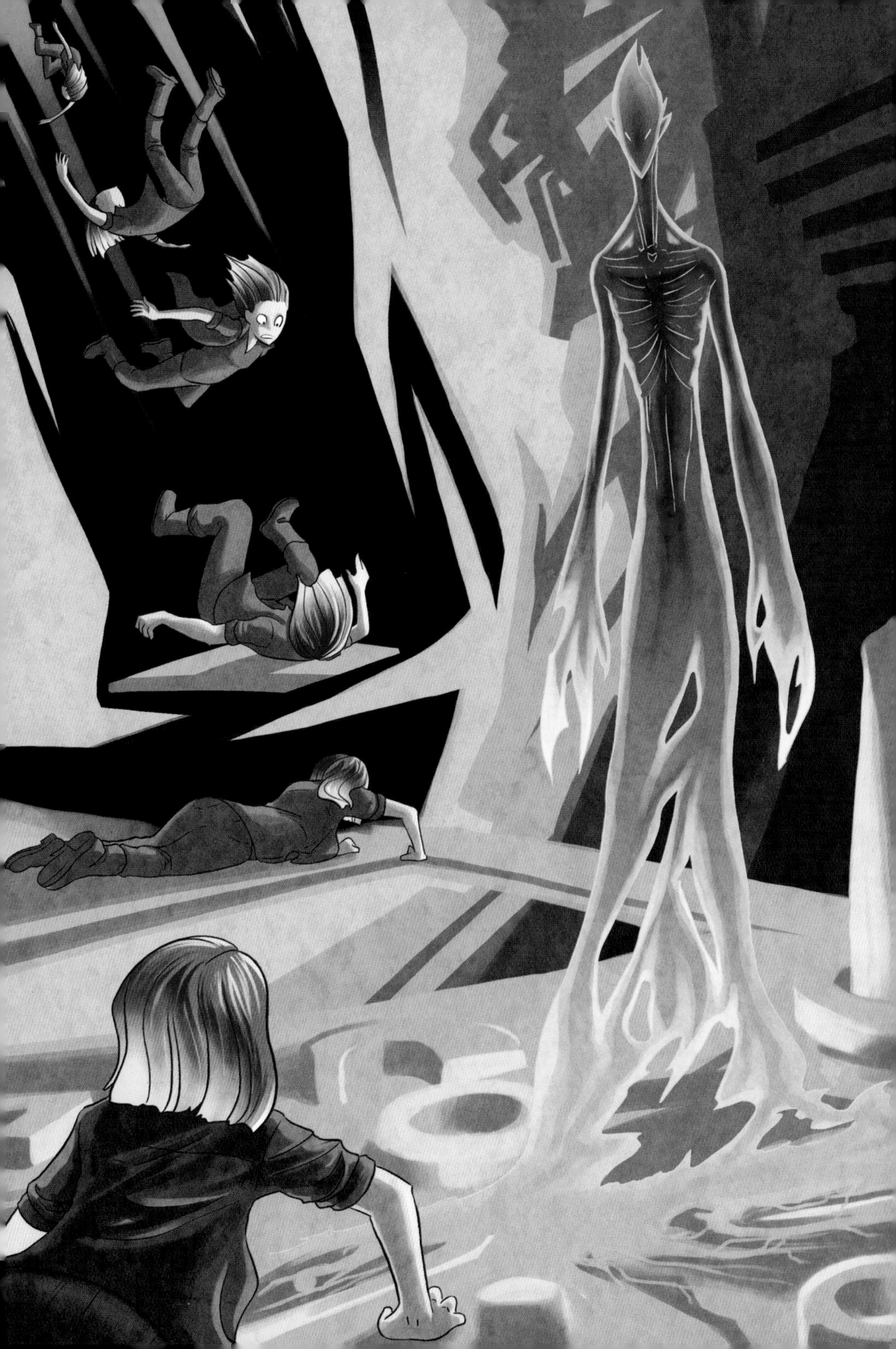

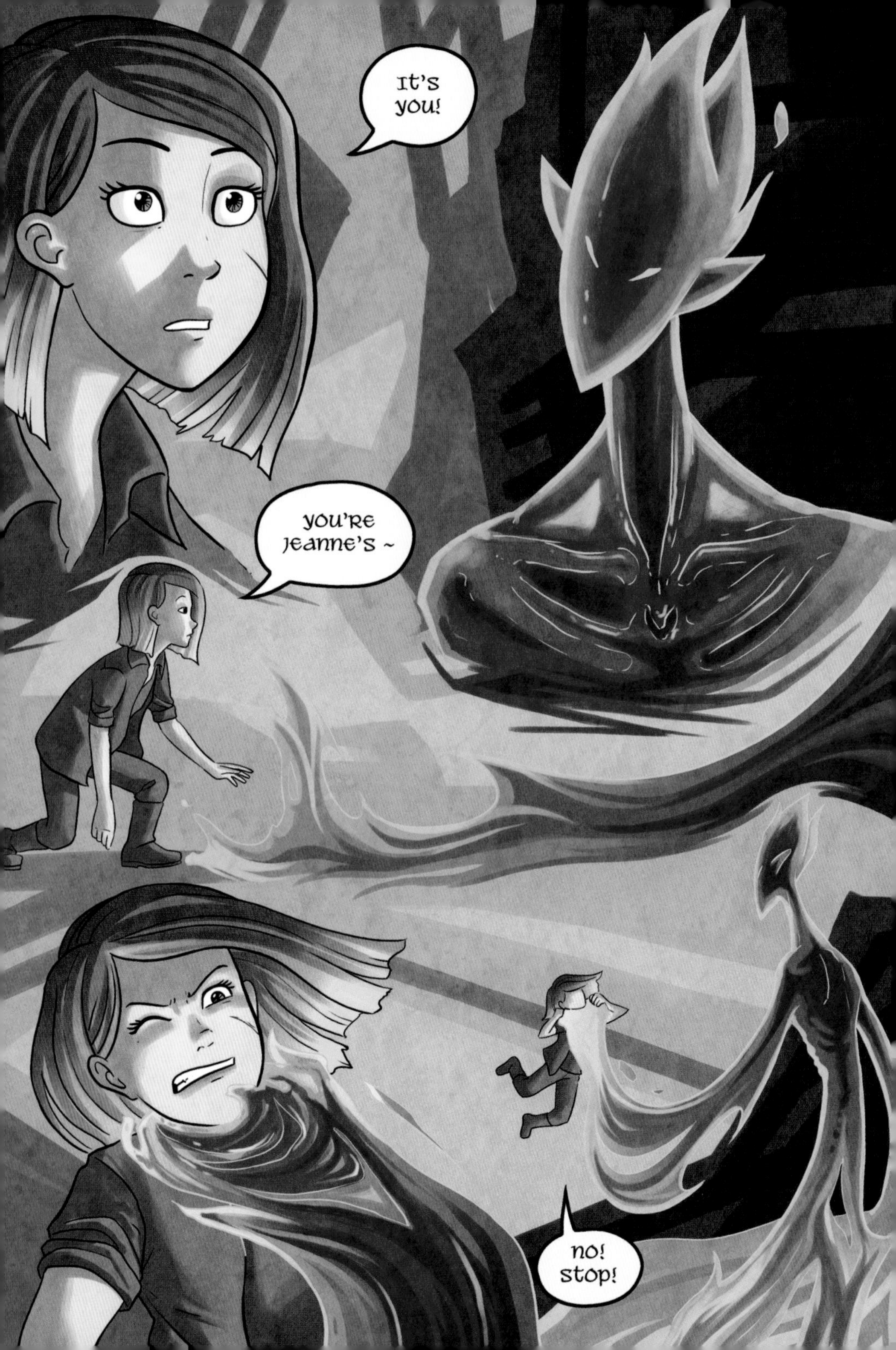
It's you!
You're Jeanne's ~
no! stop!

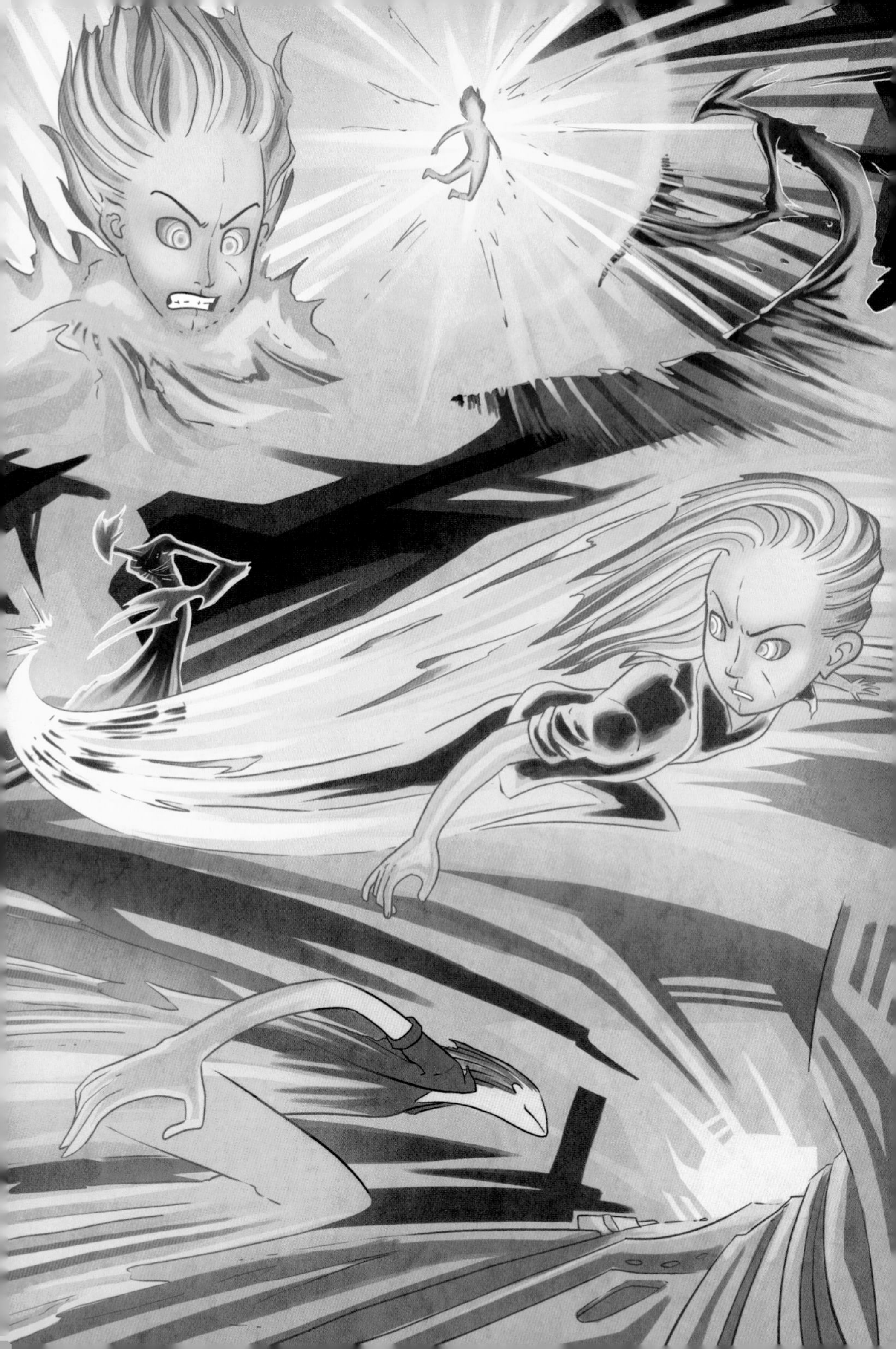

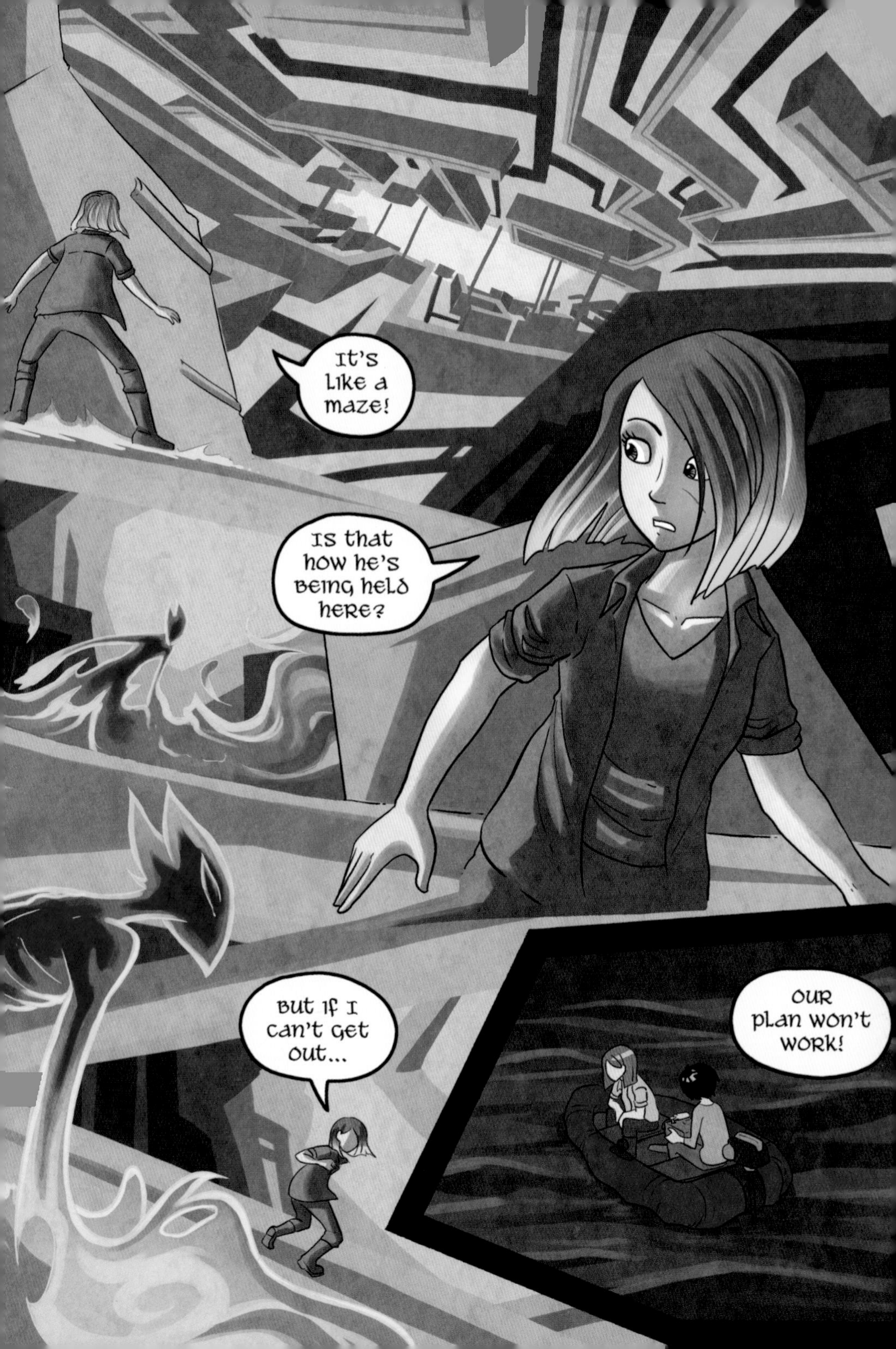
IT'S LIKE A MAZE!
IS THAT HOW HE'S BEING HELD HERE?
BUT IF I CAN'T GET OUT...
OUR PLAN WON'T WORK!

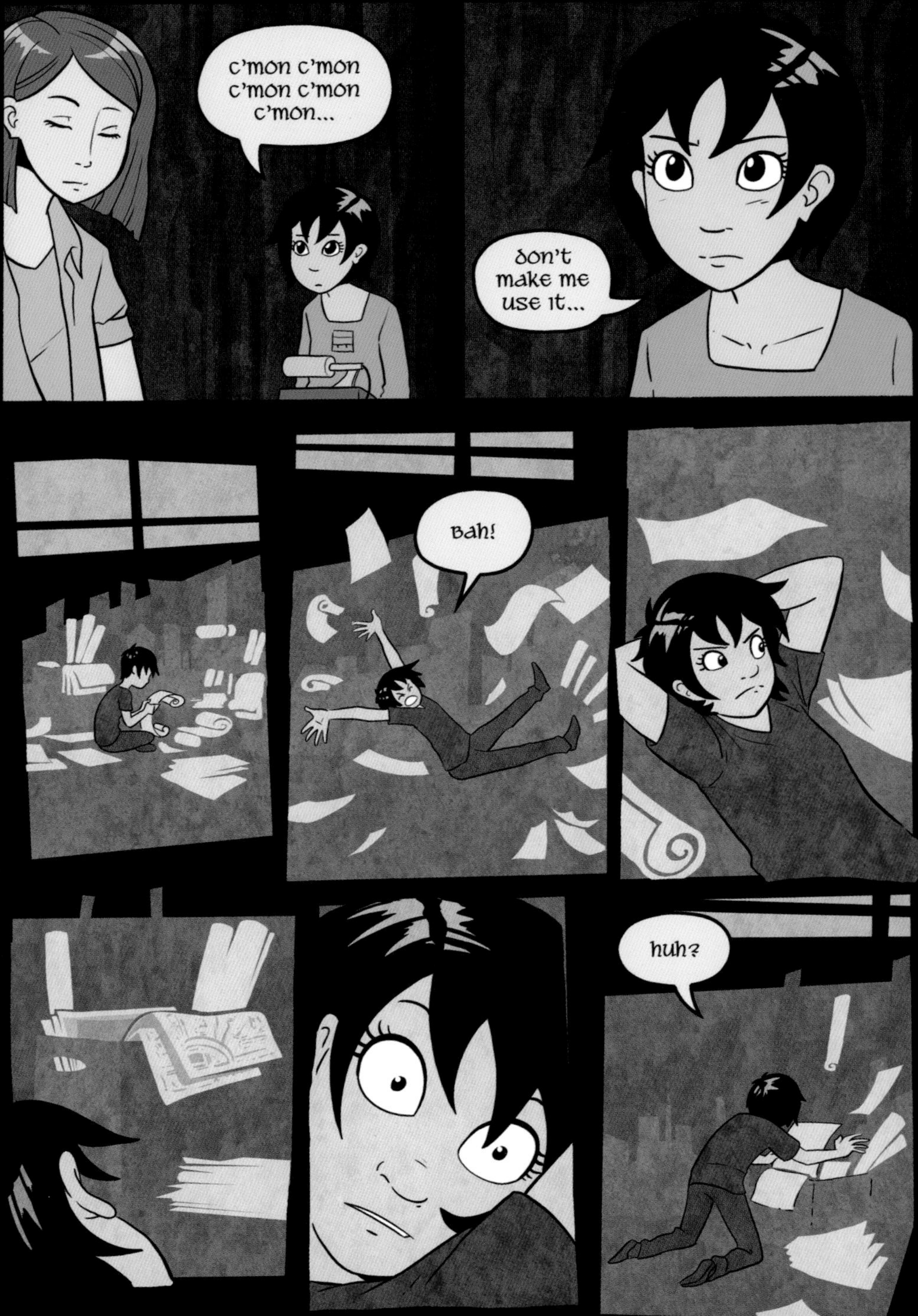
c'mon c'mon
c'mon c'mon
c'mon...
don't
make me
use it...
Bah!
huh?

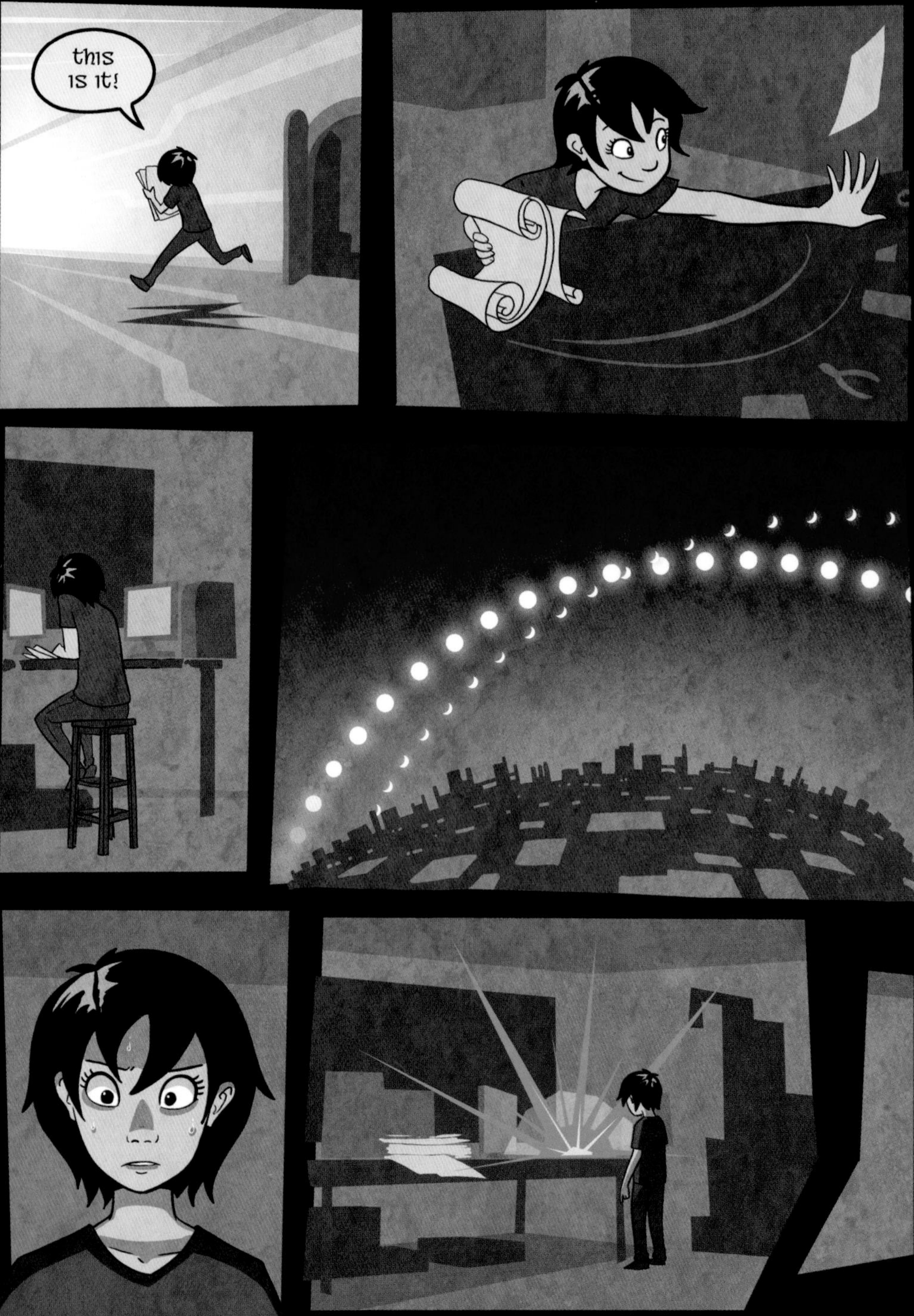
this is it!

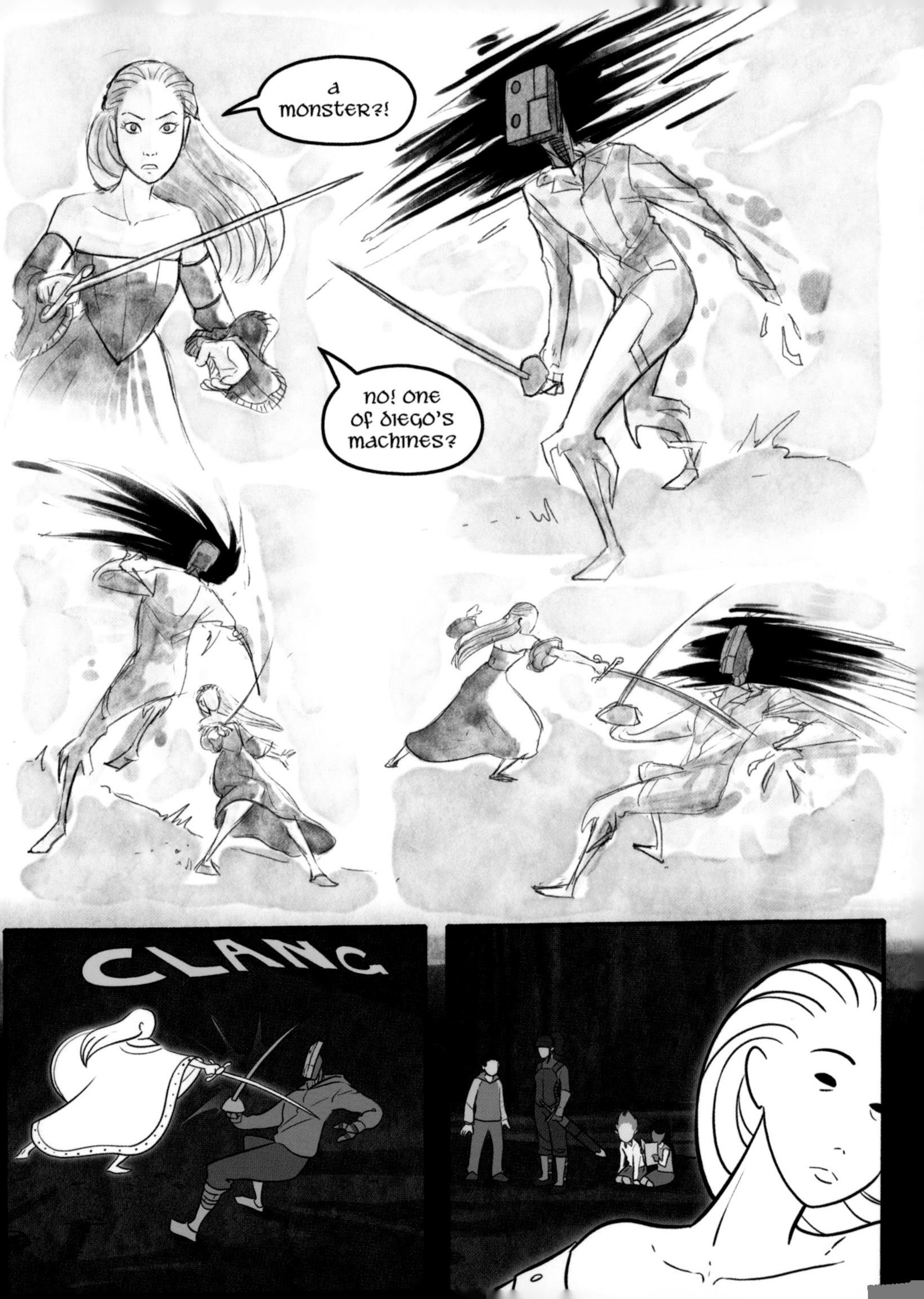
a monster?!
no! one of diego's machines?
CLANG

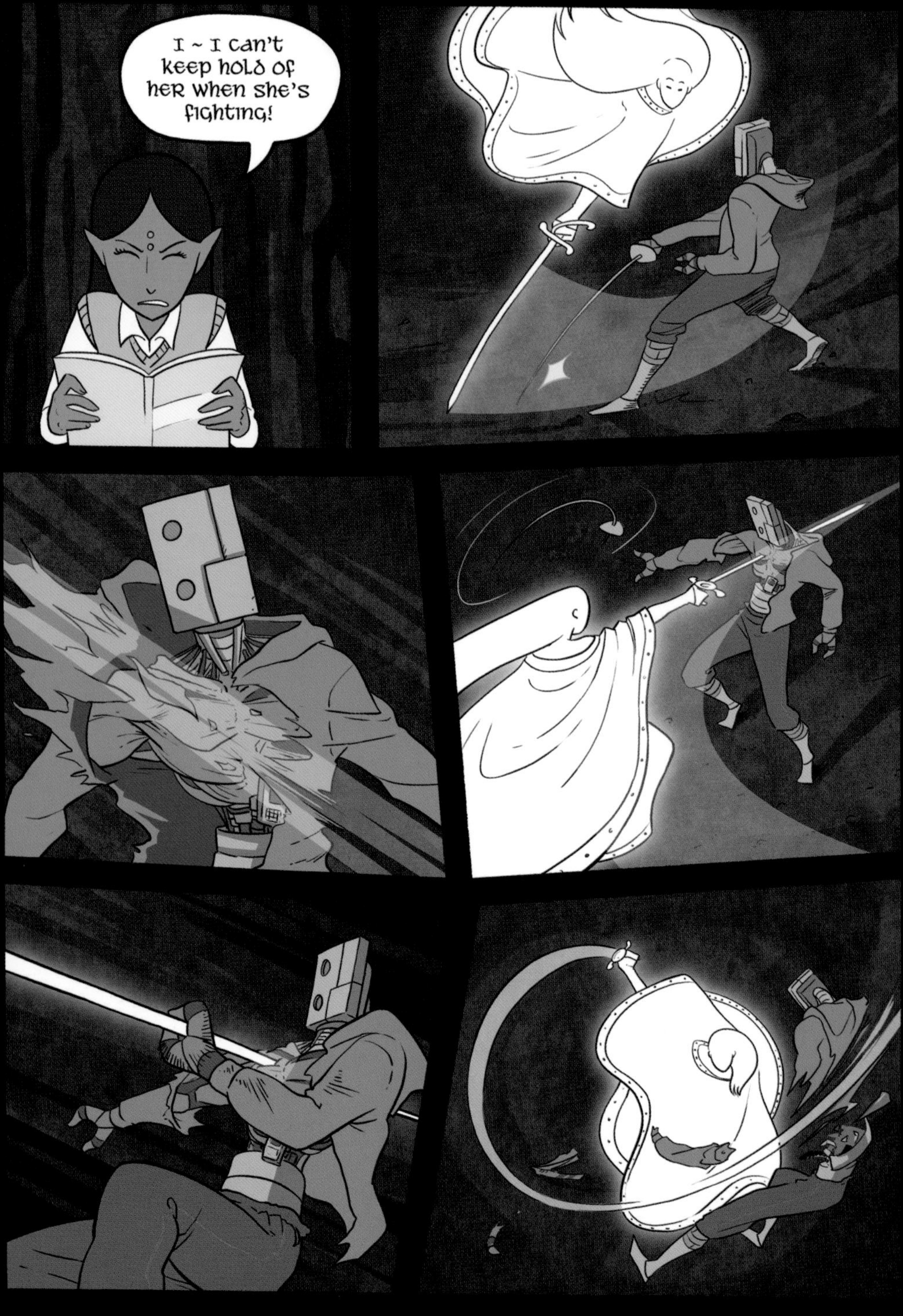
I ~ I can't keep hold of her when she's fighting!

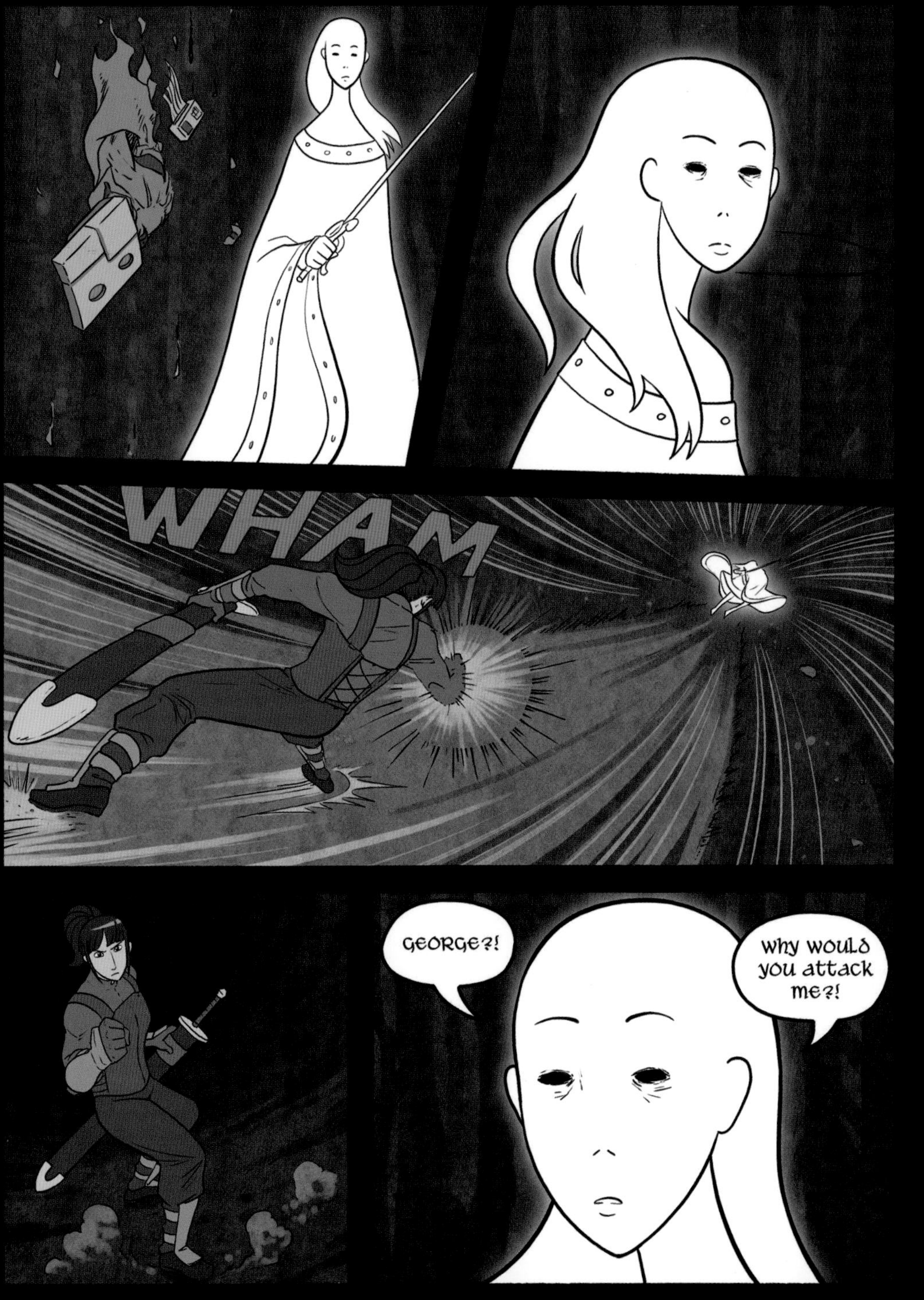
WHAM
GEORGE?!
WHY WOULD YOU ATTACK ME?!

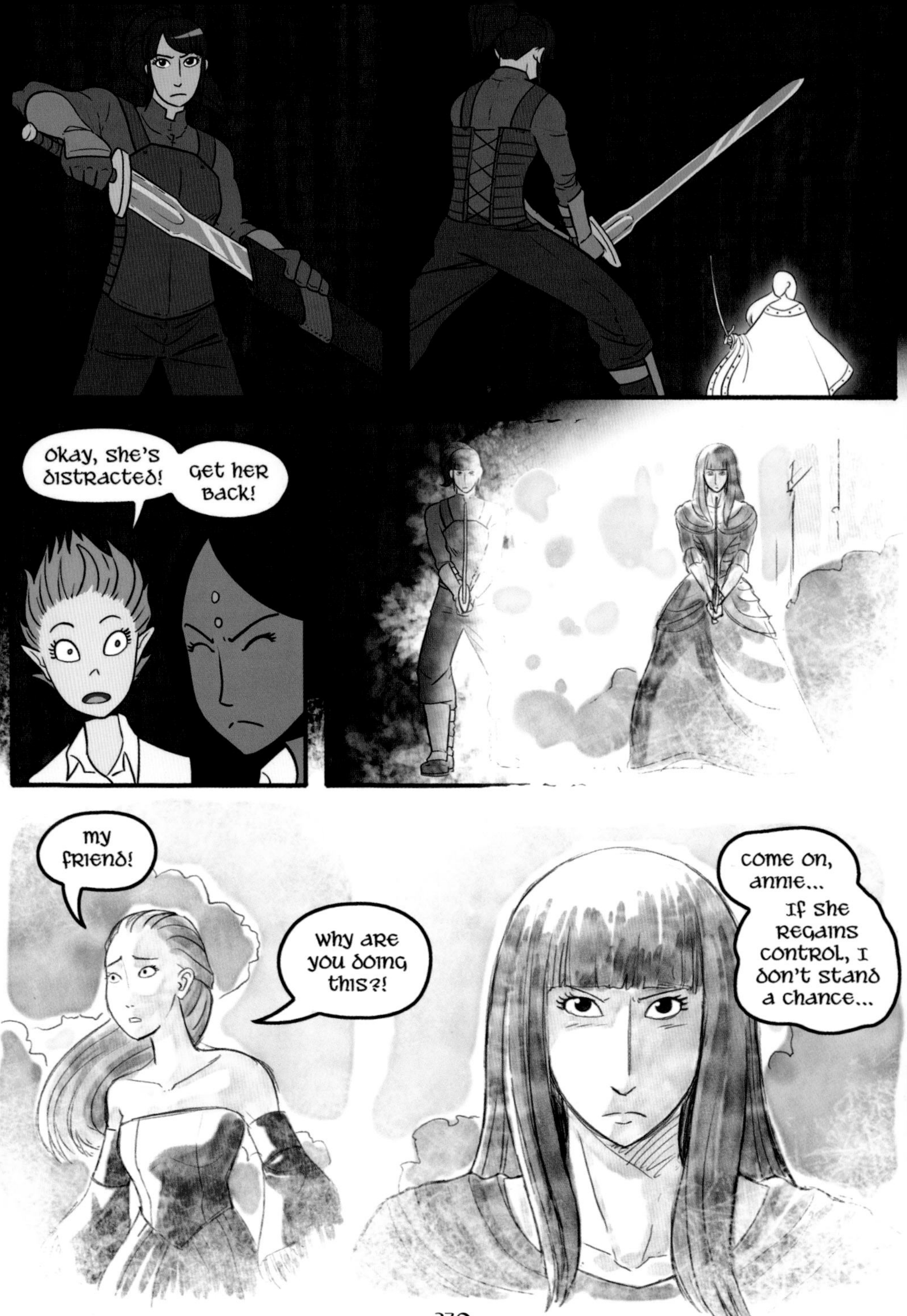
Okay, she's distracted!
Get her back!
my friend!
Why are you doing this?!
Come on, Annie...
If she regains control, I don't stand a chance...

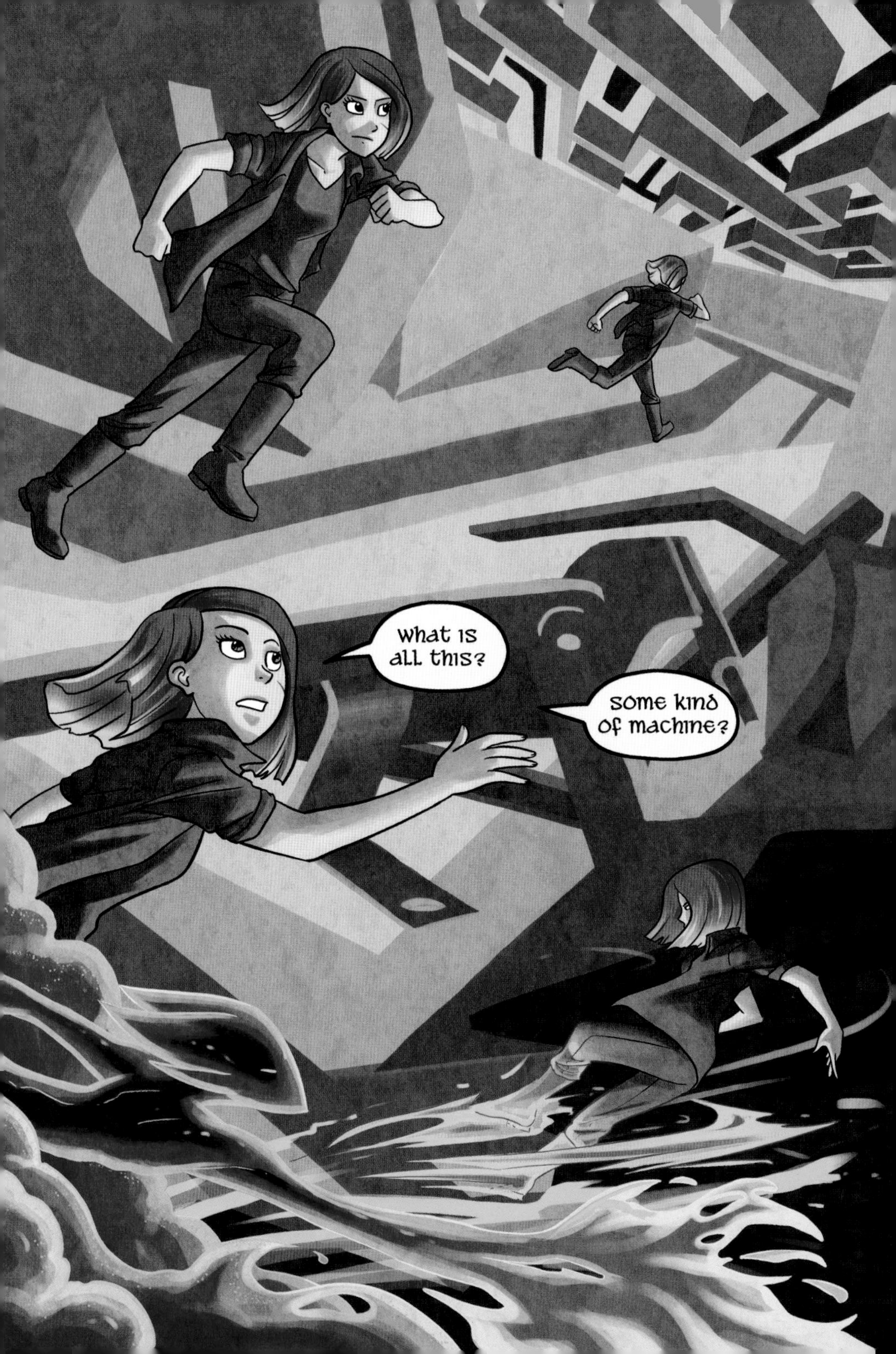
What is
all this?
Some kind
of machine?

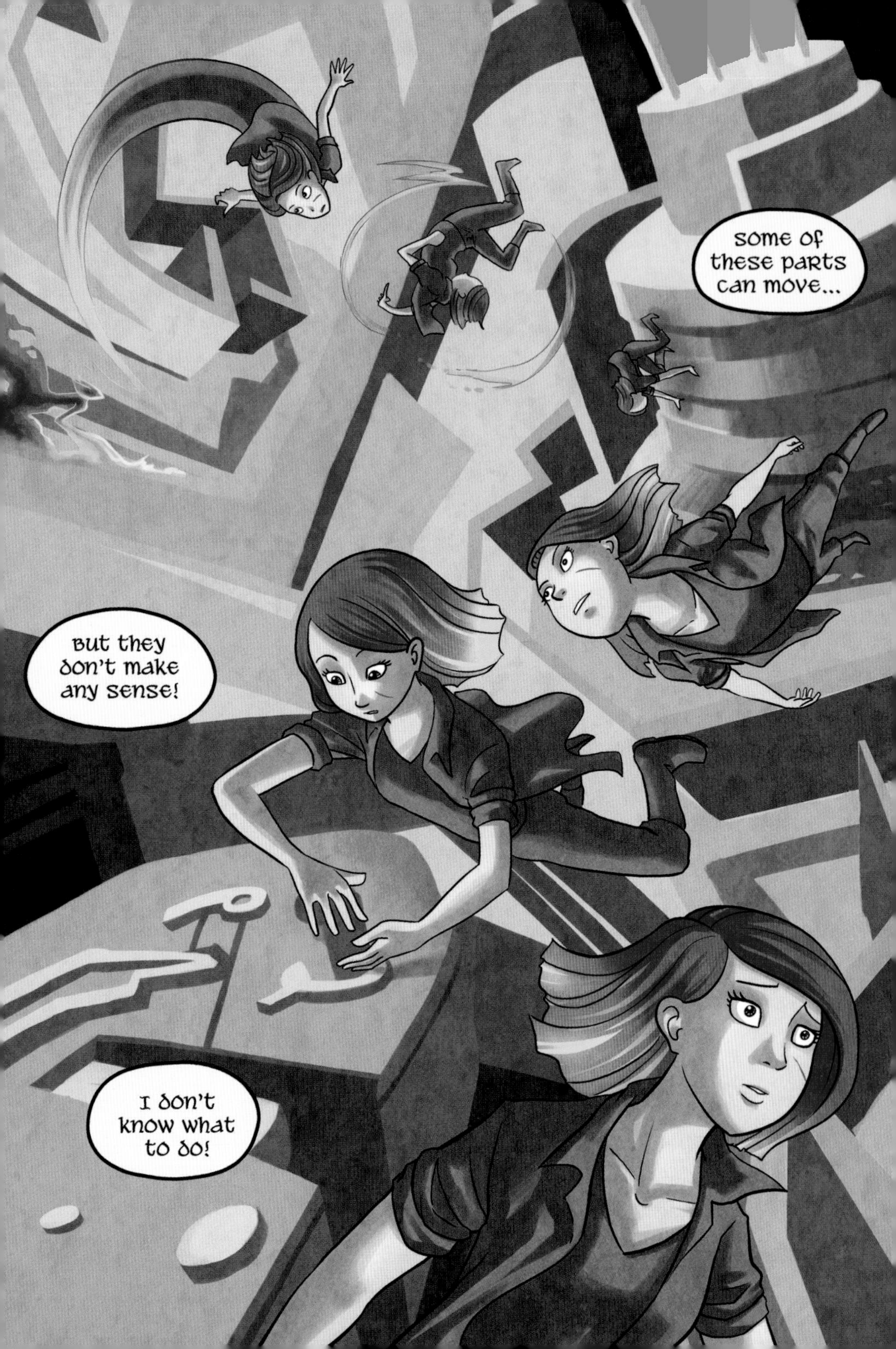
some of these parts can move...
but they don't make any sense!
I don't know what to do!

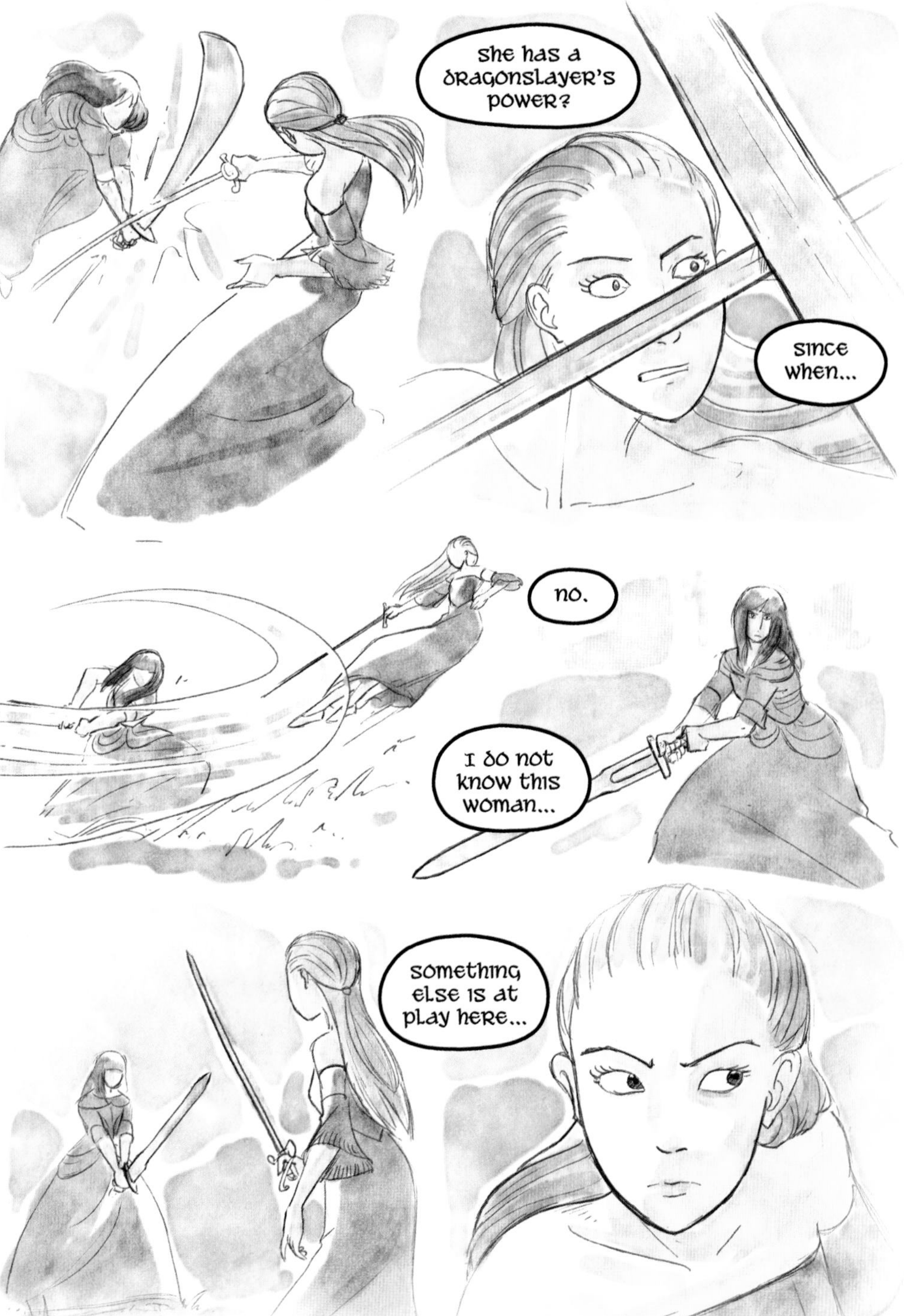
she has a dragonslayer's power?
since when...
no.
I do not know this woman...
something else is at play here...

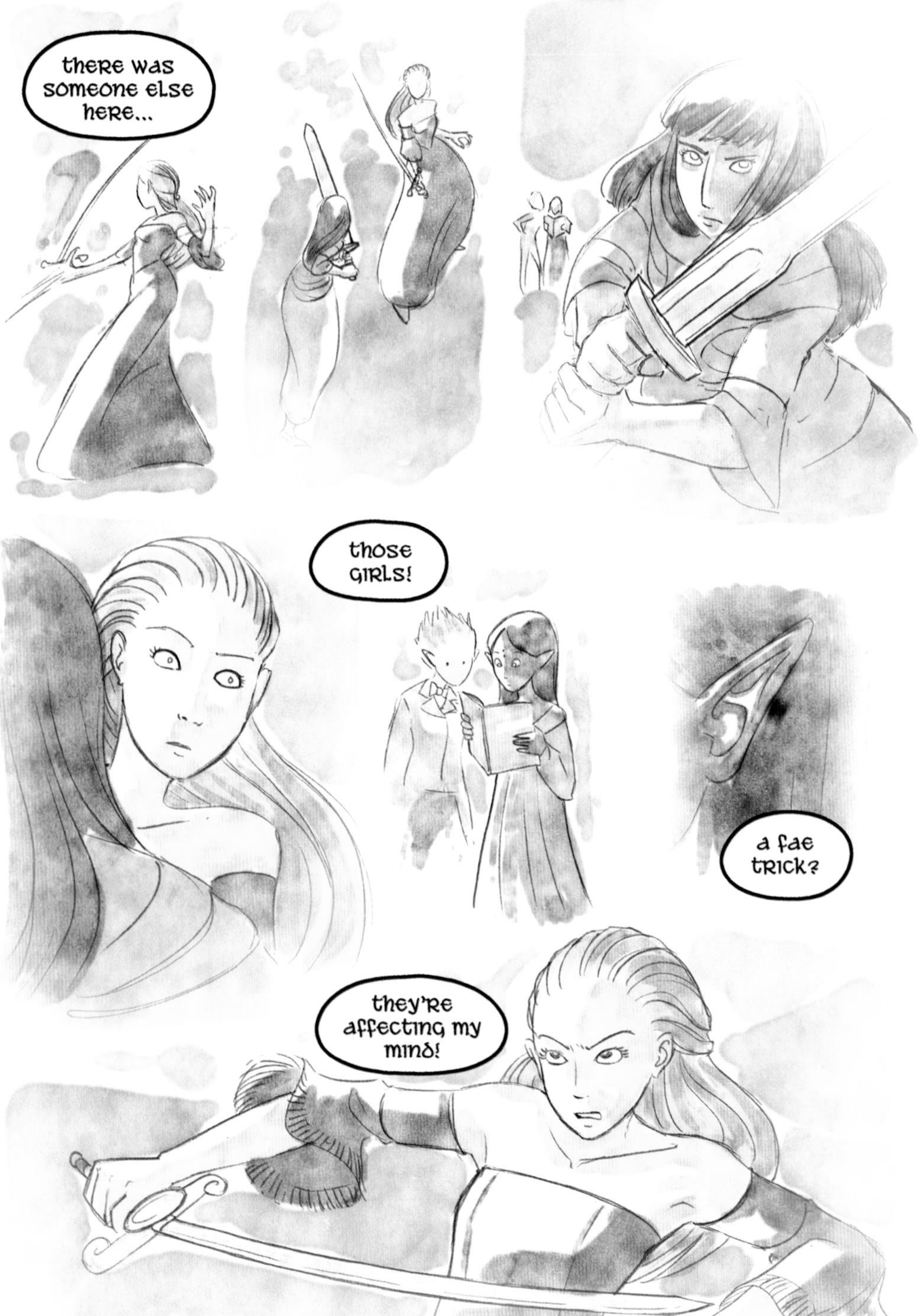
there was someone else here...
those girls!
a fae trick?
they're affecting my mind!

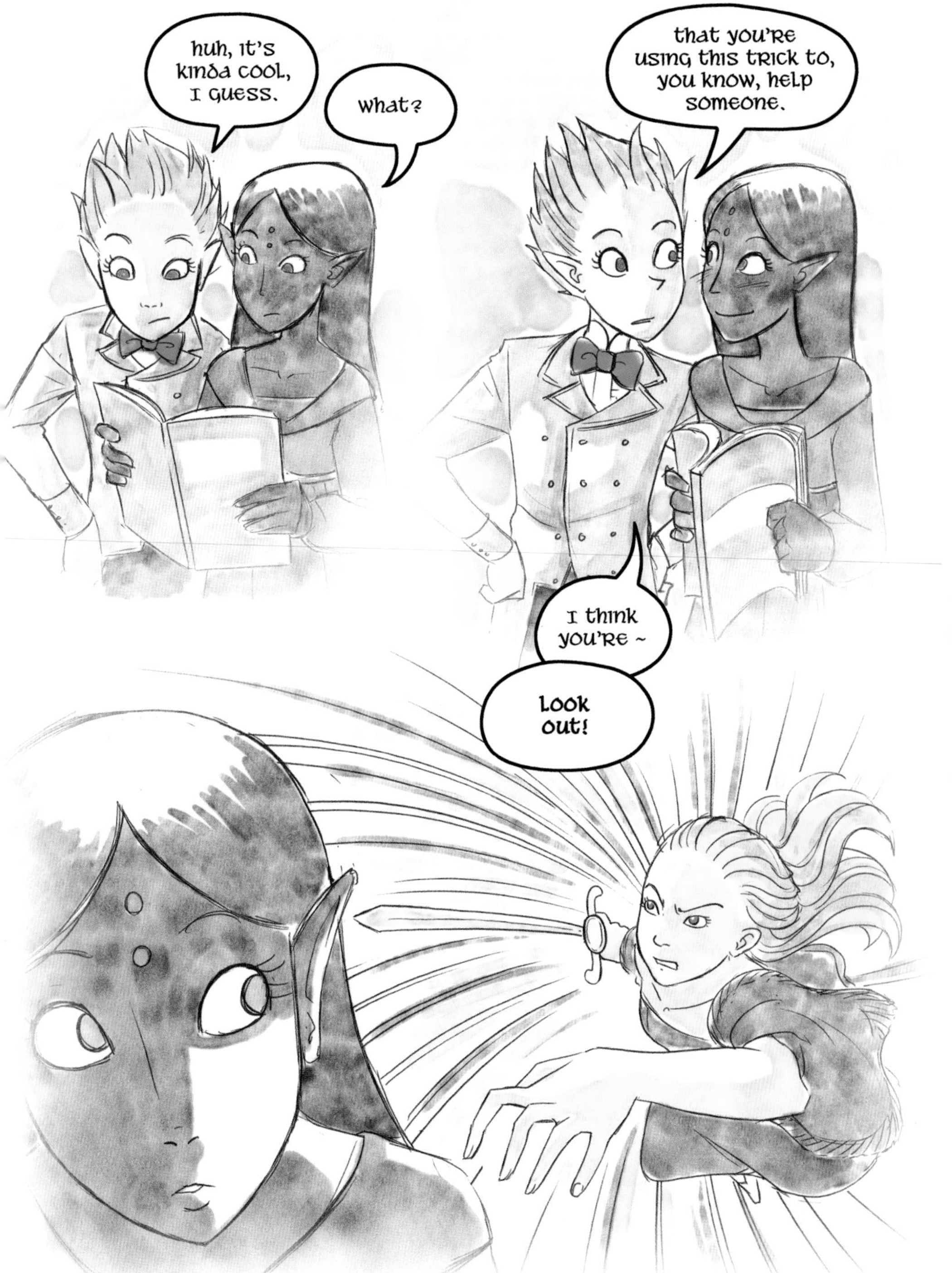
huh, it's kinda cool, I guess.
what?
that you're using this trick to, you know, help someone.
I think you're ~
look out!

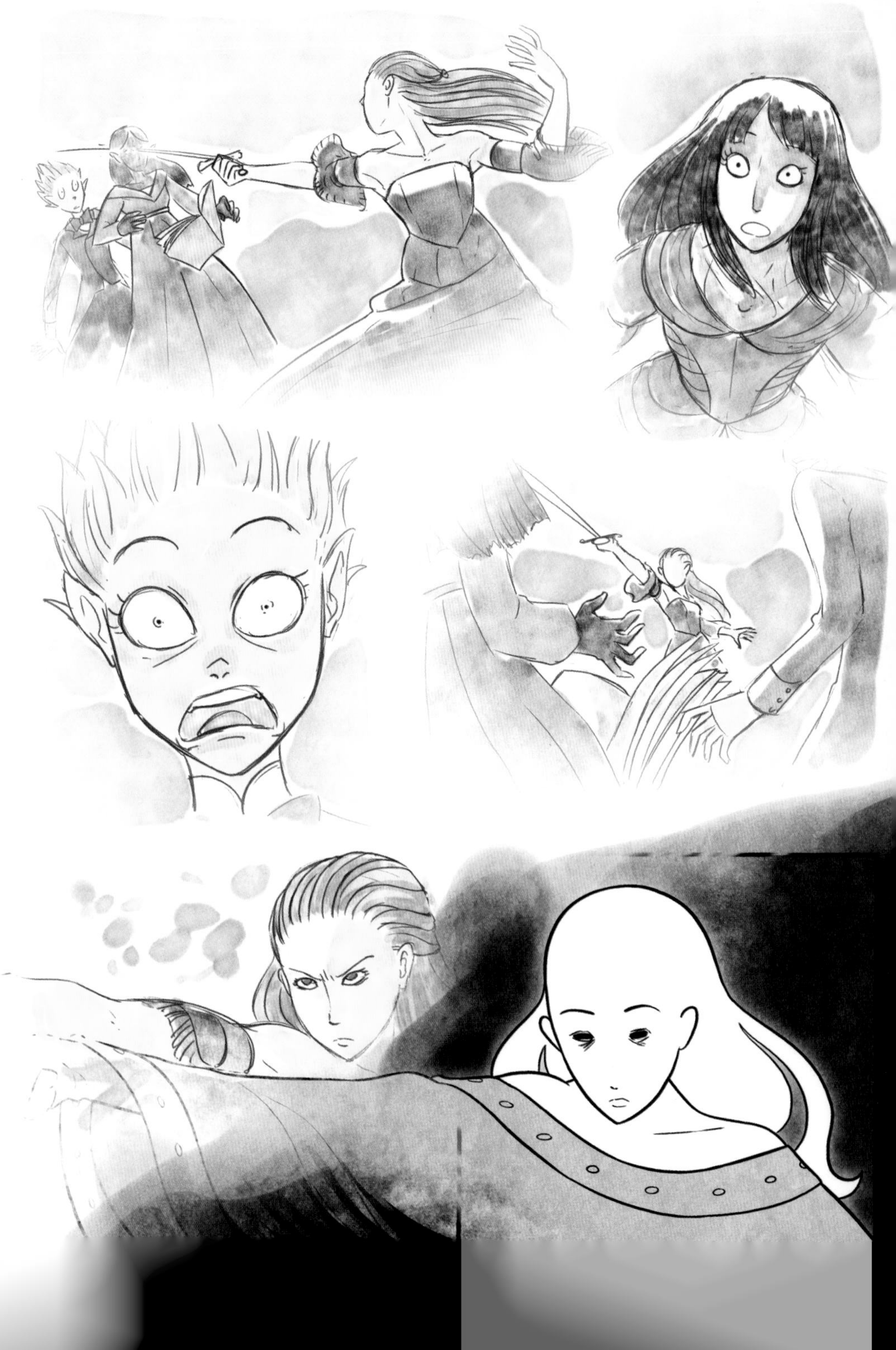

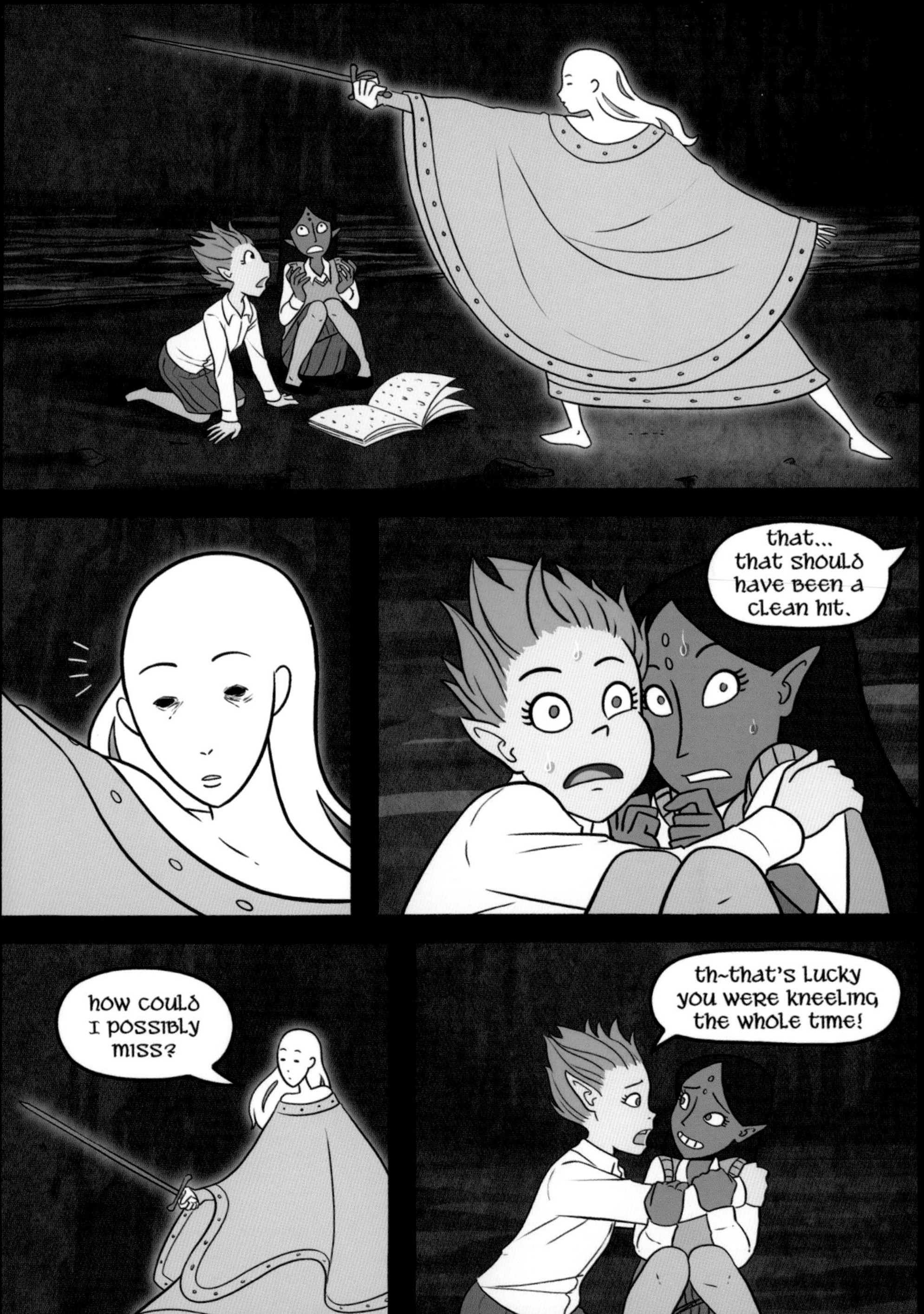
that...
that should
have been a
clean hit.
how could
I possibly
miss?
th-that's lucky
you were kneeling
the whole time!

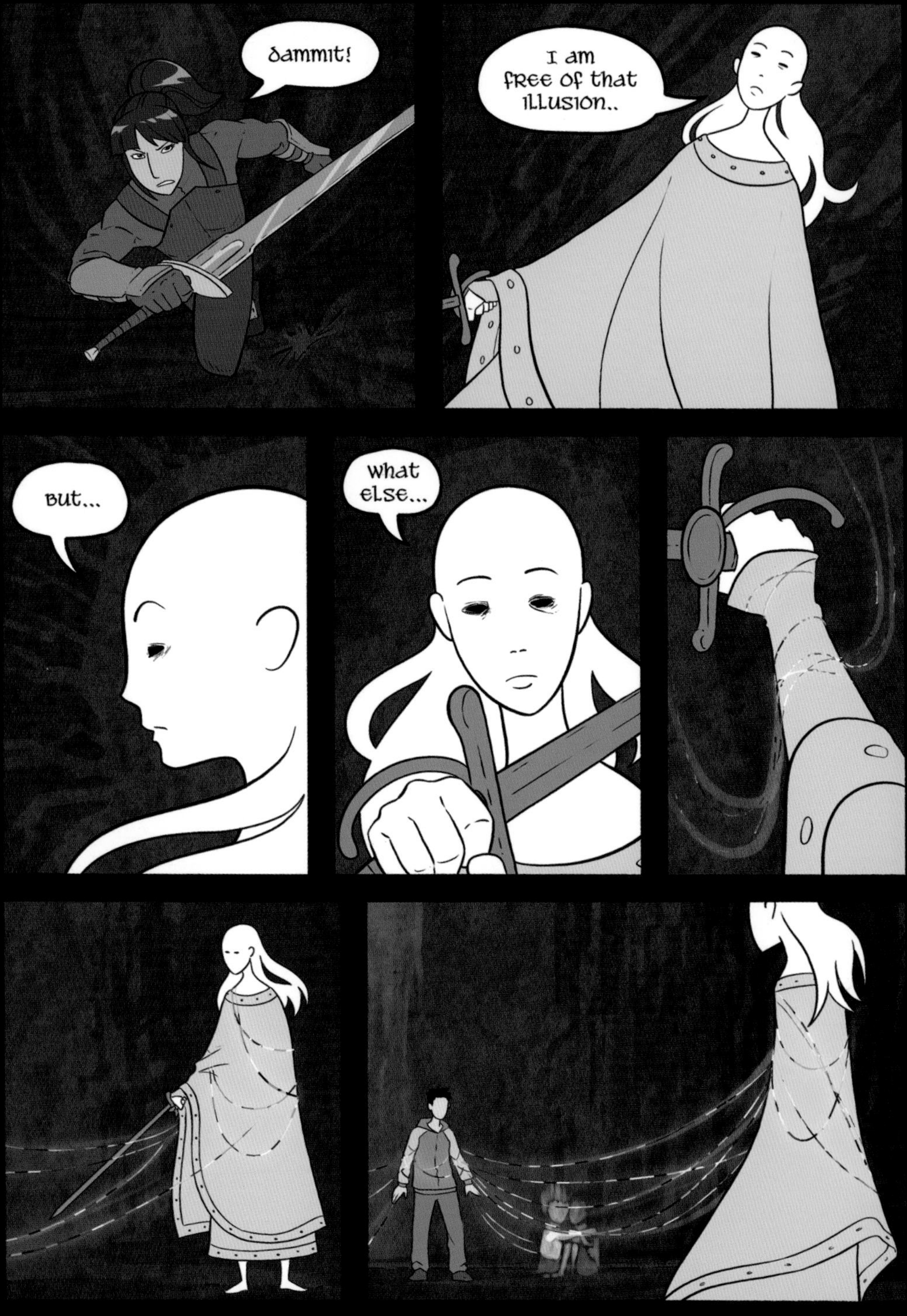
dammit!
I am free of that illusion..
But...
what else...

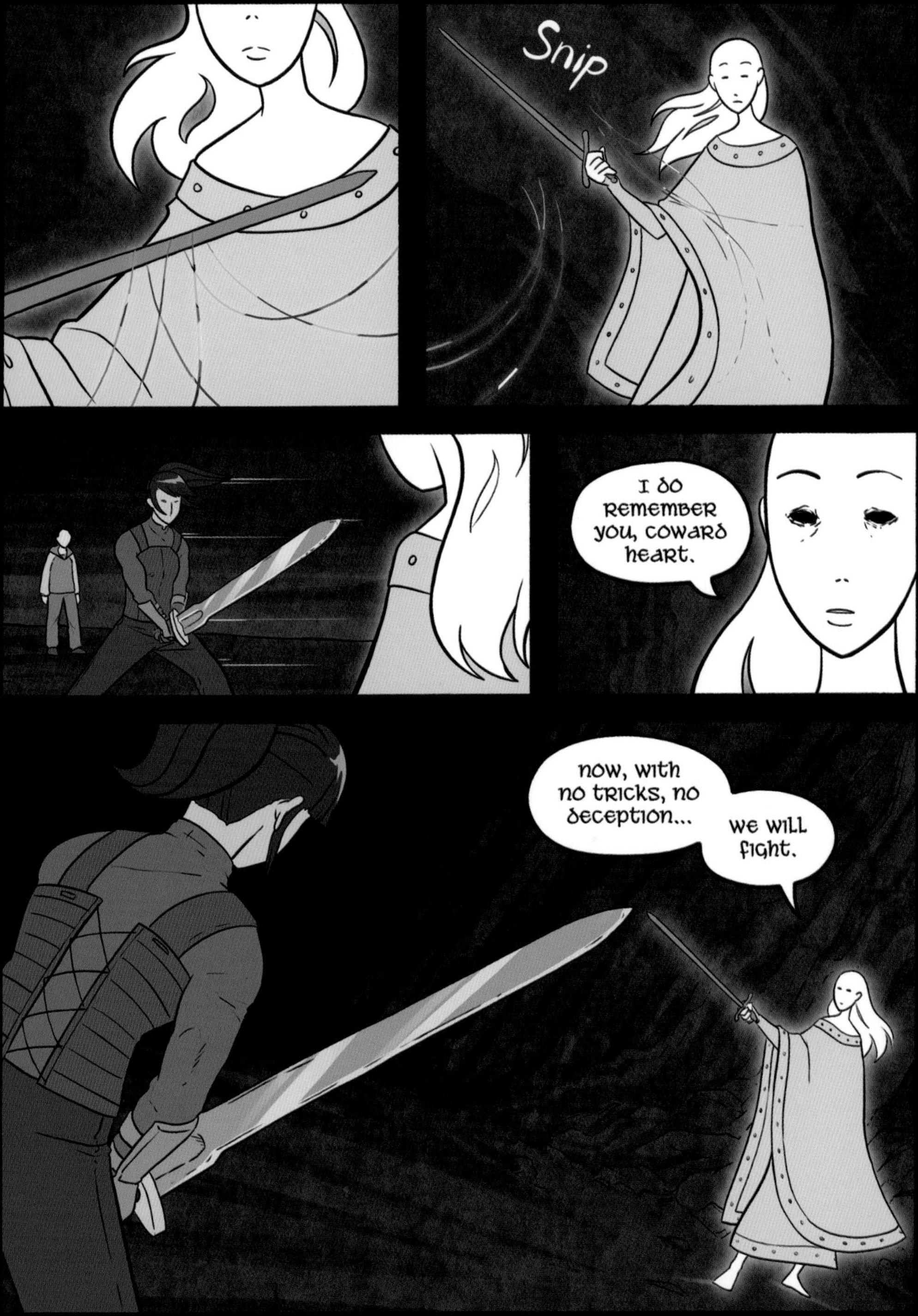
Snip
I do remember you, coward heart.
now, with no tricks, no deception...
we will fight.

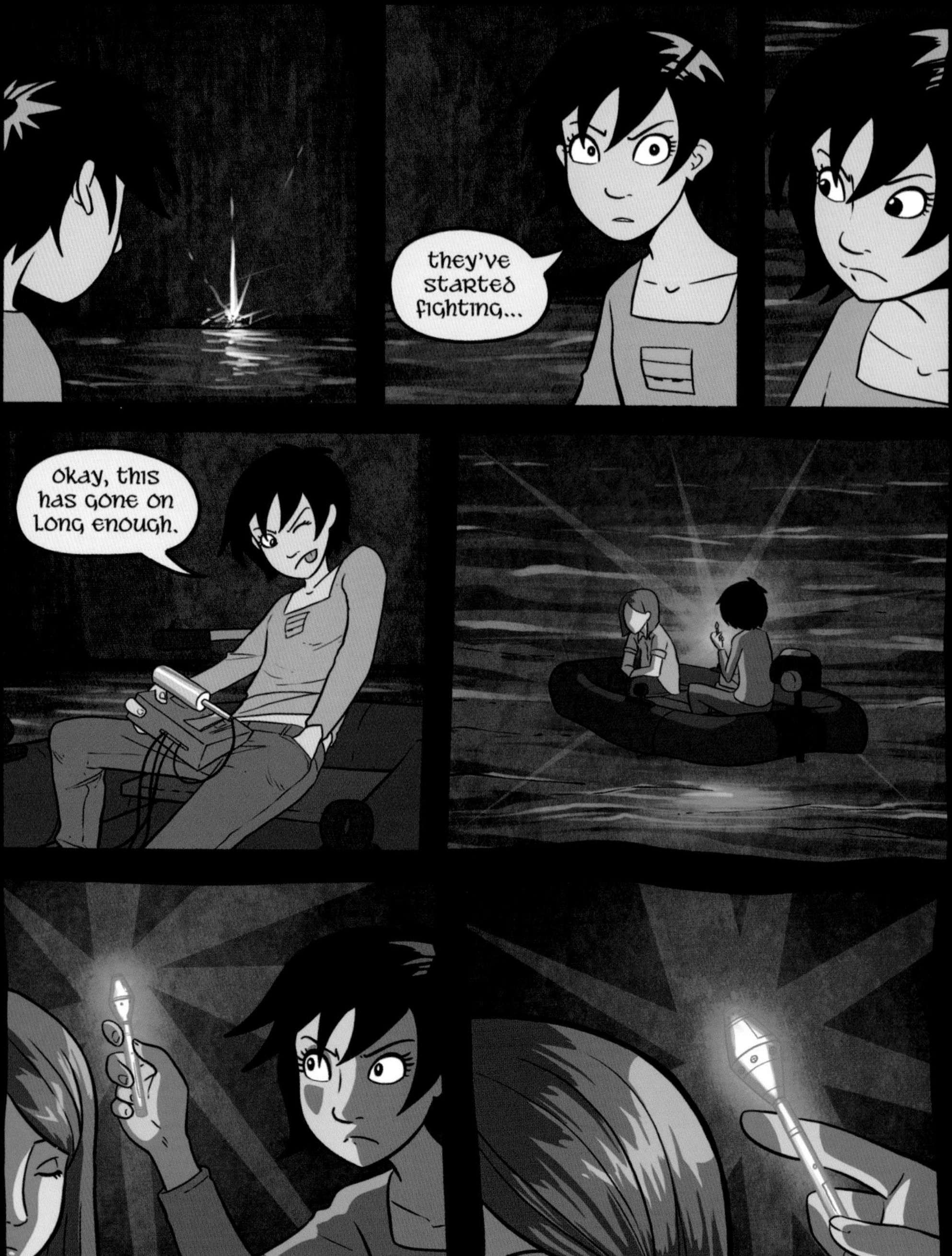
they've started fighting...
Okay, this has gone on long enough.

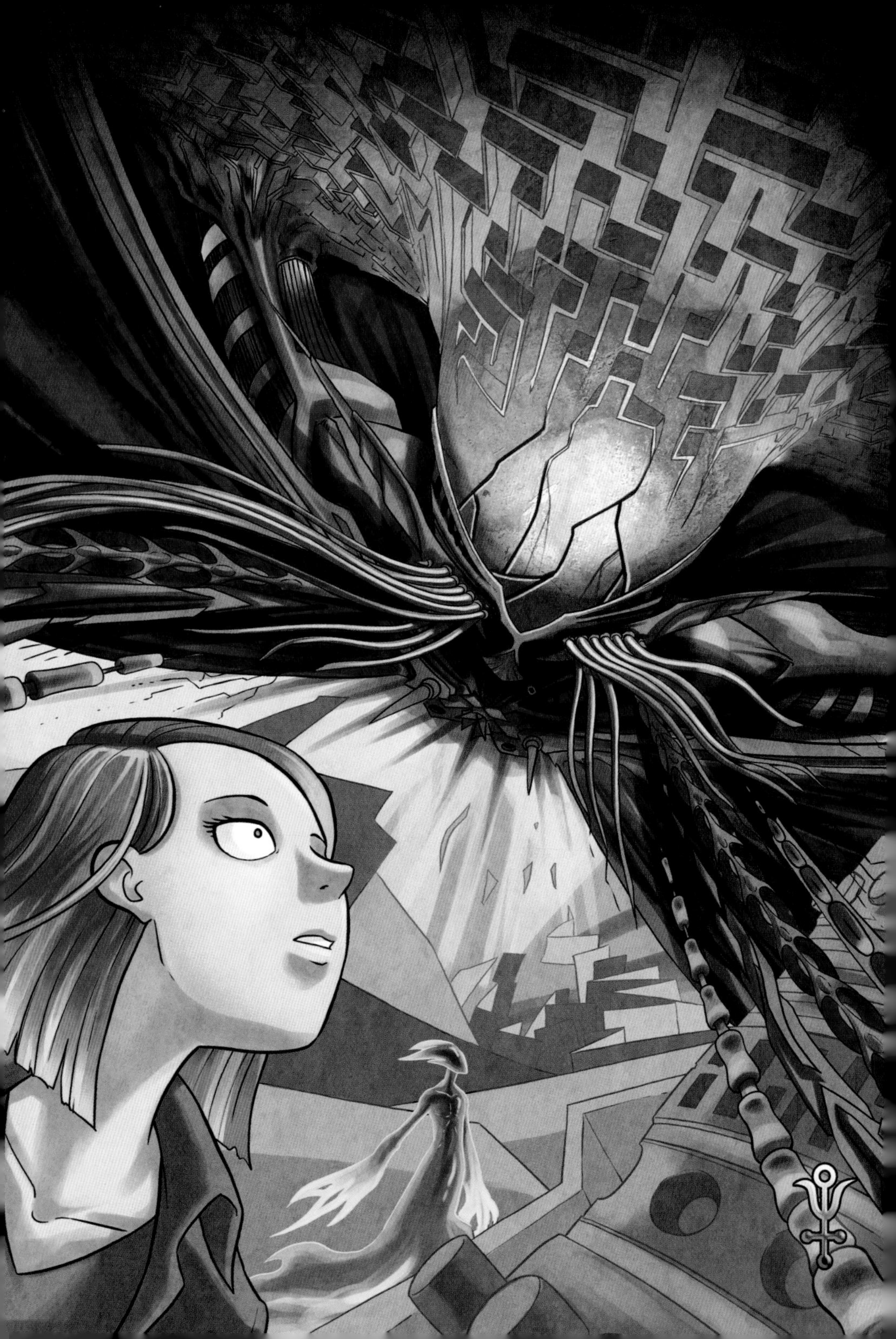

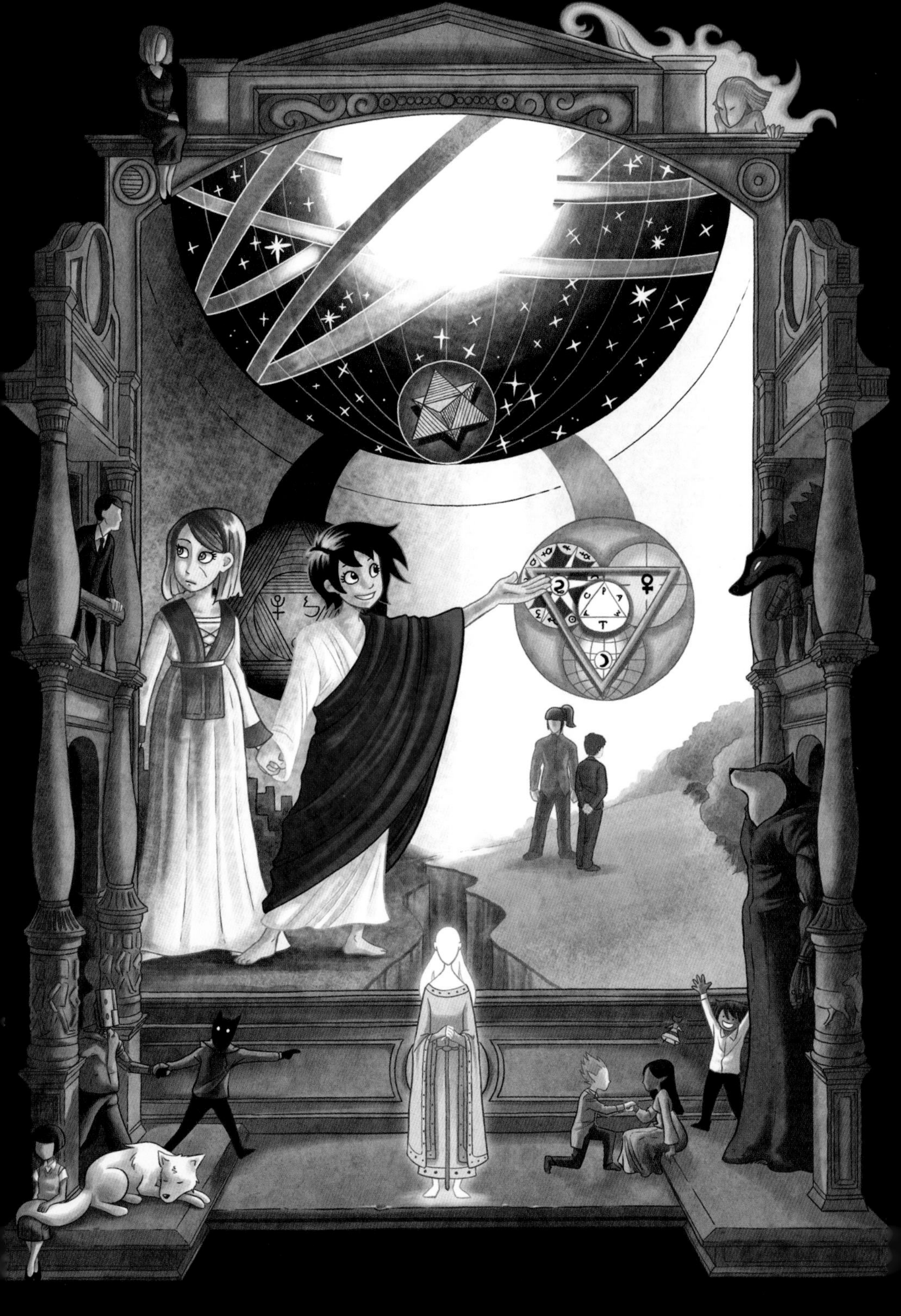

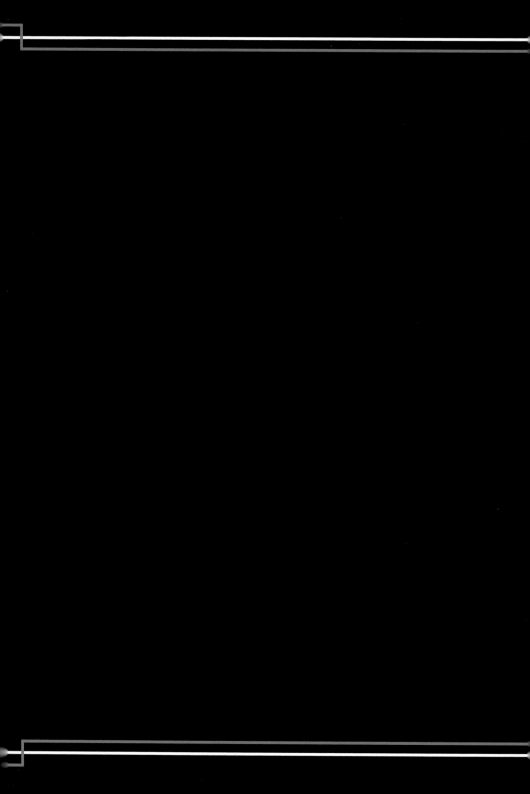

Mega Maze!

Looks like a tasty chip on the floor over there! Can you find your way away from your buddies and over to the super nice treat for your beak to eat?

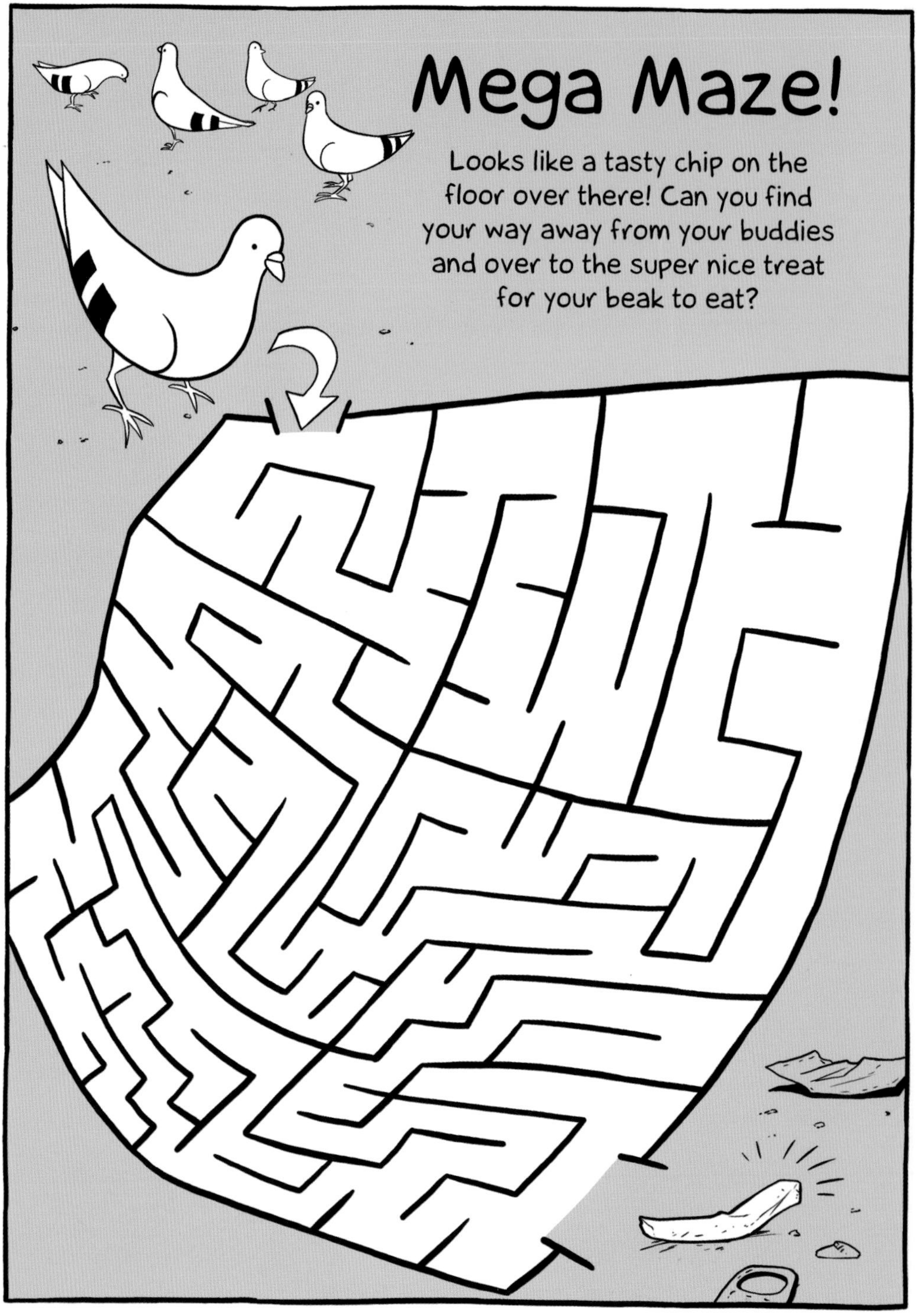

Hey!

Just look at all these cool guys! Maybe you can try colouring them with something like a marker or a stick with colour on it? Look at them all!

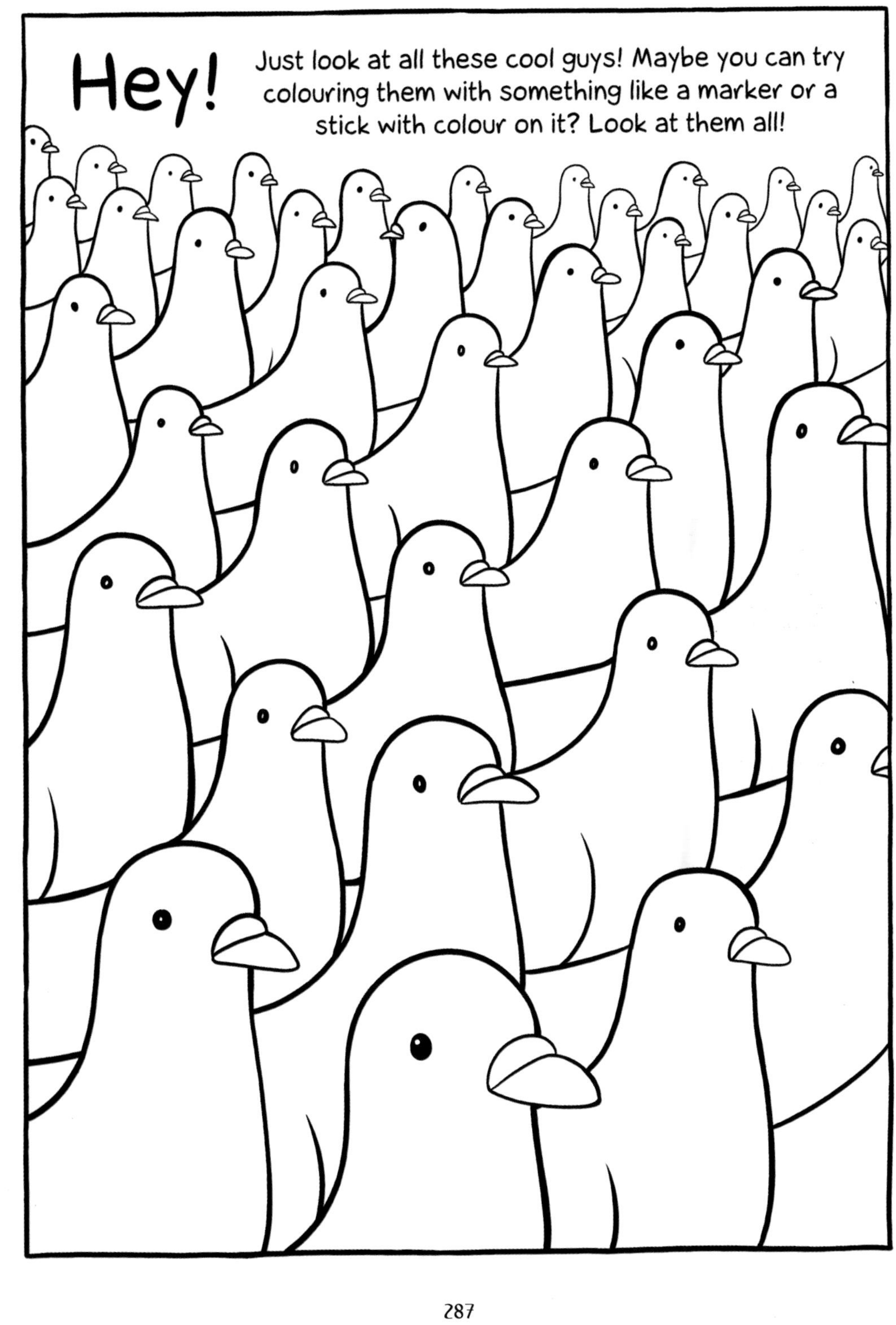

Search-A-Word!

Yikes! This looks like a bunch of letters in a box or something! Can you find the really cool hidden words in this big old mess? It's such a big mess!

D	U	E	G	E	Z	S	Z	B	N	Y	J	F	D	E
C	G	B	P	Z	Y	G	E	P	X	N	J	N	Z	V
A	M	P	Y	X	C	N	I	V	E	X	E	I	T	O
T	E	A	X	R	C	I	C	A	S	D	E	E	S	D
R	W	L	U	L	P	W	D	T	M	Q	Y	K	J	H
O	B	M	J	Y	W	I	O	U	P	L	E	A	S	E
T	B	U	A	P	B	M	N	M	P	I	G	E	O	N
S	R	H	O	M	M	K	O	B	N	U	T	Z	I	T
P	N	I	U	H	L	Z	C	L	L	A	Q	T	D	V
G	V	L	P	T	C	K	M	E	E	R	T	J	F	F
H	O	Q	N	L	T	Z	S	R	A	Q	E	E	Z	F
C	L	O	Z	Z	E	Y	T	S	A	T	E	A	X	K
U	D	U	F	S	D	V	V	W	H	D	W	D	N	V
G	U	V	F	N	B	D	B	O	J	G	S	B	Y	G
M	W	F	O	L	M	Z	T	W	S	K	O	M	W	Y

COLUMBIDAE
DOVE
WINGS
TASTY
CRUMBS

SEEDS
TRIPLE
SWEET
PIGEON
TUMBLER

PLEASE
DONT
EAT
ME

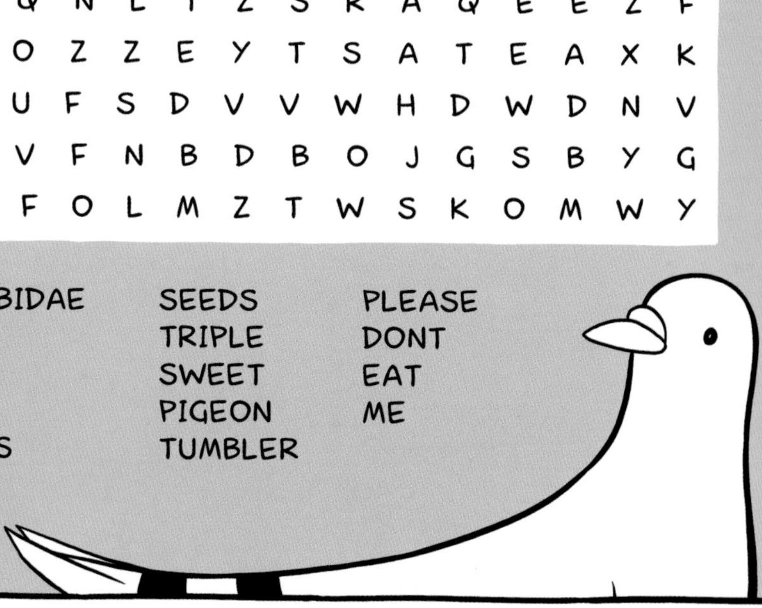

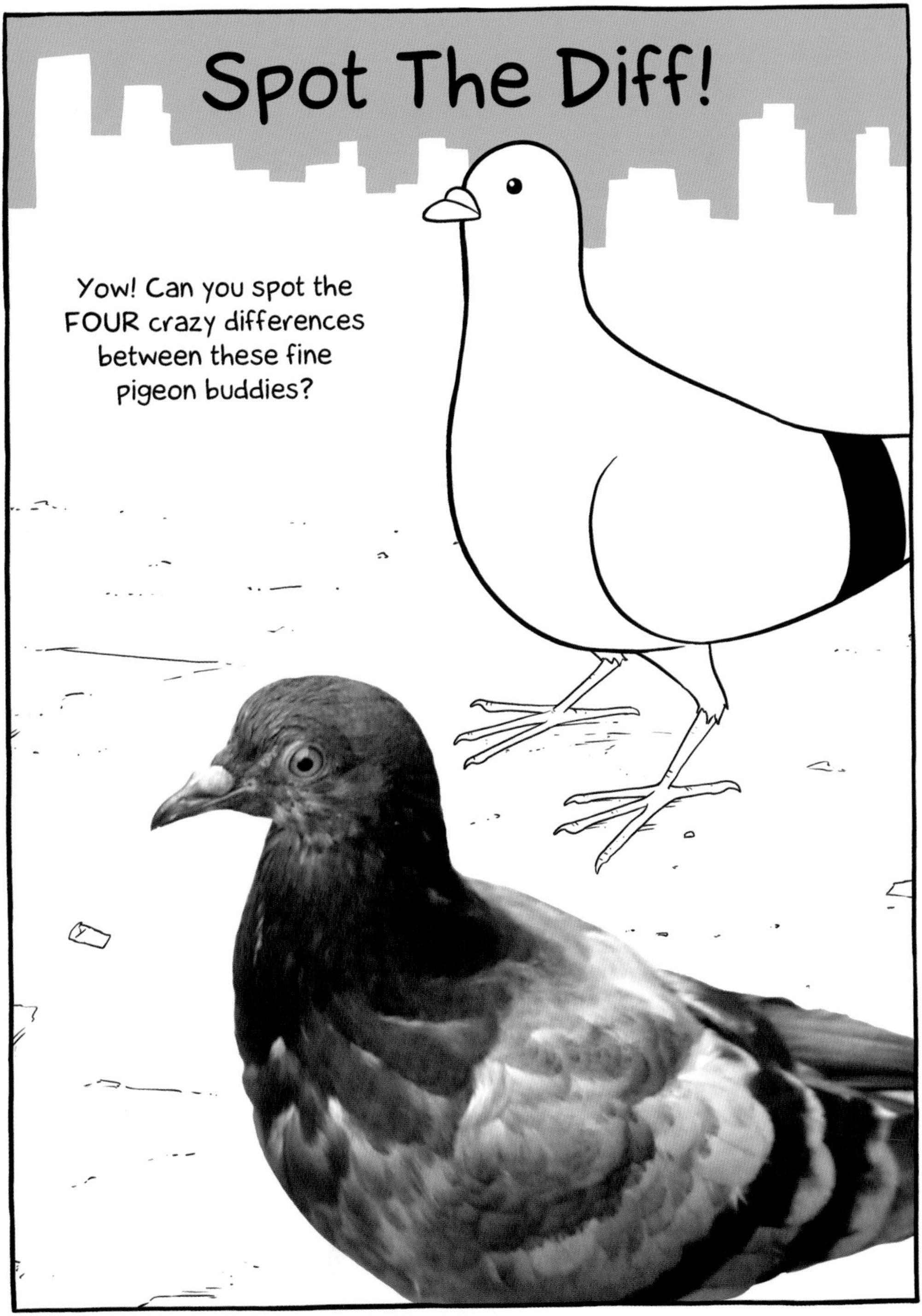
Spot The Diff!
Yow! Can you spot the FOUR crazy differences between these fine pigeon buddies?

More Words?

Well! Looks like this bunch of boxes should have letters in them? I think the cool clues below should help fill them in!

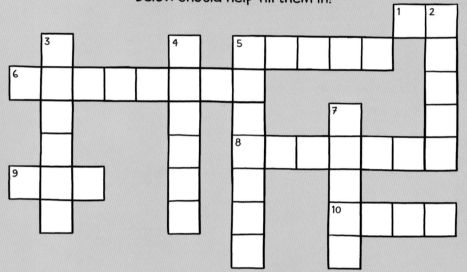

Across

1 Do humans like pigeons, yes or no?
5 I guess this is the name of a baby pigeon?
6 This is the coolest guy and also my name! (4,4)
8 Do you know the biggest bird I've seen?
9 Watch out, you might lose one of these!
10 Apparently, pigeons are just ___ with wings!

Down

2 Here comes a dove with an _____ branch!
3 We all know what bird this is!
4 A kinda tough bird.
5 This big angry bird might eat your babies!
7 Thjis magical creature loves to help!

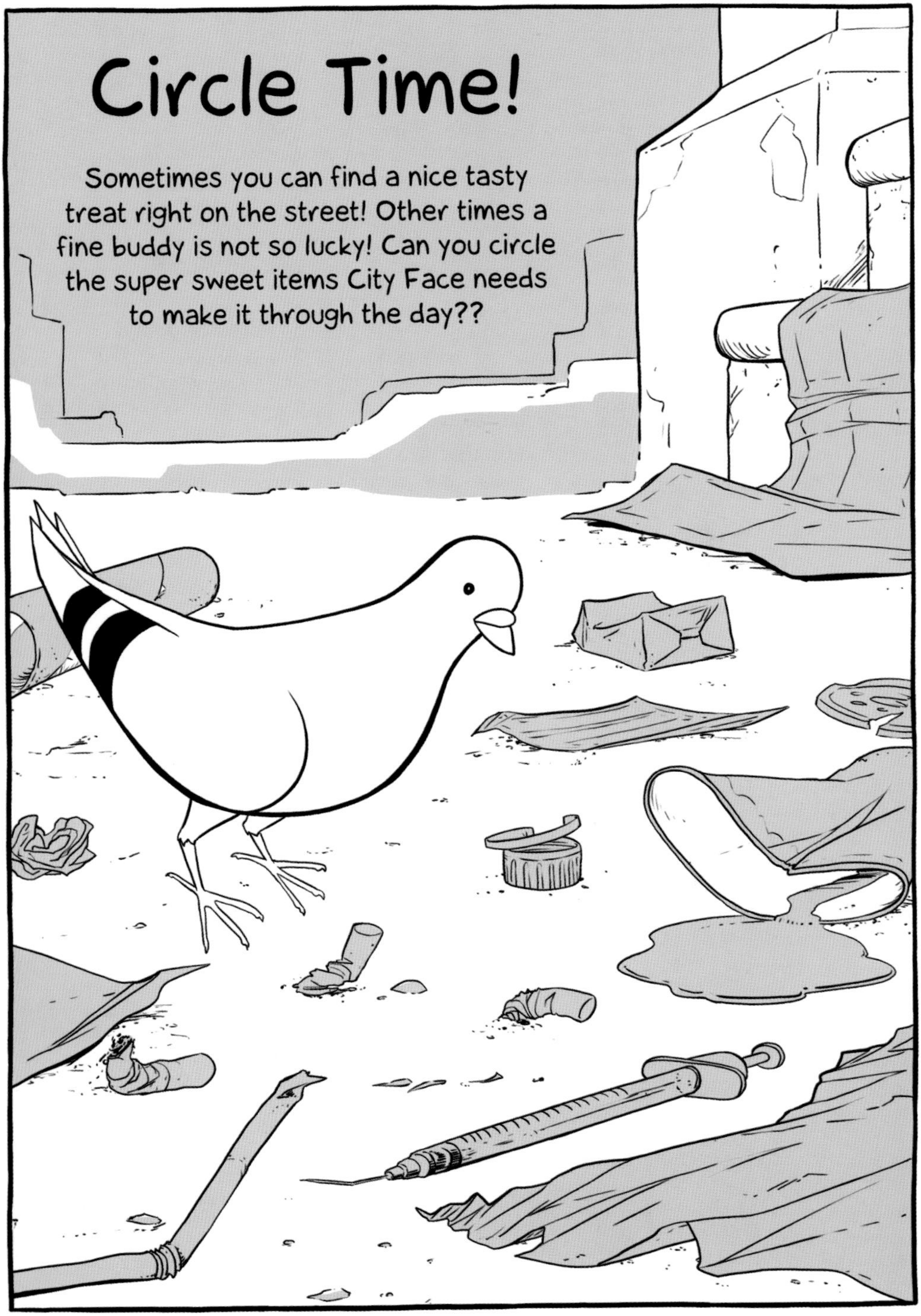
Circle Time!
Sometimes you can find a nice tasty treat right on the street! Other times a fine buddy is not so lucky! Can you circle the super sweet items City Face needs to make it through the day??

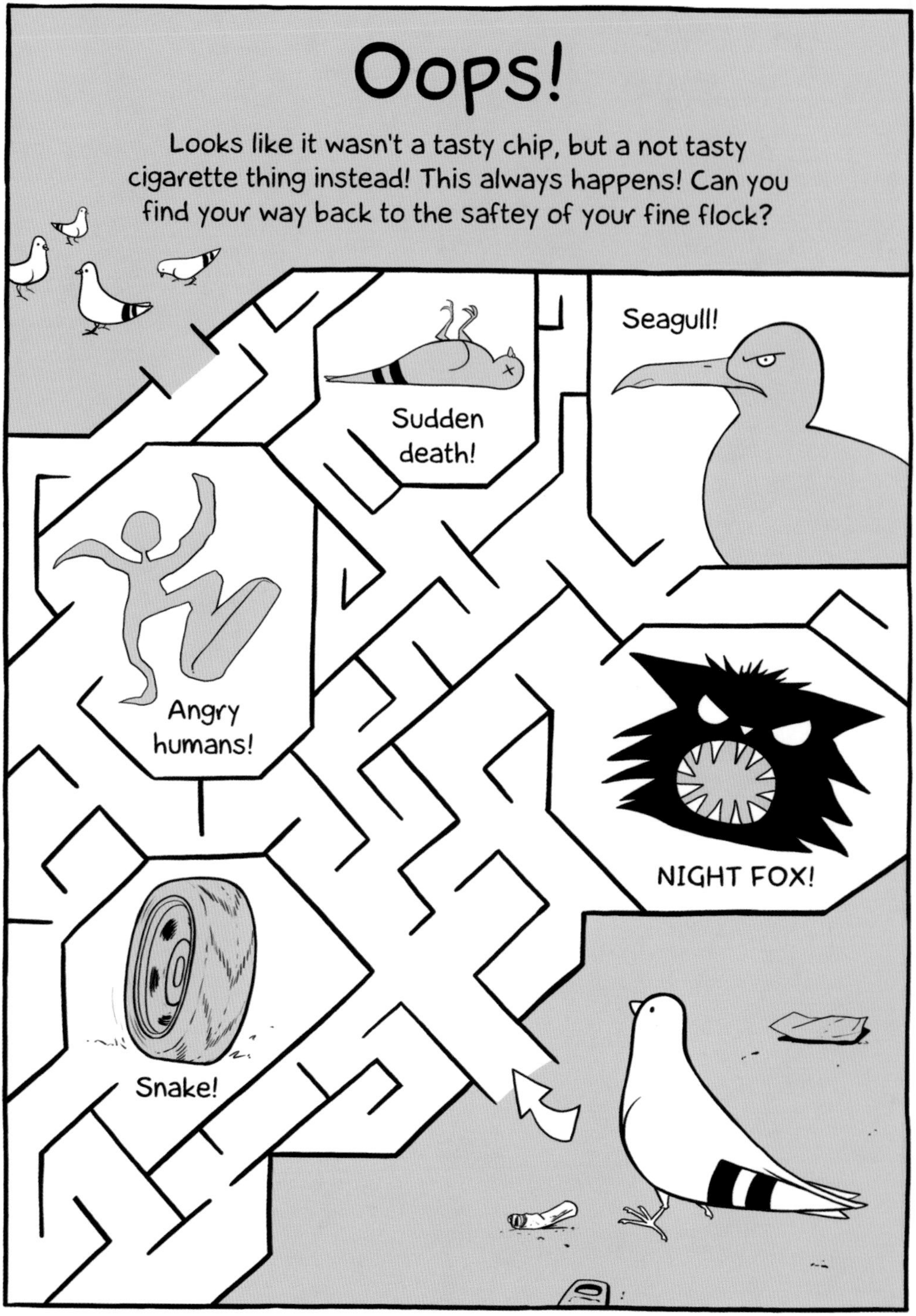
Oops!
Looks like it wasn't a tasty chip, but a not tasty cigarette thing instead! This always happens! Can you find your way back to the saftey of your fine flock?
Sudden death!
Seagull!
Angry humans!
NIGHT FOX!
Snake!

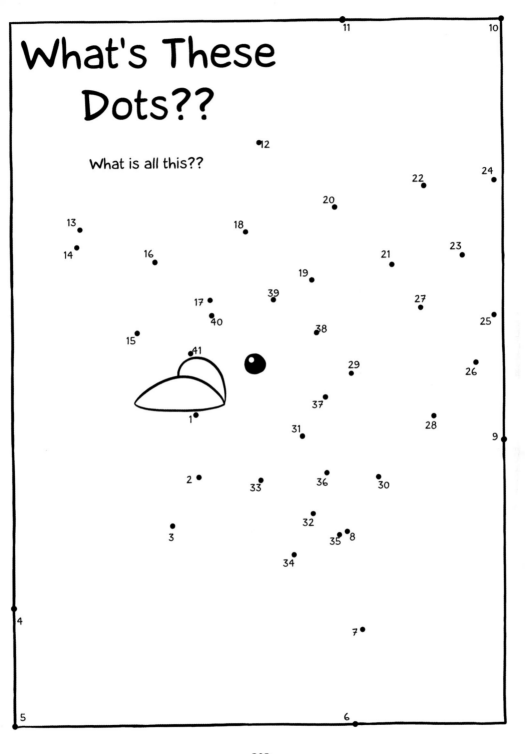

What's These Dots??

What is all this??

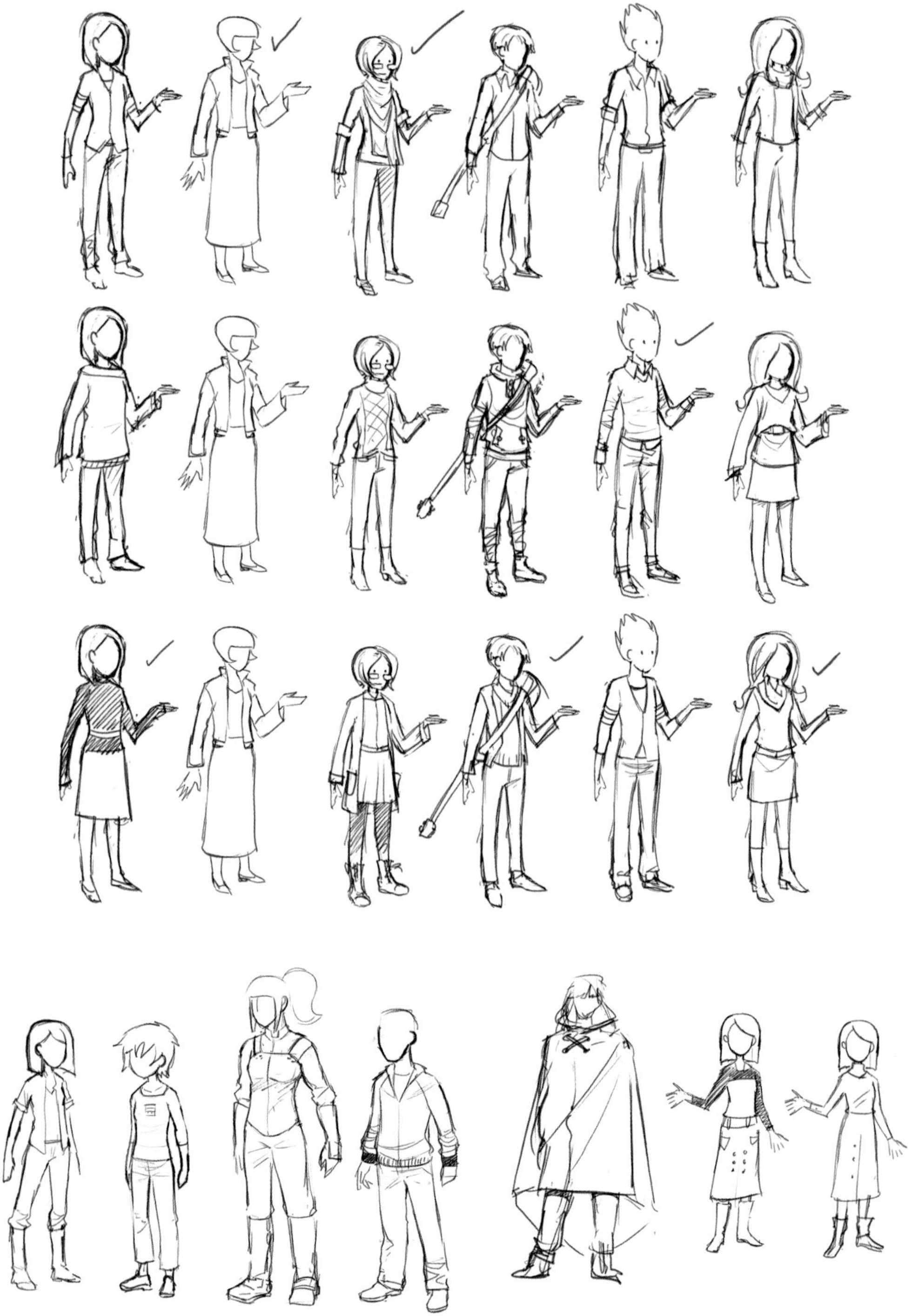

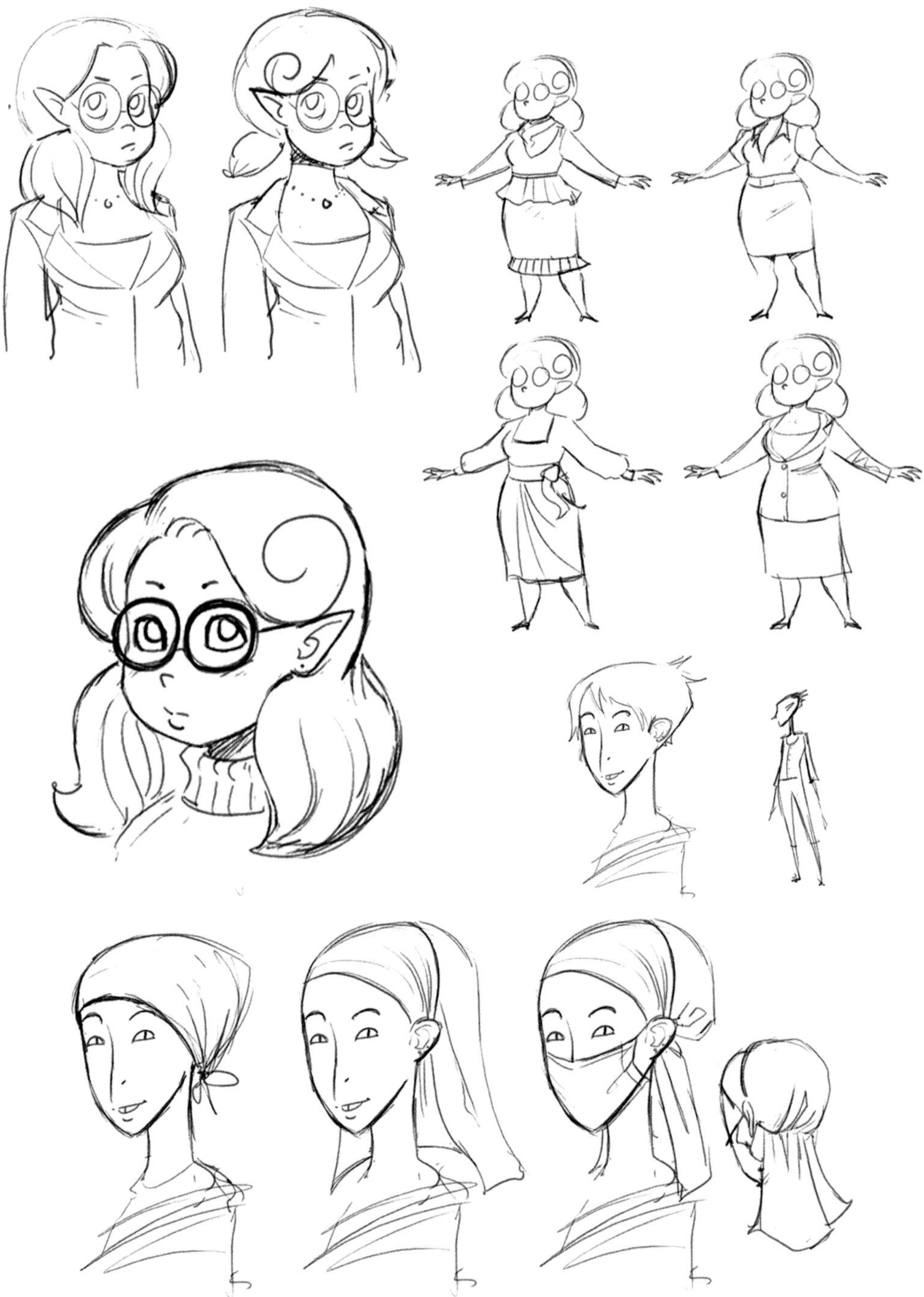

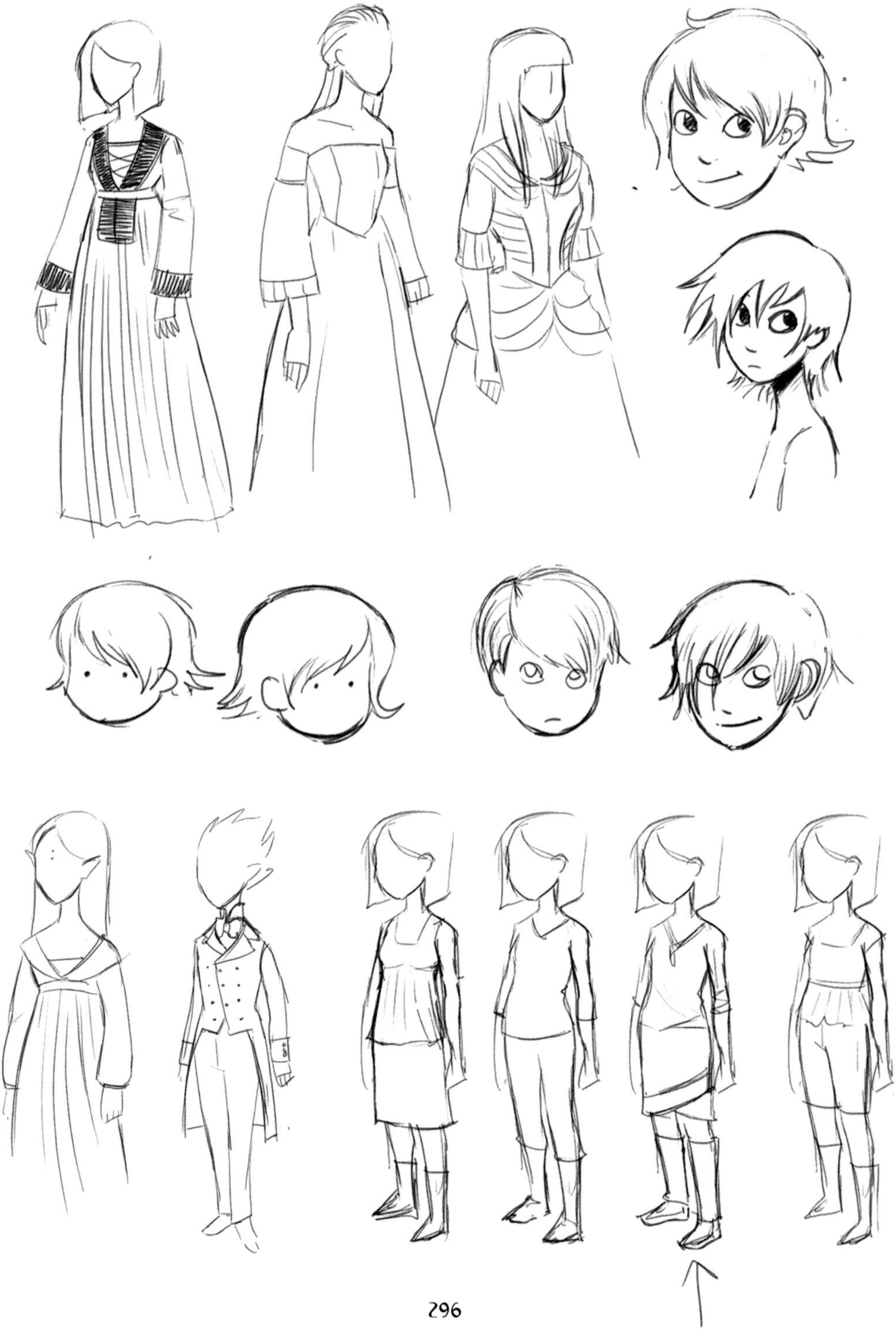

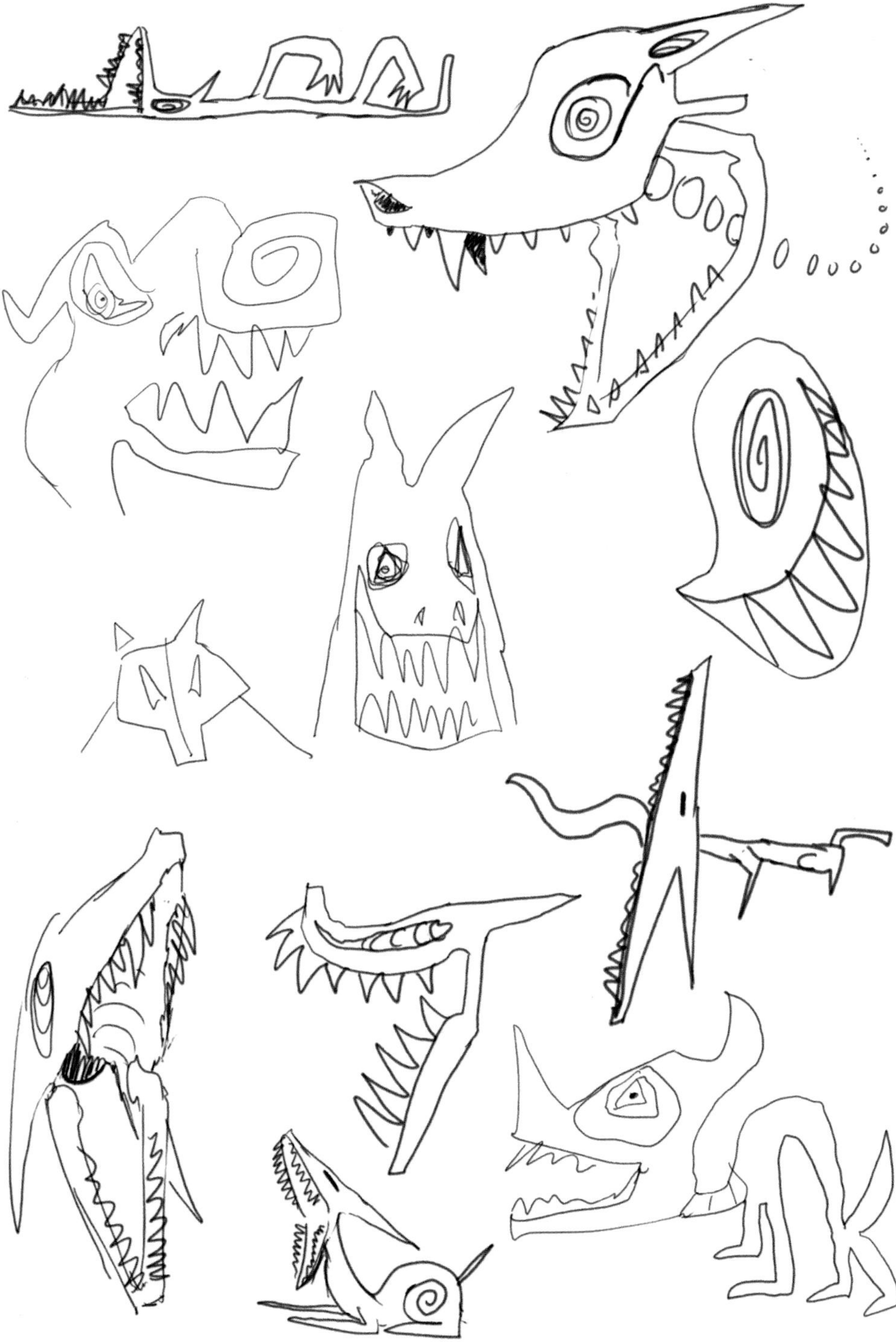

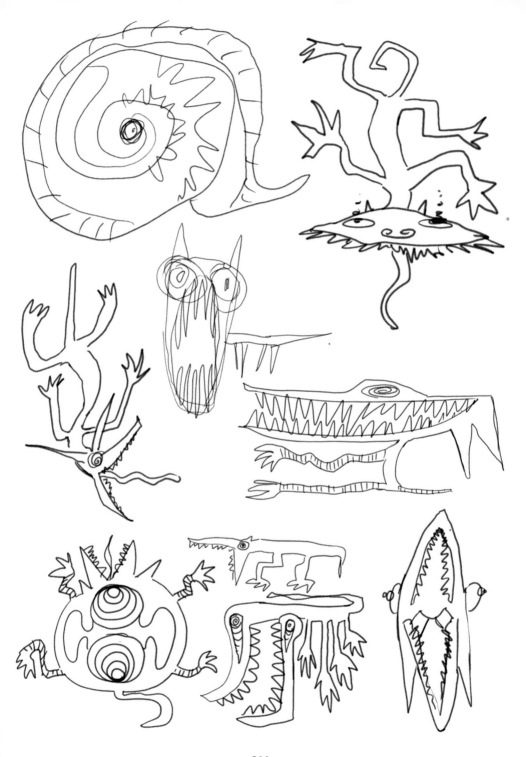

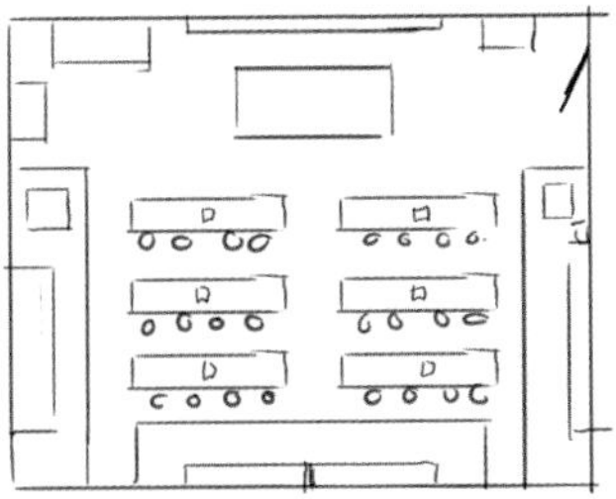
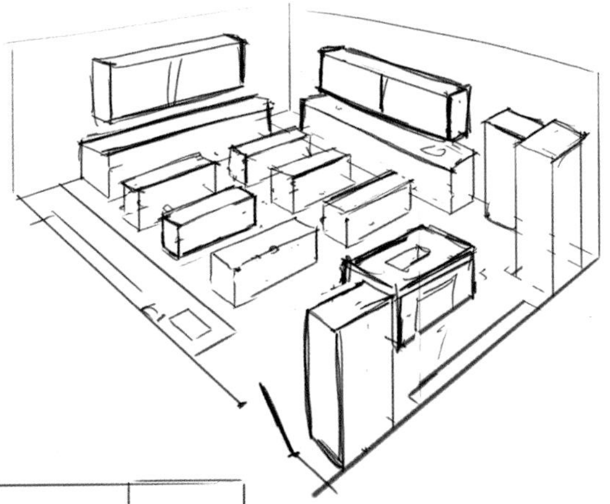
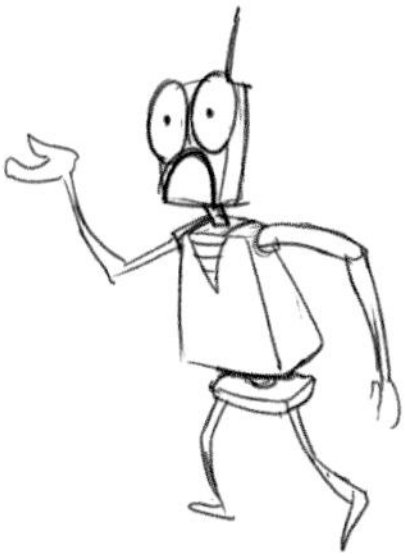
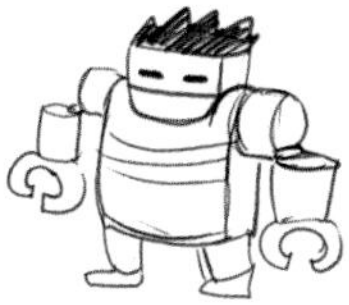
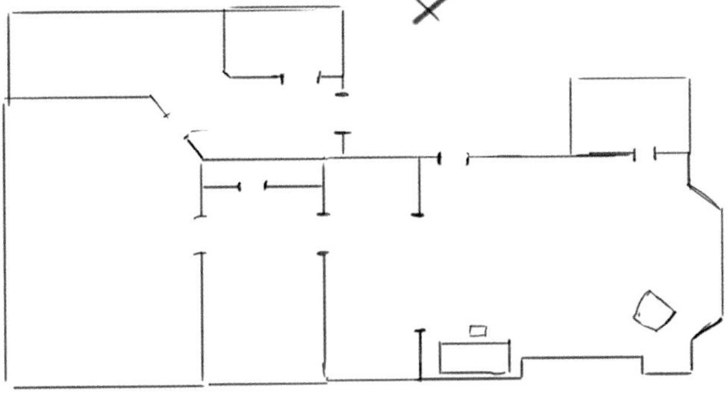
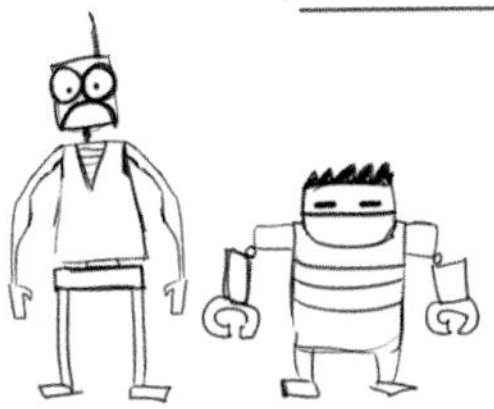
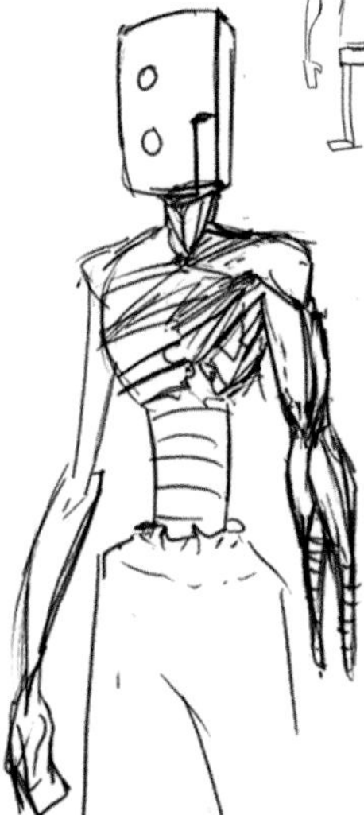
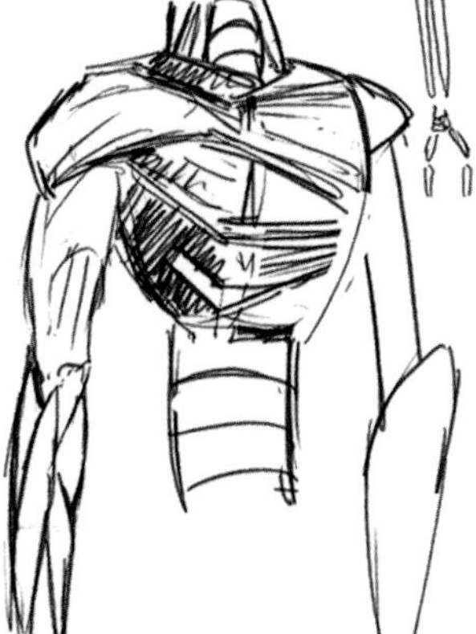
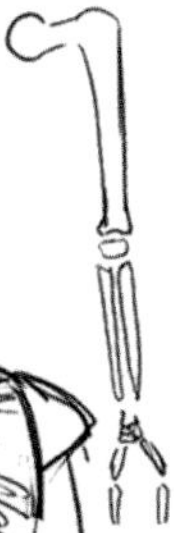
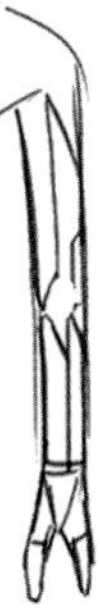
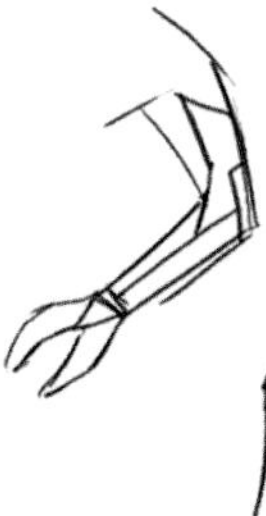
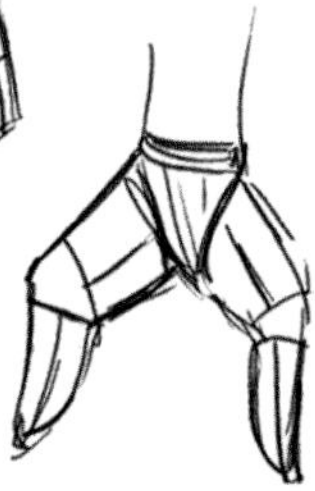
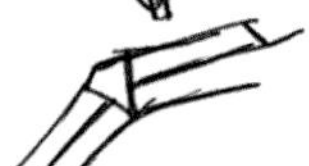
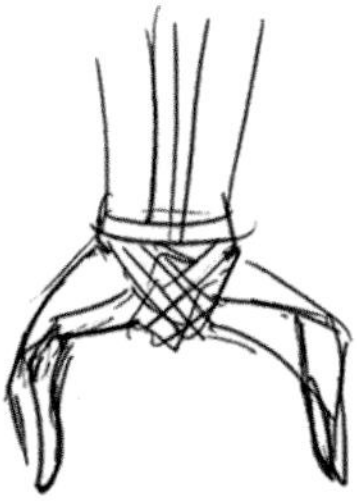

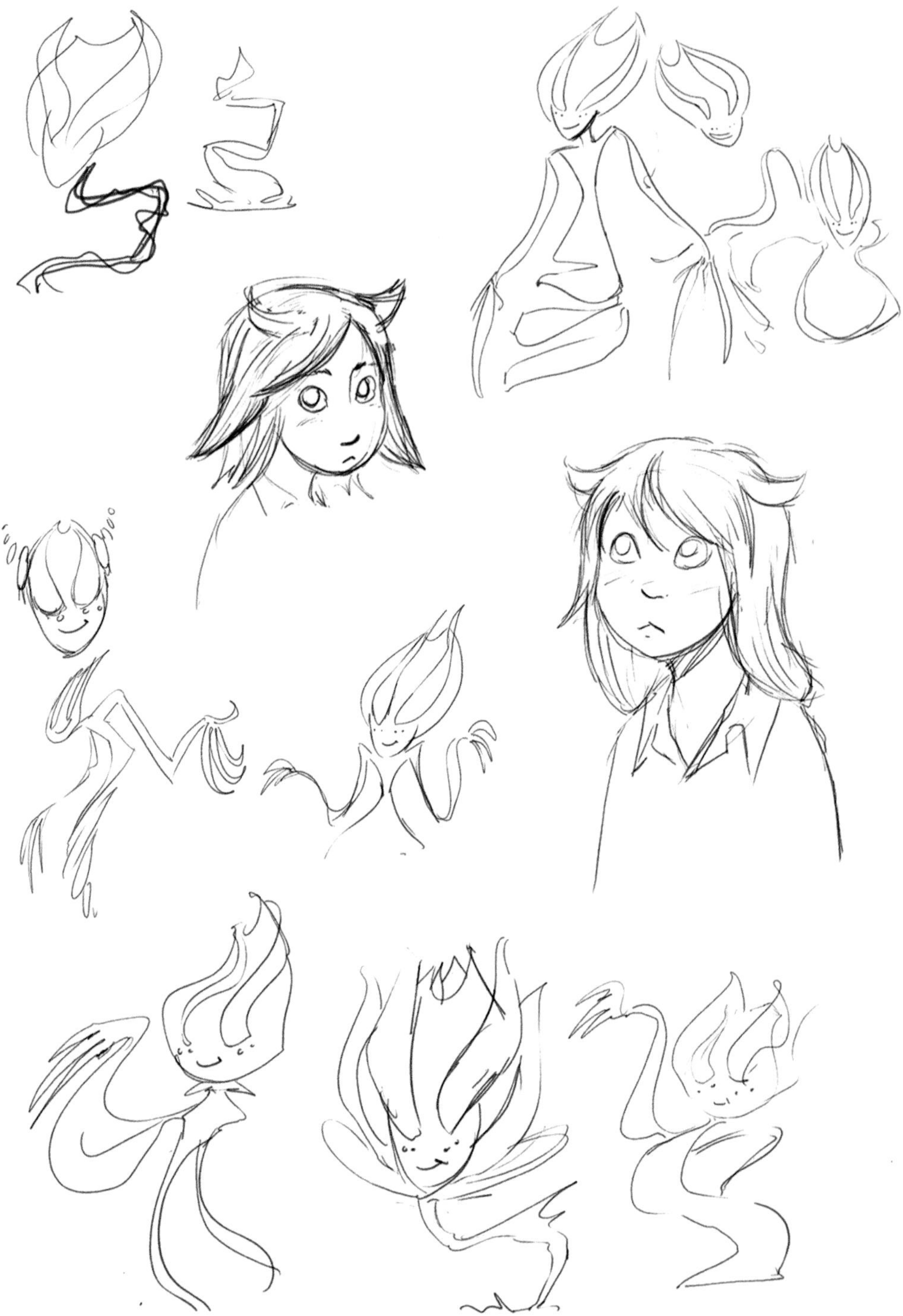

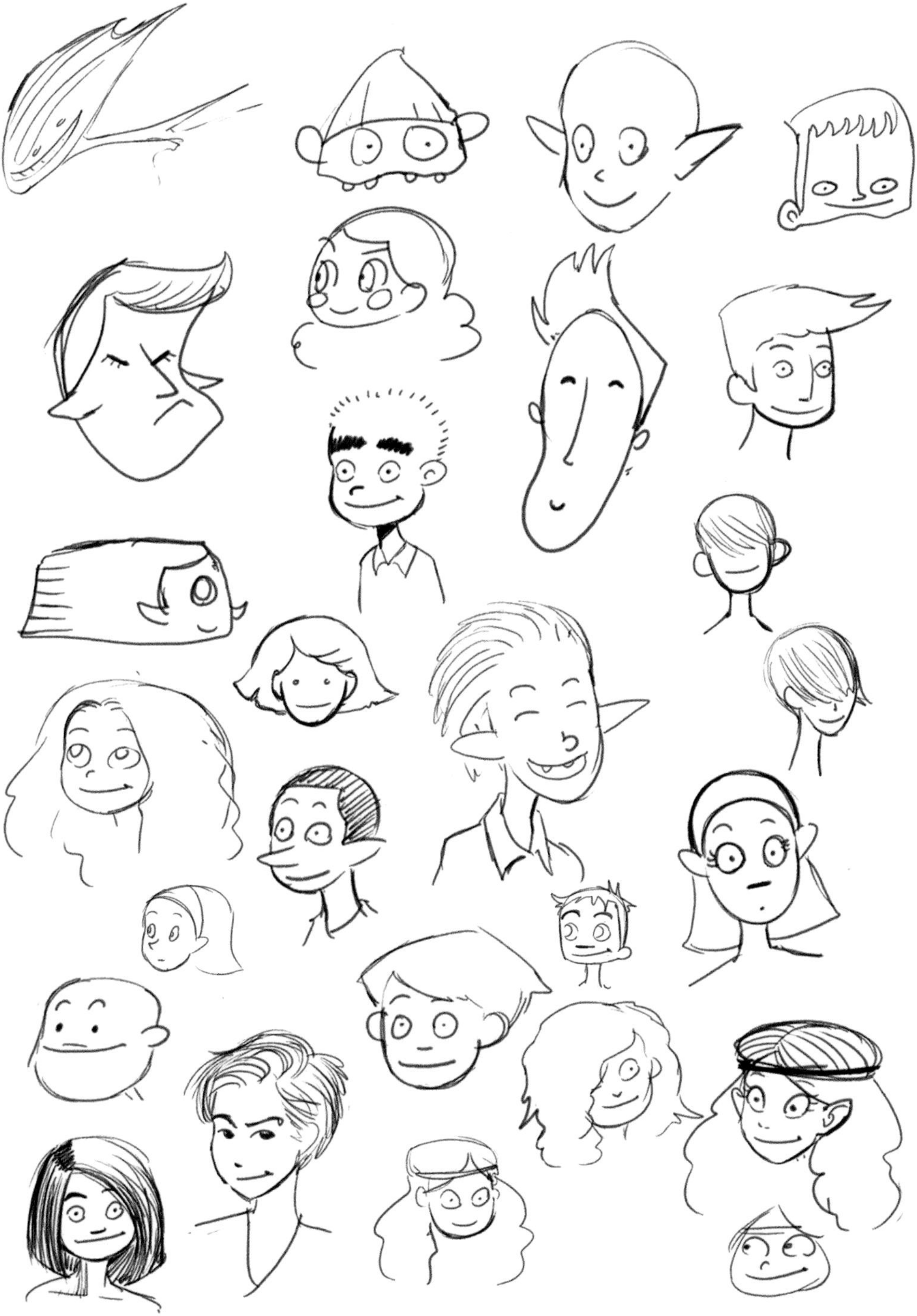

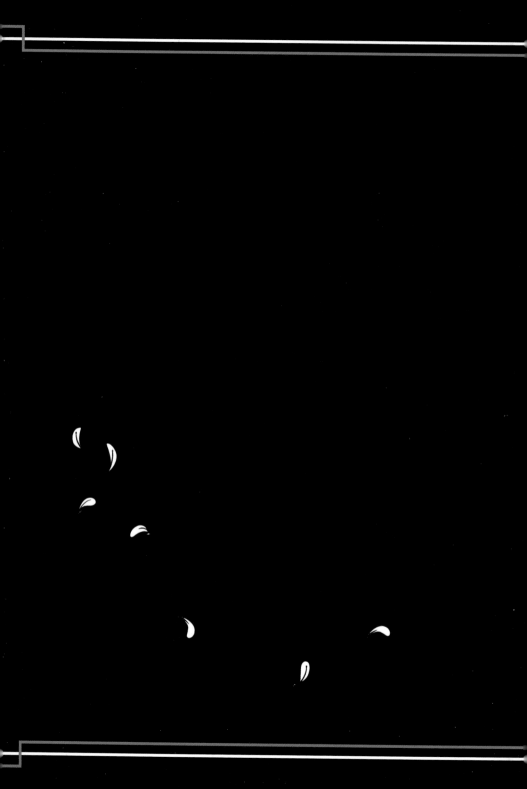

About the Author

Tom found a way out and now enjoys looking out
of the window at the trees and the pigeons.

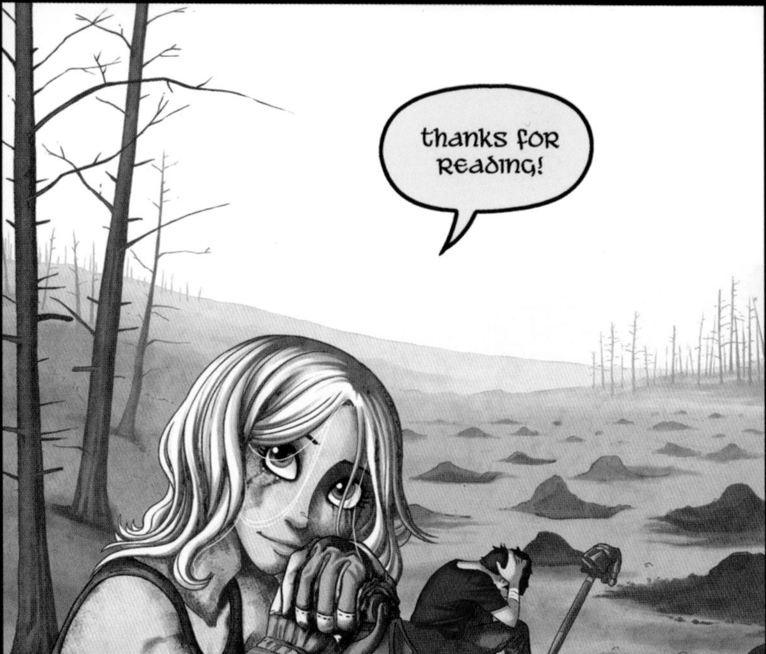
thanks for reading!

www.gunnerkrigg.com

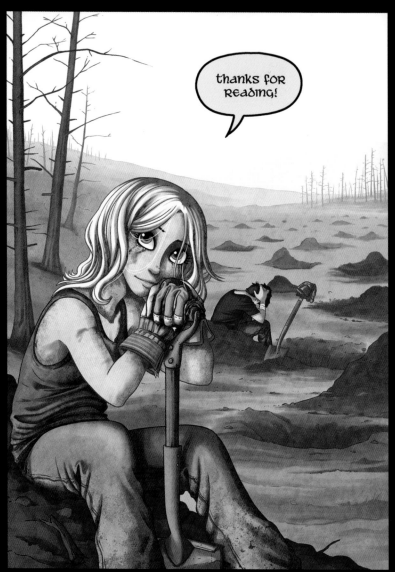